This book belongs to:

....

Praise for *Plain Bad Heroines*:

'Brimming from start to finish with sly humour and gothic mischief, *Plain Bad Heroines* is a brilliant piece of exuberant storytelling by a terrifically talented author'   Sarah Waters

'Beguilingly clever, very sexy and seriously frightening'   *Guardian*

'A hot amalgamation of gothic horror and Hollywood satire, it's draped with depth but bursting with life'   *Washington Post*

'*Plain Bad Heroines* is immersive, addictive, frustrating and highly entertaining featuring a brilliant cast of extremely eccentric, yet very intriguing, characters. A tale made for the big screen'
Swirl and Thread

PLAIN BAD HEROINES

With illustrations by Sara Lautman

ALSO BY EMILY M. DANFORTH

The Miseducation of Cameron Post

PLAIN BAD HEROINES

EMILY M. DANFORTH

HEROINES

With illustrations by Sara Lautman

b

THE BOROUGH PRESS

The Borough Press
An imprint of HarperCollins*Publishers* Ltd
1 London Bridge Street
London SE1 9GF

www.harpercollins.co.uk

HarperCollins*Publishers*
1st Floor, Watermarque Building, Ringsend Road
Dublin 4, Ireland

This paperback edition 2021
2

First published by HarperCollinsPublishers 2020

A catalogue record for this book is available from the British Library

ISBN: 978-0-00-834695-9

Printed and Bound in the UK using 100% Renewable Electricity at CPI Group (UK) Ltd

MIX
Paper from
responsible sources

FSC™ C007454

This book is produced from independently certified FSC™ paper
to ensure responsible forest management.

For more information visit: www.harpercollins.co.uk/green

For Erica,

THE HEROINE WHO HAS ALWAYS HELD MY HEART

Surely there must be in a world of manifold beautiful things something among them for me. And always, while I am still young, there is that dim light, the Future. But it is indeed a dim, dim light, and ofttimes there's a treachery in it.

—MARY MACLANE, *The Story of Mary MacLane*

To be durable and perfect, to be in fact grown-up, is to be an object, an altar, the figure in a stained-glass window: cherishable stuff. But really, it is so much better to sneeze and feel human.

—TRUMAN CAPOTE, *Answered Prayers*

Part One

. . . .

I AWAIT THE

Devil's Coming

The Story of Mary MacLane[*]

BY MARY MACLANE

....

Though I am young and feminine—very feminine—I am not that quaint conceit, a girl: the sort of person that Laura E. Richards writes about, and Nora Perry, and Louisa M. Alcott,—girls with bright eyes, and with charming faces (they always have charming faces), standing with reluctant feet where the brook and river meet,—and all that sort of thing.

I missed all that.

And then, usually, if one is not a girl, one is a heroine—of the kind you read about. But I am not a heroine, either. A heroine is beautiful—eyes like the sea shoot opaque glances from under drooping lids—walks with undulating movements, her bright smile haunts one still, falls methodically in love with a man—always with a man—eats things (they are always called "viands") with a delicate appetite, and on special occasions her voice is full of tears. I do none of these things. I am not

---

[*]   Mary MacLane. *The Story of Mary MacLane*. Chicago: Herbert S. Stone & Company, 1902.

    The book was originally titled *I Await the Devil's Coming,* but MacLane's editor refused to publish it under this title during her lifetime.

beautiful. I do not walk with undulating movements—indeed, I have never seen any one walk so, except, perhaps, a cow that has been over-fed. My bright smile haunts no one. I shoot no opaque glances from my eyes, which are not like the sea by any means. I have never eaten any viands, and my appetite for what I do eat is most excellent. And my voice has never yet, to my knowledge, been full of tears.

No, I am not a heroine.

There never seem to be any plain heroines except Jane Eyre, and she was very unsatisfactory. She should have entered into marriage with her beloved Rochester in the first place. I should have, let there be a dozen mad wives upstairs. But I suppose the author thought she must give her heroine some desirable thing—high moral principles, since she was not beautiful. Some people say beauty is a curse. It may be true, but I'm sure I should not have at all minded being cursed a little. And I know several persons who might well say the same. But, anyway, I wish some one would write a book about a plain, bad heroine so that I might feel in real sympathy with her.

ONE MACABRE AFTERNOON TO BEGIN

····················

It's a terrible story and one way to tell it is this: two girls in love and a fog of wasps cursed the place forever after.

Maybe you think you already know this story because of the movie made of it. Not so, but you'll discover that soon enough. For now, let me acquaint you with *Vespula maculifrons*: the eastern yellow jacket. If you're imagining some do-gooder honeybee humming about the pastel pages of a children's book, don't.

Eastern yellow jackets are aggressive when provoked, relentless when defending their underground home. They don't make honey, but might I offer you instead the desiccated insect paste they use to grow their masses? A given colony's workers are all stinging, sterile females who, in autumn—when they've been laid off from their busywork and can sense that the coming freeze will bring their deaths—just want to fly around, bored and gorging on carbs. (But then, don't we all?) Because they also feed on carrion, some people refer to them as meat bees. That's technically incorrect, but it sounds good.

Most crucially for our purposes here, you should know that when they're in distress, yellow jackets release a pheromone to call on potentially thousands of their angry friends to help them come get you.

In this case the *you* was Clara Broward and my God was she ever in love with Florence "Flo" Hartshorn. And my God did that fact ever upset Clara's wretched cousin Charles, who was just now chasing Clara through the thick woods surrounding the Brookhants School for Girls. The air in those woods was weighted with the scent of fern rot and ocean tide, apple mash and wet earth. And more than that, it was humming with the trill of yellow jackets. A few were probably already swirling around Clara like dust motes sprung from the beating of a rug, their buzzing pitch threaded to her pulse as her messy steps propelled her toward a clearing, and the Black Oxford orchard, where apples felled in a recent storm now spoiled in the heat.

And it *was* hot, the day humid and gray—one of those overripe summer days that sometimes linger into fall. And waiting there in the orchard with those spoiling black apples, lolled beneath a tree with juice dripping from her chin, was Flo—the love of Clara's young life. A life about to end.

Two lives about to end, careful Readers.

We know that the year was 1902, and the state the tiniest in the nation: Rhode Island. We know that the Brookhants fall term had been in session for six weeks. And we know that Clara took off into that section of woods, onto the orchard path, because several of her classmates watched her do it. She'd just been delivered back to campus after a weekend stay at her parents' house across the water in Newport, a house that they were then readying to close for the season.

Cousin Charles had been the one tasked with driving Clara to campus. More than a few students had noted this because what he'd driven her in was still something of a loud and chugging novelty, even for the wealthy Brookhants population: a gas-powered automobile. And not just any automobile, but a Winton—same as the Vanderbilts—which is exactly why Charles had gone out and bought the damn thing, along with the even stupider driving goggles that went with it. And he was, of course, wearing them when they pulled through the Brookhants gates, and then, as he slowed, he pushed them up, which smooshed his hair back into a nest atop his horrible head. Maybe some of the girls had, in fact, later said that he looked rakish and fine, but for now let's discount their certainly incorrect opinions.

The important thing to know is that Charles and Clara were arguing as they arrived. And they continued to argue, the onlookers said, as he parked his loud contraption in the circle drive before Main Hall. They seemed to say their goodbyes very unhappily, Charles lunging from the car before gathering Clara's belongings only to dump them on the ground, all the while continuing to lecture her. Then he climbed back into the driver's seat and pouted there, his arms folded tight across his chest, his dumb face bitter as a cranberry and nearly as red.

But whatever the commands she'd just been given, Clara did not stoop to gather her things and go inside her dormitory, as one might have expected of her.

As, it seems, Charles was expecting of her.

Instead, she left the pile of clothing and cases and walked a few yards to a cluster of her gape-mouthed fellow students. She then asked where she could find Flo. Several of those students, including a third-year, Eleanor Faderman,* told her to try the orchard. They told her that's where Flo had been headed earlier.

With this news, Clara started her march across the wide lawn, which ended in a playing field rimmed with woods: where began the orchard path.

During these moments, stupid Charles still stewed behind the steering wheel, his great engine chugging. But he did not then pull down his goggles and drive away from campus. Instead, he watched Clara. Watched, disbelieving, each step she took away from him and toward the tree line.

And then she disappeared completely into the dark mouth that was the path's entrance.

This is where the onlooking classmates begin to differ in their accounts. Some later insisted that Clara knew her knuckle-dragging cousin had left the car to chase after her. Those students claimed that she'd started to run even before reaching the woods, seeing or sensing Charles coming fast behind.

Others said she didn't know, hadn't seen.

And Clara herself could never say again.

Certainly, she would have been sweating, in the heavy afternoon heat of that bruised day, and this would have been part of the call to the first yellow jackets who found her. And unfortunately, ev-

---

* Remember this name.

erything about her clothing—the day dress with ruffled lace, the shoes more slipper than not—was most unsuited for an activity like running through the woods. Though it should be said that Clara often found her clothing unsuited for activities with Flo, usually just because she had too much of it on.

Flo herself solved the problem of unsuitable women's clothing by wearing the castoffs of her older brother. Or sometimes Flo's mother, when she hadn't spent all of her monthly allowance from Flo's grandparents, would even buy Flo a pair of pants or men's boots. But then Flo's mother was a sculptor, and her friends were all artists, most of them European. She liked to find ways to flout convention and usually supported the same instincts in her daughter. (When, Readers, she was remembering to remember that she had a daughter.)

Clara's parents, on the other hand, were fourth-generation Americans shaped predominately by the conventions of their gilded social class. A few smart investments—steel and timber did the trick—and they'd watched their inherited wealth grow to numbers so high that even they could scarcely conceive of them. As such, they had a fastidious respect for the orderly following of the rules and systems from which they benefited. It all made them feel quite secure in the correctness of their position within the social order, and security was Clara's mother's favorite feeling, outranked only by virtuous womanhood. (She was cousin Charles's favorite aunt, after all.)

That terrible afternoon, Charles, wanting to slow Clara, had perhaps called out to her, announcing his gaining presence. Surely his voice would have been as startling to her as the drift of a phantom, her path suddenly narrower—the low branches more like claws, her breath too shallow for her pace.

Even before what happened happened, Brookhants students had plenty of stories about those woods. They had stories about Samuel and Jonathan Rash, the brothers who had farmed the land more than a hundred years prior, stories about their spite-filled feud and its strange, resulting tower.

The students also had stories about the fog that gathered and hung in the woods, heavy as gray hopsacking dunked in a well. It blew in from the ocean only to drape itself over every leaf and briar, filling gaps and crevices, lingering for too long and hiding too much. And they of course had stories about the yellow jackets, everywhere, always, the humming of the yellow jackets, the flick of them about you. The woods were haunted, the students said. The woods were the source of sinister nighttime things that might scuttle their way across the lawns and up a vine-choked wall and in through your open window, until they were at the foot of your bed, now stomach, now pillow.

But you had to cross through the woods to get to the orchard, and usually, at least for Clara, every single time before this time, the orchard had been worth it.

The orchard, *with Flo,* and with Flo's hands and mouth, too.

It's worth mentioning that some of the Brookhants students also had stories about Flo and Clara. There were several girls who knew them well, their friends—girls who joined their club: the Plain Bad Heroine Society. And there were others, many others, who admired them. A few who probably envied them. But there was also a group, small but not insignificant, who felt quite bothered by them, who were wary of them; wary of their ideas and passions and the boldness with which they seemed to claim them.

Maybe this small but not insignificant group was even afraid of them.

The Black Oxford is an apple more associated with Maine than with Rhode Island. It was a somewhat old-fashioned and unusual variety, even in 1902, but you could still find them then in various places across New England. Brookhants was one of those places. Its orchard had nearly two dozen trees sprouting plum-black apples, like something planted by a witch in a fairy tale.* The orchard was a place that, before Flo, Clara had visited only once or twice in her previous years

---

* The orchard *was* planted at Brookhants even before the Rash brothers took charge of the land. Black Oxford apples were regionally favored both for cider-making and for their ability to store well for long periods.

of Brookhants education. But then came black-apple-eating, soft-kissing/hard-kissing, well-traveled, sure-of-foot-and-voice, fluent-in-Italian-and-adequate-in-French, and just generally delirious-making Flo. *And* came Mary MacLane's book. And everything changed.

(Though not in that order. The book came first.)

This was something else the onlookers later argued about: Was Clara carrying the book when she took off toward the woods that day?

That a copy, a much-loved and underlined and page-marked copy, was found near the bodies, is undisputed. *The Story of Mary MacLane* (the scandalous debut memoir of its namesake nineteen-year-old) had a deep crimson binding when the dust jacket was removed. A red book was not hard to spot when left almost indecently splayed against a cluster of ferns so enormous they looked like half-opened green parasols. Even in such a gruesome scene, the book stood out. Much was later made of the underlined section it was found opened to:

I have lived my nineteen years buried in an environment at utter variance with my natural instincts, where my inner life is never touched, and my sympathies rarely, if ever, appealed to. I never disclose my real desires or the texture of my soul. Never, that is to say, to any one except my one friend, the anemone lady.

—And so every day of my life I am playing a part; I am keeping an immense bundle of things hidden under my cloak.

It was no secret on campus how enthralled with that book both Flo and Clara were. (And, more broadly, with Mary MacLane herself.) As you likely already know, they'd formed the Plain Bad Heroine Society as a way to show their devotion.

But who brought the book into the trees that day isn't as certain as the fact that a copy was with them in their final moments.

Some of the onlookers said Clara was carrying nothing at all on her march from the motorcar, while others swore that they saw the book gripped in her hand as she crossed the lawn. Though she'd been seen with it so frequently that school year, it's natural to wonder if they might have imagined that part.

It was, after all, *the book*, the one that brought her and Flo together, the one that said, printed there on the page, the things Clara had once believed were her private thoughts alone. It was the book that Clara so often thought that truly, *truly,* she could have written herself. She could have had it sewn to her palm and still be unencumbered by it.

And if you asked Clara's mother, she would have told you that Clara might as well have had that vile book sewn to her hand for the length of their summer in Newport, because there it had been, day in and day out.

Later, when Clara's traveling case was searched—for it had been left there on the ground next to the car* where Charles had dumped it—no copy of *The Story of Mary MacLane* was found. This would seem to suggest that Clara Broward did take her book with her into the woods that day.

It would seem to suggest that, except for this: in a letter sent after her daughter's unfortunate death, Mrs. Broward told her sister, in great detail, of the cold comfort she had taken in burning Clara's copy of that *hateful book* in the flames of her bedroom fireplace. She wrote that she began at page one, tore it free, fed the fire, and continued on until the red binding flapped empty, like a mouth with no teeth. And then she burned the empty mouth.

Mrs. Broward certainly believed that she did this to the *only* copy of Mary MacLane's memoir that she knew her daughter to have ever owned.

Of course, all of this was only spoken of later.

Perhaps you already know that when the story of Flo's and Clara's

---

* Did I tell you that Charles had named his car America? I hate him so much.

deaths reached the press, Mary MacLane herself, then staying nearby at a seaside hotel in Massachusetts, was asked to issue a statement. She's reported to have said, "I wish I could have known those girls." This was both uncharacteristically short for a Mary MacLane statement to the press in those days and the thing that the two of them no doubt would have wanted to hear the most from her.

Before we move on, one more thing about that copy of the book found with the bodies. It was handled by faculty and police, Pinkertons and even Flo's and Clara's bereaved family members (not one of whom claimed it as belonging to their kin). And then, not so long after, it was *misplaced*. Officially misplaced, anyway. Lost. Unable to be located when it was asked after by reporters who felt sure they'd missed something the first time they'd gone through it and who now wanted another look.

Even Principal Libbie Brookhants˙ herself could not find it. She was the school's young if capable founder. She knew its grounds and buildings better than anyone else left alive, and she told those doubting reporters that she had made a point of looking for the copy in question in every place on campus that it might have conceivably ended up; it simply could not be found.

The book was gone.

This part won't get more pleasant with my stalling so we might as well get on with it. And just so you know: the facts, such as they are, get foggier from here on out, too.

We know, based on where the girls were later found, that at some point Clara veered from the orchard path. Whether this was due to Charles's gaining speed or some tactic meant to prevent that from happening, I cannot say, but it proved a fateful choice.

To be sure, that path had its own difficulties, but now a tangle of hailstorm-downed branches and thick undergrowth snagged at the

---

˙ Also remember this name, Readers.

soft fabric of Clara's dress and tripped up her steps. When she was found, her skirt was clogged with thorns and twigs, shredded from the things in the understory that had caught her.

In fact, Clara seemed to forge directly into a section of woods that the Brookhants students called the Tricky Thicket, an area of bizarrely dense growth—the trees leafier, the brambles bramblier— fed by a hot spring. It was said that even in winter, even with snow otherwise all around, the ground in that patch stayed thawed and ferns grew lush and green, and ripe blackberries might be found.

Perhaps thinking it would provide her with cover, Clara now much more slowly made her way through this thicket. And if she'd also been looking backward, every so often, checking on Charles's unhinged approach, then that too would have hindered her speed.

Though they'd left the path, the two cousins were now close enough to the orchard, to Flo, that she would have heard their shouts. Or screams. It's likely that this was why she came running toward them, hoping for Clara but finding Charles first. When that stupid man was brought from the woods, he had a black eye and a bleeding face swollen from more than stings alone.

"She charged me like a drunken bear," he told a reporter from the *Providence Daily Journal.* He was talking about Flo, who, he said, had attacked him. In an interview given from his sickbed he called her "a real she beast. More animal than girl. She had something in her hand, a stone or stick." He also said that her actions toward him had proved him right, and that what he'd previously told Clara about Flo was now made undeniably true. "That girl was no lady! She was a ruffian bastard—some foreign-born devil who exerted her depraved influence over my cousin. Clara was only too female-minded to see it."

When asked why he had been chasing his cousin in the first place, Charles had said, as if obvious: "We had not finished our conversation to my satisfaction. And before we could do so she openly defied me, playing up to her schoolmates. I knew that her mother, my beloved aunt, would want me to correct that sort of insolence at once. So I did."

Charles explained that during her weekend at home, Clara had been issued an ultimatum regarding her family's expectations for her future comportment at Brookhants: if Clara wanted to continue to attend the school for her senior year, and to graduate with her class, she would immediately discontinue her friendship with Florence Hartshorn and cease all activities related to *The Story of Mary MacLane*. (And as you now know, Mrs. Broward apparently believed that even continuing to possess a copy of that book was an activity related to it.)

Wretched Charles might have admitted that Flo attacked him, but why and how she did so was as unclear (and speculated about) in 1902 as it is today. Was it only to interrupt his pursuit of Clara? Or did Flo witness something else between them? Something worse? And when did she do it, exactly—before the yellow jacket attack or while it was already underway?

Because in the end, Readers, the yellow jackets are the thing. I told you that at the start.

What Clara did, in the middle of the Tricky Thicket, was step over a fallen log and directly into a ground nest of them. And this particular ground nest was of a size not only unusual, but seemingly impossible for a northern state like Rhode Island.

Yellow jacket colonies in places as far north as New England are supposed to last only one season. They can't overwinter, because the region is too frozen and food scarce for anyone but the queen, fed fat off the sweets of her minions, to survive. In places like Florida, warm even in January, it's not so unusual for ground nests to continue season after season—for decades, sometimes, with dozens of queens ordering around thousands of workers—the cycle of birthing and feeding, eating and building, churning along without pause. But that's not supposed to be the way in Rhode Island, which has a winter with snow and cold and frozen ground.

Just not in the Tricky Thicket.

And so here it was: a yellow jacket nest to build your nightmares from, its paper chambers stretching in underground layers until it was almost the size of three of Charles's cars parked in a row. And Clara's foot, slipping off the edge of a mossy log, landed in the uppermost layer of the nest's papery frame, where it promptly sank and sank, up to her knee it sank, wrenching her to a stop. She would have had only moments to comprehend what had happened, why the ground had given way, because now the yellow jackets were coming, furious and streaming up from the rip like a rattling chain shot into the sky.

Remember that a yellow jacket is not a honeybee. A honeybee has a barbed stinger that lodges in flesh, which means that it can sting you only once before it leaves that stinger in you and dies.

But a smooth-stingered yellow jacket can and will sting you multiple times.

And thousands of vengeful, broken-homed yellow jackets stinging you multiple times?

Charles later said that he heard his cousin's screams, but there was simply no time to reach her: Clara was swallowed up by the swarm at once, as if she now wore a writhing mummy wrap of yellow jackets, a pulsing black-and-yellow outline that smothered her until she was now them.

At some point Flo must have charged toward Clara, presumably to help her, and was at once wrapped in her own cloak of yellow jackets. And Charles—of course, fucking Charles—ran away. But not before pushing his now-useful driving goggles over his eyes. The goggles and the running away did not prevent him from being stung, nor did they keep him from swelling with hives and passing out on the path leading back to the school. But they did help to keep him alive.

Later, horrible Charles would say that he'd found great purpose and meaning in the fact of his life being spared that day. By all accounts he used that purpose to idle away his remaining days, spending his inheritance while failing at several half-hearted business ventures and in general behaving like the brutish, moneyed bowl of rancid bowels that he was. This behavior lasted for a period of several years, until he was killed on the maiden voyage of a very big ship that met a very bad end.* But thankfully this story is not about cousin Charles, so let us leave him to his turbid depths.

---

* I'm not kidding. And no, I won't draw you like one of my French girls.

Death from anaphylaxis is not known to be gentle. There were some signs, in the shape of the smashed undergrowth, in the piles of vomit found nearby, that our strong, young heroines did struggle together for a time.

How long Flo and Clara clung to each other, how hard they might have worked to move beyond the yellow jackets, the nest, is impossible to ascertain—and would, I'm sure, be quite difficult to put into words, even if we did know. Given the sheer number of stings each received—and so many of them to their faces—it couldn't have been long before they both succumbed to the thickening dark from which they would not wake.

That they might have had the chance, in their final moments, to say just how much they meant to one another, *the real desires and textures of their souls,* is a most doubtful thing given the horror of their circumstances. What is important to remember, Readers, is that they *had* said these things to each other before those circumstances befell them.

They were discovered very near to the place in the nest where Clara's foot had made the tear. There were so many angry yellow jackets still swarming the area, like a buzzing net draped over the whole of the thicket, that the responding Brookhants faculty, and soon after, the Tiverton police, determined that a controlled fire was the only way to get near enough to bring the girls out.

Brookhants students later told stories of flaming yellow jackets making their way from their now-burning nest, through the woods and onto campus, before drowning themselves, bodies hissing, in the fountain in front of Main Hall. Apparently, there were so many singed yellow jacket carcasses floating dead atop its surface the following morning that students began dipping their hands in to take them: death souvenirs. Eventually, the groundskeeper was sent to clear them with a net. Despite this carcass-skimming, the water is said to have soon turned fetid, an oily black algae growing along its sides and surface. So rank was this water, so unclean, that within days the school had no choice but to drain, scrub, and refill the fountain. This, like so many Brookhants stories, may only be the stuff of dorm-room-lights-off legend.

Brookhants students later told stories of flaming yellow jackets . . .
drowning themselves, bodies hissing, in the fountain.

But then, stranger things have happened. Even, especially, at Brookhants.

That our complicated, wonderful heroines were found twined together, hands clasped and heart to heart, has never been disputed. But given the time it took to rouse awful Charles and make enough sense of his stupid mutterings to locate them, and then to assess the situation, bring the supplies, and burn the nest—coupled with the number of stings each girl received—it is of no surprise that Flo's and Clara's mortal bodies had not fared well.

Any exposed skin was welted: their hands and necks and, the worst, their faces, which were now balloon masks of protruding lips and swollen eyes. Clara's eyes had been bleeding, the tracks of blood dried down her cheeks. The attack was so severe, so ferocious, that their topography of red hives, a telltale sign of the anaphylaxis, was quite obscured by bruising. The unfortunate students who saw them carried out of the woods—for in their makeshift planning, the officials had forgotten to bring sheets to cover them—said their faces looked like bitten and rotting Black Oxford apples. More than one girl made that comparison.[*]

I did tell you this story was ghastly.

You might think it an improvement on said ghastliness that within three years of this terrible day, the Brookhants School for Girls was closed, its buildings left empty and wanting for students who would not arrive. But you should also know that before that happened, three more heroines died on the property, each in a most troubling way.

It's true, of course, that all death is troubling to those of us left alive to bear witness, but certainly among the most troubling of all are the ugly, unexpected deaths of young people just starting to understand who and how they might be in the world. Or how they might remake the world to better be in it.

Perhaps equally troubling are the deaths of older people submerged in deep regret.

---

[*] And many who have claimed to have seen them since have said the same.

Everything else to come in these pages comprises the story of three heroines from the present and more heroines from the past and how they all collided around Brookhants, and a book, and also a book about Brookhants.

I'll say it again: Brookhants, and a book, and a book about Brookhants.

And who, you ask, am I? The voice telling you to come this way, to follow me? Some hazy apparition with a beckoning hand? A thousand yellow jackets shaped to look like a body with intention, one prone to scatter into diverging paths if provoked?

I can promise you that by the time we reach the end, you'll know me much better than I'll know you. (And if I seem to know things I shouldn't, or couldn't possibly, well that's part of our bargain. I'll cite my research when I can, but when I can't: I do now ask for your trust in me to fill in the gaps as I see fit. I can see quite a lot from this vantage point.)

Finally, let me say, right up front, how sorry I am about all the potential for puns. I cannot help that the school's name is Brookhants* and that it's said to be haunted. Whether it was, in fact, haunted even before Clara, Flo, and the yellow jackets depends on where and how you start the story of Brookhants, and for how many years you're willing to trace it.

I told you, this is only one way to tell it. And only one place to end it.

And perhaps it hasn't ended yet.

So let's begin.

---

* Don't come at me, linguists: Despite its spelling it is pronounced "Brook-*haunts*" and *not* "Brook-hantz" as in "ants." This is because that's how Harold Brookhants's last name was always pronounced, how Harold himself pronounced it. What would you have me do about it now, so many years later?

....

In the summer of 20— in Hollywood, **Audrey Wells** watched as her mom, Caroline Wells, used the wipers to try to clear a confetti of ash from their windshield. This left a gray smear across their view, a hazy blotting out that matched the smoke blotting out the California sun.

Now it was like seeing the world through the skin of a ghost.

Los Angeles was on fire: palm trees with flame canopies where there should have been leaves and hillside houses slumped into towers of char like the oversize remnants of those black snake fireworks. One blaze had jumped the freeway and missed their own neighborhood by a mile. For now. The same could not be said for the homes of some of Caroline's still-new(ish) clients. Caroline Wells: scream queen turned real estate agent.

"And dog food," Caroline was saying, still messing with the wipers and now the blue spray stuff as well. That did the trick. The ghost skin washed away. "The Chavezes have one of those poodle mixes. He's bitty," she added, "so I've never been scared of him." She looked quickly at Audrey and tacked on: "I haven't."

"Dog food," Audrey repeated as she swiped out of Instagram and into her notes app to type it. This was not an item typically found on their shopping lists. Or, like, ever before.

Audrey had only recently moved back in with her mother after three years of paying an unsustainable amount of rent for her own place in Santa Monica. Both of them had been working hard not to act like it was a concession, this living-together-again thing. (Hence this joint shopping trip.) It was a choice. An opportunity. It was surely not some sign of failure for either of them.

Audrey noticed her mom touching the thin white scars on her face, one hand on the steering wheel, one hand tracing her jaw. Caroline used to do this all the time, a tic, but maybe she did it less so these days.

Something occurred to Audrey. "Are we sure their dog is OK? I literally just read something about all the missing pets—I mean because of the fires—they escape. Do you know for sure they even still have it?"

"Shit," Caroline said, dropping her hand from her jaw as she messily merged them two lanes over, a chorus of honks in their wake. "I have no idea. I don't want to text them to ask if their dog is dead on top of everything else."

Audrey had a decent imagination for personal tragedy that blooms from a chaos of random events, both because she was an actor and it was her job to, and also because, as you might already know: she had been party to a version of it. Not a "your new house just went up in smoke and your dog died, too" version, it's true. But hers involved those scars on her mother's face and it had been, if not tragic, at least ugly in a very public way.

They were pulling into a busy strip mall with all the stores to buy all the things on this list they'd been making. Not that buying these things—bananas and bottled water, socks and hand wipes, crying chocolate (as Caroline called it), and yes, dog food for the dog that may or may not still be alive—would make any of this easier for the families with char where their houses had once been. But maybe some of it would give them at least a moment or two of comfort, a few simple needs provided for. Years later, Audrey still remembered the people who'd sent food baskets and flowers after Caroline's incident. And she also remembered the people who hadn't.

Plus, you have to do something, right? When things like this happen? You have to do something or you're left doing nothing, and that, in Audrey's experience, made you feel helpless, and helplessness was a feeling she despised. In others, sure, but mostly in herself.

"Should we split up?" Caroline asked as she parked them near a shopping cart stall. "Divide and conquer?"

"No," Audrey said. She was back to scrolling Instagram. "That never works. I can never find you where you say you'll be and then I'm locked out of the car and you're not answering my texts."

"That's a lot," Caroline said, her own phone in her face.

"It is a lot."

"If you learned to drive, you'd be the one in control of the keys."

Audrey's refusal to get her driver's license—even at the age of twenty-three—was a sticky spot between them, one that ultimately also linked back to Caroline's past public debacle. *Shouldn't I be the one too scared to drive?* was a thing Caroline had said to Audrey more than once.

"Let's do it, then," Caroline now said to the back of her daughter's phone. She waited. Nothing. "Aud," she said, "I'm leaving you." She opened her car door to emphasize her point.

At once a yellow jacket flew in through the open door, though its path sent it over the seats and to the rear window. Caroline didn't notice it because she was looking intently at Audrey, and Audrey didn't notice because she was looking intently at her phone.

More specifically, she was looking at the Instagram stories of one Harper Harper, who couldn't have been more on fire herself right then than if she'd been standing in the flame-filled Hollywood Hills. *The* Harper Harper—indie-film-darling turned celesbian-megastar-influencer. She was supposedly on a rocket ship to awards season—seemingly any awards season, all of them. The out-of-nowhere actor with enough edge to be authentic and enough talent to make a career for herself. The one who hadn't been around long enough to have that promise curdle in any of the ways it might. Yet.

Audrey had been around. Audrey's mom, Caroline Wells, the newly minted real estate agent waiting beside her, had been around even longer. Eventually that rocket ship would lose its fuel. It did for everyone, except, like, Meryl Streep. Eventually even Harper Harper wouldn't be so new, her talent seen as so *raw* and *perceptive,* or whatever other adjectives the critics were using at the moment. Soon enough, people would tire of her—the projects she chose, who she was or wasn't dating, what she posted or didn't post. That especially.

But not just yet. For the moment, Harper Harper was still on fire.

And she would be bringing that fire to her new movie, which just so happened to be Audrey's new movie: *The Happenings at Brookhants*. Because Harper was attached, it already had buzz. It might even be a chance for her, Audrey Wells, to come out from the creep of her mother's long shadow and her own childhood name.

Probably that wouldn't happen. The role of Eleanor Faderman was small, a part for a minor character actress. Whatever that meant. (Not a lead is what it meant.) But there was some meat to Eleanor, some depth—and she was to have a scene with Harper Harper herself. That might be enough to get Audrey noticed.

And more than that, there was this: for the last sixteen months, Audrey Wells hadn't been offered any roles at all. Not one. Not until *The Happenings at Brookhants* came along. Her transition from preteen to twentysomething actor hadn't quite been a transition. She was stuck in between, in the nowhere. Audrey and Caroline might have been decidedly B-list, but they did have a Hollywood past. And because of Caroline's various public incidents, that past was now often thought of as more significant than any of the roles either of them had ever played. (And that was only when anyone was thinking of them at all.)

Almost certainly this movie, like most movies Audrey had been in, would end up being disappointing. But this was still the short window she loved best: anticipating it. The promise of what the project might be if everything lined up just so and all of the usual things, like script changes or test-audience feedback or, worst of all, her own mediocrity, didn't fuck it up.

Of course, Caroline couldn't know each dip and contour in this particular coil of her daughter's thoughts, but she could guess at some of them, especially when Audrey tilted her phone enough so they could both watch the feed she was so taken with: a handheld video of a sunburned Harper Harper cannonballing into a teal mountain lake.

The whole setup was a notch too Instagram perfect to be believed, a few water droplets even landing on the lens. Then came a slow-motion clip of Harper and her little brother having a splash war in the same lake. Then another video, this one longer than the first: Harper dancing on the large deck of a lake house with a woman whose lopsided hairstyle manages to look good even while she bops her head aggressively to pop music. This person (someone Audrey had googled earlier) is Harper's current girlfriend, Annie Meng: a twenty-five-year-old visual artist who had, the year prior, sold the entirety of her first public exhibition of collages. (Two of them, said the internet, to Oprah.) They keep dancing while strings of twinkle lights blow around overhead and the real twinkle of stars stretches out behind them. And then into the frame comes a woman wearing an apron that says *World's Okayest Cook*. She waves a spatula at the camera and mouths the Roxette lyrics. Her hair is thin and her cheeks hollow, but it's clear that Harper has her mouth and chin. This resemblance is confirmed when the screen shows a series of popping pink hearts and the handwritten caption my mama can dance! Audrey can't remember ever before seeing Harper's mother in one of her posts.

"Is this Pottery Barn sponcon?" Caroline asked. "I mean I do like the apron. I thought she didn't talk to her mom?"

"I guess she does now," Audrey said. She had started the feed again, the same clips playing one after the next.

"Good for them for doing the work," Caroline said. She sounded like therapy speak in a way that made Audrey bristle, but since therapy had saved her, its argot was her default.

"It's one edited video."

"One more than none," Caroline said. She turned to really look at Audrey, who was not looking back at her, so Caroline put her hand over the phone screen until Audrey did. "What's this bringing up for you? Did she post something else about the movie?"

"Oh my God, it's not *bringing up* anything," Audrey said so quickly that she knew she didn't sound convincing. She wasn't convincing. In fact, she'd watched all of these clips earlier, before they'd left the house. Now here she was watching them again.

"I'm ready, we can go." Audrey closed the app and dropped the phone into her bag, a vintage crocodile Hermès purchased by her father, the exact kind of reckless gift he liked best to send her when he was feeling guilty about things. (Audrey had twice made arrangements to sell the bag for cash but hadn't gone through with it either time.) Her father also still held the mortgage on the house she and her mother lived in, even though they were the ones who (almost always) made the monthly payments. Even though he now lived in London. Even though he and Caroline had separated right before her scar-causing incident and divorced right after.

Caroline fished around in the cupholder—*clicks* and *clacks*—and then held her closed fist out to Audrey. "Here."

Audrey put out her own open palm and Caroline dropped two crystals into it—one pink, one purple. They were raw and jagged, each about the size of a wine cork.

"Amethyst," Audrey said, turning them over and feeling their rough then glassy surfaces against her skin. "And what?"

"Good," Caroline said, surprised. "And rose quartz. In your case it's for balancing energy and bringing calm."

Audrey nodded slowly, not necessarily condescendingly but with a deliberate effort to appear to her mother like she was humoring her. Which she was.

"Whatever helps you to let go of negativity, yeah? And maybe encourages a little self-confidence? I'm not asking you to suck on them, Audrey."

"It didn't even occur to me that that would be an option."

Caroline checked her reflection in the rearview, raking her hand through the side of her hair. "You know it's supposed to be millennials who are way into inclusive spiritual practices—so of course it's my child who rejects crystals out of hand."

"Do you see what's in my hand right now?" Audrey opened her fist again. There were red indentations along three of her fingers where the crystals had pressed into her skin.

"Now put them in your pocket."

"I don't always have pockets," Audrey said. But she shifted in her seat and put them there anyway. And then she said, in a way she hoped she delivered like an afterthought even though it wasn't, "I would just like to be good in it this time."

"Oh, honey—"

Audrey cut her off: "This one time, I want to be good and I want the movie to be good and I want it to matter. I don't want to have to make excuses for it."

I want, I want, I want, she did not say.

Before Caroline could try some other tactic meant to assure Audrey, a man called out to them from the parking lot. "OhmyGod. I'm so sorry—I know this is tacky and gauche and we don't *do this* in LA but I'm wearing your face right now. Like literally!"

Caroline hadn't shut her door since she'd opened it several minutes before and now this person—sweaty at the temples, puffy red beard—was moving even closer to that open-door access while unbuttoning his flannel shirt as quickly as his fingers would do it. "Pleasejustwaitasec," he said. "I have to show you."

"Mom, shut your door," Audrey said with more panic than she'd later admit.

Caroline did and hit the lock button, too.

"No—it's only my shirt!" the man said, his voice now muffled by the car door, so he sounded like he was talking to them through a soup-can phone. He worked the last button and then flapped his shirt open to reveal the T-shirt he was wearing beneath, which was printed with the movie poster for *House Mother 2: She's Coming for You*—the title in a garish, neon-pink font that screamed above the stalking shadow of the House Mother, her gray wig askew, a glinting knife in her hand as she came for the blonde in a bloody nightgown who was running, breasts first, as if into the camera and off the poster entirely.

The blonde was then-nineteen-year-old Caroline Wells.

"I'm a Jules Junkie! We always go when they play the trilogy at Vista. Did you know they do that?" The man now held his eyes so wide open they looked like something you'd draw in Sharpie on the side of a balloon to please a toddler. Jules Coburn was the final girl sorority sister Caroline had played in both *House Mother 2* and *3: Now She's Coming for Me.*

---

* To refresh your memories: The original final girl from the first *House Mother* movie, Samantha (Sam) Heywood, was played by Melanie Patrick. This was Mela-

Caroline lowered her window. "I was there the first time. I did the talk back after."

"Oh shit—no, I knew that!" the man said, shaking his head. "Jesus, I *saw* you there! I'm sorry I'm being so weird. I just—I'm a huge fan, which I know you must hear all the time, but I'm actually wearing this shirt today, and fucking here you are."

"I'm glad you showed me," Caroline said. She opened her car door again.

The guy now grinned a shy grin, proud that he'd won her over. He even took a step back to show that he didn't want anything more from her than what he'd gotten. "Jules kicks Sam's ass. I don't give a fuck what the neckbeards on Reddit say."

"There wouldn't have been a Jules without a Sam, though," Audrey said.

"Right—no, I know," the man said, peering past Caroline as if he hadn't realized Audrey was there until she'd spoken. Maybe he hadn't. "I mean—all respect to Melanie Patrick, of course. I'm counting down the days until my kid is old enough to watch with me. We named her Jules—shit!" He made his eyes big again. "I totally buried the lede! I, like, completely forgot until this second that my kid is named after you. Sort of named after you. You get it."

"I do," Caroline said. "Thank you. That's a real honor."

"Thank *you*! My husband's head is gonna explode when I get home. He was the one who was supposed to go to the store today and he bailed. It will drive him crazy for the rest of time that he missed you."

"You should definitely get a picture, then," Audrey said. She leaned around her mother to better see him. "To rub it in."

---

nie Patrick's first and final film role. She and her boyfriend, actor Mars Rissini (who also appeared briefly in the film), infamously died in a car accident after leaving the *House Mother* premiere party. Overnight their movie, which had been critically derided, achieved cult-classic status and became an entirely unexpected box office hit of 1987, thus launching the *House Mother* trilogy and the need for a different final girl in installments two and three—enter Caroline Wells.

The man smiled at her, but it was to Caroline that he said, "Really? I didn't want to ask but I mean I *did* want to ask. Would you?"

They all met at the back of the car. "Here," Audrey said, reaching for his phone, "I'll take it."

"You sure?" the man asked, hesitant. "Or we can just selfie it—that's classic."

"You can still get a selfie, but you'll want at least one that shows your whole shirt. That's the best part."

She took his phone, took several pictures. The man beamed. Her mother beamed.

Behind them, against the car's rear window, the trapped yellow jacket smashed itself up and down, up and down, unable to get free.

In Montana, **Harper Harper** was out on the deck photographing wildfire smoke through the pine trees while listening to her little brother Ethan tell a long story about a trick he'd pulled on his friends. The story seemed more BS than not, but Harper liked that he still wanted to impress her, especially given how infrequently they saw each other anymore.

She pulled a crushed package of menthol Pall Malls—the green box—from her back pocket. Seeing this, Ethan interrupted himself to ask, "Can I have one, too?"

"Sure," she said, tapping out her own and putting it between her lips before fishing for the matchbook she'd wedged inside the box. "You can have one the way I got my first one."

Ethan, being eleven, immediately sensed the con in this offer and wilted his thick eyebrows as he asked: "Which was how, exactly?"

"Uncle Rob saw me steal some from where Grandma kept them on top of the fridge—and before I could even do anything with them, he surprised me in my room carrying the whole rest of the carton and made me smoke one after another until I threw up." She struck the match, brought it to her mouth.

"Did you?"

She nodded. "I only got through like two or three. Grandma was pissed. At both of us."

"I can beat three," Ethan said. "Let me try. I won't throw up. I've vaped before, anyway. The watermelon kind."

"That's dumb," Harper said. "Way too dumb a move for a kid like you."

Ethan offered the inevitable response: "But it's not too dumb for you?"

"It was. It is. I just wasn't smart enough to know it then. I speak to you now from a place of regret."

"A place of regret and cigarettes."

She nodded. Fuck, he was smart. She liked him so much.

Ethan shook his head like she was a bad spokesperson for her cause—she was—and then reached for the orange soda can on the railing. He was lifting it to take a drink when a yellow jacket that had been tucked inside its open mouth pushed out that sticky entrance and flew up at his face. Ethan shrieked and dropped the can. It fizzed a geyser of orange soda that quickly turned into a pool of orange soda, some also landing on his bare feet. He was wearing only swim trunks.

"Scared ya, huh?" Harper asked. "You OK?"

"I'm fine," Ethan said, already bending to inspect the now-several yellow jackets hopping about their new orange soda pond. "I just hate bees."

"That's not a bee," Harper said. "It's a yellow jacket. You'd better be careful running around without shoes on. They're mean."

"I'm mean," Ethan said.

"Who's mean?" Annie asked as she came out the sliding door carrying bottles of beer.

"Your butt," Ethan and Harper said together. This had been their big joke for days.

"You two are very related." Annie handed Harper a bottle.

Harper smiled at the comment but also glanced through the open doorway and into the house to see if her mom was up from her nap. She didn't seem to be. "Do you mind putting this in a mug or something for me? I don't want to have the bottle out in her face if she wakes up."

"Of course," Annie said, reaching to take back the bottle. "I'm sorry, I didn't even think about it."

"No, it's fine. Just precautions."

They'd been keeping their alcohol in a cooler in their room. It wasn't like they couldn't drink, or like Shelly, Harper's mom, had asked them not to, but . . . It would have been better, Harper knew, if they hadn't brought the beer at all. But they had.

"Grandpa still has beer in the fridge," Ethan said, like he was both reading her mind and tattling at the same time. "Plus, him and Grandma order those number drinks when we go out to dinner."

"Seven and sevens," Harper said, picturing the glasses, pin-striped in yellow and pink, that her grandparents served the drinks in whenever making them at home.

"You don't have to hide it," he said. "Mom's not gonna explode if she sees it. She's been doing good."

"That's all the more reason, don't you think—if she's been doing good?"

Ethan grinned at her and she recognized the expression as just like her own minus the tooth gap because Ethan was wearing the braces she'd never gotten. (Because she was the one now paying his orthodontist bills.) Their matching grins made her melancholy, or some feeling of indistinct sadness, and to clear it away she told him to leave the bugs alone and finish his story.

Harper was right then *between projects* and on vacation in her home state with Annie, who she'd been seeing for a while in a mostly casual way that was maybe now less casual since she'd brought her there. They were at the place on a mountain lake Harper had bought for her mother as a reward, sort of, for her newly claimed sobriety (third time's a charm) and their still-recent reconciliation. You'd know this if you were following her Instagram during those days, and if you weren't: What was your problem? Supposedly everyone was following Harper Harper's Instagram during those days.*

---

* Or at least 18.6 million of us were.

Montana was also on fire. Acres and acres of the state—a million, no hyperbole, Readers, a million acres, including a swath of Glacier National Park—burned red orange to black, the sky overcast not with clouds but with smoke that wouldn't clear. Harper had posted a video where gray ash fell like strands of disintegrating clouds. Lots of someone elses had tagged shots of her and Annie and Ethan delivering bottled water to the overworked fire crews in her old hometown, the place of her previous life.

In two days, she would be due back in LA to work on *The Happenings at Brookhants*. She was a producer on this one, which was new and somewhat overwhelming, TBH. Especially because, at least at the moment, Annie at her side holding two coffee mugs of beer—not to mention the lapping lake, the falling ash, her brother trying to show off for both of them by wildly chucking rocks over the railing—was making her life in LA seem very distant. She wouldn't have particularly minded if everything off the edge of the deck, the whole country over to LA, disappeared in that smoke for another ten days or so and she could stay here and shake lake water from her ears while encouraging her mother to go ahead and turn up the Roxette mix she'd been playing on a loop since they'd arrived.

This was the dangerous thing about coming home and being with family: the collision with her previous self.

Only six summers before, Harper had stepped onto her first set for her first film role of any kind. She had tried, then, to act like she knew it was a fluke, some random one-off chance for her to play movie star, but the whole time she'd held inside her the terrifying— it *was* terrifying—knowledge that there was hope in this situation she'd dumbly lucked into. Real hope. Hope that it could potentially change things for her forever, if she didn't screw it up.

She was still young, but she was even younger then, only eighteen and pretty sure that even getting on that set was somebody else's major fuckup that would soon be discovered, and so she had better take advantage of it quick, because if she messed it up she'd have taken something away from not only her own future, but her family's future, too. (But, no pressure.)

And the most unbelievable part was that she'd pulled it off. Like, she'd ~~fooled~~ convinced *a lot* of people to believe that she was some sort of beautiful hick-town prodigy, some rare, talented bird they'd discovered in the wilds of Montana. It was too Hollywood to be believed.

And of course, that was Hollywood, exactly.

Only weeks before that first film, that first set, she'd been sleeping on her uncle Rob's couch and right on the slippery edge of a life that might have ended up eventually looking a lot like the one her mom had long been living: get fucked up to escape your days until you don't really give a shit about your days—and no one else gives much of a shit about them, either. (But only because you've made it so they can't—because if they do, you'll con them or pull them under with you.)

It was a life that Harper knew some of her friends (were most of them ever really her friends?) were living right now, in towns not far away from the deck on which she stood. In fact, if not for the smoke, she could've seen some of those towns' windows wink in the setting sun, or flash like cameras against the dark mountainside. She was that close.

But instead of that life, here was chic Annie pulling off her embroidered cover-up so she could climb into the Jacuzzi while Ethan ran to get a water gun from inside the house where their so-happy and steady and sober (for now) mother was napping.

And here was Harper Harper* herself, standing on the deck of

---

* It's doubtful that anyone reading this hasn't already heard the story of Harper Harper's name, but in case you haven't it seems essential to explain it.

Harper Harper's mother, Shelly Harper, was only fifteen when she gave birth to our future celesbian, and she was, the very week she delivered, reading *To Kill a Mockingbird* in her American Lit class at school.

And as the story goes (from the lips of Shelly Harper herself, during a podcast interview she did when Harper's first movie, *Dirt Town*, was released): *Back then I read all the time. I mean, I was a real reader. And that book was one of my favorites because Scout's such a charmer.*

the house she'd just bought, documenting her success one post after the next.

In Rhode Island, **Merritt Emmons** looked at the black rim of woods in the distance and shivered. Her brain lit up with a Henry James line as she did, one from *The Turn of the Screw*: "It wasn't a scene for a shudder." Not that she'd shuddered, really, she'd shivered, but in either case, it wasn't the scene for one, not with the popping firepit before her and Elaine roasting a marshmallow—roasting a fucking marshmallow!—next to her. Still, it couldn't be helped: Merritt shivered again. The breeze off the water was almost always cold at night. She'd been chilly enough to pull on her sweater earlier and now both it and her hair—thick with natural curls and her one physical vanity—were steeped in wood smoke and salt mist. In the shower the next morning the ghost-smoke would rinse down her body and swirl the drain. She'd always liked that aftereffect.

Merritt had what she thought was the latest draft of the *Happenings at Brookhants* script there on the seat beside her. She'd read the thing maybe seven times already, and it's not like she was even in it. She didn't need to learn the lines. (Though she had learned them.)

She'd brought the script outside, to the terrace, to read aloud the most obnoxious sections to Elaine, but Elaine had stopped being

---

Interviewer: *Did you ever think of naming her*—

Shelly (laughing and interrupting): *I know! I know! That's what everybody says. I know—I could've named her Scout. I get it, but I just didn't—that name didn't feel right. Harper Lee is the one who wrote the book and that's what I was wanting to celebrate. Does that make sense? Besides, I was young, so I thought that Marcus and I'd get married someday and then I'd take his last name and so would our daughter, so I didn't think about it, like, as being a problem or weird because I didn't think she would be Harper Lee Harper, you know? I thought she'd be Harper Lee Ridgeway. And also, for the record, I like my last name! I'm proud of my family, so why would that even bother me? Two Harpers? So what! And now, I mean, now she's made it to Hollywood so*—

(It's perhaps worth noting that Shelly Harper and Harper Harper weren't talking at the time this podcast was recorded.)

amused several lines earlier and Merritt had quit her performance. This was, after all, Elaine's home. She was the one to be deferred to.

Really, the fact of Merritt even having that script could be traced back to Elaine's involvement. That she, Merritt Emmons, rapidly aging wunderkind writer from collegetown Connecticut, would soon be getting on an airplane bound for Hollywood, where she would be assisting in preproduction work on the film being adapted from her first book, her only book, was still as unreal a thing to her as the things she'd written about in that book.

The literal ghosts of Clara Broward and Florence "Flo" Hartshorn Merritt did not think she believed in. But the story of their thwarted teenage love affair and all the weird and terrible things to come at Brookhants: those things were documented fact. Those things were verifiable. And Merritt was someone who very much liked to have things verified.

She also happened to have had access to the best in primary-source material—diaries and yearbooks and newspaper clippings—because Elaine, the woman now so carefully building a s'more next to Merritt on an oversize outdoor sectional, was Elaine Elizabeth Bishop Brookhants, and certainly one of those names should ring a bell for you, Readers, if you've been paying attention. She owned the estate, her family's estate, where what was left of the Brookhants School for Girls still stood. It was the same massive parcel of land that this, her historic ocean house, Breakwater,* was built upon.

But then, that's Elaine Elizabeth Bishop Brookhants money for you.

Merritt had been visiting the property since second grade, the year her mother received a grant from Elaine's research foundation, which kicked off a friendship between Professor Emmons and Elaine that lasted still. This happened back when Merritt's father was still alive.

He wasn't anymore.

The truth is, were Merritt's father still alive it's doubtful that she

---

* Also known as Spite Manor. (We'll get to that.)

would have written her book in the first place. What happened, or at least what she told herself about what happened, was this: her father killed himself and as soon after as she could stand to, she threw herself into doing a thing to distract herself from that fact. That thing was writing the book *The Happenings at Brookhants*. Elaine had encouraged her relentlessly. In fact, for a long time, the intensity of Elaine's belief in *her* was far greater than Merritt's own belief in the book.

"So you aren't happy with any of it?" Elaine now asked, fishing a peanut butter cup from the bag. Elaine claimed the earthiness from the peanut butter was a component so necessary as to outweigh any flimsy arguments from s'more traditionalists. She was a person like this: full of opinion and firm standing, she planted her flag in more topics than you could quite believe she could actually care about. Merritt loved this about her. Usually.

She was asking about the script and no, Merritt wasn't *happy* with it, but it's also true that her standards were both high and fickle. So many things felt so routinely disappointing to her that it seemed a shame to waste this evening on that mild unhappiness, one that she could admit to herself possibly wasn't deserved.

"It's just that it seems so blunted. But they also say you can't really tell anything from a screenplay." Merritt repeated this thing she'd heard and read and even said herself, though she did not believe it as fact when applied to her own work.

"I think it has its moments," Elaine said, offering Merritt half of the now-finished s'more. Only Elaine could manage to break a s'more so cleanly. Where were the crumbs? Where was the gooey mess of marshmallow all over her pressed black capris or the smear of melted chocolate across the collar of her white linen shirt? Elaine went on, "And it's really most useful to consider it as a means to an end, isn't it?"

"Useful how?"

"Well, if you add up the performances, the costumes, the sets and the sound effects and the score—on and on—and then all the months of editing besides, the screenplay suddenly feels quite small, doesn't it?"

"I don't know if *small* is the word I'd use," Merritt said. Her fingers were sticky and a few graham cracker shards were already down her shirt.

"Merritt, don't you think it's maybe a tad precious to be so constantly disagreeable about your success?" her mother asked from the other end of the couch, a laptop propped on her knees so that its screen lent a ghoulish cast to her face.

If it seems I've mistakenly forgotten to mention her before now, forgive me, Readers. Though you should know that introducing her this way is also indicative of the role she played in her daughter's life at that time.

"What you call preciousness I call critically informed realism," Merritt said. "And not one thing about this movie is yet a success. If it even gets made."

"What do you think, Lainey?" her mother's ghoul mouth asked, her eyes not leaving her laptop and her fingers flying over the keys. "Is sullen the new look for the young artist?"

"It's an old look," Elaine said. "But I still say the best way to get over old work is to get on to new work."

This was an even scabbier scab to pick, because Merritt was having a shit time writing anything new. She did have one idea, but—

"And *not* by resurrecting Truman Capote's worst effort," Elaine added, pressing her palms together and lifting them in mock prayer. "Please not that."

See, Readers? Nobody but Merritt seemed to like this idea very much.

Merritt thought that maybe her father would have liked it, that her taking it on would have delighted him, but when she thought things like this she never trusted them; it was so easy to make him stand in as phantom antagonist to her mother whenever she and her mother disagreed.

"You know one day soon you'll both be filled with shame," Merritt said. "You'll think, *This book is exactly as it should be and yet because I lack vision, I tried to talk her out of it.*"

"I look forward to that day, my darling," Elaine said, "though I doubt very much you'll get to it through *Answered Prayers*." She patted Merritt's leg a few times before standing.

"Ha!" Merritt's mother said. "That was perfectly placed."

"Give me the lowest form of humor and I'm the brightest star," Elaine said. Then she did some comic impression of a showgirl flouncing her curls before gathering the s'mores tray.

According to Elaine, Truman Capote's worst effort was his infamously unfinished final novel, *Answered Prayers*. Hence the pun.

She hovered. "I'll tell you what I think," she said. "You've always worked well here and you're also one to rise to the occasion, so write the thing and prove us wrong. At my age I'm so rarely proven wrong—I relish it when it happens."

"I will write it," Merritt said. "I am."

Elaine smiled. Then she and her tray were on the stone stairs that led to the upper terrace and the bank of open French doors spilling light from Breakwater's cavernous (and recently remodeled) kitchen. And then she was swallowed by her house.

Elaine's opinions took up so much space that Merritt felt their absence when she was again alone with her mother. She scrolled through movie buzz on gossip sites and feeds, her own face now a ghoul mask awash in the light of her phone screen. She returned, as she'd been doing for days, to Harper Harper's Instagram and read the comments on a post made not twenty minutes before—a shot from a Jacuzzi on a deck in the dark outdoors, *The Happenings at Brookhants* script cover page plainly legible from its perch on the Jacuzzi's rim, legible and also close to becoming script soup if it happened to be brushed by a stray appendage. Harper's caption: Taking a dip with my favorite new project.

The comments were a predictable mixed bag:

HOMOFOMO9 #GOALS 😎 ♥

kevinbranderson get me in that tub with you, mama 😎

suefirrelisonfire excuse me?! 😳 new project what? 🤯!!

design.my.life OMG I FUCKING LOVE THAT BOOK I CANNOT WAIT I WANT TO REACH THROUGH THIS SCREEN AND STEAL THAT SCRIPT S;OKFEPFLPGK[WORGJOR[IUJRPIOT GAH!

NoYourGaybot sorry. that book is so basic and you should do better. your queer fans need you to do better.

TheRealHAnniehKBarries SO MUCH THIS 👆

FeatherBirdBank #STAN #STAN #STAN

Whyureadingthisbruh$$? @neckbeard4lyfe is Bo Dhillon really into this shit? what happened to that guy?

MrsKnockKnockKnock Srsly: another round of "kill yer gays?" Could we just not?

And on. And on. And on they went—already 6,482 comments deep. Merritt typed her own comment. Edited it. Deleted it. Typed another. Edited it. Hovered over the post button . . .

She closed the app.

Then she used a garden hose to douse the fire pit, leaving it a sloppy pile of ash and char, said goodnight to her mother, and went to bed.

The guest room she slept in was on the woods side, not the ocean side, and it was dark even in the daytime as a result. Now, of course, it was night and even darker, but Merritt didn't flick the light switch near the doorway. Instead, she brushed the keyboard of her laptop, open on the desk beneath the window, and its screen popped on and lit the room with a pale white glow. The screen showed a blank Word document. This was how much of her new book she'd managed to write.

Merritt pulled on her pajamas, leaned over the desk to close the window, and then, with her hand on the window, she stopped and looked closer: there were three dead yellow jackets in the inner casing along the screen. They were all in a clump together. One was missing its head. She wondered if they died this way, touching each other, or if the wind had piled them there afterward. She wondered when the head was lost and where it went.

Merritt left the window as it was and climbed into bed. As she lay there, she worried a thought. It was hard and unwelcome, like a popcorn kernel stuck in her gums, something she could run her tongue over but not properly dislodge. Not without assistance, anyway. Not without pointy instruments and blood and pulling it out into the light, leaving a wound behind.

The thought was this: she hadn't actually been the one to write *The Happenings at Brookhants*. Elaine had been that book's *true* composer, the one with all the ideas and the know-how to manifest them and she, Merritt, had only ever been the vessel for relaying those ideas—the chimp at the keyboard.

What had Truman Capote said? *That's not writing, that's typing.*

A typist. What if she'd only ever really been the typist?

ABOUT THAT MISSING COPY OF

MARY MACLANE'S BOOK

....

Come early December, it was found with **Eleanor Faderman**. Eleanor was one of the Brookhants students said to have been wary (or was it jealous?) of Flo and Clara. When Flo and Clara were alive, that is.

Eleanor Faderman had, in fact, tried to purchase her own copy of *The Story of Mary MacLane* after it had first caused such a furor on campus the previous spring, but she'd never been able to find it in any of the bookshops she visited during her summer holiday—at least not when her older sisters weren't looking over her selections and magpieing their opinions to their mother.

Eleanor Faderman was short and slight, her features sharpened as if to points, her hair an odd sort of color, almost like it should have been brown but then most of the pigment had been leached from it, leaving it a dull tan. More importantly, Eleanor Faderman was known among her classmates to have the gift of thieving fingers and a curiously silent presence, the ability to slip in and out of spaces unnoticed. The students in her dorm made note of this often: *Eleanor, where did you come from?* Or its inverse: *Wasn't Eleanor here a moment ago?*

Given these abilities, it wasn't difficult for Eleanor Faderman to filch the copy of the book that returned with the bodies and then keep quiet about it, too. She had her chance due to the carelessness of a Pinkerton hired by Flo's mother to investigate her death. That detective had been disinterestedly thumbing through the book as he waited to speak to Principal Libbie Brookhants about the tragedy. He was new to the Pinkerton agency and unhappy with this assignment: the deaths of Clara and Flo were, of course, gruesome and terrible, but he believed they were also wholly accidental, a cruelty of nature. When the principal finally opened her door to invite him in, the detective left the copy of the book on the table outside her office.

Our Eleanor Faderman watched him do this.

And that was that: the book was now hers.

Eleanor hid it in the back of a potting cupboard in the Brookhants Orangerie,* a glinting expanse of glass and light jutting off one side of Main Hall. Seven mornings a week, Eleanor worked in The Orangerie, tending to the plants and, in the winter, feeding firewood to its elaborate and cantankerous heating system. Most mornings, she was the first to arrive there, setting its gas lamps glowing if the thin light of pre-dawn wasn't enough to see by—which it usually wasn't. (While some structures at Brookhants had by then been electrified, The Orangerie was not among them.) Once she could see, Eleanor donned her work pinafore to water and feed, treat for pests, and pluck away death and deformity from branches and stems.

Those more mundane tasks complete, she indulged in The Orangerie pursuits she liked best: cutting and bundling herbs and picking any ripe fruits to later send to the kitchen staff for preparation. She did this only if the cook had left her a note telling her how many sprigs of thyme or blades of chives were required for that

---

* In case you're not familiar, think of an orangerie as a kind of showy greenhouse/ conservatory. It was Harold Brookhants, before his death ceased his involvement in the plans for the school, who had insisted on naming it The Orangerie. (As you'll see, Readers, Harold Brookhants had a real thing for French pretentions.)

day's meals. And, despite her fellow classmates' complaints about the blandness of the Brookhants cuisine, most mornings the cook *had* left her a note, and Eleanor, snipping shears in hand, wandered the rows of herbs, fragrant and dense, relishing in her tiny harvests as she carefully twined them into bundles and left them in a basket next to the note that named them.

On some of those mornings, Eleanor Faderman also snuck a piece of fruit for herself. Not often, mind you. During the gray snowpack of winter in Rhode Island, an orange—a ripe, full-sized orange hanging from a tree branch—was a kind of miracle. Even those Brookhants students who didn't spend much time in The Orangerie could have been counted on to throw fits if they had believed one of their classmates was stealing their portion of its bounty. But occasionally, Eleanor kept her eye on a runty lime, say, one hidden by its tree's bright leaves, one she felt she could nip without anyone missing it. Save Miss Trills, perhaps.

Miss Alexandra Trills* (as dull as she was tall, which was very, thought Eleanor) was the faculty member in charge of The Orangerie. But Miss Trills would never tell. Probably. (Surely not if she believed that such an offense had only happened once.)

Though her morning tasks were many, Eleanor Faderman had them routinized and usually finished with time to herself before breakfast. Imagine, if you will, the pleasure of having a space like The Orangerie all to yourself, with no more work to be done and no demands made upon you. Especially in a place like Brookhants, with your fellow students everywhere: shouting down the hall and snoring in their beds, blowing their noses in the lavatory, whispering secrets behind you in the classroom. Eleanor Faderman went from a house filled with sisters to a boarding school filled with students, and can we blame her, Readers, for carving out a daily slice of quiet all to herself in the most beautiful place on campus? A place of fuchsia

---

* I promise it's the last time I'll ask, but please remember this name, dear Readers.

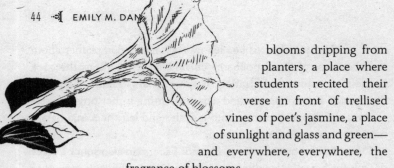

blooms dripping from planters, a place where students recited their verse in front of trellised vines of poet's jasmine, a place of sunlight and glass and green— and everywhere, everywhere, the fragrance of blossoms.

The sun now up and The Orangerie windows full of light and glint, Eleanor might take her stolen lime, or a bit of bread saved from the previous evening's meal, or even a single spearmint leaf, and wedge herself in a corner nook she'd discovered behind a massive zinc planter growing a near-to-twenty-foot *Brugmansia suaveolens*, more commonly known as snowy angel's trumpet tree.*

Here, from her wedge, Eleanor could see without being seen. Here she might suck on her mint leaf and daydream. Here she might study her Latin (what a chore, Latin), or write a letter to someone back home (probably her sister Carrie). Here she might read, often that, and pleasantly lose herself to other worlds and times—to other selves.

Here, hidden, she might observe those who came to The Orangerie without them ever knowing she was watching: Miss Trills checking on her freesias—gah, Miss Trills—or maybe Grace O'Connell, who was a morning wanderer, a sophomore the other students thought friendly and admirable. And Eleanor thought so, too. Privately she thought this.

Grace O'Connell had a wide, pleasant face and a heart-shaped mouth. Grace O'Connell had a smile she offered so easily, though this fact did not cheapen it. Eleanor thought Grace especially lovely when Grace thought she was alone, as she did those mornings she happened into The Orangerie right before breakfast, palming the weight of a lemon, or standing, eyes closed, in a warm square of sunlight.

---

* Also known as angel's tears. (A hint, perhaps, of things to come.)

If, like so many Brookhants students, Eleanor had been the type to send bags of mixed sweets and lockets of hair to her classmates, Grace O'Connell would have been the classmate to whom she'd have sent them. Or she could have easily sent her a flower message. Those were still popular among the Brookhants girls. Mary Peril, in Eleanor's dorm, had the very latest flower dictionary and was always reading aloud from it—*yellow acacia for secret love; or spearmint for a general warm sentiment; tulips to declare one's feelings*—and Eleanor, of course, had the best access to flowers on campus. But Eleanor Faderman didn't participate in the elaborate courting rituals of her fellow classmates. She did not send tokens of affection. She did not write poems proclaiming her adoration and then practice reciting them in front of the jasmine, hoping to be overheard. And she did not pick and present bouquets of flowers to suggest her secret feelings.

She kept her secret feelings secret.

There were other students too that Eleanor might see, *had* seen, in The Orangerie. Seen without herself being seen by them, I mean.

Flo.

Clara.

Flo and Clara together, thinking they were alone.

It is said that after she stole the book found near their bodies, the copy of Mary MacLane's book gone missing, Eleanor Faderman changed.

Of course, every student at Brookhants that year felt changed by what had happened to Flo and Clara. And the faculty felt the same. Some traditions, like the typically hours-long Halloween game of Witch in the Woods, were abandoned, considered too sinister to be held in the shadow of their deaths. More generally, for weeks after, the campus was hushed, the students tentative with one another and even with themselves.

But Eleanor's change was both more acute and more specific. She

Flo and Clara together, thinking they were alone.

became first enchanted by, and then rather obsessed with, Mary MacLane's words. Which is to say, careful Readers: with Mary MacLane's thoughts and prejudices, her desires and complaints. At least as Mary presented them in her *portrayal*.

No more spying on Grace O'Connell. No more fingers sticky with stolen lime juice. Now Eleanor rushed through her tasks. She overwatered, underwatered, pinched good growth with bad as she clumsily twisted rotten leaves from stems. She even ignored the spider mites and whiteflies, the mealybugs and caterpillars, each determined to eat of and burrow in the plants she was supposed to be caring for. All so that she could take the red book from its hiding spot and get back to her own behind the planter of angel's trumpet, so that she could wander the barren hills of Butte, Montana, with Mary MacLane as she beseeched the devil to come and rescue her:

> *I am a selfish, conceited, impudent little animal, it is true, but, after all, I am only one grand conglomeration of Wanting—and when some one comes over the barren hill to satisfy the wanting, I will be humble, humble in my triumph.*

What at first might have been only the call of the sensational mixed with the macabre—that is, a chance to read the scandalous musings of a scandalous girl, musings that Eleanor's two dead classmates had been wholly preoccupied with, *and* to read them from the very copy of the book found with their bodies, the copy they'd marked up and pored over—eventually became something else entirely.

The more of Mary MacLane's words Eleanor read, the more each seemed to bewitch her—causing her to see her own world, her own self, anew. The effect was as sure as had she placed a pair of Mary MacLane glasses at the end of her nose: Eleanor's vision was changed.

Eleanor Faderman had read many books in her short life. She had read books that she enjoyed and books that bored her. She had read books that made her disputatious and books that soothed her. She had read histories and poetry, philosophy and science. And she had read novels. It was, after all, usually novels that she chose, at least when choosing for herself, and so many different kinds of novels at that—adventurous orphans and brave battle-goers; careful, teasing courtships and once-ripe friendships gone to rot.

Eleanor Faderman knew many books. But never before had she read a book that seemed to know her.

By that I mean, Readers, to know her in ways she did not yet know herself, could not have named, would likely have denied, even, until Mary MacLane spoke them from her pages. And sometimes it was as if Flo and Clara were reading the book along with her. Eleanor could, if she listened past the blood in her ears, only just hear their voices saying the sentences aloud, there in her corner beneath the angel's trumpet tree. Sometimes she could almost feel the two of them pressed in against her in that small, hidden wedge—one on either side—the three of them reading together in almost unison. (Almost because Flo was always a beat behind.)

On those occasions, Eleanor couldn't even remember turning the pages in Mary's book. Perhaps she hadn't, she'd think later, fighting to stay awake at her desk in a class. Yet somehow she'd moved through the entries, Mary's true words coming one after the next.

Our Eleanor ingested those words daily. She read and reread them. She coveted them, even becoming fleetingly preoccupied with things like brown sugar fudge, Napoleon, and her fellow classmates' toothbrushes, because in her pages Mary MacLane was preoccupied with these things.

She also repeated, often, Mary's statement, *The words are only words with word meanings.* Several students later remembered Eleanor saying this—usually as a mumbled response to conversations in which she was only peripherally engaged in the first place. Or not engaged in at all until she inserted herself with that statement. I suppose it does have a kind of one-size-fits-all pliability—but rather a bleak one, no?

Even more disquieting, students recalled that during this period, Eleanor would repeat to herself—as some sort of incantation or prayer—phrases of this sort:

*From girls with sunny confidence; from the maddening interfer-
ence of mothers; from strawberries hazed in mold, surprising me
with bites of rot, Kind Devil, deliver me.*

*From the lazy opinions of my sisters; from serpents hiding in
the wallpaper; from my grandmother's preoccupation with her
silver sardine dish, Kind Devil, deliver me.*

*From the fine, blond hairs of May Hart, which are perpetually
lodged in her Tiffany hairbrush; from the smug wearers of cameo
rings; from chivalrous young men who carry old beliefs, Kind
Devil, deliver me.* [*]

As November became December and winter clenched its fist
around Brookhants, Eleanor Faderman offered these quiet incantations with such frequency that her classmates found them less and
less disturbing. Eventually they came to be seen as more tic than
threat, more background noise than warning.

Previously Eleanor's classmates might have called her capable if
standoffish, clearly intelligent if also disinterested in their affairs.
Now Eleanor often appeared to them as drowsy and unkempt,
sometimes even wearing her planting pinafore, with its soil and leaf
stains, to classes, instead of hanging it on its designated hook at the
back of The Orangerie. Students also noticed that Eleanor's black
pupils too often filled her eyes like the shiny, oversize olives she
muttered about eating correctly.[†]

Stranger yet, her limbs seemed to operate limply.

One student later remembered: "I saw her once, right before it
happened. We were out near the fountain on our way to class, and
she was ahead of me still in her work apron. There was an awful
wind that day and we were all in such a hurry. I feel that I can't quite
describe it as I should, but seeing her was somehow like watching a

* Refer to the March 8 entry in *The Story of Mary MacLane* to see Eleanor's model
for these incantations.

† Proper olive eating was another of Mary MacLane's interests, detailed in her
January 28 entry.

farmer carry a large sack of grain across a field—cumbersome and shifting. Except Eleanor herself was the sack of grain. I mean that she was carrying her own body that way. Or it was carrying her that way? I don't quite know. I only know that I noticed it and other students did, too."

Because she was so fully absorbed in Mary's world, Eleanor spent even less time in her own. By now her Orangerie tasks were entirely forgotten. No watering, no feeding, no grooming of plants. She might still bundle the requested herbs for the kitchen, but she handled even that task hastily if she managed it at all.

Despite her obsession with Mary's book, though, it appears Eleanor refused to remove the copy from The Orangerie. This, of course, meant that she spent even more hours there to be with it. Soon she was slipping from her bed and past the other sleeping girls at four in the morning, then three and two—moving like a specter down the dark hallways.

The Orangerie would have beckoned to Eleanor even before she reached it, its walls of glass letting in the moonlight, so the whole space would be washed in silver, a hue she could have seen when still the length of a corridor away. The mass of plants would be only shadows and outlines at that distance, their blooms and leaves appearing alien and dense, like a series of black explosions frozen mid-kaboom.

This all went on for more days than it should have, Readers. Eleanor's teachers commented on her tranced state in their classes, her drowsiness and confusion. She was sent to the sickroom on four separate occasions, pronounced anemic (she wasn't), and, for reasons unclear, forced to endure salves of Smedley's Chillie Paste applied to her arms, legs, and trunk. She fell asleep during supper, during lectures. She had never been particularly outgoing, had never made an outsized impression on the Brookhants world, but now she was nearly as vaporous as fog.

During this period, Grace O'Connell—whom, despite her crush, Eleanor had scarcely ever spoken to—approached Eleanor when the two were in the same stairwell after choir practice, a practice during which Eleanor had sung so many incorrect words in what was essentially a monotone that their frustrated director, Miss Hamm, eventually released them early with the parting plea: "Please get some rest, girls. Heaven knows you need it!"

Grace, her hand on Eleanor's shoulder there against a stream of departing classmates, said, "Is anything the matter, Eleanor? If you need someone to tell, it could be me."

Grace O'Connell later said that Eleanor Faderman seemed to register her hand as if she could see it without *feeling* it—as if she somehow no longer inhabited the body it was touching.

"Nothing to tell," Eleanor said, now turning to face Grace, who flinched, she couldn't help it, at the enormous size of Eleanor's pupils. And something else: a sweet scent that emanated from her.

"I only listen," Eleanor added. "And I watch, too. *People are abominable creatures*, Grace. *There is nothing in the world that can become so maddeningly wearisome as people, people, people!*"*

Grace O'Connell was understandably confused and upset by this interaction, and she did tell Miss Hamm about Eleanor's *glass bead* eyes and the way her body seemed somehow more like a *carcass* than a life, but she herself did not try again with Eleanor.

And then it was too late to try.

By all sound reason, the plants in The Orangerie should have suffered during this period. That or Miss Trills should have noticed the deficit in their care and made up for it, mentioning as much to Eleanor and inquiring about her lapse.

But during those days of Eleanor's enchantment, The Orangerie positively thrived. The fiery blooms of a once-spindly abutilon plant grew to the size of bonnets and were picked and worn thusly by some of the girls. The *Citrus limon* Ponderosa trees offered up eight- and nine-pound lemons, and the kitchen began serving lemonade or lemon pie so often that students began to expect such delights. And that expectation alone, Readers, in Rhode Island, in winter, in 1902, was plainly absurd. The poet's jasmine vines snaked themselves up

---

* *The Story of Mary MacLane*: from the January 26 and January 18 entries, respectively.

and around and over the surfaces of The Orangerie, all the while blooming obscenely—truly, obscenely—their blossoms so profuse that it became difficult to navigate the space without their petals brushing your body, their soapy scent wafting.

In fact The Orangerie was so verdant, so fragrant, that the whole campus recognized and remarked upon its change. Faculty members would group together at its doorways and say things like, "If it keeps on like this, we'll have to send Mary Kingsley in to map it."*

Of course, Readers: it could not keep on like that forever.

Of course, Readers: Eleanor Faderman could not keep on like that, either.

Please remember too that most of these things were only said about Eleanor Faderman, and were only said to even be *known* about Eleanor Faderman, after the fact.

The fact of her death, that is.

Given what you now know about The Orangerie during this time, it won't surprise you to hear that the *Brugmansia suaveolens* tree growing from the planter that provided Eleanor's hiding space was more lush with blooms than it had been since being planted there some nine years prior. Those blooms were over a foot in length, hanging in heavy clusters like suspended groups of milk glass vases.

Angel's trumpets emit a honeyed perfume, one that might have been missed for all the other flowers in The Orangerie right then, but not by Eleanor. This is because they shed their scent at night, and by now, Eleanor Faderman was largely a nocturnal creature, one who could only dimly recollect the translation of the plant's Latin name: *suaveolens,* "with a sweet fragrance." That sweet fragrance clung to her clothing and hair. For hours after her visits she carried the scent of angel's trumpet.

We cannot be certain that Eleanor Faderman knew just how

---

* Famous British explorer of the era, who, as it happens, had died two years earlier. (But not, thankfully, in the Brookhants Orangerie.)

deadly angel's trumpets are; it's also quite possible that she *did* know this. It wasn't so many years before that there had been a kind of trend that took place during the long afternoon hours in the parlors of bored women of high social standing: stirring a few drops of angel's trumpet pollen into one's tea before settling back to enjoy the rather pleasing delirium that followed. (Or supposedly pleasing delirium, anyway.) And Miss Trills did later say that Eleanor knew some of the attributes of The Orangerie's various plants better than she herself did. (Though it's possible that Miss Trills was only showing kindness to the dead when she said that.)

Brugmansia pollen might, by the pinch, produce a (dubiously) pleasant delirium. However, it's also true that when ingested in more significant quantities it produces a writhing, foam-mouthed, sticky-sweated state of violent hallucination and paralysis that can, if untreated, lead to death.

On December 7, 1902, Eleanor Faderman was found approximately two hours after she was noted absent from the evening meal. It was later discovered that Eleanor had actually been absent the whole day, but given her recent bouts of illness, she was incorrectly believed, by students and faculty alike, to be either in bed or in the sickroom (or in bed in the sickroom), and the matter was not further investigated until made mention of during the meal, which was, it must be said, a particularly bland mutton pie served with a side of roast squash. (Despite a request for tarragon and thyme, no bundles of herbs had been delivered to the kitchen that morning.)

What was eventually made clear is that Eleanor Faderman hadn't been seen by anyone then living at Brookhants since bedtime the previous evening, which was now some twenty hours before.

Of course, The Orangerie was immediately searched. Where else would anyone think to look for Eleanor Faderman? However, she was not found there, so searches continued elsewhere on campus, including those made by a warily intrepid party of lantern-carrying faculty members who agreed to take on the dark woods, starting, most unfortunately, with the Tricky Thicket.

Thankfully, despite the fruitlessness of the first endeavor, some-one thought to again send searchers to The Orangerie for another look, and it was this *second* group of pitiable students who found Eleanor's hiding spot beneath the angel's trumpet tree, and thus found Eleanor herself. Though she was, of course, no longer herself.

And now for another deeply unpleasant bit of historical sightsee-ing:

A loud first-year named Winifred Garfield, having bent low to peer beneath a potting table, spotted first the red binding of Mary MacLane's book. Moving closer, looking closer, Winifred saw, at precisely the moment she screamed, that a pale hand still gripped the book. The entirety of Winnie's view at this moment was the book, the curled fingers, and a bit of wrist and sleeve, but she knew, *she knew*, that what she was seeing was very wrong.

Once the other students looked behind the planter and under-stood the cause of Winifred's continued screaming, one of them, Nora—an older, in-charge type—took her by the hand so that the two of them could go find a teacher. This while the other three stu-dents attempted together to push the angel's trumpet planter, even a few inches, to better reach their classmate. They could not. Their efforts did, though, shake loose several of the tree's dangling blos-soms, which fell heavily upon them, sprinkling their toxic pollen as they did.

Even though the students could not move the planter, it was clear, when she failed to respond to their shouting of her name, and then when their fingers extended to touch her cold body, that Eleanor Faderman was not moving, either. That she would never move again.

Eventually, it was clever Miss Trills who rigged the lever and roller system that moved the planter and allowed them to access Eleanor without crawling in and pulling her out—which no one seemed keen to do.

By that time, The Orangerie had become the somber meeting place for all Brookhants faculty and staff other than those still in the woods (someone had been sent to find them) and the three teachers tasked with the unenviable job of attempting to soothe the riled and rumor-spreading student body, each of which had first been accounted for, and then sent to their dormitories for fitful sleep—if sleep came to them at all.

The planter moved, and many lanterns now garishly lighting her, the full measure of Eleanor Faderman's undoing was assessed, from the salt paste of dried sweat on her forehead, which matted and coarsened her pale hair so that it looked uncomfortably similar to animal hide, to the remaining bubble crusts of froth on her blue lips.

Eleanor Faderman, her cold body stiff and contorted and still dressed in her nightclothes. Eleanor Faderman, one hand gripping her stolen book. Eleanor Faderman, so many angel's trumpets dropped around her, on her, smashed beneath her (they learned, when she was carried out), that the ground was more petal than stone, the cloying scent causing headaches in several of the onlookers.

No one had words for this ugliness, an ugliness magnified both by occurring in this place of such beauty and by its nearness to the deaths of Flo and Clara.

After all, Readers, words are only words with word meanings.

Eventually, it was Principal Libbie Brookhants herself who said, "Oh dear God. I think she'd been eating them." She then carefully knelt and scooped up a handful of angel's trumpets for the crowd's inspection. The flowers she was holding were like those hanging from the branches above in every way save one: those in her palm bore clear indications of tooth marks, one or two bites missing from each, the edges of the bites browned with quick decay. The faculty now looked more closely at the blooms on the ground near Eleanor. There were bite marks in most of them, too many to count.

For the second time in a single semester, authorities were alerted, and soon members of the local police force made their way to the Brookhants campus.

For the second time in a single semester, parents were contacted via telegram with unthinkable news about their daughter and her time away at school.

For the second time in a single semester, the same copy of Mary MacLane's book was found with the dead.

TINSELTOWN

....

Audrey Wells was eating an avocado and facon sandwich with her best friend Noel at the Bewildered Hiker in Griffith Park. This was something they used to do a lot.* But first they'd run three or four miles through the park, sometimes scaring each other by pretending to see rattlesnakes because they'd seen one once before.

Sometimes they'd pretend that they *didn't* see the celebrities they actually did see heading up to the Observatory and back, or pushing their kids in jogging strollers; but there were also times that they said hi because they knew them, or at least knew them through so-and-so.

Used to be that even the Bewildered Hiker itself could be a little star clogged, though less so since social media made it a thing. Now there were too many tourists hovering around its outdoor tables and positioning their phones to take not-as-discreet-as-they-imagine pics of, I don't know, fill in your favorite sweaty, trail-climbing, vegan-chili-eating influencer here: _____.

Audrey and Noel were both on one side of a table, sharing a bench beneath a tree that kept dropping its green seedbud things on them.

"The San BernaDinosaurs," Noel said that day. "Because dino-saurs." He was squeezing agave nectar into his iced tea. There was now a small hill of buildup in the bottom of his glass.

"It feels too much like one you've already used," Audrey said.

"We haven't, though."

---

* And something they haven't done again since the day portrayed in this chapter.

"I know, but it feels like you have." She brushed green seedbuds from his arm. They'd been talking about band names for what seemed to her a very long time.

Audrey Wells had known Noel Shipler for the entirety of her life. Noel's father produced the *House Mother* movies alongside Audrey's own father (which is how he'd first met Caroline). And years later their families spent Christmas ski vacations together. (Though this was, of course, before Audrey's parents divorced and Caroline had her *difficult period*.)

Noel and Audrey were, in fact, in a quintessentially mid-90s music video together as toddlers. It's one you might remember because of the series of short-lived (and confusing) controversies it provoked. Shot for rock band the Yellow Credenzas' song "What Your Therapist Told You About Me," the video's gimmick is that Audrey and Noel are dressed up like other, more established acts of the day and imitate their more popular music videos—Oasis and Alanis Morissette and Counting Crows, Fiona Apple and Bush. You get the idea: tiny children playacting superstar make believe while alt-rockers sing obnoxiously enigmatic lyrics behind them.

Adorable, everyone agreed, the fans all loved it. Even more so once the trouble started.

That had to do with the video's closing segment, which mocked (*celebrated*, the Yellow Credenzas swore) the "Macarena" video. For this portion, Audrey and Noel were both dressed in tiny black suits paired with loud, citrus-colored ties and the fluffy fake eyebrows needed to accurately imitate Los del Rio—the duo who sang the chorus of the "Macarena."

People might have let that go as charming, but then those scenes were cut together with other scenes where Audrey and Noel were *also* dressed in the revealing 1990s club clothes and wild makeup of the backup dancers actually doing the Macarena in that famous video, the very feminine backup dancers. Our sweet toddlers nailed the song's infectious silliness—and the dance, of course that—but, as you might now be recalling, they added one additional element to the mix: a kiss. Or two, really: one while they are dressed as men in their suits and one as women in their shiny hot pants and belly shirts. These are, of course, the most minuscule lip pecks imaginable, the stuff of Norman Rockwell illustrations.

And yet . . .

Because we are a nation of spewing, bigoted asshats, these things were enough to warrant editorials and boycotts and even the odd death threat. Some people claimed that Noel and Audrey had been oversexualized in the video, while others were more concerned about its blatant genderfuckery (though those two camps of complainers sometimes aligned in their disgust). And then there were the random racists who took issue with a black Noel and a white Audrey kissing.

At any rate, soon enough the whole thing was dubbed "that controversial video" that made people angry. It went on to be nominated for Best Editing and Art Direction at the MTV Video Music Awards, among others. (It won, though, only for Viewer's Choice, and Audrey and Noel—holding hands as they climbed to the stage in matching tuxedos—accepted the statue.*

My larger point here is that Noel Shipler and Audrey Wells have always, since they can remember, had intertwined lives—more loosely strung together during some periods, in tighter knots during others. They have dated. They have hooked up. They have not done those things for a while and have then gone back to doing those things and stopped again.

Put simply, Readers: they text each other first with news. Or they did so for a long time, anyway.

"I'm not completely against Fresnomads. Or FresKnowHow? FresNowhere?" Noel paused, set down the agave bottle, and tilted his glass to check the thickening contents at the bottom.

"I know you get mad when I say this, but maybe you need to move on from California."

"Not it."

Noel wrote and produced for all kinds of musical artists, his

---

* This was undoubtedly the Yellow Credenzas' high-water mark. They broke up in 1999.

tastes and abilities wide ranging and his work ethic dogged. (His parents had started him on piano lessons right around the time he starred in that music video with Audrey.) Noel Shipler was talented, but more than that: other musicians liked having him around. They felt both put at ease by his demeanor and legitimately inspired by his suggestions. He had a knack for blending styles in ways that seemed like they shouldn't work until they did.

But Noel's passion project was his own band, which was still in the struggling-to-get-noticed phase. They'd blown up for about seven seconds for one of their YouTube videos, but they hadn't really been able to break out beyond their small (if committed) California following, one that loved them best for their live shows.*

Noel and Audrey both heard a muffled buzzing noise. It was similar to the sound of a lone yellow jacket unhappily trapped in a jar, but was in this case the sound of a ringing phone set to vibrate. It was Audrey's phone; Noel had kept it for her in the side pocket of his shorts during their run, and it was still there, and he was half sitting on it. It went silent. And then it started to buzz again.

Noel shifted his position to fish it out. "It's gonna be your mom," he guessed. "And she's gonna be in, like, some sort of kale crisis." He handed the phone to Audrey. "Kale-o-line," he added. Then he sang, reworking Outkast's "Roses" to suit his needs: "Kale-o-line. (Kale-o-line!) All the guys would say she's mighty fine. (Mighty fine!)"

Audrey's screen was bright with missed calls and texts. "Nope," she said, scrolling. "It's Gray."

Gray was Audrey's manager. She was surprised to see a screen of texts from him. They talked, of course, but not multiple texts and

---

* Even with the oversize puppets and costumes and stage antics, the band's most defining gimmick was that they changed their name every show, and always to a portmanteau involving the name of some city or town in California. They'd been Modestofu; the Santa Monica Gellers; OakLandSharks; EnciNosferatu; and, Audrey's favorite, the Santa Anais Nins.

then calls and more texts in a row, talked. At least not at this junc-
ture in her career.

His first was sent while they would have been just starting their
run: Please call me ASAP. ASAP means right now.

And then he'd sent a few more of a similar sort before ending
with one just minutes before, which read: I'm trying to convey the need
for speed here, kiddo. This is serious. Please. Answer. Your. Phone.

"What?" Noel asked, reading her confusion.

"No idea," she said, ready to press Gray's name under Missed
Calls. And exactly then Caroline texted: where are you? i'm worried

hike should be over

you need to call gray right away

Things like this—sharing a manager—made having the same career as her mother (or at least having the echo version of the same
career her mother once had) more annoying for Audrey than it
might otherwise have been. Her age and current life situation didn't
help, she knew, but she had to wonder if even when she was thirty-
seven Gray would still call Caroline if he couldn't reach Audrey fast
enough.

Audrey did not reply to her mom. But she did call Gray. He answered so quickly she didn't have time to daydream about what he
was going to say.

"Where are you?" This was his greeting.

"I'm in Griffith Park," she said. "With Noel. What's going on?"

"No, I know that part," Gray said. "I talked to Caroline. I'm here,
I'm parking. Where are you?"

"What?"

"I mean *where exactly* are you, kiddo? Where in the park? Do
I need to change into my Nikes is what I'm getting at? How far in
until I meet up with you?"

Kiddo. She was still *kiddo* with Gray and probably always would
be *kiddo* with Gray.

"No," she said, confused. "We're not—we're done running. We're at the Bewildered Hiker, the café on Fern Dell."

"Oh thank sweet Christ," Gray said. "Don't move. Do. Not. Move."

"OK," she said.

"I'm coming to you right now. Keep it seated."

"OK, weirdo," she said. "I got it. I'm sitting here, not moving." She paused to let him fill in, but he didn't, so she asked, "Do you want me to, like, order you something?" She felt stupid about it right after.

Gray was breathing harder now, probably because he was power walking in her direction. "No," he said, and then added, "Well, you know, yes. Wouldya be a lamb and get me an iced tea? Or maybe lemonade would be better. Do they have it?"

"I'm not sure," she said. "You want iced tea or lemonade?"

"Yes, that's fine," he said, with effort. "Stay put. I'll be right there."

She tapped End, shaking her head at her phone, then at Noel. "I guess Gray's here," she said, still not quite believing it.

"What, he jogs now?" Noel asked, looking over at a group of people on the trail.

"No, like, he came to find me," she said. "Specifically. He wants me to buy him a lemonade."

"Weird." Then, as if he'd just been smacked with the thought, "Oh fuck! Could you be getting fired right now? You think that's why he came here?"

"God, why would you guess that first?" Now there was a clench in her chest where there wasn't before he'd said it.

"No, I'm just saying, why would he come here? I guess he could be, like, quitting the biz and wants to tell you in person." Noel frowned. "What if he's sick or something?"

She shook her head. "He'd want to tell me something like that with Caroline." Her chest clench tightened. "Will you wait in line for the lemonade? Do you mind? In case he comes."

"Anything for normcore Anna Kendrick," Noel said, standing.

This was a joke they shared about notes she'd happened to see (OK, she'd *strained* to see) scrawled on a casting director's papers after an unsuccessful audition: *Giving good strip mall realism. Some-*

how an even more normcore Anna Kendrick. Maybe these notes had been primarily about Audrey's looks. Like Anna Kendrick, Audrey was also petite with auburn hair and, if you were straining for a celebrity look-alike comparison, had a similar facial structure, though she didn't really have the same angularity to her jaw, and her eyes were set closer together.

The uglier way to read those comments was that they had very little to do with Audrey's looks and much more to do with something essentially uninteresting, even tired, about her: the cheaper imitation. That's what made them stick. And hurt.

And it had hurt her, at first, but sharing it with Noel, making it a thing they now both privately referred to her as, all the time, had made it seem benign. Well, almost.

Noel joined the line behind several people. Audrey's mother called and she ignored it.

And then there was Gray, weaving through the crowd. His brow was glistening, the sleeves on his pink-checked button-down rolled up to his elbows. "Hey, kiddo," he said, leaning over to kiss her cheek. "How's my showing up to put a little hot sauce in your afternoon?" He took a step back, then, and patted right below his collarbone, making a kind of sour grimace as he stifled a burp. Then he covered his mouth with his hand, the screen of his smart watch lighting up as he did.

"You OK?" she asked as he sat across from her.

"I'm sorry," he said, swallowing another burp. "By-product of my power walking. Consider yourself charmed, huh?" He pulled a folder from his leather messenger bag and placed it, conspicuously, on the table between them. Green seed stuff fell on top of it.

"Noel's getting you lemonade," she said to say something. Fuck, she was nervous.

Gray nodded. Then he took a breath and said, "So listen, this isn't easy but it just is. They decided to go in another direction for Eleanor. Tim and I have been on the phone with them all morning and it's a done deal. They no longer think you're right for the part."

Tim was Audrey's agent.

She tried not to give Gray a reaction, to keep her face placid as a puddle. I mean, that was Hollywood for you, right—you're in, then you're out, and if she of all people didn't understand that by now, shame on her.

"I know it's not the news you want, but it's the news I've got and I'm sorry," Gray said. "Younger, I think—they want sixteen playing sixteen—not twenty-three playing sixteen. But it's not only that—they're changing the whole project around."

For a while they only stared at each other while green seed things floated around them.

And then, "Well, say something," he said. "Do you understand?"

"Of course not," Audrey said, brushing seeds off her shoulder and telling herself to speak calmly. "I mean, you're, like, sitting there saying this is a done deal, so OK, what's the point of arguing about it if it is, but then you're making me feel like I'm not even allowed to have a reaction. And this is fucked up and you know it—I can still play sixteen. I don't even *want* to be able to play sixteen but I can. And Bo wanted me for this. *He* told me that. I was always gonna be Eleanor Faderman, even before they cast the leads he knew that."

Gray shrugged and shook his head. "Yeah but they're making changes there, too."

"Cool," Audrey said, taking that in for a moment before full-on unloading. "So, like what? Bo has no say in his movie anymore? Did they bring in somebody who doesn't even know what they're making?" She was working herself up now. "They did, right? One of the producers is on a power trip? Honestly, Harper Harper is why this would have even worked in the first place."

"Oh, she's not going anywhere," Gray said. "Actually, she's producing."

Audrey rolled her eyes, accepting this additional BS as it came at her. "Oh right—of course," she said. "Of course she is. I hate this town. Every day I'm here I hate it more." She looked over at Noel, who was ordering. "Noel guessed that I got fired and I thought he was being a jerk."

"He probably was," Gray said. "I've found that being right all the time and being a jerk pair well."

"Cool," she said, feeling suddenly tired, like exhausted tired. She didn't want him to try to make her feel better. She just wanted him to go. "Well, I guess thanks for coming all the way over here to tell me in person. I wouldn't have expected that."

"Oh c'mon, kiddo," Gray said, revealing the start of the crocodile smile he'd been holding in. "You know I'm not that nice a guy."

Audrey took in that smile, watched it spread wider across his face, and understood, she thought, that he had only been fucking with her.

She tried to feel relief, even though she didn't. "I hate you," she said, scooping up seed stuff and flinging it at him. "You're such an asshole. What, it gives you a thrill to drive over here to fuck with me?" She had another thought. "Wait, did Noel know you were doing this?"

"Honey, don't misunderstand: you're out as Eleanor Faderman. That part's no joke." He slid the folder that he'd placed between them closer to her.

"What the hell, Gray?" She thought she might really lose it, even if there were people at all the tables around them.

He held up his hands. "Buuuuuut—you're in as Clara Broward. Probably." He nodded at the folder as if it would somehow be able to explain anything.

And that is when Noel returned with the lemonade and sat down beside Audrey. "So?"

"I have no idea," Audrey said.

"Open the folder, Clara," Gray said.

"Clara?" Noel said.

Audrey shook her head. "Don't ask me," she said. "I honestly don't know."

"Open the folder," Gray said.

She didn't.

"I'll do it," Noel said, tilting it in his direction.

Audrey grabbed the edge of the folder, pulled it back to her, and flicked it open. Her heart was clanging around, almost like it was knocking against her chest bones, and she was somehow embarrassed by this bodily reaction to news that couldn't possibly be true and would only end up disappointing her.

But the top document was an offer—a new offer—and in this offer, she saw, reading quickly, that she was to play the role of Clara Broward. And that, dear Readers, was one of the leads. In fact, it was Harper Fucking Harper's love interest. It was *that* lead.

She flipped the document over. Beneath it was a script, the Clara Broward part—and there was a lot of it—highlighted in pink.

She flipped that over. Beneath it, audition sides and another production document, this one even more confusing than the offer. She looked at Gray, who was swallowing a lot of lemonade.

"Yeah, so this part we need to talk about," he said.

"I think we need to talk about all the parts," Audrey said.

"We do, just not right this minute." He again looked at his watch and then swiped its screen, read something, swiped it again. "Clearly you can sense that Bo's decided to go in a bit of a different direction here."

"Uh, you think?" Noel said.

To catch you up: Gray was talking about the director, Bo Dhillon. Audrey hadn't actually worked with him before, but she did know him in that vague, industry way of knowing without *really* knowing. He had long expressed interest in writing and directing a different, as-yet-to-be-made movie. A movie that she and her mom would, were it ever to happen, both star in—their first together and Caroline's first in years—the second coming of the mother-daughter Scream Queens. (First there was Janet Leigh and Jamie Lee Curtis, now Caroline and Audrey Wells.)

Audrey was still trying to understand. "They changed the script?" she asked, flipping back to it.

"Some, but that's not it," Gray said. "It's a little confusing, I'll be honest—but they seem to want there to be a kind of significant improvisational element to it now."

"*Improvisational* meaning?"

He looked sheepish, which, on Gray, was particularly disconcerting. "I'm not a hundred percent on the details yet, kiddo," he said. "There's *definitely* still a script. I'm not even sure it's much different than how you last saw it—for now. I think it's more that they want you to develop some kind of bond with Harper." He made a strange face, one Audrey didn't know how to read. "And also with the girl who wrote the book."

"What?" Audrey said, then she looked at Noel, who made a *don't look at me* face in return.

"The writer," Gray said as if that explained anything, "teenybopper Virginia Woolf. What is her name again? It's old-fashioned like her book. You read it, didn't you, as Eleanor prep?"

"Merritt Emmons," Noel said.

They both looked at him.

"Calm down," he said. "I was just on her Twitter like yesterday. She's funny."

"What about her?" Audrey asked.

"She's involved, too," Gray said. "They had her do some work on the script, I guess, or they're going to, and she'll be on set. And there tomorrow too, actually."

"So that's still on?"

"Oh yeah," Gray said. "Absolutely it's on. But . . ." He paused to find the words he wanted.

Audrey didn't give him much time. "But what?"

"Well, I think they intend it to be more of a chemistry read than anything else," he said, tossing up his hands like this was to be expected. "You know, just because this is so new—so they need to see how it feels, between the two of you, especially."

"Between me and Harper Harper?" Audrey said, recognizing how unbelievable that sounded even as she said it. And daunting. It sounded very daunting to her.

"You've got the sides there," Gray said, gesturing to the packet.

Audrey flipped through them as he spoke.

"Two scenes, good opportunities to shine in both." He let her read a while before adding, "And Harper will read the Flo scene with you, so that's the deal maker-breaker."

Audrey skimmed its final page. "They kiss at the end," she said. She looked up at him.

"I know," Gray said. "So that's on the table for you two to discuss tomorrow. I mean, if you want it to be—Bo said he'd give you time to run it on your own and decide. Or you can just say no now and I'll give them a heads-up. They have no expectations either way, you can do one of those endless eye locks if you want."

"There's always the cheek brush," Noel said.

Gray nodded. "Or that. But Harper's people said she's in for it if you are. It's your call."

"What if I don't want it to be my call?" Audrey said. She felt like she couldn't catch her breath. "I'm sorry, I can't even process this. I thought tomorrow was supposed to be a table read with me as Eleanor Faderman. This is insane."

"It's not insane, kiddo," Gray said. "It's just sudden. I mean, listen, not everyone's sold on this yet. You have some convincing left to do with the producers. But Bo is firmly in your corner, so he's trying to make it a casual thing—low-key. That's why it's at his house."

"I didn't know it was," Audrey said. "At his house."

"It is. Same time, new place."

"That should be a trip," Noel said. "I'm pretty sure he's one of those real-deal horror collector dudes. Like his coffee table legs are stacks of human skulls."

"And he uses the face mask from *The Silence of the Lambs* to strain his pasta?" Gray's deadpan was solid.

"Yes," Noel said.

"Hyperbole, Noel," Gray said.

"Wait until tomorrow when he offers you a drink and then casually mentions that the glass it's in once belonged to Charles Manson."

"Stop," Audrey said, touching Noel's arm. "So what is the writer—"

"Merritt Emmons," Noel interrupted.

"Yes, Merritt Emmons," Audrey said. "*Why* is she gonna be there tomorrow? Is she producing, too?"

"Maybe?" Gray said. "Wouldn't surprise me, but mostly I think

Bo just wants tomorrow to be about seeing all the playing pieces together on the board. You know?"

"No, I do not know. What does that mean?"

Gray seemed embarrassed to say what he said next. "Bo seems to have this idea that if the three of you maybe have some *casual* time to bond it'll be beneficial. You can mine each other for feminist insight or something. I don't know."

"What?"

"Jesus," Noel said. "I think he's trying to tell you that they want to plan your playdates." He pushed at the folder. "Under contract."

"Really they just want you to hang out a little," Gray said. "It's nothing nefarious. Audrey, the prize piece of news here is that they want you to play Clara. That's the headline."

"What happened to Lily Strichtfield?" Audrey asked. This was the actress previously cast in the role of Clara Broward.

"She's out," Gray said. "You know how it is. She gets it."

"Maybe you can have her call me to explain it."

Gray sighed. "*Bo* wants you to do this. He thinks you're the right choice. Why did that fact mean something to you a minute ago when you were mad about Eleanor Faderman being taken away, but it doesn't now that we're talking Clara?"

"I think you know the difference between the parts of Eleanor and Clara in this film."

"I do," Gray said. "And when I find money on the street I smile and feel grateful and put it in my pocket. What I don't do is hold it up to the sky and demand that it explain itself."

"I don't understand that analogy as it applies to this situation," Noel said.

Gray ignored him and kept on, looking only at Audrey. "You know, when they called, I didn't try to talk them *out* of it." He offered her a face of amused incredulity. "Jesus, kiddo. How about a little excitement? They went on and on about how Harper Harper's into you, too."

Audrey laughed without humor. "Oh, I'm sure she is," she said. "Has she been catching up on my run of tampon commercials?"

"*Why does this have to be a thing?!*" Noel said, quoting Audrey's most memorable line from one of those commercials. The one that seemed to run forever.

"That job paid," Gray said. "That job pays still. Why are you making this so hard?"

"You know, you started this by telling me in such a mean way," Audrey said. "If you'd just said, 'Congratulations, here's my news,' then that would have been that—but you had to pretend I'd gotten fired and draw it all out."

"I didn't pretend," Gray said. "They did drop you from Eleanor."

"So you *did* get fired," Noel said. "I knew it."

"You're both awful people," Audrey said, already scanning the script, which felt like a whole new script because it was, really, to now see it through Clara's eyes.

It was absurd, this offer, unreasonable and enormous and hearthopingly too much. She was terrified.

It was wonderful.

HOW TO

IMPORT A MARTIAN INTO

YOUR CONTACTS

....

Merritt and Elaine were in first class on an airplane bound for LAX. Merritt had never flown first-class before, had never been to Los Angeles or even California. Elaine had done those things more times than she could remember. (But in this case, it was the studio flying them and so that was new to them both.)

Merritt had been asked to come to LA to *consult* on a range of things related to the production. She'd had, at that point, one pleasant enough conference call with its director, Bo Dhillon (a man Elaine had once referred to, admiringly, as *Hitchcock's progeny.* Because, well, Elaine). But Merritt hadn't yet formed much of an opinion on him. She thought his body of work stylish and smart, for horror movies, anyway. (Not really her genre.) And, like most everyone else, she loved that once-viral red carpet clip of him, early in his career, when he'd managed to simultaneously come out and rib a reporter for mistaking him for M. Night Shyamalan: "No, I know, can you even believe there's two *different* Indian American dudes who make creepy movies? It's crazy, right? Two of us! For future reference, I'm the gay one."

But *consult* is a baggy and nebulous term people use to mean many, many things. Merritt still wasn't at all sure what it meant when applied to what she was supposed to be doing for this movie.

What Elaine was doing for *The Happenings at Brookhants* was nominally more defined. She was, for the first time in her eighty years, the executive producer of a film. As far as Merritt could discern, thus far being an executive producer meant that Elaine wrote checks and got other people to write checks. And, of course, had opinions. And writing checks, getting other people to write checks, and having opinions were three things Merritt had always associated with Elaine, since long before her days in film production.

Almost as soon as their plane lifted from the runway in Boston, Elaine had opened the vent, lowered the window shade, and taken a green silk sleep mask from her handbag.

"Keeping to your schedule, travel be damned?" Merritt asked her. Recently she'd noticed that Elaine often disappeared to nap for several hours in the afternoon. Or at least Elaine did this when Merritt was at Elaine's house in Rhode Island.

"There is more refreshment and stimulation in a nap, even of the briefest, than in all the alcohol ever distilled." Elaine pulled the mask's elastic strap behind her head.

"From whom did you steal that?" Merritt asked.

"Ovid."

"Oh, that drunk?"

Elaine smiled as she pulled the mask down over her eyes and settled back against her headrest.

"Well you look the part, anyway," Merritt said.

"I'm told that's more than half the battle."

Now Elaine had been asleep for an hour and Merritt had read the first half of *Less Than Zero*. She'd been working her way through a list of novels set in and around Los Angeles. She felt that there was something too obvious about this exercise, too deliberate, but she had to try something. She was hoping to be inspired, and somewhere over Illinois she thought maybe she was on the verge of that, so she left Ellis's coked-up characters at yet another house party in the Hollywood Hills and pulled out her laptop and opened her book file.

She was met with the cursor blinking at the end of a note she'd left herself the last time she'd opened this file:

Answered Prayers Answered *is a terrifically stupid title.
So, so dumb.*

*You don't know how to write this book. You don't even
know if you should write this book. Certainly no one else
is here for it. It might be wise to accept these as things that
meaningfully indicate how unwise this idea is.*

Do better!

*Love,
your pal Merritt*

She highlighted the note and deleted it. Then she stared at her
ghost reflection in her now-blank screen. She had to pee, but the
light-up thing showed someone was in the bathroom and another
person was already standing in the aisle outside it, too.

She closed the file and logged into the plane's slow WiFi in order
to google *imposter syndrome.* She read six articles, one leading into
the next into the next. She did not feel soothed or seen by these articles, not even the one titled: "Your Imposter Syndrome Is Real as
Fuck. Now What Are You Going to Do About It?"

Especially not by that one.

Elaine made a kind of gulping noise in her sleep. It was loud and
startled not only Merritt, but some of the passengers around them.
Then she made another, this one a high gasp.

Worse than these noises was Elaine's face when Merritt took in
its measure: her nostrils flared and her mouth in a twitching grimace, her top lip drawing back to expose a few teeth, including a
fang, before sliding down again to hide them. Her teeth were the
color of old plaster and they sprouted from gums too red and wet.
Had they always looked like this, Elaine's teeth? The mask covering
her eyes emphasized her mouth, made it seem like her whole face.

Elaine made another strangled noise.

Merritt thought she saw . . . What had Elaine been eating in the
airport, trail mix? Or was it . . . Because she thought she saw—

Elaine's mouth opened, her fang was revealed, a low growl blew
out her twitching lips, and yes—Merritt looked closer, could feel

Elaine's sour breath on her face—she had something black stuck up on her red gums, some piece of nut or seed it must be, a black shard.

Had she been eating trail mix in the airport? Merritt couldn't remember.

The people across the aisle were plainly staring now. A woman with so many large rings on her fingers stage-whispered to her seatmate: "She's really having trouble."

Merritt did not want to be the person in charge of this moment but who else would do it?

"Lainey?" She forced herself to touch Elaine's shoulder, at first with only her fingertips and then with her whole hand, not gripping so much as applying pressure. "Elaine?" She pressed harder.

Elaine was wearing a thin sweater and her skin and bones beneath it felt soft, insubstantial. Merritt pulled Elaine's shoulder back and forth a few times, worried that she'd do damage even with so slight a move. She'd never had a reason to touch Elaine like this. She'd had no idea Elaine was so frail. Elaine did not wake, but her face eased and her mouth stopped twitching. Her teeth and horrible red gums stayed hidden. As did the black shard stuck there.

"She's fine," Merritt said out loud to herself. If the people in the seats across the aisle thought she'd said it for them, then whatever.

She closed her laptop and put it away. She used her phone to check her feeds and soon enough found herself back on Harper Harper's Instagram. Harper had just, minutes before, posted a story from the flight out of Montana she was on with her girlfriend—a doublie of the two of them snuggled together, both wearing white T-shirts with *Gal Pal* in black letters across the front, both looking rumpled and cozy for airplane seats. The caption: So cute together it's 🐐.

It felt out-of-body to be looking at that post while on her way to meet this person, both of them in their separate airplanes hurtling through the sky to the same location: Hollywood.

The last time Merritt had enjoyed talking about *The Happenings at Brookhants* at all, the last time she hadn't felt wholly like a fake, had been with Harper Harper. And the fact that that was even a thing, that she, Merritt Emmons, had had conversations *plural* with Harper Fucking Harper was preposterous.

Harper had first reached out three months ago via text, one that arrived unannounced and unanticipated. It just showed up on Merritt's phone like a signal from an alien planet that she alone had received. (Would hearing directly from a Martian really be any stranger?)

Merritt had gone to campus with her mother that day so she could work in its library. She'd checked out yet another biography of Capote and found a place at a long table to skim an article about his Black and White Ball, a lavish masquerade party he hosted at the Plaza Hotel in New York in the 1960s.* The intensity of Capote's vindictiveness was usually so tantalizing to her, but she was bothered by the group of students near her studying for an astronomy exam. She was also bothered by the graduate student—she assumed it was a graduate student, an older student, at any rate—on the chair near the windows who had nodded at her when they'd met eyes looking up from their texts. It was a nod that said *I see you—we see each other, here with our books.* But Merritt didn't want to be seen. It made her feel conspicuous, set apart rather than included. Three years before, when she was at the height of her notoriety as *wunderkind writer*, she'd tried a semester at college, a different one. Supposedly a better one. Tried and failed. She'd dropped out and come home and hadn't ever gone back. And now she felt like a cheat, an interloper, hanging around this one. (Especially because her mother taught there.)

These students in pairs and clusters, or alone with their headphones and laptops—one of them near her in a fucking U of sweatshirt drinking a green smoothie like she'd been posed by a recruiter to do so—each made Merritt feel this with a greater intensity. They weren't doing a thing to her, likely they didn't even notice her save

---

* Did you know, Readers, that Truman Capote worked on his guest list for the Black and White Ball for months? Months. He'd add a name, cross it out, and add it again, depending on his whims and a particular would-be guest's recent behavior toward either him or other guests more important to him than the wrongdoer in question.

for that one by the window, but they made her itchy and damp in her armpits. She felt rankled by their laughter, their plans to go here or there after class, their homework chatter. In this moment, she hated them.

She got up from the table and went to hide out in the stacks for a while, alone. On the way, her phone buzzed in her jacket pocket. When she pulled it out she saw she had a text from an unknown sender with a 406 area code. She had no idea where that was. She read the message.

> This is Harper Harper. You probably know by now that I'll be playing Flo in your movie. (I hope you do!) I asked Bo for your number so that I could call with some questions I have about her. This is me texting to see if it's alright with you if I do that. Think you can spare a few minutes for an actor trying to get it right?
>
> (reckoned I'd go to the black hole of voice mail if I didn't ask first)

Merritt read the text again and again. She looked over her shoulder and through the stacks to the surrounding rows to see if anyone was watching. Something about receiving it made her feel like she was on camera. But there was no one around.

She read it again.

Harper Harper (if this was really her) had texted the word *reckoned*. Also, she'd written *your movie* when they both knew calling it that was like pretending the Weather Channel was in charge of a hurricane. And if it wasn't her, if it was maybe some assistant who'd written it, well, why write it like this? What was the angle?

Merritt typed out a response. Deleted it. Tried another. Deleted that one, too. She thought it would almost certainly look thirsty to respond right away but she also had some sense (or hope) that just then Harper Harper was somewhere in the world looking at her phone and awaiting Merritt's answer.

She settled on this:

> Hi. I'm very glad that Harper Harper is playing Flo in the movie but of course I have no way of knowing that you're her. For all I know you're

just some undergrad who got my number from my mother because she thinks I should make more of an effort to connect with people my own age.

The reply came in seconds.

Bwaahahahahaha. Just a sec and I'll prove it

Merritt waited, her blood whirring with anticipation, which she told herself was not embarrassing because it was just the uncontrollable thing her body was doing in this moment. She was tired of being embarrassed by the things her body did or did not do without her conscious input in the decision.

And then her phone lit up with a new text. This one was a pic of Harper Harper, *the* Harper Harper, in tight white jeans and a loud, black-and-pink, palm-tree-printed bomber jacket over a cropped T-shirt. She was grinning her signature grin beneath one of the many slouchy beanies Merritt had seen her photographed in many times before. But the crucial items in the photograph were the two things she was holding up in front of her—a copy of Merritt's book, dozens of page marker flags sticking out from its edge, and a hand-written sign:

> *You should really make more of an effort to connect with people your own age.*

Damn. Merritt liked her too much already. Already she did. For several moments she thought about what to respond with and then texted:

You've sufficiently convinced me (killer jacket) but I'm in a library at the moment and it's no place for talking. Could you call me in an hour when I've had the chance to get back to my house?

Harper's yes please! reply came while Merritt was already texting her mother to tell her that she was going home and she'd see her there. She ran-walked the two miles or so, her head full of a new appreciation for the spring-green trees spreading their limbs overhead, this even though she and her mother had just driven under them on the way to campus. That short trip ago she'd felt nothing at all for these same trees.

She arrived home with enough time to make herself lemon-honey tea and settle in with her laptop on the porch swing, something her father had installed in the weeks before he killed himself. It was uncomfortable to Merritt when she considered how readily she now marked time this way, how every event in her history seemed to plant itself only in proximity to his suicide. She'd gotten her hair cut the day before he did it. That big limb fell from the sycamore in the backyard two weeks after he'd done it. He had taken her flea-marketing three weekends before he'd done it. (They'd bought the moth-chewed Hudson's Bay blanket with the colored stripes.)

That porch swing was really just another of her father's mostly unsuccessful attempts to make their imposing Victorian seem cozy and welcoming, which he never quite had. But now it was also somehow linked to the chain of his death, linked to the other thing he'd done. The forever thing.

After Merritt discovered her father dead in their garage, after that gaping wound of a thing, Merritt and her mother had tried to see if they could maybe talk their way into—well, if not understanding it—at least getting a handle on how they felt about it.

This was what the therapists they saw had recommended, and they'd both tried, really tried, to do what was asked of them. They had talked about it in support groups and individually with therapists, and also the two of them together with therapists, and together *without* therapists, in offices and in the car on the way to places, on stools at their kitchen island, even on this very porch swing. They'd spoken about their guilt over not recognizing some warning sign that his depression had deepened so acutely. And then about how there just aren't always signs, at least not great blinking arrows that say BEWARE NOW, SAVE HIM FROM HIMSELF—and that yes, yes, he *had* been happy and kidding around with everyone at the barbeque the weekend before he'd done it. They agreed on that. He certainly *seemed* happy. There was a Facebook post with him hold-ing corn on the cob and grinning, wasn't there?

They also talked about Merritt's mother's guilt that Merritt had been the one to find him that day. Merritt had been dropped off early when an after-school event had been canceled at the last min-ute. And Merritt felt guilty about that, too. She somehow felt guilt even on behalf of her father, who surely assumed her mother would be the one to find him, though would that really have been better? Different, yes, but better? They talked about their anger at him, oh it burned hot, and their sadness for him, and their anger at themselves. They talked about the person he'd been, how he'd been with each of them, and how they shouldn't let the memory of his death eclipse all the other memories they had of him. They talked about grief, how thick a fog it could be, how hard to see or even to imagine anything beyond it. They used a lot of metaphors and analogies: the ecosys-tem of grief, the journey of grief, the black box of grief.

And maybe some of this had made them feel better for a while.

But then this other thing happened where, because they'd done all that talking at the time, it felt like they'd used up their allotted words on the subject and it would somehow be wrong to now use more. There was, of course, a hideous hole where her father had once been, but the strange part was that it was hard not to feel like somehow *they* had contributed to making that hole. Because even now, five—could it really be five?—years later, she didn't actually feel all that much better about it. Not really—not enough—but what could possibly be left to say on the subject?

Whatever it was, they weren't saying it to each other anymore.

There on her father's porch swing, Merritt imported Harper's number, or at least the number Harper had texted from, into her contacts and paired it with a sexy pic of Harper she'd pulled off the internet. That small act made Merritt feel powerful. She thought that was probably worth examining later as potentially pathetic, but for now she relished the feeling. And then a neighbor drove by and honked hello at her. And then there was an incoming call: Harper Harper on her screen.

Merritt felt her heart wind up again, staring at the image, her phone buzzing. She thought about letting the call go unanswered. She thought about this for long enough that she could tell Harper was surprised to hear her answer.

"Well hey," Harper said back in that kind of countrified affectation Merritt had heard in her movies—all of which she'd watched by then. I mean, there were only three of them at that point if you didn't count Harper's fifty-four-second cameo in that superhero universe one, and Merritt did not. "I thought maybe I'd scared you off."

"Takes more than that," Merritt said. "Where's four-oh-six?"

"What's that, now?"

"Four-oh-six—your area code?"

"Oh shit, yeah, it's Montana. I never changed it on this phone. I like the reminder."

"Reminder of?" Merritt asked as she pushed back on the porch swing until she was on her tiptoes and could feel the strain of the swing's chains. She stayed like this, the swing wedged behind her, feet planted. She didn't want to let go yet.

"Where I come from, I guess. God, does that sound really simplistic?"

"No," Merritt said.

"I don't know—"

"So there were way too many page markers sticking out of my book in that picture you sent," Merritt said, cutting her off. "Please tell me that each of those doesn't stand for a question you have for me."

Harper laughed. "Almost," she said. "I mean, pretty much."

They talked for more than an hour that afternoon. Eventually, Merritt used her laptop to scroll through pics of Harper, posts about her, while they spoke. It made the whole exercise that much more surreal. Here's Harper Harper on a screen, looking Garbo glamorous in a slick white suit. But also, here's the folksy Harper Harper on the phone with her, asking her about Flo's relationship with her mother.

She'd done her homework, like she said. She'd read Merritt a passage from *The Happenings at Brookhants* and then ask about it. At first, Merritt thought she just wanted pointers, her thoughts about how Flo might sit or gesture or eat a piece of fudge. Eventually, though, she seemed to want to talk more about these girls *as* girls— about who Flo and Clara were (*in real life,* she kept saying) and how, through her research, Merritt had come to know them. Harper seemed especially interested in what boarding school or college life would have *really* been like for young women of Flo and Clara's day. That was one of her words: *really.*

Also: *typically.*

Also: *commonly.* She kept emphasizing these words to make her point.

"OK, but c'mon," Harper said after Merritt had spent several minutes telling her all about the Brookhants yearbooks Merritt had gotten from Elaine and their chronicles of various girls-only dances and girl-girl Valentine's Day events. "Be real with me—what about all the stuff about the courting rituals or whatever? With the lockets of hair and everything?"

"You're saying you don't give your admirers lockets of your hair?"

"Not recently, no."

"You should start. I think it would be very well received—at least until you ran out of it."

"Stop with the jokes," Harper said. "Answer my question."

"What even is your question?"

"I'm just trying to get, like, a baseline of what was expected of these girls then. I know how it happens in your book, but I mean, so, like, *lots* of girls were openly crushing on each other and making a thing of it, not hiding it? Like, was it *typical* to act like this while away at school? For most girls—not just Brookhants girls? Or was there something in the water there?"

Online, Merritt had landed on a Harper Harper fan Tumblr (one of many)—fuckyeahharperharper—and was watching a GIF of her settling in for an interview, just some random footage captured while they were setting up.

The whole of it is Harper turning toward someone off camera and grinning her signature grin while simultaneously tucking some hair behind her ear. Then a hand, an arm, slips into the shot and clips a microphone to her collar. That's the GIF, the whole thing—Harper grinning and tucking and being mic'd, grinning and tucking and being mic'd, grinning and tucking and . . . forever. This particular incarnation had 23,266 notes. It also had a string of attached commentary.

"Hello?" Harper said.

Merritt had been momentarily gifnotized. She pulled out of it and said, "They had the best slang for it back then. Much better than ours: *smashes. Spoons.*"

"I mean we do use *smash*," Harper said, sounding even through the phone like she was smiling that particular smile of hers. Merritt had seen so much of this same face in her internet searching that she'd already begun to think of it as HRF—Harper Resting Face.

"Not quite the same intentionality. Not 'I want to smash this girl.' More like 'I'm smashed on this girl.'"

"I get it," Harper said. "But, like, how many spoons were there, though?"

"Oh my God, you're not gonna let this go," Merritt said. "Young women elaborately crushing on each other, especially while away from their families for the first time, all grouped together at these schools out in the middle of nowhere, cut off from all other social spheres while they came of age romantically and physically, emotionally, was exactly as common an occurrence as I made it seem in the book. I'm talking *typical*, your word, for, like, I don't know—what, you want a fake number? How about sixty-five percent of a given student body? Probably more."

"No way," Harper said.

"Yes way," Merritt said. "But also, it was largely seen as, like, emotion for emotion's sake—or worse, some romantic ideal, like playacting courtly love. Also, it was understood as something these girls would absolutely put aside once men were again in sight. It was, like, campus tradition, not personal defect."

"It's still kind of bananas to think of, though," Harper said. "Way back then? I mean, not to be too modern or whatever, but it all seems pretty fucking queer to me."

"Sure," Merritt said, "if you were a well-to-do WASP from New England whose parents sent you off to school and you wanted to experience a few years of probably chaste but intense romantic courtship before you ended up marrying a man who would make all of your future life decisions while you birthed him many a baby and raised them up, only to send some off to war and all the others into a system of slavery-enriched US heteropatriarchal capitalism. Then absolutely. It was queer city."

Again, there was a pause. A longish one. And then, "OK," Harper said, that smile there across her words again. "I get it. I understand the limits. But also, you *know* it wasn't chaste for all of them. Stop being so sour and just admit that Brookhants was Planet Lady Love."

Merritt did laugh at *Planet Lady Love.* "They nearly put that on their crest," she said. "Now it seems shortsighted that *Esse Quam Videri* won out."

"What's that mean again?"

"'To Be, Rather Than to Seem,'" Merritt said. She'd been scrolling the Tumblr, had stopped at another GIF. This one was of a few moments from Harper's now-famous runaways-sharing-waxy-stolen-donuts-under-an-overpass scene from *Every Girl You Know.* It was a decidedly unsexy scene in the movie, but you'd never know it from this GIF, which was looped in such a way as to best show off the movements of Harper's sinewy arms.

"I feel certain that you'd have done well at Brookhants," Merritt said. "All the girls would have asked you to the dance."

"Mm-hmm," Harper said. "Only problem with that theory is I never would have gotten in. Unless they hauled their shit all the way out to Montana to hire me as a kitchen maid."

"How can you know?" Merritt said. "Maybe 1902 Harper Harper would have been a famous stage actress, then on to silent films. You still could have been one of the real greats." Merritt was just saying that to say it, but it's not unthinkable. Harper had the it. You know, *the it.*

"The 1902 me wouldn't have had the famous writer to be named after," Harper said. "Harper Lee wasn't even alive then."

"Why couldn't she be named after you?" Merritt said.

Harper didn't answer that, there was a lull, and though it was really only the first bit of silence between them since they'd started the call, Merritt didn't like it. She felt like it was the cue she was supposed to interpret as Harper's polite way of telling Merritt she'd *gotten all she needed, thanks.* So Merritt asked, "Did you get everything you needed from me?"

"Never," Harper said. "But I can let you go. I know I'm sort of fangirling you with all these questions."

"That's very funny," Merritt said.

"Why?"

"I mean that it's amusing to hear you, Harper Harper, use the verb *fangirling* in relation to something you're doing to me."

"I am doing it."

"Oh, OK," Merritt said. "I'm just thinking of your own rabid fans and this odd reversal."

"Now why would you go and say that my fans have rabies?"

"I lurk hard online," Merritt said. "You doing anything at all is apparently memeworthy—"

"Nah, now—" Harper tried to cut her off, but it was useless.

"Here's you smoking at a café in—maybe Paris? Is it too obvious to assume Paris? Barcelona?"

"Never been to Barcelona."

"OK, so smoking in Paris—check. Here's you drinking a slushee outside a perfectly suburban gas station."

"Yeah, OK," Harper said, laughing, "point made."

Merritt wasn't done. "Here's the GIF of you walking with that soccer player whose name I can never remember and you both hop over a puddle only you don't quite make it. Here's, like, seven in a row where you just take off a hat or put on a hat. You should read the comments on these. It's enough to make a lady blush."

"Not the ladies I know."

"Ha!" Merritt said. "Tell me, do you know that your fandom's hashtag is HARPEOPLE?"

"What now?" Harper said.

"Hashtag HARPEOPLE," Merritt said again. "There's a subreddit, too."

"I've never heard that," Harper said.

"Liar."

"I mean I mighta heard it somewhere," Harper said, her grin again draped over her words. This felt a whole lot like phone flirting to Merritt, Readers, but judge as you will (because of course you will).

"Well, go on," Merritt said. "You were supposedly fangirling me."

"You can't just point it out like that," Harper said.

"*You* pointed it out," Merritt said. "You used the word."

"Yeah, but now I'm embarrassed," Harper said.

"No, you're not," Merritt said. "You're miles from embarrassed. Let's have it—turn it up." She was not above being phone flattered by Harper Harper. Would you be? Really?

"I'm just saying that it's good, what you made," Harper said. "Like keeping Flo and Clara and the rest of them alive in your book—and known, that's like a legitimate thing to be proud of, you know, or have define you. I mean who writes a book at sixteen?"

"Other people," Merritt said quickly, the prickle of shame flicking along her skin like a rash. "Throughout time, plenty of them. Mary MacLane for one."

"She was nineteen," Harper said. "You beat her."

"I had a lot of help along the way, a lot of advice. I didn't do it alone."

"I'm not saying you did it alone, nobody does anything alone. I'm just saying that you did do it. *You* did. Take the credit."

Merritt felt distinctly uncomfortable for the first time since they'd started speaking. She wondered if she should now say the same kinds of things to Harper, tell her how enormous her talent was, how wonderful it was that she'd be playing Flo and how lucky it made her feel, but she also felt like those things would sound some-how too small or obvious—too sycophantic on the heels of Harper's own flattery. And so the air again hung silent between them for a few moments until there was Merritt's mother pulling into the driveway. And since her father had done what he'd done, surprises like this—anything out of the blue as it related to their home life—made Merritt rush to dread.

She could see through the windshield that her mother was not alone. One of her colleagues—a slim, man-bunned guy named Anderson—was with her. Neither of them noticed Merritt as they climbed out of her mother's neighborhood-ubiquitous Volvo station wagon.

"My mother just got home and I have to go," Merritt said, recognizing how young that no doubt sounded to someone like Harper Harper.

"Me too," Harper said. "Not my mom getting home but I do have to go. Thank you for this. I already have a clearer sense of things and it was rad just talking to you."

"You're very welcome," Merritt said. "Goodbye." She immediately regretted that sign-off, regretted not saying that she'd also liked talking to Harper. But it was too late to change it. She'd said what she'd said and that was that and why was her mother home, anyway?

If you walked from the driveway along the path that edged up against the house there was an overgrown holly hedge that blocked your view of the porch, at least until you arrived at its steps.

"Oh, you're home," Professor Emmons said with only mild surprise as she rounded that corner. "What happened to the library?"

"I decided I like the porch better," Merritt said. It was remarkable how quickly her worry over something potentially being wrong could shift into anger.

"Hi, Merritt," Anderson said. They were both standing in front of her now. "Good to see you."

She'd met Anderson before, many times. So had her father. They'd all even suffered through a dinner together once. But that was years ago. Merritt hadn't known her mother was seeing him again, at least in this particular way. Apparently, by coming home Merritt had unwittingly interrupted their afternoon tryst. God, gross.

"You know I don't like not knowing where you are," her mother said. "I wish you would have told me you were leaving campus."

"I did," Merritt said. "I texted you. Also, I'm twenty-one years old."

"Oh," her mother said, ignoring the last part of Merritt's reply as she inspected the curled leaves on a railing basket of pansies. "I didn't get it. Somehow, I don't have my phone. I went to put something in my calendar and realized. Did you see it in the kitchen?"

"No," Merritt said. "But I wasn't looking for it."

"Well, we just stopped in so I could grab it," her mother said. "Let me run and check." She slipped into the house.

Now Merritt and Anderson looked at each other.

"Any movie news?" he asked. "Your mom said they're really involving you. That must be dope."

"My mother says a lot of things that she thinks sound good."

"She's just proud of you," Anderson said. "She—"

"I'd rather we didn't speak anymore. Let's just wait together in unhappy silence."

He gave her the face she expected, one of surprise tinged pink.

She blinked at him.

Anderson might have been embarrassed to know just how much relief Merritt could see come over him as they listened to her mother approach, her boots across the wood floor of the entryway. "Got it," Professor Emmons said from behind the screen door. She was holding her phone up, shaking it at them.

"Oh thank gawd," Merritt said. "I was so worried."

"We've got to run or we'll be late for the department meeting." Professor Emmons was now walking back across the porch to the side stairs. Anderson followed a step or two behind.

"Don't leave on account of me," Merritt said.

"I think we should do kebabs tonight," her mother called back without turning around. "Can you get everything prepped and then we'll light the grill when I get home?"

"Mmmmm," Merritt said.

"Be sure to cut up those farmers' market peppers. They're getting soft. Love you!" Her car door slammed shut.

Merritt realized she hadn't mentioned the phone call, the hour spent talking to Harper Harper. (Flirting with Harper Harper? Yes. Yes, flirting.) And now she wasn't sure she would tell her mother about it at all. (She enjoyed being punitive in matters like this.)

In fact, Merritt might have almost let herself believe she'd day-dreamed the whole call were it not for the text she found waiting on her phone. Harper must have sent it only moments after they'd hung up.

Thanks again! Talking to you made me really happy. I'm off to a vintage store to find old lockets to put my hair in. You know, for the fans.

Merritt's response: ~~the fans~~ #HARPEOPLE.
And then she added, before she could convince herself not to:

talking to you made me happy, too

....

JULY 14, 2006

In bizarre breaking news, Caroline Wells (of *House Mother* fame) is being treated for life-threatening injuries after she crashed her car into a residential fence before being subsequently attacked by the property owner's dog early Friday afternoon in Bel Air. The incident was reportedly caught on two cameras within the property's extensive security system. (Footage has yet to be released.)

The out-of-work actress, age thirty-seven, mother of child actor Audrey Wells, age fourteen, who is currently filming the second season of her Disney Channel series *Class(y) Clowns*, was traveling alone on Friday, July 14, at approximately 1:20 P.M. when she allegedly swerved her Mercedes Benz over a curb and onto the lawn of homeowner Kevin Sokol. The vehicle then made its way up the lawn before crashing into Mr. Sokol's backyard fence, reports Spin-Spun. The specific cause of Wells's erratic driving is not clear at this time, though state police at the scene said they have reason to suspect intoxication.

Ms. Wells was reportedly not wearing a seat belt and sustained multiple injuries, including facial lacerations, from both the impact of the crash, which charged her vehicle through a large section of the fence, and also from the release of the front airbags.

SpinSpun reported that when Ms. Wells emerged from the vehicle, she was said to be incoherent and visibly impaired. She was also reported to be bleeding heavily from the head and face, and was screaming. At the time of the incident, the homeowner's two school-age children had been playing in the backyard with their dog, a female pit bull mix, which subsequently charged through the break in the fence and attacked Ms. Wells, pulling her to the ground. Having heard the crash, Mr. Sokol came outside and, after some confusion, was able to call off his dog. First responders arrived and Ms. Wells was transported to Good Samaritan Hospital, where she remains in critical condition.

In an interview with SpinSpun, Mr. Sokol said he believes that his dog was attempting to "protect the children," who were "upset and frightened" by the crash and the "bloody woman ranting on their lawn." Mr. Sokol added, "My kids said they thought she looked like a zombie or something. I swear to God the media better not make this about pit bulls. I'm sorry it happened but this is about what she did, not what our dog did in reaction." The dog in question, Garbo, is a rescue, age seven. Garbo remains with her owners at this time.

Last month, TMZ reported that producer Victor Castalano had filed for divorce from Caroline Wells after a series of headline-making public arguments. Audrey Wells is the couple's only child.

A request for comment from Ms. Wells's team wasn't immediately returned.

This is a developing story. It will be updated as details become available.

HARPER HARPER'S

COSTUME LIFE IN DTLA

....

One of **Harper's** cell phones, which she'd set on the counter next to her bathroom sink, buzzed with a call. Beneath the water droplets flicked on its screen, she saw that it was her manager asking where she was. They were supposed to meet with her social media team prior to the dinner she had that night (to strategize) and she was running late.

Her fingers were gooped with hair product, a purple-tinged paste. She smeared the screen as she texted him: I'm coming! I'm coming! On my way.

Her screen was now a mess, almost unreadable.

She'd gotten the hair product for free. She received so much free stuff these days. She felt compromised about it, about how it was totally true that the more you have, the more people want to give you, but when you've got nothing they find ways to make you pay for everything. Harper tried to use the things sent to her at least once or to pass them along to someone who would. Hence this paste she didn't even like—but free.

She wasn't thrilled with the state of her hair, but it would have to do because she needed to get out the door. Lateness was a bad habit from her not-so-old life, the one in Montana. It was something she'd worked on with real discipline in her new life, this Harper Harper movie star life that she still most often felt she was wearing around like a Halloween costume. Now she was someone who was on time, who kept deadlines and met expectations and seemed to do it with such effortlessness.

Harper believed that people liked this about her, this casual chill affect, best of all.

Given that it was an affect born of something once innate to her, the public expectation that she just was this way was mostly fine with Harper except she now felt that she always had to deliver it no matter what. Which, she'd realized, is the opposite of being chill.

She heard Eric saying something to Annie in the loft's main room. Annie could work like this, with intrusion. She could keep painting, or sculpting, or *arting*, even with a friend hanging around, even with a bunch of friends in and out and around. It was almost always Annie's own friends doing this, though. But tonight, it was Harper's friend Eric, in town for a week while on summer break from Brown. Harper had been the one to fly him out to LA and put him up at Chateau Marmont, which she told him was clichéd and overpriced (which is what everyone had said to her about it, even when she was in groups that nonetheless ended up there) but Eric couldn't be dissuaded. It was the sullied glamor of bad-choices-Hollywood-history he was after, and Harper was proud to be in a position to give it to him.

She pulled out her mascara (this brand one of Annie's recs). The Cigarettes After Sex vinyl started up in the main room. They were a band Annie had also introduced her to, their music like some sweetly melancholy weed dream. (Harper had recently purchased the record player at Annie's instruction as well.) Annie always worked to one band or artist exclusively until she didn't. See, so Annie did have artistic *rituals*. She just didn't let them become excuses.

Harper was starting to get used to having Annie around like this. Probably too used to it.

Eric wandered into the bathroom like a sleepy toddler about to ask for a cup of juice.

"You want?" He held out a joint to her. Eric had decided, he'd said, that he was only doing drugs the way people would have done them in the 1970s, so no vaping but plenty of joints, and no microdosing but a somewhat troubling (Harper thought) interest in cocaine bumped from the antique Laymon's aspirin tin he kept it in.

"Better not," Harper said. "This is a work thing."

"Isn't your whole life a work thing now?" He did not expect an answer to this and did not get one. Instead, he perched himself on the vanity, though there was hardly room for him there, one butt cheek slipping into the sink. This forced Harper to look around him to keep applying her blue mascara in the mirror he was now blocking. He was wearing these funny little vintage yellow soccer shorts and a white sweatshirt that he'd had on pretty much since arriving in California. He said he got the whole look from the lost and found in his dorm, which was very Eric. Knowing how to most effectively show off his killer legs was also very Eric.

"Do you want me to come with tonight since your scissor-sister bailed?" he asked.

"She didn't bail. She's working. You can see her working."

"And so," Eric said. "Me instead?"

"Always you. But not dressed like that and there's no time to get you back to change."

"I'm sure I could find something of yours to borrow."

"Yeah and then you'll look better in it than I do and forever ruin it for me."

"Life is full of these hard truths."

"Stay," Harper said. "Hang out with her. I wish I could stay. I won't be there long and then we'll meet up at whatever Annie has planned."

"That one does have all the plans." He hopped down and stood close behind her. Then he reached around to place what was left of the joint between her lips (she let him) before resting his chin on the curve of her shoulder. They both watched in the mirror as she inhaled.

"We're magnificent creatures," Eric said before licking her neck.

"Do you really not like her?"

He shrugged. "I don't like anyone. What I like is that you like her." He'd pulled the roach from her mouth and flicked it down the drain and was now opening her tub of free hair paste and working it in his palm.

"I do like her."

"I can tell." While she finished her makeup, he worked on her hair, sculpting the wave she'd made of it into something messier and more interesting. "Aren't you two just playing with each other, though? Really?"

"Did I tell you her friends gave me shit about this place?" Harper felt a pinch of regret in confessing this to Eric, because while she knew she'd appreciate his commiseration in the short term, she also knew that he would make this more than it was and hang on to it forever.

He was already set to do so. "What do you mean they *gave you shit*? What kind of shit?"

"Just, when they first came over, a bunch of them were making these comments about how nobody buys lofts in downtown Los Angeles and—I don't know—gentrification maybe, or that plus it just being tasteless, I guess. I got the feeling they think the whole place is super tacky in all the ways."

"What the actual fuck?" Eric said. "And you were hosting these people at the time? So they're literal guests here in your *home* and they can't shut their mouths for a minute while they drink your alcohol? Not to mention you're twenty-four and you bought a house, in cash, with your own earned income, so please go sit on a gold-plated tack, you fucking turd barns."

"I mean, some of them are fine."

He wasn't having it. "Oh, oh—don't temper it, Harps. I go to school with enough of them. I am intimately familiar with their ilk."

This rant made her miss him so acutely that it had the effect of a side stitch: sharp and sudden. His being there magnified all the months in between when the two of them hadn't talked like this.

"And so what did your Georgia O'Keeffe do while her megabesties were—" Eric cut himself off when Harper turned around and gave him a surprise hug.

"I love you," she said into the side of his head.

"Please tell me that you're playing with each other and it's not just her playing with you."

"*Come out and haunt me, I know you want me / Come out and haunt me-e-e,*" Greg Gonzalez sang from the other room.

"We're both having fun," she said.

"So much fun," Eric said. "A speed train of pleasure. A cruise liner of orgasms."

Harper let go of him and headed into the bedroom. He followed her, but she stopped there only long enough to grab her black biker jacket from where it was draped over the end of her bed, new and expensive—both the bed and the jacket. "Too much?" she asked him as she shrugged one sleeve on.

"Not enough," he said. "Nevertheless, you're a picture."

She shoved her other arm through its sleeve—and as her hand pushed through the material she felt her fingers brush against something strange near the cuff. Immediately after, with no time even to blink, she felt the sting: a bright flash of pain near the cuticle of her ring finger. "Fuck!" she said as a reflex.

"What?" Eric asked.

Harper kept pushing through the sleeve and her hand emerged along with the buzzing form of a riled yellow jacket. She brought her finger to her face to inspect the now-throbbing red bump there, and the yellow jacket fell to the floor, twitching, one wing bent out of place.

"This fucker stung me." She bent to look at it and Eric joined her. It made angry, buzzing circles on the polished concrete where it had landed.

"That was in your jacket?"

"In the sleeve."

"Weird."

"It really hurts."

"You're not allergic?"

She shook her head no as Eric scooted his toe toward it. Harper kicked his foot away with her own. "Don't kill it," she said.

"You can't leave it. It's irate and out for vengeance. And Annie's barefoot, isn't she? Like always since I've ever seen her?"

"It's how she paints," Harper said. "I have to go."

"What are we doing about this?" He pointed at the twitching yellow jacket.

"I'll put it out a window later. I can't now, I'm late." She put her throbbing finger back in her mouth and headed out the bedroom door.

"You'll forget about it," Eric said, following her. "And then Frida Kahlo's gonna step on it. I can see it all in slow motion, the inevitable horror to come."

They emerged into the loft's open space: living room, kitchen, two walls of brick and two walls of floor-to-ceiling windows, all of it lidded by rafters with exposed pipes and wires. *Build a Loft 101,* she'd overheard one of Annie's friends say.

Annie was crouched atop a paint-splattered drop cloth, surrounded by dozens and dozens of thick paper leaves in various stages of green from the color wash she had just finished applying to them. She was wearing the too-big Carhartt overalls she usually worked in, nothing at all on underneath. Even though it had been weeks since they'd started this, that fact still made Harper flush with desire, as it did now: coming into the room to find Annie, her hair up and a brush in hand, a flat white from the espresso machine she'd had sent over cooling on the table nearby, all of this while dressed in the brown uniform that Harper had previously associated with ranchers and winter in Montana, with wet hay stuck on the bib and mud and manure on the hems, and definitely not with seminaked queer painters whose parents owned, it seemed, most of the buildings in downtown Chicago and lived (when they were in America and not one of the other half dozen places they had property) on the top three floors of the most impressive of them.

While Harper took ice from the freezer for her finger, Eric took a bowl from the cupboard and went back into the bedroom and put it upside down over the yellow jacket. He then wrote a note on a napkin, which he placed atop the bowl: **Hostile insect enclosed. Remove at own risk.**

Harper wrapped a baggie of ice around her finger and then stopped just behind Annie, who had moved over to a table piled with several stacks of *The Story of Mary MacLane*—the 1902 edition with the red binding she'd collected from eBay and specialty bookshops. Several copies of the book were next to those stacks, already in various stages of undoing—pages removed, shapes cut from those pages: all apple tree leaves. Annie now had scissors in hand and was cutting more.

"I'm going," Harper said, kissing the back of her neck.

"Jesus, you scared me," Annie said, still cutting. "I thought you'd gone."

"These look amazing," Harper said, looking over Annie's shoulder at her work.

"Eh—I dunno," Annie said. "I'm still not sure if the thickness is what they want or how they'll stand up outside. Or how long they'll have to be outside. I'm using an ocean of shellac to bind them but, I dunno—have to wait and see."

"*We're* going," Eric announced as he headed toward the loft's main door.

"I thought you were staying to keep me company?" Only now did Annie look up from what she was doing, stalled with her scissors midsnip.

"I thought you were, too," Harper said to him unhappily. But so-chill-unhappily, Readers.

Eric maintained a facial blandness. "It's just that I haven't lolled by the pool looking thirsty at all today. And, I mean, isn't that what I came all the way to LA for? Where are my promised blow jobs?"

"Who promised you blow jobs," Harper said. "Not me."

"Those shorts do appear to offer easy access," Annie said, contemplating them, and Eric in them, for a moment before she turned around, told Harper that she looked hot, and pulled her in for a kiss, scissors still in hand.

"Careful of my jacket," Harper said. She stood very still until Annie moved herself and the scissors back into her own space.

Annie shrugged. "You show up with a slash down the back of your jacket and people will just think it's a trend. It'll be all over Instagram in two days."

"She's not wrong," Eric said as they headed out the door.

Harper knew that what Eric saw was the version of Annie who'd sent over the espresso machine and convinced her to buy the record player. What he hadn't yet had time to see was the Annie who, when they were passing through a particular neighborhood, might point to a house and say something like: "Let's move here and live out the rest of our lives in a David Hockney painting."

And when Harper said back, "Who's David Hockney?" that version of Annie wouldn't laugh or shake her head like, *Of course you don't know who that is.* She wouldn't even say, *Oh, just this painter,* and then not elaborate because it was easier than doing so. This was the way that a lot of Annie's friends treated Harper: dropping various cultural references and when she didn't immediately grasp them, dismissing them—and also, it felt like, a piece of her—before moving on.

Annie was someone who wanted to share her excitement. She'd say, "I can't wait to show you." And then she would. And not, like, on Google Images on her phone. Next thing Harper knew, she would be on her way to a Hockney retrospective at some museum, holding Annie's hand as they stood together in front of all those California swimming pool paintings and houses in pinks and yellows and greens, while Annie talked about how Hockney had achieved this or that effect, or how he imbued his work with queer sexuality. And she wouldn't lecture about it. She wouldn't perform. She'd talk, effervescent, expecting (correctly) that her enjoyment would spill over.

This was what Harper liked best about Annie: how excited she got about the things she loved and how much pleasure it gave her to share those things with others.

But Harper was also pretty certain that what Annie liked best about *her* was that she was Harper Harper—*the* Harper Harper. Of course, Annie would never say exactly that but, I mean, would they even have met if she wasn't? Where exactly, in her old life, would Harper have run into Annie Meng, a trust-funded visual artist who showed in galleries around the world and was about to embark on her third gap year? (*Gears*, Annie called them, as in, *One wasted year at Columbia, but now I'm thankfully in third gear.*) These people did not exist in Harper's old life.

Eric was a relic from that old life.

The car they'd sent was waiting in front of Harper's building. She asked the driver to drop her first.

"I'm late and you can't make me later," she said to Eric as she texted her manager to tell him she was finally heading that way. "You're not even supposed to be here—you're supposed to be getting to know her."

"I know her enough," Eric said.

"You don't."

"Will you FaceTime with my mom for a minute?" he asked. "So she can brag to all her friends and I can call it her birthday present?"

As they crept through traffic, Harper did this. She smiled her biggest smiles and mentioned her top-five most exciting recent career things to mention, those sure to most impress moms.

"It's all soooo exciting!" Mrs. Neighhardt said through Eric's phone screen. She was on a counter stool in her kitchen, the same white-and-red kitchen from Eric's house that Harper remembered from high school, and that room, even more than the woman in it now beaming at her, filled Harper with an achy nostalgia.

"Glamorous!" Eric's mom went on. "It's very glamorous. We're so proud of you, honey. And you look beautiful—every single time I see you in a magazine I cut out the picture and save it for you. I have a folder."

"Thank you, Mrs. Neighhardt."

"I can tell you both think that's stupid but wait forty years and you'll thank me, if I'm still around. You know they won't even have magazines soon enough. Every single thing will only be on our phones."

"Phones are the magazines, Mom," Eric said.

"It's not the same thing. Not at all."

While Eric was hanging up with his mom, Harper's phone buzzed with a different call. It was her uncle Rob, which was unexpected. She didn't answer.

"You're getting like the full Scrooge tour," Eric said when she showed him Rob's name on her phone's screen. "When all the ghosts of your past come a-calling. Have you been talking to him?"

"No," she said. "Not for more than a year." She stared at the screen, awaiting a voice mail pop-up.

"Oooooh. What do you think he wants?"

"I have no idea," Harper said and meant it.

"You just gave him a shit ton of money, didn't you?"

"I gave him thirty grand. But that was last year."

"Jesus, Harps. I knew you were sending him something but thirty grand is, what, an eighty percent interest rate? You were only there like three months."

"Five," she said. There was still no voice mail.

"Three months, five months, same thing."

"Not to me when I was there."

Eric didn't say anything to that.

"You know he hadn't actually asked me for anything when I sent it. I just did it. And then he took forever to cash it."

"You should have blocked him right after he did. Debt paid, ATM closed."

"I don't think that's why he's calling," she said. "It's probably something about my grandparents, something he wants me to do for them."

"You mean buy for them. So Paul and Joan are fine now? Completely cured of their homophobia?"

"I mean, no—not completely. But they're not stupid. They do understand the correlation between me being a famous lesbian and me being able to buy them a boat, so . . ."

"So they're pragmatic bigots."

"Just, you know, baby steps. God, my finger still really fucking hurts." Harper shook her hand back and forth because the motion made the throbbing quell, but only for as long as she kept doing it. Her baggie of ice was now one of water.

"You wanna bump?" Eric asked, reaching into his back pocket for the aspirin tin.

"No," she said. "I want the pain in my finger to go away. I don't want a coke rush."

"I'm wondering if we wet some down, though—made like a medicated paste?"

"Stop."

"I'm trying to help," he said.

"Are you, though?"

Eric snorted from the brass snuff key he wore around his neck, another, he said, antique. He screwed up his face in a wince, one eye watering as he rubbed his nostrils.

"You think it's maybe time to check in on how often you're doing that?"

"I'm on vacation." He snapped the lid back onto the tin. "OK, OK, be honest Sixty-forty? Seventy-thirty? What's the strap-on breakdown with Annie, for real? Lesbian tops are a myth, right? Like Sasquatch."

"You're an idiot."

"But I'm your idiot. Always, my love."

Back before this costume life, back in the not-really-so-long-ago that was her senior year of high school, Harper and Eric had formed the queer bond of being out queers in a place where others weren't, mostly.* They'd known each other since elementary school, but be-

---

* The moment that sealed the deal on their friendship came one afternoon when they'd been seated near to each other at a school assembly. A girl named Amber Blankenship had, to the great amusement of her friends, called Harper a *man-dyke*. Harper responded simply enough with "That's an oxymoron." And that might have been that, but Eric then turned to the girl and offered this: "See, Amber, you're such a fucking moron that even your insults fall under that category."

fore coming out, they'd never had cause to confide in each other. They just didn't have that much else in common. Eric was a GPA-tracking, overachieving (when he wanted to be) type. His mom was on the city council. He did concert choir and competitive speech and drama and already had a college scholarship waiting for him. He'd earned it. And his parents expected it.

Meanwhile, Harper had half-heartedly googled some community colleges in the tri-state area. She kind of liked the dorm options at one in North Dakota. (At least how they showed them on their website, which was probably misleading, she knew.) She had a job at a grocery store four afternoons a week and had thought, quite a lot, about spending at least her first year after high school still doing that job—only hopefully with more hours. This plan felt manageable to Harper. Reasonable. And best of all: largely self-sufficient. Her grandparents would be disappointed, but then she'd been disappointing them a lot that year already.

She'd been living with them (again) since her mom, Shelly, had (again) lost a job due to her drinking. It had been a revoked driver's license that did it this time. She'd needed to have one as a condition of her employment and had lied about losing it (due to a series of DUIs she'd accrued). They got behind on their rent, then more behind, then evicted. Ethan went to stay with his dad (who was not Harper's dad) in Deer Lodge and Shelly and Harper moved in with Grandma Joan and Grandpa Paul, as they'd done a few times before.

Harper's grandparents had always functioned more as a second set of parents than not. Harper even looked like her mom, a lot like her—the *you two could be sisters* remark wasn't far-fetched—at least when Shelly was taking care of herself. Sometimes it seemed to Harper that her grandparents saw her as a chance to correct some crucial parenting error they'd made with her mom. A do-over.

For years, Harper's grandfather had called her *my tomboy* with pride. During the summers she'd go along with him when he went junking: helping him to haul things from the muck and weeds of outbuildings and then spending long afternoons in his workshop while he fixed those things for resale. Her grandfather was anything but a showman. Even still, Harper thought his skills were a kind of magic. It's not everyone who can take a broken hunk of metal that's been sunk into the ground for years and make it work again. He could.

"This one don't mind getting her hands dirty," he'd say when people asked about her tagging along, snapback on her head and dirt on her T-shirt. But tomboy chic had apparently stopped being so charming to her grandparents once she'd reached an age where it didn't just speak to her haircut or her clothing, but also to who she brought home to their couch on a date—or who she wanted to bring home, anyway.

Harper hadn't been *at all* prepared for how personally they'd take her coming out. They weren't religious and they weren't political, even if they did watch Fox News. She couldn't remember them ever having much at all to say about queer people before she said she was one.

And they still didn't have much to say about queer people. Well, that's what they *said*: that they didn't want to talk about it and didn't want her to, either. Leave it alone.

But her grandparents' silence on the issue was confusing, because while they made clear that they didn't want to discuss it with her, the fact of her being gay now seemed to make them unhappy with every *other* thing about her too, even stuff they'd let slide before. It was like a kind of eclipse that darkened the whole of her for them: her clothing, her friends, her smoking—which they'd known about for a while. They acted like being around her *this way* was too much to ask of them. Hadn't they suffered enough with Shelly? Did Harper really have to go and add this, too? It was selfish, as they saw it, attention-seeking.

Harper's mom, for her part, was fully supportive. But Shelly didn't hold much sway with her own parents right then.

Then came January and the start of Harper's final semester of high school. And since she still didn't know what she'd be doing *after* high school, this semester had taken on a terrifying weight to her. She both wanted to get it over with and wanted it to slow down.

Shelly was doing the *new year, new you* thing she'd done lots of times before and was supposedly getting her shit together, drying out. She'd found a job cleaning rooms at a motel in Butte. But she was also seeing this guy from that job who Harper did not like at all and she wasn't around much. And when she was, Harper didn't think her shit seemed so together.

The final straw: her grandparents ran into Harper while she was with Eric at a gas station. For whatever reason—because why the hell not—he'd been wearing pink sunglasses and this cheap, white net wedding veil they'd just found caught in the branches of a tree. Harper's grandparents wouldn't even acknowledge her. They pretended not to know her when she said hi, actually turned their faces away and ignored her, which was so absurd and dumb. She made a big joke of it later with Eric, but fuck: it gutted her. When she got home that night, they tried to issue an ultimatum about who she could and couldn't spend her free time with and what she could spend it doing. If she was to continue living under their roof, that is. This was Montana in 2009 and not Rhode Island in 1902, and yet, astute Readers, this ultimatum wasn't so far removed from the one Clara Broward's mother had once issued to her.

And just like Clara, Harper wasn't having it.

She loved her grandparents as they were, and she hated that they couldn't love her the same way. And so long as Ethan was fine with his dad, and he was, she really just wanted to finish her senior year in peace. It was appreciably efficient, Harper's desire (and ability) to compartmentalize her life this way. Call it a coping mechanism if you want to. She called it an asset. At least at that age.

So she went looking for her mother's brother, Uncle Rob.

"You must be feeling pretty sorry for yourself if you scrounged around long enough to get to me," he'd told her when she'd asked if she could stay with him for an undefined *while*. She'd been waiting for him on his concrete stoop, trying not to smoke all her cigarettes as she sat in the dark and cold, her backpack and a scuffed-up wheelie suitcase beside her.

At the time, Rob seemed not at all surprised to pull up in his

Camry and find her there waiting for him. Not surprised, but not pleased, either. He'd just gotten home from work and they went in the door together, Rob immediately unbuttoning his blue button-down to expose the undershirt beneath. He liked to keep his house very warm.

Rob did tech support at an area hospital. He'd held his current job for five years, even buying himself this square house with its square of dead lawn. And he paid his electric bill on time, had car insurance and a meager retirement plan. So in Harper's family he was the success story: the steady, reliable, asshole Rob.

Mostly, she used it as a place to sleep and shower. She had school and the grocery store and the rest of the time there were her friends and their houses, especially Eric's house and his mom's red-and-white kitchen. (Harper sometimes got the sense that the Neighhardts didn't like her very much. Or they didn't like her as an influence on Eric. They couldn't see that it was mostly Eric influencing her and not the other way around.)

Rob kept a steady schedule. There was food in his fridge. He did laundry on Sundays. He pulled in the driveway after work like he said he would and got up and left again in the morning, locking the door behind. All of this was something.

But also: sometimes he would come home in a bad mood, or want to show off to his friends, one of whom always made a point of telling Harper she was *too hot to end up a lezzie for real*. On those nights, he might watch the TV with the volume turned up stupid loud, or be watching porn on his laptop and not trying very hard to hide it.

This was when his small house, which he kept too damn hot—half of the windows painted shut and a kind of vile, carpet-cleaner-and-sour-milk smell spread over its insides—felt the most treacherous to Harper. So she tried not to be there, even if it meant staying out in the gruesome Montana winter wind, wandering around with Eric—if he could get away from his own house, which was trickier for him than it was for her.

If Harper had known of Mary MacLane then (she didn't) she

might have seen herself, with Eric, as philosophers of *their own peri-patetic school*—hour after hour spent walking around and talking about their *dull, dull life*—and *the pageant of the Possibilities*˙ in their future. Eric could talk cleverly about anything. Sometimes he quoted his favorite Tumblr accounts verbatim. He was funny and cutting—downright mean, a lot of the time—and Harper liked hearing him go off, especially about people in her own life: her grandparents, Rob-the-Slob. She let him have almost all the soliloquies. He did them better than she did, anyway.

She felt like Eric saw her the way she wasn't yet but wanted to be, the way she hoped she'd grow into. Other people called her hot, sometimes—creeps at the grocery store, Rob's friends—but Eric said she was *cursed by queer beauty*, which he could manage to say in a way that didn't sound dumb. It made her feel seen. Eric talked about queerness as an asset. She'd never thought about it like that before. Sometimes she thought that she could almost feel her brain learning new ways to think when she was around him. She liked it.

When people asked about what she was going to do after high school, even when Eric asked her, she grew fidgety and agitated, avoided their eyes as she told them that she didn't know yet, she'd figure it out. She couldn't admit to these people (pity or doubt on their faces) that her dreams were bigger than whatever lesser option she knew they were imagining for her. Sometimes she couldn't even admit this to herself. It felt daunting to believe in those dreams. And naive. Picking up hours at the grocery store felt much safer. Slippery, but safer.

But the truth was: she *could* see a shiny version of her future, without having any clue how to get there. She only knew that how not to get there was to let herself sink into the easier life, the one that was all around her here, beckoning: rolling down its window in the grocery store parking lot and asking if she wanted a ride, if she wanted to party.

˙ *The Story of Mary MacLane* January 15 entry.

She'd been at Uncle Rob's for five months when the casting call and the movie being filmed in Missoula changed everything forever. One bleak and barren Mary MacLane winter, one that pushed Harper up against the dark void of that other, waiting life—the wrong one, the slippery one. And then a miracle. And then the exact kind of luck that was unfathomable, it was so big.*

There's no business like show business, there's no business I know.

---

* Mary MacLane herself had this kind of luck to go along with her talent. If we're calling it luck, and Harper herself always called it that when telling her own story.

BODIES PILING UP.

SNOW PILING UP.

BUT WHERE TO PLACE THE

BLAME AT BROOKHANTS?

....

It's now past time that I pull you back to 1902, Readers, to the angel's trumpets and glass of the Brookhants Orangerie, where Eleanor Faderman still lay dead and gripping the once-missing copy of Mary MacLane's book. The copy now again accounted for.

And oh had it ever been accounted for. The unlucky students who found Eleanor had already told their classmates about it, which meant the whole of the school knew. Now, while they waited for help to arrive from town, most of the faculty had come to see for themselves. In fact, a few of them seemed almost as concerned about the presence of the book as they did the body.

And it was up to **Principal Libbie Brookhants** to do something about that.

Do it now, she told herself. Take it from her now before someone else does, before they all notice. And talk.

Principal Brookhants stood in a swarm of her colleagues, still gathered near—but not *too near*—to Eleanor's body. A few were even standing atop the bitten blooms. Some were weeping. All were stricken with horror. Around them fogged the cloying scent of the angel's trumpet at night.

You must do it now, Libbie told herself, sliding around Miss Lawrence and closer to Eleanor.

Libbie Brookhants was still a relatively young woman and looked it in the flush of her cheeks and the shine of her gingerbread hair. There were, it's true, the beginnings of crow's-feet at the edges of her eyes, but only the beginnings. She still looked young enough to be mistaken, on occasion and from afar, for one of her students.

What's more, she felt young, felt it acutely in moments like this one, with so many other women waiting for her judgment and instruction. She was the youngest of her many siblings, all of them brothers with a surname to uphold. Or better yet, outdo. At the age of twenty-two, she'd married a very old man only to almost immediately become his very young widow. And for the last eight years, she'd been the young principal and proprietor of this school, her school: the Brookhants School for Girls.

"I can't think how we'll go on now," Miss Larson was saying to Miss Hamm as Libbie managed to position herself behind Eleanor.

"We can't and we won't," Miss Hamm said. "It would be indecent to. It's indecent to even be gathered here."

Libbie didn't disagree. She was now within reach of the book, if only she could bend down to retrieve it. But even as they pretended to look away, she could feel the eyes of her colleagues upon her. They were watching her, waiting to remark upon her handling of this moment, waiting to catch her out and place the blame for this—and for Flo and Clara, too—squarely at her feet. Perhaps she should let them. Close the school and . . .

And what? What then?

Libbie had been crying. She'd stopped, now. Mostly. But the water in her eyes bubbled her vision. It made her almost seasick: the crimson book below her puffed like sailcloth and the crowd of grim faces before her as warped and strange as gargoyles stuffed into shirtwaists. All except for Miss Alexandra Trills. Alex, *her* Alex[*]—a head, two heads, in some cases—taller than any of the other women in the room and as familiar as ever, even now. Libbie wiped her eyes

---

[*] Alex to Libbie and Alex to us. Always.

and held them to Alex's own until she felt them lock together in silent conversation.

Miss Trills and Mrs. Brookhants were suited to this kind of intimate exchange because of the intimacy of their relationship. It was an intimacy known, while also sometimes deliberately or ignorantly misunderstood, by their colleagues. In the language of the day, Mrs. Brookhants was a young widow and Miss Trills was her devoted companion. Her *very, very* dear friend. Her confidante.

Her bestie.*

However, Miss Trills and Mrs. Brookhants had no time to find much comfort in their friendship on this night. At least not in this moment. In fact, perhaps it was only more fuel to the fire. For when, emboldened by Alex's presence at the back of the crowd, Libbie carefully knelt to retrieve the book, the music teacher, Miss Hamm, struck like a coiled serpent:

"And so what is your excuse for it this time, Mrs. Brookhants? Or will you now finally condemn it?" Miss Hamm pushed her way to the front of the unhappy group. She was both the most doctrinaire and the most dramatic of the Brookhants faculty. She pointed a finger at the book as if she were on the witness stand and had been asked to indicate to the court the presence of a murderer. Leanna Hamm did love an audience. "There's a known wickedness in that book and our girls won't leave it alone. I don't think they can. I don't think they *want* to." She spoke this last bit with hushed alarm lacquered over her words.†

The group looked at Libbie for her response. She had not yet removed the book but was still kneeling to do so. She gathered herself before speaking. "We're all as devastated by this as you are, Leanna. But I won't pretend the devil himself lives in this book." She used

---

*   But, like, with benefits.

†   Here's how Libbie Brookhants characterized that moment in her diary: *It was almost as if Leanna didn't want the book to hear what she was saying about it.*

this as her cue, it was as good as any, and lifted the book from Eleanor's grip. She was very gentle.

Even still: a few teachers gasped or turned away. But not Miss Hamm.

"It's every bit as real a culprit as a knife or a jar of poison. It *is* a poison!" Miss Hamm was now sniffing in indignation. "It poisons the mind."

"The flowers Eleanor ate are the only poison here," Alex said as she moved nearer to Libbie.

"And *why* did she eat them?!" Miss Hamm asked as if Alex had proved her point rather than countered it.

"They were all in that club," Miss Cullen said quickly, hoping to egg on Miss Hamm, which was Miss Cullen's way. "We had that group of them reciting it: *Kind Devil this and Kind Devil that.*"

"Eleanor Faderman was never in that club," Alex said. "She wouldn't have been asked."

Miss Hamm ignored her. "I said at the time we shouldn't allow it on campus—the book or their awful group."

"And certainly forbidding something has never before encouraged our students to pursue it," Libbie said. She now held the book—as casually as possible, given the circumstances—against the folds of her skirts. Alex, ever perceptive to her Libbie's unstated desires, moved carefully alongside her and took the book from her hand, holding it low against her side, then her back.

"They would go out into the woods, remember?" Miss Hamm said, her excitement mounting now that she sensed others were backing her up. "And come back feral and rude, full of bad ideas."

---

* It was Miss Hamm (who felt she had bonded with Clara's mother during a campus visit) who wrote a letter outlining her concerns about the hold she believed Mary MacLane's book had over the girl. In fact, it was the receipt of that letter, in concert with cousin Charles's ravings, that was the cause of Clara's last-minute trip to Newport, so that Mrs. Broward could issue her ultimatum about ridding Mary MacLane, *and* Florence Hartshorn, from her daughter's life.

"But that isn't the same copy, is it?" someone asked from the back. "It's not the copy we found with Florence and Clara?"

"That copy was previously disposed of," Libbie said firmly. This was a lie.

"At least there's that," Miss Lawrence said.

"You're certain?" Miss Hamm asked in side-eye. "I understood it to be lost. That's what we were told—that's what Clara Broward's own mother was told."

"I am very sure," Libbie said. She softened some. "There *is* more than one copy of this book in existence."

"It broke sales records, didn't it?" Alex said. "For weeks it was everywhere."

"And what a poor commentary on the state of things *that* fact is," Miss Hamm said.

Libbie tried to speak now with the firm authority of her position. "If any of you would take the time to read it," she said, looking pointedly at Miss Hamm, "as *I have,* you would know that it's primarily the purity of feeling expressed that our girls are responding to. The author is about their age and so earnest in her passions, so forthright and unabashed. She seems to them like someone who could be their bright-brash friend. Some of our girls even seem to think they could be her."

"Heaven help us if that's true," Miss Hamm said.

"Why don't we help ourselves instead, Leanna?" Libbie said. "I think we're quite capable of it. The book is nothing more than a young girl's diary."

"Nothing more than a diary?" Miss Hamm scoffed. "Let me ask you, Mrs. Brookhants, did *your* childhood diary cause a group of girls to make a suicide pact in"—she turned to Miss Mercado to ask—"where was it that I told you?"

"St. Louis, I think it was," Miss Mercado said, like she was hoping for a gold star.

"I did not keep a diary as a child," Libbie said.

Miss Hamm ignored her, playing to her crowd. "And now they'll be telling the same stories about Brookhants and our girls. And they should!" She turned again to Libbie. "We've all granted you considerable room to test convention here, Mrs. Brookhants. Time and again I've said nothing, even when I thought your educational methods dangerously liberal. Slipshod—"

"Now, Leanna—" Miss Mercado tried to slow her, but Alex was more forceful.

"You've *granted* Mrs. Brookhants nothing, Miss Hamm," she said. "Not one thing. It is simply not in the realm of your authority to do so."

Now Miss Hamm was spitting her words. "Since coming here, I've excused the goings-on at this school more times than I can count. I've made excuses for *every sort* of accusation imaginable—the things I've excused—but you can be sure that I will do it no longer. And I will not be told that a bad book is a good one and pretend to agree." She gathered herself again. "We've failed these girls. Three deaths and *we're* to blame. How many more will it take?"

"I don't—" Libbie began, but again there was no point. Leanna Hamm was too competent a performer to give away the last word.

"I feel very unwell and am going to bed now," she said, pushing her way back through her colleagues. A few of the others said and did similarly. But only a few. The crowd reshuffled around Libbie, awaiting their instructions.

"I don't feel as strongly as Leanna does about that book," Miss Lawrence said. "But it does seem to me, at *this* moment, rather foolish to waste your breath as its defender."

"I wasn't defending the book," Libbie said. "I was defending reason against superstition."

"I'm sure that's what you believe you were doing," Miss Lawrence said. "Even still, what will you do with the copy you took from Eleanor?"

"I'll take care of it," Libbie said. "It won't be seen here again."

She meant this.

※

Much later, once various officials had arrived and questions had been asked and answered—answered primarily by Libbie Brookhants and without any mention of the book—and after Eleanor's body had been examined by the physician and collected by the undertakers, and after a decision had been made to cancel regular classes for the following day to allow the students the time needed to reflect and begin their mourning, the remaining faculty members, in puff-eyed pairs or groups, also left for their beds. It was now well after midnight and there had been considerable talk of the weather turning bad.

"I think we should stay here tonight," Libbie said when she and Alex were finally alone in The Orangerie. "Whatever's left of tonight." Through the windows they might have seen their carriage waiting, but Libbie wasn't looking through the windows. Instead, she was staring at the place where Eleanor's body had been, so many bitten blooms still smashed there. "These need to be removed before morning," she said, swirling some around with her foot. "Or girls will be gaping at them."

"Collecting them as souvenirs," Alex said, taking Libbie's hand. "They'll be gone. Miss Lawrence said she'd have it done before breakfast."

"Must we kill the tree, you think?" Libbie asked as she looked up into the branches of the angel's trumpet. "To stop tongues wagging."

"Killing it won't do that. Besides, there are thirty other plants here that would have the same effect. Eaten in this quantity, maybe more than thirty."

"I don't want to kill it," Libbie said.

"Neither do I," Alex said. "It's a beautiful tree."

Libbie looked where Eleanor had been and asked, "What could she have been thinking?"

"I wish I knew," Alex said. She then lightly pressed her lips to the hand she was holding before pulling it, and Libbie, to her and finding her mouth. It was a kiss given and returned simply, a comforting act of normalcy during a most distressing time.

"You're asleep on your feet," Alex said. "Home will be best. We'll have Caspar bring us back in time to join the girls for breakfast."

Libbie nodded. She was grateful for Alex's care, for the routine of it.

And yet: between them thrummed a chord of discontent that reached far beyond the immediate trouble here at Brookhants.

Alex bundled Libbie into her coat and scarf. They were headed, by carriage, to Breakwater, Libbie's ocean home, which is where Alex would also be spending the night. Indeed, despite her small but private quarters on campus in the Faculty Building, Breakwater—beyond the woods and overlooking the ocean—was where Miss Trills spent most of her nights while she was a teacher at Brookhants, there in Libbie's bed.* In *their* bed.

"Do you have the book?" Libbie asked as they were at the door.

"I nearly forgot it," Alex said. "Thank God you didn't." She crossed the room and took it from behind a large watering can where she'd stashed it earlier.

Libbie had to keep herself from grabbing for it as Alex again came close. It is enough, she told herself, that she has it in her hand and it's coming home with us.

On a clear night, the journey from campus should have lasted about twenty minutes. But now the hour was late, the clouds were thick, and the storm had arrived.

In the cold closeness of the carriage, surrounded by the even colder sound of its wheels squeaking over the snow-packed road, Alex continued to hold the red book between them: their party's third, and unwanted, guest.

"I wish I'd thought to take this from her sooner," Alex said, her warm breath creating a fog that would soon mist the carriage windows. "If I'd managed it before the others had noticed . . . This book has only ever been bad for us."

"Not you, too, darling," Libbie said. Casually, so casually, she took

---

* This was the very same house, astute Readers, that Elaine Brookhants Kessler now owned, the house where Merritt Emmons wrote *The Happenings at Brookhants*.

the book from Alex in her gloved hand and thumbed its pages. "If I had read this as a girl of Eleanor's age, I would have thought it the whole world. And if I'd known you then, I would have asked you to read it so that we could talk about it being exactly right in all its glinting feeling."

"You would have *told* me to read it," Alex said. "And I would have, to humor you."

The carriage jerked and they were tossed together, hard, against a sidewall before it was righted—and now no longer moving. Caspar, their driver, shouted his apology. "Hit a drift and they lost their footing." He was off his perch, down on the ground and talking soothingly in an attempt to settle the horses as he dug at their legs halted there in the snow. "It will have to be the sleigh tomorrow," he yelled.

That drift wasn't helping matters, but you should know that the horses were often spooked in this particular patch of road as it cut through the woods—the trees tall and dense on either side, too many of their low branches stretching out to scrape the carriage with a horrid sound like bone fingers finding a coffin lid.And now there was more snow, the flakes sudden and angry.

As Caspar worked, the carriage shuddered with his efforts, and Libbie said, quietly, "You do know that when you say this book is *bad,* you sound like Leanna Hamm, and that should frighten you very much."

"I think I am a little frightened," Alex said. "And it hasn't a thing to do with Leanna Hamm." She paused. Considered. "I did not say the book itself is bad."

"You didn't?"

"I said this business with the book, the way it keeps turning up in tragedy and the stories they're telling, already—that's what will be bad for Brookhants. It already has been."

"*We* are Brookhants."

Alex nodded. But then she said, "And so was Eleanor Faderman."

Caspar called that he thought he'd solved the problem and he must have, because now they were moving again. They rode in somber silence while the wind howled at them.

That is, until Alex said, "You know, it doesn't matter if this book is the cause."

"How can you say *if*? *If* it's the cause? Do you hear yourself?"

Alex shook her head. "What matters now is that people believe it to be."

"Leanna Hamm believes it," Libbie said.

"There were others. And tomorrow there will be more. These things build like avalanches." Alex was not looking at Libbie, but out the fogged carriage window, which she now wiped with the sleeve of her coat. "They start off with a few flakes and gather force, tumbling down and down until they smother you."

Libbie shook the book at Alex. She'd had enough. "At least Mary MacLane has the excuse of her tender age to account for her theatrics. Tell me, what is yours?" She did not wait for an answer. "No, don't. I don't want to talk any more about it tonight." She looked out the newly clear window and saw the bundled figure of their maid, broom in hand. "What on earth can Addie be doing? She's mad to be outside in this."

They'd rounded the last bend and there was Breakwater,* the

---

* The fact is, Readers, that despite its official name, and no matter how many times that name was repeated back to them, none of the locals (or Brookhants students) referred to this house as Breakwater. Instead they knew it as **Spite Manor**. This was because of its then architectural innovation. The Providence firm that designed the house had, at Harold Brookhants's instruction, incorporated into it a strange, hexagonal tower, wide enough to hold its own staircase and not much else until you reached its top, where it expanded into a domed room. Most resembling a lighthouse or a windmill—but offering none of either of those structures' services—the tower was originally constructed in the 1700s, when a fight occurred between the brothers who then owned and farmed the land.

Not long after, with the brothers no longer speaking, the younger of the two, Jonathan Rash, took great pains to construct this odd tower in a precise location in relation to his brother's home. As the tower neared completion, its primary purpose was discovered: he'd built it to block his brother's best views of the ocean. And in this Jonathan Rash was successful. The elder brother, Samuel Rash, could now see only slices of blue, slim lines of waves, from his home's windows—mostly he saw just trees. And tower. Eventually, Samuel sold his portion of the farm and left the state. But the tower, now known by locals as the Spite Tower, remained.

By the time Harold Brookhants purchased the property in the 1870s, both of the windows at the top of its odd tower lit yellow like jack o' lantern teeth.

"I'm sure she's doing whatever she thinks will please you most," Alex said, watching as the maid finished her final sweep of the porch—it was down to bare wood, for now—and hurried back inside the house.

"Please not that tonight as well."

"Not tonight or any night," Alex said as Caspar pulled them up the drive, the still-recent addition of electric porch lights casting yellow egg yolks of illumination across the snowy ground.

Libbie kept Breakwater running with the same minimal staff she'd inherited from her now-dead husband, Harold. Save for large and irregular repairs, and unless Libbie was hosting, it was really only a single family, the Eckharts, who made the house function: Caspar, whom you've met and who in addition to driving the carriages tended to the meager livestock and grounds; his wife, Hanna, the head housekeeper and sometimes cook; and their son Max and his new wife, Adelaide, who had recently moved from Harold's Pittsburgh estate and who took care of all else.*

---

original Rash farmhouses had—through the destructive modes of abandonment, time, and weather—crumbled to their foundations and been overtaken by the creep of the woods. The Spite Tower, however, which was watched over and tended to by Little Compton residents proud of their local history of Rash actions done in the name of spite, still remained. And Harold Brookhants was also quite taken with the tower's story, so he had his initially puzzled architects incorporate it into their plans.

Once the build was complete, and if you were viewing the house from its front, the tower looked like some kind of turret jutting up from the structures' right side. This was, thanks to good design, somehow less incongruous with the home's traditional New England shingle-style architecture than you might think.

* Years before, the Eckharts had also come to Rhode Island from Pittsburgh, from Harold's much grander estate there. In the Pittsburgh house, the Eckhart family had accounted for just three of many more household staff. But they just so happened

Perhaps, Readers, this doesn't seem so small a staff to the presumably staffless you and me, but compared to other members of Libbie's social set and the personpower required-desired to run their massive mansions across the water in Newport or Jamestown, hers was indeed a skeleton crew. And the truth is: they were all still getting used to the addition of Adelaide to that crew. Even the Eckharts themselves were still getting used to it, but especially Alex.

However small in number, the Eckharts were a capable bunch, and even despite the lateness of the hour, the house was warm and lit when Libbie and Alex pulled in that night. This was especially welcome, because here, at this house of windows, perched, as it was, above the ocean, the wind was terrible—moaning as it crashed the waves and whipped sheets of snow upon the women.

Working with effort against the wind, Adelaide managed to open the wide front door for them. She still wore her outdoor things, which were wet and heavy with snow. "I'm so glad you've made it back to us," she said, taking their coats and hats. "I was worried about you." She chanced a look at Libbie before crossing to the hall closet, nearly running into her mother-in-law, Hanna, who had just then come into the room from the kitchen.

"We are all so sorry to hear about the girl. What a thing to happen." (Caspar and Max had been sent for earlier to help with the search for Eleanor.) "She couldn't have been in her right mind, poor thing."

"I can't stop thinking about her," Adelaide said from inside the closet.

"We all feel that way, Addie," Libbie called.

"Is someone with her now?" Adelaide asked, joining them again in the front hall, her eyes wet with tears. "Surely someone will stay the night with her? One of your teachers?"

"I would have," Libbie said. She nodded at Alex. "We both would have. But the men from Graynam's have already come to take her."

"Where is the child's home?" Hanna asked.

---

to be three of Harold's personal favorites, so once Breakwater was complete, he'd brought them with him to Rhode Island to run it.

"Baltimore," Alex and Libbie said, unintentionally, in unison.

"What an awful trip," Adelaide said. "Even to think of it, in winter. It's so terribly lonely to imagine her making it now as a piece of cargo. I wish we could keep her here on the grounds with us, make a grave for her somewhere among the trees."

"It won't be like that," Libbie said, bothered by the image Adelaide had conjured. "No one will be treating her like cargo."

Outside, the wind screamed at them. At first it was a chorus of pitches, but eventually those shaped into a single low and breathy moan, one that wouldn't end when it seemed it should have.

"Do you know how long the storm will last?" Alex asked. The four of them looked warily out the windows at the waves of pelting snow lit in yellow from the porch lights.

"I didn't know it was to come at all," Hanna said.

"That's because it wasn't expected," Adelaide said. "Not like this. I think it's for her." She paused, then added, "For your Eleanor," though it wasn't necessary. They all knew who she meant. Adelaide sneezed, then. And once more.

"Oh, Addie, you should have come in from the cold sooner," Libbie said. The maid did look pale. "The clearing could have waited for morning."

"There'll be plenty more to clear in the morning," Hanna said. "There's more even now."

"Should you stay here tonight?" Libbie asked, looking between them. "The four of you? Where is Max?"

"Tending to the radiator in your bathroom," Hanna said. "It was giving him trouble earlier. And that's very good of you, ma'am, but I'm sure we'll manage." She traded an unreadable glance with Adelaide. "It's not so very far and Mr. Eckhart will want his bed."

"No one can say he hasn't earned it," Alex said.

Both couples lived in small cottages on the property. And Hanna was right, they weren't so very far away. But then, it wasn't usually so very late and so very terrible out when they headed to them.

After stabling the horses and again clearing the front path, Caspar Eckhart joined them in the entrance hall, a layer of snow on his shoulders and hat. When asked about staying the night he said,

It was snowing so hard that it was difficult
to tell it was snowing at all.

without hesitating, that he certainly did want his own bed. And then agreeable Max came in from the back hallway to announce that they had enough coal to last at least a week and that he was confident the radiators would remain steaming through the night, whether or not this damned blizzard kept at it. And then the four of them insisted again, as they bundled themselves for the trek, that their cottages were not too much trouble to get to if they huddled together and moved with haste.

Even so, the wind smashed against the heavy front door with such force that the group had trouble closing it behind them. It was snowing so hard that it was difficult to tell it was snowing at all. It just *was* the air, like mist or a swarm of yellow jackets: the flakes hovered across the landscape in a constant, buzzing mass.

Even after the swing of the foursome's hand lanterns had been lost to the swirling dark, Libbie, still looking out the window in the direction they'd headed, said simply: "I wish they had stayed."

The Eckharts had never before chosen to stay the night at Spite Manor, not that there was often cause to ask them to, but even still. They'd rather make the trek through the woods, in the dark, *in a blizzard*, than stay the night in Libbie's home.

"Do you wish that all of them had stayed, or is there one in particular you're thinking of?" Alex asked.

"I'm thinking only of the storm, Alex."

"Of course." And then, by way of half apologizing, Alex added, "They're just glad to be alone together. In their own homes."

"I remember when we once felt like that," Libbie said. She was immediately unhappy with how churlish she sounded, even if she meant it.

But then Alex made it worse: "I'm not sure we ever have. Not here."

Outside the wind moaned like a wailing phantom and Libbie shivered. Again.

ACROSS TOWN, A SCUTTLE

Audrey was spooked. Just a little. It was preaudition nerves, probably, but the book wasn't helping. Neither was the script.

Caroline was out showing houses, so right now Audrey was home
alone in theirs, the final stretches of daylight thin and watery across
the living room floor. Soon she'd need to get up to turn on the
lamps and close the now-open patio doors.

Spooked or not, she was glad for the alone time. She had to prep.
She'd settled in on the couch, a bowl of peanut butter M&Ms (her
mom's old line-learning reward system) on the coffee table, her script
on her lap. And the book, Merritt's book, was there too, though the
ghostly black-and-white photograph of Flo and Clara on its cover
was unsettling enough that she had just covered it with a folder.

Earlier, after Noel had dropped her off, Audrey had come in the
door to find Caroline in the middle of a twice-weekly juicing session: kale, lemon, and green apple. She was serious about this. Intense, even. Green glass bottles lined one side of their fridge.

They'd hugged with the juicer still whirring in the background,
Caroline teary eyed with pride. Audrey didn't even get to spill her
big news, not really, since Gray had already filled her mother in.
Fucking Gray.

Still, Caroline wanted to go over everything again, which they
did while she fed pieces of fruit to the masticating machine on the
counter: what Audrey should wear and how she should do her hair
and the kiss. The kiss! Should she do it? Caroline said yes, so long
as the run-through with Harper went well beforehand. And why
wouldn't it? Of course it would.

At some point, Audrey had tried to explain the part Gray had stumbled over, this *improv-but-not* business, or whatever it was, this staged bonding exercise with Merritt and Harper.

But Caroline was momentarily distracted. She was tasting her mixture, frowning, adding more lemon.

"Mom? It's weird, right?" Audrey asked again.

"Well, I think it's more last minute than it is *weird,* honey," Caroline said. "Who knows why Lily is gone. She might even be the one who dropped out, and they're spinning it now to make it seem like they have the upper hand." She added a scoop of turmeric paste to her batch.

"That's not even what I'm saying is weird, though," Audrey said. "I meant this part about all of us being forced to hang out—me and Harper and Merritt Edmunds or whatever. The writer."

"I could've guessed that about Bo," Caroline said. "These come-up-from-indie dude directors all want to prove themselves with their elaborate methods." She was whisking a little cayenne into the juice, still distracted. "They're always so desperate to remind you that they've been to film school. And that they alone have *the singular vision.*" Audrey laughed at *the singular vision* and then Caroline did, too.

"But why focus on the negative of it, anyway?" Caroline said. "It might actually be nice, you know, to have an opportunity to get to know them like this. I mean, and I don't think it can really hurt your process, can it?"

"I mean, no," Audrey said. "I hope I'm not that precious."

"You're not," Caroline said. "At all. That's my point." She wiped her hands and turned to face Audrey, a coppery smear now across her shirt collar. "I think it's an incredible opportunity and you should run into it with your head high and your arms open. I think the universe wants this for you."

"I know you do," Audrey said. "And you got turmeric on your shirt. For the three hundredth time this year."

"Oh, I didn't, did I? Where?" Caroline looked down but did not see it.

"Collar."

"Crap," she said. When she pulled her collar out for a better look she added yet another dose of turmeric, this time in the form of a coppery fingerprint. "I knew I shouldn't have put this on yet. Now I need to run and change." She assessed the mess on the counter, in the sink, the juice left to bottle. "Do you think you have time to clean this up for me, honey? At least to get it in the fridge and the juicer cleaned out? You know how gross it gets when it sits." She was now drinking from a glass Audrey had refused.

Audrey sighed at the mess, at her mother. "Wouldn't it maybe be easier just to list the house for sale? I know an adequate realtor."

Caroline was already on her way to change. "Adequate? Jerk." She called back, "I'll owe you! I'm sorry for leaving it."

"No, I know," Audrey said. "I've got it. I'll do it. Leave it to your charming housemaid."

"I owe you!" her mother called again. She left, in a clean shirt, soon afterward.

But now it was hours later and Audrey still hadn't finished the cleanup. She'd bottled the juice, put it in the fridge, and composted the eviscerated remains of kale stalks and lemon rind, but the juicer's components were all soaking in sudsy water in the kitchen sink. In water long since gone cold.

The smell of smoke from the surrounding fires blew in the patio doors and wafted over to where Audrey sat on the couch.

Shit. The doors were still open.

First she'd been watching clips of her favorite onscreen kisses. Then part of an interview with the writer, Merritt Emmons—*not* Edmunds. Audrey needed to remember that for tomorrow. Now it was film footage of Manhattan street scenes from 1903, digitized but still scratchy and splotchy, as if infested by bugs. It was unreal to her that such footage existed. That she could sit on her couch in Los Angeles and watch these people from the past avoid getting clipped by a hackney cab while buying peaches from a street vendor. There was something mesmerizing about it, all of them now dead, just trying to get to work, or to keep their hat from blowing off, avoiding the horse droppings near the curb—most of them not even realizing that a camera had picked them up to store them for the future, for Audrey's own consumption one hundred plus years later.

This black-and-white footage—with its blisters and hop-skips, its shadowed faces—was starting to strain her eyes, but the clip she'd selected still had three minutes to go and Audrey didn't want to turn it off. She was doing the unreasonable thing that she sometimes did; the superstitious thing she didn't like to admit to. She'd made a rule about this video: she had to finish it or. Or else. Or something bad. She was in that kind of edging-on-truly-frightened state where staying still and silent seemed best. Where she knew she could give herself over to fear, but that she could also resist if she only put some effort into doing so.

But there was so little daylight left, now. And the room was filled with shadows.

Before she'd turned to the videos, Audrey had read the scene in Merritt's book where the Brookhants girls told stories about yet another campus *quirk*: the way shadows lengthened and thickened into shapes, into creatures or specters, or most often, the girls said, into swarms of yellow jackets. Then she'd read the script's version of that scene.

If they didn't get too CGI with it, Audrey supposed that it would be both beautiful and creepy—a combination Bo Dhillon was known for.

It *could* be both. Or it could just be creepy.

The street scene footage ended and Audrey told herself to stop pretending to be scared. The breeze from outside was full of smoke. It was time to close the doors.

She stood, moving her body with resolute intention. She walked the nine steps or so to the doors and slid them shut. Then she locked them and looked out past her reflection to the glitter of pool lights, yard lights, and headlights up and down the lumpy, shadowed hills.

A noise behind her made a catch in her throat.

She turned to look. There was nothing—not that she could see, anyway. It hadn't been a particularly loud noise—and not one that was immediately discernable to her. It wasn't the sound of the door opening. That had a security-alarm chime. And it wasn't something being knocked off a shelf or a drawer being rifled through. It wasn't human or even animal. It was—

She heard it again. Faintly. For some reason it called to mind the footage she'd just watched, its scratchy movements.

It clicked for her then, what it sounded like, something like dead leaves being blown by the wind. It's a distinctive noise, one you know when you've heard it. It's best named by an equally distinctive and creepy—it *was* creepy, she thought—word: *scuttle*. A thing that spiders do. And rats. And leaves wind-tripping across gravestones in horror movies.

Audrey had heard a scuttle in the otherwise quiet house, a house that she was supposed to be alone in.

Now she felt her pulse speed up as she stood, still and silent, trying to control her breathing.

Carefully, slowly, she looked through the rooms, cursing all the open space and high ceilings, especially the big, uncovered windows. So many windows. Anyone outside who wanted to, who put in a little effort, could see her through those windows, alone in the house.

But what if they weren't looking from outside? What if they'd already come in?

She listened hard. She heard nothing but her own breathing.

Did it seem too smoky? It was possible, she guessed, that so much smoke had blown in the patio doors, but she hadn't noticed it beyond the smell. Now it was like the rooms were not quite themselves— distorted, somehow, too full of thick shadow and hazy gray.

"C'mon, Audrey, don't be a baby," she said. But she didn't like that, either. Didn't like the sound of her voice—which seemed both too loud and too indicative of her fear—in the otherwise empty quiet.

From where she stood, she had a dead-on view over the couch, into the kitchen—the mess she'd left in the island sink still waiting for her there. She decided she'd march over, a firm and in-charge march, pick up the sponge, and finish the stupid dishes. And then, when that was done, maybe she'd let herself call Noel and ask him to come run lines with her. Or she'd call a Lyft and go get some frozen yogurt. Or she'd lock herself in her bathroom, which had only a skylight for its window. Caroline should be home soon, anyway—like any-minute soon. But the thing to do right now was to stop playing statue in front of the sliding door.

So she did. She walked toward the kitchen. And as she reached the couch, got a single step behind it, a girl's voice, so loud and awful in the quiet, began a terrible song.

Whaaaaaat's the ra-cket, yel-low ja-cket?
Broooook-hants is your home.
When you get a taste of us—
you won't leave us a-lone.

Audrey screamed. The voice was undeterred.

Footsteps, footsteps falling fast—
sweets will bring you, too.
And upsetting even one,
will call forth each of you. *

The voice was Merritt Emmons's, and she was reading (or, more properly, singing) from her book, and it was coming from the fucking Wi-Fi speakers. They were all over the house—turned up loud because Audrey had been playing music earlier that morning.

She spun back around to the couch, to her phone. It was shoved between the top cushions (had she left it there?) and she struggled to free it without making it sink farther between them. It kept

---

* Written by Brookhants students and added to and kept alive by area locals, the Brookhants yellow jacket chant was originally seven stanzas long. Over the years—especially during and after the tragedies—verses were added, modified, dropped. One of the more controversial verses was:
  You stung their arms, their legs, their backs—
  Attack! Attack! Attack!
  The lips where our dear girls would kiss—
  you were sure not to miss.

sliding down and the awful song played on until finally, her fingers curled around the phone.

Its screen showed—sure enough—that the audiobook of *The Happenings at Brookhants* was playing from the middle of chapter 3, which made no sense, to pick up there, but neither did the fact of it playing at all.

She tapped Pause. Merritt Emmons's thin voice cut off midword.

But now it was too quiet in the house. Such a cliché, but in this case, Readers, please allow it. Audrey scrolled to a playlist, music that was subdued but not too quiet, certainly not too somber or emo. She played it. She turned the volume lower. She already felt better. A little better.

The speakers, that app, had acted strangely before. Not anything like this, of course, but the system sometimes cut out or switched playlists; occasionally sound poured from speakers in locations she hadn't meant to turn on. She thought she'd seen something online about an Amazon Alexa laughing in the middle of the night for no reason. She guessed this was maybe like that. A creepy fluke. Something to make a story of. Bo Dhillon would like it, probably; if she was presented with the right moment, she might tell him about it tomorrow.

Audrey tried to stand still, to catch her breath and calm her thudding pulse, but the nighttime shadows twitched and flickered around her, and the smoke seemed thicker yet.

She watched the shadows across one of the high walls—thirty-foot ceilings, Caroline liked to say. The shadows seemed to pool and fill and gather themselves into shapes more dimensional than they had any right to be.

Enough. She'd had enough.

She turned on the kitchen lights, all of them, the big brass-and-glass lanterns over the island and the perimeter cans and the under-cabinet lighting, too. This light was bright and strong. Audrey wasn't sure they'd ever, since moving in, had all of the kitchen lights on at once. She would finish the dishes, there in that intense light. She would run hot water and add more dish soap and clean the stupid juicer really, really well. And by then Caroline would be home.

Would be almost home?

Would be on her way home? Surely.

"Stop it, Audrey," she said to herself. "Stop it. You're not a nine-year-old. It's an audiobook. Grow up."

She leaned her elbows on the island and texted Noel a quick summary, explained that she was freaking herself out alone with her script and *her demon speakers*. Even though his reply wasn't immediate, she felt better having sent it—the sense of perspective that came from making fun of her fear.

She tried to hold on to this perspective as she went around the island to the sink side, opening the lower cabinet door as she bent down for the dish soap, shutting the door, rising back up. And that's when she saw that something was wrong with the dishwater.

There was something—there were, in fact, many somethings—floating in the sink.

She looked closer. It wasn't juicing scraps.

It was—they were—yellow jackets.

There were dozens of them. Most of them were dead, their bodies floating atop the green dishwater. Worse were the few that were only just alive, their thin wings and thinner antennae akimbo, their shiny black eyes searching and their bodies twitching as they struggled to find a surface they could cling their sticky legs to.

Audrey took an unconscious step back from the sink, her hand over her mouth to ward off, what? Another scream? A spew of bile? She wanted to run the tap full blast and flick the garbage disposal and whoosh them away into its crunching metal mouth. But to do this she'd first need to reach her hand into that cold green water to pull the sink stop. And there was no way she was doing that.

She couldn't stay in the room with them, but she didn't want to go anywhere in the house that the scuttle might have been coming from, either. She FaceTimed Noel on her way out the front door. He answered before she even got to the bottom step outside.

"So I'm freaking out," she started, and then launched into a recap of her last several minutes as she paced between their two avocado trees. Those trees were Caroline's favorite thing about the yard.

"Aud, breathe," Noel said. "You're making me dizzy."

Noel was calming. He told her it was all *some fucked-up shit* and that she should stay outside and on the phone with him until he got there, that he was heading over now. But then, not even two minutes later, there were Caroline's headlights in their driveway. Audrey hung up and lunged at her mother's door handle.

At first, Caroline, who was still putting the car into park, seemed to think Audrey had more good news she just couldn't wait to tell her. But then, as her daughter pulled her into the house, not even letting her grab her things from the back seat, she realized otherwise.

Now the two of them stood in the kitchen and looked down together into the water. "Is it plugged or something?" Caroline asked at first glance, still confused. Then she recognized what she was looking at. "Oh, gross! Yuck." She used the dish sponge to push through the mucky water, launching a wave of cascading wasp carcasses. "God, there's so many of them."

"Don't touch them!" Audrey said, though she didn't really know why she felt quite so repulsed. She had never been particularly squeamish about bugs.

"Hey, hon, it's OK," Caroline said, taking note of the sharpness in Audrey's voice and dropping the sponge; it floated like a raft among the bodies while she put her arm around her daughter and squeezed. "Maybe we have a nest of them. Sometimes people get them in their walls." She scanned their walls for some obvious sign of infestation that of course wasn't there. "They can be expensive to get rid of, I know."

"I don't think that's it," Audrey said. She was still shivering.

"Audrey, what's up? Why are you so upset about this? Did you get stung?"

"No, it's—the whole night it's been—" She tried to say what it had been, exactly. But now, with her mom in the kitchen beside her, the house felt more like itself, their neighbors' lights on the hillside brighter and closer, the rooms less smoky. And the wasps in the sink? They seemed smaller and more reasonable a thing to find there. Gross, sure, but not somehow tied to the scuttle, the song.

"Did you leave the patio doors open, honey? Because with all the fruit scraps—you know we actually get wasps in here a lot."

"No, I know," Audrey said, feeling increasingly stupid. "They were open."

"I mean, I killed a couple the other day. I've never seen this many at once, but with all this stuff sitting here for hours . . ." Caroline looked again at the sink. "I think they just got too close to the water and drowned." She had a sudden thought; it blinked on her face and she added, "Or what about the fires? I bet that's it. I bet it's something to do with the fires burning up their nests."

"Probably," Audrey said without meaning it. "I didn't notice any coming in, though."

"Well you wouldn't have," Caroline said. "It's not like they all came in a swarm. You don't notice one at a time. And if you were already scared."

Audrey nodded. It could make sense if she let it. "There's all this yellow jacket stuff in the script. They burn the nest."

"I know," her mom said. "You said it was creepy."

"Yeah," Audrey said. "And I'm just anxious about tomorrow."

"Well, that I know allllllllll about," Caroline said. "Plus PAD. So, so much PAD."*

Later, while Audrey sat close, perched on the island counter, Caroline made for them her really good lemongrass soup and told a bunch of stories she'd told Audrey many times before about shooting her first lead role in *House Mother 2: She's Coming for You,* and all the practical jokes they always played on each other on set, part of which encompassed a big old house that the production had rented in Pasadena. And Audrey smiled and laughed at the right times, and the events of the previous hour seemed smaller and sillier and less worthy of consideration the further away from them she got.

Especially once the dishwater was drained.

---

* In the parlance of the Wells household, Readers, *PAD* stands for *preaudition diarrhea.*

PLAYING DRESS-UP DINNER

....

Across town from the sink of dead yellow jackets, **Merritt** was sweating. A lot. Enough that she worried she might smell of it, the rank stink of nervous BO. She was glad that at least it was only Elaine sitting next to her. For now.

They were on one end of a stiff banquette that curved around their table, with Bo Dhillon, Heather the executive producer, and two, for your purposes, interchangeable movie studio people, squished awkwardly around to the other end. It was a tight fit, with all of them brushing thighs and arms. Their table was in front of a glass wall of wine bottles and all around them people in designer clothes ate squid ink pasta and first-of-the-season white truffle pizza (for the grotesque price of $135 a pie).

Now add to that, this: Harper Harper was late.

But at least there was soignée Elaine in her crisp, popped-collar shirt and thin cashmere cardigan, one strand of antique pearls peeking through. Elaine Brookhants is someone who perpetually rides atop the crest of a wave of her own confidence and calm. It's the kind of assuredness that comes from having always had what Mary MacLane called the Money, and she certainly fit in well there at Spago in Beverly Hills. This is where they were having their dinner: Bo Dhillon's hammy surprise for Merritt. You can't make it more than thirty pages in *Less Than Zero* without someone snorting coke in the bathroom at Spago. (Bo couldn't deliver the actual restaurant from the novel, the 1980s version, but this was his deliberate nod in that direction, one he said he'd come up with after seeing Merritt's tweets.) She guessed she was flattered that he'd made the effort. At least a little.

"Not all cheeses need be smoked," Elaine was saying as she removed the mascarpone from her veal tartare, an appetizer she'd chosen for the table. They'd decided to order drinks and "a bite to fortify us," (said Elaine, naturally) while they awaited Harper's arrival.

"Smoked cheddar, certainly," Elaine went on. "Gouda and mozzarella, yes. This, no. So easy for these celebrity chefs to forgo taste for theatrics."

"I think it's freakin' fantastic," Bo said, reaching across the table for another piece. Elaine made a face at that reach, but Merritt was fine with it—he was welcome to her portion. Until Harper got there, she didn't think she could eat. Maybe not after Harper got there, either.

Not that Bo wasn't trying very hard to keep things casual. Or maybe he wasn't trying at all and was always this casual. (Though Merritt doubted it.) Unlike the other studio people at the table, who were all dressed in suits or partial suits—white teeth, intentional hair—Bo was doing, like, a Paul Bunyan–meets–James Dean thing. He wore old-fashioned leather work boots with dark blue jeans. His fitted T-shirt seemed, on first glance, to be standard-issue white Hanes, but was actually the kind of no-label designer tee meant to be recognized by people in the know. (It had one thick, vertical line of green embroidery up from its bottom hem. Merritt had later googled it.)

And then, well, what to say of his hair?

Bo Dhillon had a large forehead—one made larger by his only-just-sort-of-receding hairline. On the sides of his head, his hair was short, neat, but he kept the top longer and parted to the right and back in a kind of oiled wave of Jazz Age nostalgia. You could see the tracks from his fingers in that hair, where he'd raked through it with some expensive, artisanal pomade, no doubt, one made of an unreasonable combination of ingredients: orange oil and beeswax and juniper sap.

Once you left the surface of his head and traveled southward down his temples and to his cheeks, this hair (black veined with silver) exploded into a mutton-stache, one that was only just starting to become unkempt—as if he'd once put effort into maintaining its shape but hadn't lately. The overall effect was more handsome than not, especially because he had a good smile beneath those whiskers. And he'd been offering that smile quite a lot, asking about their flight and their plans while in town. Stalling for Harper . . .

Some brisk member of the waitstaff had placed two chairs in front of their table, but for the first thirty minutes or so, those chairs remained empty. *Harper's bringing someone,* Bo told them, while explaining she'd be late. (He offered no excuse for said lateness.)

Though all of the movie people were friendly enough, it was also clear they were waiting on Harper. They were all waiting on Harper. No one more than Merritt. She snatched looks at the door when she could. (But then so did the rest of their group, save for Elaine.) Merritt checked her phone for texts that weren't there. She even tweeted things she wasn't proud of.

Things like:

Merritt Emmons @SoldOnMerritt
Tonight it's Spago a-go-go. You'll know me because I'm the one not kissing @BoDhillon's ass.

Bo immediately retweeted that. (Are you surprised?)

Mostly, Merritt felt young. She felt like she looked young and sounded young when she spoke. And the wrong kind of young, too: the *no need to take me seriously, go ahead and dismiss me, I'm forty-five pounds too fat and not nearly connected enough to anyone in this town for you to know what to do with me* variety.

She also alternately hated and was fine with, happy with, even, what she'd decided to wear: high-waisted, wide-legged navy pants and a silk T-shirt screen printed, then hand painted, by a designer she'd first found on Tumblr. The image was this kind of washed-out, sinister-looking motel in the desert, lots of pinks and oranges and sand colors, with the words *A Bag of Boiled Sweets* hand lettered in tiny purple across it.

She'd piled her hair up loosely, letting her curls fall out where they may. That night she still had many strands of color. She'd dyed them herself. It took a dumb amount of time to do, but she'd created an entire spectrum of pinks, from pale prom carnation to fuchsia. She also wore long, copper vertebrae earrings; they were intricate, delicate, weird. She was hoping that in concert she looked stylishly disordered.

But the longer she sat there not eating the veal appetizer and having little to add to the semigossip the studio people were batting about, the messier she felt. Not interesting messy—not Holly Golightly, messy-zany chic—but four-year-old with sticky hands wearing her mother's lipstick and things from her sister's closet messy.

(And just to be clear here, Readers, I'm talking about Truman Capote's Holly Golightly—the one from his novella—*that's* the look Merritt had been going for, which is decidedly different than the Audrey Hepburn movie version of the character made so popular in all those black-and-white posters hanging in dorm rooms.)

Merritt also didn't know how much longer she could effectively tread conversational water without making clear that she loathed being forced to do so. She'd already managed to successfully skim over the requisite discussion about why she wasn't in college without actually mentioning her single, failed semester at Holyoke or her breakdown and subsequent weeks-long hospitalization—and that had taken some real maneuvers. It was, maybe, somewhat impressive to have entered college with a book under her belt. It was certainly less impressive to then almost immediately drop out and go into a hospital. And then to come home and stay home for the next three years and not write anything else worth mentioning in that time.

"So the real question," Heather-the-producer said, "is what are you working on now? Assuming you are." Heather had a badass (Merritt thought) power-woman bob of shiny hair that shimmered when she moved her head, which she did a lot. Enough so that Merritt assumed she must know how cool it looked when she did so. Heather also had the right mouth to pull off the red lipstick she wore.

"Oh no," Elaine said, patting her mouth with her napkin. "Here we go."

"What?" Heather asked, turning to Elaine, her bob shimmering. "Is that a bad question?"

"Not a bad question. But you'll get a bad answer."

"Now I'm intrigued," Bo said.

"Don't be," Merritt said, glancing at the door, hoping again for a Harper who wasn't there. "She's overselling. It's not even really worth talking about—I'm not done."

"Then you're in good company," Heather said. "All we do in this town is talk about the things we're making that aren't done."

"That probably never will be done," a studio person added.

"Come now, dear," Elaine said. "If you're determined to sail such ruinous waters you might as well boast about the voyage."

"Boast away," Bo said. "We want you to."

Merritt sighed. She did not like the pressure of this setup. "Do you know Truman Capote's unfinished final novel?"

Bo nodded and Heather said, "Maybe?"

"So I'm finishing it," Merritt said. She stopped. Waited. They didn't give her much to work with in the way of reactions. "Kind of. It's hard to explain if you haven't read it, but I'm rewriting parts and adding my own story lines—it's like a companion novel more than it is a true completion of his."

"That's because Truman's was never actually a novel," Elaine said, twisting the band of her simple watch. "It was a face-painted collection of tawdry gossip columns done up as literature."

"Sounds promising," Heather said.

"When we do the one-name thing, the Madonna, Beyoncé thing, for Truman Capote, don't we say Capote, not Truman?" Bo asked. "It's confusing otherwise because of President Truman."

"I don't know what you do," Elaine said. "But I always knew him as Truman."

"Wait, *did* you know him?" Heather asked. She seemed excited about this, which Merritt found endearing given that they were in the town that made name-dropping an art before simply relegating it to a fact of existence.

"Not well," Elaine said.

"Oh, now *you* c'mon, Lainey," Merritt said. "You did too know him."

Elaine used both hands to smooth the tablecloth in front of her. "For a number of years our social circles overlapped," she said. "I was living in New York then, predominately, and society there is of course just one elaborate Venn diagram." She shrugged. "Well, it was once, at any rate. Often enough, Truman and I found ourselves in one of these troubling intersecting regions." She made two small circles with the thumb and pointer finger of each hand and held them up to her face, almost as if she were about to do the goofy upside-down-hands-into-a-party-mask thing that everybody's uncle teaches them at some point, but instead she placed one circle behind the other and peered through the space where they overlapped.

"Right in here," she said, still looking at everyone at the table through that overlapping section, "in the stuffed pied-à-terre of this person or that, worlds colliding and all the rest." She undid her fingers, raised her eyebrows once, and when she lowered them, tipped her head as if to say, *You know how it is.*

"I love that," Heather said, though her face was one of both pleasure and bemusement, as if she was reconciling Elaine anew compared to the vision of Elaine she'd formed previously. "I love all of that."

If you're wondering why Merritt wasn't reacting similarly, it's because she already knew about Elaine's brief history with Mr. Truman Capote and had previously teased out every detail of personal knowledge that Elaine would relinquish to her. It was Elaine, after all, who gave Merritt her first Capote book (the first novel he'd published), *Other Voices, Other Rooms,* inscribed to Elaine thusly in black ink:

> *To sticky-rich, violet-eyed Lainey-Janey: What troubles have you seen this week? Tell me, but first let me fix me a drink.*

> Yours,
> Truman

Merritt had spent more time than she would admit running her fingers over that inscription, sniffing it, trying to take in some lingering essence of Capote.

"Are you one of the ones he wrote about?" Bo asked. "That's what he got in trouble for, right? Gossiping about you society ladies?"

"He got in trouble for all kinds of things," Merritt said.

"Oh, I never made it into print," Elaine said, waving her hand once as if to shoo that notion from the air hovering over their table. "Remember, he was ten years or better my senior. When Truman was skewering his swans I'd yet to ring up enough transgressions to be worthy of his pen." She paused, thinking, and added with a slow-blooming smile, "Now if he'd waited for another decade or so to smash his sandcastle, maybe by then my stories would have suited his tastes." She held that smile there for them to enjoy before she said, "Well, but then he died, as people tend to do. It's consistently disappointing how consistently that happens."

"What does that mean—*smash his sandcastle*?" a studio person asked.

"Would you prefer *poop on his doorstep and complain about the flies*?" Merritt said.

Elaine clapped her hands once and laughed a real laugh. "Truman's is a very old, very brief tale," she said. "You can tell it in two words: *he told*." She took a drink and let them consider that.

"Told what?"

"What didn't he tell?" Elaine said, "Murder, adultery—"

"Vindictive menstruation," Merritt interrupted.

"Well come sit next to me," Heather said, laughing.

"Everything awful he could fit on a page," Elaine said, ignoring them. "Truman told the world what he'd been trusted to keep to himself. He'd been welcomed into the homes, which of course means the extraordinarily private lives, of a certain social set." She paused to shake her head. "He called those women his swans. Isn't that plainly infantile? Who on earth wants to be someone's swan?"

"The ugly duckling, for one," Merritt said.

Elaine smiled and raised her eyebrows at Merritt before continuing. "Of course this was not Truman's *own* bracket, let's say—he was a guest—he would have told you that he was their court jester, that's what he told everyone at the end, that they wanted him to entertain and then leave them be, close the door on the way out and pretend to forget what he'd seen and heard. And I suppose that's more accurate than not. They were his swans, you know, but he was *their* pet. Whenever I saw him, one or two of those women would be huddled around him, on his arm, at his side on the divan, devouring his attention and all the scraps of gossip he tossed them like so many chocolate-covered cherries."

"Do swans eat chocolate-covered cherries?" Bo asked.

"These particular swans did," Elaine said, her eyes, I swear it, Readers, twinkling. "And they grew fat and contented with the way Truman fed them. But of course, they'd open their mouths to feed and while doing so tell him *everything*." She shook her head at the idea, seemed to be increasingly bothered by her own story.

"*Every*thing, everything—all their secrets told to a sharp-tongued, filthy-minded storyteller with a worldwide audience. And worse, one who thought that it was his sacred duty—I really do believe this—to take us all down a peg, or more, as soon as he had enough material. And such temerity, such gall, to believe he'd keep us as friends while he did so." She seemed to rest, then, on this thought, shaking her head and again smoothing the tablecloth.

Elaine was more worked up than Merritt would have thought she'd let herself get. Merritt was surprised to hear her use the word *us* rather than *them*. In all the times they'd spoken of Truman Capote, Elaine had never seemed to Merritt very invested in what he'd done. That pronoun—*us*—bothered Merritt. It seemed an embarrassing slip, for Elaine, to be so consumed by such old, peripheral memories.

"But, Lainey," Merritt said, "why does it matter anymore? Especially since he's the one who got the worst of it in the end."

"Do you think that's true?" Heather asked.

"Well he certainly thought so," Elaine said. "And he was cast out. His swans changed their numbers and forgot his name. After he published those first stories it was as if he simply ceased to exist. Oh, it was a nasty business." Her eyes were unfocused, her mind on the past. "And he never recovered. Not really." She seemed to be done, but then she added, somewhat conspiratorially, "Do understand, it was all just gossip. This was the kind of slimy stuff better left oozing in the pool drain than published in the pages of *Esquire*."

"Gossip containing more truth than fiction," Merritt said.

"So late-stage Capote was America's warm-up for TMZ?"

"No," Merritt said, before Elaine could. (Though she wasn't sure Elaine even knew what TMZ was.) "You can't erase the fact that he knew these people. He really did consider some of them his friends, like *real* friends, and they'd have said the same about him. Before he did it, I mean. Besides, Truman Capote was an artist."

"We'll agree to disagree, as we always have, about the level of *art* on display in that book," Elaine said.

"Yes, we will," Merritt said.

"I believe it's what ruined him," Elaine said. "I do. He published the short stories but he never finished the novel, did he? All that bluster about how we would hail it as his greatest book and he never even finished it. And now it's part of his legacy, and such a sad part. Even you must see that, Merritt."

"See, you *could* ruin your reputation before Twitter," Bo said.

"Just not as fast," Heather said.

"Mmmmm," Elaine said, shaking her head no. "It was much more than that. I think he let all that spite be the vinegar that stewed his talent, so much so that he could never wash it clear and start again." She turned to Merritt and said this last part pointedly: "You can't ever turn a pickle back into a cucumber, Merritt."

"But sometimes you need a pickle, Lainey," Merritt said. "Sometimes what you're after is brine and bite."

"Hear! Hear!" Bo said with that good smile of his.

"I think it's a significant mistake," Elaine said, shaking her head and taking a drink from her cocktail, though it was mostly melted ice in the glass. She swallowed and said, "But you're still young and that is the best time to make them."

"I think it sounds great," Bo said.

"Makes me want to read his version first," Heather said. "To set the stage." She was back on her phone.

"You'll need a tetanus shot after you finish," Elaine said.

"Well now I *have* to read it," Heather said.

"I'm on its Wikipedia," one of the studio people said. "It says some people think there are long-lost chapters in a bus station locker here in LA."

"Yeah, they don't exist," Merritt said. "People love a treasure hunt."

"I dunno," the studio person said in singsong while holding up their phone even though it was pointless—Merritt couldn't read its tiny print from where she sat. "Some editor swore that he saw them back in the day."

"Wikipedia sure knows a lot of things," Merritt said.

"Does it know where the hell Harper Harper is?" Heather asked.

Everyone half laughed at that, but you could tell their patience was wearing. The sommelier came to ask about wine selection and Elaine chose for the table. "Sparkling to celebrate?" she asked without waiting for or wanting an answer.

The studio person started to read aloud something else from Wikipedia and Merritt thought she might excuse herself for a moment, but right then Harper Harper came strolling into the restaurant. She stopped on her way over to greet people at another table, but they saw her. They all saw her. She'd made her entrance at last.

WHATEVER HAPPENS:

KNOW THEY'LL ALWAYS HAVE

THE DUMPSTERS

....

So now let's have at it, shall we? Really there can be no more keeping it from you. Let's do now talk about the striking, the stunning, the hot-damn-arch-eyed-strong-jawed-lip-stung-long-limbed-celesbian elephant in the room: the looks of one Harper Harper. I mean, everyone else is always talking about them. Why not **Merritt**? (And so why not me?)

That night at Spago, Harper was alone. The aforementioned date was just that: mentioned, but not present.

Instead, she was alone and smiling, saying something to another table of stylish people, then tilting her head toward her waiting party, her strawberry-blond hair (could it actually be that color all on its own?) the kind of purposefully messy that Merritt had been going for with her own, only Harper succeeded. Hers had that tousled look of a hero in a surfing movie. Do you get what I'm saying here? Pieces this way and that, but all of it light and textured and sportily, attractively rumpled. Let's not just say *bed head* to be done with it. Let's get our collective mental picture where it needs to be. This was Brad Pitt in *A River Runs Through It* meets *Rosemary's Baby*—era Mia Farrow meets Tintin by way of k.d. lang divided by Twiggy. This was Harper Harper, leather jacket and everything. (Everything being the cigarette tucked behind her ear, Merritt saw, as she reached them. Perhaps an inch gimmicky, that, but let's not hold it against her, Readers.)

They'd been talking about Truman Capote, and Merritt had already been thinking about Holly Golightly, so this line from *Breakfast at Tiffany's* flashed across her brain: "For all her chic thinness, she had an almost breakfast-cereal air of health, a soap-and-lemon cleanness, a rough pink darkening in the cheeks."

Bo got up and slid from his position behind the table to give Harper a hug. Then the two of them stood before their group (most of the restaurant now watching, by the way, pairs of eyes turning toward them, waiting for content as though they were opening an app on their phones—the Harper Harper Meets and Greets app).

"Sorry, everybody," Harper said, a little breathless but not in an overdone way. "I'm a real goat to keep you waiting." She paused, seemed to think over her words, grinned. She had that matchstick-sized gap between her two front teeth. Merritt saw it then and something twitched inside her, some flinch of recognition at seeing this famous attribute up close.

Then Harper said, "Actually, my grandpa says you should never show up anywhere hauling a sack of *I'm sorry*s and I just did. But now if I apologize for that I've added another sorry, so there's no fixing it."

By now Heather and the others were also standing, but they just leaned across the table to bestow their greetings. Someone's camera app flashed at them. This surprised Merritt. It seemed too obvious for the crowd. But then she wondered if it was part of the night's plan, if the image captured would be strategically placed on some industry-frequented website before Merritt's group had even finished their sparkling wine.*

"Where's Annie?" Bo asked as he sat.

"Working," Harper said. "Do not disturb." She reached across the table to shake hands with Elaine, and while doing so they said brief nice things to each other. Merritt's impressions got muddled here, because she was focused on the fact that Harper would be turning

---

* It would.

to her next and she'd have to say something as well. And why hadn't she prepared?

It was too late now. "Hello," Harper said to her, leaning over for a hug.

Merritt wasn't expecting this—that hearing Harper say hello would make her a little melty, and also quite a lot embarrassed about that meltiness. And she certainly wasn't expecting the hug, which she returned awkwardly, half standing into it and feeling like a sack of sand while she did.

"I love your hair," Harper said as they pulled away and she pushed her chair back to sit.

"Thank you," Merritt said, dazed and very conscious of the other people at their table, and in the restaurant, watching them. Everything seemed to buzz—the table, the wine bottle wall behind them, the air. Starstruck they call this, Readers.

About then the waiter came around to take their order. Merritt went with a pasta, because that seemed easy enough. Harper ordered off menu. When she asked, "Can they do those fries again? The bacon fat ones?" she was answered with an "Of course. For you, always."

As the waiter took the other orders, Harper leaned close to Merritt, close enough for Merritt to feel the breath of Harper's words on her face, and said, "I really need to smoke. Wanna come put yourself in harm's way?"

"Not particularly," Merritt said.

Harper smiled without teeth. Waited.

"I guess I just won't stand too close to you," Merritt said.

"My mother loves that song."

"I don't know it," Merritt said.

"Really?" Harper said. "The Police?"

Merritt shook her head no.

"I think we somehow already found the one thing I know that you don't," Harper said as she slid back her chair.

People watched as they stood up from the table. There might have been another phone flash.

People watched as Merritt followed Harper, who clearly had done this before, in a zigzaggy path around the other dining clusters of so-and-so VIPs.

People watched, Merritt hoped they did, as their twosome was separated by a member of the waitstaff cutting between them. Once he was out of the way, Harper grabbed Merritt's hand until they were out the hidden rear door next to the kitchen. And Merritt let her.

Who does that? And with such ease? Grab the hand of a near stranger and make it feel like an expectation and not an intrusion?

They stepped down into a kind of walled courtyard behind the restaurant. In other towns, in my town and maybe in yours, it would have been just stinking dumpsters and concrete back there, but this was Beverly Hills. There were polished cement squares edged by neat, thin lines of green ground cover speckled with tiny, blue, star-shaped flowers, and the dumpsters themselves were, of course, well dressed, hidden away in a massive modern box of wood and metal. Even more impressive was the wall of herbs—dozens of herbs planted in rows of copper pots, hanging vertically. And despite the dark, there was still SoCal sunbake coming off the pavers, and a kitchen door open to let fresh air in and the busy chatter of staff out.

"This one of your usual haunts?" Merritt asked.

"Smokers have to learn where to do it," Harper said. She cupped her cigarette to light it, took a drag, held it, exhaled, courteously, over her shoulder and away from Merritt. "Do you want?" she asked. "I have more." She produced a mashed pack from the pocket of her jacket.

"No," Merritt said. "I don't smoke. It's never occurred to me."

"Well you should know they're now saying it might not be good for you."

A prep cook, his kitchen whites splattered with many splattery somethings, came out the door, a pair of shears in hand, which he sort of lifted in their direction as a wave before proceeding to cut a mass of herbs from the herb wall. The fresh scents of mint and tarragon lifted up from the snipping of those shears and across the way to Harper and Merritt, mingling, not unpleasantly, with Harper's cigarette smoke. The streets surrounding them spilled their city noises—a honk here, a car stereo seeping Drake there, people talking about people things as they walked past—into the otherwise quiet space the two of them now shared with the snipping cook, his shears scraping the soft scrape of sharp metal with every scented cut.

There was something about the wall of herbs, the thick waft of its scent and the impossible amplification of those shears, that both of them recognized as unusual and familiar at once. It was something akin to a shared spell of déjà vu, though that wasn't it exactly. But there was, between them, the whir of some unknown enchantment that had cranked the volume on their senses, and while they were both cognizant of this, they didn't know how to name it, or quite how to say it aloud to the other, or if it would somehow ruin it to say it aloud. So they did not mention it.

"What'd I miss in there?" Harper asked.

"Me defending Truman Capote and a baby calf appetizer," Merritt said.

"Fuck," Harper said. "That's what I get for showing up late." She exhaled, tilting her head behind the plume of smoke. "Did Bo tell you about tomorrow yet? Audrey Wells?"

"Who's Audrey Wells?" Merritt asked.

"She's an actor," Harper said. "I'll let Bo catch you up. He was probably waiting on me to go over it all."

"So we should hurry back in there, you're saying," Merritt said, pretending to start in that direction just so Harper would pull her back.

It worked. Harper grabbed her hand again. "You fail at reading the room."

"We're not in a room."

"You're even worse at reading the alley," Harper said. "Fuck." She put the ring finger of her noncigarette hand into her mouth and sucked before pulling it out again and shaking it back and forth like a dog flicking water from its back.

"Everything OK?" Merritt asked.

"No, it is not," Harper said. "I got stung by a fucking wasp."

"Just now?" Merritt asked.

"No, earlier tonight," Harper said. "It was in my coat sleeve."

"How strange," Merritt said. Some small, dark discomfort at this news flicked on inside her. But it was very small and easy enough to ignore.

"Yes, it was," Harper said. She tongued a fleck of tobacco from her bottom lip and blew it gently away from them. Then she dragged again. The cigarette was smaller, now. It did look fitting, there in her mouth. The cook went back into the kitchen as Harper carefully flicked ash into the supplied receptacle. Merritt didn't like how even that pedestrian gesture, one associated with something she loathed—smoking—made her fidgety, so inescapably aware of being in the presence of the Harper Harper.

Harper took one deliberate step closer.

Despite what Merritt had said in the restaurant about avoiding Harper's secondhand smoke, they'd been standing close. Now they were standing *very* close. Merritt could appreciate how tall Harper was, the long, thin shape of her there in the soft electric light of Spago dumpsterville.

"I'll show you how weird it really was," Harper said. "Weirder than you're guessing. I just got new ink."

Merritt couldn't make sense of those sentences. She wasn't sure she was supposed to. "Well, I have seen your old ink," she said. "Actually, I think there's an Insta devoted just to your tattoos."

"Promise they don't have this yet," Harper said. She flipped her right arm to face palm up and presented it. She was so close to Merritt that she had to bend her long fingers back toward her own body to make her arm fit there in between them, and even then, the back of her hand, the curl of those fingers, rested against the top of Merritt's sternum.

There, on her forearm, placed within Harper's famous sleeve of flora and fauna, was a yellow jacket.

It had been rendered in a style that was something like asking Edward Gorey to interpret it. Merritt could tell there were words embedded in its thin wings, as if they were growing there, but she had to lean into Harper's hand and tilt her head in order to read them:

esse quam videri

Merritt was not someone who regularly blushed. She was like Mary MacLane that way. But if she did blush, she would have right then. "Does this mean your tattoo artist couldn't manage *Planet Lady Love?*"

"I'm saving that for my backpiece—shoulder to shoulder," Harper said. Then she asked, "So you like?"

"I think you just went and added yet another anachronism to production," Merritt said. "Flo was, by all accounts, fair skinned and tat-free."

"I'll have to get in good with the makeup department," Harper said.

"I doubt you'll have any trouble with that."

They were still standing very close, Readers. Harper had righted her arm, put it back at her side, but Merritt was there in the full strength of her magnetic pull, and also within a kind of bubble of clingy cigarette smell and snipped herbs.

Merritt really didn't know what to do with any of this, what Harper had shown her, even the fact of Harper standing there beside her like this. But then she didn't have to say anything because Harper did instead. She ducked her head to achieve optimal eye contact and said, "Did you know that everyone used the same word to describe you to me?" She was not quite smiling but held her face there on the precipice of it. "I mean they're wrong, I think. I *think* they are. But they all used it anyway."

Merritt felt a flutter of panic but shoved it down enough to say, "Sounds like everyone could use a thesaurus."

"*Prickly*," Harper said.

"What?"

"*Prickly*. I remember because everyone said it about you and I can't hear it without, like, imagining a cactus—like a legit old-school cactus in a Western with the sunset behind it."

"Saguaro," Merritt said. "That kind's a saguaro."

"See, and I love that you know that."

"Those are the exact kinds of things I know," Merritt said. *Prickly* wasn't so bad. *Prickly* she could deal with.

"Nowwwwww we should probably go back in," Harper said.

"Do we have to?"

"Yes," Harper said. "But tomorrow, when we're done at Bo's, come out with me." When Merritt didn't answer right away, she added, "I promise we'll do something you can be all kinds of prickly about."

"I can be all kinds of prickly about anything," Merritt said, glad to be back in the realm of sarcasm and deflection, sure footing for her. "In fact, I dare you to find an activity that challenges my ability to be prickly."

"Game on," Harper said.

It was again Merritt's turn to say something. Preferably something clever, but she'd used up her stores. The magnetism thing, Harper's proximity, the enchanted world of the courtyard, it was all eroding her abilities. "Lainey might have something planned for us," she said. This was an easy lie.

"Whatever it is you'll skip it," Harper said, again dropping her face so that it was close to Merritt's. "I never get to be the one who shows anybody LA. Ever. Everybody's always showing me. So you have to let me play tour guide."

"I'm not sure that I *have to,* have to," Merritt said.

"I think you do," Harper said. "I think it's in my contract, actually."

"Shouldn't it be in *my* contract, then?"

"It is," Harper said. "It definitely is. You need to read that thing more carefully."

Merritt might have kissed her. I don't know. I can't say, because she didn't do it. But she might have. I can't properly explain that *might have,* either. Who could explain that? Certainly not Merritt. They didn't really know one another. And Merritt didn't kiss people she didn't know. She didn't even kiss people that she did know. And she was with *the* Harper Harper, with all the Harper Harper neon about her, in her leather jacket, with her somehow-wave-tossed hair and her chic, badass, but still lemon-soap ways. With her Gal Pal Annie apparently off painting in the night. And Merritt was the unknown, prickly, rapidly aging wunderkind from Connecticut in the perhaps regrettable, trying-too-hard T-shirt and dangling vertebrae earrings.

It was like she'd already breathed in too much of the movie-magic fairy dust that seems to sometimes hover over that town, and now it was in her nose and lungs, the effects of full-on Hollywood hay fever setting in and leaving her sticky eyed and brain fuzzed and on the perpetual edge of something like sneezing. Which, as you know, my dear sneezing Readers, is actually a very vulnerable state: chest muscles compressing, throat closing off, and a powerful rush of air building inside your body.

It's not a state you want to linger in. You just want to sneeze and get it over with.

Still in this daze, she followed Harper back to their table, where things were a bit awry. Well, not awry *at* their table proper—in fact, their food was already there—but things were awry elsewhere and those things were being reported on back at their table.

"We were just sending out the search party," Bo said, smiling in a knowing way that Merritt did not care for.

"What'd we miss?" Harper asked, but Merritt was looking at Elaine, who was on her phone with someone, talking quietly, but still, she was talking on it right there at the table, which was not Elaine Brookhants behavior.

"Life imitating art?" Heather said.

"Oooooooh-weeee-oooooh," one of the studio people said, doing a purposefully crappy kind of ghostly yodel.

Merritt was trying to catch Elaine's eye, or her words, but Elaine was turned toward the high back of the banquette and her conversation was too hushed to hear. "Did something happen?" Merritt asked the others.

"Yes," Heather said. "But not something that can't be fixed."

"The moment I go away," Elaine said, tapping End on her phone screen and looking up at the table. "I do apologize for taking that call. I needed to make sure they'd put it out completely—there was some confusion."

"Put what out?" Merritt asked.

"The fire, dear," Elaine said. "At home. Someone set fire to The Orangerie."

"Shit," Harper said. "No way."

Even in her state of confusion, Merritt thought this reaction adorable—mostly because Harper had never even seen The Orangerie.

"Who did it?" Merritt asked.

"They don't know yet," Elaine said. "Probably bored teenagers with summer on their hands."

"Your rebel friends?" Harper asked Merritt.

"I don't have any friends," Merritt said. "Rebel or otherwise."

"My money's on the ghosts," a studio guy said as he spooned some sort of sauce over his dinner.

"How much was lost?" Bo asked Elaine.

"That is what I was trying to ascertain. Though I'm still not clear." Elaine looked again at the screen before sliding her phone back into her purse. "They said they'd send me some pictures, but it's probably too dark to see much now. There's no light. They haven't finished their rewiring and now this has destroyed most of what they had done. What's been done in the last few weeks, anyway, is apparently what got the worst of it."

"Of course it is," Heather said, rapidly texting someone. "Meaning everything that's been done for the sets."

"Again," Elaine said, "I'm not yet sure how bad it is. We'll have to wait and see in the light of day."

"I'm telling you," the sauce-spreading guy said glibly, "it was Flo and Clara."

"Were they only in The Orangerie?" Merritt asked. "Whoever did it?"

"Carl didn't know that for certain yet," Elaine said. "But that's what he thinks."

Carl Eckhart did a little bit of everything for Elaine, from groundskeeping to security. As long as Merritt had known Elaine, there'd been Carl in the Red Sox ball cap with a snow shovel or a pair of hedge trimmers, season dependent, in hand.

"He was off to get his son and a flashlight to do a sweep of the buildings," Elaine said. "But I doubt there's anything else to see. I think it was just kids being a touch rotten."

"Have you had much vandalism there?" Heather asked. "Over the years, I mean."

"Not much, no," Elaine said. "Certainly not arson. Every so often someone breaks a window or gets into one of the buildings and spray-paints something." She took a drink of her wine and then added, "Sometimes a group of high schoolers tries to stage a séance, or who knows what they think they're doing, out there."

"Having sex," Bo said.

"You don't wind up there accidentally," Merritt said, ignoring him and thinking of the campus. Its remoteness was one of her favorite things about it. "Now there's only one road in and it's not marked—and it starts from her land, anyway." She tilted her head at Elaine. "And then the gate to the campus proper is locked. And the fence around that part is fifteen feet tall with barbed wire at the top, so unless you have a key, you pretty much have to go in or out through the woods—and that's a hike. I'm just saying that you have to want to get there."

"I wonder if it was somebody who knows about the film," Heather said. "Maybe that was part of the intrigue."

"Maybe it's the ghosts who don't want us filming there," the studio guy said. "They're camera shy."

"Let's hope so," Bo said, twirling his pasta around his fork. "That would call for a little method acting, yeah, Harps?"

"Whatever it takes," she said.

"Speaking of," Heather said, turning to Bo. "Tomorrow? You want to catch Merritt up? Or do you want me to?"

Bo made a kind of *have at it, I'm still chewing* gesture.

"Merritt," Heather said, pulling her plate closer and taking up her fork and knife. "Did Lily Strichtfield ever get in contact with you? About playing Clara?"

"Not really," Merritt said. "Her assistant sent me an email saying she might have some questions for me at some point. But I haven't heard anything else." She started to say something more, stopped, then said it anyway. "I sort of assumed she would be here tonight."

"Us too," a studio person said.

"She has a scheduling conflict—" Heather started.

"Is that what we're calling it?"

"Will she still be there tomorrow?" Merritt asked.

"No, I'm sorry," Heather said. "That wasn't very clear. She's actually left the production. Our shoot schedule wasn't working for her—"

"It was a little more than that," the ghost-obsessed studio guy said.

"The point is that she has another project she's committed to and we tried to rearrange"—Heather paused, cutting at her food—"but we couldn't make it work. She can't do both."

"We *could* have made it work," Bo said. "Probably. But we're using it as an opportunity to go another way."

"Which is what way?" Merritt asked, trying to remember the name Harper had said out by the dumpsters. It hadn't been the thing she'd most wanted to pay attention to out there.

"Do you know Audrey Wells's work at all?"

"No," Merritt said.

"She's great," Harper said. "She's really great."

"She is," Bo said. "But she's not known. We had cast her as Eleanor, but we're thinking of her now for Clara."

"Huh," Merritt said, processing the news. Eleanor Faderman was no Clara Broward. The roles were nothing alike.

"Audrey's been at this since she was a toddler, literally a toddler. She knows her way around a movie. And I think there's something there." He pushed his chin out, extended his neck, and scratched at it roughly. "More than competency, I mean," he added. "I think she might be our dark horse."

Harper was fiddling with the cigarette refill she had at some point placed behind her ear. "I don't think she's ever really had the chance to do something better," she said. Then she seemed to realize that she held the full attention of the table. She dropped her hand from her ear and said, more loudly, "Before now, I mean. She's been good in whatever she's been in, but it's all been sort of . . ." She let the thought trail away.

"Low rent?"

"Cheese bucket?"

"No one's arguing that she's a bankable name," Bo said. "This is part of the allure. She's fresh."

"Yeah, but the thing is that she's *not*," studio person said. "Take a look at her IMDB page sometime."

"Right, fine," Bo said, shaking his head. "I think we've established that she's been in a lot of crap before now. This would clearly be a role that would ask more of her."

"Yes, and I don't see it," Heather said. "I don't see Audrey Wells making a leap like this. Even if she could, the risk outweighs the reward. And then there's Caroline to factor in."

"Caroline is no factor at all," Bo said. "Not in this."

"That is what you keep saying," Heather said.

"Who's Caroline?" Merritt asked Harper, which, in that moment, was like asking the whole table.

"Caroline Wells," Harper said. "Audrey's mom. She's an actor, too."

"I don't know her," Merritt said.

"You probably do," someone said. "She's an eighties scream queen. She did the *House Mother* movies?"

"Not my genre," Merritt said.

"She was also on that weird, like, half-animated dramedy that the critics loved but nobody actually watched. Remember, the *Fern* thing? I think she might have won an Emmy for it."

"*Fern Feldstein Loves You, Baby,*" Harper said.

"Yes! It was funny. I heard—I didn't watch it."

"No, that's not how you'd know her now," Heather said, turning to Merritt. "She's the actress who got attacked by the dog . . ."

"Oh yes!" Elaine said, clapping her hands once. She was clearly excited to be a part of the conversation again. "After she crashed her car. She was on something, wasn't she? Or sauced? And she drove up onto the lawn where there were children playing and when she got out the dog attacked her? They put out the surveillance tape. It was horrible." Elaine didn't say any of this like she thought it was so horrible.

"*That's* Caroline," Heather said.

"Caroline Wells is neither here nor there," Bo said. "*Audrey* Wells, who we're talking about, has done a little of everything. Lots of television, but she's done some features, too."

There was a pause where it seemed like the other studio people might have things to add, but none of them did.

"Well, she's not her mom, right?" Merritt said. "People do have their own identities."

"Yes they do," Bo said.

"I'm excited about her," Harper said, her lovely face turned toward Merritt. Hers really is a lovely face, and I'll tell you: I don't throw around that kind of BS. Right then her eyes were bright and big, as if she could maybe hypnotize with her level of sincerity.

"Listen, I'll make sure you've seen her clips before tomorrow," Bo said. He tapped at his phone then, busily, making a show of making this happen for Merritt.

"I'd like that," Merritt said. And she did want to see them, sure. But she didn't know why he was acting like her thoughts on the process, the way she would or wouldn't ultimately weigh in, would make a difference to anything he was deciding. They hadn't consulted her before casting Lily Strichtfield, or apparently before parting ways with Lily Strichtfield. Why bother now?

She didn't know how to accurately read any of this. Her pasta was congealing before her. She'd yet to take a bite. "So she's coming tomorrow," Merritt said, "but you'll still be making your decision about her?"

"Yes," Heather said.

"My decision is already made," Bo said. "She's Clara."

"It appears that you're not on the same page about this," Elaine said.

"No, we're not," Heather said simply.

"Right," Bo said. "Tomorrow, if the both of you could just spend some time with her, I think that would be really useful."

It took Merritt a moment to even realize he was speaking to her.

But Harper said, "Yeah, I would have anyway. Of course."

Merritt didn't know what she would have done *anyway*. She didn't even know what the next day would look like. This was not her world and she felt that acutely. But what Bo was asking seemed a small enough thing. I mean, what else was she in town for?

"Whatever's helpful," she said.

"I'm really glad you're here," Bo said. "We all are."

"I know I am," Harper said before eating a fry. Her off-menu food looked, it must be said, fantastic. Fries *and* mashed potatoes and a small green salad with grated lemon zest atop its leaves like cartoon gold dust.

The business portion over, they ate their cooling dinners quickly and said their goodbyes.

Not even an hour later, Merritt would be in her hotel bed looking at Twitter and Instagram and other places the photos from their evening had already popped up online. She thought her eyeliner looked gunky but her earrings were on point.

While she was scrolling and evaluating (and mostly avoiding the comments) there came a brand-new post: Harper Harper at some party with her arm around Annie Meng, their foreheads sweaty, their bodies nested in a way that suggested their comfort holding such a pose together.

There Merritt was in her baggy pajama shorts, stray minibar

cookie crumbs on her pillow, and Elaine sleeping in the room next door, while Harper Harper's night hadn't even finished yet. Which made Merritt's part in it, what? A pit stop? A speed bump?

Don't say *obligation,* Readers. Don't even think it.

And back at Brookhants, someone had tried to burn down The Orangerie.

Unreal, this life. Completely unreal.

GRAY DAWN,

BLEAK MO[U]RNING

....

The night Eleanor Faderman was found dead it snowed thirty-one inches at Brookhants.

And it was still coming down the next morning.

The blizzard spread across New England, but Rhode Island received the worst of it and the Brookhants estate seemed to hold the storm's heart. And it wasn't only the snow, it was what the wind had done to it. Overnight it had formed drifts that reached up, like arms in cloaks, to hang from the bottoms of windows, and worse: drifts that crested into frozen waves that blocked doorways, forcing those inside to tunnel out and those outside to tunnel in.

Snow curled, like prying fingers, into the spaces between window and sill, and it slithered through the gaps between door and thresh-old, depositing white snakeskins on entryway rugs.

At Breakwater, enough snow had managed to scuttle indoors that it was noticed by **Libbie Brookhants** as she made her way up the twisting Spite Tower staircase. Some even dripped over the spines of the shelved books that lined the stairwell, as if it was hanging from the eaves of a roof. She shivered seeing it.

So much snow had blown against the tower's many windows that it seemed they'd been covered in mourning shrouds, so even as the day filled with light, the windows let little of it inside.

Gray Dawn, Mary MacLane called it in her book.

Gray Dawn, Libbie Brookhants said to herself as she settled at her desk in the center of the round tower room, the peak of its ceiling high above her. It was like sitting beneath an open umbrella, the rafters its ribs.

As you may know, Readers: it's bad luck to open an umbrella indoors. And in Spite Tower, the umbrella ceiling was never not open.

And the glass eyes from Harold's stuffed birds and furry things mounted about the room were never not watching. The talking boards stacked on the shelf never more than half asleep, never not waiting for the scrape of charcoal to wake them up. The spoils of his strange travels, canes and statues, urns and books, all on the precipice of vibration should Libbie stray too close.

She shivered again. She set the book on the desk and stared at it. She was tired.

She'd barely slept, it's true, but she'd not meant to sleep at all. She'd intended to wait only for Alex to fall asleep before she could, alone and unobserved, do *something* with the book. (Though she had no idea what that something should be.)

But Alex didn't fall asleep right away. Too much had happened that night, too much had happened before that night, and so too much climbed into bed with them, sat heavily upon them, and kept them up and thinking, even if they did not say the things they were thinking to each other.

Especially because they did not do that.

And so while she had waited for Alex to fall asleep beside her, Libbie herself had drifted off. Into what seemed at first a happy dream—until it slithered into nightmare.

Libbie Brookhants had dreamed of a bright summer day there at Breakwater, the sun enormous and yellow in the cloudless sky. A group of her friends walked in a row down the steep wooden staircase that led from the terraced lawns and gardens to their private stretch of beach. They all wore wool or flannel bathing dresses—bulky and buttoned and built for modesty—but at least their legs and arms were exposed and some of them, like Libbie, had left a few of those top buttons undone as well.

In this dream, Alex was jovial and still young—Alex the Flirt, as she'd been when they'd first met in college—soon splashing and smiling in the waves, her shoulders warm from the sun when Libbie touched them, which she felt free to do many times. Everyone was laughing and relaxed, easy with one another. They drank tart lemonade from their picnic basket before kissing with puckered mouths in the surf. They did not hide these kisses. At some point, Alex's strong hands were on her, there in waist-high water, wave-hidden hands pulling Libbie in and holding her close against the throb of the tide before moving slowly down the front of her sopped flannel costume before eventually, teasingly, resting between her legs. Libbie almost melted at the pleasure of their closeness in the sun and salt, their friends on the shore watching, until that pleasure melted into something else—the way it happens in dream time—the mood shifting as abruptly as the turn of a kaleidoscope lens, the colors jumbling to form a new pattern from the same elements, this one bleak and wrong.

Now wave after wave of seaweed tumbled toward them, thick and stinking, black seaweed like matted nests of hair or piles of rotting snakes, until the waves were more seaweed than water and everyone fled to the beach.

Everyone except Libbie, that is. She was stuck in place.

She called helplessly to her friends as they stood onshore, their toes just out of the water's reach, silently watching as she was pulled farther and farther out, struggling against the waves and the black tangles until this unhappy scene flowed to another, and the beach and her friends drifted away, and Libbie, still in her bathing costume, wet and shivering, was standing in fetid water, oily and rank and up to her knees, the bodies of hundreds of wasps floating around her, there in the fountain in front of the Brookhants Main Hall. All of the students and faculty—and Flo and Clara and Eleanor Faderman, too—circled the fountain and stared grimly while a man in a smart suit, a man who most resembled her dead husband, Harold, sat casually on its rim, smoking a cigar while he instructed Libbie to *clean herself*. He tossed a cloth and a bar of soap at her, which she did not move to catch. The items bounced off her stomach, and when she looked down to see, that stomach, *her* stomach, was pregnant and stretched obscenely in her bathing dress. The bar of soap and cloth lay atop the black water until they sank into it as if sucked down by some unseen mouth. Into the fountain not-quite Harold threw his cigar, which hissed unnaturally as it went out, and then he reached down to the ground and pulled up something Libbie couldn't see until it cleared the rim: a large tub of bathing salts with a garish pink-and-white-striped label, *Dr. MacLane's Arsenical Bath Salts—Guaranteed to Restore Virtue in All Ruined Women*. A pen-and-ink drawing of Mary MacLane in a fashionable hat smiled coyly from the label's bottom corner.

Then the drawing moved. It winked at her as its mouth stretched to say, "Time for a bath, Libbie!" And then again and again until the gathered students and faculty joined in, until it became a chant: *Time for a bath, Libbie! Time for a bath, Libbie!* And shadow Harold opened the tub and began pouring black salts into the fountain. But as they streamed out, right before they hit the water, they snapped into yellow jackets and were upon her.

Libbie Brookhants had woken to a room creeping with thin light. It was nearly seven. She was shivering with sweat and tied up in her nightgown.

But Alex, thankfully, was now asleep beside her. At least there was that.

She slipped from the bed and washed her face at the sink in her dressing room, making only whispers of noise as she dressed quickly in the half dark.

She then quietly, oh so quietly, took the copy of Mary MacLane's book from where she'd hidden it from Alex: beneath her pillow.

Had there ever been a more obvious cause for a nightmare?

By the time the Eckharts arrived that morning and tunneled into the house, their noses and cheeks red, their coats and hats as if frosted with grainy buttercream, Libbie Brookhants had been at her desk in the tower for hours—groggy and addled and not yet solving the problem of Mary MacLane's book.

The Eckharts were loud. They had to push back the snow that tumbled in with them. They stomped their feet and brushed the

She then quietly, oh so quietly, took the copy of Mary MacLane's book.
Had there ever been a more obvious cause for a nightmare?

buttercream from their shoulders, sounding like people very glad to again be indoors.

They were also, Libbie saw, as she came down the tower stairs to greet them and ask about their trek, conspicuously without Adelaide.

Max reported that she was feeling poorly. He said she'd had some trouble even getting to their cottage the night before, though given the storm, they'd all had some trouble with that, and he'd hoped sleep would cure her. But then during the night she'd woken him, shaking his shoulders and calling his name. He'd found her up and out of bed with her coat over her nightclothes: pale, fever soaked, and talking nonsense about needing to come back here, to Breakwater, at once.

"Here?" Libbie asked. "Why on earth?"

"We don't need to go into all of that, do we, Max?" Hanna, who had already seemed unhappy with her son's storytelling, called from the dining room. She was on her way to the kitchen to fetch a mop. "Mrs. Brookhants doesn't need the bother. Between her fever and this lack of sleep, is it any wonder Addie can't keep her mind fixed on what's real?"

"It really was only nonsense, Mrs. Brookhants," Max said. He lowered his voice a little. "She had some idea about the storm causing the tide to rise and it carrying you off. I told her, 'Addie, it doesn't matter how much it snows—the water can't come all the way up those rocks in one night.' But she said it would. She wanted us to come see that you were alright, even though I said you were sleeping warm in your bed and that we'd be the only thing bothering you. I'm sure it's the news of the girl that's done it. My mother said it got in her head funny as soon as she heard." Great clumps of snow had fallen from the sides of his boots and he stooped to gather it in his hands, which made no sense, as it was melting even as he did so.

"Oh, Max, please leave it," Libbie said, watching him now awkwardly attempt to hold the dripping clumps, like a child who's hauled snowballs indoors.

"Sorry, Mrs. Brookhants," Max said, dropping it again.

"I think it might be best to send for the doctor," Libbie said. "Just to be cautious. For a fever to be causing her such confusion so quickly—"

"Not today we won't," Caspar said. Libbie hadn't realized he was still lingering in the entry hall with them, snow in his dripping beard.

She turned to him unhappily. "We won't?"

"None would make it," he said. "Anthony Harton's crew will come when they can to help clear the school road," he added. "But it won't be passable today."

"Not even by tomorrow if it keeps on like this," Max said.

Libbie hadn't expected this news. She could, of course, see that it was very unpleasant outside, but she'd been thinking the storm would only delay her arrival at Brookhants, not prevent it entirely.

Hanna was back, already swishing the mop through the snow-melt on the floor. "Adelaide didn't know what she was saying," she said again. "She needs only to rest."

"It seems she's been given just the day for that," Libbie said. She tried to sound cheery about this, but it rang false. She had to get to Brookhants.

There were, of course, logistical matters that needed her atten-tion, meeting with the trustees, drafting a formal letter to all parents apprising them, in official terms, of the bad news. And they would have to handle the newspapermen, hopefully better than they'd done with Flo and Clara.

But it was the immediate aftermath of this peculiar tragedy that Libbie was most concerned with, especially as it pertained to any gossip about the book, any questions raised or alluded to. It made her itchy and sour to be kept away from her school, unable to control its goings-on. No doubt Leanna Hamm would right now be in the dining hall, riling her colleagues as they tried to eat their toast, or worse: asking the somber and sleep-deprived students what they remembered about *The Story of Mary MacLane* and its influence on Eleanor Faderman, and on Florence and Clara, too. Soon Miss Hamm would be rounding up any lurking copies for some rash action she was planning. Perhaps a bonfire in the winter-drained fountain? Libbie could easily imagine the worst from Leanna Hamm and now she couldn't even get to campus to counteract it.

"I shouldn't have left my girls last night," she said. "I'd be there now."

"We did not *leave* the girls," Alex said, coming down the wide staircase from the second floor. (Never to be confused, Readers, with the twisty, cramped, and book-lined staircase leading to the tower.)

Libbie had been hoping she wasn't yet awake.

"They have every other instructor at their disposal." Alex smiled but her tone did not match it. "It snows here each winter, and yet each winter we're all so surprised to find it unpleasant."

"I've never known it to snow like this," Caspar said.

"Addie mentioned her snowshoes," Libbie said, thinking aloud.

"When did that come up in conversation?" Alex asked. "And why?"

Libbie ignored her and turned to Max. "Do you think they might fit me? Well enough for just one trip?"

"I think they would . . ." Max said. It was clear there was something else he wasn't saying. Max's face was usually a signal flag for his thoughts.

"Adelaide would rather I not borrow them," Libbie said. "Is that it?"

"Oh no, that's not—" Max said, shaking his head with wide eyes in an effort to be most convincing. "Addie would want you to use them as much as you like. It's just—" Again he stopped short of saying the thing he wanted to say.

"It's bad out there, Mrs. Brookhants," Caspar said. "Very." Max nodded at this.

"I can see that," Libbie said. "That's why I thought of the snowshoes."

"Yes, ma'am . . ." Now it was Caspar trailing off.

"They're trying to tell you that it's worse than what even Adelaide's magical snowshoes can solve," Alex said. "It's not a trip we can make today."

"Is that it?" Libbie asked the men. "Is that what you're telling me?"

"I think Miss Trills has it right," Caspar said. "It isn't a day for travel, even on a short road."

"Here we are in the great twentieth century and I can't get across my own land to my students," Libbie said. "Is that the full of this morning's report?"

"I might go for you, Mrs. Brookhants," Max said, determined to be the one to offer a solution.

"That's an idea," Caspar said.

"And why would it be right for you to do so but wrong for me?"

Max started to answer, but Libbie cut him off with a wave of her hand. "No, please don't say. If I could go, that would be the thing. You in my stead does me no good. Though I thank you for the offer, Max. And with Addie ill."

"Adelaide's ill?" Alex asked. "What's happened to her?"

No one seemed interested in going through that again, and so she was answered by Hanna with: "Only a touch of fever. She'll be right as rain tomorrow if she gets the sleep she needs today."

The day's disappointments now dispensed, Hanna and her mop and Caspar and Max all went about their work. Other than Libbie, only Alex remained, looking out the window at the swarming snow.

Libbie turned to slip up the tower stairs, but as she did, Alex said, "You didn't sleep."

"If you know that it must be because I kept you awake."

"You didn't," Alex said. "I couldn't sleep thinking of Eleanor and the angel's trumpets. She knew the risk. I'm sure she must have."

"That they're poison?"

"Yes, but more than that—that they would kill her, all that she ate."

"You mean to say what?" Libbie would not be the first to use the word.

Alex shook her head as if to clear a thought. "What have you done with the book?"

"Which?" Libbie asked.

"You know which. I think it's past time I read it and now the snow's given me a day to do so."

"Is your memory so short as that?" Libbie asked, trying for nonchalance. "We read it only this summer."

"That was your diversion," Alex said. "Not mine."

Now Libbie was indignant. "Surely even you can remember Sara Dahlgren reading aloud its most relevant entries?" She gestured toward the dining room. "Right here. At dinner? She stood on her chair. Katharine was laughing so much she choked on her cocktail."

"Isn't Katharine often choking on her cocktails?"

For a moment, Libbie considered the worth of continuing in this vein. She decided that it was better to try than not to do so. "Later that night I recall us both being quite inspired by what we'd heard. Sara teased us the next morning about how quickly we'd rushed off together. Or have you no memory of that, either?"

"Vulgarity has never suited you, Libbie," Alex said, her voice a notch lower and her eyes casting about for Hanna. "And yet you're so determined to keep trying it on."

"I'd say that I wear my vulgarity better than you do your priggishness, but I'm no longer certain that's true. It quite suits you."

They looked at each other unhappily. Outside the wind snarled to match.

"We're both tired and quarrelsome," Alex said, as if she was now being the reasonable one. "Let's not give in to it. I don't want the copy from Sara Dahlgren's performance, anyway. I want to read the copy we found last night with Eleanor Faderman. Where is it?"

"It's on my desk," Libbie said, sighing and again starting up the tower stairs. "Come fetch it."

"Yes, I think I will," Alex said, taking a step or two in the same direction. And then she stopped, fully planted herself, and looked up the narrow tower stairs as they twisted into dim light. "Are you working now?"

Libbie had anticipated this reaction. Unlike Harold, Libbie's departed husband-of-happenstance, Alex did not find the story of the Rash brothers and their Spite Tower charmingly representative of ye olde New England. Truth be told, Alex had always found the tower unsettling—a place to avoid in the otherwise well-appointed house. Because of this, she left its dominion solely to Libbie. Which Libbie was grateful for, and sometimes took advantage of.

Like now.

She stopped climbing and turned to face Alex below her. "I still have to write the Fadermans—and I don't know what that will take from me. If you'd prefer, I can send the book with Hanna when she brings my tray."

"Yes, that's fine," Alex said, retracing the steps she'd just taken. "I'll be in the parlor."

Libbie was pleased by the success of her deflection, however momentary. The tower stairs were as good as a drawbridge and moat, she thought as she climbed the rest. Any additional time granted to her was necessary. The book was there on her desk, just where she'd placed it hours before, and she still didn't know what to do with it.

She pulled the shawl from the back of her chair and wrapped it over her shoulders before sitting. It was much colder here in her perch atop the tower, the world outside its windows still a swirling white void. She flipped through the book, letting the pages fall against each other until she found what she wanted: the March 5 entry.

Again, she stared at it. Alex was far too clever not to notice it. And Alex, being Alex, would also understand how to read it. Sara Dahlgren was a lot of things, but cunning code maker was not among them.

This entry, one of the book's controversial anemone lady passages—*this* was proof of Libbie's lie. It showed what she had done, right there on the page in ink. A Pinkerton might be able to handle the book and not discern her culpability, but the same could not be said for Alex. Her Alex. This was the page that connected Libbie to the book, because it *was* her book.

Or it was once, at any rate.

Before she gave it to Flo and Clara.

They'd come to her office to ask permission to form their club: the Plain Bad Heroine Society. It was the morning after the hailstorm and she'd been busy with the groundskeepers, sorting out the damage, so she'd been unable to make time for them. They'd instead made an appointment for the following day. They were so excited!

And smitten, it was clear. In the giddy rush of their pink-cheeked crush, they so reminded Libbie of herself and Alex, once upon an earlier time.

Charmed by these students, Libbie had, at some point during her busy day, thought to bring them her personal copy of Mary Mac-Lane's book. She'd surprise them with it. She knew that copies of the book were scarce at Brookhants, that some teachers (like Leanna Hamm) had even told students that they were banned from campus, though that wasn't true. (At least not at the time.)

If Flo and Clara were surprised by this gesture, by their own Principal Brookhants not only owning such a book but giving it to them, they did not show it. At least not to Libbie.

But even as she handed it to the girls—and before that, when she'd plucked it from the bookshelves lining the tower—Libbie knew Alex wouldn't approve. It was one thing for their students to be such champions for the book. It was quite another for their principal to seem to endorse it, and the things it said.

And now, of course, and now . . .

Well, someone like Leanna Hamm would make much out of the bad fact that it was Libbie's own copy that kept turning up with dead Brookhants students. And perhaps it wouldn't only be Leanna Hamm who felt that way.

Libbie knew it wouldn't.

She'd been so pleased with herself and her decision, her secret support of these girls in crush, that she'd quite forgotten about the book's March 5 entry and how it exposed her. She'd forgotten about it, that is, until her copy was found in the woods with Flo and Clara and the questions about who had brought it there had bloomed, and with them the examinations of its marginalia.

And then she'd remembered.

Under any other circumstance, Libbie would have been disappointed with what the students had done to her book. It was positively filled with scribbles—in ink and pencil both, passages underlined and circled, others marked with stars or hearts or cryptic notes written above or below the print.

Perhaps they had never intended to return it to her, but under the strange and terrible circumstances that *did* return it, Libbie Brookhants was grateful for those markings. If they hadn't been there, her connection to it would have already been discovered. The book had been handled by many people before Eleanor had stolen it. But as it was, Libbie was still the only one who knew. And now that she had it again, she planned to keep it that way.

⁂

Last August was only the third time that their friends—the friends who were most like Libbie and Alex—had come to Spite Manor to visit. This was just a few months prior, but now, with all that had happened since, it seemed impossibly long ago: a full week of sun-bake and salted skin, of sand in their hair—sand all over the house, really, on the floors and in the bedsheets—all of them eating too much peach ice cream out on the porch because they could not stop themselves from doing so. It was rich and sweet and deliciously cold. It made their teeth and temples ache.

The night Sara Dahlgren had read those passages from Mary MacLane's book the lot of them were, Libbie remembered, a little bit drunk and a lot sun silly from their day. The Eckharts were away at Max and Adelaide's wedding in Pittsburgh, so Libbie and her friends had enjoyed the full run of the staffless house and were already stripped down to their nightgowns and silk robes, nothing at all on underneath. Sunburned Alex had even deigned to wear the striped boy's nightshirt Sara bought for her in Spain, though she'd blushed and laughed at it when Sara had given it to her.

It was meltingly hot, each of Spite Manor's windows open with the ocean crashing outside, all of them lolled around the dining table, goading each other on.

Their friends* had delivered to them all manner of gay surprises from the Continent: poems and novels, a book of nude drawings,

---

* Really, Readers, it was primarily Sara Dahlgren who had brought them these things. And she'd brought them mostly for Libbie.

and a set of *artistic* stereo cards purchased from the private stock of a prominent Parisian photographer. In those images, women in top hats and tails had their arms around each other, and women in far less clothing had their mouths upon each other.

"Good thing I decided not to invite Anthony Comstock,"* Libbie had joked when the stereoscope† was passed her way and she had the chance to view the most explicit of the photos.

"Can that whiskered rhinoceros really still be at it?" Sara had asked.

"He's even worse than before! They gave him an ounce of power and he's spun it into a pound of tyranny."

"Have I ever told you that I had the great displeasure of meeting him once at a benefit?" Sara asked.

"We know!" Katharine said, trying to cut short the story they'd all heard, which never worked with Sara.

"Although that particular evening did also then offer me the very

---

* The truly priggish creator and enforcer of the New York Society for the Suppression of Vice and namesake for the term *comstockery* (censorship). In 1873, Congress passed a law named after him that made transporting "obscene, lewd, or lascivious" material a crime.

† A stereoscope was an instrument that allowed its user to view specially made cards in 3D. Think first-gen Instagram, Readers.

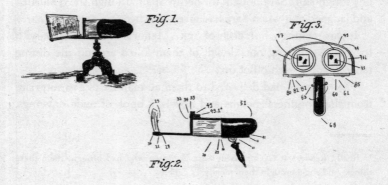

great pleasure of voicing a number of new obscenities in Mr. Comstock's pitiful presence. I don't think he even had time to write them all down for his records, so many came his way at once."

"We've heard this before!" Katharine shouted again.

More drinks were mixed, more Comstock-condemned materials passed around.

However, for once the biggest success of the evening's sapphic show-and-tell did not belong to the fashionable Europeans and their artistic photographs. On this night the winning item was as young and brash as its country of origin: American Mary MacLane's portrayal, a book Sara told them she'd sought out as soon as she'd arrived stateside the month before.

"And that was all *quite* fortuitous," Sara had said. "Something out of a novel. Did I tell you? My regular bookseller didn't have a single copy left in stock—and I'd gone there especially for them. He said he would have to order them for me and I didn't know if I'd have them before I had to leave New York and I was most vexed about that and was walking up Lexington, pouting, trying to think where else to look, and I ran into the most interesting woman selling them from a folding table right there on the sidewalk. Can you believe it? I practically stepped on her."

"You think every woman you meet is the most interesting woman you've met," Alex said, to the group's particular delight because Alex did not usually speak this way, not even to Sara Dahlgren.

"Not *every* woman, Alex." Sara blew her an exaggerated kiss before continuing. "As it was, *this* interesting woman sold me five copies. I would have taken more, and I told her that, but I couldn't carry them, and unlike my regular bookseller she did not offer delivery."

"You don't say," Alex said. "How remarkably uncouth of the woman on the sidewalk with the folding table."

"What a queer thing to be selling on the street," Katharine said. "Where do you think she came from?"

Sara smiled like this was the best part. She shook her head. "Clearly a woman with a head for sales. Anyway, you should be very grateful that I was so willing to play pack mule, because I am now giving you one of the copies that I hauled up Lexington that day."

"Aren't we the lucky ones?" Libbie had said, squeezing Alex's leg beneath the table and then leaving her hand there on Alex's bare thigh.

That night, the group of them had first giggled, then howled, as Sara read aloud Mary's continued beseeching of the devil. Fed by this audience of rummy women, Sara grew more and more animated in her performance. Eventually she climbed atop her chair and practically sang the entries she'd been saving for her finale: Mary's erotic desire for Fannie Corbin, her anemone lady.

At first, they all also pretended to find these passages worthy of more titters. But this was only to save face. They were, each to a listener, stirred.

For Alex and Libbie in particular, Mary's bold declarations of lust kindled a shared longing. It was a longing additionally charged by the company, the photographs, the cocktails—but its greatest fuel came from their own memories of who they had been, and what they had been to each other, all those years before when they were Mary's age, or just about: the year they had discovered the previously unmapped landscape of their desire.

They had believed, then, that they were charting new worlds with their bodies. Surely the arch of Alex's back, the jut of her hip bone, the flush of her cheeks when Libbie moved atop her were each more beautiful than the sunsets or mountain passes or banal wildflowers Libbie had previously gushed over, never guessing at their mere adequacy. She could almost (though not quite) blush to remember the hours—hours!—they had spent together in the narrow, squeaking bed of an empty Wellesley dorm room (one with a leak in the ceiling that had yet to be repaired), using their hands and mouths to explore the territories of each other's bodies. And most importantly: those bodies when they were fitted together.

Mary MacLane's words were now like an echo of that lost time. And that echo had lasted for more than just a single night of lovemaking to be overheard and remarked upon the next morning by their pretending-to-be-scandalized friends.

In fact, Readers, it seemed to Libbie that it had lasted all the way into the fall and the start of term. She and Alex *had* been better.

They had been more like what they once were to each other—more like the couple they'd been, like the people they'd been—before this life at Brookhants.

Until, that is, the tragedy with Flo and Clara.

And now Eleanor, too.

And so here was Libbie, at her desk atop the tower, the book before her, and what to do with it?

Sara Dahlgren and her games, everything a chance to play.

Her very personal inscription to Libbie was buried in the March 5 entry. She'd made boxes around letters and underlined words until the passage read as follows:

To library*—
   I feel a strange attraction of sex
   a certain strained, tense passion
   And this is my predominating feeling
   It brings me pain and pleasure mingled in that odd, odd
fashion.
   Love,
   Your sara

Sara had written beneath in her own hand: *P.S. Hasn't your Alex ever learned to share?*

Libbie sighed. She looked out the windows at the snow still coming down and thought she might let herself be hypnotized if she stared long enough. It seemed almost to hum. She could hear it beyond the shivering windows. Perhaps she should just give the book to Alex as it was, even leave it open to this entry when she did. Then they would finally have to talk about the things they'd rather not. Wouldn't they?

---

* Sara Dahlgren's pet name for Libbie.

The clock struck the half hour and startled her, its chime filling the room like a warning bell. Hanna would arrive with her tray at any moment.

Libbie picked up her pen. She did not want to talk to Alex about the things they did not talk about.

So for now, she would add more brackets and boxes to confuse the issue. That's what she would do. She'd thought of doing it earlier but couldn't, for whatever reason, make herself mark the page. But she would do it now. It would hide Sara's original code in plain sight. If almost everything in the passage was marked, then who could read it and make any sense of it—who could discern the original message or its sender?

Libbie put the pen to the page. And, she would have sworn it, the buzz from outside grew louder. Her eyes wobbled. She refocused, tried again. Her markings looked so obvious to her—so tellingly new, added after the fact.

She drew boxes and circles. She underlined and crossed out.

But the more of her own markings she added, the more Sara's original message seemed to stand out. She couldn't explain this, but it was almost as if Sara Dahlgren's lines were now darker.

And that buzzing from outside had come in. Libbie looked up into the umbrella ceiling and then behind her at the shelves lined with Harold's collections. She almost expected to see the mounted taxidermy, the broken pieces of ancient pottery, the framed photographs and sky charts and maps vibrate. The buzzing moved through it all: from the floorboards up through her desk and the walls to the rafters above.

And now Sara Dahlgren's message was practically glowing. This was so stupid, *so stupid a thing,* and yet Libbie was so frustrated that she was now near to tears.

And Alex would read it and Alex would know. Another wrong between them.

She could hear Hanna saying something below. She was on the landing, on her way up.

Libbie had waited too long and now her only choice was to remove the page. Its absence would spark other questions, yes, but the evidence that connected her to the book would be gone.

Libbie bent the binding back, heard it break as she did. She found a ruler in the drawer—quickly, quickly now—and set its thin edge against the inside fold of the page. She fit it there exactly and then applied pressure.

Now there was the rattle of Hanna and the tray of dishes up the twisting stairs.

Using her right hand, Libbie tore the page from the top.

Never before in her life had Libbie Brookhants so neatly removed a page from a book: no jagged edges or remnants left behind. There was a chance, slim but possible, that Alex wouldn't even notice it was gone. Or if she did, she might think this hop from page 180 to page 183 merely a printing error. (Though given that it occurred in one of the most explicitly sapphic entries in the volume, this was doubtful, Readers.)

Libbie now slid the leaf that was pages 181 and 182, the evidence against her, beneath some other papers on her desk and closed the book just as Hanna came up the final stair and into the room, the coffeepot and saucer rattling with her efforts. "A bit late this morning, aren't I?" she said. "But my jam will make up for it, I hope." She placed the tray at the edge of the desk and turned the cup over so that she could pour into it.

Libbie felt like she'd been slapped hard across her face. Or maybe it was more like she'd ducked away from a slap at the last moment. She couldn't tell.

"Hanna," she asked, as even the scent of the coffee warmed her, "do you know the cause of the buzzing? Is Max doing something else with the radiators?"

"What is it, now?" Hanna asked, adding a ghost of cream.

"The buzzing sound," Libbie said as if it should be obvious. It should have been, but now that she had said it, she noticed she could no longer hear the noise.

"I haven't the least idea," Hanna said, turning her head as if to listen.

"It seems to have stopped," Libbie said. She took a drink of her coffee. It was bitter and rich, a combination she favored.

"Oh good," Hanna said. "Max has fixed it, then. He is clever about those radiators." She set a plate with toast and fruit in front of Libbie, mentioned again that the blackberry jam had turned out well, if she did say so herself, and then asked, "Is there anything else, ma'am?"

"If you could bring this to Alex," Libbie said, handing her the book. "I think she's in the parlor."

"Yes, I just saw her there," Hanna said.

So it was done.

Hanna was carrying the book away and it no longer showed Libbie's secrets. She would have to do something with the page, of course, but it was only a single piece of paper. She might drop it in the kitchen fire or confetti it with scissors. Or she might keep it. She might. Because it was from Sara and because she wanted to.

But she had a little time to decide about that, anyway. For now, Libbie wanted only to finish this cup of coffee and then put her head upon this desk and rest her eyes.

She was so tired.

THE (UNOFFICIAL) CHEMISTRY READ

· · · · · · · · · · · · · · · ·

Audrey had not slept well.

Over breakfast, Caroline had blamed preaudition nerves. "Yeah, but with a part like this, I'd be—"

"I'd be nervous if you weren't nervous," Audrey cut her off.

"Exactly. Hey, maybe think about bringing the crystals I gave you." Caroline put up her hand. "And you don't need to have a big reaction to me saying that."

Audrey *was* nervous. Anxious, too.

But those things didn't account for the twitching shadows on the walls of her bedroom as she'd tried to sleep, shadows that seemed to skitter and shudder with pointed wings and pointed bodies. Shadows with black-black mirrored eyes.

And nervousness didn't account for the noises she'd heard, buzzing that became almost a hum, as if her bed was itself atop a yellow jacket nest, or as if the whole of her room was somehow inside of one. It was a sound that was only there when she didn't try to listen for it. And then it was constant. And sometimes it seemed as though there were whispers laced in with that hum-buzzing: girls' voices talking low. She'd spent most of the night—before a few anemic hours of sleep claimed her, anyway—stiff beneath her covers, an icy skein of fear coiling around her spine even as she told herself she was being truly silly and to grow up.

Now, in Noel's truck, on their way to Bo Dhillon's house, the gold sunlight on the windshield helped to thaw the previous night's chill. Audrey told people she hadn't made the time to get her driver's license. But the truth was that the idea of operating a vehicle in California traffic plainly terrified her. Terrified. Even as a passenger, her inclination was to imagine accidents—to see them, always. She anticipated the slam of metal on metal, the way it would twist and bend and the air would fill with screams and tire screeches. And though the fact of her not driving was becoming increasingly cumbersome in her day-to-day, right now it was welcome. She was glad to have Noel at the wheel.

Some other good news, they eventually saw as they pulled up the drive, was that Bo Dhillon's bungalow turned out to be like the So-Cal version of a storybook cottage. (The woodcutter's, Readers, not the witch's.) It had a porch with river rock pillars and wide railings and was set back within landscaping made to look more natural than manicured.

"I don't see any skulls yet," Audrey said.

"Just wait," Noel said. "You can't leave that stuff out in the yard."

Gray happened to arrive right as they did, both of them pulling into a pea gravel side lot where several other cars were already parked in a jumble.

Audrey breathed out a long breath. She tried to remember anything at all about Clara that might help her to Clara better. She turned to officiousness as a calming technique.

They watched Gray unsuccessfully nose his car in one direction, then another.

"You should try to have fun in there," Noel said.

"Thanks, Dad."

"I'm serious," he said. "You're already their choice. So go do the thing."

"I like it so much better when nobody expects anything from me and then I surprise them by delivering anything at all."

"That bar's so low you're gonna stub your toe on it."

Gray had given up with parking maneuvers and stopped behind someone's gleaming Audi. He rolled down his window and waved at them to pull alongside.

"I'm getting out," Audrey called to him.

"Isn't Noel staying?" Gray asked.

"He wasn't," she said, confused.

"Well, he can," Gray said. He leaned out his window a little so he could better speak to them both. "Up to you. They said the more the merrier."

"Weird," Audrey said. It was another odd thing about this already odd situation. Bo Dhillon's *elaborate methods*. She looked at Noel.

"Up to you," he echoed, shrugging.

"Stay," she said. She didn't know if that was the right choice, or if it would mark her in some way, make her seem amateurish. She didn't feel like she had time to contemplate it.

They ended up blocking what was left of the drive. Once Audrey was out of the car, she looked more closely at the house. On one of those wide railings now sat Harper Harper. She was smoking a cigarette and looking at something in her lap. A book, Audrey saw, when Harper turned a page.

And then she looked up and at them and waved. They all waved back.

It was shady under the eaves where Harper Harper was sitting, and Audrey watched the circle of her cigarette end burn orange as she inhaled. Then Harper turned toward the house and shouted something through the screen door that Audrey couldn't make out. She turned back to them, to Audrey, and called out, *"There are few things that annoy me so much as to be called a young lady!"* She seemed to be reading from the book.

"Seems reasonable," Gray yelled back. He was the first in their procession to reach her.

Harper kept reading. *"I am no lady—as any one could see by close inspection, and the phrase has an odious sound. I would rather be called a sweet little thing, or a fallen woman, or a sensible girl— though they would each be equally a lie."*

"Mary MacLane," Audrey said.

Harper grinned. "She's such a weirdo Montanan," she said. "She's like my personal brand ambassador. Have you read it yet?"

"Not yet," Audrey said. "I will."

"You have to," Harper said. "Then we can, like, book club it to- gether. We'll get Merritt to explain it to us."

"What do you have me doing?" Merritt asked from inside the house as she pushed the screen door open. Audrey first saw the bold shape of her hair, its impressive color and curl.

"You're gonna run our Mary MacLane book club," Harper said, gripping the pillar beside her so she could lean back and look at Merritt as she walked from the shadow of the porch roof and toward the sunlight. "You're the president."

"Don't tell me," Merritt said, putting on her huge sunglasses as she stood next to Harper at the railing. "You meet in the woods, right? And you call yourselves the Plain Bad Heroine Society? And you're in love."

"This is Merritt," Harper said to them. "She wrote us."

"Hello," Merritt said with a wave like a windshield wiper.

Audrey echoed that hello and waved back. She could tell already—between Merritt's hair and those sunglasses, even with just the one comment she'd made—that Merritt was the type of woman in her twenties who most intimidated Audrey. She seemed so confident in her affect: erudite, particular, and unimpressed. (Actually, Audrey had formed this opinion the previous night, watching the video interview of her. Now she was just having that opinion confirmed.)

Gray lived for introductions. He stepped toward Harper with his hand partially extended. "I'm Gray Wright, Audrey's manager. And I couldn't be a bigger fan of yours." He seemed to be done and then thought better of it, looked at Merritt, and added, "Of the both of you, I mean. Of course."

"Of course," Merritt said without smiling.

Harper unfolded herself and jumped down into the shiny driveway pebbles. She pinched out her cigarette, hid it behind her ear, and shook Gray's hand, all as one continuous move. "Thank you," she said. "It's nice to meet you."

"Gonna go say my hellos," Gray said, halfway up the porch steps and seemingly unsure of how to navigate Merritt after her comment, so he just left it.

Harper was now standing before Audrey and Noel. She wore a white T-shirt with a Renaissance-oil-painting-style image of a silver tray heaped with pears, grapes, and pomegranates. Over it were the words QUEER FRUIT.

"Great shirt," Noel said before Audrey could.

"Thank you," Harper replied. "I just got it at Slap Happy. In Los Feliz. You know it?"

"I don't think so," Audrey said.

"Let's add it to my tour," Merritt called from behind them, inserting herself from the porch.

"Are we even doing that?" Harper asked, turning back to Merritt, who was now leaning over the railing, her head and shoulders in the sun and the rest of her in shade. "I didn't know you ever said yes."

Merritt shrugged. "I didn't ever say no."

"It's good you're wearing jeans, then," Harper said inscrutably. She turned again to Noel and Audrey. "Shit, I'm sorry. Hello," she said, holding out her hand. "I'm Harper. And I am very glad you're here. And excited."

Harper's hand was cool and dry. Audrey was trying to remember the last time she'd shaken hands with anyone her age. "I'm Audrey," she said. "I'm really glad to be here." She hated how introductions make everyone sound like parrots. Or at least they made her feel her worst parrot self.

"Noel," Noel said, kind of waving, "professional third wheel."

"Nah, c'mon, I know about you," Harper said. "This Malibu girl who was sweet on me for two seconds is so into your band."

"Was *sweet on you*?" Merritt said, now coming down the stairs to join them. "Was this happening in an episode of *Father Knows Best*?"

"Yeah, were you there?" Harper grinned at her then turned back to Audrey.

There was something about the intensity of Harper's focus, when you had it all to yourself, that was both unsettling and almost-but-not-quite pleasant. Audrey noticed this even in those first few minutes of interaction. Maybe it's because Harper could seem somehow both earnest and sort of fake, put-on. Audrey couldn't decide how seriously to take this whole thing she was doing, this Harper Harper shtick, or even decide if it was a thing she was *doing* at all.

Audrey also thought it was strange how much Harper looked like Audrey had expected her to, like the movie version of herself. All of that style (or maybe not style, but persona) that you've heard about: it was there.

Audrey was an industry kid through and through. You couldn't surprise her with horrifying and revealing photos of this or that celebrity because she intimately understood all the ways in which there was the human and then there was the movie star—especially when we were talking about the film-carrying, high-voltage talents. She knew, from experience, that when you met the action hero, he was gonna be skinnier and shorter and have worse skin, maybe— still handsome, of course, absolutely—but not the guy on the screen.

I'm telling you this so that you'll believe me when I say that Harper Harper surprised Audrey because she seemed to carry with her *all* of the stuff Audrey had seen onscreen and more. She couldn't quite see the flaws, the cracks that were supposed to reveal where the movie version ended and the human began.

"Hey, hey, the gang's all here," Bo Dhillon said, opening the screen door and stepping outside.

He bounded down the stairs and over to them, to Audrey, stepping around Harper to grab her shoulders, a hand on each, before he kissed her cheek, his big moustache smashing against her face and neck.

"Really good to see you, girl," he said as he pulled back, still holding her shoulders. He was in olive jeans and a T-shirt with one of the posters for the original *Black Christmas* printed on it in all of its 1970s vibrancy—the discord of a happy red-and-green holly wreath as the outline for the black-and-white photo of a dead girl in a chair, her mouth a gaping scream and her head encased in a sheen of cellophane. It was a grotesque image and now directly in Audrey's sight line. "I'm so amped about this."

Audrey nodded. "Me too. Thank you so much for thinking of me."

"I didn't think of anybody else."

Merritt was behind them and off to the side a little. She said something then that Audrey didn't quite hear.

Apparently neither did Bo. "What's that?" he asked, dropping his grip from Audrey's shoulders to turn and look at Merritt.

"Oh, I was just saying, except for the other actor," Merritt said, smiling like they were all in on something together.

"I'm sorry, what now?" Bo asked her again.

"You couldn't think of anyone but Audrey to play Clara . . . except for Lily Strichtfield, who was playing her until yesterday." Merritt was still smiling plainly, as if she hadn't just said the thing she'd said.

"I mean, ouch," Audrey said, trying to make it a joke though it did not feel like one.

"What's your point?" Harper asked Merritt exactly as Noel said, "Wow, kid."

"I'm not your kid," Merritt said. Her voice wasn't sharp, exactly, but her smile was gone. "Just getting used to how this all works. Hollyweird." Now she did smile again. Sort of.

Bo jumped in. "No, you're right that it takes getting used to." His tone was as jovial as a party clown. "Lily was great. She *is* great, but she didn't work out for this and I say we're all the luckier for it. Sometimes fortune blooms from the muck of happenstance." He turned now, formally, to Noel. "I'm Bo, by the way," he said. "I know your dad."

"Hey, I know him, too," Noel replied.

"Funny guy," Bo said.

"Don't tell him that," Audrey said. "He'll never stop reminding me." She tried to join in with a joke, but whatever had just happened with Merritt had made her wobble with doubt. What the fuck was that?

Bo looked around at all of them and said, "Cool. Alright, well come on—everybody's in the back. There's a shit ton of sushi." He started up the porch stairs and then turned and said, "I'm sure it seems otherwise, but this is all very relaxed today, Audrey. Really. More than anything we just want to gauge the energy between you."

"Our chemistry," she said.

"Yeah," he said, running a hand over his moustache, "that's part of it. But I'm talking energy, too. This one's only gonna work if the actors make it their own—that goes for you and Harper especially. I'm not saying full-on improv—you know, like toss-out-the-script bullshit. We like the script."

"I do, too," Audrey said quickly.

"Yeah?" he said. "Good. But I still think we're all going to have to really live inside this one to pull it off the way it deserves. You know what I'm saying?"

"Yeah," Audrey said. "I think so."

But, Readers: she did *not* know, not really, what he meant by that.

THINGS ARE NOT

ALL THAT PLEASANT OUT BY

BO DHILLON'S POOL

....

I'll not soften the blow (nor will I season the gristle or bubble wrap the bullet): **Merritt** did not want Audrey Wells to play Clara Broward.

Early that morning she'd watched Audrey's clips.* They all seemed to Merritt, truth be told, notably average. Shoulder shrug. Fine, I guess.

Merritt had then searched for Audrey's social media, thinking maybe her feeds would somehow show that this person was personally interesting enough to play Clara, that she had Clara's spark and life force. But there weren't any feeds to stalk—none at all. Instead, Merritt found plenty of posts about Audrey's mother, Caroline, and her series of past public *debacles*. She'd watched that leaked security footage of the car crash and the dog attack a few times—it was especially haunting because it was in black-and-white and from a weird angle—Caroline looking like a ghost-zombie, the dog leaping at her in a flash of muscle. Merritt could see why it had achieved back-in-the-day virality. She did find some lingering evidence that maybe Audrey had once maintained a public Facebook profile. Or someone

---

* In case, like Merritt before watching Audrey's, you've never seen any, think a self-promotional commercial for actors featuring some of their best scenes. Best being subjective, Readers.

had, in her name, when she had been in that tween TV series; but that was years before. And now: nothing.

And *Fine, I guess, shoulder shrug,* couldn't ever be enough to play Clara Broward, who was brash and vain and clever.

Audrey Wells was iceberg salad with a side of banal.

Now Merritt took a drink from her second (third?) iced coffee of the morning and tried to avoid making eye contact with Harper, who seemed to be studiously attempting to make eye contact with her. Thankfully, she had her face-eclipsing sunglasses on, so she didn't think Harper could tell where she was or wasn't looking. They were now out in Bo's backyard, on the stone patio next to his pool, beneath a massive pergola draped with bougainvillea vines of showy pink flowers and a few strings of unlit globe lights, their wires droopily crisscrossing the space.

All around her people were mingling, producers and other studio people and a few crew members, Harper's massive entourage of agents and managers and assistants, whatever they were, hangers-on, and Elaine, of course. Merritt had last seen her in the kitchen telling Noel a long story about her husband and his career as a political cartoonist. It was charming. It was also a story that Merritt had heard before, like most of Elaine's stories. Everywhere there were people eating stupid-expensive sushi, drinking cucumber and mint water, telling gossipy inside jokes, talking about so-and-so who went here and there doing this and that.

Merritt had tried, a little, to participate in some of this talking, but as it did not suit her talents, she was happy to eventually settle in on one end of the outdoor sectional with her phone in front of her face.

Oh, she wanted to talk to Harper Harper, Readers. Of course she did. She wanted to sit next to Harper and pick up where they'd left off the night before. But Harper had her squad with her today—so many people who seemed to fill such distinct roles—and Merritt now doubted her own recollection of what had happened the night before, what she had felt and what she felt certain Harper had felt, out there by the Spago dumpsters. Everything today had her feeling almost seasick with wobbly uncertainty, and somehow disappointed. Disappointed already.

Part of that disappointment: Audrey Wells, who, it really must be said, was no Clara Broward. Of this Merritt felt quite certain. But it was an impotent certainty, the worst kind, because who would listen to her about it? Who would care?

Merritt looked up from her phone at the people gathered around the patio. Audrey was now standing with her manager next to a long outdoor dining table covered in food. The manager was reaching for a handful of edamame while talking to Josh, a guy Merritt had earlier been introduced to as one of Harper's agents. She'd already decided she didn't like him. It had taken her only a few minutes of being around him for that to happen.

Bo's pool smelled strongly of chlorine, like something was off with the chemicals. He probably rarely swam in it. Somebody cracked a joke in reference to the pool scene in the *House Mother* movies and Merritt again wondered what it was she was even doing there, how any of this really had anything to do with her at all. She scrolled through phone pics of the now-fire-damaged Orangerie. Carl the caretaker had texted a new batch right before they'd left the hotel for Bo's, these taken in the summer sunshine of that very morning in Rhode Island. The char was relegated to the new construction within those glass walls, like a massive shadow plant blooming outward from its center, the black burn reaching and ready to take over had it not been stopped.

As she squinted at the images, trying to see them in the glare of sunlight across her screen, a text lit up her phone. She was amused, and, TBH, rather thrilled, to see it was from Harper.

> other than t-shirt shopping, whatchu thinking for our date? can't
> decide if you'd be into touristy LA (because irony) or wanting to avoid
> all of that . . .

Once she'd read it and looked up, she found Harper Harper looking at her.

So Merritt texted back:

New phone, who dis?

Harper smiled when the text landed on her screen. Then she took a minute or so, searching for something online, copying and pasting, before sending:

The saguaro (/səˈwaroʊ/) *(Carnegiea gigantea)* is an arborescent (tree-like) cactus species in the monotypic genus *Carnegiea*, which can grow to be over 20 m (70 ft) tall. http://en.wikipedia.org/wiki /Saguaro

So Merritt wrote:

Wikipedia as your source? Really?

Merritt liked this. She liked it probably too much, given those Instagram posts she'd seen the night before with Annie the artist. She texted:

Is it a date? Aren't you seeing someone right now?

Harper's fast response:

yes. she's seeing other people, too. are you OK with that? (this is kind of new to me)

To which Merritt wrote:

~~I don't know if I'm OK with it.~~

But what she sent was:

I've been thinking, for a while, that I want to get my eyebrow pierced. Can you make that happen today?

Harper:

nice. nobody does that anymore—which eyebrow?

Merritt:

The left.

Harper:

ITC i know somebody.

good thing it's the left or we'd be SOL

Merritt felt nearly giddy.

Even though she knew, she *knew,* this was just what Harper Harper did—that it was who she was, *how* she was—Merritt was still keeping alive one tiny whit of hope that maybe it was something more than the same charming performance that pretty much everybody received a greater or lesser version of. She really needed that to be true because she was, despite herself, feeling quite like a Brookhants girl of yore. She was smitten. She was smashed on Harper Harper *and* she wanted to smash Harper Harper. Both versions worked, in this case.

"You're into the CrossFit-type stuff then?" she overheard Harper's agent, Josh, say to Audrey as their cluster headed into the seating area, blocking Merritt's view of Harper.

"Sort of," Audrey said. "I don't belong to a box or anything. But I do functional training. My trainer makes me do a lot of HIIT."

"Nice," Josh said. "Go hard and get it done. It's the only way."

"What is that?" Merritt asked, her constant desire to know things getting the best of her. "What's HIIT?"

"High-intensity interval training," Audrey said, right before Josh said the same, so that his words became her echo.

Merritt raised her eyebrows at them. "I'm not familiar."

"It just means you, like, go all out in short intervals, with rests in between," Audrey said. "Like push-ups and squats and stuff, fast and focused—but, like, with everything you have. It gets your heart rate up, then you slow it down, then you bring it back up."

"High intensity, Merritt," Elaine said, surprising her by joining in from behind. She and Noel had come into the yard. "That sounds right up your alley."

"I don't think so," Merritt said. "I don't even want to walk to my alley. There's no way I'm doing a bunch of push-ups once I get there."

"Well, whatever you're doing," Josh said loudly to Audrey, as if trying to wrestle the conversation back, "keep it up. You look great."

Merritt thought this comment creepy, but somehow also expected, given their surroundings and Audrey's job. Case in point: no one else seemed to think it particularly strange that this older dude was so openly appraising Audrey's body.

Well, except for maybe Audrey herself. "Thanks," she said stiffly, nodding a couple of small nods.

Merritt started to say something, stopped herself, then said it anyway—under her breath but loud enough to be heard. Her specialty today. "Maybe you're even a bit *too* fit. For Clara."

"What do you mean *too fit*?" Josh asked, turning toward her. "I've literally never heard that."

"Just in terms of accuracy," Merritt said. Both Josh and Audrey were now looking at her unhappily, expecting an explanation. "We have photographs of Clara Broward. We know what she looked like." She paused, stared hard at Audrey. "I mean you look lovely, as you are, just not accurate for Clara Broward and her curves. You could always gain weight."

"Yeeeeeah, I don't know about asking Audrey to do that for this role," Bo said quickly, joining them from wherever he'd been. Everyone in the backyard was now listening to this conversation, even if they were maybe pretending not to. Bo propped himself on one arm of the sectional. "What you're saying is interesting, something to keep in mind, but there are convincing things we can do with the costuming. A killer corset."

"And that's fine," Merritt said. "I'm just saying that you'll be manufacturing your version of a look that Clara wore around for real. She was heavier than Audrey. This is a fact. It's not a shameful fact, it's just a fact. If you're going for accuracy." Merritt knew she had a point, but even still: she was not usually one to make judgments about anyone else's body, even in service of a valid argument. And that's not what she was trying to do now, either, but maybe it sounded like she was. She was ready to let it go, but then Bo said:

"Well, there are different shades of accuracy, right?"

"I don't know what those words mean the way you're using them," Merritt said.

"An audience wants what it wants from its lead actresses is what he means," Harper's agent said, smiling a smile that showed his blue-white teeth.

"Oh, so you're that guy?" Merritt said, barely turning her head to appraise him.

"Come again?" Josh said.

"This doesn't seem a bone worth chewing at the moment, Merritt," Elaine said.

"That's also not what I was saying," Bo said. "What I was getting at is that there are lots of ways for an actor to inhabit a character, to get them to feel *accurate*—your word. *Truthful* is my word."

Now Harper was standing, smiling, commanding attention. "Josh's just acting like an asshole," she said to Merritt. "He's messing with you. He's *not* actually that guy. He reps me, right?"

Merritt definitely had a response to that—she had opened her mouth to make it, even, but Bo got there first. "That's not the movie we're making here, anyway. You know that."

"Do I?" Merritt asked.

"You should," Bo said. "I *want* you to know that. It's why we brought you out here."

"It's not about me," Merritt said, even though that wasn't true. "It's not my story. It's Flo and Clara's story. And all the other Brookhants girls. They were real, which in this case means not made for Hollywood."

"Exactly," Bo said. "Like I said, that's part of why we've got you here—to keep us honest."

"Well, that's a mistake," Merritt said. "I don't often keep myself very honest. It's not necessarily a priority."

Heather, the well-coiffed producer from the night before, moved from the food table toward them, a bottle of sparkling water in her hand. "You should know now that while everyone wants to get this right—and I mean that sincerely, so keep speaking up—there are also *always* concessions we have to make in order to get a movie finished in such a way that we're *all* feeling good about it. It's a collaborative process, lots of people with lots of opinions. Nothing would ever get made otherwise."

"Maybe things shouldn't always get made," Merritt said.

"No, they shouldn't," Bo said, clearly over this discussion. "But since we are trying to make this movie, what if you three adjourn to my office for some prep time? Everything's already set up to record in there and it'll give you a little privacy." He turned to Audrey and asked, "You good with running them a time or two with Harper and bouncing any questions you have off Merritt before we come to watch? Take twenty minutes, half an hour? Whatever you three think you need."

"That sounds good," Audrey said.

"There are copies of the sides on the desk," Heather said.

"And sides are?" Merritt asked.

"Parts of the script you use for auditions," Heather said.

"But is this an audition?" Merritt asked. And Audrey, for one, seemed interested in the answer to that question, though in the business of getting up and gathering things and leading the three of them to Bo's office, no answer came.

THE HAPPENINGS AT BROOKHANTS—

AUDITION SCENE 2

....

INT. L'ORANGERIE—NIGHT

Lightning strobes outside the walls of glass and skylights. Hard rain streams like snake trails. Flo enters, wipes water from her face, and shakes her hair. She is shutting the door against the storm when Clara's presence outside startles her. She comes inside and they stand apart for some moments in the dark, dripping, the rain falling hard on the glass and the lightning spitting. Already there is tension between them.

                          CLARA
Am I intruding?

                           FLO
      (still surprised to see her there)
No.

                          CLARA
Would you say otherwise?

                           FLO
Yes.

                          CLARA
Ha! You wouldn't. Never to me.

FLO

I would say it. I'm glad you've come.

Flo hangs her coat and lights lamps. She knows her way around. There is now a warm glow that better shows the row of large tables down the center and on either side of the space, as well as the citrus trees and other exotic plants.

FLO (CONT'D)

Though I don't know why you have.

CLARA

That's not what I gather from the poems you write. On paper you claim to know so many things about me.

FLO

(hesitant)

The paper doesn't answer back when I write on it.

CLARA

So you prefer me silent? You want only a vessel for collecting your pretty words?

FLO

That's not at all what I want.

The first pings of hail land upon the building. The girls are uncertain of the noise.

Clara approaches the exterior glass wall to peer outside and more hail hits, louder. She backs away.

CLARA

(delighted)

Hailstones—some like a tennis ball!

EXT. OUTSIDE L'ORANGERIE—NIGHT

Various shots of the hail piling up, hitting the windows.

INT. L'ORANGERIE—NIGHT

A large hailstone hits a glass pane right over their heads; they look up to see the glass crack and furiously spiderweb.

FLO

(grabbing Clara's arm)

Come under with me!

She pulls the lamp and Clara beneath the center table, where they crouch and then settle into sitting, facing each other, the lamp between. The hail is loud and they listen to it smash against the building, some of the glass cracking but not yet breaking.

CLARA

Will the glass hold?

FLO

I don't see how.

CLARA

We could leave.

FLO

We should.

They don't. Hail thuds and pings above and around them and Flo is still holding Clara's arm. It is intimate and delicious in its thrill.

CLARA

Was this your plan all along?

FLO

Even at Brookhants, the weather
doesn't listen to me.

*They huddle and brace during additional crashes
and flashes of lightning. A pane cracks, then another, but the glass has yet to shatter.*

CLARA

Mmmmmm. It smells of orange blossom.

(beat/raises eyebrows)

Imagine, in L'Orangerie. And it's so private
here, isn't it? Even if it is a world of glass.

FLO

It isn't always so private. I'm turned
away more than I'd like.

CLARA

The groundskeepers? Oh, Eleanor?

FLO

(coyly shakes her head no)

CLARA

Who? What won't you say?

They both wince at a boom of thunder.

FLO

Miss Trills.

CLARA

(bored)

Oh yes, Miss Trills and her
freesia. Eleanor Faderman says
she's smashed on it.

FLO

Eleanor Faderman has it wrong.

CLARA

Does she?

FLO

(with weight)

Miss Trills and Principal Brookhants.

CLARA

(knows without knowing)

Tell me.

FLO

Miss Trills isn't smashed on
her freesia. Her heart belongs
only to Principal Brookhants.

CLARA

(pretending to misunderstand)

I'm sure they're very familiar
friends. Mrs. Brookhants is still
a young widow—

FLO

(interrupting)

The young widow of an old man.

(beat)

I've heard.

CLARA

A very rich old man. Even so, to then
be left out here with all of us, day in and day
out—ugh, only imagine it.

                         FLO
I don't think she minds.

                        CLARA
I would.

                         FLO
   (with significance)
I saw them here—together. When they didn't know
anyone was watching.

                        CLARA
   (delighted)
You were spying on them? What a sneak you are!

                         FLO
   (embarrassed)
I didn't mean to catch them.

                        CLARA
Catch them?
   (beat)
I don't think you know what
you saw.

                         FLO
   (pointedly quoting Mary MacLane)
Do you think a man is the only creature with
whom one may fall in love?

                        CLARA
You know Mary's book as well as I do.

                         FLO
I think better.

CLARA

(dismissively)

I think not.

FLO

(again quoting MM)

I feel in the anemone lady a
strange attraction of sex. There
is in me a masculine element that,
when I am thinking of her,
arises and overshadows all
the others.

CLARA

(continuing that passage and adding
another)

"Why am I not a man," I say to
the sand and barrenness . . . certain strange,
sweet passions stirred and waked somewhere
deep
within me.

(beat)

(bravely, as a challenge)

If you saw them as you say you
did, tell me what you saw them do—
Miss Trills and Mrs. Brookhants?

FLO

Telling you won't be enough.

It's evident that both girls know what she means by
this, but Flo hesitates, and it seems like maybe
the kiss won't happen.

So it's Clara who takes the lead. She kisses Flo
with certainty—in a rush. But after she begins,
their mouths together, her courage dwindles in

*the reality of the moment and she begins to pull
away.*

*Flo, sensing Clara's uncertainty, pulls her back,
validates this thing they both want. It is not a
perfect kiss, but it is true in its intention.*

*They allow what they've done to become real to them
before they kiss again.*

OUR THREE HEROINES ALONE

TOGETHER AT LAST

....

Harper, first into the room, hopped up onto the edge of Bo's desk—an industrial mass of a desk, wooden slab top with metal legs, solid enough to have been built for the rollicking of a pirate ship or the pound of a butcher's mallet—and settled herself there, touching the cigarette behind her ear. She would have happily smoked it right then, but this was her job, even if sometimes, like now, it didn't really seem like one. Bo didn't like people to smoke in his house. (Bo's husband Ozzi especially did not like it.) And right then, Bo needed the three of them to be in his office, just as they were. He was counting on her to make this work. And she was counting on herself to make this work. She was, after all, now an officially credited producer: she was supposed to have insights and know-how.

Bo's office was large, though made smaller by the camera and lighting equipment set up along its perimeter. Audrey sat at one end of a green velvet chesterfield as Merritt headed to a wall of bookshelves. She inspected the spines. "Decorator," she said to no one in particular, "do be a lamb and stage it to look like I read."

Harper laughed. "Checking to see if you're there?" she asked as Merritt slid out a Peter Straub novel, *Ghost Story*, thumbed its pages in a paper purr, and put it back.

"I'm not," Merritt answered.

"How do you know already?" Harper asked. "That's gotta be three hundred books."

"I know mine," Merritt said. "It's not here."

"That's because he's got it on his nightstand," Audrey said. "Right? Stuffed with Post-its and weird notes in the margins."

"That's it," Harper said, smiling at Audrey for trying with Merritt. "You're Bo's own Mary MacLane. He's obsessed." She said this last part as reinforcement to Audrey's kindness.

But Merritt would only have it her way, which was to now look over her shoulder at them while gesturing to the framed, vintage movie poster she was nearest. "This is the one your mom is in, isn't it?" she asked Audrey. "That's her?"

Audrey didn't even have to look. She seemed to have clocked the poster when they'd walked in the room. "Yeah, that's Caroline giving fright face."

"Campy," Merritt said, her nose nearly against the poster's glass.

"That pool party scene," Harper said. "It might be what made me gay, if I, like, trace it back." She studied Audrey's face. "Sorry, is that fucked up for me to say? About your mom?"

"I mean, it is a thing I've heard before," Audrey said. "Not the make-you-gay part, necessarily, but the formative nature of that scene."

"Can I ask you something else?" Merritt asked her. "Since we're on the subject."

"Sure," Audrey said.

Harper couldn't read that *sure* at all.

"I mean, feel free to tell me it's none of my business," Merritt said as she settled into a club chair, "but is there any particular reason you're not online? *I* couldn't find you, anyway. Not at any of the usual haunts."

"Oh," Audrey said. "No, I'm not on." She paused, seemed to be considering something. Then, "Wait, are you asking if that's *because* of my mom?"

"Is that why?" Merritt asked.

Harper thought Audrey looked like she was now silently sorting through possible answers, not very excited about any of them: like rummaging through a laundry basket for the least-dirty socks.

She settled on: "It's why I got off in the first place, but that was a long time ago now—during all the tabloid stuff over the accident. And my parents' divorce."

"That shit was fucked up," Harper said. "I mean, obviously I don't remember it like you do but, Jesus—that was way too much to try to wade into."

Audrey nodded. On her face you could see a light turn on in some room from her past. It was there without being a show for them, which is probably why Harper noticed it.

"How old were you?" Merritt asked.

"Fourteen," Audrey said. "But it basically kept going until I was, like, seventeen, I guess. Anytime she went to rehab or did a red carpet or did anything at all, for a while. Then it stopped." She tilted her head. "Mostly."

"Fuck that shit," Harper said.

"Yeah, and now I—anytime I've seriously thought about going back on, or someone tells me I should, it seems not worth it. It all just feels like ads or gossip." She stopped, seemed worried she'd offended them, and quickly added, "I mean, I know it's not that way for everybody. Just, I refuse to pay someone to do it for me, but, like, when I've tried to dip my toe in, it feels like I'm eavesdropping on people. I hate that. And I hate how constant it is."

"No, I get that," Harper said again. "I get all of that. I feel like, even with the trolls, I've been able to find my people online and, like, come into my own *because* I've found them. Whereas you were having to hide from people really early."

"So these sides?" Merritt said. Even though she was the one who'd started this discussion, apparently she was now ending it, too. "What are we doing with them?"

Together they skimmed the pages.

"I'm already so obsessed with this place," Audrey eventually said. "L'Orangerie. I remember going with my parents to a premiere party or something at the restaurant L'Orangerie. I mean, like, I was really, really little but—"

"You speak French?" Merritt interrupted.

"Oh," Audrey said, surprised. "Yeah, sort of. I had lessons for years. My dad thought it was important for some reason. I still make a mess of it, though. I learned that the one time I was in France and trying to show off."

"Huh," Merritt said.

"I keep trying to learn languages with apps but not committing," Harper said.

"I don't think I could do it with an app, either," Audrey said.

"Let's hope *L'Orangerie*'s still standing when it's time to film there," Merritt said. Her French was unnecessarily sharp.

Harper remembered. "Oh shit, that's right. Some asshole set it on fire last night," she explained to Audrey.

"That's terrible. What happened?"

Merritt did not respond to these prompts so Harper raised her voice a little and asked, "How does it look this morning, Merritt? Did you hear anything else?"

"Just that it's a mess," Merritt said, flipping through her phone and then handing it to Harper. On its screen was a picture of the burned-out middle of The Orangerie: glass walls enclosing a heap of wet ash.

"Oh fuck," Harper said, the thinnest of shivers along her spine. It was worse than whatever she'd imagined. Though, truth be told, she hadn't worked that hard to imagine anything about it at all.

"They just took those," Merritt said. "There's more. Scroll forward."

Harper did. There were several shots from various angles, but at the center of each, the soppy mess of charred wood and ash was like the black nest of some horrible thing, empty and awful and waiting for its tenant to return. No one had been hurt in the fire, she knew, and the damage seemed relatively contained. And yet these images were somehow gruesome. Maybe it was the contrast of the ripe green Brookhants lawn in the background, there beyond the glint of The Orangerie's glass, while in the foreground this black hole of burn and wet almost looked to be alive. The pictures, one after the next, made her feel a little nauseated.

"Can they fix it in time to use it?" Audrey asked, now beside Harper on the desk, leaning over to see the phone screen. "Or will it delay things?"

"No, they say they can fix it," Merritt said. "Elaine keeps saying it's not as bad as it looks. But I don't know who's telling her that."

"Who did it?" Audrey asked. "Do they know?"

"I believe the consensus at dinner last night was ghosts," Merritt said plainly.

Audrey's face opened up in, was it hope? "Do people really think that?" she asked.

"No," Merritt said, reaching to take her phone back. "Not really. It was a dumb joke."

Audrey tried to smile like she was also in on the joke. "Oh, for sure. Right."

"Do *you* think it was ghosts?" Merritt asked like Merritt would.

"I guess I wasn't totally sure," Audrey said. She was clearly embarrassed, even blushing a little across the bridge of her nose and the tops of her cheeks. "I think I have ghosts on the brain."

"How's that work?" Harper asked.

"I'd like to know," Merritt said.

"No," Audrey said, blushing harder. "Last night—" She shook her head. "It's a lot of nothing. It's dumb."

"What is?" Harper asked.

"Nothing," Audrey said, smiling. "Really. It's nothing."

"We can't possibly move on until you tell us what *ghosts on the brain* means," Merritt said.

"It's really not anything," Audrey said again. "And now I'm embarrassed that I brought it up. There was just a bunch of weirdness at my house when I was reading the script." She spoke like she was attempting to shrug off what she was saying even as she said it. "Like I creeped myself out, which is a total compliment to your book, but I think it primed me to be willing to believe in the supernatural today or something."

"So you do believe in it?" Merritt said. "In *ghosts*?" Her nostrils ever so slightly flared, as if the word itself was malodorous.

Audrey was flustered. "I mean, not like hovering with sheets, but I guess I think I could be convinced, sometimes—at least that places can be haunted. Weird energy. I don't know."

"I believe," Harper said. "And anyway, ghosts don't care if we believe in them or not—I mean, in order for them to be real."

"I think the opposite is true, actually," Merritt said. "Like most things with no scientific evidence to support them, their existence depends entirely on our belief in it. Magical Thinking 101."

Harper turned again to Audrey. "Ignore her. What happened last night?" She wanted to hear this, which meant that she needed Merritt to stop with her needling.

"It's kind of *about* her is the thing," Audrey said, smiling at Merritt.

"Well now we have to know," Harper said.

"Please tell us," Merritt said. "I won't interrupt."

Audrey did. She told them about the videos she'd watched, and the scenes she'd read. She told them about the open patio doors and the night shadows and the scuttle she'd heard behind her in the house. Harper nodded along, made a point to do so—it did all sound sort of creepy—but then Audrey got to the song surprise-playing on their speakers.

"Oh shit," Harper said. "Wait, the chant thing? No way. That thing freaks me the fuck out. I'd have lost it."

"I did lose it!" Audrey said. "I screamed and then I, like, flailed around like an idiot trying to get it turned off. And then when I did, it seemed like the rooms were foggy or something. It just felt wrong, like something was there with me inside the house that shouldn't be there." Now she seemed to be losing confidence again, rushing through the rest. "And then later there were all these dead wasps floating in dishwater in our kitchen sink, but I mean like dozens, and I didn't see them come in anywhere. Some of them weren't even dead yet." She looked between them, embarrassed. "But when I say it now, it also just feels like a bunch of coincidences that I've strung together."

"You don't have to play it down," Harper said. "That sounds scary as fuck to me. Jesus."

"Move over, clowns in the storm drain," Merritt said.

"Don't even joke," Audrey said. "Last night I would've taken a clown in the storm drain."

Harper hopped from the edge of the desk. She felt wired. "Listen, that fucked-up chant thing comes on at night in my house when I didn't tell it to? I'm losing my shit. It would be weird not to lose your shit over that."

"No, I know," Audrey said. "I did lose my shit." She smiled, took a breath. "So hey," she said, looking at Harper. "Because I am mortified that I told you all of that and don't want to talk about it anymore, and also because I'm a little nervous that we're wasting time: I had this possibly dumb thought that we could use the desk to stand in for the Orangerie table—in the scene. I mean get under it together? What do you think?"

Harper liked the idea a lot. Audrey Wells was gonna work for this, she could feel it. "Totally," she said. "When the hail comes. I love that."

Harper thought she maybe then heard Merritt make some small noise to indicate her displeasure over the idea, some signal of disapproval or judgment, but if so, it was a very small noise, with no follow-up, and besides, this was not Merritt's specific area of expertise. In this instance, Harper would not defer. This part, this letting a character swallow her up, this fitting of herself into the self of another, it was the best part of all of this—the part people sometimes said she was such a *natural* at.

Merritt's potential judgment over their acting choices notwithstanding, Audrey's story seemed to have worked as kind of a conversational bridge to get them past their earlier tension: maybe because it both made Audrey seem vulnerable and let Merritt feel superior. Whatever the case, now Audrey was asking Merritt a question about the shorter of the two scenes—the one with cousin Charles—and Merritt was actually being helpful in her answers.

She told Audrey that, in her opinion, Charles was always more taken with Clara than was appropriate for cousins. But it's possible he might not have even realized how deep her infatuation with Mary MacLane's book ran (Charles was no reader) except for the crucial fact that Mary MacLane herself had visited Newport, Rhode Island, during the summer of Clara's obsession. And Clara's family, of course, summered in Newport. For a week or so in August it was a common topic of societal discussion there: Mary MacLane would be coming to attend a wedding and write an article for the *New York World* about what she called "the pomps and vanities" of those with "the Money."

Unsurprisingly, Clara Broward had become every bit the 1902 fangirl at the prospect of actually meeting her idol, and cousin Charles, egged on by the gossip around town, took notice of this. Mary MacLane suddenly seemed worthy of his daft attention. So he stole the book from Clara, read it (let's be real: skimmed it), and declared it, and Mary herself, an affront to decency. And Charles got Clara's mother riled about it too, convincing her that Mary MacLane was the most vile of influences and that Clara must be protected from her dangerous way of thinking.

As a direct result of his meddling, Clara was not allowed to go to Bailey's Beach and meet Mary MacLane when she came to Newport. And for this, Clara would never forgive awful Charles. Or, if eventually she might have in the distant future, there just wasn't any time to—she died not two months later.

Merritt knew her stuff, and even though Harper had heard her say some of these things before, she was glad she was now saying them to Audrey. As she listened, and without really thinking about what she was doing, she headed to the wall of windows behind it, touching the cigarette at her ear as she went. The view was of Bo's side yard and then on into the neighbor's backyard, where a mom and toddler were in the garden. As she looked through the glass at them, Harper could suddenly smell lilacs that shouldn't even be there this time of year—ripe and heavy with blossom, full of perfume.

"Clara locked herself in her bedroom the whole time Mary MacLane was in Newport," Merritt said. "She did try to sneak out once, but a maid saw her and called for her mother, and Charles caught her in the garden. I mean, he basically tackled her is how she wrote about it after. So here she was, Mary MacLane right there in her town—I mean, *right*, right there, down the street and visiting with the sole purpose of observing people like Clara's family, like Clara herself, even—but she couldn't go meet her. It's fucking heartbreaking. In her diary entries from that week Clara talks about having these really vivid dreams—or daydreams, it's unclear—that Mary would come through her open window at night."

"Come through her window and what?" Audrey asked Merritt.

Her voice sounded like it was a greater distance away than Harper knew it to be. "Wait, do you mean like sex dreams?"

"I do mean like sex dreams," Merritt said. "I mean, we're talking more subtle than *50 Shades of Mary MacLane,* but yes."

Audrey was now asking about maybe seeing the diaries, more than just the entries reproduced in Merritt's book. Harper had wondered about this too, was going to turn and get in on the ask, but she felt magnetized to the scene out the window. She couldn't pull away, though she couldn't say why.

The woman out the window was now picking tomatoes and the toddler happily stomped around, her purple jumper cladding a body built for cumbersome, destructive movement; her mother clearly exasperated. Harper smiled, leaned closer to see which of the crops would be harassed next. And then, in a flinch, the scene changed. The child was crying—Harper could just hear the shrieking through the window, and now the little girl was clutching her cheek, screaming. The mother shot up from her crouch and tore off one of her gloves to cup the same place on the child's face that the child was holding. The mother's other arm reached around, picked up the screaming toddler, and carried her off and into their house.

The child had just been stung. That was the explanation Harper's brain filled in for her. A bee, maybe. Could be.

But Harper knew it wasn't.

As she stared, in the space between window and garden, she saw several small things drifting in the air—could be ash, caught on the breeze, or insects. Whatever they were, they caught the glint of the sun as they drifted. And now there were even more, their soft forms collecting on the air as if hovering there. And now still more and more until, as if some wrong lens had been placed in front of the window, the scene changed, and it was snowing. It was impossible, but it was. The world outside the window was white with snow—the trees caked in it, the garden killed by it—its plants stiff and gray, frozen, the tilled ground mounded white, and footprints, from garden to house, showing the path the mother had walked with her screaming child. Though somehow the tomatoes remained bright red, now almost like shiny Christmas tree ornaments—much too red against the snow. And in the moments, for they were only moments, Readers, when Harper tried to make sense of this change, it was as if a white hand crept up the window, and now there was snow and ice clinging to it too, reaching across its panes and forcing Harper to peer through gaps in order to continue to see the garden.

In the span of these queer happenings, the room had grown prickly behind her. Prickly between Merritt and Audrey, that is, some line apparently crossed, judging by Merritt's current tone. Harper could sense that—she could feel it tickle at the back of her neck, palpable tension—even as she continued to blink at the strangeness outside the window.

Somehow, she knew that if she turned away, the winter scene would be gone. If she spoke of it aloud, called to Audrey and Merritt to come see, or even tapped at the window to try to knock free some of the snow, or to feel the ice and cold collected on the other side of the glass, then it would all return to the way it was before, the way it should be: sunny and hot and SoCal in summer. And she didn't want that to happen yet, though she couldn't say why. She felt a bit light-headed. She could smell the lilac again. And then—

"That is not what I'm asking about at all." Audrey's voice, its strained tenor, pierced Harper's snow world, its whites and grays swirling away, leaving glinting sun and green and brown—shiny cars in the driveway, one corner of a blue swimming pool. All as it should be.

Audrey's voice, however, said otherwise: "It's not the fact of the kiss," she said, "it's what you just said about us doing it today."

"What I said is that you seem really uncomfortable with it," Merritt said. "Based on what *you* just said."

Harper's bare arms prickled with gooseflesh. She couldn't tell for sure if it was from the scene out the window or the one developing behind her. "I just watched this kid outside get stung, I think," she said, turning to find both Merritt and Audrey staring at her, neither of them happily.

"Are we supposed to kiss today?" Audrey asked. "I mean, is that what they're looking for with this whole setup?"

Audrey's question was enough of a surprise to Harper that whatever had just happened out the window was shoved below it. At least for now. "What do you mean, with this whole setup?" Harper asked. She came around the desk to join them again. "I'm sorry, catch me up—I must've missed something."

"In the scene," Audrey said. She held her sides up like a placard. "The kiss at the end."

"There's a lot of kissing at the end," Merritt said. "They spend the entire scene building to that action." She made a line with her mouth, almost the pure emoji form of that expression. Then she broke that line to say, "Clara *wants* to kiss Flo. She's into it. I'm thinking the actor playing her should probably not be weirded out by the idea of women kissing."

"I don't even know where you're getting this," Audrey said to Merritt. "That's *not* what I said."

"Huh. Clearly I got it from *something* you said."

Audrey was back on one end of the chesterfield, her body in a knot. She shook her head to herself, like a bobble doll, and then turned to face Merritt full-on. "Yeah, so I'm bi," she said. "Not that it's really your business, but no, the idea of kissing a woman does not make me uncomfortable. Not as a person, not as an actress. I don't—"

"Actor," Merritt said flatly.

"What?" Audrey said. If a word can sound like an eye roll, that one did.

"Why does it have to be *actress*? Is it still *poetess*? Do you go to a *doctress*? Actor. One word for all humans who do the thing."

"Last time I checked, they still give awards for best actress," Audrey said.

Merritt sniffed. "Well if they give awards for it, I mean: holy shit."

"OK," Harper said, trying on what she hoped was like a reasonable but chill counselor voice. "Come on—Audrey's not in charge of naming things. I mean, plus *heroines*, right? Like the whole namesake of our purpose." By now she'd caught the thread of their disagreement and was considering how to say the next part without Merritt storming from the room.

"Yes, in 1902," Merritt said.

"Just so you know, Merritt," Harper said, "this is like standard practice. We always talk about anything physical, you talk it through with your scene partner and decide how to do it or if you even should. I mean, especially for an audition. It's never a given. Or it shouldn't be."

Merritt blinked at her. "Yes, and all of that makes sense," she said. But she said it as if nothing Harper had just said had anything to do with whatever was pissing her off in the first place and now she was additionally annoyed to have been educated about their process. "It just seemed to me like there was some real subtext in what Audrey said earlier. But forget it. I must be mistaken."

"I really don't know how this got so confused," Audrey said. She looked at Harper to make her case. "I wasn't even saying that I don't think we should do the kiss—I just wanted to talk about it, see where we're at."

"Totally," Harper said. "We still can do that, right?"

"Right, yeah," Audrey said. She paused, then added, "And I would ask that no matter the gender of the person I was doing this scene with." She looked at Merritt. "I really am sorry if you thought I was saying something else. I wasn't."

Merritt shrugged, noncommittal. "I misunderstood. Mea culpa. I just wanted this movie about queer women to actually have some involved."

"Well if they cast me, I'll count for one of them," Audrey said.

Merritt offered no reaction to this.

But Harper said: "Fuck yes you will."

Audrey Wells was gonna work for this. She could feel it.

THE (REAL) CHEMISTRY READ

········

Audrey tried to tell herself that she was now feeling very determined to do the kiss and to do it well. To do the whole thing well; blow them out of the water with her talent at being Clara Broward. Because fuck Merritt Emmons and her nonexistent subtext. Fuck her, sitting there in Bo Dhillon's club chair, watching them.

While Merritt watched, Audrey and Harper sorted their blocking. They practiced getting under the desk and working through where their bodies would settle next to each other, what made most sense in this scene for their characters and the shifting provocation between them. Then they choreographed the kiss, how it would start and end. They rehearsed that choreography twice. It felt fine to Audrey, not mortifying, definitely technical and definitely being clocked by judging Merritt, but fine. It was fine. Harper's lips were dry, on the first go, but she noticed that herself and applied minty balm and now they were shiny with it. The kiss could work, Audrey thought, they could manage it like the professionals they were.

Right now, what they were lacking in all this choreography was the context of the scene that would deliver that kiss, land it, so that it made sense and wasn't just a thing they were practicing. They needed to run that scene in full.

So they did.

The first time through, Audrey played Clara as more aggressive and in command than she did in the next one, but in neither did they kiss.

They were tight, under that desk, their arms near to being in each other's lap and their faces close, but the scene called for Clara to kiss Flo when she sensed that Flo wouldn't kiss her. And Audrey did not do it. Both times Harper said her final line, "Telling you won't be enough," and then she turned her head, their mouths hovering, Audrey practically tasting cigarette, but after a moment or two of lingering, she ducked out from under the table and said, "Should we run it again?"

Both times she did that.

But then they ran it a third time. And this time Audrey felt better. She didn't rush the lines she'd rushed the two times previous. She felt like she'd found about the right place to settle Clara, somewhere between tentative and flirtatious, knowing and unsure. And she felt, in the way Harper responded, that she too thought they were improving. And so that time Audrey thought, *I will kiss her.* And she felt totally good with that decision, with trying the kiss out once and then, depending on how it went, doing it for Bo and the others, too. She felt like making that decision, to herself, even brought a kind of correct momentum to the scene, a kind of accurate tension for what was to come, something Clara herself would have been feeling as she prepared to do this thing for the first time.

But then, about six lines before the end of the scene, before she was going to do it, *she was,* it was like sound effects delivered a *knock-knock-knock* on the office door. Harper and Audrey stopped, and looked, and Merritt said, "Yes?" And the door opened and Bo was standing there grinning at Audrey and Harper under his desk and saying, "Hey—nice blocking. You two 'bout ready to kill it?"

"I think so," Harper said to him, and then to Audrey she said, "Yeah? That was feeling really ready to me."

And so Audrey said sure. Sure. Because what was she gonna say? *No—stay under here and let's kiss first to make sure I can do it in a minute.* I guess she could have said that, Readers. She could have said exactly that. But she didn't, and now Harper was ducking her way back out from under the desk and offering Audrey a hand to help her up, and Bo was telling them that he would gather the masses. And that's what he did. And in the very brief amount of time it took for that to happen—since they'd all been waiting around for this, they came quickly—Harper asked, "So, the kiss. Yes? Or no? Or? Where are you with it?"

"Yes," Audrey said, saying it confidently to try to help herself to feel confidently about it.

"You're sure?"

"Yes," Audrey said again.

"Cool, I think so, too," Harper said, flashing her Harper Harper gap-toothed smile. There was no more time to linger on it anyway, because people were already entering the room. Soon Bo's office was fairly stuffed: Merritt had moved to Audrey's old seat on the couch and now Elaine Brookhants was there next to her. And two of the suits in the club chairs. Bo standing in one corner with Heather and somebody else. Josh the agent and two others from Harper's entourage against the bookshelves. And other people too, scattered among them, plus Gray and Noel in the doorway, barely even in the mix.

It was bizarre to have it be so many people for this.

It was also time.

They asked her to do the short scene first, the cousin Charles scene (Heather read for him). Audrey did it well. Maybe she wasn't quite settled at the start, but then she really nailed a particular zinger and earned a few honest laughs from her cramped audience. And she finished strong, channeling the indignation and displeasure Clara always felt when forced to contend with Charles.

When she was done, everyone clapped politely, but not like they were clapping only to be polite. And Gray nodded and gave her a subtle thumbs-up. Noel saw him do this and shook his head no and quickly gave her, instead, two thumbs up while also making a, like, rock 'n' roll *fuck yeah* face at her.

Merritt was not smiling, of course, but she didn't look disgusted, either. Disinterested, maybe, but not overtly disappointed or horrified.

And then people were shifting in the room so that Harper could get by, could get up to the desk and next to Audrey. "Crushed it," she said quietly as she approached. Then she winked. It was a move that suited her.

It was only then, as Harper positioned herself for the start, that Audrey noticed she didn't have her sides in hand. She'd had them minutes before, as they'd been rehearsing, and it had seemed like she was using them. But now her hands were empty, so she must have memorized her lines. This revelation threw Audrey a little.

And then, while she was processing Harper's off-scriptness and telling herself it didn't matter (*Who cares, just do what you did before, do it like that*) there was Heather, reading from a text lighting up the screen of her phone and saying, "Oh, wait—wait a sec. Don't start yet—your mom's here."

At first, Audrey didn't think she could possibly be talking to her. Other people in the room seemed to understand right away that she was, but Audrey did not. She only half heard her and was like, *Whose mom?* and then continued to concentrate on Harper and what she'd be able to do in this scene that Audrey herself plainly couldn't yet, because she still had to read almost all of her lines. But then somewhere in those same seconds, she noticed that most of the people in the room had stopped their chatter and their phone-poking to look at her. And she had to think again about what Heather had just said, and then ask, "Wait, *my* mom? Caroline?"

"Yeah, she just texted," Heather said. "She's walking up right now so we'll give her a minute."

"*My* mom?"

"In the flesh." Heather smiled.

Audrey still hadn't even quite latched on to this when there was Caroline, her just-manicured hand on Noel's shoulder as she slid around him and into the room, people turning to greet her.

She looked good. She usually did these days, Readers—but these days people didn't see her everywhere like they used to, either, so they were more surprised by it. She had this kind of glamorous-natural thing going, where, for instance, she got a manicure, but just to buff her nails and keep them short and shaped, a hint of shine, noticeable only if you looked close. She wore a sleeveless navy jump-suit with a thin belted sash of the same material around her narrow waist. It fit her very well. But Audrey also thought she could feel other people in the room staring at Caroline's scars: the remnants of the bite wounds that the many reconstructive surgeons couldn't make disappear, the thin seams running up from the top of her lip to her nose, the dent, it was kind of a dent, in her right cheek. Or maybe not the scars themselves, but what they represented—the big ugly thing. Probably they weren't doing this. She was beautiful and once famous and possibly that's what they were staring at. But Audrey didn't think that was all of it.

Caroline managed to look around the people now walking over to greet her to find Audrey staring back at her and smile and shrug an *I'm sorry,* mouthing *I didn't know*—right as Gray half shouted, by way of explanation: "Sorry, hon, it was me—I texted her earlier."

Audrey stared at him, wholly confused. And angry.

"I texted her before, I mean," he said. "Because we're running a little late and I'm gonna have to go soon and I didn't want you not to have anyone here after I left, to drive you, but then Noel stayed anyway, so it didn't matter." He turned to Caroline. "Plus, I texted you back to say don't come."

"I didn't get it until I pulled in," Caroline said. "Audrey makes me use the Do Not Disturb app when I drive."

As explanations go, this one did not make sense.

"But no matter," Bo said, now standing next to Caroline, his arm around her. "Right? More the merrier. You didn't even miss the show. She's still got one to do."

Caroline nodded and smiled again at Audrey, and Audrey smiled back because what else, Readers? What else? The room shuffled around to fit Caroline. She ended up, no kidding, standing directly in front of her own *House Mother* poster. Of course she did.

I don't know, gentle Readers. Audrey was thrown, yes, but she might still have managed something resembling decent if she hadn't happened to look at Merritt right then. She'd lost track of her in the unexpectedness of Caroline's arrival, hadn't seen her specific reaction to it, but if Audrey had to guess, she'd say that it was probably pretty similar to the reaction Merritt was having now. Which was a smirk. Like, an all-knowing, all-mocking smirk of disapproval and pity and maybe even contempt. Wouldn't put it past her.

And then, right then, they started the scene. And she was completely awful in it. I mean, think of all the bad acting you've ever witnessed and imagine Audrey Wells giving you some of all of it in this performance.

She flubbed lines. Badly enough that she had to repeat them. In fact, they restarted the scene not once but twice. Bo called for it, tried to give her time to re-collect. It didn't help. She didn't play off anything Harper was doing. She felt no emotion, no connection to the material, so she tried to compensate by going big, overacting. And then, when she realized that's what she was doing and inwardly cringed about how awful it was, she tried to pull back, to go small, but what she gave was flat and empty instead.

She was aware of the people watching her, their eyes on her— their breathing and movements in the room. She was aware of her mom, and her mom's poster, over to the left. She wasn't *in* the scene at all, she wasn't Clara.

She was Audrey Wells, an actor in front of a room of judging people while she poorly read lines from a script. There was nothing there that wasn't decidedly amateur at best and just plain bad at worst.

And the flop sweat—her nervous system pumping out perspiration on her forehead, her neck—came and it came in a rush. The beads and shine were noticeable to everyone watching, including Harper Harper. Especially to Harper Harper, crushed under that desk with her.

And then, because Audrey knew all of this as it was happening, as she was doing such a shit job, she thought (and you're probably already guessing at this, because it's exactly the kind of terrible decision a person makes when they're trying to save something that can't be saved, when they're desperate): I can make this better with the kiss. If I do the kiss well, if I get it right, that's the thing they'll remember most. It's the closer.

Audrey had been told before that she kissed well. I mean, the people telling her that had their various reasons for doing so, yes. But still, she had been told it before. More than once, in fact, and by different people. So she thought, Do *that*, now. Kiss her well, with all of Clara Broward's kissing intention, and she'll respond as Flo would because she's Harper Fucking Harper and she can act and at least you'll have that. At least you can say, I blew the read but I nailed the kiss.

But she didn't.

I mean, not at all.

Because the thing is, the scene had gone so poorly that Harper couldn't possibly have imagined that Audrey would even want to do the kiss. There had been zero chemistry, zero spark or *energy* (thanks, Bo) between them during that read. There had been nothing at all, and now here Audrey was with her lips stuffed so closely to Harper's that it was impossible to misread her intentions. I mean, they'd run it twice and Audrey had never positioned herself quite like this. And yet, Harper probably still believed there was just no way. Not with things going so poorly.

But oh, there was a way, Readers: Audrey kissed her. She leaned in and crash-landed her mouth onto Harper's, who was not expecting this move. How could she have been? It takes skill to deliver to an audience a kiss that's meant to read as passionate but also new; committed, but also questioning. Good acting was the believable embodiment of a character—of a life. This was face-mashing lip wreckage.

What Audrey later remembered most specifically about that kiss was *knowing,* even as she pushed her head toward Harper's, even before the crash landing, that it wasn't going to work. And then it didn't work. And then she didn't want to pull away because, fuuuuuuck, then what? Then there was a whole room of disappointed and embarrassed people who'd just watched this disaster go down was what. And the only thing left to do was face them. Bo and sneering Merritt and Noel and Gray and *her mom.* And so even though it was terrible—oh, it was so bad—Audrey kept kissing her.

And because she was a good actor, Harper tried to sell it. For Audrey's sake.

But, Readers, trying to sell this kiss was like trying to sell a sack of bloody pig lips outside your local vegan grocer.

It wasn't working. It didn't work. So then, with no grace, or skill, or sense of delivery, Audrey stopped kissing Harper and pulled her head away.

To their enormous credit, the people in the room did not polite clap. If they had, Audrey might have started crying. She was
already on the brink of it. But everyone assembled understood her
shame in those moments. Some of them offered kind smiles. Some
of them looked away, pretended to take notes or read things on their
phones. Somehow she managed to avoid looking at Merritt, but
Noel's attempt to not look mortified on her behalf, to look caring if
not cheerful, wasn't at all successful.

"So that's it, right?" Heather eventually said to Bo. "We've got
what we need?"

"Got what we need," Bo said. He looked at Audrey. She looked
away first.

And then Heather, now talking like synthetic sunshine, said, "OK!
Great. Lots more food in the back, everybody." She had a smile on
her face and her hand out as she approached Audrey. "Thanks so
much for trying this out with us last minute."

Audrey scurried out from under the table and found words to say
as they shook hands. "Of course," she said. "Thank you so much for
asking me to."

Heather nodded her shimmery bob once in this very final *yep,
really didn't work, don't ever, ever call us* kind of way. So before she
could escape the room along with the other people hurrying out,
Audrey asked her, quietly, "Is the other part? I mean—is Eleanor—
have you cast somebody else in that role?"

"Yesterday," Heather said. "Esme Oates. Do you know her? She's
great."

"I don't know her," Audrey lied. "But thank you."

After that it was just a not-that-prolonged shuffle through uncomfortable goodbyes to get out of there. People were busy navigat-
ing the awkwardness of professionally stepping around so stunning
a failure, while also not going overboard with phony cheer. It was,
in a word, Readers: weird.

Harper gave Audrey a one-armed hug and said something like
It was so great to finally meet you. Merritt managed to shake hands,
a better greeting than she'd given Audrey out front, and even said,

quietly, "Sorry again about earlier. I genuinely didn't mean to doubt your queer cred." She seemed earnest enough about this, but even still: fuck Merritt Emmons, Readers.

Soon enough it was only her people—Gray and Caroline and Noel—and Bo and his assistant left in the room. And Bo and his assistant were deep in quiet conversation. So Audrey had to wait.

She knew she wasn't good enough for this part. She had known it right away, the day before at the table with Gray and Noel, there in the green-seed rain. But it still sucks, a lot, to have that kind of knowledge—your sense of your own inadequacy—confirmed for you. And in this case confirmed for you in front of an audience.

Shame burned in Audrey's chest and behind her eyes. Really all she wanted to do now was get out the door to the privacy of Noel's car, where she could cry. But Bo and his fucking assistant were blocking her exit path. So she waited, trading glances with her people, trying not to cry, not to cry, not to cry. At some point she locked onto that stupid *House Mother* poster and had a stare-off with the fake-bloodied Caroline, the one who had been about her age. *Why did any of this ever seem like a good idea?* she wanted to ask that version of her mom. *And has it ever really been worth it?*

Eventually, not soon enough, Bo finished his conversation and his assistant left, shutting the door behind her.

He didn't make Audrey wait. "Well, *that* was very bad," he said, leaning up against the edge of his desk where Harper had been earlier. "*Quelle horreur!*" He gestured for everyone left in the room to sit as well. "I mean you went for it, didn't you? Can't say otherwise."

"I know," Audrey said. She didn't want to sit. She wanted to make with the pleasantries and get the hell out of there. "I don't even—"

"You really let Merritt get under your skin, huh?" he said. Was he smiling? He *was* smiling. "Or was it your mom showing up?"

She felt off-balance. Wind-knocked. "No, it wasn't—"

He cut her off again. "Either way, it's what we want. And what we'll want more of." He again gestured for them to sit.

Audrey didn't think she'd heard him right.

But then Gray said, "I think so, too," as he settled himself, comfortably, in the seat Merritt had been in earlier. Now he was kicking out his legs, even flopping one foot over the other, as if he was in a deck chair on a cruise. "I think it might actually be *better* that it was such a horror show. It'll unquestionably further antagonize the whole thing with Merritt. Stir the pot."

"I thought you had to leave," Audrey said to him. This addressed just one of the many things confusing her at the moment, but it seemed the easiest one to put into words.

"No, I'm good, kiddo," Gray said. "Part of the ruse: the mother intrudes. Come on, sit down."

Audrey looked at her mom, at Noel. They weren't smiling wide, like they'd pulled off the *surprise!* part of a surprise party, but they weren't confused like she was: they clearly knew whatever it was that Bo and Gray knew. She felt drugged or maybe asleep. Mostly she felt like she might scream at them. Like she'd start to scream and not be able to stop, to scream and scream and scream.

"Let's talk," Bo said.

FIN DE SIÈCLE MEET CUTE

....

My dear, anticipating Readers, before I tell you what Bo and Audrey talked about that day in his office (and I *will* tell you, of course I will) we have a date to get to. Two dates, in fact.

You already know, don't you, that we're set to venture out into the smoky wilds of Los Angeles with Harper and Merritt, but first I'd like to turn your attention to a different girl-on-girl scene from more than one hundred years before: how Miss Alexandra Trills and Principal Libbie Brookhants first came to be Alex and Libbie, *our* Alex and Libbie.

It seems to me—given the horrors you've already experienced with them, and also the dreadfulness still to come in these pages— that we owe them at least that. After all, their particular subplots of this unwieldy story didn't make it into Bo's screenplay. (Though I won't apportion all the blame for that to Bo Dhillon. Alex and Libbie scarcely made it into Merritt's book on the curse, either. Or at least Merritt's first book on the curse.)

Of course, young Mary MacLane herself might have briefly appreciated that this was to become the Hollywood way of things: nubile bad girls meeting in the woods beat out middle-aged domesticated sapphics every (screen) time.

And so, before this bad tale subjects them to more trouble, please allow me to linger, for a few moments, on a better time.

They'd first met while students at Wellesley College.

Principal Brookhants was then only Libbie Packard—a sophomore, class of 1893—and Miss Trills a junior and captain of her crew team, known widely among her peers as Alex the Flirt. Wouldn't Eleanor Faderman have been surprised, Readers, to think of *dull* Miss Trills as the campus flirt?

Libbie Packard had certainly seen (and heard of) Alex(andra) Trills at various times during the school year previous. However, back then she'd been only a fresh frosh, and even the idea of approaching Alex had seemed a mountain too tall to scale. Now that Libbie had one year of Wellesley under her bicycle bloomers, she decided to take a closer look.

Her first chance for doing so came at the Class Colors ceremony near the start of the fall semester. Alex had been chosen to wave the junior class flag on the shores of Lake Waban, which she did with a kind of unforced and elegant athleticism, while alternately smiling and ducking her head at the attention. Like several of her classmates, she wore a straw hat and necktie with her bright white blouse and a long, pleated skirt that caught the breeze off the water like the stiff petals of a tulip might. She was so slim it was as if her clothing covered only angles and not actual flesh. Still, she was strong with that flag, capable and aware of the attention she drew.

Half of the Wellesley campus was then smashed on Alex the Flirt, and she on them, so who could keep track of one smitten sophomore pinching her cheeks for color and hoping to be noticed in a sea of such girls, some of whom seemed—to Libbie, anyway—to require no cheek pinching at all to appear flushed and vivacious?

And so it was, that very day, that Libbie Packard made a plan to get Alexandra Trills to notice her. And you should know, Readers, that Libbie Packard's plans to be noticed tended to be successful.

Her whole life (thus far) she'd felt she'd had to find ways to make herself seen. This was because she was the youngest child in a Chicagoan family tree with success at every branch: her father an influential architect; her mother a society maven and (occasional) campaigner for social reform. Not to mention her brothers, one of them only a few years away from being elected to the US Senate. (And there were countless uncles and aunts, cousins and close family friends, all with somehow even shinier shines on their Great

American Dreams.) So our Libbie Packard had grown up learning how best to get herself a little attention when she needed it, sea of red-cheeked competitors or not.

She was meticulous in considering her options for approaching Alex: something subtle and clever, or brash and bighearted? Or could she achieve clever and bighearted both—an infinitely trickier pairing?

While she bided her time, Libbie joined a campus club, the Waggish Rogues. They performed skits at assemblies but were better known for their gotcha surprises—think something like early flash mobs—the fifteen or so of them suddenly descending on the library in masks and gowns to stage a scene from *A Midsummer Night's Dream*. Or, while their more sensible classmates slept on the eve of Halloween, filling the dormitory hallways with cornstalks and pumpkins to greet them come morning.

All that fall and winter, Libbie kept quiet tabs on Alexandra, who was making her rather loud rounds as Alex the Flirt. She was paired briefly that school year with Jane, and then, for months, with Hazel Two.* Libbie completed an informal polling of several juniors and seniors, Alex's classmates, to glean the details of the smashes that had come before. And there were so many of them—Evie and Ida, Kitty and Violet—canoodling on the tennis courts, sharing a bag of lemon drops in the library. But so focused was she, so certain of coming success, that these stories inspired not jealousy in young Libbie Packard, but fortitude.

As you've no doubt surmised, this quest was less about the particulars of the attraction Libbie had to Alex—whom she did not even know, not really—than it was about the attraction she had to achieving Alex+Libbie status. Soon it would be she who would accept a nectar drop still warm from Alex's hand, and as it spread

---

* There were three Hazels enrolled at Wellesley at that time, and though the calculations used to determine their ranking was rather unclear, everyone seemed to agree on said ranking—including the three Hazels themselves.

its sweetness on her tongue, the two would sit against each other in some conspicuous place on the College Green, tasting sugared peach and being envied by all who were not them.

It wasn't until May Day—her second year at Wellesley nearly finished—that Libbie Packard felt ready to be seen by Alex Trills. To make certain that she'd be seen by her, that is.

Libbie made her move at that evening's students-only Follies, an event hosted by the Waggish Rogues. She was adequate in the ensemble skits, but it was really only her solo performance that she cared about, especially once she'd confirmed that Alex was in the audience, pleasantly near to the front and sans Hazel Two.

Libbie was dressed as Nike, the Greek goddess of victory, complete with paper wings strapped uncomfortably to her back and a golden laurel wreath (really just painted branches from campus shrubs) atop her head.

To open the number, two of her fellow Rogues pushed her onstage in a squeaky wheelbarrow. This action, combined with her costume, drew the first giggles. Then the Rogues positioned themselves stage left, where an oversize title card was waiting. They now held it between them to set the scene for the audience:

NIKE, GODDESS OF VICTORY,
RECOUNTS HER ROLE
IN THE VICTORIES OF THE HEART
OF OUR OWN ALEX THE FLIRT.

This drew more giggles and some whoops, too. Libbie watched as Alex straightened in her seat and pretended to be embarrassed by the attention: classic Alex the Flirt head-ducking.

Standing tall in the wheelbarrow, downstage center, Libbie Packard as Nike began her song in just about the sweetest sotto soprano you've ever heard. Part of the gag was that, despite ostensibly being the brash goddess of victory, our Nike was a little stage shy. However, as she sang on, listing Alex's lengthy history of campus crushes—and her own role in bringing them about—she gained confidence:

> . . . *Sitting pretty with Kitty, all due to my charm.*
> *Then Mary's heart went pitter-patter when you had her on your arm.*
> *Oh Alex, sweet Alex, that you're a flirt we know is true—*
> *but you must now give credit to whom the credit's due.*
> *I've been there behind the sunsets*
> *you brought your girls to see.*
> *I've been the cause of the red-rose bloom*
> *that sealed your victory.*
> *In all these earthly crushes,*
> *it's been me at the strings.*
> *Why there have been so many conquests—*
> *you've quite worn out my wings!*

Libbie had a fairly limited range as a performer, but she'd created this character to maximize her skill set—soft and sweet building to winkingly brash—and she delivered with relish. The audience was hers, but it was Alex's appreciation she was after, and with the glare of the footlights and rows of grinning faces before her, it was difficult for Libbie to discern what Alex thought of her tribute.

The song reached its crucial final turn, where Nike makes her challenge:

> *After Evie, after Hazel*
> *and after Violet, too.*

At this point, a fellow Rogue delivered a scripted interruption by running onstage to correct Nike with the pun "I think you mean Hazel Two." She held up a card to the audience that read: ~~Violet, too~~ **Hazel Two.**

Libbie continued with her song, now amended:

After Evie, after Violet,
and after Hazel Two.
I'm bored with bringing triumph—
I've done what I will for you.
Now it's your turn, Alexandra—
to prove your abilities.
Why not try your hand at Nike?
Can you weaken goddess knees?
No, I won't be there to aid you—
I won't assure your victory.
But if you can claim my lofty heart,
you'll have the best of me.
Come get me, Alexandra—
our dear Alex the Flirt.
Come test your mettle with a god—
if you're to know your worth.
You can find me in the Pantheon.
That's where I live, it's true.
But you'll need more than disrepute—
to make me fall for you.

Unquestionably, many a heart went pitter-patter, and several cheeks may have even been pinched for Libbie Packard that night. A few students threw flowers onstage and there was one particularly stellar whistle that came from the back of the theater and cut across the applause in its intensity.

But our Nike was after only a single victory, not dozens of them.

She claimed it out on the lawn, at the cast party, which was as much the reason for the popularity of the Follies as were any of its skits. It had rained earlier but now it was clear. The night was drunk on the liquor of late spring, on wet grass and pale moon, on air still warm even after the sunset, air now scented by the rain-smacked lilac bushes planted at the back of the theater, their branches so heavy with blooms and moisture that several were bent against the ground.

The audience was hers, but it was Alex's appreciation she was after.

Libbie was being served her second glass of punch, something made with too little wine and too much sugar, but she was glad to have it still. Her mouth was rimmed in grape stain, her shrub wreath slipping down her forehead.

"I hadn't heard they'd moved the Pantheon to Wellesley," Alex the Flirt said, approaching her from behind. "Fine work by the trustees."

Hackneyed or not, Readers, Libbie's heart lit like a match, and she turned, smiling. It was dark out there on the lawn, difficult to see well, so she couldn't tell if Alex was smiling, too.

"You know you might have sent me a note," Alex said. "Or come to find me. I would have met you, if you'd asked me to."

"There wouldn't have been any applause for me with just a note." Libbie's crown was now tilted over one eye.

"How can you be sure?" Alex asked, stepping closer. Now there was almost no distance between them at all. She held out her hand and softly, steadily righted the wreath, gold paint coming off onto her fingers as she did, though she wouldn't notice that until the next morning. "*I* might have clapped for you, alone with my private note."

"It's not too late for that," Libbie said. She heard her blood in her ears. It had started a moment before, when Alex had touched her temple, fixing the crown, Alex's soft fingers against the even softer skin at her hairline in the warm, scented night—the kind of distinct memory that would plant itself in her to be recalled for much longer than she could have guessed right then.

"How do you know me?" Alex asked, her tone more serious. "I mean, do we know each other?"

"I'm trying to know you," Libbie said. "If you'd let me."

"After all this effort, seems I have to," Alex said. She *was* smiling. "You did borrow a wheelbarrow. Now it's Miss *Nike* Packard of Chicago, do I have that right?"

"I'll let you call me Libbie," she said, victorious.

HARPER AND MERRITT
GO ON AN IMPOSSIBLE
LOS ANGELES DATE

··················

Anybody have money on *motorcycle*? As in, twenty bucks says Harper Harper was driving a motorcycle that day, and that it would serve as the pumpkin coach for her and Merritt's Los Angeles dream date?

Because if so, Readers: it's time to collect.

She had driven some rare model of Moto Guzzi to Bo's. It's the kind of bike that people who know about such things, people who care, care about. I am not one of those people, but that bike was a beaut: cream and green, chrome and oil-rubbed leather.

She'd also brought with her a glittery blue helmet for Merritt and a more elaborate black one for herself. She had them propped against the bike's tires there in Bo's stuffed driveway. And draped over the seat was a black leather jacket very much like the one Harper wore herself.

"Is this gonna be OK for you?" Harper asked as she bent to retrieve the helmets and hand Merritt hers. "It's cool if not. I mean it. I'll get us a car."

"Oh wow," Merritt said. "Fuck. OK." The closest she'd ever been to being on a motorcycle was briefly riding a Vespa as part of a tour group in a hill town in Italy and let's face it: that wasn't very close at all. "I should have expected this. Since it's such a known thing about you."

"Doesn't mean it's your thing," Harper said.

"Oh, it's not," Merritt said. "But today I did sign up for the full Harper Harper experience. Is there even room for us both?"

"There's room," Harper said, patting the seat in the back. "This is where you go. But also, we really don't have to do this. I mean it. I want you to be comfortable."

"You just need to tell me every single thing I need to know to not get in your way and to keep you alive, by which I mean to keep you keeping me alive. Everything—spare me nothing. Where do my hands go, where do my feet go, how do I sit, how do—"

Harper laughed and said, "I wouldn't let you get on otherwise. You're sure?"

"Stop asking," Merritt said. "Teach me."

So Harper did.

Once Merritt was seated behind her, but before she had started the engine, Harper leaned back and asked, "Piercing first? Piercing last?"

"It's your show," Merritt said. "This is supposed to be your California dream come to life for me."

"So no pressure, then," Harper said.

"All the pressure," Merritt said. "Every ounce of it." It felt to her like they were escaping, leaving the bungalow of botched auditions in their dust.

And yet somehow, Readers, somehow, taking off with her arms at Harper's waist, feeling the bike's whir, its metal churn—feeling it, not just hearing it—latched to their bodies while the wheels roiled beneath them and heat bloomed from the engine, somehow all of that was only the cheese and crackers before dinner, the not-so-memorable opening band before the headliner.

The least of it.

First Harper took Merritt to Metal Mug, a piercing place in West Hollywood. It was bright and modern, its big windows streaming gobs of California sun into the lobby and two fiddle-leaf fig trees in cement pots making the most of that light, their leaves huge and too green to be believed. So while they waited—for no time at all— Merritt dug her sharp thumbnail into a couple of them to be sure.

They were not only real, they were now wounded by her: black crescents weeping plant matter.

The place was so smartly designed and sterile that the only vestiges of punk-days-past came from the soundtrack and the staff. When they'd entered The Clash was playing but now, as Sloane, their piercing professional, readied her station, it hopped to Billy Bragg singing "A New England." Sloane's own face was an archipelago of metal adornments. You could tell she was pleased Harper had requested her, but she certainly wasn't gonna go on about it.

"I don't get to do eyebrows very much anymore," she said, having selected two so-thin gold hoops from her jewelry case.

"She's gonna bring them back," Harper said. "Single-handedly."

"As close together as you can get them," Merritt said. She was now seated in a big chair, almost like a dentist's chair.

"You'll wear them well," Sloane said. It felt like the whole thing had just been notarized by that statement: Sloane's official seal of piercing approval.

"You will," Harper said, her face closer to Merritt's ear than it needed to be for her to say it and for Merritt to hear it. Her breath, the soft impact from those words, linked up with the nerves in Merritt's spine and traveled her length.

Billy Bragg sang, "I saw two shooting stars last night / I wished on them but they were only satellites."

Soon Harper and Sloane joined him, singing the part about looking for another girl.

And then, because the song was so soon over, Sloane called to someone in some unseen part of the shop, "Ayyy! Mimi! Play that one again." And hidden Mimi did. And the needle went in above Merritt's eye with a pressury pinch, not really pain, just sharp pressure releasing a stream of tears but only a couple quick drops of blood, which Sloane didn't let linger.

She was efficient, in her purple-gloved hands. She was fast. Merritt had barely comprehended the addition of those tiny hoops to her eyebrow, to her face, in her reflection there on the hand mirror they'd given her, when Sloane said, "A few for our Insta," and she was posing with Harper, their warm cheeks pressed together.

And oh my gawd: Merritt was smiling. Her eyebrow throbbed like she'd been stung there, was *being* stung there. But she was smiling.

Then Harper took Merritt's hand, as she had the night previous at Spago—hand in hand with her leading and Merritt following with almost all the willingness to do so that she then possessed—and they were leaving, they were out of there, and as they reached the front of the shop again, up near those fiddle-leaf trees, Merritt said, "I need to pay." But that wasn't true, it turned out. Harper had already, or they'd pierced her for free, for the publicity: Harper Harper, valued and frequent patron of Metal Mug. Or perhaps it was a little of both, but whatever it was, there was no money owed by Merritt and no one to pay it to, Sloane and Mimi probably busy hashtagging those pics they'd just taken.

And then they were again outside in the full of that California sun, more of those too-postcard-to-be-true palm trees above them. But in front of them, immediately in front of them, were paparazzi and fans. Some of them were #HARPEOPLE, but others had gathered because they saw other people gathering, something to see. There was a buzzing swarm of humans from Metal Mug's doorway all the way to the Moto Guzzi and a few squeals, a few gasps—yes, gasps—as they now walked through the swarm. As Harper Harper came into its midst.

Later Merritt learned that Harper had posted their location, likely right as Sloane was swabbing Merritt's eyebrow with iodine. This meant good attention for the shop, sure, but Harper also knew, had to, what it would do. The chain reaction it would cause. And how fast. Minutes. It had only been minutes since:

Harper Harper @HarperHarper
Getting new hardware for brilliant/gorgeous @SoldOnMerritt @MetalMug so she can be gorgeous X 2.

And people had come to find them, and more would come, still. "So who's she, anyway?" one of the paparazzi guys asked, gesturing his ostentatiously oversize camera at Merritt. "Who the fuck's Merritt Emmons?" He was reading her name from his phone.

"Who the fuck are you?" Harper asked him back.

And he smiled as he said, "I'm the guy who keeps you paying for this sick bike." She seemed to know this particular jerk, seemed to have an affable thing going with him.

"This the lay of the week?" another guy asked. He was filming them on his phone.

"Of the day," someone else called, because of course they did.

Now almost all of them, fans and paparazzi alike, had phones and cameras and one iPad too pointed at them.

A woman with endless legs stuffed at their shapely bottoms into black combat boots and sprouting at their shapely tops from denim cutoffs so cut off that their white pocket innards were the lowest hanging fabric on her legs walked toward them. Over the rest of her svelte frame she wore a thin white tank top (no bra) and a green-and-blue flannel shirt, unbuttoned, sleeves rolled. Her brown hair was big and messy, her sunglasses as large as Merritt's own. She said, as she reached for Harper's other arm, the arm that didn't end with a hand in Merritt's: "Hey, I want a ride on that bike."

"Only fits two," Harper said, winking at her. "Next time."

"Come on," this stranger said. "Take me instead. I'm better for you. And I love you."

Readers, she said it like maybe it was so. She might as well have been Mary MacLane, standing there, reading from her diary: *Oh, my dearest—you are the only one in the world! We are two women. You do not love me, but I love you.*

Actually, maybe not that *exact* passage, or at least not its final line, because then Harper said back to this woman:

"I love you, too."

And I don't know, Readers, maybe she did. Maybe she meant it. Maybe Harper Harper loved that girl in the flannel, the girl with the enviable legs. She said it like she meant it, but also like it was something she said and meant a lot. And then she kept moving, while keeping Merritt there beside her, as the crowd thickened around them.

She'd resituated their closeness, reached her right arm across her own middle and put that hand into Merritt's right hand so that her left arm, the one with the hand that had been holding Merritt's, could go around the small of Merritt's back and she could better steer and shield Merritt with her own body. And when Harper did that, pressed up close against and around her, Merritt wanted, as she had the night before, to turn her head and kiss Harper. There was that Harper Harper magnet pulling them together. And Merritt knew, she *knew*, that if she did it, Harper would kiss her back. Merritt knew it the way she knew how to tie her shoes, her dad's middle name, how to flick a light switch. Simpler things, even, more known to her, as if always known to her: how to scratch an itch or close her eyes, how to sneeze.

And I bet you know, already you know, that Merritt did do it. She turned her head and raised her eyebrows and asked, "Shall we?" so close to Harper's mouth that she might as well have kissed the words into it. Harper smiled in a nod and Merritt did kiss her, there in the throng of paparazzi. And Harper Harper did kiss her back, as Merritt, heartbeat certain, knew that she would. You've seen the videos. You've seen the pictures. It looks, in some of those videos, like maybe that decision was Merritt's answer to Hollywood legs and her query. A kind of smug affirmation of her position. And how did it feel? Like the kiss equivalent of her first ride on Harper's Moto Guzzi: whirring, fast, and could-be dangerous. She even felt it in the throb of her eyebrow.

I can tell you, though, that Merritt wasn't anticipating the cheer from the crowd that went up around them. Who gets one of those for a kiss, other than just-married couples and those prodded into performing on the jumbotrons in sports arenas?

And because they found themselves in that kiss so easily, I bet you, online viewer, didn't guess when you watched that clip that this was their very first ever kiss, out in front of Metal Mug, in the pool of paparazzi and #HARPEOPLE, onlookers and tagalongs.

And I bet you didn't guess, wouldn't have known, that this was also Merritt's first kiss since a two-week trip with some fellow eighth-graders to a university research facility in Upstate New York, where they did STEM work with solar power and Merritt blissed out in her nerdom.

During that trip, Merritt had broken off with Travis Zienkowski a bunch of times, into the side hallways and dark corners of the dingy dorms they were housed in, and they'd made out elaborately and fumblingly, with more tempo and energy than real passion.

But still, those sessions had seemed to Merritt, at the time, like the starting point of all that would be soon to come, the kisses of her almost-immediate future. Travis Zienkowski as gate opener.

Travis wasn't her first-first kiss, mind you. That had been down-the-street Kathleen, in her upstairs bedroom, while they were not actually playing with Kathleen's ZhuZhu Pets. And then Merritt had kissed Alexi, a kid she met only once, at her cousin's wedding in Ohio.

But Travis, dear Travis Zienkowski and his oversize Adam's apple and dry hands, his supervillain T-shirts and truly profane sense of humor—Merritt had thought *he* was the starting gun for all the adolescent kissing to be racing toward her soon.

Turned out not.

Turned out that she tuned in to him the way you sometimes—when at a place like Brookhants, say—happen on a radio station for the length of a song, the end of a weather report, and then that station goes static and not only can you not find it again, you can't find any others, either.

Instead of a string of Travis Zienkowskis—and Merritt would have been happy for Tawnya and Tara, Timothy and Trevor, T-whatever Zienkowskis, too—she'd skipped another grade and transferred to a different school, one meant to more adequately challenge her. And it was a challenge, it certainly was, not knowing anyone there, especially during that awkward bag of ages.

And then, not so long after that, there was her father and his suicide and whatever it was she and her mother had become together—their particular version of a family. And then there was her homeschooling, which meant a lot of alone time. Which she said she wanted. And maybe she did. But still, she grew, as you well know, prickly. She grew into the majestic saguaro you read before

you today. Mostly, she lurked and she hid and she refused to connect. Even more so when her book came out and her brain wouldn't
turn off about it.

Then she took her saguaro self to college and instead of shedding
her spines she grew more of them. She grew cactusier by the class,
by the interaction, the few she managed, anyway, that one semester.
She grew prickly in more than her countenance—even her thinking
felt prickly to her—sharp and caustic and not only when applied to
others, but when applied to herself.

And so between sweet, profane Travis in that dorm, in eighth
grade, and that day in California with Harper, the kiss you all witnessed on your own screens, there had been no other kisses at all.

For Merritt, that is. For Merritt there had been no other kisses.

While for Harper Harper there had been—it seemed to Merritt,
anyway—everyone; everyone she might want to kiss ever. Including,
that very day, Audrey Wells.

Oh, not the same kind of kissing, to be sure. I'm not conflating.
But Harper and Audrey *had* kissed, and also for a crowd, not even
two hours before.

It may surprise you to know that, as they finally reached Harper's
bike, their helmets on, the *whir-chug whir-chugging* engine going
and people mostly clearing out to let them through, Merritt thought
of Audrey.

It might have started, that thought, or series of thoughts, a little
smugly—a lot smugly: a private comparison of the success of her
kiss with Harper and the, nearly exquisite in its awfulness, failure
of Audrey's. But as she again latched her arms around Harper, as
they gained purchase over the parking lot and hung a right out into
traffic, palm trees aligned along either side of the streets like state-
sponsored tourism sentries, those smug thoughts gave way to a feeling of—it wasn't pity. It wasn't. It was empathy for her, I guess, a
breath of thanks for the kind of remarkable day Merritt was having,
and also a breath of regret, truly, for the kind of day Audrey was having. Merritt knew she was. And she also knew that she'd contributed
to some of that badness. And Audrey hadn't deserved it. Not really.

While Merritt was offering Audrey her silent regret, small and useless though it was, Harper cut them through traffic, her bike a knife slicing that stretch of road, until they easily lost the two paparazzi determined to have more of them, even, than they'd already given.

You should know, Readers, that the things that happened next on their date can't actually all be true. I know that, even as I prepare to tell you about them. I know, with all the good and sound logic of my narrator's mind, that there were not, there could not have been, the hours needed to do the things the two of them did that late afternoon and evening and into the night, both the tourist stuff (Merritt was one, after all) and the not: the Sunset Strip, the Walk of Fame, rainbow sprinkle ice-cream cones and fizzy water at the outdoor tables of some West Hollywood queer restaurant they only stopped at long enough to be seen licking those cones and drinking those drinks.

Then on to Harper's childhood friend Eric's rented bungalow at the Chateau Marmont, because Harper said they haaaaaaaaad to at least stop in. Eric had just started grad school. He wasn't "in the industry" at all—Merritt was told—but he certainly seemed to know a bunch of people who were. Despite Harper's promise that he would share embarrassing tales from their past, it was still intimidating for Merritt, walking into that space of shapely, disenfranchised Hollywood types—everyone appearing so lazily stylish, everyone seeming to already know everyone else. But it's true that Eric was warm, and he did seem delighted to see them: shrieking and smiling and climbing over people on a couch in order to reach them via the fastest route possible so he could bestow hugs and offer drinks.

And, crucially: Merritt was there with Harper Harper. They had come together. This was a fact that seemed somehow both known and readily accepted by the people in that bungalow and it calmed her. Some.

There, in the private garden, in the heat bake of early nightfall, hot wind blowing the flowering vines around them, Merritt had a lot more to drink than she usually did—which was really about nothing ever. Harper did not. She was driving and unwavering in her thoughts about sobriety behind the wheel. (Or behind the handlebars, as it were.) She did, however, have a cigarette; two of them, actually. They stayed there for the length of two cigarettes, and Merritt still disapproved, even if it made her a prude, but her disapproval of this essential element of Harper's existence—that she was a cigarette smoker—was not the order of the evening.

Besides, the smoke from the fires, and the almost-always smog, and the efforts of the late-setting sun had proved to be the exactly right Los Angeles alchemy to wash the whole sky lilac to pink. And how could they not drive off again into that? So they did. Back out into the night and on to other places—places they couldn't possibly have traveled in the space of those hours—probably not in two or three such nights: the various homes of Harper's friends, a spin around Griffith Observatory, a taco stand, the Venice Canals, a quick pull-in to the fluorescent white light that rectangled beneath a massive gas station overhang, where they filled the bike's tank, a prolonged stop on the side of a road so they could watch the fires in the distance before Harper grabbed Merritt a clump of white blossoms from an orange tree, the two of them taking turns mashing them to their noses in mockery *and* celebration of Brookhants girls of yore.

Smoke (fire and cigarette) and orange blossoms: the evening's scents.

Eventually, Harper drove them slowly and meanderingly through what Merritt thought was just another random residential neighborhood in Silver Lake, to end them up at another friend's house, she assumed. But then they made a turn and up the street Merritt could see the glow in the branches without yet understanding what it was she was seeing: the Chandelier Tree.

Do you know about it, Readers? Merritt didn't. Not before that night. A large part of its magic lies in its location, which isn't a theme park or even a city park. It's a big, old sycamore tree with an enormous canopy studded with more than a dozen lit chandeliers, several of them in boughs overhanging the street. And it's growing in the corner of the smallish front yard of a smallish house in a random LA neighborhood. There's even a white picket fence.

Harper pulled up to the tree's wildly painted parking meter, used to collect donations toward the house's electric bill.

There were a few other people standing around taking pics. These people noticed them and seemed to figure out that it was Harper Harper once she removed her helmet, but they were too cool to make a thing about spotting her. And once they left, there were only the occasional dog walkers nodding hello. Those hellos surprised Merritt but I'm telling you, Readers, the Chandelier Tree engendered warmth and good feelings.

I mean, it was filled with glowing chandeliers with all their attendant chandeliery accoutrements—crystals and bangles and brass. They belonged, of course, in gaudy mansions or hotel lobbies. But instead, here they were outdoors in this random tree. And when the lights were on, the leaves glowed and the branches glowed and they cast shadows, and sometimes those dripping crystals sounded like wind chimes—clinking and tinkling.

Fuck, I hate the word *tinkle*. What a terrible word. It's so knowingly, boastfully saccharine. But it is the right word for the sound those chandelier crystals sometimes made.

Anyway, Readers, it was beautiful. The whole thing was beautiful.

And Harper was beautiful showing it to Merritt, pointing out her favorite chandeliers, there from the street below. And Merritt was beautiful being shown it, her face a kaleidoscope of light and shadow as she looked into the branches. And the night was beautiful. The quiet of the street was beautiful. And all of this beauty was so good. And it also came with its own soft ache because they both knew, perhaps better than many others their age, that it was so precarious, so prone to dissipate.

As they stood there, looking up into the branches, Merritt told Harper that she hadn't been sure before, but now she was: Harper was the perfect John Fante character.

"What now?" Harper asked, keeping her head back and eyes up in the tree.

"Local novelist," Merritt said. "Screenwriter, too—in like the forties and fifties. I just read his big Hollywood novel: *Ask the Dust.*"

"Did you read it because you were coming out here?" Harper asked. "Like as research?"

"Yes," Merritt said.

"I love that," Harper said, turning her neck so she could look at Merritt and shake her head. "I love that you would do that." She then ran two fingers along a few strands of Merritt's hair, the pink strands. "Say again who I am?"

"You're two characters rolled into one," Merritt said. "You're Arturo *and* Camilla." She pulled out her phone and searched until she found the exact passage from *Ask the Dust*. She had it in her notes. It didn't take long.

She read it to Harper.

Los Angeles, give me some of you! Los Angeles come to me the way I came to you, my feet over your streets, you pretty town I loved you so much, you sad flower in the sand, you·pretty town.

It made Harper laugh, somehow, the strange delight of having Merritt read that to her beneath the glowing canopy of the Chandelier Tree.

Her laughing made Merritt laugh, too. Then Harper took Merritt's phone and read the passage to her. And then they read it together. They shouted it, screamed it out into the neighborhood around them. They did this like moon-raving maniacs until a man walking by with his two agitated Boxers on a double leash stared long and worriedly enough to bring them back from outer space.

It was impossible then, Readers, for them not to be kissing.

For all of their closeness that night, all of their touching and movement and bike situating, they hadn't done that again, kissed, I mean, since their first, out in front of Metal Mug. Though I swear to you, Readers, it seemed like that had happened on Saturn during the previous century and not a few hours before, and not more than twenty miles away, from where they now stood beneath the spread of those branches.

These kisses beneath the chandeliers were of a different variety than their kiss that afternoon. That kiss had a kernel of show-and-tell to it—of bravado and silliness and parking lot antics. But these kisses were started up by Harper, her fingers firm on the soft skin of Merritt's chin, tilting Merritt's head and guiding her mouth to her own sure lips, her smoky tongue and her breath hot like the wind they'd shouted into.

Merritt recognized just what a stale romantic gesture another version of herself would have seen this as: Harper driving her to that tree to then kiss her beneath it.

Of course she recognized that.

But she didn't mind. In fact, right then she felt ready to embrace every stale romantic gesture she'd ever before mocked. Isn't that what the swell of a crush is, after all? Recognizing the flush of truth in all the love clichés?

In fact, let me add even another cliché to the mix: she'd never before been kissed like this.

And if the echo of the motorcycle whir in her legs, and the dull throb at her eyebrow, and the remaining scent of orange blossom mashed in her nostrils, and the glow of those sycamore chandeliers around them were all part of making that sentence true, then so what? So be it. She wanted it, and more and more and more besides.

The Vegas-style parking meter at the Chandelier Tree was rigged to take credit cards, and so after they'd kissed and kissed again, Harper gifted it plenty in digital money as their thank-you. And then they were off.

This time they ended up at their final destination: Cinespia and the midnight movie at the Hollywood Forever Cemetery. Yep, movies in a graveyard—grass and headstones, shaggy palm trees above and bodies all around, the sky only managing a silver dark even then, even that late, because of the light from the screen.

They were showing *The Blair Witch Project* for the midnight horror feature. Merritt didn't think about it then—she wasn't really there for the movie—but now, if she considers that night, it does pinch at her: those young and terrorized filmmakers not quite realizing just how bad things had gotten until it was too late for them to do anything about it. The filmmakers onscreen, I mean, in that movie's fictional story line. The characters: they're the ones who are ruined. But the people behind the screen, the people who made *The Blair Witch Project*? Well they did very well indeed. Laughed all the way to the bank, as they say.

Harper took Merritt's hand and they meandered the headstones to eventually settle in the grass at the back of the crowd, their view of the screen somewhat obscured by a marble angel. It wasn't likely they'd be noticed back here.

"Have you seen this before?"

"Once, maybe. I think," Merritt said, not wanting to talk or watch the movie or do anything more, right then, than continue to lean against Harper in the hot breeze on the lawn and just be. Just be there, at the movies, in Hollywood, with *the* Harper Harper as her date.

They did that for a while: leaning, kissing. Harper smoked, which she probably wasn't supposed to do there, but managed all the same. Sinister things happened on the screen. Those poor, unknowing student filmmakers meddling where they oughtn't. One of the characters mentioned his mom, his mom missing him, hoping that maybe she'd take action to find him, and Merritt all at once thought of her own mother, and Elaine, and of the lateness of the hour.

While Elaine had seemed rather delighted that Merritt had plans to go out with Harper, she must have by then, Merritt knew, been expecting her back at their hotel.

So Merritt dug her phone out of her bag. She hadn't looked at it since finding the *Ask the Dust* passage. There were many texts, one missed call: Elaine. Her mother. Elaine. Her mother, her mother, her mother. Elaine.

> Just checking in!
>
> Getting a little late and wondering if you're still planning to stay at the hotel tonight. Just text me to let me know you're back safe.
>
> Merritt? 4 people have now sent me the same link.

At first, Merritt thought this mass of missed attempts at reaching her had to do mostly with the fact that it was now well after midnight and she'd left Bo's bungalow hours and hours before—and on the back of a motorcycle to explore a city wholly unknown to her.

But Harper, who'd also pulled out her own phone, now reminded Merritt about the scene they'd caused earlier. The one captured on video. Believe me or not, Readers: Merritt had almost forgotten it in the laughing-gas time that had passed since.

"We're trending," Harper said.

"You're joking."

"Nope. Well, in limited markets. The queer ones."

"Explain yourself."

"Both #KissMeHarper and #PiercingPuckerup. That one's really stupid. And just #HarperHarper, too."

"Right—so *you're* trending," Merritt said.

"I'm not kissing myself in this video."

"*You're* not kissing anyone in that video," Merritt said. "I kissed you."

"If you say so."

"There's an easy way to settle this," Merritt said. "We'll go to the instant replay."

They watched together on Harper's phone. There were several versions to choose from, and in almost all of them the footage was clear. Those photographers had all been so close to them, and their kiss, when it happened, filled the screen. You could see, well, that it was intentional and enjoyed; you could certainly see the specifics of what they'd done—but Merritt was relieved, she was, to see that it didn't play as lurid. And that it lasted only a few seconds. It had felt longer to her in the doing.

That relief drained away once they started scrolling the comments.

Most of them, on the particular post they'd landed on, anyway, seemed to be positive, calling their kiss *sweet* or *cute* or both. *#goals* showed up in a few comments, too. And *awwwwww*. But Harper eventually got to a string of them about how much better she could do than Merritt, about how unattractive and fat and gross Merritt was. And what had happened to Annie or the soccer player or that actress from the superhero franchise? And as Harper continued to scroll, those comments seemed to multiply like Gremlins in water: one begetting another that was even uglier and meaner, and then a still-uglier one after that.

A tame example: Since when did HH start volunteering for Save the Whales?

Another: Q: How many dykes does it take to kill my boner?

A: Just the ugly fat one.

Harper flicked fast to her home screen. "Fucking garbage humans with keyboards," she said. "I'm sorry."

"It's OK," Merritt said, wanting that to be true, but instead feeling much more wrecked by what she'd read than she was willing to show Harper. She kept talking to save face. "You don't have to protect me from the internet, you know. I've been there before."

Merritt realized who she was saying this to and the unfathomable enormity of what it must be like, daily, to be Harper Harper, Online Public Person. How silly Merritt, with only her tiptoes in fame land, probably sounded to her. How naive. "I mean, not like this, obviously," she added. "Like with this many people paying attention. I'm just saying that I've seen that shit posted about myself before."

"Then I'm sorry about that, too," Harper said. "That it's business as usual just makes it worse."

"Hashtag no shit," Merritt said. She didn't want to be, but she was thinking of all the comments of a similar nature (and worse, probably much worse) that she'd not read, those Harper had spared her from. For now.

It clicked for her, somewhere in there, that some of her missed calls and texts had to do with these videos, with this captured footage of their kiss now bouncing from page to page, click to post. Her mother would have surely seen it by now: Merritt's pierced face a surprise, their kiss a bigger surprise, and that it was all available for repeated online review and mockery and meme-making the biggest surprise of all.

"I missed a call from Bo," Harper said then, as much to herself as to Merritt.

Harper's phone, Merritt had come to realize, was its own self-perpetuating electric storm, her many followers and squad members and employees, old flames and new flames, family too, probably, lighting it up, making it buzz and rattle and whistle and play music, and all manner of other noises, relentlessly, when she left the sound on, which she seemed, wisely, not often to do. Even still, her screen was always ablaze with notifications.

"Does he usually call you so late?" Merritt asked.

"No," Harper said. "He doesn't really call me at all. He texts, sometimes." She seemed to wonder at whatever she saw then, there on her screen. They'd shifted positions and Merritt could no longer read it. Harper typed something back to whomever had made her make that face. "He coulda lost track of time," she added as she did so. "You work really weird hours on film sets. It's easy to forget that other people don't."

"Yeah but he wasn't on a set today," Merritt said. "He was at his house, eating sushi."

Harper ignored her. "I dunno, I guess I should call him back. It's gotta be about *Brookhants*."

"You're going to call him right now?"

"Yeah, probably," she said. "It is pretty weird that he would *call* me. And you're right—it's late." She said this as though the fact of the hour had only just taken hold for her. "Maybe it's something to do with the plan for tomorrow." She scrolled her screen for a while, reading things. "That's probably it," she said. "I missed a call from my manager, too."

"Maybe it's about who they're bringing in for Clara now," Merritt said. She nearly added something ungenerous about bringing in someone better and more equipped for the part than Audrey Wells, but she didn't. Instead she said: "I think you should put him on speaker."

"Whaaaaaaat?" Harper said, her HRF back in full form. She liked the idea, Merritt could tell.

"Come on," Merritt said. "Give me something to remember about this date."

"You're saying I haven't done that already?"

Merritt shrugged. "The question is: *Have you done enough?*"

Harper stood and reached to pull Merritt to her feet as well. Then they moved even farther away from the crowd, until they were standing against a tall hedgerow studded with yellow flowers.

"If this gets me in trouble," Harper said, touching Call, then Speaker, "I'm throwing you under the bus."

"I'll only pop its tires," Merritt said.

Harper made an unsure face and then said, smiling, "Because cactus." She gave Merritt a quick kiss for that, and Merritt marveled at how unreasonably comfortable it was, really, in the span of a single night, to just accept the fact of casual kisses from Harper Harper.

"You've been busy," Bo said as his greeting. "Piercing Pavilion and the Case of the Canoodling Writer."

Harper laughed. "She's here with me," she said. "Like on the phone, I mean. You're on speaker with us."

Merritt groaned at her for telling him so soon—or at all.

"I hate being on speaker," Bo said. But he didn't actually sound upset about it. "Hi, Merritt," he said. "I like the eyebrow rings."

"They look really good on her," Harper said.

Merritt would be embarrassed for you to know how 😍 that compliment made her.

"So, real quick," Bo said, "as you two are presumably otherwise occupied—"

"We're at the cemetery," Merritt said, not intending to explain.

"At the movies, she means," Harper said after.

"Oh shit," he said, "I haven't done that in forever. Good for you. You should soak up all your LA good times while you can because we're off to Brookhants in two months."

"You got the rehearsal time?" Harper asked. "All of it?"

"We compromised at a week, not two, but that ain't bad," he said, real mirth in his voice. "Gonna make it work."

"That's awesome," Harper said.

"I think *necessary* is the word," Bo said. "We'll need every minute of it."

"But how, though?" Merritt asked.

"How what?" Bo asked back.

"I mean I thought it was all a scheduling nightmare," Merritt said.

"I thought you had to confirm the role of Clara before you could lock anything in."

There was background noise before he answered. He was talking to someone there with him, but Merritt couldn't make out what he was saying to them.

"Well, that's why I called," he said, coming back to them.

"We called you," Merritt said.

"Before," he said. "It's why I called Harper before. I wanted her to be among the first to know, and now you, too, Merritt: we *are* going with Audrey for Clara. We settled it all up here in the last hour or so, the t-crossing, i-dotting stuff, anyway."

.

Clearly, Readers, there were no appropriate words of response to what he'd said. Not for Merritt, anyway. I mean, what he'd told them was fundamentally incomprehensible to her.

So it was Harper who spoke first. "Oh wow, no way," she said. "Sweet."

"Audrey Wells, you mean?" Merritt said. "From today."

"Yeah, turns out we can't get Audrey Hepburn," Bo said. "She's already committed to a different project. Something very grave." When neither of them laughed, he said, "Come on, you're in a cemetery: that was astoundingly on point. Yes, of course. Who else? Audrey from today. Audrey Wells."

"Cool, OK," Harper said with her requisite ease. "And she's in for the rehearsals, too?"

"Completely," Bo said. "One hundred percent."

"So she must have come back to your house, after we left," Merritt said.

"Who?" Bo asked. He'd again been talking to someone there with him.

---

* White space, here, intended as visual representation of the vat of wholly bemused and angry (for Merritt, anyway) silence following Bo's bewildering news.

"Audrey," she said, making sure not to look at Harper because she didn't want to see the face of concern or annoyance that she was pretty sure Harper was about to make at her. "She must have come back and done a completely different audition than the one she did in your office today," Merritt continued. "Different than the one we were there for, I mean. Because *that one* was embarrassing. I mean even to watch it was embarrassing, I can't imagine having been the person who did it."

"That wasn't an audition," Bo said.

Harper said nothing. Nothing to rein Merritt in. So Merritt leaned even closer to the phone's speaker, there where Harper had it held between them.

"OK, but so anyway, she came back and she nailed her *nonaudition* the second time, huh? Gawd, now I wish we hadn't left so early so we could have witnessed her triumphant second take after the spectacular failure of her first, when it was completely clear to everyone in the room that—"

"Take me off speaker, Harper," Bo cut in. "Now."

Harper did, right away, putting the phone to her ear. Now all Merritt could hear was Harper's end of the conversation, which went: "Yeah, for sure. No, yeah—I know. Yeah." Silence for a while. Then, "Yeah. OK. Sounds crackerjack. Thank you, Bo."

It's important that you understand, Readers, that Audrey's nonaudition had been, it seemed to Merritt, anyway, so purely awful, so all-the-things wrong, such an epic and total #FAIL, that it had scantly even been discussed after the group of them had filtered from Bo's office and, briefly, back to the patio. I mean, at least during the time while Merritt and Harper were still there. There was nothing *to* discuss. There was no need to go on and on about it, reveling in Audrey's wretchedness.

So instead people had said things like:

Well, change of plans, I guess.

And:

I didn't think that kiss was ever going end. Hand to God, I thought Bo was gonna have to legit yell cut.

And:

Hey, what about Quenby Birk? You know, redhead? Plays the daughter on that noir thing HBO just did? She's fantastic. I don't know about her availability but . . .

This was the chorus that surrounded them as they made for the Moto Guzzi, and there was no need for Merritt or Harper to add to it, especially with their date waiting just beyond the edges of Bo's driveway—so close—if only they'd go.

And so they had, Merritt assuming there was no need to discuss Audrey Wells as Clara ever again because Audrey Wells herself had silenced that discussion.

Now, in the graveyard, Harper ended the call with Bo.

She looked at Merritt, hard, and said, "That was so fucked up. He's the director. We still have to work with him."

"No," Merritt said. "Not me."

"Listen, I get that this isn't your world and you obviously look down on it or whatever," Harper said. "But it is mine. And what you just did is not how I am in it."

"What is happening right now?" Merritt asked, waving her hand up and down in front of Harper's face a few times like you do when trying to test someone's field of vision. "Are you having some version of soap opera amnesia? You were there today, too! I mean, it was you who she attacked with her mouth, I'd think you'd remember."

"You've got to stop."

"I haven't started," Merritt said. "This decision makes absolutely no sense and it's infuriating and condescending that you'd pretend otherwise. I mean, if she was, like, a bankable name or whatever, *maybe,* maybe you could make a case. Or if she'd done some other major part before and just had, like, the most off of off days of all time, fine. But it's neither of those things. She's not famous and she's not particularly talented. The reasons for casting Audrey Wells in this part are zero."

Harper shook her head, like it almost pained her that Merritt didn't get it. She scrolled her phone for a few seconds and then said, resigned, "Bo's actually a pretty smart guy and I think he knows what he's doing, and he definitely knows what he wants for this." She stopped scrolling to look at Merritt. "It's his movie."

"Really?" Merritt said. "Because just in the last twenty-four hours I've been told that it's *your* movie, that it's *my* movie, now it's *Bo's* movie."

"That's what Heather was trying to explain earlier, though," Harper said. "That wasn't BS—that's how this works. It's *everyone's* movie, in the end. If we ever get it made."

"Oh not a chance in hell," Merritt said. "Not mine. Not with her as Clara."

There was yelling and manic breathing coming from the sound system. Onscreen, the herky-jerky handheld camera captured the filmmakers as they ran, terrified, through the dark woods.

Harper and Merritt stood uncomfortably in the wash of that on-screen terror for a minute or so. Stewing. At least Merritt was stewing, Readers.

Harper was doing a lot of texting or posting. As Merritt watched her thumbs move over her keyboard, her practiced ability, she was additionally rankled by how calm and steady Harper was being about this decision. She was trying to sell it as the professional and necessary response of a serious actor hoping to keep her head down and do her work, presumably so she'd consistently get offered more work. And maybe that was a part of it. But, Readers, Merritt sensed, she just had this back-of-the-brain tickle, that it was something more.

And the longer she considered Harper's cool calmness, her unreasonable reasonability—those *Blair Witch* speaker screams more panicked and constant than ever, and Harper Harper so intent on her phone screen and her *tap-tap-tapping*—the more Merritt knew that she was lying to her.

"When did you find out?" she asked.

"Find out what?" Harper said, convincingly surprised or confused, sure, but she's an actor so grain of salt and all.

"You already knew they were giving Clara to Audrey," Merritt said, convincing herself of this even more as she said it aloud. "You didn't learn about it just now over the phone like I did."

Harper gave Merritt no real expression to work with, nothing there on her face to read effectively. But she didn't tell Merritt that she was wrong, either.

"So when?" Merritt asked. "Who tipped you off?" But then Merritt knew. She knew exactly. "Josh the creep, right?"

Harper nodded. "He texted me that it looked like it was going through, they just had to work out some contract stuff."

"When?" Merritt asked.

"Earlier," Harper said.

"No," Merritt said. "Nope. When specifically? Earlier as in when we got here?" She gestured around them. "Or *earlier*, earlier, as in the Chandelier Tree earlier?"

"Earlier," Harper said, touching the cigarette behind her ear. Merritt had already come to recognize this as a thing she did often.

"Oh cool—so you've let me be the fool all evening," she said. "So when? Gas station earlier?"

"What does it have to do with you *being the fool*?" Harper asked.

"Fuck," Merritt said in an angry one-snort laugh. "Just say it. When did you know they were going with her?"

"At Eric's thing," she said. "Out in the garden."

"The garden—" Merritt said, swallowing. "Of course."

She remembered, now, that Harper had been on her phone some while they were at the Chateau Marmont, while she smoked there outside and Merritt drank too many drinks too fast and those flowering vines blew around them. Harper hadn't had it out for long, her phone, and Merritt thought she'd taken it out to get pics of the two of them, which she had also done. It made her cringe with embarrassment to now remember that that's what she'd thought at the time—it seemed so unbelievably naive.

And so this meant Harper had known about Audrey-as-Clara for hours and she'd not said anything about it to Merritt.

"I knew you would be unhappy about it," Harper said, explaining even though Merritt hadn't asked her to. "And I just wanted to keep having this like it was."

"Having what?" Merritt asked.

"Our date," Harper said, smiling. Not grinning but smiling.

"Whatever tonight has been. I knew you'd be mad after you heard and I didn't want to bring that into the middle of this."

Merritt already felt foolish. But now Harper had made her feel immature, too: Harper had been protecting her from this news all evening. She chose her next words carefully. "I don't know why you were so concerned about my reaction. I think what's quite clear, in all of this, is that it absolutely does not matter what I think about this decision, or what I think about any presumably disastrous future decisions that might be made about *our* movie."

"That's not true," Harper said. "Like at all."

"OK," Merritt said, as a text from Elaine landed on her phone. Now this is really too late and too long without hearing from you. It's unkind. Please PHONE IN NOW.

"Don't you think we should try to let the movie stuff be the movie stuff?" Harper asked. "Business? And then we can have our own thing, too. Our own separate thing?"

"No," Merritt said. "I don't. The *movie stuff* is us."

"Why?" Harper asked. "How we met doesn't have to be who we are to each other."

"*We* aren't anything at all," Merritt said. "Except two people connected to the same doomed movie."

"That's just more prickliness," Harper said. "I'm trying to know you. I want to."

"Well, you should know that I have to be going now," Merritt said. "Also, I want to be going now."

After a moment, Harper said, "This is a really shitty way to end this great night."

And at that, Readers, Merritt could have offered a truce. She could have agreed with Harper. She could have said any number of banal things, like It is. Or Yep. Or even just a nod. She could have nodded.

Instead, she said: "I wish you were actually the person I thought I was here with before, like, ten minutes ago."

"Yeah," Harper said, right away. She seemed to wonder if she should say the next part, and then she did: "I'm sure you do. Come on, I'll take you back."

"Don't trouble yourself," Merritt said. "I can get where I'm going without you taking me there." She made a show of opening a ride-sharing app on her phone.

"Really?" Harper said. "This is how we're leaving this?"

"There's nothing to leave," Merritt said, still tapping at her phone. "Do drive safe."

LIBBIE BROOKHANTS TAKES A BATH

······················

It wouldn't stop snowing at Breakwater.

The constant howl of the wind outside was cold and hollow, the white on white on white out the windows dizzying if you looked at it for too long.

Snow fell so ceaselessly from a sky hung low that it seemed like the clouds were disintegrating. And there was no keeping up with the shoveling. Oh, you could try, Readers: but you would fail.

The snow came and came. Perhaps it wouldn't ever stop.

During those long hours of waiting out the storm, such a chill settled over the house that I suppose I might as well, hereafter, go ahead and refer to Breakwater as Spite Manor.

Because let's be clear: this is what the house has always wanted to be called, what it has always deserved to be called.

And **Libbie** had never felt more trapped inside it. She was still waiting for Alex to finish the book, to come see her with fresh complaints about it. Or with questions Libbie would not want to answer. If she let her mind drift, it lingered on Brookhants and the trouble she suspected was marinating there without her. And those thoughts filled her with a buzzing dread.

She wandered the hallways, but somehow Hanna seemed to be around every corner—polishing this or putting away that. Libbie wasn't someone who minded having house staff so much as she minded being reminded about the many things those staff did for her. So she found herself needlessly adjusting the portraits on the walls or pulling threads from a carpet fringe, if only to appear that she too was contributing to the running of her home.

She had finished her first cup of coffee, then drank another right after, and part of another after that. Now she had a stomachache and a headache, too. She tried to have a longer conversation with Max about Adelaide's health. He had been thawing a pipe in the cellar and she caught him in the kitchen warming himself over the stove. But he refused to elaborate on Addie's strange symptoms and it was soon clear to Libbie that she was not only being intrusive, but also keeping him from his work, and he was too polite to say so. She apologized for holding him up and he looked most relieved to slip back down the stairs away from her.

Libbie couldn't even spend these hours with Alex, because as soon as Hanna had delivered the doctored book to her, she'd positioned herself on a settee in the parlor and hadn't left it, though she did keep sighing—more so if Libbie crossed through or even near to that room. So much sighing. Eventually, Libbie decided to stop being bothered from afar. She found a novel she'd been looking forward to, Maugham's *Mrs. Craddock,* and chose a chair near the fire. (And near to Alex, too—the room was small.) Libbie did manage to read a few pages but found she couldn't focus. The words slipped into each other, the lines blurred, she lost her place. And then a sigh from Alex. And another.

Libbie had already told Hanna that they'd have their supper at seven, and so with more than two hours to spare, but night already descended—wretched, wretched winter!—Libbie Brookhants went upstairs to draw herself a bath.

Expensive and modern plumbing innovations were the exact kind of thing on which Harold Brookhants could spend hours ruminating. So it's no surprise that he'd been particular about these elements of Spite Manor's design. The house had three full bathrooms, each with a large bathtub, two of them with separate showers as well. These were in addition to the built-in sinks in the dressing rooms. When their house was being built, Libbie had found Harold's preoccupation with things like exposed nickel plumbing very dull indeed, though she did now appreciate how modern and convenient the bathrooms were.

But they were also cold. Even with the radiator scalding to the touch, Harold's insistence on marble flooring and marble panels for the walls left the rooms with a chill in the winter. Especially on a day like today.

And so now Libbie Brookhants let her bathwater run hot. Great clouds of steam swirled up from the tap as she waited for the cold tub to fill. It would be a wait—the tub was large. If Adelaide had been present, she'd have readied the room for Libbie, drawn the bath, helped with her disrobing if she'd wanted, which she often did not.

Adelaide was such a curious addition to the household. Welcome (at least for Libbie), but curious. Max had met her the previous spring, when he'd been asked back to Harold's (former) Pittsburgh estate to run a small landscaping project for Harold's sister, Cecilia Brookhants Taunton, who now owned said estate.* Max had been rather adorably proud to be asked back, so even though Libbie wasn't much a fan of Cecilia, and even though it *was* a bit of a strain on things to manage for a month without him—Libbie had been happy enough to let him go.

And then, surprise! Max returned home engaged to Miss Adelaide "Addie" Trevert, who was then employed as one of Cecilia's housemaids. And oh was Max ever in love with her. They'd had their engagement portrait taken together before he'd left Pittsburgh, and for weeks after, Max carried the cabinet card of that photograph with him at all times, happy to find a reason—or invent one—to show it.

Also, there was this: Cecilia had offered him full-time employment, if he wanted to move back to Pittsburgh that is.

"Of course, I'd rather stay here at Breakwater, Mrs. Brookhants," Max had said when he'd presented this dilemma to Libbie. "But I wouldn't want you to feel that I'm forcing your hand."

---

* Well, or who now lived there, at any rate. The distribution of Harold's assets, after his death, had been prolongated, litigious, and unpleasant, to say the least.

(*If that isn't forcing your hand, I don't know what is* had been Alex's response to the matter.)

At any rate: Adelaide had joined them in August, mere weeks before the semester began.

Right from the start, Alex hadn't liked her very much. She claimed that Adelaide was lazy, even spoiled. She said that Addie did as little as she could get away with doing (or not doing), and that Libbie didn't see it only because the maid was always playing up to her; because Adelaide was pretty and sensitive and doted on Libbie.

For her part—at least at first—Libbie thought that Alex was just catching Addie at the wrong times, and that she hadn't settled into her position within the household yet.

And so what if Addie did dote on her a little? So what? It was nice to be doted on.

Libbie also sensed, from a few surprising remarks that had passed between them, that Adelaide was much more intelligent than she always let on. Libbie had even wondered about asking Addie if she'd like to sit in on a class or two. Or perhaps to be tutored occasionally in subjects of particular interest to her. Of course, Alex would surely object, not only because Addie was older than the Brookhants students, even the seniors, by five or six years, but because Alex—though she was loath to admit it in mixed company—thought that Libbie should hire more house staff, not fewer. Certainly, she wouldn't like the idea of Adelaide skipping her work to visit campus. And Hanna probably wouldn't like it, either. Though perhaps Max could be persuaded: anything and everything for his still-new wife.

Libbie dipped her hand into the bathwater to test its temperature. She crossed the room to a cabinet to retrieve a bottle of salts, but upon opening the door and seeing them on the shelf, the memory of her nightmare—the fountain, Mary MacLane's laughing face—shivered within and she changed her mind about using them. She did, however, unwrap a new bar of soap: lilac scented and hand milled in Marseille, another summertime gift from Sara Dahlgren and crew, who had spent much of the previous year in

France and were now likely there again, living *une belle vie* even in winter.*

As Libbie slipped into the bath—the exquisite burn of entry taking her breath—the displaced water almost, but not quite, crested the rim. She'd filled it too high. She turned off the faucet, and as she settled, she flitted between these thoughts: Adelaide and her untapped smarts, Sara Dahlgren and her Parisian women, the reason for the chill between herself and Alex, and poor dead Eleanor Faderman, carried as frozen cargo to Baltimore only to soon be buried within its frozen ground.

Libbie stretched the length of the tub. She soaped herself until the water clouded and the scent of lilacs filled the room. That scent returned her, as it almost always did, to the night of the Follies, the night she claimed Alex as her victory. How fine and strong Alex had seemed to her then, how assured. Even now, though years and years had passed and each of them was far too known to the other to sustain that kind of flame, Libbie's distinct memory of that previous Alex, Alex the Flirt—the one who had been built as much of rumor and notion as flesh—made the version of Libbie now in the tub warm with desire.

She rolled a hand towel and placed it at the nape of her neck, wedged it there against the tub's wall under the weight of her resting head. She closed her eyes. She let the soapy, scented water slip in and out of her mouth. It almost tasted sweet, but that was surely a trick of the scent. When her hand eventually met the pulse between her legs, she no longer thought of young, brave Alex, but of Adelaide. Adelaide in her cleaning bonnet, reaching high to dust a ledge; Adelaide asking if she might borrow this or that book; Adelaide bringing her coffee early in the morning, when neither Alex nor even Hanna knew that she, Libbie, was in fact awake and at her desk atop Spite

---

* Libbie hoped it was beautiful, anyway. She thought about France often, in all seasons, and needed to believe that it was beautiful and better there at all times. Better than here, at any rate.

Tower. But Adelaide knew this and would visit her sometimes. "I
brought you this," she'd say, leaning close to Libbie in order to set
the coffee down before her. "I thought you might want it."

"I do want it," Libbie would say. "Aren't you wonderful to think
of me?"

But it wasn't this vision of Addie leaning close at her desk that she
lingered on. Libbie had moved on to a much stronger memory, one
she didn't allow herself to peek at very often because she didn't want
to diminish its effect.

That August, shortly after their friends had left and before the
students had returned, while Adelaide was still new to her employment at Spite Manor and while Libbie and Alex were still in the
thrall of their reenchantment with one another, Libbie had noticed
Adelaide watching them from the dressing room.

Each of the dressing rooms linked to the bathrooms proper—
this had been one of Harold's design specifications—and so at first,
when, from her bed, Libbie noticed a presence there, she assumed
that Adelaide had simply slipped into the room from the bathroom
side in order to put away laundered garments and would slip away
again just as quickly, likely even *more* quickly, and with great embarrassment, once she realized that the bedroom was currently being
privately occupied. Very privately occupied.

If it had been Hanna, Libbie would have stopped Alex at once
and they would have pretended, however awkwardly, to be only taking the afternoon nap they had said they'd each be taking.

But it wasn't Hanna in the dressing room. Hanna's steps were
heavier and her shape, even in shadow, thicker.

And then, Readers, a curious thing happened: Libbie sensed that
Adelaide *wasn't* leaving in a hurry, embarrassed to have caught them.
In fact, she seemed to linger in the dressing room.

At first, Libbie couldn't be sure she was seeing what she seemed
to be seeing. The light in the bedroom was dim, its heavy curtains
closed against the brightness of the afternoon.

And yet a person again moved behind the gap in the dressing
room door. She was still there.

And now the shadow figure—Adelaide, *it was Adelaide*—seemed to be right up against that door, looking through the gap and into the bedroom. Libbie felt she could practically hear her breathe!

She was watching them.

Surely she knew by now what it was she was seeing—even if chancing upon them had been, at first, an accident.

Alex—her head between Libbie's pale legs—knew none of this. But Libbie, her own head resting upon the bed pillows, had a clear sight line to the dressing room and its door gap. Adelaide mustn't have thought that Libbie could also see her. Adelaide must have believed herself to be hidden behind the cover of that almost-closed door.

It *was* quite dark in the bedroom.

But now that Libbie knew Adelaide was there watching, the thought of her continuing to do so, *choosing* to watch, thrilled her so completely that Alex soon commented on how quickly her pleasure had come.

Libbie could never tell Alex about Adelaide watching. Something like this would only pinch at, provoke, the discomfort already between them. And what's more: Alex had believed that Libbie's excitement that afternoon was due to her efforts alone. She would be embarrassed and angry too, to learn otherwise.

Truth be told, Readers: Libbie liked keeping this secret. She liked it very much.

And there was also this: right before she'd reached her peak—for in the rush of those moments she closed her eyes—she'd felt the sudden certainty that Adelaide herself *knew* that Libbie had discovered her presence. Which meant that they were, in fact, watching each other. Libbie couldn't confirm this without asking her, which of course she would never do, but she knew it in a deeper place than the answer to such a question could get at, anyway.

The thought of that day, now in the tub, was enough to bring Libbie there again.

After, she drifted into hazy sleep. The bath was hot. The steam in the room was thick and scented in lilac. And she was so tired and momentarily contented. It was easy to give herself over to it.

❦

It was the choke of salt water that woke her.

As she slept, Libbie's towel pillow had slowly, slowly slid down the wall of the tub—and her head and neck and shoulders along with it—until her mouth reached the surface of the water and some of it slipped in past her lips. This was the exact danger of napping in a bath and Libbie Brookhants felt it as water reached a throat not prepared to swallow. She coughed and spit and shot her eyes open, yanked from sleep and panicked, splashing water out and over the edge of the tub as she jerked to sit upright.

And to breathe.

For a few moments she could only cough and take clogged breaths and assure herself that she was fine, she was safe. For a few moments she couldn't make sense of where she was.

The bath. She was still in the bath.

Only, the room had gone dark. Hadn't she switched on the light?

The snow through the window did cast a pale white, but the room was the color of coal smoke anyway—the sink and the cupboards only hulking shapes as she tried to settle her eyes.

And then there was the buzzing, steady and low, almost like the hum she had heard in her study that morning.

She licked her lips, her throat sore. Why did she taste salt?

She pulled a hand from the tub and sucked her fingertips. Salt water: exactly as if she'd brought it in from the waves below.

The buzzing now hopped off, hopped on, hopped off again. Louder each time it returned.

She squinted. It seemed to be coming from somewhere above her, maybe along the crown molding. It was too dark to see anything there.

The buzzing stopped. It started.

Bad wiring? It could be that she *had* put on the light but then it had gone out with this buzzing as its cause or symptom. Maybe something to do with the storm?

Libbie reached to pull the plug, to drain some of the water before she moved to climb out of the tub. As she did this, her fingertips skimmed something around the stopper. She jerked her hand away. Then she felt again, more tentatively, primed for revulsion.

Again her fingers found it: a thick coating of algae—slimy feathers of it—and not only around the stopper, either. As fast as she could feel for it, it seemed to spread, until it coated the bottom of the tub, until she was sitting on it, her naked skin pressed against its awfulness. And now, even as she watched, it climbed like a shadow up the sides of the tub's enameled walls.

It could not be, but it was: algae spreading like a heap of skittering spiders, its black legs reaching and racing.

She screamed for Alex, but the buzzing was on again and now so loud—so much louder than before—and Alex a floor below and several rooms between. Libbie knew she wouldn't be heard. She needed to stand. She needed to get herself out of this mad bathtub.

She tried to grip its rolled rim, but the algae was already there, thick and noisome but with a distinct note of former sweetness gone bad. It was the scent of lilacs left too long in a vase, the water growing rank—a miasma of rot and perfume both, like the fountain from her nightmare. She pulled her hands back and turned them over, saw black algae on her palms and fingers. She dunked them back into the tub, but as she tried to scrub them clean, the buzzing grew louder still, until she could place it exactly. Yellow jackets.

The sound was the horrible buzzing of a swarm of yellow jackets.

Libbie again attempted to grip the rim of the tub and plant her feet hard against its bottom in order to pull and push herself up. But the algae was too slippery, so thick with slime, she couldn't gain purchase. Her thrashing movements spilled great arcs of water onto the marble floor. It smacked hard there.

And then Libbie Brookhants watched—squinting to be sure, trembling when she was—as the antennae and black, mirrored eyes of a yellow jacket emerged from the dripping end of the bathtub faucet. Its head twitched as it felt the air.

Soon after came the rest of its pointed body and cellophane

wings—its yellow stripes somehow incorrectly bright, almost as if glowing there in the dark. Now it used its sticky, jointed legs to spring from the faucet and fly in a line just over the top of her left ear. She swatted her hand at the awful buzz of it, the hideous flick of it through the air, as another yellow jacket emerged from the faucet. And then another. Until there came a stream of them.

Now, Readers, Libbie Brookhants screamed and screamed, and not only for Alex, but for anyone who might hear her, who might come. The wretchedness of the rot-sweet scent was stronger too, and the buzzing, the buzzing was everywhere, joined by the sounds of the faucet-sprung yellow jackets now careening between the bathroom's walls.

And now, oh God, she sensed some dark presence in the dressing room, a scuttle, a shift of shadows, there beyond the gap—the door not quite closed. There was only a line of space through which to see, but just as in the memory she'd used to pleasure herself, Libbie was certain that someone now stood in the dressing room, watching her.

"Let me help you, Mrs. Brookhants," Adelaide said, opening wide the door.

Maybe Libbie, at first, felt a brief ripple of relief, but if so, it ended in cold dread as Adelaide Eckhart took her first steps into the room—strange, stilted steps. This was because, Libbie strained to see, to be certain: Adelaide was wearing her massive snowshoes. They were like dinner platters strapped to her feet. It should have been a comic thing, Adelaide indoors in her snowshoes, being blithe and merry and making Libbie like her even more. But in these moments the effect was only additionally unsettling, especially as she neared the tub and Libbie saw her in full.

She looked very little like herself, at least not like any version of herself that Libbie had ever encountered, nor any version of *any* person Libbie had ever encountered. She wore one of Max's dark wool work coats; it was still flaked with fresh snow and hung open garishly, revealing that her too-thin nightgown was all she had on underneath. Her hair was up, pinned at random, as if she'd done it in the dark, sections of it stuck to her scalp and matted with sweat.

"Let me help you, Mrs. Brookhants," Adelaide said,
opening wide the door.

Adelaide's face, though, was the most wrong. Even in this half dark, Libbie could see that it was discolored and swollen, but only in patches, as if someone had inflated one eyelid, part of her bottom lip, the soft skin beneath her chin, and then had painted those flesh balloons in reds and purples.

"The girls told me to come to you, Mrs. Brookhants," this false Adelaide now said through her strange, stretched mouth, her words also misshapen. "They said you'd tell me how wonderful I am to think of you."

"Addie, you're not at all well," Libbie said slowly. "You must be half frozen!" Adelaide's uncanny approach, her obvious illness, the awful warp of her face—as if behind a papier-mâché mask—had shocked Libbie into momentarily disregarding the terror of the bathtub, the yellow jackets. "Why aren't you in your bed?"

"I like watching you, Mrs. Brookhants," Adelaide said, now bending and reaching her arms toward Libbie as though to pull her to standing. "I think you like me watching you."

Adelaide's arms were also marked with welts. Libbie shuddered to see the black muck deep beneath her fingernails. She couldn't let them touch her. "I'll need a towel, Adelaide! You know where they are," she said sharply, the latter part only to buy herself time.

"I'm sorry, Mrs. Brookhants," Addie said. "Of course I do. I know where everything is here." She turned to the cabinet, began her cumbersome, slapping steps there, and Libbie used these moments to thrust herself up and out of the tub. She didn't care how much of the horrible seawater—a wave of it, Readers—splashed out over the side. She *did care* that some of the black algae wedged up and under her own fingernails with her effort, but she wanted only to be out of the water, over the rim of the tub, and standing, though as soon as she set one foot on the puddled marble it slipped out from beneath her and she crashed down, hard, smacking her hip against the tub's edge before smashing her naked body against the floor.

"Oh, my dearest darling Mrs. Brookhants," Adelaide said as she turned to see, towel in hand. "What have you done? Now you must let me help you." She didn't seem to notice the yellow jackets beginning to swarm her—five or six of them, surely in her field of vision—landing on her face, hopping from her hair to her shoulders to her chest and around and back.

Addie didn't notice them, but Libbie Brookhants certainly did.

And the buzzing, the awful buzzing, it was everywhere: vibrating in the air and through the marble panels too, up and down the walls and along the floor, as if it was trying to force itself inside of her. Libbie watched the black algae spreading fast across the floor, like someone unrolling a carpet of it. Everywhere the bathwater had sloshed it now spread. And then there was Adelaide again standing over her and Libbie's breath catching hard in her throat.

"Addie, am I dreaming?" she asked.

"Oh no, Mrs. Brookhants, no," Adelaide said as she bent toward Libbie with a dirty towel stretched between her arms. "You're dying."

The towel was some filthy, rancid thing stained with every awful substance that might bleed or leak or spray, and there would be no saving Libbie from this. Adelaide bent closer still, and now the towel would wrap her up, Addie would see that it did, that it covered her, that she couldn't escape it, that it was pulled around her tight and—

The overhead light turned on.

It was as if its electric glow simultaneously snapped off the worst of what was wrong. The buzzing ceased at once. Libbie was still on the floor, still in pain, but the spilled water around her was now only water: there was no creeping black algae. And while Adelaide remained standing above Libbie in her strange costume, the towel she held was clean and white and fresh from the cupboard. Adelaide's face *was* red and puffed with welts, but she was also recognizably Addie and not some stretched skin mask formed from her features.

"Libbie?" Alex asked from the doorway, clearly trying to make sense of a scene that refused such an effort. She'd come to talk about Mary MacLane's book—she still had it in her hand, in fact—and had heard the commotion from the hall, had opened the door and reached in to turn on the light. "What's happened? Adelaide, why are you wearing your snowshoes in the house?"

"I slipped getting out of the tub," Libbie said, reaching to take the towel Adelaide was still holding above her. She quickly covered herself. "I'm fine, but Addie isn't. You need to find Max or Hanna and bring them here."

"Let me help you," Alex said, coming into the room, slipping a little as she did. The sloshed bathwater had spread across the length of the floor. Now inside the bathroom, closer and under the light, she took in Addie anew. "Oh! What's happened to her face?"

"Alex!" Libbie said. "Please find Hanna. Now."

Alex did so unhappily, giving Libbie, as she left the room, a look that suggested they would certainly discuss all of this later, and the book in her hand, too—but in private.

Libbie managed to stand, though her hip was throbbing. Adelaide had not moved. In fact, she held her empty arms stiffly before her, as if she were still holding the towel that was now wrapped around Libbie.

"Come with me, Addie," Libbie said, taking her by the elbow.

Between the wet floor, and Libbie's hurt hip, and Adelaide's absurd shoes, they moved very slowly. Once they were finally through the dressing room and into the bedroom, Libbie sat Adelaide on the edge of her bed. She held her hand to Addie's temple and found it flushed with fever as she'd expected, but when she went to pull her hand away, Adelaide clasped her own cold fingers overtop, holding them there while attempting to nuzzle her face against them. The towel, Libbie's only cover, slipped down, and she had to sloppily maneuver it back around herself with her one free hand.

"Stop this, Adelaide," she said, firmly pulling away from her reach. "Let me help you, now." Libbie's hip throbbed as she bent to remove the snowshoes. She saw, then, that their woven netting was variously studded with leaves and brambles and even a single delicate harbinger of the spring season then still months away: a blue windflower.* It could not be, but it was. As Libbie began to unfasten the snowshoes' topmost leather straps, she asked, choosing her words carefully, "Adelaide, where have you been walking? What path did you take to arrive here?"

"Through the orchard, of course," Addie said simply. "The girls told me it would be quickest, because of the snow."

The orchard was not along even the most indirect route between the Eckharts' cottages and Spite Manor. In fact, it was in the direction of campus.

Before Libbie could ask for an explanation, Adelaide said, rather cheerfully, "Did you love your dead husband, Mrs. Brookhants?"

And where was Alex with Hanna or Max? Earlier the house had seemed so full.

"Shhhhhhhhh," Libbie said. "Be still now. You have a fever and you aren't making sense. I'll get these boots off and I'll bring you a glass of water." She now had one snowshoe removed. The other, the one with the flower twined up in it, awaited her efforts.

"I don't think I love mine," Addie said simply. "Not that he's dead yet."

"No, he certainly is not," Libbie said.

"My sisters tell me what a catch I've made in Max," she said, performing some kind of a simpering imitation of their voices. "And his mother tells me—she tells me all the time. *Oh, he's just so terribly sweet and good.* He is, isn't he, Mrs. Brookhants?"

"He does seem it," Libbie said, still undoing straps.

"But I don't want him to be," Addie said. "I don't want his sweetness. It makes me almost sick to have him touch me. Sometimes I want to scream and scream at him."

Libbie had both of the snowshoes off now, and so she started on the laces of Adelaide's boots. "Addie," she said carefully, "is Max to blame for your face?"

"Oh, my dearest, most delicious Library," Adelaide said, "you

---

* Also known as a wild blue anemone, Readers.

know better than that." She giggled, an awful giggle. And then she
began to sing:

What's the racket, yel-low jacket?
Far afield you roam!
But you'll never leave these grounds
for Brookhants is your home.

"Enough," Libbie said. She shivered. She was still wet beneath her
towel but that wasn't the cause: it was Adelaide's perfect knowledge
of a song she should not know.

Just one sting will make us smart.
With two, we might be brave.

"Quiet now!" Libbie said.

Three will buzz inside our hearts.
With more, we're in the grave.

"Adelaide, stop—" Libbie started, nearly in tears at how wrong
this all was, but she was interrupted by commotion in the hallway
and then—

"What in heaven!"

Hanna, her skirts rustling with her efforts, rushed into the room
followed by Alex, who was still carrying the book, and who would
have likely still been pouting over being sent away earlier, had she
not just caught the final lines of Adelaide's song.

"Dear girl, why are you here?" Hanna asked as she reached the
bed. She did not wait for an answer before adding, "Why did she
come?" She looked at Libbie to explain.

"I don't know!" Libbie said, finally pulling free one of Adelaide's
boots. "She won't tell me anything that makes any sense. She came
in from the dressing room while I was taking a bath, still in her
snowshoes."

"But you're leaving out so much, Mrs. Brookhants," Adelaide said, grinning.

"It's her fever," Hanna said quickly as an apology. "She doesn't know what she's saying."

"Yes, I do!" Adelaide said. And then, as if giving a formal recitation, she clasped her hands to her chest and spoke brightly: "*There is the element of Badness in me. I long to cultivate my element of Badness. Badness compared to Nothingness is beautiful.*"

"You see, it's pure nonsense," Hanna said. "It's her fever talking."

"It isn't nonsense at all," Alex said, her face gray. "It's Mary Mac-Lane."

And, Readers, it was. Addie had just offered a partial recitation from the final lines of Mary's March 19 entry.

"*Oh Kind Devil,*" Adelaide said, looking between them and giggling, "*deliver me.*"

Interlude

....

SIDE TALKS WITH GIRLS

A side talk with girls means a word here or

there about things that are interesting—

a little discussion of this or that which provokes

a question.

—RUTH ASHMORE, *Side Talks with Girls**

---

* The opening sentence of the preface to the popular advice book *Side Talks with Girls* (1895).

Ruth Ashmore was the pen name of Isabel Allderdice Sloan Mallon. Though it should be noted that the concept of respectable lady-advice columnist Ruth Ashmore came from the male editor of a newspaper who wrote the Ruth Ashmore columns himself until he could find a "woman-writer" he judged as up to the task. (Of course he did, Readers. Of course he did.)

To give you a sense of the book's intended audience (WASPs), the topics covered, as named in the chapter titles, included: "Girl Life in New York City," "The Girl Who Uses Slang," "The Elder Sister in the Home," and "The Girl Who Goes A-Visiting."

Of particular interest here: chapter IX, "What Shall a Girl Read," and chapter XI, "Your Own Familiar Friend," which details the dangers of girl-on-girl crushes.

·············

BO DHILLON MAKES HIS CASE

If you'll allow me to return you now, Readers—as I promised you I would—to Bo Dhillon's office on the day of the chemistry read, with Audrey still sharing your confusion about this scene unfolding before her. The scene of which she was a crucial part, even if she seemed to be the only one in the room not to understand it. This scene:

"I know you can give us a bang-up Clara," Bo said from behind his big-dumb desk. He folded a stick of gum onto his pink tongue, whereupon it lay like a stiff piece of cardboard until he closed his mouth and spoke around his chews. "I'm not worried about that."

"How could you not be worried about that?" Audrey asked. She felt unsteady, and like she couldn't quite catch her breath. "I mean I know how awful that was. I *know*."

"Nah," Bo said as he waved his hand as if to wipe her concerns out of the air. "We'll get you the best coach. Somebody who's worked on other period stuff—I have people in mind. And you've still got time to get a handle on her." He paused, smiling like he knew he was about to confuse her more and relished in it. "What I want to talk about is getting a good Audrey out of you."

"Audrey's maybe had enough riddles for today, Bo," Heather said. She'd slipped back into his office at some point, but Audrey hadn't even noticed until now.

"Why is that a riddle?" Audrey asked. Her face felt hot while simultaneously her flop sweat was cooling beneath her clothes, leaving her chilled.

By then, almost everyone had left Bo's house. But Audrey was still there with Gray and Caroline and Noel—and Heather—and Bo was still trying to explain his grand concept, which was improbable enough that she couldn't quite believe it.

The (admittedly confusing and potentially hokey) gist was this: the movie Bo Dhillon intended to make was both the scripted drama about cursed heroines at a Gilded Age boarding school that Audrey had always thought she was signing up for, *and also* the docudrama of the three contemporary heroines—Audrey Wells, Merritt Emmons, and Harper Harper—who were involved in making that movie. Something a little like putting all the making-of, behind-the-scenes extras *into* the movie itself, found-footage style. But better, ideally much, much better, because it would be done under Bo's artful eye and arrangement, with his distinctive sense of mise-en-scène and his penchant for films that slowly and deliberately curdled the beautiful into the terrifying, so you couldn't quite see the seams in between.

"I know we all tricked you and I get you being mad about that," Bo said. "It was clearly a fucked-up thing to do." He waited for her to respond.

"Yeah," she said to the windows behind him. She couldn't meet his eye.

"Yeah." He paused again, this time as if searching for the words he wanted. "But I guess my explanation is that I needed to see if it was even *interesting* to have the three of you alone in a room together. If there was potential there. And if you'd known about this you would have been trying to be interesting, which is not the idea. It's the opposite of the idea."

"So you were watching us today?" Audrey asked. "Like, the whole time we were in here?"

"Oh, for sure," Bo said, not at all embarrassed by this fact. "That was the whole point of today." He nodded at the large video cameras at the back of the room. "Two of those were running as soon as you guys came in here, and then there are also cameras there and there." Now he was pointing at the bookshelves and a plant in the corner. "And mics here, here, and here." He gestured to other objects in other places, one of them on the desk beside him. It looked like a container for holding writing utensils.

"Out front, too," Noel said. He, at least, did seem embarrassed by these revelations.

"Yep," Bo said again. "That was great stuff, actually. Much more tension in the meet-and-greet portion than I was anticipating."

"Merritt doesn't like me," Audrey said, shaking her head. She was nine parts embarrassed to one part impressed by his orchestrations.

"Ehhh, maybe," Bo said. "I'm not sure that's it." His smirk was like that of a ten-year-old finally being discovered in the best hide-and-seek spot. "Have you ever heard of Thomas de Mahy, the Marquis de Favras?"

"No," Audrey said. His question felt like a trap. Another one.

"Riddles, Bo," Heather said again.

"No, it's not a riddle," Bo said. "He was an aristocrat, got caught up in French Revolution drama and publicly executed as a martyr. But he's most famous now for his last words, which he spoke immediately upon reading his death warrant: *I see that you have made three spelling mistakes.*" He shook his head to himself, clearly still delighted. "Dude's about to be offed and still it's: *I see that you have made three spelling mistakes. That's* Merritt. That's Merritt exactly. It's not about liking or not liking you."

"Hmm," Audrey said. Even if he had a point, she wasn't convinced by it.

"And that moment between the two of you, out front, read beautifully on camera."

Audrey didn't know where to look, or even who to say this to, really, since they had apparently all been in on it. "I feel like such an idiot."

"Honey, you're not at all," Caroline said.

"You're not," Bo said fast, swallowing his smirk. "How could you know? Look at all the people I recruited to pull it off."

Audrey nodded. His explanation didn't help much. She got conned. But also buried somewhere in there, if she was being honest with herself, she was intrigued by Bo the Magician explaining his tricks. And that curious part of her asked: "So was it worth it? Were we interesting?"

Gray had been looking at his phone. Now he looked up. "Yes. Decidedly."

Bo took it from there. "I didn't even know about whatever this Merritt/Harper thing is until last night. If it even is a thing. But I mean, couldn't be better, really—and we've barely even stirred the pot." He looked at Heather, practically winked at her. "I mean, better than stirring the pot: we haven't even added the main ingredient."

"Who's the main ingredient?" Audrey asked. She felt like she'd lost her capacity to be surprised.

"*Where's* the main ingredient," Bo said. "Brookhants."

She stared at him without changing her face.

He kept going. "I mean, I know I don't need to tell Jules Coburn's offspring this, but part of the appeal for a lot of these real-deal horror nerds is the narrative of the curse *surrounding* the movie." Bo was animated about this: big gestures, voice full of ambition and excitement. He was also clearly speaking from his wheelhouse. "You know, all the stories that leak from sets about how it felt like something supernatural kept interrupting production, because an evil force didn't want the movie to get made. People eat that shit up." He added, "Don't get me wrong, *I* eat that shit up."

"I think we have a little familial experience in that realm, huh?" Caroline said.

"I guess," Audrey said. She still wasn't ready to look at her mother.

Unsurprisingly, Gray and Noel now chimed in with their own additions. Location shoots in haunted places, chaos and calamity following particular actors or directors, movies in jeopardy and those never finished or those that perhaps shouldn't have been (cue a Dracula cackle here): *The Exorcist, The Omen, Rosemary's Baby, Poltergeist, The Texas Chain Saw Massacre, The Town That Dreaded Sundown,* and of course, *House Mother 2.*†

---

* To remind you: the character Caroline played in the *House Mother* movies.

† Some of the details are just as disturbing as you probably want them to be, like

It should be of no surprise that horror movies tend to collect more of these stories than other kinds of films, even though there are supposedly curses in other genres: *The Wizard of Oz* and *Waterworld* and even *Superman* (some of its earliest versions, anyway). However, it's obviously scarier (contextually) for a movie about a ghost to supposedly have an authentic ghost on set, or for the devil to mess with a production about, say it with me, Readers: the devil. (Though surely not Mary MacLane's Devil. That guy's too busy being charming.)

"So how is this not just *The Blair Witch Project*, though?" Audrey asked. "Or *Paranormal Activity*? Or any of the other found-footage stuff?"

Heather laughed at that question with particular relish, though Audrey hadn't intended it as pointed so much as genuine.

"Not you, too!" Bo groaned and leaned back in a huge stretch, his shirt riding up in front, which exposed a fold of fuzzy belly. He resituated himself, pulled his shirt back down, and said, "I mean, a lot of the recent found-footage stuff is tired, I hear you—shaky cam and a bunch of jump scares. But *Blair Witch* is the better analogue here anyway because of its meta making-a-movie thread. And listen, nobody loves *Blair Witch* more than me. I cut my teeth on that movie. I saw it six times. I mean, I'm talking back-in-the-day six times, like in a movie theater in a mall."

"Only six?" Noel said.

Bo chucked a pad of Post-its at him. "I think it's very fair to call it formative. OK? *The Blair Witch Project* will forever hold a formative place in my cinema psyche. But a crucial difference here, as you might recall, is that they're only *pretending* to make the documentary about the witch in that movie. It's not its own viable, stand-

---

the series of bizarre incidents surrounding the film *The Omen*. Here's just one of them: the girlfriend of the special effects engineer—the man who rigged the film's elaborate decapitation scene—was later decapitated herself in a car accident in Belgium while the engineer was driving. It happened near a road sign that showed 66.6 kilometers to the next town.

alone thing, it's just part of the fictional plot—that witch is a fucking fake. We'll actually be making our scripted movie based on a very real, *nonfiction* curse." He picked up one of the sides from his desk and shook it around at them. "And we'll be making it as a film that *could* hold its own were we asking it to. Flo and Clara will get their due. But while we're doing that, we're gonna do this other thing, too. And then my job is to figure out how to cut those things together without ruining either of them."

"Or both of them," Heather said.

"Always the champion for my cause," Bo said.

"You should tell her what you mean by *stir the pot*," Noel said rather solemnly. "I mean, what we've already done."

"I was gonna do that, Noel," Bo said. "Thank you." He was still trying for affable, but it had just cracked. It was clear he didn't especially love this guy telling him what to do, and probably wouldn't have gone along so easily were he not in salesman mode. He ran his hand over his moustache a couple of times. "Listen, Brookhants will give us plenty to work with. I was out there a few months ago and it's unreal how beautiful and enchanted, I guess, it is." He glanced at Heather quickly, looked away. "Everywhere you point your camera, there's something better to shoot."

"But," Noel said loudly.

Bo gave him a *back off and let me do this* look. "We will have a few things in place to get you three talking or reacting." He sensed, rightly, that Audrey was bothered by this admission. She had stiffened into a starched-shirt posture.

"This will not be anything over the top, Audrey," Bo added, like he thought he shouldn't have to. "Nobody will be chasing you through the woods with a chain saw."

"Just maybe with a cursed book," Noel said.

"Dude," Bo said. "Give it a rest a minute, yeah? I've got this. I don't need you to do the subtitles."

"You sure?"

Bo paused pointedly, staring hard at Noel with his mouth partially open and his shoulders pushed forward in a kind of boxer-at-a-post-weigh-in-press-conference hunch. When it seemed clear that Noel wasn't going to chime in again, Bo relaxed and said to Audrey, "Think stuff like sound effects or props, you know, maybe we add some fog to the trees."

"OK," Audrey said, unsure.

Heather shook her head and said, "If we're coming clean, let's go the distance." She smiled at Audrey like a parent attempting to explain away the bad behavior of their child. "Some of it will absolutely scare you, we hope. That's the point. But it's nothing that will put you in any kind of danger."

"Of course not," Bo said as if even the insinuation was distasteful.

"But it might feel really personal," Noel said. "Especially because it will mean you're never really alone when you think you're alone. Not while you're there."

"Not true," Bo said. "Bathrooms and bedrooms will be off-limits entirely."

Audrey ignored Bo and looked at Noel, trying to decipher his meaning. Something in his expression made her understand without really understanding. "What did you do, Noel?"

"I'm sorry," he said. "They asked me, it wasn't my idea."

"I told him he had my blessing, honey," Caroline said.

"Last night . . ." Audrey said, still knowing without knowing.

Noel half sang, "Whaaaaaat's the ra-cket, yel-low ja-cket?"

"You're an asshole," she said. She shook her head, felt a blush rise up her neck.

"It's just an app," Noel said quickly. "It gave me remote access to your phone. I really thought you'd figure it out sooner." As an after-thought, he added, "Gray asked me to do it."

"I was only the messenger," Gray said, his hands up.

"How did you do the yellow jackets?" Audrey asked, feeling stupid, just so stupid, but also relieved. "Oh my God—were you in our house? I thought I heard something but I couldn't—"

"I wasn't," Noel said. "I swear to you. I wasn't there. I installed the app to play the book—earlier, I mean, when I had your phone. I didn't have anything to do with the yellow jackets."

Even as Audrey looked in her mother's direction, Caroline was already saying, "Me either, honey. None of us planned for the bugs. It was a fluke."

"Or part of the curse," Gray said.

"Wouldn't that be something?" Bo said.

Audrey looked around his office, still trying to avoid eye contact. Again, there was that vintage *House Mother* poster of Caroline mocking her from the wall. She couldn't let herself believe any of them, not right as they were admitting that they'd all been in on this together. Also, because a big part of her really wanted the yellow jackets in the sink to be just another piece of the setup.

"Wait, were you filming me last night, too?" She knew the answer and it was bad. This was all bad.

"Just with our own security cameras," Caroline said, as if this was somehow not an invasion. "I didn't let them add any others—I only shared the footage with him. That's all."

They had cameras in the living room, in the kitchen, one that caught the front yard, and another the driveway. Bo would have seen all the angles of her terror.

He seemed to sense that his pitch was getting off course. "Listen," he said, "I know this is a ton to take in, but the thing to focus on here is that it worked, right? It was an effective method of eliciting a stellar performance."

"I wasn't performing," Audrey said.

"Fair enough," Bo said. "But now you know."

"That it's all fake, honey," Caroline said.

"Exactly," Bo said. "Just like anything else on a set. So, I mean, Heather's right, you'll still have moments of genuine fear, because you won't know the specifics of what we have planned for you, but you won't be, like, incapacitated by it because you'll be in on the larger operation."

"But you can't let on that you are," Heather said.

"Right," Bo said. "That is the crux of it."

"And you're saying Harper and Merritt really don't know?" Audrey said. "About any of this?"

"Not until after we wrap," Bo said. "If we can keep it going for that long. Big if—knock on wood." He actually rapped his knuckles on his desk.

"How is that even legal?" she asked. "I mean, is it?"

Heather took this one. She seemed very ready to. "Rhode Island allows for one-party consent in all video recordings unless they're taken in places where a person can reasonably expect privacy—changing rooms, bathrooms, locker rooms."

"So *I* would be that consent?" Audrey asked. "The one party?"

"No," Bo said quickly. "That's not—don't look at it that way. We're all getting recorded all the time, every day. Brookhants already has security cameras running 24/7, that's before we even get there to add ours. Harper and Merritt *will* know eventually, Audrey—just not out the gate. We need to let things marinate out there a while."

Audrey had piles of questions about how this could possibly work, how Harper's contract could even allow for it and what it would look like in the day-to-day, how they could keep it a secret for so long—or if they *should* do such a thing, even if they could.

What were the ethics of being one of the magicians if you were doing tricks for people who didn't know that they were not only at your show, they were in it? They were part of the act?

But that afternoon she asked only one of those questions. It was the question that had been blinking before her since Bo had started his explanation: "Why not pick Harper for this? She's the better actor and the name."

"Bingo," Bo said. "That's why it can't be her."

"Explain that to me."

Bo was delighted to do so. "Because Harper's natural, and somehow mostly endearing, instinct is to post every fucking thing that happens to her—which her fans want and expect her to do, by the way—and when she goes to make this movie some spooky shit is gonna happen to her. We're banking on her sharing it. Harper's our leak. And she can't be in on the fix if she's the leak. I mean she's good, but she's not that good."

"I don't know," Heather said, "she might be that good."

"But why risk it?" Bo said. "This way whatever she posts about what's going on will be as authentic as anything on socials can be. Otherwise it would just be bought and paid for."

"Isn't that a distinction without a difference?" Noel said.

"Who even invited this guy?" Bo said. He was less aggressive than he'd been with Noel before, but he still said it not so much like he was kidding.

"You did," Audrey said. She wasn't kidding, either.

Bo went on to explain some of how they planned to pull this off: the hidden cameras and recording equipment strung up in all kinds of places, the plant and body mics, the video drones, the separate crew dedicated to following the three of them around in order to get *behind-the-scenes* footage that would end up being much more than that. Audrey tuned in and out of his explanation. She felt embarrassed and disappointed, but she didn't feel this way entirely, or even predominately, because she'd been tricked.

Instead, it was because she felt like her original thoughts about all of this, about being asked to play Clara, had been validated. Of course they had never really wanted her to act in a serious dramatic role opposite Harper Harper. Of course she wasn't actually good enough for Clara and Clara alone. They'd picked her because they thought she'd be desperate enough to be their pawn, the sucker stooge tasked with making sure the more important leads hit their marks in scenes they didn't even know they were in. This was the rare case, she'd already decided, where being kept in the dark was preferable, where it meant that you were the more valuable party.

Audrey would have forty-eight hours to make her decision, per the agreement made as she and her group left Bo Dhillon's bungalow that day. But—in the car on the way to her house, in the kitchen with takeout, Gray and Noel still tagging along, even as Noel scooped dan dan noodles with one hand and pulled up various examples of cinema verité on his phone with the other, and they all tried to voice the potential career benefits of taking the job— Audrey had her mind made up. She was a no. It was a pass. Put her in the back with Lily Strichtfield because this wasn't the project for her. She even suggested, when Gray eventually said that he really had to be going, that they call Bo now and tell him no deal. Get it over with. She was that sure.

"At least sleep on it," Gray said, waving his hand over the motorized trash can until the lid flipped open its plastic mouth. "You don't have to take the full two days, but please at least sleep on it. It's much too big an opportunity not to do at least that." He'd started to dump his leftovers when Caroline sped over to stop him, taking the container right out of his hand. "I plan to recycle it, Caroline," he said, rolling his eyes.

"Yeah, but we compost, too," she said.

Audrey thought Gray looked rather pathetic in that moment, the trash lid smacking shut next to him, his shirt wrinkled, a dribble of sriracha down its front. She said, "Fine. I'll sleep on it." She had every intention of calling him the second she woke up to say, "Nothing's changed—please tell them no."

After Gray left, Audrey and Caroline and Noel settled outside on the patio furniture and rehashed it all again, around and back and over. It was impossible for Audrey, now sitting on the other side of the doors she'd had to will herself to close the night before, not to keep thinking of how frightened she'd been and how the two people sitting beside her had helped to pull it off.

"You're totally sure it wasn't anything other than the audiobook last night?" she asked. "Like maybe they put a fog machine out here or something? Or maybe Bo got somebody else to do the bugs if you two didn't?"

"I really don't think so, honey," Caroline said. "It was a rushed deal—we weren't planning this for weeks or anything." She scrunched up her face—a move she used a lot in the *House Mother* movies—before asking, "Are you so mad that we helped him? I went back and forth and back and forth, but I didn't want you to miss out on this because I wouldn't do my part."

"I am mad," Audrey said. She waited a few moments before adding, "Which doesn't mean I don't get why you did it. Was the Lily Strichtfield thing fake, too?"

"No, I think she really did back out," Noel said.

"Smart girl," Audrey said.

"Maybe," Caroline said. She hesitated, and then, "It's an interesting concept, though—isn't it? I mean *I* think it is. You're not even a little bit curious to see how he puts it together?" Caroline didn't sit still well. She was again out of her seat, pulling the patio table to the right, resituating its chairs. She was always staging things in the house to make them look more like the TV-renovation-reveal house she kept in her head.

"I don't think it's as interesting as he's saying it is," Audrey said. "Bo's acting like he's Orson Welles and he's inventing some bold new cinematic approach. But he's not."

"Right?" Noel said. "I kept thinking that, too. Orson Welles is the perfect example, because he *did* shit like this ninety years ago."

Caroline was now tossing and retossing the throw blankets onto the chaise longues so they looked more casual in their drape. As she let one flutter into place she asked, "Did shit like what?"

"I mean, not *exactly,* exactly the same," Noel said, "but *The War of the Worlds,* right? That was a radio play before it was a movie, but they broadcast it like it was a news bulletin—they kept interrupting with these fake breaking news alerts. Didn't some white people even call the police because they thought aliens were attacking?"

"Sounds like us," Audrey said.

"Even if they did, that doesn't seem like this to me at all," Caroline said.

"Really, you can't see it?" Audrey said.

"I think what Bo's proposing is more like a William Castle move," Noel said.

"Oh perfect," Audrey said, "that guy."

"Remind me," Caroline said.

"You know him," Audrey said. "Dad's super into him."

"He was king of the horror movie gimmick," Noel said. "Especially if it broke the fourth wall. Involving the audience was Castle's whole thing. So like for *The Tingler,* which was about this parasite that attached to your spine and fed on your fear, Castle had motors installed on the theater seats so that they shook during certain scenes. And he had this countdown clock come on the screen before the ending of *Homicidal*—which, like, gave people time to leave the theater before the final scene, if they were just too terrified to watch it. I mean, it was sort of dope in its day, I guess. Entertaining."

"None of that stuff is really the same as this though, you guys," Caroline said. She sounded annoyed. She'd moved on to turning the hand crank to raise and lower a striped shade umbrella so that it closed more neatly. "I think you're both reaching."

"Not that far a reach," Noel said. "Bo's just proposing a twenty-first-century version of it. Even if it's something as simple as the opening of *Texas Chain Saw Massacre,* the narrator telling us that the film we're about to see is the true *account of a tragedy,* it's just part of the history of the genre to make the fiction onscreen seem as real as possible to the audience."

"Yes, because it's scarier that way," Caroline said. "This is not a grand conspiracy." Finally, she had the umbrella how she wanted it, and after one final chop to a throw pillow, she sat back down to survey her adjustments.

"I don't know," Audrey said. "In retrospect some of that stuff looks really corny. Castle was like a schlock director. That's not at all what I thought this movie was supposed to be. I doubt Harper Harper does, either."

"Yeah, but that doesn't add up, either, does it?" Noel asked. "If she's producing? She knows something about this. She has to."

"I don't know," Audrey said. "He was so adamant that she doesn't but—"

"But why would you believe him?" Noel asked. "I mean, why believe him about anything now?"

"That's a really broad brush you're both painting with," Caroline said. "Bo Dhillon isn't William Castle. He's not a used car salesman." She was tracing her chin scar with her fingertips as she turned to Audrey. "We both thought *Big Yard, Quiet Street** was so great. Remember? Just original and weird and so good. And you told me Aimee Barambo loved working with him on *Five Blocks*†—said she'd do it again, first chance she got. And look what that movie did for her."

"*Five Blocks* wasn't like this. It wasn't built around a gimmick."

"That's *your* word for what he's trying to do," Caroline said. "I hardly think it's Bo's."

"I mean, everything about making a narrative film is a gimmick, though, right?" Noel said. "It's all make-believe meant to trick you into investing in it. Or rejecting the act of investment for one of analysis or abrasion."

"I don't need you to be the Kind Devil's advocate here, Noel," Audrey said. "You've already done that part."

"He's right, though, honey," Caroline said. "That's all it ever is. Some of the gimmicks are just more subtle."

"So you both apparently think I should do it, then? This is your endorsement."

Noel shrugged as Caroline said, "What matters is if you want to do it or not. I just don't think you should base your decision on a Bo Dhillon track record that doesn't actually exist."

"That's fair," Noel said.

"I also don't know why you wouldn't do it," Caroline said, standing and immediately turning to wipe invisible wrinkles out of the cushion she'd just been sitting on.

"Really, you don't," Audrey said. "After today, you don't."

---

* Carlos Burr's review of *Big Yard, Quiet Street* happened to contain Bo's personal favorite summary of his style: "Think Wes Anderson directing a remake of *The Shining*, only set it in suburbia and ask Shirley Jackson to consult."

† From its IMDB description: "When a precocious child goes missing on the short walk between home and her grandmother's apartment, her father retraces her route and discovers an increasingly terrifying and macabre world hidden beneath the veneer of the commonplace."

"Yes, really—it's incredible. It's an incredible opportunity. Two great parts in one movie made by a real horror auteur." She threw up her hands. "But you have to want it, not me."

Her mom was already halfway to the kitchen to look for something sweet when Audrey noticed the folded bit of paper on the seat next to her. It had fallen out of Caroline's pocket. Audrey used her fingertips to unfold its tiny folds. It was a torn piece of envelope with writing in blue ballpoint: *Don't wait. Your life is now, today.*

Audrey looked up from the note to find Noel watching her. She passed it to him, carefully—it was so small that it wouldn't take much wind to carry it off. He read it and said, "She's better than a fortune cookie." He handed the note back.

Audrey worried the paper between her thumb and pointer finger, rolling it into a scroll. "When they delivered her dry-cleaning last week there was a sandwich bag of these stuck over the hangers with a note that said they'd taken them out of the pockets and weren't sure if we still wanted them or not. There were like a dozen."

"Did she still want them?"

"I don't know," Audrey said. "I hung the whole stack in her closet. She didn't say anything about it to me. For all I know, this could be one of those they sent back in the baggie."

"If it works, work it," Noel said.

Audrey smiled at him. "I'm mad at you."

"I know."

"Do I do this movie, Noel?"

"I don't know. I mean, I can see all the ways it could be total shit. I mean, like, for you, on set, but also just as a film. A fucking mess. Like, worst-case scenario, it's what—one of those ghost hunter reality shows on cable meets gay period piece?"

"Yes," she said. "In other words: a thing which no one wants."

"Yeah, but . . ."

"What?"

"I just don't think the guy's suddenly a hack, either. That doesn't make sense. And Caroline's right that his body of work doesn't bear it out." He started to say something else, but changed to, "Do you think you'll regret it if you do it?"

"Right now all I can see are regrets lined up in both directions—regrets for yes and regrets for no." She made herself ask, "Why do you think he wants me for this? Really?"

"Part of it is because you're scream queen royalty," Noel said without hesitation. "To pretend otherwise is stupid. He has to market the thing."

"Yeah," she said.

"But I also think it's because Bo thinks you can do it. He trusts you to deliver both badass Clara Broward and also Audrey Wells, normcore actress-next-door. That *is* part of it."

She wasn't so sure she believed him on this point.

"That's part of it, Aud," he said again. "I'm sorry I fucked with your phone and lied about it."

"Me too," she said.

"You forgive me?"

"Not yet."

He nodded. "What about now?"

He went home soon after. Audrey lingered outside in the red wash of sunset and fire haze, chewing on that slip of paper from her mom's pocket, its sentiment bleeding blue onto her gums. She'd taken Caroline up on her offer to go buy them slices of coconut cake from a vegan bakery they both liked, so now it was only her, alone again and tired and reconsidering her last twenty-four hours, wet axiom mash in her molars.

And then Bo was calling. Audrey thought about not answering, but she did.

As soon as she picked up, like in that moment, he said all of the following: "I think we somehow got too bogged down in the bullshit this afternoon. That's my fault and I'm sorry. I was trying to save face, and because of that I didn't do a very good job of explaining why I need to make this movie this way and why I need you in it. Can I try again now?"

"OK," she said, trying to decide if he sounded sincere or like he was just trying hard to sound sincere.

"So when I was figuring out what to say when I called you"—he was rustling paper around, Audrey could hear that clearly on her end—"I wrote some notes. I was actually gonna send you an email but that seemed cowardly. I've got stuff here about docufiction and pseudo documentary and meta horror. I can give you my thesis on the flaws and successes of films like *Berberian Sound Studio* and *Lake Mungo*—or we could skip it."

"Skip it," Audrey said. "I was just talking to Noel about all of that. Sort of."

"That guy knows things," Bo said. He seemed almost nervous.

"He does," Audrey said. "And he thinks your concept is kind of tired."

"He's wrong," Bo said. Any nervousness—feigned or real—was gone with those two words. "But that's at least half my fault. Probably more. Listen, I'm pretty sure the problem here lies in euphemisms. I can tell you that Brookhants is special, or has an energy, or is fucking, what—*touched* or whatever I said earlier. But I'm only doing any of that to avoid saying the word *haunted*. And I'm not doing it anymore. I think Brookhants is haunted, Audrey. I experienced that when I was there. I swear, I even felt the breath of it when I was *reading* about it after I left. And I am not some crystal-carrying believer in the paranormal. I don't give a shit about ghost hunters or séances or whatever. I don't read my horoscope even though I'd get some real points with my husband if I did. Brookhants is haunted. You can feel that, I mean, like, in your marrow feel it, when you go there. You *will* feel it."

He paused, maybe to take a drink of something. Then he was right back in it. "OK, so now's the part where you don't laugh. OK?"

"OK," she said.

"This is you promising?"

"This is me promising," she said.

"OK. When I was there a few months ago, I went out to the orchard to shoot a little and take photos. There were other people with me—Nick Woodyard, you know him, right, our production designer—and Heather was there, too. But they were still back in the buildings on campus and I was alone when I got to the orchard, which is through the woods and in this clearing where, like, the trees finally open up to sky again. It's this spring afternoon, warm day. I've got my jacket off. I'm looking around, sun on my face and feeling good, shooting this and that—and then it's like somebody starts lowering a black shade down over my vision. I know how that sounds"—he hurried his speech even more, as if he anticipated her interruption—"but it wasn't like I just felt some indistinct ghostly presence. And I definitely didn't see a pair of rotten-faced dead girls in ratty dresses. It was like a blackness was laid over that orchard—and this was on a beautiful, sunny fucking afternoon with fucking apple blossoms blowing around—but I started shivering and, like, tunnel-visioning on the weird fungus climbing up the tree trunks, and this, like, guts-exploded dead robin on the ground near me that was covered in maggots. Probably those things had already been there when I arrived, but now it was like they *were* the place. Does that make sense? And there was this really messed-up buzzing underneath it all, too— like it was coming from banks of fluorescent lights."

Audrey knew the sound exactly.

"It wasn't that anything had actually changed about the orchard, I don't think. It was that something in that place made me see the orchard differently. It, like, infected me—it got *in* me. And it got in the photos," he said, excited, like he was just remembering that detail. "I mean, not like fucking *orbs* or whatever dumb proof people try to show in photographs of haunted places. This thing, this, like, creeping blackness, it changed the way *I* looked through my camera. It made me take these dark, really messed-up pictures. It didn't, like, add anything bad to the scene, you get what I'm saying? It made *me* the bad thing in the scene—like the conduit or something."

He paused again, took another drink.

"I wanted to get out of there. Like, I felt bad and sort of scared of myself, and I wanted to go find people and not be alone, but then when I walked back into the woods, almost as soon as I did, the trees were just trees again. I, like, snapped back into myself. But I felt alive, too. Really alive. It was that feeling you get when you're a kid and you finally come up for air after holding your breath for too long in the deep end of a pool, but now you've got, like, that chlorine burn in your nose and at the back of your throat and you made it up and out—you can breathe, go get a popsicle from your friend's mom or whatever. I ran, like for real ran, back to campus to get everybody to show them, but then when I went back to the orchard with Nick and Heather, I couldn't make it happen again. And it didn't ever happen for them while we were there. Or me either. Not again."

Audrey wasn't going to say anything in response to this, but it seemed like Bo thought that she was and decided he needed to get in a defense, quick. "But it *did* happen once. Brookhants is haunted. That's what I believe. And it's also the thing I couldn't bring myself to say earlier today, which I'm sorry about. And Heather is, too— because she was expecting me to do it and I chickened out. I'm still trying to figure out how to, like, come out as believing in this stuff. It's so fucking embarrassing. I mean, I make horror movies. I'm supposed to know better."

"People believe in all kinds of things," she said.

"Yeah and mostly we judge them for it."

"I believe you," she said. She wasn't sure that she did. She wasn't even sure that he believed—or that there was anything *to* believe. She just wasn't sure.

"But . . ." Bo filled the word in for her.

"I still don't feel like that explains why you have to keep it a secret from Merritt and Harper. Why not tell them this too, like you're telling me?"

"Because I don't want three performances," Bo said. "I want three people having the kind of experience I had without *acting* like they are."

"Yeah, but now I know," Audrey said. "So how does that even work?"

"Well, *you* will have to give the performance of your lifetime," Bo said. "That's what this is: a chance for you to do that with a project worthy of it." There was no humor in his voice.

"Oh right," she said. "Just that."

He spoke quickly again, now fully in pitch mode. "Audrey, listen, break it down with me: Merritt isn't even an actor, right, so if I did tell her, I'd have to worry about what we'd get from her. She'd be on the whole time—like way on, super conscious of how she was coming across."

Audrey thought this was probably true, and might have conceded that, but Bo kept going. "But the much bigger concern is that I don't think Merritt would even agree to do this. In fact, I'm sure she wouldn't. Which means I have to film first and ask permission later. Once I have a movie to show her, she'll come around. I know she will. She's smart, she's got taste. She'll respond to the art, even if she balks at the process it took to get it. And I'm willing to sort that out when I have to, because I think she's gonna lend something crucial to this that we wouldn't have without her. Especially now, with whatever's maybe going on between the two of them."

"OK, fine—even if all that's true about Merritt: why not Harper?"

"Yeah, so Harper could probably deliver, even if she did know. But what I said earlier about her as influencer is true and we need that—we need her posting every goddamn minute about how haunted Brookhants is. And I still think those posts will be better if they're coming from someone who doesn't know that there's any reason to doubt her experiences as authentic."

"Or doubt the people she's having them with," Audrey said.

"I *knew* that was your hang-up," Bo said. "I said it to Heather. You don't want to be the one conning them, right?"

"It's a pretty major invasion of their privacy," Audrey said. "Not even just invasion—exploitation. I mean, it's gross. I know the whole time and they don't and we're all tricking them into being scared and filming that? It's really fucked up."

"You get out there, you're gonna see for yourself that this isn't a trick. It's not about it being a trick. I wouldn't be doing this if it was."

"But you're making it a trick," she said. "You *are* doing it. What really happened to Lily Strichtfield?"

"I can assure you that hers was not a moral objection. Don't think she took some phony high road and so you have to, too."

"I think she decided she didn't want to be the one who sold everybody else out."

"Not it at all," Bo said. "You're wrong. She got scared. She was in until I told her about what happened to me in the orchard. Then she looked the place up and read Merritt's book and it was a deal breaker for her. Apparently, she's already a big believer in ghosts. She said—and I quote—*I don't fuck with that stuff.*"

"Maybe I don't, either."

"OK," he said. Then he waited like he was expecting her to say more.

She didn't.

"Listen," he said. "I have no idea how you personally feel about ghosts. I'd love to hear more if you want to tell me. What I *do* know is that I made a mess of it this afternoon and so I thought, fuck it, Heather is right: coming clean is the only way. You're in or you're not—with all of it. It's gonna be too many moving parts when we get out there for me not to just cop to it all now."

"You said this afternoon that I'd know for sure that anything happening to us was fake," Audrey said. "Like, that it would only be practical effects to get our reaction. But now you're saying the opposite. You're saying it's really haunted."

"Yeah."

"So which is it?"

"Both," he said. "It could be both."

"Cool."

"Listen, that's the truth," he said. "It's me playing my one Brookhants hand to my every advantage. I don't see any other way to approach this."

"Then how do you know for sure it's not dangerous out there?"

"I guess I don't," he said. "But I do know we'll have eyes on you guys pretty much every second you're there. Unless you're in the bathroom."

"Yeah, that doesn't make me feel better."

He groaned. "For real now, Audrey. Doesn't any of this sound even a little bit fun?"

"No."

"Really?" he said. "I mean, I can put on my serious director voice and tell you that you'll never get another opportunity like this again, but I'd rather lead with our collective sense of wonder. Just step back for a minute from all this minutia about who knows what and consider this: we'll be out there in New England on the ocean, start of fall, telling curse stories in the haunted woods. I mean, what could possibly be more glorious than that? Don't life experiences count for anything anymore?"

"I don't have to go to Rhode Island and lie to a bunch of people in order to have life experiences."

Bo laughed. "Now you sound like Merritt."

"She does it much better than I do."

"I know!" he said, still laughing. "This is why we need her. And hey, and I really don't mean to hard sell you with this—"

"Yes you do," she said.

"Yes I do," he said. "I was talking with Heather and we were thinking it might be something if your mom played Clara's mom. I mean, it's like one scene, you know, but the wink of it—you as Clara, your mom as your mom—it might . . ." His words drifted off, his attention clearly grabbed elsewhere. "Ho-leeeee fuck—I think we just got our confirmation that Harper and Merritt are a real thing. Or a thing that kisses, anyway."

"What?" Audrey was still trying to process the offer he'd maybe just made to cast her mom as Mrs. Broward. He had made it, hadn't he? Caroline would flip. She'd be so excited.

"Go to Twitter," Bo said. "They're trending."

"I'm not on Twitter."

"Yeeeeah, but I bet you know how to get there."

She went. She watched a few versions of Harper and Merritt happily kissing while encircled by fans and paparazzi, Bo offering commentary as he continued to watch from his own screen.

They kissed like it was the only thing in the world for them to be doing in that moment and they were both so totally into that. They kissed like they knew the world would soon be watching them on repeat, and they had two middle fingers and two sets of thumbs up for those viewers. They kissed like they were entirely oblivious to what had just gone down at Bo's house, this weird and confusing and messy movie project that had now been the centerpiece of Audrey's own past twenty-four hours.

They kissed and they kissed on a loop.

The anger and envy their seeming obliviousness kindled in Audrey was not at all rational, but there it was, smoking away in the pit of her stomach. And it was *this,* Readers, that ultimately changed her mind. Bo's reasoning, his ghost story, his hard sell had helped, no question, though she doubted any of it would have been enough on its own. But now paired with this—

"OK," she said. She gave him the credit even if it wasn't entirely deserved: "I think you might have convinced me."

"I did?" He sounded unsure. "Really?"

"I think so," she said. "My mom will be so, like—she'll be beside herself to do this. I know she will."

"It's a cameo, Audrey. Caroline can't be the only reason you say yes."

"She's not. I—it's not about her. I have a lot of questions. I want you to please tell me everything you just told me again, even your orchard story. I'll probably want to hear it a lot more times after today, too."

"Sure," he said. "Right now?"

"Yes, if you have time," she said. "Explain it all again. How it's going to go."

"But, just to be clear, you're saying you're in for the whole thing, you and Clara both?" Bo asked. "I want confirmation of your total commitment, here."

"Yes."

"OK, so let me tell you the deal about Brookhants," Bo started. He started again. He told her everything again. And more.

And while she listened, Audrey watched that clip of Merritt and Harper kissing again and again and again.

HAROLD BROOKHANTS MAKES HIS CASE

Alexandra Trills's mother died during childbirth.

Alex's father, Ogden, who was the first to call her Alex, had been diagnosed with melancholia even before his young wife died, and his condition only worsened after.

Ogden and his newborn daughter moved into a somewhat shabby house across the street from his parents' grander house. Despite once having more ambitious plans for his career, Ogden settled into a regional sales position within his father's millinery business. This position required him to often be away on travel, which meant that Alex was largely raised by nursemaids who, as she grew, switched out for governesses. Alex was quite fond of these women, even when her cleverness outpaced their own. (She was a serious and obedient child who rarely complained.)

Alex's father encouraged her scholarly aptitude, even despite any social conventions it brushed up against regarding her sex, and even despite his parents' claims that he was making an odd duck even odder. When Ogden was home, father and daughter often read together after supper, or simply talked to each other about what they were reading. It was Ogden who first put thoughts of college into his child's mind, where they grew into plans for college.

Until, that is, Ogden Trills hanged himself in his hotel room in Maine. Alex was then eleven. She was moved across the street and into her grandparents' house, one of elaborate customs and rules. Her father was rarely mentioned, and what he'd done was *never* mentioned, except as a dark mark upon her.

Her grandparents fretted openly and often that she had inherited *the melancholy*, as they called it. They worried about how tall and slim and masculine she was. They worried about how much time she spent reading, and the things she said—*when* she said things— and how on earth she'd find a husband. Who would have her? She was such a peculiar girl. The very attributes her father had once celebrated in her were now topics of constant concern.

Perhaps Alex's grandparents worried themselves to death, because by the time she was seventeen, both were gone, one after the next. Later, Alex would consider this the greatest kindness they had ever shown her. For once they, and their objections, were cleared from her life, she had freedom to set its course.

Her only other close relative—her father's brother, Uncle Lawrence—was glad to let her. He now had his father's millinery business to run and no time or interest to spend on the hands-on rearing of a bookish niece entering her late adolescence. Ogden had left her enough money to pay for an education at the college of her choosing—and not very much more than that—and so Uncle Lawrence sent her on her way.

Which is how she eventually ended up at Wellesley. Where, as you already know, Readers: she thrived. And in that thriving, *because* of it, she met our Libbie Brookhants, who was then Libbie Packard.

Despite Alex's reputation as Alex the Flirt, her previous courtships at Wellesley had been just that: romantic farces full of high ideals and vaguely courtly gestures. After years of her grandparents' admonishments about her looks, she had happened into her desirability quite by accident in college. Something about her studiousness (which was never performed) and her sincerity, enclosed within the long, thin shape of her (a shape then dressed in fitted jackets or her rowing costume) produced the right alchemy of attraction for her classmates during those years.

Once she recognized this desirability, Alex played into it, certainly; but she had not planned for it and in many ways was still quite naive about its strength. She understood herself to be rather more stoic than the girls who fawned over her and she very much liked that contrast, liked thinking of herself as the object of desire, one who was desired precisely *because* she did not invest too much of herself in the matter.

This changed with Libbie Packard.

By the time Libbie made her move at the Follies, the semester was all but finished, so they were forced to acquaint themselves via a vigorous exchange of letters—which suited them both. As the summer ticked by, these letters moved from conventional to revealing, to increasingly, teasingly intimate, always with Libbie as the one to first cross the next threshold, Alex following tentatively along.

Whatever boundaries they pushed against, they did so only with ink and paper, their desire sealed up in envelopes and shipped off to await a private response.

However, when the two of them came back together in the flesh for fall semester, they promptly combusted.

Before Libbie, Alex had believed that all carnal pleasures outside of marriage were base. She felt they were an affront to her high esteem for women as the fairer sex and beneath the pure sentiment that might only exist between two ladies who loved free of concupiscence.

After Libbie, Alex didn't know what that earlier Alex had ever been thinking.

But only—and this is crucial to understanding Alexandra Trills's mindset, eye-rolling Readers—because she knew that she and Libbie Packard were truly, *truly* in love. Alex came to understand their shared carnality as an expression of that love, which, she believed, did more than absolve it. It sanctioned it.

Although they were not so very apart in years, Libbie seemed then, to Alex, so terrifically young and bold, so refreshingly modern in her way of seeing the world and her place in it. Modern *without* being unsavory. Despite that Libbie came from far more money (however new that money might have been)—and with it its own great burdens of expectation—she simply did not seem noosed by convention in the way Alex so often did. Indeed, she was so free and easy that it was quite natural for Alex to feel more free and easy when with her.

Their most significant dilemma was that by the time they finally coupled up at Wellesley, Alex was a senior, and Libbie only a junior. So they spent their last overlapping school year drunk on each other, and then had no choice but to sober up and separate.*

Libbie took this well. Alex did not.

Libbie felt ready to woo and pursue others, many others, she hoped, within her lifetime. Men and women—probably more women than men, but who could say for certain? She might marry. She might not. She might move to Paris with Sara Dahlgren and disappoint her parents when news of her exploits reached them. (Or disappoint her brother, the senator; for he would surely be the most disappointed.) All around her, she saw young women like herself striking out as originals. And she wanted to be one, too.†

Alex had no such plans. For Alex, Libbie Packard was it. Libbie Packard was all. At least when it came to matters of the heart. Libbie Packard had wanted her. *Her*, peculiar Alexandra Trills. (And not *only* to wear on her arm as they crossed campus.) It was as if Libbie Packard had somehow gotten inside of her, with more than her hands or mouth, I mean. To lose her now would be like cutting off a part of herself. She'd no longer be whole. When they'd read Henry James's *The Bostonians* together, hadn't they laughed at Verena choosing Basil Ransom? And cursed it? *Of course* the great love affair of that novel belonged to Olive and Verena and *not* to Verena and Basil.

But what could Alex do now, while they were apart? Write letters, for one. Which she did. She wrote the longest, most confessional letters of her life. Were they desperate, these letters? A bit. But Alex

---

* They tried, for a short while, to again exchange their constant stream of letters, but Alex did not easily digest the news of Libbie's various exploits, and soon there remained only an inconsistent trickle of correspondence between them.

† It is perhaps worth asking, Readers, if one is truly an original if one only seeks to be so in the likeness of other originals.

then felt desperate for Libbie. For *her* Libbie, still away at Wellesley and no doubt pursuing her new conquests with aplomb. Libbie did write her back. But inconsistently, and with little of the passion she'd once put to paper.

It was a spectacular and particular cruelty, Alex thought: for Libbie Packard to be the one to make her feel more desired, and more complete, than anyone else ever had, and then for Libbie Packard to extinguish that desire at will.

She'd had her heart broken, Readers. Perhaps you're familiar with the state.

And that state could have been the end of their story. Their story together, I mean.

Alex and Libbie's separation might have lasted for years longer than it did, maybe for always, if there hadn't come a carnival of marvels that set the world talking and made Libbie—and the rest of the Packards—more proud of their hometown than even they could quite believe:* the World's Columbian Exposition of 1893. (Perhaps better known to you as the Chicago World's Fair.) If ever there was a site more rich with spectacle, or which provided a better reason for hosting the passionate reunion of two young American lady WASPs of the future, I do not know of it.

After months without any words at all between them, Libbie wrote to ask Alex to come visit that summer, to take in the city and, of course, their fair fair. Mr. Packard would pay her way. (First class. Naturally.)

As I'm sure you've already guessed, Readers, our Alex said yes.

She arrived in Chicago in the full scorch of August. She'd come on the train from Providence, where she'd recently finished her first year as one of only a handful of female graduate students then enrolled at Brown University. She'd bought a new skirt and shirtwaist

---

* Which is saying something, Readers, because the Packards had always been rather insufferably proud Chicagoans. Go Cubs.

and two new dresses and hats for this trip (she'd asked her uncle Lawrence for money, something she hated to do, so you know it was important to her), and she felt wonderfully independent, if occasionally also a notch too bold, traveling alone on the train.

Back in Rhode Island, Alex had been living quite contently (and chastely) with a companion, grade-school teacher Edith Hays, nursing her heartache all the while, and from the moment she spotted Libbie at the train station—Libbie in her pale blue summer dress, standing on her tiptoes atop a shoeblack box that she borrowed for the purpose of scanning the crowd of recent arrivals—Alex had wanted nothing more than for the two of them to wind themselves together like a jasmine vine in The Orangerie.*

Libbie hopped down from the box and ran through the crowd to reach Alex. They embraced and Alex thought: We'll fall right back into what we were. She's called me to her and I've come.

But then, during their hansom ride to the Packards' impressive home, Libbie was distracted, giving half answers to Alex's questions. Here they were together in Chicago, which was just then electric with current to spare, but Libbie seemed preoccupied with something, or someone, else.

Alex wanted to ask her about it. She wanted for them to shut themselves up in Libbie's massive corner bedroom overlooking a park—was *everything* so grand and green and new in Chicago?—and talk and talk. And then maybe to do much more.

But there was no time.

At the house they were met by Libbie's parents, two of her brothers and their wives and loud children. Alex dutifully toured the property and admired the art she was expected to admire. Then she freshened up in her guest room (which was several rooms and a long hall away from Libbie's own) before late-afternoon cocktails, and then they were off again, this time in the three separate carriages it

---

* Only the Brookhants Orangerie did not yet exist, though I think you get my meaning here.

took to carry them all. They were expected at a reception honoring Libbie's father's contributions to the success of both the fair and, more broadly, the city of Chicago.

The Packards had been coming to the fair since its opening day. Mr. Packard was even forced to miss Libbie's Wellesley graduation because of it. But more than this: the World's Columbian Exposition simply was her city that summer.

However, other than a few lines in Libbie's invitation letter, and what she'd read in newspapers, Alex had no real sense of what to expect when they swept in the dignitary entrance that night: the glittering dreamscape that was the White City. And she wasn't in the mood for it, anyway. She was tired from her long journey and now worried about the strain between them, Libbie's preoccupation.

They disembarked their carriages and even in their rush to the reception hall (all of this old hat for the rest of the party) Alex could see that the scale of the fair was overwhelming and its crowds the same. It was also very hot outside, in this late stretch of evening, and she felt like a wrung-out rag. She hadn't expected to do so much so soon and rather wished she'd stayed behind at the Packards' house to rest.

They hurried along as a group, escorted by an official with a red rose in his lapel and a walk that was nearly a jog. Once or twice, Libbie pointed out this building or that, but Alex had no time to really take them in, and then it was up and into the hall where Mr. Packard was to give a speech. A glass of champagne was put in Alex's hand, and as the room swelled with swells, she felt like she might faint. She needed to eat something and to sit down, preferably, while she was doing so.

Mr. Packard said bland things about industry, but those things were wrapped in the always-pretty sentiment of promise for America's bright future. People applauded. People toasted and drank.

Alex then met a group of Libbie's very stylish childhood friends, including, for the very first time: Miss Sara Dahlgren. Certainly, she was pretty, Readers. The sum of her features almost uncannily encompassed the preferred look of the moment: head of blond hair pinned into a (deceptively) simple chignon that topped her thin, pale neck; her smart evening dress fashion-plating over the most desirable S-curve shaped by her corset. But Alex also found her to be too loud and too dominating, always looking for the chance to cut in with something witty. (Or Sara Dahlgren herself at least seemed to think the things she said were witty.)

Libbie had told Alex previously that when they were younger—before Libbie had gone to Wellesley to study and Sara had gone to Europe to play—the two of them had shared an intimacy. It had been Libbie's first love affair. Alex believed Libbie when she said she no longer had such feelings for Sara Dahlgren. She did *not* believe Libbie when she said that Sara Dahlgren felt the same about her.

And she was right not to.

"I didn't know old Harold was going to be here," Sara said through her teeth. Alex could see that she was looking at whomever Mr. Packard was talking to right then. "Ooh la la—all the way from Pittsburgh to glad-hand your dad." She turned to Libbie. "Is *she* with him?"

"I'm sure she must be," Libbie said, glancing toward those in question without interest. "Somewhere. He so rarely travels without her."

Alex could already tell that Sara Dahlgren savored moments like this, when she had the ability to translate some social interaction for the person in the party who could not speak the language. Meaning she could therefore decide if, and how, to do so: whether to give them the full translation, or only her selective interpretation.

What Sara now said to Alex was, "Of course you've heard of Harold Brookhants."

"Have I?" Alex said.

Libbie smiled at her and squeezed her arm and said, "You have. He's the Brookhants behind Brookhants Lumber and Steel. But everyone loves to talk most about his séances."

In the space of just that smile, that touch, Alex felt better about them spending the next two weeks together than she had since she'd first arrived at the train station. So much so that she almost didn't hear what it was that Libbie had said about the man.

"Oh, I'm sure I have heard of him," she said, looking at him again. His wide forehead and crown were shiny with perspiration, and the froth of hair at the back of his head washed brick red into gray, matching his beard. (Though somehow, the well-kempt—if massive—moustache beneath his nose was hanging on to true ginger.) He had the paunch of an epicure, which he was apparently known to be, and his tan summer suit and tie were of the latest cut and style. Harold Brookhants might have been old but he was not without taste. Alex thought he wore the self-satisfied look of a man who has just played an impeccable prank on someone who deserved it. Or perhaps a lot of someones who deserved it.

"I see her," Sara hissed. "To the left of the ice sculpture. Don't everyone look at once—she'll know! With the necklace."

"She's talking about Harold's personal soothsayer," Libbie said dismissively.

"Seer," Sara said.

Alex couldn't tell if Sara was taking any of this seriously or not. She looked where they were looking, across the glittering room to the dessert table, where a woman wearing an amethyst gown set off by earrings and a choker of the same gem was fussily selecting strawberries from a platter. The cascading stones in her chandelier earrings were surely large enough to produce a clicking or tinkling noise when she turned her head, like wind chimes for the body. Alex thought such an effect would give her a headache.

The Spiritualist turned to speak to someone behind her, and then she turned back to the desserts. When the woman was viewed from the side, Alex thought her facial features were rather unfortunately squashed together at the middle, rendering her profile lumpy. But when Alex saw her face straight on, it seemed scrubbed of definition, difficult to get a handle on. Slippery. This save her eyes, which were very keen indeed.

"Who is she?" Alex asked.

"Madame Verrett," Sara said. "Of the French Verretts."

This meant nothing to Alex. "And how does your father know Mr. Brookhants?" she asked Libbie, though at this point she didn't really care.

"I'm not entirely sure," Libbie said. "Everyone knows Harold

Brookhants." She paused, smiling a charmed smile at Alex. "I mean everyone except you, of course."

Sara Dahlgren didn't like this. She turned to Alex as if she was really pondering something and then said, "From what Library tells me, you might have more in common with our Harold than you know."

Alex was beginning to think she might really dislike Sara. "Oh, I doubt that very much. I don't go in for rapping on tables and lecturing in a trance." She held up her hand as if taking a solemn pledge, and said, "I promise hereafter that all of my lectures will be delivered when I'm fully awake—even if my students say otherwise."

Libbie squeezed her arm again.

"I wasn't talking about Harold's spiritual beliefs," Sara said. "I was talking about—"

"Sara, look who came," Libbie said, cutting her off and pointing toward a group of loud revelers who had just entered by the stage.

"Ashley Marcum!" Sara said. She crossed the room like a hummingbird in a dress, flitting through the crowd to her destination.

"She's an acquired taste, I know," Libbie said. "But she's my—"

"Oldest friend," Alex said. "*I* know. I can try to expand my palate. For one night, I can."

But all that night, as their otherwise happy group rode together on one of the massive cars of the exhibition's great modern machine, the Ferris Wheel; and as they tossed pennies (and a few nickels too, because all but Alex could afford to be so wasteful) into the tiered cascade of the Columbian Fountain; and as they pretended to be frightened by the dancing cobras drifting to the music of the shirtless snake charmers—Sara Dahlgren played the role of instigator. She was always touching Libbie's arm, grabbing her hand, pulling her off into the crowd to whisper secrets in her ear.

Sara Dahlgren knew what Alex was to Libbie. Libbie had told her. And yet it seemed to Alex that Sara took great delight in pretending that she did *not* know. Or that if she did, that it meant nothing to her.

As strings of colored bulbs lit up like boiled sweets around them, Alex watched Sara pull Libbie toward her yet again, this time telling her to close her eyes and stick out her tongue. Libbie did this with no questions, only trust. Sara then looked right at Alex, a knowing look, as she unwrapped a stick of the much-hyped Juicy Fruit chewing gum being debuted at the fair. Sara continued to look at Alex, her face now clearly in a leer, as she placed the gum on Libbie's pink tongue, whereupon it lay like a stiff piece of cardboard.

At least until Sara squealed, "Chew it, Library! Chew!"

Once Libbie did, her eyes still closed, but a smile drawing over her chewing lips, Alex again felt a tug of unease.

Libbie said, around her chews, "Fruity!"

The faces of Libbie's encircled friends, especially the teeth in their wide, laughing mouths, were then colored so strangely by the lights: jagged patterns of red and orange and green making stained glass windows on their bodies. The scene looked and felt wrong to Alex, nearly malevolent: Sara's leering, Libbie's chewing, the awful laughing of the circle. It seemed as if a darkness was right then scuttling about the group of them, these brash, young, moneyed Americans, with no one the wiser but Alex. And even she couldn't quite bring herself to believe it. She thought she must be a touch delirious from such a long journey ending in this night of too much spectacle. She was in need of calm and quiet and sleep.

Near to where they'd stopped was a vendor's tent. The young woman behind its counter was selling something she was calling Matryoshkas—intricately painted papier-mâché dolls, shaped somewhat like bells, that opened to reveal smaller dolls nesting inside, until came one no larger than a thimble. The vendor had been regularly calling out to passersby to get their attention, but she'd stopped hawking when Sara had circled their group next to her booth.

The vendor had also watched Sara feed Libbie the gum. She'd watched intently, but she did not cheer as the others did when Libbie began to chew. Instead, she'd turned to look at Alex and watch for her reaction.

Now, as Libbie's friends continued on through the twisting aisles of booths selling scarves and marionettes, ornate knives and hand mirrors, the woman with the Matryoshkas reached out across the counter to brush Alex's arm. Alex was then trailing her party, still disturbed by what she'd seen and felt, and the woman's touch was as light as a wraith's.*

When Alex slowed to turn and look at the vendor, she wasn't even entirely sure if she *had* been touched.

"This you need," the woman said, taking her chance now that she had Alex's attention. "For you." Though the dolls she was selling were Russian in origin, the woman's French inflection was thick. She gestured to the doll on the polished wood counter before her, though she did not pick it up. She only held her open palm behind it so that Alex would look there.

It was awful, what Alex saw when she did.

While the other dolls in the booth were painted with serene or even beatific expressions, the trim on their dresses intricately detailed with flowers and hearts and curlicues, this doll was a grinning skeleton. Her cunning smile—for it *was* a smile, Readers—formed only of bone and teeth and her violet eyes narrowed. She still wore the headscarf and clothing of the other dolls, but blackberry brambles wrapped her throat like a noose, and her flesh was stripped from her body and painted as a pile of folds of peach and red at her feet.

And in her hands she held a book, bound in red. This detail was particularly striking.

The vendor had her dolls displayed in various states of undoing,

---

* Today, due largely to the success of Erik Larson's book *The Devil in the White City*, the Columbian Exposition is often discussed alongside Chicago's then-lurking serial killer, H. H. Holmes, and his nearby murder hotel. However, many types of crimes, both violent and petty, were committed at and around the fair. Perhaps this is why it did not attract too much attention, at the time, that a Russian couple, Gleb and Irina Belevol, who were listed as running vendor booth number 117 (painted dolls), were reported missing by the fair's end. Multiple witnesses saw the Belevols retrieve their badges and vending license and set up their booth. Some even remember them working there during the first weeks of the fair. But then, Readers: poof. A dual disappearance. The Belevols were gone.

some arranged with all the versions in a row, from big to little; others only partially unnested. But the doll on the counter in front of Alex thankfully still had all of its selves shut up within it.

"Oh no," Alex said quickly, turning to leave, "not for me." She felt seasick even looking at it.

"It is for you," the woman said, her voice like a music box. "Maybe not for now but for days to come."

Alex looked more carefully at her. (She was happy to look anywhere that wasn't the doll.) The vendor seemed quite young to be alone in this booth at the great fair. She certainly wasn't as old as Alex, perhaps not even nineteen, though her face had a curious way of looking like one thing and then another, older and then much younger, in shadow and then in light—a sharp nose, a round chin; a flat nose, a pointed chin. Which was it?

It must be the colored bulbs that were confusing Alex, and the heat, the whir of this mad fair around them—for now the whole space seemed almost to buzz. The sound filled her ears and thickened her thoughts.

"I don't want it," Alex said, making a point of turning away from the booth completely before raising up onto her tiptoes so that she might look over the crowd in the direction Libbie had traveled. But it was a useless effort. She couldn't see Libbie or Sara or any of her party.

"You will want it," the woman said. "And I'll give you a fair price."* She'd put on a pair of green-tinted pigskin gloves so quickly it could have been a magic trick.

In her periphery, Alex could see her now pick up the doll. She did not want to move her head to look, but felt she could not help herself, and turned in time to watch the woman carefully pull off the doll's top portion to reveal the face and torso of the next inside.

This doll was at least a girl and not a skeleton. Despite herself, Alex now peered at its pale, painted face.

---

* Did she intend this as a pun, Readers?

"See how beautiful?" the woman said. She tipped the contents from the bottom of the largest doll into one hand. The wooden pieces made a tapping noise as they fell against each other. She connected the now-empty halves of the first doll, the largest doll, and set it back on the counter where it had been.

Alex could see the second-largest doll in full. She was also painted with cunning eyes, a red book in hand. About her flitted a swarm of insects, the hem of her dress clogged with leaves and brambles.

Alex did not want to stay at the booth any longer. She did not want to see more of the doll's selves revealed, but she felt as if in a trance. The woman's hands were gentle, purposeful as they pulled the doll into halves, the clicking of the wooden pieces like a metronome.

The faintest trickle of music, a song Alex knew but could not place, wafted over and around the booth, until the chaos and color of the fair seemed to dim, and it was only the clicking Matryoshkas, the young-old woman showing them, and Alex watching.

The next doll wore pants and a boy's shirt, even despite her feminine face and curls. She was holding a branch dotted with apples. At her feet were still more apples. And a red book.

The next had stunned eyes like black seeds, her mouth slack and dark. Large white trumpet blooms twisted into a crown over her hair and cluttered the bottom of her dress. She held a red book.

The next had eyes opened wide in fear, this because her mouth was sewn shut, the stitches painted to look like they'd been done in thick, black twine. Her head was painted as if slopped to one side. She held a red book.

The next was washed out, its colors pale and its details faded, almost as if it had been submerged in water. Indeed, it was shellacked with a mange of coarse sand coating its form, the red book painted as if waterlogged.

"Now the last," the woman said. She had the final doll hidden in her hand. It was small enough to be enclosed entirely in her fist.

Dunnn-duh-dun daaa-dun-dun du-hun flowed the music. Alex might have been one of those dancing cobras from earlier, held in the sway of this vendor and her show.

The other dolls now formed a macabre chorus line at the counter's edge. Their gruesome finale was still hidden tight in the woman's gloved hand, which she now held out before her—so close she was almost touching Alex.

Alex shuddered, backed away a step. But she did not leave. She couldn't. She had to know. She had to see it.

Dunnn-duh-dun daaa-dun-dun du-hun.

The woman uncurled her fingers like a spider stretching its legs.

There, on her gloved palm, a doll the size of two acorns stacked together.

This doll did not leer, or scowl, or smirk. She was not bloodied, or drowned, or made of bone. She *did* appear younger than the others, a little girl of maybe nine or ten. She was pretty. Smiling. Her eyes curious, but not quite cunning.

Alex bent closer, her face now right above the woman's outstretched palm. She squinted. This doll looked a little like her Libbie, her eyes and mouth. Or, maybe not quite, but—

"We've found you!" shouted her Libbie, her *real* Libbie, who was now behind her. "Where were you?"

But Alex could not turn away from the doll. There *was* a resemblance.

"Alex?" Libbie said.

Her name from her Libbie's mouth, that's what broke the trance.

"I'm sorry," Alex said, standing up from the bend she'd been in to better see the doll. She turned around, blinking her eyes as if waking from sleep. Sara Dahlgren was still at Libbie's arm.

"How did we lose you?" Libbie asked. She was concerned, but also a tad put out.

"How did *she* lose us?" Sara said.

Libbie seemed only now to take in the vendor, the booth. "Is this what's kept you?"

"She was showing me," Alex said, trying to form an explanation but discarding her words even as she said them. Instead, she gestured to the French woman as if to say, *See what she has there,* but the vendor was putting the doll back together as if that was her only focus, as if, only a moment before, she had not been wholly occupied with selling it to Alex. In fact, she was acting as if she didn't know the three of them were even watching her or talking about her—as if their stopping in front of her booth had nothing to do with her at all. Four of the doll's selves were already renested.

"Oh no! Was this for Library?" Sara asked Alex with mocking concern. "Did you think you'd surprise her with one of these, only now the surprise has been ruined?"

"No," Alex said. "I don't want one."

The woman in the booth had worked with unnatural speed and precision and the doll was fully back as one. And now, just as quickly, she hushed it away somewhere down below the counter and out of sight.

"They're pretty, aren't they?" Libbie said, really considering the booth's displays for the first time. "Very clever," she said to the vendor.

The woman nodded without looking at her. "Merci," she said, but then she turned around and moved to the shadowy back of her booth, bending over some stacked crates to dig at their contents. She gave every signal that she did not intend to engage them further.

"Can we please move along now?" Sara said. "Unless you have other dolls to visit?" she asked Alex.

"I think I'd like to go," Alex said. "To leave, I mean."

"Now?" Libbie asked. "But it's still so early."

"You could stay," Alex said.

"Yes, you must stay, Library," Sara said, again latching herself to Libbie. "It's been days since anyone's even seen you here."

But Libbie pulled away from Sara and moved toward Alex. "Do you not feel well?" she asked.

"I'm only tired," Alex said. "And I seem to have picked up a headache somewhere."

"Probably down your glass of champagne," Sara said.

Alex had mentioned a headache mostly as a further excuse to leave, though once the words had left her mouth, she found them to be true. Too true. Her temples pounded. She didn't know how to explain to them—or to Libbie, really, as she felt no need to explain herself to

Sara Dahlgren—what had just happened with the vendor and her awful dolls, and even before, with Libbie and her friends and the colored lights. How could she possibly explain her larger sense of foreboding? How chewing gum and children's toys had so disturbed her?

There was no explanation.

"Of course you're tired," Libbie said. "Of course you are. How inconsiderate I've been. After your trip, you must be exhausted. Let me take you home."

"We could send her—" Sara began.

"I'm taking her now, Sara."

Alex did not wear her triumph on the face she showed Sara Dahlgren as they parted, but this required real effort on her part.

In the back of the hansom, Libbie took Alex's hand and held it the length of the way to her parents' house, her body curled toward Alex. They kissed, the first time they'd done so in more than a year. Alex felt some of her worry ease. She *did* have a headache and she *was* tired from her trip. Perhaps that was enough to explain it. If she slept well, maybe in the morning . . .

But then, when they were climbing the stairs to the bedroom wing—the Packards' grand house empty save for staff, everyone else still back at the fair—Libbie said, "I won't do it tonight. God knows you need your sleep. But I do need to tell you something. First thing tomorrow. I was hoping we could have one night together before you knew, that *you* could, before I said it out loud, but now I don't think that was right, either."

Libbie was a stair or two ahead, and Alex touched the back of her dress to slow her, then said, "I knew there was something. You'll have to tell me now or I won't sleep at all. Not after that."

"I haven't been, either," Libbie said. "Sleeping."

"What is it, Libbie?" Alex expected to hear something about Sara Dahlgren in response.

She did not expect to hear what Libbie did say, which was, "I'm pregnant."

Alex was glad she didn't tumble back down the stairs, she felt so unsteady. She gripped the railing as she said, "Oh, Libbie. You're certain?"

"I am."

"Tell me how," Alex said, even though she didn't want to hear.

❦

Later, much later, once she was the principal at the Brookhants School for Girls and **Libbie Packard Brookhants** would remember how she'd gotten there, she wouldn't start her story with her impressive family in Chicago, or with her time at Wellesley, or even with her marriage to Harold Brookhants. Not when she was telling her own story to herself, anyway.

Instead, she returned again and again to the decisions of a single summer night at the Columbian Exposition. What amounted to a few moments, really, spent by a fence on a man-made island so lush with fragrant plantings that Mary MacLane would have thrilled to describe it.

She'd had too much champagne. Sara Dahlgren saw to that. The only excuse anyone needed to pour more was that it was finally feeling like spring and the fair, *their* fair, was here at last.

The spectacle of the fair, its very life and vibrancy, seemed to grant permission for all manner of excesses and eccentricities. And Libbie Packard, now a college grad with a Wellesley degree and at least a few months to herself—*she hoped*, oh she hoped—before her mother would start in again, in her committed and tireless way, about marriage prospects, well: she was determined to use that permission any way she saw fit. After all, if one couldn't be a sensualist (or even a hedonist) in the White City, where could one?

Our Libbie Packard put this question to the test on the last night of June. She'd been home from commencement activities at Wellesley for only a handful of days, and thus far she'd spent more time at the fair than anywhere else. In the nearly two months since it had first opened, Libbie's fashionable Chicago friends had learned how best to exploit their connections to curry favorable reservations or invitations.

Which is what they were doing this night.

For hours, Libbie had been flirting wildly, obnoxiously, with

Mr. Simon Everett III. He was Sara Dahlgren's distant cousin, visiting from San Francisco and a real cad (or *sport,* if you were feeling generous). But Simon was also very handsome, and charming
enough for one night.

Libbie had danced with him at a dazzling party held at the Electricity Building and then strolled arm in arm with him through the
vendors. (Where he bought her a bouquet of paper flowers she soon
misplaced.) On the boat ride across the lagoon, as they neared the
Columbian Fountain and felt the spray from its rushing water, she'd
pressed up against him, knowing full well the effect of her cause.
And so when, soon after, they'd gone ashore to spread their picnic blanket on a field of mint, and Simon had led her away from
their party to the nearby fence and behind it—where piles of cable and hulking machines were hidden to keep them from spoiling
the Wooded Isle's pastoral effects—it hadn't seemed significant so
much as inevitable. Libbie had even tried to remember, at the time,
lines from *Madame Bovary* that seemed particularly relevant: *He
drew her farther on to a small pool where duckweeds made a greenness
on the water. Faded water lilies lay motionless between the reeds. At the
noise of their steps in the grass, frogs jumped away to hide themselves.*

Mostly, she felt happy to be young, and adventurous, and desired
in just this way.

There was then the elaborate loosening and shedding of clothing,
the scratch of Simon's moustache paired with the wetness from his
mouth, the far-too-brief pleasure of his hand, which came before
his somewhat skillful entry, his less-skillful thrusting, and his not-
at-all-skillful withdrawal—for this was the manner of contraception
most accessible and favored. From that messiness on, Libbie had
wondered what the appeal of this encounter had really been, for her.
Why she'd entertained it. There was now left only Simon's huffing
and dribbling, the stain on her dress, the sound of the croaking
frogs at the shoreline, which was no longer literary or even particularly pleasant, only loud.

The situation seemed suddenly unnecessary to her, from the
thick wrap of mud on her shoes (she'd sunk down into it while he'd
thrusted) to Simon himself, who was now straightened up and tend-

ing to her in the most careful and unfortunate manner, petting her hand and nearly cooing at her, as if she were a baby elephant at the zoo or some delicate thing on display in a shop window that he might take home and keep all to himself. Libbie dismissed his tender musings and led him back to their picnicking friends, who shared looks. Knowing looks.

And that, Readers, should have been that. Libbie knew that Simon Everett III had no intention of calling on her again. And even if he had, she wouldn't have received him. They did a thing, the thing ended. It should have remained as only a very small dot on the very large map of her life. Nothing more.

Libbie then continued on with her summer. She saw her friends, especially Sara, who was just then enamored with an opera singer and always full of chatter about that. She wrote to invite Alex to come visit in August and was thrilled when she responded yes. She concerned herself with preparations for her fall trip abroad, first with her mother and then, for two months, with Sara and co. She would see Paris, finally, really see it: live within it as a young woman in full bloom. Something would happen in Paris, she felt so certain, something that would make clear to her what to do next. Who to be.

And then, in the middle of August, some seven weeks after her night at the fence with Simon, Libbie experienced a collection of bodily impressions so inchoate that she only became certain of them *as a collection*. It took them all for her to notice: the miss of her monthly time, her finicky appetite, the nausea that swept in to overwhelm her, and then dissipated almost as quickly. By week eight she was certain. She was pregnant.

And Alex was to arrive in three days for her grand summer adventure in Chicago.

For those days, Libbie lingered alone with this very bad knowledge: the knowledge that she'd let herself get pregnant with Simon Everett III's baby.*

And also the very bad knowledge that she did not want a child.

---

* Simon Everett IV?

And she certainly did not want Simon Everett III's. She never wanted to see Simon Everett again.

For three days, Libbie went over and around this and back around.

And then, that night on the stairs, the night of Alex the Flirt's arrival, she told. Not in all that detail, but the short of it: who the man was and how she'd allowed this to happen. And Alex, her Alex, looked like she might sink under the tide of this news. And there they were standing in the middle of a staircase, so that wouldn't do at all. And then—

In through the big front door came Libbie's parents and a train of people behind, people they'd invited back from the fair for an after-party. They were loud and gay and champagne drunk.

"Oh, you are home!" Libbie's mother said when she saw her daughter on the stairs. She came up to meet them. "Oh wonderful! You're not thinking of going to bed, are you? We've brought the celebration back with us."

"I see that," Libbie said, looking past her mother and the people still filtering in through the front door. She dared not look at Alex next to her. She could not.

If Mr. and Mrs. Packard were this merry train's engine, then its caboose was none other than Harold Brookhants, *the* Harold Brookhants, with *the* Madame Verrett at his side.

"Well at least come and say hello to everyone and introduce Alexandra," Mrs. Packard said as she turned to join her guests. "Before you again abscond in the night. Everyone said they barely saw you at the reception, you were stuck in the corner."

"Hardly that, Mother," Libbie said, starting down the stairs with Alex coming, too. What else could they do now? It would cause such a scene to ignore everyone when here they were plainly awake and still dressed and standing in the middle of the staircase.

"It's wonderful to see you again, Mr. Brookhants," Libbie said, as Harold took her hand and kissed it.

"It's much more wonderful for me to see you," Harold said. "You look radiant tonight, Miss Packard—full of the force of life."

"Well I don't feel it," Libbie said. "I'm afraid my mother guessed right and we were headed to bed. Miss Trills only arrived today by train from Providence, and I haven't let her sit for more than five minutes since she got here."

"Oh, but she's so young and strong, she can manage," Madame Verrett said, plainly appraising them both up and down with her violet eyes.

"Have we met?" Libbie asked her.

"Not formally," the Madame said. "I came here tonight to meet you."

"You did?" Libbie said, surprised. She smiled at the Madame as if in on her joke, but the woman did not smile back and did not seem to be joking.

"Forgive me," Harold said. "What a goat I am, never fails. Miss Libbie Packard, this is the Great Madame Verrett of Gascogne and"—Harold now looked rather helplessly at Alex—"I'm afraid I didn't catch your name, miss."

"Alexandra Trills," Alex said. She was clearly still so stunned from the news on the stairs that she hadn't quite returned to form. "Libbie and I met at Wellesley," she added.

"Ah, college sweethearts," Madame Verrett said. "So chic, so American. Though of course your way cannot produce a child. Not yet."

Libbie's heart shuffled like a deck of cards. She could not find words of response.

Alex had some: "What a peculiar thing to say."

"Was it?" the Madame asked.

"Yes," Alex said. "Very."

"I'm sure I have no idea of your meaning," Libbie said.

"I should think you have every idea of my meaning," Madame Verrett said.

"Odette," Harold said. "Not now."

"Why else have we come here?" the Madame asked, her earrings clinking with the force of her indignation. "Never say *not now* to me again, Harold."

"Everyone's moving into the garden for ice-cream floats and cherry brandy," Mrs. Packard called as she swept back into the foyer. "Darling, why have you stalled our guests at the front door?" she said to Libbie as she plucked a curl at Libbie's neck. "Your hair has gone so limp in this humidity. You can't say you get that from me."

"No, your style stays very firm, doesn't it?" Madame Verrett said to her.

"Yes, it does." Mrs. Packard seemed unsure if she'd been complimented or insulted.

"We were just meeting Miss Trills," Harold said in explanation. "Who is understandably worn out from her long journey. We'd be beasts to keep her awake one moment longer."

"Yes, I suppose that's true," Mrs. Packard said as if this had not previously occurred to her. "You know, both of you girls do look tired. Run along to bed. I'll make your excuses."

"You do need your sleep," Madame Verrett agreed. "Now more than ever." She looked only at Libbie when she said this.

"Why do you say that?" Mrs. Packard asked her.

"Because the great fair is here, of course," Madame Verrett said, taking her host's arm. "And it takes so much from all of us to take it in as we should."

"I haven't heard it put quite like that," Mrs. Packard said.

"Oh, then you must stay close to me," Madame Verrett said. "I know all the best ways to put things. Now will you show me the way to this brandy?"

Once they'd left the room, Harold said, "You go on to bed now, girls. And tomorrow, please come see me for lunch. Both of you. I'll send my driver."

While Andrew Carnegie might have set the standard for businessmen who had done well by Pittsburgh, he was only the guy at the top of that ladder. It was a ladder with many, many rungs, and on one of those rungs, within reaching distance of Carnegie's trouser hems, stood Harold Brookhants.

Although, and this is worth noting, Harold Brookhants's standing did not begin and end with the vast sums of money he had made in turn-of-the-century Pittsburgh. Harold Brookhants could trace his American lineage back to before the Revolutionary War, and he could additionally trace the starting point for his substantial familial holdings to the years after that war.

In fact, had he settled more firmly in Manhattan (he had a château-style house there, but was not often found in it), married earlier (and a bit more carefully), and worked with any diligence at it, he could have out-Astored the Astors in a quest for social preeminence. But securing and maintaining a position within the Four Hundred* was of no interest to Harold Brookhants. His interest was in securing and maintaining a position within the afterlife.

Did I mention, Readers, that Harold Brookhants was old? I mean *really* old. Sixty-six to Libbie's then twenty-two; a chasm of more than forty years between them.[†]

So Harold Brookhants was very rich, an American blue blood, and now quite old. Because all three of those things could be said truthfully of him, he was allowed considerable leeway when it came to his eccentricities, of which there were many.[‡] You should know

---

* Mrs. Caroline Schermerhorn Astor's attempt at drawing the gates around the, in her mind, true blue bloods, the old-money and manners names in New York society, as opposed to the gate-crashing new-money crowd. (If you're thinking that it's all rather stupid, Readers, so did Harold Brookhants.)

† He commanded for the Union in the Civil War, for fuck's sake.

‡ For now, let me try to condense the full of Harold Brookhants's oddities into a single story that illustrates how rashly he would spend his money to fulfill even his most unconventional desire. Though history (incorrectly) gives the credit for the following dubious scheme to William Waldorf Astor (or Lord Astor, as he was known in Britain, where he lived), it was actually Harold himself who came up with the idea, which was to have a giant redwood tree, one that had grown for centuries in Northern California—and was nearly thirty-five stories tall, with a base forty-four feet in diameter—felled. Harold did this with the sole purpose of having a table-sized slice cut from the trunk and then shipped all the way to Pittsburgh so that he could have it lowered by crane into the home he was constructing, obviously before its roof was put on. For years after he used it as a séance table, one that could comfortably seat up to fifty guests. And he used it often.

So while Lord Astor *did* later make a drunken bet about the size of Californian redwoods, and then had a tree of his own felled, and a table-sized section of its

that before marrying Libbie Packard, he was a confirmed bachelor. And not just any confirmed bachelor, but the kind of *confirmed bachelor* the very term was coined to elucidate.

The other thing you should know about him, the thing he told Alex and Libbie the next day at lunch in the private dining room at the block-long Palmer Hotel, is that he was dying.

"Should be dead already," he said. "Ought to be, but Madame Verrett has me feeling fine."

"For now," Madame Verrett said. "And not for much longer." She was consulting a menu.

"The lemon ice," she called out to a waiter across the room, though her rudeness didn't matter to anyone but Alex and Libbie. The dining room, with its mirror-shined mahogany paneling and enormous coffered ceiling dripping crystal chandeliers, was empty: Harold had rented it out for their party. Which, with the fair at its peak, must have cost a fortune.

They'd been there not half an hour, and Madame Verrett had thus far ordered, seemingly at random, eleven different items off the menu. Of those, she had pronounced two *fair* and another *edible*. The rest she had declared an embarrassment.

"I'm very sorry to hear that you're in such poor health, Mr. Brookhants," Libbie said.

"Well, but I have lived a full life, haven't I?" Harold said. "In this world."

"I'm also sorry for your news," Alex said. "Though I'm still not sure why you've asked us here to tell it."

"Yes, you are," Madame Verrett said. "None of that."

"I'm in a position to help you, Libbie," Harold said. "We can help each other."

"Miss Packard doesn't need your help," Alex said.

"Does your sweetheart always speak for you?" Madame Verrett

---

trunk shipped to his London house (the ocean voyage probably adds to the appalling excess of the story, which is why Astor's version gets remembered), it was actually Harold Brookhants who set the precedent.

asked as she produced a small blue vial and tipped several drops of some fragrant liquid into her wine.

"Isn't that something you should already know?" Alex asked her. "As a clairvoyant?"

"Of course I do know," Madame Verrett said. "This is why I'm making mention of it—so that she also notices."

"I want to hear what you're suggesting," Libbie said to Harold. "I want to hear what anyone can suggest to me about how to unmake this mess I've made."

"An unmaking, my dear, is but one of your options," Madame Verrett said. "And not the one Harold is interested in."

"All of this is *mad*," Alex said. "It's mad for us even to be here right now. I—"

"You can say that as often as you like," Madame Verrett said. "But only naming it as such does not make it true. You have to believe it. And you don't. You know why you're here and so does she."

"I think we should leave now, Libbie," Alex said, putting her napkin on the table. "I think we shouldn't have come at all."

"I want to hear what Mr. Brookhants has to say to me," Libbie said. "I'm sorry if that hurts you, but it's my decision to make."

"It's a man you scarcely know who's the cause of this," Alex tried again. She lowered her voice, though it was impossible to speak to Libbie privately at this moment. "You don't need the counsel of another strange man. *We* can find a solution together."

"But we haven't found one," Libbie said.

"We've had all of one morning to discuss it!"

"What solutions are there, really, that you could help her with, child?" Madame Verrett said to Alex. "If marrying the father is out of the question."

"It is," Libbie and Alex said together.

"Yes," Madame Verrett said. "So, you see, don't you? Infinitely more complicated. All of this is not *mad*, as you put it, it's fate. I see you at the fair yesterday when you're trying so hard for me *not* to see you, and Harold sees you and understands at once what you are to each other, a living line from Sappho—and with Harold so in need, and you so in need. It's fate. So we'll sit together here until you lis-

"I'm in a position to help you, Libbie," Harold said.
"We can help each other."

ten, and I'll try to find even one thing to eat. I'm so hungry, always, in this country. I hate it."

"I'm listening now," Libbie said. "Please go on, Mr. Brookhants."

He nodded, seemed to gather his words again. "We're alike," he eventually said. "I think you know that already, don't you?" He smiled at her, almost shyly.

"I'm not sure I do know," Libbie said.

He gathered more words. "In the way we love, that is—our own kind. I love men as you love women."

"Well, at least one time she loved a man as you love men," Madame Verrett said. Then she took a very loud bite of the very large lemon ice that had just been served to her in a sweating silver chalice and added, "Here we are, after all."

Harold ignored her. "I've always wanted a child, but—with the way I am, I didn't know quite how. I didn't want to marry, not even as a ruse. I don't think you do, either. Am I right about that?"

"You are," Libbie said. "For now. Today I don't."

"It's much simpler for a man not to, of course. Not *easy*, always, for a man like me. But much simpler than for a woman." You could tell he was building up to something: one eye had gone twitchy and he'd puffed up his chest a bit. "But if *we* were to marry—"

"You could be her grandfather!" Alex said. "It's preposterous."

"It does seem very unlikely," Libbie said as if there were many other crueler words she could have chosen than *unlikely*.

"It's obscene," Alex said. "If Libbie's going to marry someone to hide this, she'll find someone her own age. Or closer to. She'd have choices."

"Not many, in her condition," Madame Verrett said, scooping another bite of her ice. "This I like," she said. "It's tart and cold."

"I don't think—" Libbie said.

"Please," Harold said. "Please let me finish."

She nodded at him to go on.

He did. "I have money. I have more of it than you could spend in twenty lifetimes. I have a beautiful house in Pittsburgh and one in New York and one in France, of course." He smiled at the Madame, who was still looking at her ice. "But the one I've been building on the ocean in Rhode Island is the most special of them all. Or it will be, when I'm finished with it. It comes with land—it's touched, this land. Madame Verrett led me to it and it's full of the most magnificent vitality. It hums with it. I want to establish a school there, that's what this land wants—I feel so sure of it—a school for young women, and now I know the woman to run that school. The *women.*" For the first time since he'd begun his pitch, he looked at Alex.

She looked away.

Harold didn't let this deter him. "I don't have much time left in this realm, Libbie. Or on this earth, if you prefer. You could let me do this for you before I leave. I could give you such a beautiful life in this special place. It's a remarkable place, you'd need only visit once to know that. And you both could live so happily there. It would be private, entirely your own, and you'd soon be a very young widow with the protection of your husband's name and could run it for years and years with the money I'll leave you. Even with no students, you could stay open. But of course you will have students, too many even to take them all, I imagine."

"No need to imagine," Madame Verrett said. "It would be so. For a time."

"Why would you do this for me?" Libbie asked him.

"I like you," Harold said. "I always have liked you. But this I'd be doing for me as much as for you. I told you, I've long wanted a child of my own."

"Yes, but I don't and you're dying," Libbie said. She only seemed to realize the force of what she'd said once she had. "I'm sorry, Mr. Brookhants, I am. I don't mean to be cruel, but you're saying I'd be a young widow there in a house on the ocean, and now I'd be a young widowed mother."

"Her child wouldn't be your child anyway," Alex said. Unlike Libbie, she no longer cared how she sounded to either of them. She'd had enough of this nonsense. "It would be Simon Everett's bastard."

"That is not *entirely* correct," Madame Verrett said. She burped into her napkin and then added, "There are things that can still be done. Quickly, very quickly. You're two months along?"

"Yes, about," Libbie said. Madame Verrett's accuracy prickled her skin.

"It's not what we'd call ideal," Madame Verrett said. "But it is still possible to effect a change. Possible." She picked at her teeth and looked, frankly, quite bored with the three of them.

"Yes, so here we are at the troubling bit," Harold said.

"Oh, is *this* the troubling bit?" Alex asked. "Oh good."

"It all gets rather complicated from here and I'm not sure how much you would even want to know about my beliefs, or where to start to help explain this in a way that you could understand. I have some books I might lend you, but for the purpose of—"

Madame Verrett held up her hand. "Harold, Harold, Harold—no. No, no, no. Please. I did not come here for the food." She pushed her sweating silver chalice away and now faced Libbie and Alex as their teacher, a position that suited her. "In the natural world," she said, using her hands for emphasis, there in the air above the table, as she spoke, "there is energy that can be transmuted even as it is forming. This is common enough, if you know where to look for it. Harold is too old now to have a child without *some form* of assistance, anyway." She looked closely at him for a moment or two. "Yes, I think so. It would be difficult. So now, instead, I will give the same kind of assistance to him *after* a child has already been conceived. It's different, but the same, in the end it's the same—it becomes Harold's child, too."

"*Assistance*?" Alex asked like the word itself was rotten.

"It is a single ceremony," Madame Verrett said. "Only a matter of hours, at least at the start—to make the necessary change. It will be done at my house in France, with my sisters near. There are two nights we might choose from, though one is better than the other, for reasons you cannot understand so I won't give them to you. And then you'll hide your pregnancy there, in France. None but we would know. And after, you'll come back to your new home, and school, on the ocean."

"After?" Libbie asked.

"After you deliver the child," Madame Verrett said, as if she should not have to do so.

"This is preposterous," Alex said. "It's—"

Libbie interrupted. "I don't want a child. Whether or not you could do any of what you just said, whatever it is you just said." She looked forcefully at Madame Verrett. "I don't want to be a mother. I don't want a child."

"I know!" Harold said. "That's why it's so perfect. She would be *my* child, not yours. Not if you didn't want her to be."

"I don't," Libbie said.

"She?" Alex said. "So now you're certain of that as well?"

"It would be a girl," Madame Verrett said like she'd just told them it was a Wednesday, which it was.

"This is a farce," Alex said. "It's a farce. That or I never woke up this morning. Maybe I'm still asleep on the train crossing Ohio."

"Aren't they funny?" Madame Verrett said to her. "They don't match at all."

"Aren't what funny?" Alex said.

"The things you say aloud," the Madame said. "Compared to the things you think, I mean."

Alex stood with such force that her chair nearly toppled behind her. It rocked on two legs before settling. She touched Libbie's shoulder. "I'm going. You stay if you want to hear more of this."

"No, I'll come, too," Libbie said. She also pushed her chair away from the table, but then seemed to hesitate over her decision, unsure.

"Of course," Harold said, standing. "We don't have to cover everything in one luncheon, after all. Such big decisions. And I know it's so much to think about when you're already thinking about so much. I want you to know that I do understand your skepticism, dear girl. And your reluctance."

"I appreciate you—" Libbie said. She stopped, started again. "I don't know quite—I—it's very kind of you to have offered me so much, Mr. Brookhants." She stopped again, shook her head. "I don't understand your offer, I don't think. But I can see how generous it is, under the circumstances, and I want you to know what that means to me."

"Please think carefully about this, Libbie," he said. "Please? You still have time to consider what's best for you."

Madame Verrett squinted her face in disagreement as her un-stated objection, and then decided to go ahead and state it. "You have a little time. You do not have endless time."

"No one on earth has endless time," Alex said as she took Libbie's hand to pull her away.

"Ahhh!" Madame Verrett said, smiling. "Now you see, this thing you *do* believe, and you've said it out loud. Good for you! This is progress. Unfortunately, this thing you believe isn't true. There *are* some with endless time, both on this earth and elsewhere. And there are others, like Harold, who use their lives to make more time. But as you don't know that, or didn't until I just told it to you, at least it's not yet another thing you were thinking while you said the opposite."

"I'd prefer it if you never spoke to me again," Alex said.

"Aha! Another true thing! I am indeed the miracle worker they call me in the papers!"

Part Two

....

THE

HAPPENINGS

AT

BROOKHANTS

Now I will send my Portrayal into the wise wide world. It may stop short at the publisher; or it may fall still-born from the press; or it may go farther, indeed, and may be its own undoing.

That's as may be.

I will send it.

What else is there for me, if not this book?

—MARY MACLANE, *The Story of Mary MacLane*

Woodrow kindly said: "So, you've started writing again. Novel?"

"A report. An account. Yes, I'll call it a novel. If I ever finish it. Of course, I never do finish anything."

—TRUMAN CAPOTE, *Answered Prayers*

WHAT TO MAKE OF THIS ARRANGEMENT?

....

Despite having grown up on and around film sets, **Audrey Wells** shivered as they rose over the crest of a hill and she caught her first glimpse of Spite Manor and its infamous tower. Even at this distance, there was something deeply disquieting about the way it shot up from the house like an arm raised in distress.

It's a mistake to be here, she thought.

The more Audrey tried to sink that thought, the more buoyancy it gained, floating to the surface of her consciousness and bobbing there.

I shouldn't be doing this.

Carl (the driver) had picked her up at T. F. Green airport in War-wick and they had been in the car together—one in a fleet of SUVs and vans that would be used by *The Happenings at Brookhants* production—for longer than she'd anticipated.

At first, the traffic was dense ("Weekendas headed to the cape," said Carl), but then, as they left the freeway for a two-lane road replete with tar snakes, the landscape turned to sections of shady woods that merged into lush farmland and back again, occasional glimpses of bay or bog throughout. Soon the road narrowed until farm stands cluttered along its side, bearing rows of cucumbers and squash, corn and potatoes. Patrons stood squeezing the tomatoes they would eventually purchase, place in their canvas bags, and take back to their coastal homes (or end-of-summer rentals).

Eventually, the road cut through a town square that was part Currier and Ives, part Instagram bait: an ice-cream stand, a strip of antiques dealers, a deli housed in a renovated 1800s mercantile with patriotic bunting hanging from its windows and pots of geraniums flanking its entrance. Audrey recognized the deli from Merritt's book. She'd interviewed locals there.

When Carl turned again, it was onto a road with a security booth; a gate blocked their path. The gate slid open for them with only a wave to the guard working the controls.

Now, and for the last several minutes, they'd been on this private road. Rhode Island was supposed to be a tiny state, Audrey knew, and yet the Brookhants property managed to feel quite isolated.

And then they came through a copse˙ of trees and their view was dominated by the flashing blue of the water to one side and Spite Manor to the other. Audrey couldn't help herself. She let out a *wow.* If not for the production equipment trucks parked beneath the shade of a spread-limb maple tree, she might have let herself believe that Carl had been tasked with driving her into the past.

"Not bad, huh?" he said.

"Yeah, no, definitely not bad." She smiled at him.

"It's a pretty spot." Carl, Readers, was most adept at understatement.

Audrey rolled down her window. The wide view of the water was lovely, but she was a California girl and had seen similar a time or two. But the house, Spite Manor, was what Carl might call *really something.* Charming in a glimpse, perhaps, at least until you really looked at it and realized its various components added up to something slightly off: the wiggling worm in your farm stand tomato.

The house was clad in weathered shake siding, a skin of gray scales, its many windows and doors trimmed in crisp white and deep green. It wore its enormous shake roof like a straw hat, eaves extending to shade its low porches entirely, as if those porches were the house's face, its window eyes hidden under the roof's brim. The porches held antique wicker rocking chairs and hanging ferns. Spite Manor was anchored, on one side, by an impressive, vine-covered fieldstone chimney, and on the other by its even more impressive tower.

˙ Troubling, isn't it, what the addition of an *r* does to that word?

As they pulled up the driveway, the expanse of the house filled the windshield, and Audrey noticed a distinct shift in the noise beneath the wheels. They were now driving on crushed seashells, thousands of pieces slipping and spraying over each other.

"Just put these down and they stink like it," Carl said.

He was right. The shells smelled like dead fish in a dirty ocean. But Audrey fixated on their sound, the way they chimed as they fell against each other, like someone gathering a sack of broken dishes. It's true she was drowsy from lack of sleep, *and* from the flight, *and* from the drive in the summer heat, but Audrey felt certain this sound could hypnotize her if she let it.

She tried to focus on something else, looking up into the row of glinting windows at the top of Spite Tower. She flinched, startled. There was a person standing behind one of them.

Audrey squinted and decided the dark outline belonged to Elaine Brookhants, still as a stuck scarecrow and staring, watching the advance of this Hollywood invader from her perch. Audrey held up her hand as they neared the base of the tower. She couldn't tell if Elaine acknowledged her or not, because the window kept glinting and they kept on driving.

They continued on to the back of the house, the trees soon dense around them, canopied above them, their roots stretching across the road, which was no longer shell but knobby dirt.

"Bet you're gonna like these, too," Carl said as the SUV bounced in the ruts. "They're cute. That's what Pete said when I brought her, anyway." Carl had already told Audrey that Pete was his nickname for Harper Harper, apparently his refashioning of the joke *I'm Pete and this is my brother Repeat* in recognition of her double name.

The cute things Carl had been referring to were the tiny houses production had hauled onto the property. And Pete was right: they were cute. They were also strikingly modern when compared to the house they'd just passed. Three in a row, identical, tall and narrow and abundant in black metal windows; each was capped with a small roof deck that fit two Adirondack chairs and a shade umbrella. The drop down to the bay was not more than twenty yards from their front doors.

They were also—and this was the second time in less than twenty minutes that Audrey had considered this word—*isolated*.

"There's Pete now," Carl said. Clearly Harper had won him over.

She was hanging half of her body out the front door of the tiny house nearest to where they'd parked, her arms braced hard against the doorframe to keep from falling into the grass. She smiled and squinted in their direction. Then she went back into the house and when she popped out again she wore purply-teal sunglasses with mirrored lenses. She was down on the grass and approaching them as Carl opened his door.

Along with those sunglasses, Harper was wearing pale pink swim shorts spread with green alligators and a green bikini top, her stomach flat and one shade tan. And she was barefoot with the requisite cigarette behind her ear. Audrey felt suddenly overly attired, even in her simple white-and-blue summer romper.

"Surprised you didn't get her lost," Harper said to Carl.

"Who told you I didn't?" His grin was now the size of his face.

Harper came around to Audrey's door. "I've been in there waiting on you," she said, pulling Audrey into a hug. "How was your trip?"

"It was good," Audrey said to the back of Harper's neck, which smelled of sunscreen and cigarettes. "This place is unreal."

"I know, right?" Harper said. "And you haven't even been over to the school yet. Or have you?"

"No," Audrey said. "We came right here."

"This is where they told me to bring her," Carl said. He was hanging back, letting them talk, but he wanted this point made.

"Well you can't trust this guy," Harper said, jerking a thumb in his direction. "I bet he *was* supposed to take you to campus first. You're probably missing something crucial right now."

"She always laying it on this thick?" Carl asked Audrey.

"I feel like I can say yes," Audrey said, again marveling at how quickly Harper seemed to have bonded with him, which prompted her next question: "How long have you been here?"

"Like *here*, here?" Harper asked.

Audrey nodded.

"Just a day. I came out this way early because I did a week in Provincetown with my mom and my little brother. Then we were in Newport yesterday. It's over there." Harper pointed across the water. "I could see the lights from the mansions last night. We should buy binoculars and watch the Vanderbilts drink champagne."

Carl snorted at that. "All you'd see is tourists with their phones out."

"Carl's not a big fan of tourists," Harper said. "We the evil summer people."

Carl shrugged like he didn't disagree.

"Is your family still here?" Audrey asked her.

Harper shook her head. "They left this morning. Ethan's gotta get back for school. It's just been me and Carl ever since, so you know I'm glad to see you."

"The lady of the manor hasn't asked you over for lawn tennis?" Audrey asked.

"What now?" Harper smiled like she knew there was a joke in there but couldn't decipher it.

"I just meant Elaine," Audrey said quickly. She gestured through the trees in the general direction of Spite Manor, feeling self-conscious about her attempt at humor. "Brookhants. You haven't seen her?"

"No, I don't think she's even here yet," Harper said. "She's still traveling or something." She lowered her voice to a goofy, caper-planning register, and said, "But we've gotta get into that house, right?"

"I thought I just saw her," Audrey said. "When we pulled in."

"Maybe she's back," Harper said.

"She's not," Carl called. His head and shoulder were submerged inside the open hatch of the SUV. He was gathering pieces of Audrey's luggage. "She won't be here until Friday."

Audrey made a *how does he know* face at Harper, who explained, "Carl's family's worked here since back in the day. He's, like, connected to the curse by blood."

"Wait, are you an Eckhart?" Audrey asked, another dumb shiver fluttering along her spine.

"All my life," Carl said. He stood in front of them now, his arms loaded with Audrey's various bags. "Which one is yours?" he asked her, nodding at the tiny houses.

"I don't know," she said.

"I think they stocked the fridge in the middle one for you," Harper said. "But otherwise they're all the same and you can for sure have the one I've got my stuff in if for some reason you like it better."

"Oh, no, I'm fine with whatever," Audrey said. "And the other one's for Merritt?"

"Yep," Harper said.

"But she's not here?" Audrey said.

"Nope," Harper said. "Not yet. Maybe not at all."

Audrey wasn't unhappy about this news.

Between the three of them, they decided that Audrey had probably seen some member of the crew up in the tower. According to Carl they'd been there all week, readying the rooms for filming. He drove away as soon as he'd hauled the luggage inside. And after touring her around the immediate area and giving her the Wi-Fi info, Harper left Audrey alone in the surprisingly airy main room of her tiny house. She was now supposed to settle in for a few hours before they joined up again to head over to the campus proper, where Bo would meet them.

Audrey liked the house she'd been given, at least in the bright afternoon light. Its many windows let in the crash of the ocean in front and the sounds of the woods behind. Its fridge was filled with her (contractually specified) favorites—cartons of fresh berries and cashew cheese, grapefruit seltzer and glass bottles of real-sugar Coca-Cola—and there were jars of pretzels and peanut butter M&Ms on the counter. There was also a bouquet of rather ostentatiously large and blue hydrangeas on the dining bar. The card attached read:

> So glad/lucky to have you here. Can't wait to get started making something real.

> —Bo

(P.S. When MM visited Rhode Island she called its hy-drangeas "fascinating and false—like many, many other things in Newport-by-the-sea.")

Audrey texted Noel, Caroline, Noel, Noel, Noel. She unpacked. She listened to a long, encouraging voice mail from Rachel, the acting coach she'd been working with pretty much nonstop on how to Clara Broward better. She read two emails from production with various complicated instructions. Then she thought about wandering down to the private beach where Harper had said she was heading. But sleep, or an attempt at it, sounded better. Audrey had not slept easily since that day in Bo's home office when he'd said he was putting all the cards on the table about this movie and his plans for her part in it.

Actually, remembering Readers, it was for one night even longer than that, since she'd not slept well the night before that had happened, either: the night of the yellow jackets in the kitchen sink.

Now that she was here, on the property, now that it was all actually starting, she hoped that maybe sleep would come.

It did not.

And it would not.

ALEX SEES THINGS IN STEREOVIEW

··················

Alex the Liar* hadn't been sleeping, either, Readers.

She struggled to keep her eyes open in The Orangerie's oppressive heat. They felt like they'd been wrapped in starched wool.

She yawned. She blinked and blinked again. Then she brought the stereoscope to her face and looked through its lenses at the image she'd selected. She squinted and it grew blurrier, so she pulled back, repositioned, and relaxed her eyes until the photo shifted into its crispest three-dimensional form. She couldn't be careless. She had to be certain.

She *was* certain. The image had changed. Even since yesterday.

She pulled the card from the viewer and placed it at the bottom of her stack. These were the very same *stimulating* stereo cards that (galling) Sara Dahlgren had brought over from Paris last summer. Had brought over from Paris for Libbie. They'd become infected, Alex had determined, after she'd stupidly used them as bookmarks in Clara Broward's copy of *The Story of Mary MacLane*.

That was a mistake she'd not soon make again.

Although perhaps nothing at Brookhants happened by accident anymore. Perhaps it never had to begin with, not since Harold had lured them here.

(Not since Alex had encouraged him to.)

There were fourteen infected images in total, which meant Alex still had nine to go.

----

* For reasons that will soon become clear: this is how Alex had been referring to herself in her head since Eleanor Faderman had died.

A fat drop of sweat rolled off the end of her nose and landed on top of her notepad. It briefly magnified the final *o-n-e* of the word *anemone* before absorbing into the paper. Another bead of sweat rolled into her right eye, leaving it stinging as she picked up her pen to add the following note, avoiding the sweat spot so as not to tear the paper: **Woman standing has blue anemone tucked behind ear. Woman kneeling has blue anemone stem between teeth.**

Alex had been checking the cards since February 6. Today was the seventeenth. In that time, the image had changed from showing one blue anemone in the bouquet at the base of the curtain to now containing *only* blue anemones.

She fanned herself with her notebook, though it did little good.

To Alex's knowledge, no one had formally tended to The Orangerie's plants since the start of the spring term some weeks before, but they seemed to prefer this. There was now something unquestionably depraved in their growth, something abhorrent. They smothered the windows, so that from the outside one could no longer see in, and the daylight that filtered through took on the eerie green of swamp gas. Vines had tangled into knots that could school sailors, and the citrus trees, though still producing enormous fruits, no longer had enough students to eat them. Instead, they fell to the ground and rotted there, leaving a cloying stench in the air and calling to the ubiquitous fruit flies, which sometimes swarmed so thickly that Alex could swipe through the air and come up with a palmful of them.

And all of this was to say nothing of the heat. It was, after all, winter at Brookhants. Even with The Orangerie's cantankerous heating system operating at its fullest ability, it should have been drafty inside these walls of glass, even downright cold in places.

Instead, Alex now flicked more sweat from her eyelid.

She knew that soon enough she would have to stop this unnatural takeover. No one else could be counted on to see it for what it was and to take action. But for this moment, she was grateful for the privacy offered by The Orangerie.

Alex also felt that she owed it to Eleanor Faderman to spend time in the place where the girl died. It was important not to let herself forget that Eleanor had died. And how. Sometimes Alex thought she should be trying to spend time in the Tricky Thicket too, since that's where Flo and Clara had met their ends. But it was harder to reach the thicket in winter. And the truth is, Readers, while Alex mourned their deaths—of course she did—she simply did not feel for them the same level of sorrow and regret that she did for Eleanor.

Lonely and alone Eleanor Faderman: Alex had failed her.

Whereas Flo and Clara had brought Mary MacLane's book to Brookhants. And they'd started that club—and whatever wrong went with it out in the woods. Some of the blame for all of this surely wreathed their necks, too.

Alex believed that if Flo and Clara were somehow victims of the book, then Eleanor Faderman was most a victim of them—of their bad influence. *They* were dynamic older girls with campus stature. Eleanor Faderman had been only a wispy ghost mooning about in their shadows.

So what if Alex gave the bulk of her sympathy to poor Eleanor? Someone should.

Alex slid the next stereo card into place. This was the image of the woman in top hat and tails holding hands with the woman seated before her on a settee. The two of them grinning so garishly at each other that they seemed to have fish bones jammed cheek to cheek to stretch their mouths.

But something had changed: the wallpaper.

Where there had once been fuzzy fleurs-de-lis now were angel's trumpet flowers, long and white with gape-mouthed ends, popping from between the stripes in mocking clarity.

Alex wiped more perspiration from the nape of her neck. She slid the card to the bottom of her stack, added another from the top. She needed to finish and get outside to meet the carriage before she was missed.

If Libbie would miss her. Rather hard to say, at the moment.

She forced herself to stay on task, noting new putrefaction in each image, all fourteen. Some cards revealed only small changes or ad-

ditions, such as a cloud of black smoke on a window, or the creep of rot down a curtain, a few black specks hovering in the air that might be yellow jackets, but several of the images were now altered with monstrous significance.

Image #9: Scene painted on the three-paneled screen in background depicts an orchard of gnarled trees bearing black apples. Previously that screen bore a painting of healthy, fruitless trees.

Image #13: In the original, uncorrupted incarnation of this image, two women lounged together on the bed reading a magazine that the smaller woman held for them both to see. Now, that woman is holding a copy of *The Story of Mary MacLane*. Although the book's title is too minuscule to read, its binding is clearly tinted red. This while the rest of the image remains in black-and-white. *

---

* Despite its simplicity, to Alex, this was the most egregious change of all.

When, some weeks before, Libbie had started her unnecessary tutoring of Adelaide, Alex had used those newly free hours to start, in earnest, her evidence-gathering. She would document the foul things afoot at Brookhants, maintaining a careful record, until she'd not only convinced herself, but had enough proof to convince Libbie as well.

She already had Flo and Clara's copy of *The Story of Mary Mac-Lane,* and it was surely the key item, but each day she found yet more corroboration that she could not rationally explain. Like these stereoscope cards, for instance. She'd slipped several inside the book to mark the entries she wanted to discuss with Libbie. Only Libbie had become so cross when Alex had broached the subject, so dismissive. (At the moment she was unwilling to talk about it at all.) So Alex was left to do the work herself, to scan its marginalia for clues and to guess about its missing page.*

One night, doing this, she'd noticed a black growth in the corner of one of the cards she'd been using as a bookmark. She could see it even without the stereoscope, but *with* the viewer the problem became so much clearer to her.

Alex's working hypothesis was assembled from bits of local lore, which held that Brookhants had been cursed since the days of the Rash brothers, owing to the brothers' unnatural means of assuring their farm's success. Alex thought that perhaps, over time, that curse's efficacy had diminished. That is, until someone or something came along and allowed it to take root again. Someone like Harold Brookhants, for instance, with Madame Verrett stoking his belief.†

---

* Alex had several pet theories about the missing page, but the most likely of them (she thought) was that it contained handwritten instructions for some Plain Bad Heroine Society ritual or invocation, and that it had been deliberately removed by one of the club's remaining members to keep it from being discovered after the book was found with the bodies. That or Eleanor had simply taken it, for purposes unknown.

† It's true, Readers, that Harold Brookhants had never hidden his interest in the Rash brothers and their famous feud. As you know, he'd incorporated that feud's resulting tower into his otherwise modern home. It's also notable that, though money

Wasn't it at least *possible* that Harold had stirred up a wasp nest of trouble here by poking into things that he should have let be, and that even now, years after his death, that trouble still hadn't subsided? And then a certain desperate book, written by an arrogant and wanton girl, made its landing on campus. A book that other desperate and misguided girls placed far too much stock in.

A book ripe to carry a curse.

Mary MacLane had written her portrayal with the purpose of escaping her dull domestic life as an unhappy daughter in Butte, Montana. She not only made no secret of this, she shouted it from the page. And what's more, it had worked. She'd become famous and, at least for a time, financially independent, with a means to procure more money as soon as she was willing to write another book of the same sort. (Or worse, Alex guessed. Her next book would almost certainly be worse. It would have to be, wouldn't it, to make anyone notice?)

Was it really more inconceivable to believe that Mary MacLane herself might have made some dark deal to ensure her astounding success than it was to believe that she hadn't? That such unexpected, nearly overnight great-good fortune had fallen out of the sky and into her lap? Over and again in her book she called out to the Devil—her *Kind Devil*—to end her drab loneliness: *It hurts—oh, it tortures me in the days and days! But when the Devil brings me my Happiness, I will forgive him all this.*

Why should it be so impossible to believe that this Kind Devil would welcome the chance to trod his hooves around a school such as theirs, one filled with girls who thought themselves to be the same as their beloved Mary MacLane?

Mary MacLane really wasn't *so* remarkable or talented or genius. Not really. It's just that she put to paper the things that other girls

---

was certainly no barrier, Harold chose to purchase land in Little Compton for his summer estate. This when nearly all of his friend-enemies were building their much grander homes in more fashionable Newport.

had the good sense not to, the *moral courage* not to. Whereas Mary MacLane only had her Devil egging her along toward notoriety.

Alex saw very clearly how dangerous a book like Mary's could become in the hands of such impressionable girls, such privileged girls: girls who kissed and fondled and laughed as they read each other passages out in the woods; girls whose parents' social standing had taught them that there was nothing at all in the world they could not subjugate, purchase, or ignore; girls who set fires only to watch as others tried, and failed, to put them out.

What could be the harm in destroying this single, festering copy of such a book? For if there was even the slightest chance that it was the cause or conduit of their current troubles, wouldn't it be better to do so? Even if some people might believe the action rash? Or benighted. (Even if Alex herself would have always thought the same. Before now, that is. Before now she would have . . .)

And anyway, hadn't Alex lost all authority to argue such things when she'd come here to be with Libbie? When her Libbie had agreed to Harold Brookhants's offer? (Or had agreed to enough of it, at any rate?) Here Alex was, after all, on Harold's land in Harold's Orangerie. She could hear Madame Verrett laughing all the way from France: *I know what you're thinking, Alex. And it's not what you're saying out loud.*

What Alex the Liar had never confessed to Libbie, what she'd never been able to, was that *after* she had spent her remaining days in Chicago working to convince her that no matter how bleak her situation might seem, surely there were other, better, *sounder* options than Harold's mad offer; and *after* they had sorted through these options together, discussed them and weighed them and tried to think of still more; and *after* Alex had watched from the window of her departing train as Libbie stood weeping on the platform watching her, watching her leave, Mr. Harold Brookhants had found her.

He'd found Alex, I mean.

Right away, Readers, he'd found her, there on the train, before it had even cleared the outskirts of Chicago. He and Madame Verrett had schemed it down to the minute. Alex hadn't even been particularly surprised to see them coming up the aisle toward her. This trip had depleted her capacity for shock.

They had her trapped like a yellow jacket under a bowl. At least until the first station stop. (But even then, they could simply change their tickets, too. Harold Brookhants had the means to do whatever he liked. Except, it appeared, to convince Libbie to take his offer.)

For miles chugging across the country, Eastward Ho!, they worked to convince Alex that Harold's option was the *only* option, and not just for Libbie but for her as well—if she wanted to be with Libbie, that is. Harold painted his imagined Brookhants School for Girls as a paradise awaiting its tenants. And owners. A place where she and Libbie could live as openly as the Ladies of Llangollen.*

If Harold sold Alex the dream, Madame Verrett sold the nightmare, the one she said would be sure to come true for Libbie if she refused Harold's offer. If she, for instance, told her parents of her pregnancy, or sought out Simon Everett III—or any other suitor—or attempted some horrible method of ending her pregnancy herself: all of which were options Libbie and Alex had discussed. Anything but Harold's offer, the Madame said, would seal her fate.

And what a wretched fate it would be. That much was certain. Madame Verrett enumerated a host of dreadful futures for Libbie Packard, all of them avoidable, of course, if she'd only marry rich old Harold and partake in a ceremony or two, in France, before delivering her child there.

Alex did try to argue with them, to counter their assurances with her own ample doubts and misgivings, but together, over those miles and miles, they wore her down.

---

* Lady Eleanor Butler and Miss Sarah Ponsonby, who lived together for fifty years at the end of the eighteenth century and into the nineteenth. During that time, their cottage and gardens were visited by a host of authors, thinkers, and doers, some of whom wrote poems and other tributes to them. And since that time, more authors, thinkers, and doers have argued about what, precisely, Lady Eleanor and Miss Sarah were to one another, except for two women who clearly braided their lives into one.

After all, she *did* want to braid her own life to that of her Libbie. Was she so wrong for wanting this, Readers? Libbie herself didn't seem to know what she wanted. Couldn't Alex want enough for them both?

And if Harold was going to die soon, anyway—and both he and Madame Verrett were so adamant that he *would*—then so what if he tried a few more of his nonsense rituals before he did?

Because of course they would be nonsense! What else would they be?

From the train, Alex wrote Libbie a letter. In it, she explained that she'd perhaps been a notch *too rash* when she'd so stridently condemned Harold Brookhants and his plan, too motivated by her own stupor over Libbie's distressing news. Alex didn't perform an about-face on the matter—that would have been suspicious—but she did begin the process, one furthered by many more measured letters between them, of allowing room for the idea of the future Harold Brookhants had conjured.

Alex let that idea of future in the door, spun it around, and told Libbie, gently—ever so gently—to take a good look, to consider it fully. It did have an appeal, didn't it?

She, Alex the Liar, had done that. She'd done it so they'd end up here.

And now here they were.

And Alex the Liar had work to do.

TYPIST'S BLOCK

....

Merritt hadn't spoken to Harper since the Hollywood Forever Cemetery the night of their date, even though they'd seen each other the very next day at the production office on the studio lot. There, Merritt had made a short speech wishing them well with their efforts and excusing herself from further ties to *The Happenings at Brookhants*. Elaine had protested. Bo and Heather had offered (subdued) words of disappointment. Merritt would not be dissuaded. She said she felt like they all better understood the movie they wanted to make than she did. And so they should make that movie. Without her. Then she flew home from LA, sans Elaine, three days early.

In the hours and days following, Harper sent her several unanswered texts ranging from conciliatory to explanatory to (almost) poetic. The final of them: Really did not expect the silent treatment from you, Saguaro.

Merritt's mother was off doing research in a London archive. She'd invited her, but Merritt had said no without even considering the offer. She was glad to have their house to herself, living, for the first ten days or so, in her own campus-movie-inspired fantasy of frat life: letting takeout containers pile up on the end tables, Netflix-binging, searching for porn that didn't make her hate herself for watching it. (Maybe seeking out ethical porn wasn't so much part of the frat fantasy.)

And then she grew bored with her antics, cleaned up her mess, and spent the next several days *doing things*. She painted the flaking front porch swing. She weeded out closets and donated stuff, a lot of it once belonging to her father. She moved through the house, room by room, until she reached the garage. Then she stopped. She didn't ever go into the garage anymore, hadn't been in there since the day she'd found him. And even that day, her father had tried to tell her (well, or to tell her mother, whom he surely expected would be the one home first) not to go in.

He'd left a note taped to the outside of the door. It read: DO NOT ENTER! DO NOT OPEN DOOR! CALL POLICE! CARBON MONOXIDE INSIDE!

Almost as soon as she saw the note that day, Merritt had heard the music. Loud, coming from inside—over the whir of the car engine, even, she could make it out.

Dave Matthews Band, "Ants Marching."

And what the fuck do you do with that? What are you ever supposed to do with that supremely fucked-up fact from your life? The fact that your psychologist father was playing the DMB song "Ants Marching" on repeat as he killed himself? The fact that the song contains numerous instances of situationally on-the-nose lyrics?

People would want to visibly wince or laugh or both, if she told them, but they couldn't: they'd be monsters if they did. So then that would leave them looking at her in that icky, steady-faced, not-laughing-but-yes-judging limbo, asking themselves why on earth she would share with them such an upsetting detail. And what are *they* supposed to do with it?

Anyway, Merritt stopped her clean out at the garage.

Around that time, Bo called and the two of them had their longest conversation to date about his vision for the film and why he wanted (*needed,* he said) her to be a part of it. When he was finished, Merritt thanked him for elucidating, but she also told him that her mind had not been changed. Bo said he was disappointed but he understood.

She'd then tried to throw herself into her writing. She now had notebooks and Word docs full of timelines, sketches, and asides, both about Capote's original *Answered Prayers* pages and the real-life people on which he'd based his characters. She also had a nearly twenty-page outline. What she didn't have was a book.

Part of it was that she'd spent too much time researching and obsessing over Truman Capote's own inability to finish that novel. But the bigger part of it was that she didn't think she really knew how to write a book, at least not when she wasn't at the desk atop Spite Tower, Elaine trading her snacks for paragraphs.

And then Elaine doing much more than just reading those paragraphs, those pages: asking astute questions about them and offering insights, suggesting edits, bringing her additional documents to round out her research.

Elaine Brookhants, the true keeper of the story. Always.

But Elaine wasn't around now and she didn't like this story anyway, so . . .

While Merritt *wasn't* writing, she spent hours watching Harper Harper content, which included sometimes tracking down internet chatter devoted to their kiss. What was left of it, anyway. The online gossip tide turns so quickly and there were plenty of other grrrls paired, or at least photographed, with Harper in those days: a Bollywood star attempting to break into the American market, a professional beach volleyball player, the youngest of four siblings in a popular folk-pop band, an internet-famous chef known for her elaborate cakes and punk aesthetic.

For Merritt, keeping up with Harper's Instagram that summer felt a little like pulling the lever on a slot machine of enviable queers with interesting professions. Which pairs will come up today?

When Merritt's father had been alive, he'd more than once made the observation that their campus neighborhood became a ghost town in the summer. Students vanished from the Victorians turned apartment houses and FOR RENT signs grew like clover on their lawns. The businesses downtown suddenly had plenty of available parking and you didn't need to make reservations for dinner.

Partly because she couldn't sleep at night—her mind buzzing with Harper's various feeds and her own inability to write a sentence that didn't make her wince—Merritt started personally haunting her ghost town during the small hours. It got her out of the house without forcing her to interact with anyone who might ask after her mother, the movie, her life. It made her feel connected to the people around her without requiring actual contact. In this way, it wasn't entirely unlike her internet lurking.

She'd nap in the afternoons and evenings, set an alarm to be up by midnight. Some nights she'd sit on the porch swing for a while, but once any remaining interior lights turned off in the houses of her immediate neighbors, she'd leave her home to wander.

Often, she liked to walk right down the center of a street, where there was a gap in the limbs that reached out from the trees planted on either side—a line of stars and sky between the leafy tops. If a car came, its headlights loud like a scream, she'd move enough for it to pass by, acting like it was the thing in the way, not her. She looked in display windows and read, really read, the flyers on telephone poles: yard sales, lost pets, cash for ugly houses.

She'd pass a flooring place and imagine her life selling carpet. She'd pass a beauty salon and imagine her life doing hair. Mostly, she tried to imagine contentment: the state of being content. She didn't think it was something she'd ever been before, so it was difficult for her to accurately imagine how it might feel. But she did try.

Eventually, Merritt got to know which house would have a blue TV glow in its upstairs bedroom window, no matter what time she passed; and which would have the handsome husbands (or that's how she thought of them) just off shift and still in their hospital scrubs, sitting in their kitchen eating a late-late dinner or an early-early breakfast. A few times they waved at her. She wondered how she looked to them out that window, there in the cast of the street-lights with her humidity-poofed hair. Like a ghost?

Probably more like an escapee of some kind.

After a couple of hours, sometimes longer, she'd return home from her haunting, make coffee, and complete the ritual by logging in to Harper's feeds. Harper Harper on the West Coast, living a life three hours earlier and a thousand times busier than her own. At that hour Harper would inevitably still be out on the town, still getting tagged in pics and posts.

It was an exquisite kind of torture, cycling through those posts. Merritt judged the clothing, the poses, the captions, the hashtags, all with a level of snark and bile that embarrassed her. She felt immensely sorry for herself, and then immediately congealed that feeling into one of self-loathing. Why the fuck did she care? What was any of this for and why couldn't she leave it alone and do something worth doing?

But she didn't. She'd eat some things. Fall asleep for a while. And the next night she'd haunt again.

One day, close to the time Merritt's mother would return from London and Merritt would have nothing but clean closets and a thorough knowledge of the town's lost pets to show for her weeks of solitude, Harper texted her:

> If you think, fine world, that I am always interesting and striking and admirable, always original, showing up to good advantage in a company of persons and all—why, then you are beautifully mistaken. There are times, to be sure, when I can rivet the attention of the crowd heavily upon myself. But mostly I am the very least among all the idiots and fools. I show up to the poorest possible advantage.

The words were, of course, Mary MacLane's. And they were just about the perfect thing Harper could have chosen to send, enough like an apology to be interpreted as one, but with all the Harper Harper glitter.

This time, Merritt waited a few hours, then she texted back:

> I never learned to sew, and I don't intend ever to learn. It reminds me too much of a constipated dressmaker.

These words were also Mary's. And they earned her what she thought they might:

> **Harper:** LOLz. I've missed you.

Merritt: What, pray tell, have you managed to find to fill your time if not our repartee?

Harper: Masturbation.

Merritt: Heavens! Are we sexting? Is this the sexting the internets have warned me about?

Harper: Get ready. I'm sending something super erotic your way.

Merritt waited. It would be a lie to say that it wasn't anticipatorily, Readers.

And then, there on her phone: a picture of Harper's knees and bare feet, the camera held above, probably midthigh or so. She was wearing jeans.

Merritt sent back a picture of her elbow.

Harper sent one of her earlobe.

Merritt sent a close-up of her eyebrow piercings.

Harper: no fair. that I was there for.

Merritt: Look again, this time with all the sexual heat of a sexting session.

Harper: OMG. I seeeeeee it. yes! YAAAAAASSSSSSSSSSSS.

They carried on like this for a while.

Until, at some point, Harper texted:

only a few days until we see each other for real and I get to see all these parts in person.

Merritt: Nice try. Not happening.

Harper: you're not even gonna come show me the black apples?

Merritt: No. May they fall from their trees and rot rotty deaths.

Harper tried to call her then, her image showed on Merritt's screen.* But Merritt didn't answer. Instead she dismissed the call and texted:

> **Merritt:** I don't want to have a conversation about it. But if you want to text me about other things, I'll do that.
>
> **Harper:** uggghghghghghghghgghghhghghghghg. you're impossible, Saguaro. but I vow not to give up on you.
>
> **Merritt:** Your inevitable defeat. Tell me about something I'll like.

And, Readers, Harper had. For days she had. They started one of those endless text threads that picks up at random and continues that way, sometimes intensely, with rapid back-and-forths, and sometimes with hours-long pauses in between, one of them waiting for the other's reply. Merritt would send Harper lines from Capote correspondence and Harper would send back candid pictures from a fashion shoot. Harper would tell Merritt about the pile of really shitty scripts she'd been sent and Merritt would tell Harper about the gruesome details of the true crime podcast she was currently listening to even though it was freaking her out.

Without planning for it or even commenting on it, their texts grew increasingly personal and revealing: Harper told Merritt about her worry that her mother was drinking again and hiding it well, managing it until she didn't—which was something she could stretch for months into years, Harper said. Annie had told her to confront her mother but Harper hadn't. Not yet.

This mention of Annie had eventually trickled into an exchange about open relationships, during which Merritt revealed to Harper that, for most of her own life, anyway, her parents had been in one. Harper seemed really interested in this, especially as the concept

---

* Merritt had taken the time to pair pictures with exactly four of her phone contacts. Harper Harper was one of them. Merritt's father, who hadn't had an active cell phone number since three weeks after his death, was another.

applied to old straight people, so Merritt told her the basics: that her parents had sat her down and explained it to her in the most clinical and nonshamey way when she was ten or so. She also told Harper about how occasionally one of her parents' friends might join them for dinner, or they'd vacationed with other couples a few times, but that they didn't have the kind of situation where anyone ever moved in with them or anything. Mostly, it did not affect her day-to-day, Merritt said. Via text, it was easy to make it seem both amusing and banal.

Merritt did *not* share with Harper that she sometimes thought her mother liked the marriage this way better than her father did. She did not share this because she didn't always believe it, she only sometimes did. And when she did, it made her hate her mother. And she didn't want to. And she didn't think it was necessarily fair to.

Even if Merritt didn't share these specifics, it was still really nice to talk this way to someone she wasn't paying to listen to her talk this way.

But whenever Harper tried to bring up the movie, Merritt would shut down and refuse to reply until Harper offered something else. And then Merritt's mom came home from London. And then it was time. Enough days had piled up and it was August and it was time. One of the studio assistants cc'd her on all the relevant emails and sent her schedules and travel options and asked her to call them, to get in touch about her plans.

Merritt ignored those messages.

Soon Harper texted:

I'm here. I'm fucking here at brookhants and it's unbelievable and I can't believe you aren't here with me. We could be acting out our favorite flo/clara scenes by tonight. Get your ass here.

Merritt: You'll soon have Audrey there for that. She is Clara, after all.

She knew it was small and tacky to respond this way. She did it anyway.

Harper, no doubt a frequent recipient of jealousy-tinged texts, did not respond for a few days, and when she did it was with a picture of the crew working on The Orangerie, which Merritt almost didn't recognize, given its face-lift.

Harper: it's still incredible and you're still missing it.

Merritt didn't respond to that. Well, let me put it another way, Readers: she didn't text a response to that, but she did respond by poring over Annie's Instagram, scrolling through pictures of all of Annie's angles at Art Basel Hong Kong, clicking through the links to her latest exhibitions and reading reviews in various online forums. They were predominately positive. And it seemed she was donating 100 percent of the proceeds from a recent auction of her work to disaster relief in Puerto Rico. So she was talented and beautiful and good, too. Certainly, she was not plain and bad.

That night at dinner, Merritt's mother said, as she passed Merritt a huge wooden bowl of salad, "So you're still not planning to go to the set?"

"Nope," Merritt said, using the tongs to pick around the salad components she did not care for.

"Why do you think it's baby and bathwater with you, Merritt?" her mother asked. "Since you were little. Your impulse is always to toss out the good with the bad if it's not going exactly your way."

"Gosh, I wonder. Wherever might such an approach have been modeled for me?"

"But not when I was in my twenties!" The professor poured herself a lot of white wine from the sweating bottle she'd set beside her glass. "I calcified along *with* my experiences, not before I'd even had any."

"It's telling that you think I've not yet experienced anything worthy of changing me, Mother," Merritt said, shaking her head. "I knew you'd talk to Elaine about what happened in LA."

"She's my friend, too. It wasn't behind your back."

"It certainly wasn't at my front."

"You do know that she has a diagnosis now," her mother said. "Or did you not know that? Have you even thought to ask her?" She seemed to ask that question like she wanted an answer but continued before Merritt could give one. "They're calling it mixed dementia. She's getting a second opinion but—she did have that stroke last year, too. It's not good news."

"I didn't know," Merritt said.

They looked at each other. Her mother took a drink of wine.

"But I also don't know what Lainey's diagnosis has to do with me and this movie."

"I think you do." Her mother sighed. "I had hoped to do this with a little more finesse."

"Do what?" Merritt asked.

Her mother sighed again. "She's coming to pick you up." She looked at her watch. "She should be here within the hour. She shouldn't even be driving, certainly not on 95, so Carl's following behind her—but Lainey doesn't know and so please don't say anything. *My* job was to see that you were packed for Brookhants, but honestly—really and truly—I don't want the fight, Merritt. I don't see the point. You're an adult."

"That we agree on," Merritt said. However, her mother's news had surprised her.

"Good, so then you talk to her. And when you do, remember that she took—she's taking!—a huge gamble on this, too. Because she believes in you."

"Right, so now with the guilt approach," Merritt said. "Check and check." But she had been thinking a lot about this herself—Elaine's substantial role in the production.

And as you might have sorted for yourselves by now, Readers: all paths lead back to Elaine Brookhants.

She'd started by wooing young Merritt early, with fire-pit tales of the curse.

Soon enough, Merritt had grown accustomed to picnicking at Brookhants, on the campus proper, at least once a summer. By then it hadn't operated as a school for over a hundred years, but Elaine paid to keep the grounds half-heartedly maintained and the buildings from falling down.

She had tried, she said, on various occasions, to donate the whole place—buildings and land—to this organization, that endeavor, but its relative remoteness, and especially the potential costs of its upkeep, kept any of those deals from ever going anywhere. (Its cursed history maybe didn't help.) And Elaine refused to sell it to the developers who wanted to knock it all down to build some rich person's summer home—or *homes* plural, more likely. Or condos—gah, condos! The idea of this ever happening particularly bothered Elaine. The nerve of building summer homes in Rhode Island for rich people.

Merritt could remember Elaine convincing her fully, at that tender age, of the deplorability of such an action. Elaine convinced her even as they rolled away from campus in the hunter-green Jaguar convertible that Elaine had recently imported from the UK. She convinced Merritt even as she continued to drive said car in the direction of her own sprawling summer house there on the coast: Spite Manor.

It can, dear Readers, be difficult to appreciate blatant hypocrisy when one of your ten-year-old arms is hanging out in the space where the passenger-side window should be (but it's not, because it's rolled down, of course), your skin touching the sun-hot slick metal of the curve of a mint-condition Jaguar's door, your hand holding a fast-dripping strawberry ice-cream cone, the road clicking beneath you, green leaves twittering the sunlight above you, and the summer day pressing against you ever so gloriously as Elaine speeds you into it.

Merritt loved Brookhants. I mean she really loved Brookhants, from her very first visit. And she loved it even more, as a place of escape, after her father died. She fell in love with it. Fell in love with the feeling she got there, the one that began to seep its way into her even on the road to campus, the trees so tall and dense that the sky became branch and leaf. If she stared just beyond their trunks as they sped by it was like turning pages in a flip-book, like anything, glorious and terrible too, might appear in the darkness beyond.

And then those woods would open up and the campus would fill the windshield's expanse. Merritt loved the limestone-and-brick buildings, the overtaking ivy, the clover-choked lawn, the dried-up fountain, the tangled jumble of a once-manicured garden, and especially, most especially, the tall but narrow Orangerie jutting off the side of Main Hall.

She'd thought she was being clever when she'd known to refer to that long structural expanse of grimy and mostly broken windows and weeds as a *conservatory,* but Elaine had immediately corrected her.

"No," she said. "That won't do. It's specified as The Orangerie on the original blueprints. Naming it that was fussy even in the 1890s, and of course Brookhants wasn't ever really fashionable enough to warrant it, but that was a sticking point for Harold. It was always The Orangerie. He even helped devise some magnificent heating system to keep it temperate and humid through Rhode Island winters. Can you picture that, dear?" Elaine had asked, settling her gaze on the structure, which made Merritt do the same. "Can you fully imagine the wonder of coming in from a blizzard to the tropical warmth of an Orangerie, and then picking a grapefruit from one of your trees, seeing the snow piling against the glass? Can you imagine doing that, Merritt? In 1900? In Rhode Island?"

Merritt could imagine that, yes. She could easily hold that picture in her mind. And she thought it was such a wonderful picture, too: one filled with wonder.

Because of that wonder—and because of all the other things about Brookhants, too—despite its infamous deaths and the umpteen resulting urban legends about its curse, visiting the campus, back then, never scared her.

But the locals at least got it half right: there was always something hovering there, something in the color of the light and the shift of the shadows. And whatever that something was, it was as intoxicating to Merritt—at ten, eleven, twelve—as any potion peddled by an old beggar woman in a folktale. Keep your magic beans, your shimmery vial of purple liquid, your enchanted rose: give her the crumbling Orangerie and empty fountain and Black Oxford orchard.

During all of her falls, winters, and springs, Merritt longed most for those brief weeks in summer when she knew they'd be back visiting Elaine, who let her picnic and roam and lean against the low stone walls and imagine, of course she did, what her own life might have been like had she been a student there. She could make the visions as romantic as she liked. *Of course* 1902 Merritt would have had scads of friends. *Of course* she'd have been more Clara than Eleanor, a founding member of the Plain Bad Heroine Society. Of course.

As she grew older, Merritt took her off-season infatuation online to the boxes of ephemera Elaine had gifted her: yearbooks (*The Brookhantsian*[*]), personal letters and business correspondence, newspaper clippings, and the prize peacock: Libbie's diaries.

Eventually, Merritt had started her blog: *The Happenings at Brookhants.* You shouldn't think that this was any big deal. No one cared that she was doing this except Merritt herself and maybe Elaine. She wrote and posted in solitude for months, think maybe eleven hits in sixty days. (And don't pretend that you were one of those eleven. You didn't read her Tumblr back then and we both know it.)

At some point, a freelancer who was tasked with building a "Scary Places" listicle happened upon *The Happenings at Brookhants* and liked what she read and linked to it. And then that link got used in a half dozen similar lists and articles: "Abandoned Haunts"; "Wicked New England"; "Do Not Enter: Fifteen Cursed Locales." All of that upped Merritt's traffic considerably.

Soon after, Elaine suggested that Merritt stop giving her research away for free and instead turn it into a book.

It would be wrong of me, Readers, not to admit to you how serious and wonderful and, yes—the truth—*adult* that sounded to Merritt at the time: to hear Elaine say that this thing she was muddling around with online could be, she thought, a published book. (It didn't hurt that through Elaine's various machinations, a literary

---

[*] Yeah, so perhaps not the students' best work.

agent soon contacted Merritt about such a plan, which made the whole thing go from fantasy to not.)

And then Merritt's father killed himself, and in the aftermath of that, writing the book—which was something she could do largely in private, alone atop Spite Manor with her laptop and notebooks and one of Libbie's diaries open before her—took on an obsessive urgency. One she was happy to give in to. It was this massive thing she *had* to do—*was doing*. It had nothing to do with her father or her mother or even the world of the present day.

She could almost hear their voices as she wrote—as if all of them, Alex and Libbie and Flo and Clara and Eleanor—had crowded in with her, around her.

And of course, there was Elaine and her astute advice, constant and so necessary.

Before *The Happenings at Brookhants* was even published, Elaine was already talking about how wonderful it would be as a movie. She said she wanted to back it. She said she'd wanted to finance films for years, but that Hollywood was a *grubby business to break into*. So they arranged for Elaine to buy the film rights. This was an unusual deal, as Elaine, at that time, didn't own even a piece of a production company, didn't have one toe, really, in Hollywood (though she did have her toes everywhere else: two casinos, a pile of hotels, rights to mines in various places near and far).

But Elaine paid well, Merritt's agent said and the internet seemed to confirm, to become holder of the film rights to a relatively quiet nonfiction book about long-dead sapphic WASPs, which meant that if any filmmakers were interested, they'd have to deal with her.

It turns out that this was maybe a very shrewd move on Elaine's part, but at the time it seemed most like a gamble.

Or maybe just a kindness, even an act of protection.

So what to do with all of this backstory, Readers, now that Elaine was no doubt speeding her way toward the very house in which Merritt sat alone at the dinner table, her mother a vibrato of sighs as she fed the dishwasher. What to do with Elaine's belief in her, which was sometimes terrible to Merritt because it seemed so wide and unending, impossible to live up to. Especially now that Elaine was older and too often showing that age. Especially now that she'd been diagnosed. Merritt was no solitary genius, no self-made success. She was acutely aware of the debts she owed others—most especially Elaine.

She felt, sometimes, like that debt had been carved into her bones.

She left her mother in the kitchen and wandered out the front door to the porch swing only minutes before Elaine turned down the block in, you knew it: the green Jag. She had a periwinkle-and-cream-striped scarf tied over her hair and as she pulled up, she tapped the horn twice and then shot both arms high as if she were in the front car of a roller coaster taking its first steep drop. By the time she reached the brick path to the porch she was already talking to Merritt as though they were midconversation. "It shouldn't take us much more than two and a half hours to get there—even *if* we stop at Gray's for ice cream, and I don't know why on earth we wouldn't stop at Gray's for ice cream if we're driving by. Coffee cabinet for you. Pistachio in a cone for me." She was on the porch stairs now, elegantly peeling her leather driving gloves from her hands, one finger at a time.

"So I do hope you can pack quickly, dear," she said. "In miniature too, as cargo space is at a premium. But haste is really the order of the hour."

She crossed the porch to Merritt, who slipped from the swing to give her a hug.

As they pulled away, Elaine said, "How about you don't fight me on this, Merritt? What if, for once, you just let it be easy?"

"Not in my nature."

"It could be," Elaine said. "If only you'd allow it."

"You made good time, Lainey," Merritt's mother said, pushing her way out the screen door, a dish towel over her shoulder.

"Yes, but you've made no progress," Elaine said, tilting her head at Merritt.

"Did you really think I would?" her mother asked.

"I had hopes," Elaine said. "Also, I do know that Carl's been tailing me the whole ride. The man's no James Bond."

"I don't think anyone would ever confuse the two," Merritt said.

"No one's forcing you to come, darling," Elaine now said to Merritt. "I'd tie you up and put you in the trunk but there's simply no room for it." She stepped forward and laid one soft hand on Merritt's cheek, moved Merritt's face so it was right in front of her own, very close. "Merritt, I'm getting to be an old woman—"

"No way," Merritt said, interrupting her. "The dying-wish angle won't work on me."

Elaine laughed a big, openmouthed laugh that showed off her teeth in a way that made Merritt shudder. "Am I dying? What do you know that I don't?"

"Jesus, Merritt," her mother said. "Lainey, how *are* you feeling?"

"Today I feel like I'm thirty and flirty and ready for drama. Last week I couldn't get out of bed for three days." She slid past Merritt and onto the porch swing. "How goes the book?"

"Like it hasn't been able to get out of bed for three months," Merritt said, the two of them now pushing the swing back and forth.

"I had a feeling," Elaine said.

"Well I'm so glad you could make the trip to gloat."

"Merritt, really," her mother said. She now stood with her arms crossed. "I'm sorry, Lainey."

"Not at all," Elaine said, waving her away.

"Stop apologizing for me," Merritt said.

"Stop giving me reasons to," her mother said.

Merritt braced her feet hard on the painted floor to stop the swing. She turned to Elaine and said, "I would think you of all people would want me to be someone with artistic convictions. And not just to have them, but to keep to them."

"Convictions, yes," Elaine said. "Excuses, no." Then she thought for a moment before saying, "I'm told she's doing well in the rehearsals." She held up her hand to stop Merritt from interrupting her before she could get the next part out. "And it's not only Bo who's saying it. Audrey is holding her own. She might even end up being quite good."

"Lainey, can I fix you a drink?" Merritt's mother asked. "Perhaps you require a double to talk to my daughter?"

"Water, no ice, would be perfection," Elaine said. She waited for the screen door to thwack shut before she started them swinging again. She said, "Tell me what's stopped your progress with your book."

"Maybe that I was never really making any to begin with."

"And why do you think that's the case?"

It seemed to Merritt like Elaine was daring her to say it, to admit that she hadn't done it the first time. Not really. "I don't know, Lainey—why do you think it is?"

"Well, I don't think it's the book you want to be writing," Elaine said. "But I've already told you that and you don't want to hear it."

"Maybe I can't write fiction."

"I don't buy that for one minute, and it shouldn't stop you, anyway. Truman wasn't writing fiction in that book. That's why he had all the trouble with it in the first place."

"No, I know, but turns out I'm not so intrigued by the gossip he was intrigued by."

"Of course you're not," Elaine said. "It's been decades. It's too stale now—and it was too tawdry to begin with."

"And I don't have my own petting zoo of swans to feed in order to find something fresher."

"That's very rich, Merritt," Elaine said.

"Why?"

"Now where on earth might you find famous"—Elaine paused, smiling—"or fame-*ish* people with scads of time on their hands? People to whom you could be in the closest of proximity for the next several weeks?"

"Not at all the same."

"Really?" Elaine asked, the word dripping with incredulity.

Merritt smiled a real smile at her. "I do love that your solution to my writer's block is for me to Capote your movie."

"I'm only reminding you of something you wrote," Elaine said. She offered this next part as if in recitation: "Brookhants is more haunted by its ghost *stories* than by its ghosts."

"*Did* I write that?" Merritt said. "Mawkish much?"

"Not mawkish," Elaine said. "True. Not the full of the truth to *me*, of course, but it *is* the truth to you. And you said it well. So why not go there and see where more Brookhants stories lead?"

Readers, let me be clear: it wasn't that this idea had never before occurred to Merritt. Of course it had. Something like it, anyway. How could it not? Especially since Harper Harper already had something of a Kate McCloud* about her. But it felt like it was a bridge too far. Merritt had no ethical problems building on Capote's now-historic gossip, but drumming up her own felt pretty fucking cheap.

"You hate what Capote did," Merritt said. "Why would you want me to do it, too?"

"Because I'm confident you won't do it the way he did," Elaine said quickly. "Burning all your bridges until there's no way back across the water." This time she was the one who stopped their rocking. She turned to Merritt and took both of Merritt's hands in her own, which were soft and cold. "Merritt, please at least let me offer you one solitary pearl of old-lady wisdom."

Merritt shrugged as if to say, *Do it.*

"Don't find yourself regretting this. You're much too young to haunt your own life."

Merritt blinked at Elaine. It wasn't the first time she'd found Elaine's advice to be oddly intuitive, peculiarly in the know. She said, "I don't know how to be around any of them."

She was admitting to more in that sentence than it seemed like ten small words should hold.

"I know," Elaine said.

---

* Capote's too-charming-and-beautiful-to-be-believed tragic heroine in *Answered Prayers.*

"And I know I'm not good enough to do it as well as it should be done, and it'll show."

"I know you think that," Elaine said. "Even though it isn't true. And I also know you like the movie star more than you'll admit." Merritt tried to shrug a *whatever* at that, but Elaine wouldn't have it. "You do," she said.

"What else do you know?" Merritt asked.

"I know you need to pack now, and quickly, if we're to get there before dark. I'm tired and I'd like to. If the trip here was any indication, the Massholes are out in full force."

"But what about the Connecticunts?" Merritt smiled at her.

"The worst!" Elaine said. "The very worst. I'll let you drive. You'll stay with me tonight, start fresh in the morning. We can surprise them. I love a surprise."

Merritt said, "If I come with you now, I want you to know that I might just turn around and come home again tomorrow."

"Of course," Elaine said. "But you won't."

"No, I won't," Merritt said.

THE PLAYERS ASSEMBLE

....

The next morning, **Harper Harper** found herself in the increasingly common position of being the one doing the waiting.

She'd already been waiting, for days, for Merritt to change her mind and come to Brookhants, and now today she was waiting for Bo and Audrey, who were twenty-plus minutes late meeting her to rehearse a scene in The Orangerie.

Harper, never one to stand around, had been helping the crew stationed there unload their trucks. Some of the teamsters hadn't liked this very much, but they also weren't used to giving orders to the talent. It wasn't even nine A.M. and everyone was already sweating off their mosquito spray, Harper included.

She gripped one end of a massive wooden table, a table built for kissing beneath, and carefully walked backward on a narrow path between potted trees and rows of big-bloomed plants intended for placement in The Orangerie.

A crew member named Kae carried the other end. Kae was one of a handful of locals who knew better than the Los Angelinos on crew who had tried, at least at first, to be exclusively organic and handmade about their bug repellent selections, opting for creams that made them smell like cupcakes but did nothing to keep the Brookhants mosquitoes away. Now they were all showering in great clouds of the MAXI-DEET stuff. (Consider the gasoline-and-metal taste it leaves on your tongue part of its charm, Readers.)

One of Harper's phones dinged in her pocket. Then again. Cell service was shifty at Brookhants, and sometimes a bunch of stalled notifications would land at once.

"You need to check that?" Kae asked. "We can set it down." The table was heavy. Kae's forearms strained with its weight.

"Yeah," Harper said. "Let's just clear the door." She stepped backward and down into The Orangerie as her phone dinged again. They set the table down as soon as Kae was also inside the door.

The text was from Uncle Rob. Harper could picture him sitting on his lumpy couch, sending it to her. (Or maybe he'd upgraded that couch since cashing her check.)

He'd written:

Thought you might want to keep an eye on this

Then he'd sent several screenshots from her mother's Facebook page. It was two hours earlier in Montana, barely seven A.M., but Rob was already up and tattling about the pics that Harper's mother, his sister, had posted from the party she'd had at her lake house the night before.

Harper used her lurker profile to go to her mother's page and sure enough, there were more pics posted there and her mom had been tagged in her friends' images, too: red Solo cups and beer cans and sunburned faces.

And on top of this, her mom was apparently again seeing (or something?) ex-husband Paul, Ethan's dad. Here he was with his arm around her, and here he was at the grill flipping an ear of corn, and here he was grinning in the Jacuzzi with his pink chest and polarized sunglasses.

The thing is: Harper liked Paul. She'd always liked him, and he'd been sober and steady for years and years, so maybe this wasn't necessarily such a worrying development.

Maybe.

"I can grab somebody else," Kae said tentatively. "If you need to be done now."

"No," Harper said. "I'm good. Just give me one sec." She didn't text Rob, but she did text Ethan to tell him to have a good day at school and also to fish for info on where he'd spent the weekend. She hoped it was with their grandparents. She guessed it probably was: he wasn't in any of the posted pics. Then she put her phone back in her pocket and together they moved the table away from the doorway and into place.

Harper watched as Kae pulled a green bandanna from their back pocket and wiped their forehead and neck.

"What, are you trying to take my job?" they asked.

"You wanna trade?" Harper said.

"I dunno," Kae said. "I haven't actually seen you do much of anything yet, so I don't even know what I'd be in for."

"Fair enough," Harper said. She knew Kae was joking but she could also see how it might seem that way, especially since she and Audrey had spent these past few days rehearsing with Bo away from the curious eyes of the crew. Harper wasn't sure yet how things were going.

They were going is how.

The beeping of another delivery truck backing up to The Orangerie made Kae say, "Uhhhhhh, how can there be more tables left in the world?"

But the truck turned out to be filled with plants. There were dozens of them crammed together, their leaves and tendrils spilling free, like green hands reaching, as soon as the hatch was lifted. Kae and Harper watched as another crew member situated the unloading ramp—it was steep, the truck was big—and Layla, a greenskeeper,* started up it with her iPad checklist at the ready.

They continued to watch as Layla's inspection took her deep into the mass of plants. By the time she reached the back of the truck, she was no longer visible to them. That's when they heard her yell, "Fuck. This. Shit."

"Yuh-oh," Kae said quietly to Harper. And then, much more loudly, they called to Layla, "Anything I can do?"

"Yeah, you can find me fifteen orange trees that aren't dead," Layla

---

* Harper had never before heard that specific term, but the *Happenings at Brookhants* art department boasted two greenskeepers: crew members tasked with dealing with horticulture and landscaping. Layla's specific domain was all things Orangerie.

said, emerging from the greenery and starting back down the ramp.

"Are they dead or are they—" Kae started.

"They're dead," Layla said. She was already on her walkie-talkie, searching for somebody to help her fix this. *Above my pay grade* is a phrase she used.

"So you want the dead ones off the truck too or no?" Kae asked, already partway up the ramp.

"Off, I guess," Layla said, trying to hold the walkie-talkie while also looking at her iPad. "No, leave them on."

Kae was handing plants down to Harper when Layla changed her mind again. "No, you'd better take them off. This truck isn't going back to that greenhouse tonight and I can just see somebody trying to say we killed them by leaving 'em on it." She was already walking toward the gardens to check something else, but she called back, "Just put them in The Orangerie, inside the door—to the left. I'll deal with them tomorrow."

"To the left, to the left," Harper sang, her arms wrapped fully around the heavy pot of a massive sword fern, its leaves blocking most of her view.

"All the dead trees in a pile to the left," Kae picked up the song.

"Nice," Harper said.

They plantified the lyrics to other Beyoncé songs as they worked.* At least until they reached the dead trees at the back of the truck.

"Well these won't do," Kae said.

"Somebody fucked up good," Harper said as her phone dinged again. And then again. It was Ethan, on his way to school (with Grandma) and grumpy because it was Monday morning. Harper

---

* Samples:
Come on, flowers, now let's get in formation.
And
You know you're the shit when you need all that pollination.
And
'Cause if you like it, then you probly should have watered it—
Don't be mad because you didn't fucking water it.
Yeah, they weren't great, Readers. Calm down about it.

asked to see this day's sneaker choice and he sent a pic in exchange for hers and then she put her phone away, satisfied. For now.

Harper and Kae were each able to carry two trees at once because they were so parched. The trees were even more pathetic once they were off the truck and in the sunlight. Grouped together in The Orangerie, they looked like the Addams Family's idea of container gardening: a potted forest of brown leaves and stunted fruits faded to ghost colors, dead and shriveled on their branches. Several of them seemed to be nothing more than sticks stuck into the center of a tub of dirt.

Harper took a vape out of her pocket and put it between her lips, inhaled.

"My nephew just got in-school suspension for using one of those in class," Kae said, rather adorably excited about this fact.

"Yep," Harper said as she exhaled a cloud. "Me and every other fourteen-year-old you know." She pulled again and then said, "Only they're all just getting hooked and I'm trying to use this thing to quit."

"Is it working?"

"I have no idea. You want?" Harper extended it in her fingertips.

Kae took it, pulled once, exhaled, and said, "Weird. Is that supposed to be cucumber?"

"I think maybe," Harper said. "I got a variety pack. But really I just want a cigarette."

"Won't bother me," Kae said. "Maybe not in here, though. They told me it almost burned down once already."

"Oh shit," Harper said. "Yeah." She remembered what Merritt had shown her—blooms of char growing right where they'd left those dead trees. The memory of that day in Bo's office, what had happened out his window, felt sour inside her. "I'll stick with this for now," she said, and pulled on the vape again.

Kae used a pocketknife to open several massive bags of potting soil. "We're filling these," they said, nodding at a pile of smallish (compared to what they'd just been hauling) planters stacked near them on the floor.

"Cool."

"Hey, can I ask you something? If it's not too weird." They tossed a pair of gardening gloves to Harper before putting on their own.

"Yeah, but only if you make it weird," Harper said, trying to guess what it would be. Something about someone she'd dated? Or maybe about someone famous she'd worked with or what projects she had lined up next.

Kae slid-heaved a bag of soil over to Harper and, handing her the knife to open it, said, "Is the story about how you were discovered true? Like, that's actually how it went down?"

"I don't know," Harper said. "How do you think it goes?"

The bags were cumbersome, shifting and heavy. Kae gave up on pouring soil out, at least while it was so full. They scooped it with a bucket instead. "Just that you were at a friend's audition, like not there for yourself or anything—that you'd never even acted—and you met Arden Cleary* outside smoking and Arden was like, *Hey there, movie star*." Kae paused, then added, "And that you didn't tell your parents until after you'd already shot the whole thing."

Harper pulled a final time on the vape, then slipped it back in her pocket. "Parent," she said in her exhale. "Just my mom, but close enough otherwise. I *had* acted before, though. I was Sneezy the Dwarf in fifth grade. Which was epic."

"I mean, of course."

Harper cut the seam on her bag before closing the knife and handing it back to Kae. "*Hey there, movie star*," she said. "That's funny."

"How was it really?"

"Unreal," Harper said. "Mostly it felt fake. My friend Eric was hyped on this casting call where he said they needed a ton of teenagers to play bit parts—or probably just be extras, in the end—and it was, like, the weekend before graduation and my finals were over so I was like, *Bring it*."

Harper scooped the dark soil as she spoke—it smelled rotten, like it had been wet in the bag too long. "It was for an indie that was supposed to shoot in Missoula that summer. Not that at the time I

---

* As in Arden Cleary, the Academy Award–nominated director of *Dirt Town*.

really knew anything about what indie versus any other kind of film meant. But Eric did. He'd been in this regional theater thing and so he was our big high school star, and he really wanted to do it, so I went with him, mostly to fuck around in town while he did his thing. He, like, had an audition piece worked up, a headshot—the whole deal. And it was taking forever, and I wasn't really that into it. To be honest, I didn't want to wait in line. I went and saw some people, got my hair cut, bought this rad T-shirt with some graduation money—I was really feeling myself—and then I came back, and he still hadn't gotten in. And now the people running it were, like, on a break and so I was outside the building where they were doing the auditions and texting with him about how I was gonna ditch him if he didn't hurry the fuck up, and I ended up bumming a cigarette from the casting director. And then Arden—who I definitely did not know at the time, like, I mean, I'd never even heard the name Arden Cleary, so I'm for sure not gonna know that person was the casting director—and a couple producers came back from wherever they were off getting food. And they were like, *What's your deal? You seem weird.*"

"*You seem weird?*" Kae repeated like they didn't believe it.

"No, I mean basically," Harper said. "Unlike everybody else waiting to audition, I wasn't trying to be anything to them right then, so I stood out more. Do you know what I mean? Because I wasn't acting like anything. I mean, I think that's really what it was. I didn't want to be there, so they were into me. Reverse psychology or whatever. I wasn't doing anything all that special—"

"Probably didn't hurt that you're gorgeous," Kae said, wadding up their spent soil bag and pulling over another.

"Oh no," Harper said. "I really wasn't. Right now you're looking at the Hollywood version of me, where I can pay somebody to do my eyebrows. Please believe that I looked mangy as fuck that day."

"I do not believe," Kae said. "But go on."

Harper shrugged. It wasn't true, anyway. Within about forty seconds of meeting her, one of the producers had told her that she had a face built for close-ups. (Even at the time she knew what a cliché that was and because of that didn't take it very sincerely even though it was offered that way.) "They brought me in the back way with them and I'm texting Eric and he's like, *Whaaaaaaat? The. Fuck.* He was pretty mad, actually." She smiled at the memory. "Then they had me read a couple of scenes. The weirdest thing was they wanted me to smoke."

"Seriously?"

"Yeah, they made me, like, sit up on top of the back of a desk chair with my feet on the seat, smoking and talking bullshit into the camera for five minutes." She scratched at the back of her neck with the glove and could feel the dirt she'd left behind on her skin.

"But like what, though?" Kae asked.

"I don't know," Harper said. "Like how I thought of myself or something. How I saw myself."

Kae was serious, earnest. "How did you?"

"I don't know," Harper said, shrugging and feeling like she'd somehow let this story she'd told more times than she could count edge into personal territory. "Just some A-plus bullshit, I'm sure," she said, dodging. "The whole thing felt like a game. It definitely didn't feel like it would end up meaning anything real in my life. Even when they took all my contact info and said they were emailing the script and working on connecting me with an agent, I still bought it, like, zero percent. I was mostly worried about whether or not we were gonna have time to go get burritos before we left Missoula."

There was some small commotion outside The Orangerie, and a couple crew members jogged by, toward the garden, one of them talking loud on his walkie-talkie. Both Kae and Harper watched through the glass as they went.

"Yeah but now here you are," Kae said.

"Here I am," Harper said.

And then she added, "Actually, I think Arden got cold feet about me, at one point. I know she did." Why was she telling this part? She never told this part. "We Skyped a bunch of times, before we were gonna start filming, and as we got down to the wire, I could tell she was like, *Oh shit—what did I do?* She asked me to make videos like working my shift at the grocery store or fucking around town with Eric, which is all I ever did anyway. Just on my phone, I mean. Those seemed to reconvince her, but by then I was worried that they'd made a huge mistake."

"Turns out not," Kae said.

"I've still got them fooled," Harper said. "For now."

They finished filling the smaller containers, and Kae showed her where to dump the rest of the soil: into the massive, currently empty zinc planter that would soon be holding the angel's trumpet tree. There were four bags left on the pallet. That amount probably wouldn't even fill the planter halfway, but it was a start, so the two of them hauled the bags over, knifed them open, and heaved them up to the flat, square lip, in order to pour them in. They'd emptied two bags, and Kae was currently dumping in the third, when Harper noticed that something weird fell out of the bag alongside the soil. Before she could even really comprehend what was happening, it was covered. But then came another weird thing—something of a different size and coloring than the dirt and falling at a slightly different rate of speed, like it weighed less.

There were several of these somethings mixed into the soil.

"Maybe plant matter that didn't decompose," Kae said when Harper tried to explain what she'd seen. Kae wadded up the bag they'd just poured and made to grab the last full bag and heave it to the planter's ledge. "It's dirt. It's got a bunch of crap in it. Like actual crap."

"No," Harper said. "This was something else. Hold off a sec." She reached both arms down into the container. She had to rest her hips over its flat lip and let it swallow the top half of her to do this, it was that big. She moved the dirt around with her gloves, fast at first, and then more methodically, until she found one—though she still didn't know what she'd found. She teeter-tottered back over the edge to a standing position, brushed the thing off with her finger-tips, which didn't work very well because her gloves were too bulky, so she took one of them off in order to do it more gently.

It was round, about the size of a ping-pong ball, and light in her

---

* *By end of day tomorrow*, said Layla the Greenskeeper.

hand. Fragile. She pulled off her other glove and continued to wipe away the dirt. She even blew at some of what remained, which made Kae laugh.

"Buried treasure?" they asked.

"I think it's supposed to be an apple."

"What?" Kae asked, leaning in for a better look. Harper tenderly held the thing aloft in her palm like it was the Hope Diamond.

It *was* an apple: a tiny papier-mâché sculpture painted, rather realistically, to look like a Black Oxford apple. There was even a minuscule brown stem and green leaf at the top.

"You think there's more?" Kae asked, already leaning over the edge of the planter. Harper did, too. Together the two of them clanged heads as they fished out delicate, papier-mâché sculptures of the following items: a blue flower, another apple, and, oh yes, Readers, a yellow jacket. The second apple had torn and its insides were now exposed. Once Harper cleared the dirt from it, the honeycomb pattern of the paper used to fill it and give it shape was evident: the gray chambers of a wasp nest.

Harper and Kae laid the objects in a row along the lip of the planter. They seemed brighter there, richer, in a line against the zinc edge.

Kae unwadded the soil bag and scrutinized its label. "Maybe they're for some kind of promotion?"

"What would they be promoting?"

"They're all garden stuff," Kae said, flipping the bag over and scanning the back. "Flowers and bees—it's about their brand."

"I don't know. They look too handmade for that. And old."

"I mean, they're really beautiful," Kae said. "I just don't know what they're for." They looked closer, glancing their fingertips over the top of the yellow jacket. Harper had the same impulse. There was something about the pieces that made you want to touch, to covet them.

"Do you think maybe you're supposed to plant them?" Kae asked. "You know that thing where they embed seeds in paper and you can water it to grow flowers or whatever. They do it with grass and it looks like insulation." Kae picked up one of the apples, the one

It was an apple: a tiny papier-mâché sculpture painted,
rather realistically, to look like a Black Oxford apple.

that wasn't torn. "I bet that's what this is." They held it up into the streaming light and inspected it for seeds.

"Maybe," Harper said. It wasn't completely unreasonable, what Kae was saying. It was no more unreasonable than finding the things in the first place. But it was obvious too that all of these objects represented Brookhants and its curse.

She pulled out her phone, ignoring its screen of notifications and going right to her camera app. She then took several pics of the sculptures from different angles. Kae was right, they really were beautiful, especially there in a row in the brilliant light of The Orangerie.

Somebody talented seemed to have taken their time making them.

Harper was captioning her post* when Bo and Audrey walked in. They were talking in that kind of feigned hush that isn't actually all that quiet but straining to appear like it's a whisper—the voice people use for both gossip and genuine alarm.

Audrey wore a striped Oxford shirtdress, a double-wrapped skinny belt at her waist, and pink canvas shoes dotted with gold pineapples. She should have been the picture of effortless summer, but as she pushed her sunglasses up onto her forehead, Harper saw how unhappy she was. She said to Bo, "His mouth looked really bad."

"It didn't look great," he said. "Good thing he had it on him." He looked at Harper. "Sorry about the wait, we got sidetracked on the way over here—Brookhants strikes again." He wore denim cutoffs and another of his horror movie T-shirts, this one for *The Uninvited*.

"What happened?" Harper asked.

"The crew in the garden hit a ground nest," he said.

"Of wasps," Audrey added.

"Yellow jackets," Bo said, raising an eyebrow at her.

"One of the landscapers, like, *literally* hit it with his shovel,"

---

* That caption: Just found these in a bag of dirt at Brookhants. Beautiful, but cursed?

Audrey said, her eyes wide, "and a bunch flew up at him and stung him in the face and neck. And he's allergic."

"Oh shit," Kae said, stepping into their cluster. "Do you know if it was Marco?"

"That's exactly who it was," Bo said, as if noticing for the first time that Kae was there.

"Is he OK?"

"I think so," Bo said. "Or he will be."

Audrey jumped in: "Only because he had his EpiPen on him and he injected it right after. Like immediately."

"He was just telling me about how he's allergic," Kae said, turning to Harper. "I mean, just this morning he was telling me, at breakfast."

"His face is pretty fucked," Bo said. "They're taking him to the ER now to get checked out."

"His lip," Audrey said, shaking her head. "His top lip looks like it's a water balloon."

"That's so scary," Harper said.

"It's for sure losing us time," Bo said. "They were already supposed to have the garden finished and now they can't work in there until they get the nest cleared out." He looked at his phone. "Brookhants keeps on giving," he said, scrolling. "Whose idea was it to shoot here?"

"I should probably go over that way and see if they need me," Kae said.

"We'll be in here for the next hour or so," Bo said, not looking up from his phone. "Everyone should already know that, but maybe you can be the one to do any necessary reminding."

"No problem." Kae made a kind of *good luck with this guy* face at Harper and Audrey and left.

"These are beautiful," Audrey said. She'd wandered over to the papier-mâché sculptures and picked up the blue flower. "What are they?" She turned it over in her hand.

"No idea," Harper said. "We just found them."

"They're props?" Audrey asked.

"No," Harper said. "Like in the dirt. They came out of a bag of soil." Harper laughed, both at hearing how dumb it sounded and also at Audrey's reaction face.

"Let's get to this," Bo said, looking up from his phone and spinning around, considering the space. "So if we orient ourselves from here," he said, gesturing to the zinc planter, "Eleanor's hidey-hole." He backed up to reconsider, and as he did, knocked his heel into a container holding one of the citrus trees Harper and Kae had just hauled in.

Bo turned to see what he'd run into and took in the cluster of them, flicking one of the skeletal trunks with his fingers. "What's up with these?" he asked like he didn't expect an answer.

"They're dead," Harper said. "They came off the truck like that."

"Jesus Christ," he said. "We get twenty sticks in pots when it's supposed to be the Amazon in here."

"Layla's on it," Harper said.

"I don't even know who the fuck Layla is," Bo said, texting something to someone in a rather furious way. "Oh, yes I do," he added absentmindedly, before slipping his phone into his back pocket. "OK," he said, clapping his hands together hard and again looking up at Harper and Audrey. "The Faderman discovery scene. Flo's got the—"

"I think we should maybe wait a minute," Audrey interrupted. "Sorry," she added quickly.

"What?" Bo was clearly near to reaching his limit of tolerable interruptions.

Audrey pointed behind him. He turned, and they all looked together through the glass at the vintage green Jaguar convertible that had pulled up alongside the building, Merritt Emmons at the wheel and Elaine Brookhants as her passenger. Elaine was now waving in at all of them.

"Well, shit," Bo said, but he sounded happier than he had all morning. And he was smiling.

AN UNDESIRABLE MORBIDNESS

....

After another hour spent working in the humid cloister of The Orangerie, Alex was now shivering as she waited outside Main Hall for Libbie to come down from her office, or for Caspar to arrive with the carriage, whoever came first. She had the stereoscope and cards hidden in her bag, along with the other items she now kept away from Libbie: a small, corked jar of dead yellow jackets scooped from the bathroom floor; two dried and flattened angel's trumpet blooms clearly marked by Eleanor's teeth; a handwritten version of the student song she'd heard Adelaide so wrongly sing a verse of; and, the real prize, Clara Broward's personal copy of *The Story of Mary MacLane*. The copy curiously missing a page.

Cold wind cut through her coat and dress. Alex felt the sweat that had pooled in her chemise while she worked in The Orangerie chill against her skin. That chill ran the length of her and she looked again for the carriage but did not see it. Caspar hadn't quite gotten the run of this new routine, either. She and Libbie used to nearly always stay on campus through supper; now, it was so empty and quiet, so morose, that they'd stumbled into the habit of taking their evening meal at Spite Manor. Which meant additional work for Hanna.

Alex glanced back at the entrance to Main Hall, its wide double doors, to see if Libbie had emerged from one of them. She had not. As Alex again turned around, she took note of the fountain. It was drained for the season, a layer of unmarred snow inside, though that had melted some in the dull sun, pulling it away from the rim and exposing a black ring.

Alex stepped closer, put one hand against the fountain's stone and felt the cold seep through her gloves.

They'd had to drain and refill it after Flo and Clara had died— something foul had been growing in the water. It had seemed unimportant to Alex at the time. There was so much going on and all so dismal, the scummy fountain had seemed the least of it. But now, as she ran her (thankfully gloved) fingers along the thin ring of black growth, it returned to her—the flaming wasps that had drowned in it. The black water that had followed. What remained was something almost like pasted ash. Whatever it was, this black ring, it appeared to run the entire inner top edge of the fountain's basin. Some of it flaked off as she pressed her fingers against it.

She'd seen this before, or something similar, rimming their tub at Spite Manor the night Adelaide had come, sick and wearing those snowshoes, while Libbie was taking her bath. What was left in that bathtub hadn't been dried and frozen like this, but it was otherwise the same. Alex knew this because she'd been the one to scrub it off the next morning.

There were things about that night that Alex felt sure Libbie had not told her. Things said between Libbie and Adelaide, dark things that had happened in that bathroom—before Alex had arrived, and again after Libbie had sent her away to find Hanna.

But this was how she and Libbie were: they stepped around their secrets in silence, afraid to disturb them. Perhaps they should be afraid.

Alex looked at her hands, the fingertips of her tan gloves now black.

She turned again to search for Libbie at the doors. She was not there. Alex considered going back up the stairs to wait inside the entrance, but then she heard the horses and soon after saw Caspar and the carriage coming on the Spite Manor road.

At the same time, across the snow-packed lawn, at the rim of the dark woods, there was movement and color.

She squinted to better see. Her eyes were tired from their exercise with the stereoscope, so maybe this was only a trick of the trees. But—no, she was correct. The colors were brighter, the picture clearer: two girls had come from the orchard path and were now slowly crossing the lawn in her direction. At this distance, she couldn't yet make out who they were.

There were now so few students remaining at Brookhants that Alex had made a point to study up on each girl who was left. She hoped to never again be caught unawares about their interests and activities, how they were spending their time.

As Caspar slowed the carriage before her, giving a nod, Alex ignored him and stepped around it so that she could keep watch on the students moving toward her across the lawn.

In the immediate aftermath of Eleanor's death, it seemed like they might have done enough to calm the parents and the trustees: Libbie's many letters and telegrams, the meetings she'd held with prominent families in Boston and Baltimore, Philadelphia and Hartford. Oh sure, they'd lost maybe a dozen students at once, as soon as the snow was cleared enough for their parents to send drivers to fetch them. And a few of the faculty, Leanna Hamm included, had resigned, leaving behind scathing letters of condemnation as they did. (None more scathing than Leanna's.)

Even still, as they sent the students off for their winter holidays, Alex had told herself that they'd made it through the worst. That since they'd located the book (and Alex had corralled it to her own keeping) and had somehow reached the end of such an unimaginably wretched year, the dawn of 1903 could only be an improvement.

But oh, my sage Readers: not so.

Most of the student body simply did not return to Brookhants. Arrivals day came, as always, in mid-January. The rooms and halls were cleaned and waiting, smelling of citrus polish and wax. To start them off on the *goodly path,* one family, the Bentons (their daughter Aimee was in year ten) had shipped copies of the newest edition of Ruth Ashmore's *Side Talks with Girls*—one for each of the students. Mrs. Benton had even bookmarked what she believed to be the most relevant chapter: "Your Own Familiar Friend."*

Libbie thought the book full of facile advice for girls who were meant to look pretty and say little, but to appease the Bentons and their wide circle of influence, she'd agreed to have one placed on each student's nightstand, and there they awaited readers in those lemon-scented rooms. Only readers did not come for them.

Some of the parents didn't even feel the need to account for their daughter's removal from the school—they simply sent for her belongings.†

And then, even worse: upon recognizing the bleak state of things, a number of the girls who *had* returned in January promptly contacted their bewildered parents, explained their unease at the situation, and turned around and left again. Left for good, this time.

---

* A telling sample of the kinds of advice given in that chapter: "I like a girl to have many girl-friends; I do not like her to have a girl-sweetheart. There are but two people in the world to whom a girl should give her confidence—the first is her mother, the second is her husband. When two girls are very intimate, and count out of this intimacy not only their own sisters but all their other friends, they are apt, unconsciously, to cultivate the faults of selfishness, of meanness, and to cause an undesirable morbidness to spring up."

† What was there to say, really? The cause was so widely known that two of the less-established and academically rigorous regional prep (finishing) schools for girls—including Mrs. Hutchinson's (in Newport) and St. Catherine's (in New Bedford)—had apparently used the recent deaths at Brookhants (and also, of course, the whispered rumors of a curse) to drum up business for themselves. It's worth noting that while Mrs. Hutchinson's and St. Catherine's were maybe rather short, in those years, on academic excellence, they believed that they made up for any deficits in that area with their offerings in the *domestic arts,* and in their extensive religious requirements, including mandatory classes and church services. These had always been (notable) gaps in the Brookhants curriculum and tradition.

Which in turn left Brookhants at somewhere around 35 percent capacity for the spring semester of 1903.* This was even lower than in the school's first years of operation, when Libbie and Alex were still trying to establish Brookhants's reputation as a place for the *modern girl* to become *thoroughly prepared and mentally mature*—enough so that she might succeed at any women's college.†

Alex did not spare worry for the students who had left. She did not plot and plan ways to convince them to return. That could come later, once Brookhants was again safe. For now, she believed those students were better off wherever else they'd landed.

Her focus was to keep steady watch over each of the girls who remained.

Such as the girls who had just emerged from the woods, who were now clutching at each other so that they moved as one. The combination of their hats and flapping coats, with the wind billowing and sucking at their long, black skirts, made them appear, from this distance, as a grotesque, two-headed bird.

They seemed to notice Alex standing there with the express purpose of watching them approach. One of them, sophomore Camille Andrews, Alex could now see, held her hand in front of her mouth and leaned in to whisper something that the other, Josephine Narse, found amusing. She doubled over in a perfect fit of laugher.

As far away as they were, and with the wind, whispering was most unnecessary. Alex clearly could not hear them. It was a performance meant to annoy her.

And then, as the girls continued to clutch and giggle, and seemed to additionally slow their steps, Alex thought she saw Camille slip a

---

* Even Aimee Benton returned home, leaving her copy of *Side Talks with Girls* behind.

† Brookhants culled its faculty from the likes of Barnard, Bryn Mawr, Mount Holyoke, Radcliffe, and Wellesley. It's perhaps no surprise, then, that its curriculum was heavily skewed to best prepare students to pass the entrance exams at those institutions.

book, a *red* book, into the opening at the front of her coat, which she then bundled around herself to conceal.

"Josephine Narse and Camille Andrews," Alex shouted into the wind, "who gave you permission to be in the woods?"

Camille called back, or pretended to, but Alex couldn't hear what she'd said. She felt the girl was making her voice purposefully thin.

"Students are no longer allowed in the woods without permission," Alex shouted. "You girls know this! You've been told time and again!"

Camille again pretended to answer with something Alex could not make out. She'd had enough. She started toward them, her boots crunching the snow. Its top layer was a crust of ice that held each step until it didn't and she sank into the dry snow below, which forced her to pull up and out so that she might step again. And promptly sink again. Snow and ice fell inside her boots. Her hands were in fists as they swung at her sides. She was suddenly furious with these girls and their galling impudence. She stepped again, sank again. Stepped again, sank again. Camille and Josephine whispered and laughed before her. She hated these girls, she really hated them, she would—

"Alex?"

Alex stopped, then turned. Libbie stood beside the carriage, her face puzzled, though even as Alex watched, Libbie took in her stance, the girls coming behind, and her features shifted into disappointment.

"Where are you going?" Libbie asked.

Alex could hear the girls behind her now, no doubt hoping this interruption would spare them their punishment.

"I saw them come out of the woods," Alex called. She knew she sounded like she was tattling, but she *was* tattling. "And I believe Camille Andrews is hiding something in her coat."

The girls took another tentative step or two. They were slight enough to walk atop the snow crust, not to sink down through it. Now they were nearly in line with Alex, who flicked them a scowl, something she immediately regretted for its lack of composure.

"Girls," Libbie called to them. "Are you both alright?"

"Yes, of course, Principal Brookhants," Camille said. "We were just on a walk. It's so awfully dull here with everyone gone. We only wanted to take the air before supper."

Take the air. Now that was Camille putting it on thick, Alex thought, the same way Camille's older sister had behaved when she'd been at Brookhants. And *she,* the older sister, had once been friends with Clara Broward.

"And have you something in your coat?" Libbie asked. "Something you're hiding from Miss Trills?"

"It's only a novel," Camille said. "I've lost my gloves and my hands were cold, so I tucked them up into my sleeves and couldn't carry it." She reached in and pulled out the book. It was bound in red, was the correct size and shape. Camille started toward Libbie but Alex grabbed for the book instead.

For one wonderful moment, Alex was dead sure that here was the proof that Mary MacLane's book still held sway at Brookhants, even after all their troubles with it. And now, Libbie would be unable to refute it, herself having just witnessed two of their so few remaining students walk a copy out of the woods.

But alas, as she looked down Alex saw that she held Richard Marsh's novel *The Beetle*, a vivid, color illustration of that ugly insect crawling across its front. It *was* a lurid tale of horror. But it was not *The Story of Mary MacLane.*

"It's *The Beetle*," Camille said, speaking not to Alex, but to Libbie. "I've read it so many times."

"It's *very* scary," Josephine added stupidly.

Alex turned the book over in her hands. It did look like it had been read many times, its binding stained and marred. There was also a slip of paper wedged between its pages, a few inches sticking out the top. Perhaps it was only a bookmark but it flicked at some vague core of dread inside her.

"I'm not sure it's wise to work so diligently to frighten yourselves, girls," Libbie said. "But I have heard that if that's the result you're after, then you've landed upon the novel to do it."

"Oh, it's deliciously awful," Camille said. "It's one of my favorites because it's so gruesome."

Alex had been about to look at that sandwiched piece of paper, to make certain it wasn't something it should not be, but Camille's comment rekindled her anger and she thrust the novel back at the girl, asking, "Why would you *choose* to fill your minds with fresh horrors? Haven't we had quite enough of those here, without also seeking them out in books?"

"They've already set the tables, girls," Libbie said, interrupting with false cheer, "so you'd best hurry."

Camille and Josephine did not wait for additional instruction. They scooted around Alex like she was a panting tiger on a short leash.

"I'm told there's gingerbread for dessert," Libbie added. "Will one of you see about saving me a piece for tomorrow?"

"I will, Principal Brookhants," Josephine said as both girls reattached themselves to each other. They even waved at Caspar and fawned over the horses as they went.

But once they reached the Main Hall steps, Alex, who was still stopped in the snow, watched as Camille turned and looked right at her in order to grin like a devil—the girl's mouth mirroring nothing so much as the mirthless stretch of lips Alex had seen earlier in the stereoscope image, as if Camille now had fish bones jammed between her cheeks. It was the same awful smile. Camille turned to follow Josephine inside and Alex shuddered.

Libbie had been waiting to mount the carriage, unhappily watching Alex watch the girls. "Was any of that necessary?" she now asked her. "Did you get what you were after?"

Alex, still stunned by Camille's smile, took a few moments to process Libbie's displeasure. Then she said, "They were coming from the woods on the orchard path." She felt that should be more than enough to explain.

"Well if that isn't cause for a scene."

"It's very suitable cause for a scene," Alex said, feeling, as was often the case now, that she needed to defend herself. "They've been told not to go into the woods. More than once, they've been told. And those two are no good for each other, anyway. Not so long ago you would have agreed with me about that."

"It feels long ago," Libbie said, taking Caspar's hand as she mounted the carriage.

"Yes, it does," Alex said. "That we agree on." Her stockings were now sopping and there was so much snow in her boots she could curl her toes around it. She felt additionally displeased when Caspar did not hold out his hand to assist her into the carriage and instead moved himself back into the driver's seat. This was almost certainly because Alex had refused his assistance so many times before, but no matter: today his lack of deference rankled her. It was her right to refuse but he should nonetheless offer.

As Alex heaved herself into the carriage, Libbie said, sounding very defeated, "This really can't go on."

"It won't," Alex said simply. She meant it.

ROAD APPLES

Audrey did not want to be in an SUV on the way to a strip mall in Tiverton. They were now six days into filming—six messy, not particularly successful days, if you asked her—and tomorrow both she and Harper had five A.M. call times.

And yet here she was: in an SUV on the way to a strip mall in Tiverton. With Merritt along, too.

Only Merritt did not have a five A.M. call time. She would likely wander onto set the next day whenever (and if ever) she felt like it. From what Audrey could tell, and to Bo's annoyance, thus far Merritt had spent about half of her time at Brookhants in front of her laptop. The night before, in fact, when she'd been brushing her teeth for bed, Audrey had looked out the open window of her tiny house and through the window into Merritt's. Her cottage was dark except for the cool wash of light from her laptop screen, which was wrapped around her like a private fog. If Audrey listened for it (and silenced her electric toothbrush) she could even hear the *tap-tap-tap* of Merritt's hands over her keyboard. Audrey had wished for binoculars so she might read the screen.

She should ask Bo for a pair. If she did, she felt certain they'd show up on the counter in her cottage, probably with a little note attached. Just now there was yet another *little note* from him on her phone screen in the form of a text:

Something coming up ahead in the road. Get out of the car to look.

It was dusk, and Carl Eckhart was driving them through the woods surrounding Brookhants on a dirt road reopened by production only days before. There was tree canopy above and they were enclosed on either side by tall trunks and looming dark, some patches deeper than others.

Audrey was in the seat Bo wanted her in, left side behind the driver. Harper was up front with Carl, because of course she was—the two of them having apparently already attained their mutual ride-or-die status—and Merritt was next to Audrey. Audrey happened to know that this particular Range Rover was rigged with cameras and microphones aplenty. (And she was wearing her own concealed mic.) Bo had been sending her rushed texts about blocking, about how best to incorporate this or that when she played this scene. Because that's what it was, for Audrey: a scene. One that had come up earlier, apparently, than Bo had been planning for, but *he was capitalizing on the opportunity.*

For Harper and Merritt, it was a spontaneous trip, happening only because Harper had said she was craving a Cherry Coke slushee and some greasy pizza and Carl had overheard and said he knew where there was a convenience store in Tiverton with an Icee machine.* And it happened to be in the same strip mall with a, as Carl put it, "pizza joint."

"So Caspar and Hanna were what, your great-great-grandparents? Great-great-great?" Harper was now asking Carl. "I can't ever do family math right."

"Not grandparents," Merritt said, her face in her phone, but not missing a word. "Can't be. Max and Adelaide didn't ever have children. Remember, Hanna—"

"My relation to them is a lot more distant than that," Carl said.

---

* Which is *not* a slushee, careful Readers, but in this instance, it would have to do.

Audrey smiled at Carl not caring whether he cut Merritt off.

"Well, you got the last name anyway," Harper said. "That's what matters."

A fresh text from Bo landed on Audrey's phone: Get in there! Ask him about what he knows about the curse. Something!

Her heart rate ticked up. She played out a few options in her head, thought them each stupid, and decided to go with what she hoped was the least stupid. She took a breath, leaned forward a notch, and asked, "Carl, does your family believe in any of the curse stuff? I mean, did you, like, grow up thinking of it as real?"

She thought she sensed an eye roll from Merritt, but to be fair, it was only a sensation. And this Merritt, the one who had shown up with Elaine in that green convertible, was notably changed from the Merritt Audrey had met back at Bo's bungalow of horrors. She wasn't kind, exactly. But she wasn't outwardly cruel and needling, either. (At least not yet.)

Carl scratched at the back of his hairline, pushing up his Red Sox baseball cap as he did so that it now sat crooked atop his head. "I don't know," he said. "Me and my sister would sometimes scare each other about things we pretended to see in the woods that we didn't. Least I didn't."

"Like what?" Harper asked. She appeared to revel in this line of inquiry.

"Oh, like witches around their cauldrons, I guess. Or ghosts. One time I told Sue, that's my little sister, that I'd found a skeleton buried by the hot springs. She didn't quite believe me, but she still came with me to see it. I waited until she was bent over looking for it and then pushed her in."

"Sounds like you were a jerk," Harper said. "Does Sue even still speak to you?"

"She does, in fact," Carl said. "She's a better human than I am."

"Not hard," Harper said.

And it seemed like that was it, they were moving on from the topic of cursed Brookhants as it pertained to Carl Eckhart. Audrey waited for somebody to ask something else, except everyone but Carl had their eyes on their phones; it was again quiet enough to make out the seventies soft rock playing on the satellite radio station.

She had to be the one to do it. Again.

"But did you ever talk about, like, the girls who died?" Audrey asked, again leaning forward in her seat so that Carl would be certain she was speaking to him. "Or anything about the curse—I mean, in specific?"

She felt so obvious, desperate. She wasn't any good at this.

"I can't honestly sit here and tell you that it came up a whole lot," he said. "But you're right—somebody must have told me some of the history at some point, because I know it now."

"Maybe other kids?" Merritt said. "I interviewed some locals for the book and most of them had at least one Brookhants story that they thought was better than their friends' one Brookhants story."

"That could be," Carl said, looking for her in the rearview, but Merritt's face was still tilted down to her phone, so he found Audrey's instead. "Probably my friends knew some of it better than I did. I was never into that stuff." He winked at her. "Not the answer you were looking for, huh?"

Audrey responded quickly, "No, it's—I didn't have one I was looking for. I just wondered what you thought of all this. I mean since it's the reason we're making this movie and you're connected to it personally."

"I think they're paying me too much money to drive you three around, so I'm fine with it."

"Not the hero we want but maybe the one we need," Harper said.

Another text from Bo: Keep it on this track.

Audrey did not have anything else to ask on this track. Nothing. She was tired. This was dumb and she was bad at it. Plus, she had a real scene, a Clara Broward scene that would ask a lot of her, the following morning. That's what she should be thinking about now. Not this.

They'd been rounding a bend in the narrow road, the trees so clogged and heavy around them that they formed a kind of tunnel. And as soon as the road straightened again, there was something in the middle of it.

"Shit!" Carl's sudden braking lurched them forward with enough force to be snagged by their seat belts and jerked back. Audrey's phone flew out of her hands and into the front of the SUV, where it smacked hard against the windshield. Merritt shrieked and the four of them, to a person, rubbed their necks at the whiplash.

"Everybody alright?" Carl asked. They were now fully stopped in the road.

"Not so much!" This from Merritt. "What was that?" She made a *can you believe this guy?* face at Audrey.

"There's something in the road," Harper said. She had already undone her seat belt and now popped open her door to climb out.

"What's in the road?" Merritt asked, leaning forward to better see out the windshield.

"Bunch of boxes of something," Harper said.

"I'll go look," Carl said. He opened his own door. "You stay—all I need is to be the one who gets you run over."

"Oh c'mon," Harper said. "Who's gonna run us over? This road didn't even exist until, like, yesterday." She hopped down to join him even though he kept arguing with her about it.

Audrey stretched between the front seats in order to reach her phone where it had dropped onto the floor. As soon as she touched it, she could tell that its screen was shattered.

"Was that your phone that flew past my face?" Merritt asked.

"Yeah," Audrey said as she sat back and looked at it: it wasn't working, like shards of glass popped from its spiderweb black screen not working. "Unfortunately, I think Carl just killed it." She tilted it at Merritt so she could see the shattered screen.

"Fuck," Merritt said. She'd been charging her own phone and now handed the cord to Audrey. "Maybe try this?"

A piece of glass fell from the phone's screen even as Audrey plugged it in. Nothing happened.

"I'm sorry," Merritt said, watching the screen stay dead. "Tell Carl he has to buy you a new one."

Outside, Harper and Carl laughed together at something.

"So are you participating in this inanity?" Merritt asked.

This was Audrey's moment, but how to play it without Bo on her phone? "I guess so" is what she went with. She opened her door but didn't move.

"OK. Let's forgo all reason and get out of the car here in the darkest part of the woods to look at the thing in the road that's not supposed to be there." I bet you know, Readers, exactly how Merritt said this. But she did undo her seat belt and open her door.

Outside they were submerged in the green light from the leaves overhead. The dense mugginess added to the feeling of being underwater in a pond. Or a scummy fountain.

Audrey joined Merritt in front of the SUV and they walked together. Carl and Harper were blocking their view of the things in the road. And then Harper bent over them. She was already using her phone to take a video of whatever it was.

Carl turned as he heard them approach. "Apples," he said, as if he didn't know the meaning of the word he'd just used. "I got nothing."

Merritt and Audrey peeled apart, moved around Carl and Harper to see what he meant.

Apples is what he meant: three antique wooden crates of Black Oxford apples, two placed side by side and one centered on top of them to form a small pyramid there in the middle of the road. A few yellow jackets made lazy swoops above and around these crates, and now around the four of them as well, though not enough to pay much attention to. It was a reasonable, even expected, number of yellow jackets for autumn and crates of apples.

"I have no idea what these are doing here," Carl said.

"Well, obviously somebody put them here," Merritt said. "They didn't bounce out the back of a truck into this nice stack of three."

"Or what if they did?" Harper said. With her nonvideoing hand, she took an apple from the crate atop the pyramid and held it up to her phone's camera lens. Then she situated her face into the frame and took a bite.

"Harper!" Merritt said, though even she seemed surprised by the force of her reaction. She regained her detached voice to add, "That seems ill advised given that you don't know how these road apples came to be."

"*Road apples* are what you call horse droppings," Carl said.

"I did not use the term by accident, Carl," Merritt said.

"It also seems *ill advised* given every fairy tale ever," Audrey said. This comment earned her a nod from Merritt, which pleased her a stupid amount.

"It's a good apple," Harper said, chewing as loudly as possible for her video. She then took another large bite, because of course she did. "Like, really good."

"I mean, they have to be from Brookhants, right, Carl?" Audrey asked. She had to stop saying *right, Carl* after every question, but this was what came from making her be the screenwriter, too. She wondered how they were even filming this. External cameras on the SUV, or drones? Or did Bo have a crew camouflaged somewhere nearby in the woods?

"Could be, I guess," Carl said. "This is what's in the orchard, but nobody I know uses these kinda crates anymore. And we haven't picked ours yet, either. It's still too early."

"Spooky," Harper said, midbite. She seemed to be done with her video, her phone no longer held aloft.

"Is it?" Merritt said. "Seems like someone's idea of a prank. One that's too enigmatic to mean much of anything."

"I think she looks like Mary MacLane," Audrey said. She kneeled to examine the smiling lady holding the apple on the crate's paper label, *Black Oxford* printed in script over the image's bottom. Audrey did actually think this, but she also knew it was the kind of thing Bo would want her to say.

"Oh shit," Harper said, kneeling, too. "Yeah, she does." She looked up at Merritt for confirmation.

"I mean, she doesn't *not* look like her," Merritt said. "Her style is from the right era, anyway."

"So do we bring them with us or just move them to the side of the road?" Carl asked.

"Bring them," Harper said.

"Side of the road," Merritt and Audrey said exactly together.

"You're outnumbered," Carl said to Harper.

"Not if you make it a tie."

"I can't," he said. "I'm also for side of the road."

"Nerd," Harper said, but she slipped her phone into her back pocket, tossed her apple core into the woods, and bent to lift the top crate. Carl went for the one nearest to him, but Merritt got to it sooner, and before he could reach the crate in front of Audrey, she had bent over and lifted it, too.

"Well this isn't right," Carl said, his arms still empty.

So it was that our three heroines walked the apple crates to the side of the road and moved them just off its edge, into a spread of massive ferns, their fronds growing up from the ground like too many webbed fingers reaching.

As the heroines stood, a breeze stinking of rank ocean came through the trees and made them look into the woods beyond.

Merritt saw it first.

"What is that?" is all she asked. Now the others looked where her face was pointed and saw it, too.

Though what it was they were seeing was unclear.

It was a vertical shape, like a shadow made of static, maybe forty yards off into the trees and trees and darkness. It drifted behind trunks and back out again, hovering and pulsing.

Now that they were silent and watching they each, to a person, could hear a kind of low hum emanating from it.

"Jesus fuck," Carl said between his teeth. "It's a swarm of wasps."

"Yellow jackets," Harper said like a reflex.

"Let's back it up slowly now." Carl was already doing the thing he instructed—one step and then two.

"Why are they going up and down like that?" Harper asked. She took the same number of steps Carl had taken, but instead she took them forward, into the woods, toward the drifting swarm.

"Harper, you don't mess with these," Carl said, his voice sharp. "I've seen them take down a deer." He'd now moved another few steps back and

"Yellow jackets," Harper said like a reflex.

down the road in the direction of the SUV. "We can get a good look from behind the windows when we drive by."

"It isn't coming toward us, I don't think," Merritt said. "It seems like it's hovering."

"For now it is," Carl said. "They can move whenever they want. Fast."

"Why are they in that shape?" Harper asked again. She was still walking, slow step by slow step toward the mass, and now a couple of yards off the road and into the woods.

"It doesn't matter," Audrey said, letting panic infect her voice. "He's saying it's not safe. Please don't go any closer." Was that too much concern? Was she overdoing it?

Even if it was too much, Harper seemed to listen. She stopped moving in the swarm's direction but pulled out her phone again to start filming.

Though the shape did not appear to drift any closer, its hum was somehow denser and stronger, the notes low and pulsing like plucked strings through the trees. Audrey could now feel that hum in her body, settling in her blood and bones where she did not want it to be.

Carl wasn't even with them anymore. He was back at their vehicle, climbing in.

The shape drifted in and out of shadow. Sometimes its outline was clear and sharp, then it would muddle and fuzz, its contours smudged. It seemed to make the very air around it vibrate.

"I've never seen anything like this here," Merritt said. They were standing close now, Audrey and Merritt, shoulders brushing—with Harper those couple of yards in front of them, in the woods. Carl was, for the moment, forgotten.

"I thought there were always yellow jackets here," Audrey said in a near whisper.

"There are," Merritt said. "But *I've* never seen anything like this here. Not firsthand."

The hum churned on like an incantation while the smell of sick seawater clogged their noses.

And then—

The SUV's ignition startled them. By the time they turned to look, Carl had it nearly behind them. As the passenger-side window rolled down he said, "Your ride, ladies."

Merritt did not wait for further instruction to climb in, and Audrey, without her phone, didn't know if she was supposed to or not. So she did. Just in case it wasn't a Bo trick. (But it *had* to be. Of course it was.)

"We go now, Harper," Carl said, his voice raised and firm. "Please—I'm asking you."

Harper lowered her phone after he added the *please* and turned and walked to the car, too—though she took another couple of apples from one of the crates as she passed.

"God, I hope my video turned out," she said when she got in. "That was bananas." Harper set the apples she'd grabbed in the front cupholders and turned around in her seat to face Merritt and Audrey. "My heart's going a mile a minute. Did you see its arm?"

"What do you mean *arm*?" Merritt asked.

"That thing, like, raised its arm at us—like it was saying *Come here*." Harper's face was flushed and her eyes seemed even bluer than usual, glittery with excitement.

"How does a swarm of yellow jackets raise its *arm*?" Merritt asked.

"How did you not see it do it?" Harper asked. "Audrey, tell me you've got me here."

"I couldn't really see it that well," Audrey said. "I mean, I didn't see any arms but—"

"Oh come on," Harper said. "*Come. On.* Fine. I can show you." She climbed over the armrest and into the back and found a perch between Merritt and Audrey.

"Not safe," Carl said.

"Look, look, I'm buckling in," she said as she did. "Sorry, Carl." Harper grinned as she held out her phone and hit Play.

They must have watched the video a dozen times. They watched it until they had just about arrived at the strip mall that was the reason for the trip. They watched it until Harper and Merritt *agreed to disagree* about what they were witnessing—the beckoning arm Merritt refused to see, no matter how many times Harper pointed it out or even traced it for her on the screen. Audrey thought she could kind of see it—or at least see what Harper meant—if she *let herself* see it, that is.

They watched until Harper finally had enough cell service to post it. Well, to post the apple crates that had come before the swarm first, and then to post the more frightening thing.

Her caption: After we moved the crates, this happened. Turn your volume waaaaaaay up and tell me those yellow jackets don't look like a floating woman in a dress telling you to "Come here, child. Come here."

Tell me you don't see her arm reaching toward you through the screen.

"Pure poetry," Merritt said, reading Harper's post from her own phone's Instagram feed.

"So you're gonna treat this like you did the orange trees?" Harper said.

"Oh my God," Merritt said, throwing up her hands in overdone exasperation. "Please get over the fucking orange trees."

"I can't," Harper said. "I was there. I know what I saw. And so I know what you saw, too."

"I saw sickly trees get better with appropriate care," Merritt said. "I'm sorry, but there's no magic in that. It's basic botany—take a plant off the back of a windowless truck and give it some good light and water and it grows. Jinkies, Daphne! Must be the work of a ghost!"

"Audrey, please chime in here anytime," Harper said.

Audrey did not want to chime in. Audrey had already done so, several times during the days previous, since the very day, in fact, when the orange trees that had been brought into The Orangerie as brown sticks had been found bursting with leaves and flowers and, on two of them, the green pearls of newborn fruit. She hadn't paid all that much attention to the trees when they'd come off the trucks— she hadn't been the one hauling them in like Harper had—but she had seen Bo's anger about them being dead, and so agreed that their unexpected health and vibrancy was, well, unexpected. She'd agreed to that despite Merritt's eye-rolling and shoulder-shrugging. Audrey was pretty sure this miraculous botanical recovery was another Bo

Dhillon touch. She couldn't be certain, of course, but it did have the feel.

"Those trees were dead, now they're not. How many things like this have to happen before we melt your frozen, unbelieving heart?" Harper asked Merritt.

"Things like what?" Merritt said.

"Unexplained occurrences," Harper said.

"How about one thing that really does defy explanation?" Merritt said. "Let's set the bar at one real thing."

Carl was now parking them halfway between the pizza place and the convenience store with the Icee machine. Before they got out, and without much hope, Audrey checked her phone again. It still wouldn't turn on.

So much for further instructions on this night, Readers.

TRIFLE WITH THE TRIFLE

....

Alex sat alone at one end of the long table not eating her supper. She was the only living thing then in the dining room.

The bouquet of purple freesia she'd brought home from The Orangerie the day before and placed at the center of the table (in Libbie's crystal wedding vase) had already died. Not drooped or wilted. Died. Some of the bouquet's dumped appendages now lay shriveled across the table's surface, which was so painstakingly polished by Hanna that it would cast your phantom reflection as you passed by. Alex told herself that the carriage ride in the cold could have contributed to the freesia's demise, but she didn't really think so. She felt it more likely that anything just then thriving in The Orangerie simply could not live beyond its cloister.

It *was* peculiar, though, that Hanna had not yet seen to remove the bouquet and its mess.

This night, Alex had been served haddock. She was not an admirer, but she wasn't hungry anyway. Hanna was clanging things around in the kitchen next door, and if Alex listened intently, she could hear the voices above her in Spite Tower, where Libbie and Adelaide were having their Thursday evening tutoring session.

Why there should be so much laughter during a rigorous discussion of *Macbeth,* Alex could not say.

This was now the way of Spite Manor on Tuesdays and Thursdays. After a ride like the one they'd had that day—silence save for the noise of the horses and road, and the awful scrape of branches across the carriage top when they passed through the woods—they would arrive home. Alex would then sit down to supper alone in the dining room and Adelaide would bring a tray for two up to Libbie's office, there atop her terrible tower.

A tray for the two of *them,* that is—for Libbie and Adelaide.

For several weeks, all during Adelaide's prolonged recovery from her strange and sudden illness, Libbie had been tutoring her in the tower. Even with the Brookhants enrollment at its dismal 35 percent, Alex had expressed her strong disinclination to allow Adelaide to attend classes on campus—as Libbie had guessed she would—and so they'd come up with this arrangement instead. Although now that she had accrued a pile of lonely suppers, Alex would have preferred the former. And would have most preferred for Adelaide not to be tutored at all, though her best arguments went limp against Libbie's reasoning that with so few students currently at Brookhants, she had plenty of time to teach anyone who wanted to learn. And Addie, she said, so wanted to learn. And had the mind for it!

Alex hadn't personally witnessed any evidence of Adelaide's impressive aptitude, but Libbie seemed lately convinced that they were employing some kind of undiscovered savant as one of their maids.

Alex poked at the fleshy haddock. It had gone cold in its wan puddle of oil and its smell was most unappetizing, particularly when mixed with the fetor from the murky freesia water sitting spoiled in the vase. She pushed her plate away, running it into and over some of the discarded flower droppings. She scanned the room's dark corners. The whole expanse, starting from the Turkish rug on the floor and pressing up to the coffered ceiling, seemed to her now clouded with the miasma of decay, thick and nearly as vaporous as Tricky Thicket gas.

She caught the trickle of a tune she recognized but could not place. Hanna was humming to herself as she worked in the kitchen. Strange, Alex couldn't recall having ever heard Hanna do that before. Not once in seven years.

Hanna, Alex believed, did not like this tutoring arrangement between Adelaide and Libbie any better than she did, though certainly Hanna had her own reasons for that. Probably they had to do with Addie's (sudden) convergence of peculiar ailments—ailments that apparently overtook her completely before they seemed to retreat just as fast.

After the queer night in the bathroom—Adelaide's snowshoes, the black algae scum in the tub, the six yellow jacket carcasses Alex later found strewn on the floor like ominous confetti—Libbie had insisted that Adelaide stay in her bed at least until the roads were cleared and they could send for the doctor. Libbie had not thought to consult Alex in this decision, despite the fact that for the past seven years she had also been sleeping in that bed. That Alex technically had her own room down the hall, where her clothing and belongings were stored, and where Hanna regularly changed bedding that had not been slept upon, was not the point.

Libbie had decided, and so it was that in her bed Adelaide remained, sleeping on Alex's side—and also sometimes giggling, moaning, and talking nonsense—for two days. During this time, Alex and Libbie slept apart, Libbie in a guest room and Alex in her technical bedroom. This was primarily because Hanna had unexpectedly stayed on at Spite Manor as well, tending to Adelaide and seeing everything, always. (Except, Alex thought, when she found it convenient not to.)

When Alex checked on Adelaide the first morning of her confinement, she did so early enough that she thought only Hanna would be about. She found Libbie instead. She was sitting on the edge of the bed, holding the maid's hand while the two of them talked quietly about something, likely about what had really gone on in the bathroom the night before. But Alex couldn't be certain of this, because they stopped talking once they'd noticed her in the doorway. And then Max had come in right after, pushing past her with a bowl of snow he'd just gathered. They'd been using it to numb the swollen portions of Adelaide's face. Max was ruddy with concern for his wife, and in the wound dressing and general fussing that had followed, Alex couldn't seem to find the right moment to ask Libbie and Adelaide what they'd been so intently discussing.

As soon as the roads were passable, Caspar had gone for the doctor. By the time he arrived back at Spite Manor with him, Adelaide was already sitting up and drinking bone broth and behaving just about as she should. She claimed her fever had finally broken and that she was now feeling *so much more like herself*. And she had looked rather beautifully pale and serene right then, Readers, propped there against Alex's own pillows like some fresco of a wounded angel done on a crumbling plaster wall. Addie's face—especially her lip and eye—was still swollen, though far less so than it'd been the night it had happened. And the intense reds and purples then tinting her skin had settled to an almost-fetching pink.

Adelaide had little to say about the cause of her injuries. She claimed that she couldn't remember putting on the snowshoes, leaving the cottage, startling Libbie in the bathroom with her strange approach and even stranger speech. She said those fever-dream hours were lost to her, that she couldn't quite believe everyone when they told her what had happened, what she'd done.

The doctor, for his part, believed her facial injuries to have been caused by an insect, probably an arachnid. He said that despite it being winter, he wouldn't rule out some particularly aggressive poisonous spider lurking in their cottage's floorboards and suggested that Max complete a thorough inspection for nests or webs.

But, as Alex recalled, the doctor couldn't seem to find much else wrong with her.

Thinking of her propped there on Alex's side of the bed, surrounded by her doting attendees, pinched at Alex as she now sat alone in the dining room with her spongy haddock. She strained to hear fresh sounds from the tutoring lesson in the tower, but couldn't make any out over Hanna's song, which had grown notably louder. In fact, it was right on the other side of the door, coming toward her.

Alex almost had it—the tune—*dunnn-du-dun du du du du-un*—it was . . .

The song cut off as Hanna pushed open the door and came into the room carrying what appeared to be an unnecessarily large serving of trifle. "We used Brookhants's own apples for this," she said as she placed the towering portion on the table before Alex and cleared the fish plate.

Alex watched as a hunk of the fruit-and-nut mixture, sticky with syrup and flecked with so many dark spices, slid down the side of the serving to land in a mass of thick yellow cream. She thought she might be sick if she continued to look at it.

"Was the fish not good, miss?" Hanna asked from the doorway, her question clearly an afterthought.

"It was cooked well," Alex said. "I'm afraid I have no appetite this evening."

"That's been the case all week, Miss Trills."

"Has it?" Alex asked. She couldn't remember if she'd been eating or not.

"That's why Addie asked if I would make trifle for you," Hanna said, nodding at the dish. "I know if there's one thing you have a taste for, it's trifle made with my almond cake. I didn't have the time for it today, so Adelaide made it for you herself. It's what's there with the apples."

"Oh, wonderful," Alex said, refusing to look at her serving. "This will be the thing, then."

Hanna nodded. She turned to leave.

"Hanna, what song is that you've been humming?"

"I didn't mean for you to hear me," Hanna said, turning back around again. "Didn't know I was so loud."

"You weren't at all. It's just that the house is quiet tonight."

"It is," Hanna said. "And if I hear that song even once, it's with me for a month."

"Which is it?" Alex asked again.

"'Annie Lisle.' I can't imagine where I heard it."

---

* "Annie Lisle" is a rather mawkish American ballad about a fair young maiden who dies from some unnamed ailment. It was written in 1857 by New England songwriter H. S. Thompson. A few choice lyrics:

On a bed of pain and anguish / Lay dear Annie Lisle, / Chang'd were the lovely features, / Gone the happy smile.

Even if those lyrics are new to you, I bet many of you are more familiar with this

Hanna had the kitchen door pushed open and was partway through when Alex asked, suddenly, "Hanna, where did you hear it, do you think?"

Her face, now only partially turned toward Alex, was caught between the dim light of the kitchen and the even dimmer light of the dining room, washing it in shadow. Alex could not read her features as she said, "I really couldn't say for certain, Miss Trills. Must be Adelaide. Max calls her his songbird."

"I didn't know that," Alex said.

"Oh yes, she's always with a tune in her mouth," Hanna said. Then she kept on to the kitchen, letting the door *whish* closed behind her.

It wasn't proof. Not wholly. The Brookhants students sang their yellow jacket song to a number of different tunes. Sometimes they didn't even use a tune, instead offering it almost as a skip-rope chant. But Alex most certainly had heard them sing it to "Annie Lisle." That was one of the melodies they favored for it—and their lyrics fit it well.

Once (with the doctor's blessing) they'd finally gotten Adelaide out of Libbie and Alex's bed and back to her cottage—Spite Manor momentarily emptied of all Eckharts—Alex had tried to talk to Libbie about what they'd both heard Addie sing: lyrics belonging to a student song that she simply had no right, and no honest way, to know. But Libbie wouldn't acknowledge how wrong it was for that song to issue from Addie's mouth.

Instead, she said that Adelaide might have overheard students

---

song than you think. In 1870, its tune was borrowed for the Cornell University alma mater, "Far Above Cayuga's Waters." (Which, as you might recall, is proudly sung by the character Andrew "Andy" Bernard on the sitcom *The Office*.)

Since that melodic reincarnation, the tune has also been used as the backing to the alma maters of more than a hundred other schools. Or, if you prefer to dig even deeper into the annals of twentieth-century popular culture, it was used for the Kellerman Resort closing celebration song in the 1987 film *Dirty Dancing*. (Which is where I first heard it, judging Readers.)

It *is* catchy. And it certainly has staying power.

singing it in any number of places, at any number of times. Out in the woods maybe, with Addie close by, going to or from her cottage. Or perhaps she'd been in the orchard when she'd heard it. Or working in the garden when a few of the girls had happened along. Libbie said that Adelaide herself probably didn't know why she knew the song, or what it meant—she'd just picked it up.

Alex did not believe this reasoning sound. Adelaide had only been with them since August and, to Alex's knowledge, had never yet had occasion to meet any of the students, who would have had to roam through the woods for quite a long time in order to get close enough to Spite Manor to be overheard. But Libbie said she would not discuss the matter further, and when Alex had tried to reposition her argument—to make it again, and better—Libbie had simply refused to take it up.

The mound of trifle on the table before her now seemed to slide and bubble, folding in on itself like the ground in the Tricky Thicket. Watching it made Alex bubble up too with a sour burp she hid behind her hand. She did not want to eat even a single bite of this dessert. But Hanna was right: almond cake, which apparently made up one of the trifle's layers, was usually a personal favorite, something she even requested from time to time. Hanna and Adelaide both would be hurt or would act hurt—Adelaide especially—if she did not seem to make at least a little progress with it.

She was sure this dessert was some attempt at a peace offering from the young maid.

Alex picked up her spoon and nudged at the trifle. The cake was so spongy it trembled. She imagined the rank vapors from the haddock and the dead bouquet draping themselves over it, forcing her to ingest them as well.

She wondered where she might hide a portion. Just on the other side of the sliding door, in the hall, were two large ferns in brass pots. If she was sure to clear the contents as soon as Hanna and Adelaide left that night for their cottages, Alex thought the plants' long fronds would disguise her dumping grounds for now.

But as she listened for Hanna at the door, and already gripping the edge of the trifle dish in anticipation of moving quickly, Alex thought, quite suddenly, of her stern grandparents and their dining table, with its elaborate rules and procedures and endless, to her child's mind, dinners. After her father's death, while she was still getting used to the run of her grandparents' household, she had often done something similar: hiding bits of unwanted food about the room as soon as the meal was finally over.

Alex told herself that she was no longer that silent child, the nuisance with oyster oil dribbled on her skirt. *This* was where she lived now, where she had made a life with her Libbie, and she would not hide unwanted food in the plants in her own dining room.

She did not wish to remain at the table a moment more. She set down her spoon and readied to push back her chair. In the center of her vision, the dish of trifle remained untouched.

And yet, Hanna had said that Adelaide had made the dessert especially for Alex. She *would* be disappointed if Alex did not eat any. And Hanna too would notice and remark upon it. Hanna was often so strained with Alex. Always, really—there'd been a strain with Hanna, because she was Harold's servant first and to Harold her loyalties remained.

Alex again picked up her spoon. She would not hide the trifle in the ferns. And she would not refuse it. She would eat three large bites, each followed by a hearty swallow of water, and that would be that.

She managed the first well enough. The cake layer was good, the same flavor as always, but the custard was too thick and the syrup on the apple-and-nut mixture too generously spiced—the flecks of clove and cinnamon, allspice and nutmeg were large and overpowering, as if they had not been properly ground. Even after she'd chewed and swallowed the bite, she could still feel their bulky remains speckling her tongue and lodged in her molars.

She took several sips of water, swishing them about her mouth before swallowing. As she scooped her next bite, she tried to think of something other than what she was doing. What came to her was the scene that afternoon with Josephine and Camille. There was something about the book—the red book that Camille had concealed—that was amiss.

Alex wished she'd held on to that copy of *The Beetle* and not handed it back over to trying Camille Andrews. She replayed the moment when she'd seen the girl slip it into her coat. She wondered if perhaps Camille actually had two books tucked away beneath her clothing—*The Beetle* and Mary MacLane's—but she'd shown Libbie and Alex only the one that wouldn't get her into trouble.

And why hadn't Alex pulled the slip of paper from it, or opened to the page that held it? Now it felt like that paper had quite literally been a warning flag flapping from the book. What if it was the missing page from Flo and Clara's copy of the MacLane? It might have been! And how would Alex ever know now? She couldn't trust Josephine or Camille to tell her the truth.

She brought the second bite of trifle to her lips, over her lips, into her mouth. She meant to swallow it without chewing but found she could not do so. Always before she'd thought the Brookhants Black Oxfords the best variety of apple for winter-keeping she'd ever known, but those used in this dessert were mealy and dry. They seemed to wrap around her teeth and suck the moisture from her tongue. And then there were those too-big spices again, even more of them in this bite. Only, when she crunched one between her teeth, a very hard piece, like a jagged pebble, it did not bring the sharp taste of nutmeg or clove. It did not taste like a piece of burnt walnut or peppery cinnamon, either. Instead, it released the botanical taste of wood pulp, or that of a particularly bitter seed.

She drank more water. She drained her glass, in fact, and got up to refill it herself from the pitcher on the sideboard. As she sat back down, her stomach gurgling unpleasantly, she thought again of the novel Camille had produced that afternoon.

Alex flashed upon that moment: the book in her hand as she looked down at it, after she'd taken it from them. It had that awful illustration of a large beetle crawling across it, one with thorny mandibles and a shiny exoskeleton tinted with glinting green.

At once Alex knew, though she could not let herself believe it. She scooped from the trifle a portion of the fruit-and-nut mixture, one with an ample coating of syrup. She stood, holding her spoon up toward one of the electric sconces that jutted from the wall.

She held her breath and squinted, letting the light shine through the mixture. Just as if she were holding some prehistoric piece of amber, the syrup lit up in the incandescent light and magnified its holdings: a jointed leg, a section of glassy black eye, one portion of striped thorax. Not spices at all, but bits of crushed insect.

She dropped the spoon. It made only a hushed thud against the thick carpet. Its contents bounced off, some landing on the toe of her house slipper. Almost as a reflex, she stuck her index finger into her mouth, running it along the channel on the inside of her bottom lip, up against her gums. She scooped out a portion of the unchewed *spices* that had lodged there and held them to the light. On her finger was a wet mash of striped abdomen. And somehow even worse: a single yellow jacket wing in full.

The vomit bubbled up in her throat. She wanted only to avoid the carpet, but it had been made to cover the whole floor, save a few inches along the walls, so Alex leaned over the table and did it there, rank bile and trifle splashing against the freesia droppings.

Right after, she felt dizzy and weak. Emptied out. It was as if her whole body was made of that spongy almond cake. It couldn't possibly keep her upright. And it did not. She slumped into a messy pile on the floor, her view of the room blurry, as if she needed to reposition the stereo card.

She sensed the dark shape of someone at the door, footsteps coming toward her, a rustling of skirts. Then there was Hanna next to her saying, "Oh, Miss Trills—you really *aren't* feeling well!"

And then her blurry vision gave up for black.

EVEN IN EAST BUMBLEBUZZARD,
RHODE ISLAND

....

The convenience store in Tiverton, BETTY'S, according to the yellow-and-purple sign hanging above its door, smelled like astringent lemon floor cleaner and fresh popcorn. But it was the too-bright fluorescent lights that **Merritt** noticed first as she entered. They were abuzz. The whole store hummed with them.

Audrey followed Harper straight to the churning neon slush of the Icee machine—ostensibly what they'd come for—as Merritt drifted down the candy aisle. She wasn't looking for anything in particular but still found it uncomfortable to be this close to Harper without either of them having resolved whatever it was between them. If there ever was anything between them. And Merritt was sure that there had been. Right?

There *had* been, Readers.

"I don't know," Harper was now saying to Audrey. "I wouldn't go for a blend on your first Icee voyage. Go simple, you know? Get to know the beverage before you get custom with it."

Merritt rolled her eyes for an audience of candy bars, all the shining cellophane and rainbow foil. She didn't know how to do this with these two. She felt like she wasn't doing it right and she hated that feeling. And the swarm in the woods? What was that, really?

The door dinged as three people entered the store together. They were late teens or just tipping over into their twenties. The one in front had a John Waters moustache and a sky-blue tank top and skinny joggers covered in pink roses. The other two had on wispy white beach coverups, their bikini straps poking through at select

places. They smelled of sunscreen and pot, a lot of pot, Merritt realized as they passed her in the aisle, their flip-flops slapping—sand
sprinkling onto the floor.

"God, it's cold in here," the one trailing the other two, the caboose,
said as they went around Merritt. That one still wore sunglasses—
despite being indoors and despite it being night outside, anyway.
The sunglasses now looked Merritt up and down, an obvious ap-
praisal. "You have great fucking hair."

"Thank you," Merritt said.

"You do!" Harper yelled from over by the Icee machine. "I've said
it myself."

The group of pot-smoking beachgoers laughed at something privately funny as they made their selections in the beverage cooler:
two grapefruit and one lime seltzers.

"Hot Cheetos yes, hot Cheetos no?" Moustache asked the other
two.

"What a question," Harper answered for them, her mega-cup
Icee in hand, red straw at the ready. "Always yes."

"Oh my God!" Sunglasses said, doubling back toward her in disbelief. "Oh my fucking God. You're Harper Harper!" Sunglasses now
turned toward Merritt and asked, "It is, right? It's her?"

Merritt wasn't sure if she should—

"Oh no way," Moustache said, coming down an adjacent aisle
so that he shot out near to where Harper was standing, which was
right about in the middle of the store. "No way, no way. We were
just watching your ghost post—like in the car before we came in.
Terrifying."

"You don't even know how much I love you right now," Harper
said, stepping forward and clapping Moustache across the back, as
natural as could be. "Did you hear that, Merritt? My *ghost* post."

"Oh absolutely," Moustache said. "Hundred percent it was a
ghost. It was one of the dead girls."

"It was!" the beachgoer next to Merritt said to the two of them.
And then to Merritt, more quietly, "I'm, like, shaking right now. You
know her?"

"I do," Merritt said. She'd lost track of the other one and then saw her walking down the chip aisle with her phone up and recording. Of course that.

"Hi, I'm Asha," that one now called, waving with her nonphone hand. "I hope this is OK! I cannot believe you're here right now."

"I am here," Harper said, waving at Asha's phone as she held up her Icee. "A toast to Betty's in Tiverton, Rhode Island," she said into the camera.

"Thank you from Betty," the woman behind the front counter said, deadpan as fuck.

"Shit, are you really Betty?" Harper said, turning toward her. "As in *the* Betty from the sign?"

"None other," the woman said. "You must have a sign somewhere," she added. Then she gestured to Asha, who had moved a few steps closer but was still videoing Harper. "They seem to know you like you do."

"Her sign is Scorpio and she's got twenty-two million followers," Moustache said.

"Huh," Betty said.

"Is this still real life?" Sunglasses asked Merritt.

"No," Merritt said.

"I didn't think so," Sunglasses said, drifting to the center of the store to join the other two in orbit around the blazing sun of Harper Harper.

They took a lot of selfies. Or quadruplies. Harper talked them into Icees and insisted on serving them up, the largest size for each.

Merritt knew how this worked. She'd been in the Metal Mug parking lot, after all. So while selfie station was happening, Merritt and Audrey joined up to hover like maiden aunts at a bridal shower. It wasn't that Harper didn't try to grab them to pose too, it's that they both shrank from her gestures of inclusion. And Harper being Harper, she didn't make a whole thing about it, which was good, especially since the three beachgoers didn't seem to notice.

As Audrey was paying for the Icees, Betty at the counter—her hair a cascade of black curls, her contouring flawless, and her hoop earrings the width of Starbucks grande cups—asked, "She's one of them making the movie over at the school? The devil thing?"

"Yes," Audrey said.

"Really it's more of a curse thing," Merritt said.

"And how are you two involved?" Betty asked.

"Just part of the production," Audrey said, answering for them both, which Merritt was, in this instance, grateful for. Above them the fluorescent lights hummed.

"Hey, any chance you're a local?" Audrey asked Betty.

"I guess so. People around here seem to want five generations' worth to count, but I've got thirty-plus years here, so."

"You definitely count," Audrey said. "What do you know about Brookhants? I mean, if you don't mind saying. Like what have you heard about it being haunted or whatever?"

Merritt was surprised by Audrey's tenacity in this line of questioning.

"I mean, like I said, I only know it's bad vibes over there," Betty said. "I had friends in high school who went out there to mess around, or they said they were, but I never did it. I don't play with devil stuff."

"So you heard it was like demonic or something?" Audrey asked.

"I mean, yeah, I guess. People would go light black candles there on Halloween and play Bloody Mary or whatever. Or Ouija boards." Betty nodded as she remembered. "That was it—they'd bring a Ouija board and try to talk to the dead girls. I'm not trying to mess with dead girls."

"OhmyGodIloveyousomuch!" one of the beachgoers said to Harper, like they were making a wish.

"She's a big deal, huh?" Betty asked. It seemed to delight her to be puzzled about how and why that could possibly be true.

"Harper Harper," Merritt said. "When you have a sec, google Harper Harper."

"That's her name?" Betty asked. "Harper Harper?"

"Just google it," Merritt said. Betty pulled her cell phone out from somewhere behind the counter and Merritt took that as her cue, or their cue. She didn't think she had the wherewithal for another parking lot paparazzi fest with Harper tonight. "Shall we?" she asked as she turned from the counter toward Harper and her fans. "Ready to go, Harper?"

Harper was just then signing Moustache's tank top. "I can be," she said, finishing. "Asha, Mackenzie, Bryce, it's been a pleasure."

It was almost too much, Merritt thought. All of this was really too much.

"This is the best night of my life," Asha said. "You are a dream human."

"Love you!" Harper said, pushing the door open to the night. After the air-conditioning of the store, the asphalt under their feet seemed to throw its heat up at them.

"Even at a convenience store in East Bumblebuzzard, Rhode Island," Merritt said as they reached the SUV.

"Even what?" Harper asked.

Farther down along the strip mall, Carl spotted them and pointed the key fob in their direction. There was a beep and a click as the doors unlocked.

"Even what?" Harper asked again, like she was anticipating liking Merritt's answer.

But before Merritt could give it, the beachgoers—Asha, Mackenzie, and Bryce—came running at full force out of the store and toward the SUV. Toward our heroines.

They'd been momentarily entranced, Merritt thought, by the total surprise of this movie star in their local haunt—and maybe by the pot they'd smoked, too—but once Harper had left, that trance was snapped and they'd realized their missed opportunity. They wanted more. Fans always do. And Harper was still right here, standing in *their* parking lot.

"We know you, too!" Asha yelled at them, her flip-flops slapping across the asphalt. Merritt assumed she meant Audrey until Asha added, "You're the one who kissed her! You wrote the book!"

"Oh Jesus," Merritt said, her heart rate ticking up as she opened the door nearest her and pushed herself inside. Audrey was close enough behind her that they pretty much climbed in as one. The smell of the apples Harper had brought in from the road was surprising in its intensity: cider sweet and trapped like a gas in the car. It nearly made Merritt gag.

"You saying this is too much attention for you?" Harper asked, laughing from the front seat as she slammed her door shut.

The fans were amped up, now. The three of them shouting and laughing and one-upping each other, taking selfies, trying to angle so they could get Harper through the window.

Carl had made it back to the SUV. He put the pizza in the cargo area while the beachgoers asked him questions and he responded with things like, "You kids go on home, now. These gals don't need the bother. They're working out here. This is their job. Do you kids have jobs?"

"Brookhants has more security than just the booth and the gate, right?" This from Audrey.

"Are you really scared of Mackenzie, Asha, and Bryce?" Harper asked, turning around in her seat again.

"Am I scared of people doing stupid people things?" Audrey asked. "Always."

Carl opened his door to get in and the overhead light came on and the stalkers in the parking lot screamed to see their heroines again. "Well there's your Rhode Island welcome committee," he said, starting the engine.

He pulled out slowly, the three fans still standing there, still shooting with their phones. "That pretty typical for you?" he asked Harper. "In the real world?"

"Sometimes," Harper said. "Depends."

Carl shook his head like this was end times.

Harper went to put her Icee in the cupholder. She had to remove one of the apples she'd taken from the road to do it. As fast as she picked it up, she dropped it onto the floor, shaking the hand she'd held it in back and forth, flicking her fingers. Wet sludge flew off them and spattered about.

"Gross!" Merritt said as some of it landed on her cheek.

"What's the problem there, touchy?" Carl asked Harper. "Had a bug on it?"

"No, it was mush," Harper said. She poked at the apple still in the other cupholder and then jerked her hand back like she'd discovered that it was a coiled snake. "Fuck, this one's like that, too—it's like they melted."

Merritt was still wiping her cheek even though there was no longer a need. "Well, you left them in a hot car in a parking lot." She lowered her window to clear the sweet stink.

"It's not *that* hot," Harper said. "And we had the air on. These are like applesauce in wet skin."

Audrey reached to touch the apple still in the cupholder. "Gross," she said as she pulled her hand back. "I think it's rotten."

Carl turned on the overhead light again so they could all look. The apple *was* rotten. It was soft and sunken in on itself, its skin leached of color and wet, sweating like it had a fever. You could see where Harper and Audrey had poked it, the pocks in its rubbery flesh.

"You sure picked bad ones," Carl said. "A bad apple knows its kind, I guess." He seemed very pleased with himself for this observation.

"They were fine when I took them," Harper said. "I *ate* one. You all saw me do it."

"I told you not to," Merritt said.

"They were *fine,*" Harper said. "All of them were completely fine. They were not rotten skin sacks."

"I already called in for somebody to go pick up the crates we left there," Carl said, turning off the light. "They can take another look and try to figure out where they came from."

"It's another weird thing, Merritt," Harper said. "For your list."

"It's your list," Merritt said. "Not mine."

The rest of the ride they were quiet. The return trip was a little shorter, since they didn't have to go through campus proper but instead went around to the Spite Manor side, where their tiny houses sat all in a row. This also meant they didn't have to travel the apple-crate road, though it's unlikely they could have seen anything, even if they had. The roads they traveled were dark now except for the SUV's headlights, which revealed the slither of white fog that was beginning to gather low across their path. Carl turned up his rock station.

There was a curious energy around them. It was like they'd trapped some of the excitement from the convenience store fans in with them—like it was buzzing about them now, brushing their bodies with flicks and twitches. Nobody mentioned it, but Merritt thought they could all feel it.

When they reached the entrance gate, Carl stopped, rolled down his window, and said, "Hey, I've got the semiprecious cargo here," to the bald guy in the security booth, who pushed the button to slide the gate back and open the road.

"This really is it for security?" Audrey asked.

"No, we've got some guards patrolling, too," Carl said. "A few of them."

But then, before the gate had even made it all the way across, from behind them came headlights and shouts, a beeping horn. They turned, all of them—even Carl, though he put his head out his open window to do it. The fans had followed them—because of course they had, Readers—and were now idling behind the SUV in their *beatah* (the way Carl says *beater*) car, a massive land yacht with a black cloth top and a white body and a front hood panel that had at some point been replaced, apparently, because it was blue.

"We wanna party with you!" Asha was screaming while hanging out the front passenger-side window. "Let me kiss you, too!"

"Me too!" Bryce yelled. He was the one driving and he pounded the car horn in several short blasts.

"Amateurs," Harper said as she lowered her own window and waved at them, which made them scream louder. "They played this all wrong. They should have snuck in through the woods. They could've done it quiet that way."

"That's comforting," Audrey said.

The guy from the security booth stepped outside. He told Carl to *drive on through* and that he'd *take care of these frickin' idiots*. He radioed another guard and turned on the bright beam of his long-handled flashlight, pointing it at the fans' car. "Seems like you mighta took yourselves a wrong turn," he said as he approached the land yacht.

"No, we took all the exact right turns!" Mackenzie shouted back as the other two laughed.

The gate slid back across the road, closing the SUV into Brookhants. Carl drove on, leaving the fans behind in the thickening fog, which soon swallowed them up.

"You were saying, about security?" Audrey said.

"It worked, didn't it?" Harper said.

"For now," Audrey said. "But they'll have to do more than this."

"I think you might be right about that," Carl said.

"Don't encourage her, Carl," Harper said.

"I'm not," he said. "Not at all."

Merritt added nothing to this discussion, but privately she thought that the things they should most worry about at Brookhants had already been invited in.

A TOWER TOUR, A CARPET PICNIC,

A SOUND IN THE NIGHT

....

By the time the road rounded to Spite Manor, the fog had intensi-
fied so much that they could only hear the chime of shells beneath
their wheels without actually seeing the change in surface. With the
house, and its tower, looming before them, Harper mentioned, as
casually as she could—though she did not feel casual about it—that
she still hadn't seen the inside.

"You want to go now?" Merritt asked.

"Um—yes," Harper said, turning around in her seat to best perform her enthusiasm for Merritt. "You're serious?"

"Can we?" Audrey asked.

"I don't see why not," Merritt said.

"You check in with Elaine about this?" Carl asked.

"I think I can handle any necessary check-ins with Lainey, Carl,"
Merritt said. "Let us out here, please."

Carl didn't stop, though he did slow down. "Let me turn around,"
he said. "I'll drive you back." They'd already gone around the back
of the house and had just entered the canopy of the woods, the dirt
road's skeleton of tree roots rumbling them along.

"No need," Merritt said in her Merritt way. "Please stop now."

Carl did as he was told. Even still, he added, "Here? You really
wanna get out here?"

"Yes," Merritt said, opening her door to the dark and the fog. "We
can cut across the terraces."

"*This* is the kind of Brookhants event I've been waiting for," Harper said. She turned to Audrey and said, "Tell me you're down for this?"

"I mean," Audrey said, "how can I say no?"

"Like this," Carl said. "*No.*"

The three of them ignored him and climbed out, the woods at once crowding them with shadows and sounds. As Harper went around back to get the pizza, Carl craned his head out his window to look at the dark shape of the house in the distance. "Not very many lights on in there," he said. "Just in the tower is all I can see." He sighed. "If you wake her up, you'd better tell her I said for you not to go in."

"It's fine, Carl," Merritt said.

"I'm gonna tell her you told us to make ourselves at home," Harper said. "And to be sure to turn on all the TVs and run the vacuum."

"You would," he said.

Soon the red glow of his taillights grew fuzzy with distance and darkness and fog. It blew in from the water and swirled about, hanging from branches that stirred uneasily, their leaves fluttering like the wings of bats. Or maybe they were the wings of bats.

"This is terrifying, right?" Audrey said. "It's at least a little bit terrifying."

"No," Merritt said.

But there they stood in an unmoving knot on that dark, uneven road in the fluttering night woods while they breathed and listened.

And then—

"This way," Merritt said, her voice and steps sure as she took off in the direction of the house. Neither Harper nor Audrey let her get very far ahead. She cut them back out of the woods and down through the walking paths of a rigidly ordered vegetable garden. "We'll go around to the front and then you can imagine I'm Sara Dahlgren giving you my very best come-on."

"No need to imagine that part," Harper said.

"Really?" Merritt said. "If anybody here's a Sara Dahlgren, it's you." She said this happily.

The fog was even thicker in front of the house, sometimes almost like they were walking through sheets on a line or along the edge of a velvet stage curtain. And with the damp grass a sponge beneath them, the whole world felt soft and out of focus—as if it was intent on hiding parts of itself from them.

"Yeah, OK, so this is creepy, though," Audrey said.

"I think it's beautiful," Harper said. She meant it. But she also kept catching flutters at the corners of her eye, things that moved too quickly, especially in the fog, to catch in full. They almost could have been people. She couldn't decide if these moments actually scared her, or if she only liked the idea of being scared right then.

"It's like this a lot this time of year," Merritt said. "There's a beach not far from here called Fogland. But it is particularly dense tonight."

Near the house, they hit a patch that was thinner than what they'd just walked through, and in the glow of strategically planted outdoor lighting, they could take in some of the impressive banks of hydrangeas, their blue blooms the size of infants' heads.

Spite Tower was now above them, its lit windows a row of teeth.

"Is this still real life?" Audrey asked.

"No," Merritt and Harper both said.

They climbed the stairs and crossed the porch, the painted floorboards groaning with their steps. Harper caught a glimpse of her ghost self in the dark window glass and felt her heart skip around, and again when the ocean breeze jostled the hanging ferns, and again when Merritt gripped the knob to open the front door.

"Hey, maybe she is asleep," Harper whispered, surprising herself as she did. "We could just stay out here. It's nice out here."

"Are you scared, too?" Merritt asked over her shoulder. "That I did not expect."

"No, I just . . ." Harper trailed off as Merritt pushed open the door. Unlike the floorboards, it didn't squeak at all, having been recently oiled by production. The dark house now stood open, its heavy silence seeping out like its own kind of fog.

It was so cliché even to think it, but that didn't stop Harper from doing so: it felt like the house was waiting for them.

Compared to the fog world they were about to leave, this house seemed too solid, too sure of itself. Harper found herself wanting to stay in the land of impressionism. Spite Manor, she knew, would be an experience in photorealism.

But then, this is what they'd come for.

Merritt stepped in first, clearly comfortable with the drill— flicking on the entrance-hall light and slipping off her shoes. "Shoes-off house," she said, pushing her sandals with the toes of one foot until they were in a neat twosome off to the side. Audrey followed next, doing the same with her flip-flops. By the time Harper was even inside the door, the two of them were already well into the foyer, Merritt saying something to Audrey about the bouquet of blue hydrangeas on the highly polished table at the room's center. Other than the whisper of their voices, all around them was heavy stillness.

Harper, with the pizza box, felt that she had to move quickly. She did not want to let them get too far ahead of her in this house. It bothered her to imagine them no longer in her sight, even though the fact of that bothering her bothered her, too. But she was wearing her vintage Jordans, and even with the laces half undone she couldn't just slip the shoes off like they were a pair of sandals. Still, she tried to use the toe of her right shoe to push down on the heel of her left and pull her foot free from it. But even as she did this, she noticed Merritt move into an adjoining room, disappearing from view, and Audrey following her.

"Hey, wait," Harper said, trying to whisper but still be heard, trying to sound chill and definitely not panicked, trying to hold the pizza box steady while also getting her foot out without losing her balance. She did not. She fell over, hard, onto the antique entryway runner, crushing the pizza box as she went down and sending a puff of dust and sand up into her face, which made her sneeze. Loudly. So loudly.

"Good gawd," Merritt said through her teeth as she came back from wherever she'd been. "Can I bring you a trumpet, too, Tank?"

"Sorry," Harper said from the floor, where she now pulled off her sneakers. (Which is what she should have done in the first place.) Then she stood with the now-smashed pizza box, her feet in socks.

"This is it, right?" Audrey was saying quietly. She was on the other side of the foyer, her neck craned to look up a dark staircase. "The tower?"

"Yes," Merritt said.

"So right here is where . . ." Audrey didn't finish, but instead looked down at the floor beneath her feet.

"Yes," Merritt said. "I was planning to save it for last, but I can see there's no point."

"We don't have to go up there right this second," Audrey said, but Merritt had already moved past her and was on the first stair.

"Yes we do," she said.

Harper hurried across the room to join them. Her socks were slippery on the tiles but soon they again found rug. She hit the first stair, pizza box in hand, thought better of it, and left it on the table with the hydrangeas, moving fast to catch up to Merritt and Audrey. She took Audrey's hand as soon as it was near enough to grab.

"Don't let go," Audrey said quietly when she did.

Harper didn't. She didn't want to. The stairs were steep and unevenly spaced, awkward, and the walls so strange and crowding with their lumpy rows of books, the light from the sconces too dim to do much but throw gothic shadows around them. Somewhere near the middle of their climb, Harper's sock snagged on the rough tread and she felt herself, momentarily, get pulled back—until the thread broke, that is. But that split second of being stuck, being *claimed* by the tower stairs, was enough to rattle her—deliciously so.

"You OK?" Audrey said as Harper shoved even closer behind her.

"Oh for sure," Harper said. "Loving every minute." This was not untrue. She felt young in a way she hadn't for a while, and a little silly too, in her stocking feet scaring herself. She liked it.

The air in the stairwell was heavy and hot. Her palm was sweaty where she held it together with Audrey's. Soon more light spilled from above and they came up the final turn and into the round expanse of the study. Merritt was waiting for them.

It was just as Harper had imagined it—somehow almost too

much like the thing it was supposed to be: the windows lining its curved walls, the high ceiling shaped like a circus tent, the taxidermy staring at them, and the shelves stuffed with books and maps and pictures. A room-sized cabinet of curiosities.

"Is this all set design?" Audrey asked.

"No," Merritt said. "This is how it's always been since I can remember it." She looked more carefully at Harper, and said, "Did you drop the pizza again?"

"No, I left it downstairs," Harper said. Merritt stared at her like she needed more of an explanation. "I felt like maybe we shouldn't eat up here or something," Harper added. "I don't know."

"That's adorable," Merritt said. "I'll go get it."

"Just because it's like fancy up here or whatever," Harper said to further explain, but Merritt was already slipping past her to the stairs, their bodies glancing as she went.

"It's the least fancy room in the house," Merritt said from the stairs.

"This view's unreal," Audrey said, looking out a window.

"This room is unreal," Harper said.

"This whole place."

Harper nodded. She thought that something was about to happen, or was already happening, something that she couldn't quite get a handle on. Like the day in Bo's office, at the windows—the toddler in the garden, the snow that couldn't be—but now it was happening to all of them, *for* all of them. She pulled out her phone, started recording: a circular sweep of the room with close-ups on the reflective eye of the taxidermy hawk and also a few of the antique book spines: *Psychography—Marvelous Manifestations of Psychic Power, Book of Mediums: Experimental Philosophies of Mediumship, The Society for Psychical Research*. She entered the frame in the video's last moments to do a surprise-mouthed-emoji face with a thumbs-up, and then uploaded it to her stories with the (rather uninspired) caption: MotherFing Spite Tower!!!!

Then she joined Audrey at the window to take in the view. The fog, or the mist, whatever it was, was low hanging. From this vantage point she could see beyond and through it. She could see the gaps where the water rolled itself toward the shore. And across that water, a smear of black land and smudges of yellow lights in windows.

"Some of these are really beautiful," Audrey said, now from behind her. "I never knew there were so many kinds."

Harper turned. Audrey was flicking through a crate of talking boards, one after the next—*click, click, click* as they fell against each other.

Click, click, click Harper's pulse went in her chest.

"Have you ever played with one?" Audrey asked.

"You don't really play with those, do you? I mean, if *The Exorcist* taught us anything."

Audrey laughed. "God bless Linda Blair, but I think it probably depends on how seriously you take it." She'd pulled one of the boards from the stack and was examining its lettering.

"I wouldn't even know how to work some of those," Harper said.

"I do," Merritt said from the top stair. "But not with pizza grease hands. Those are all antiques. And I didn't bring any napkins. But I did bring this." She set the pizza on the desk and pulled a bottle of red wine from where she'd had it wedged under her arm. "No way I could carry glasses, but I did manage a corkscrew."

They had a floor picnic atop yet another antique carpet. The pizza was cold, and a lot of the cheese had to be scraped from the lid of the box from where Harper had smashed it, but nobody cared. The ocean crashed outside, the breeze coming in was cool, and *there was that in the air which is there when something is going to happen.*

"Did Elaine grow up here?" Audrey asked, pulling the crust from a slice and leaving everything else. "In this house?"

"Really only during the summers," Merritt said. She was working the corkscrew on the bottle of wine. "Otherwise, it was the Upper West Side. And France." She pulled the cork, its whistle low and long. Then she took a swig from the bottle.

"I can't really imagine spending so much time here as a child," Audrey said. "I mean, if you know anything at all about its history—"

"I was a child here," Merritt said. "I was a guest, but still a child guest. And I knew its history."

There was that in the air which is there when
something is going to happen.

"Yeah and you wrote a book about it first chance you got," Harper said. "I think you were very infected."

"Did you ever manage to fall asleep here?" Audrey asked.

"Yes," Merritt said. "Always."

"I know I wouldn't have," Audrey said.

"You might have, if you'd come into it like I did." Then, after a moment, Merritt added, "I can't quite imagine having had your childhood."

Audrey shrugged. "I guess it's whatever seems normal to you at the time."

"*Did* it seem normal to you?" Merritt asked.

"A lot of it did," Audrey said. She looked like she was thinking. "Not all of it. Not what happened after the crash. But I was older then, too. Are you sharing." She nodded at the wine.

"Of course, sorry." Merritt passed the bottle. Her top lip and the skin just above it were now purple.

Audrey took a drink and then stood, wine bottle in hand, to again inspect the contents of the busy shelves.

"How goes the book?" Harper asked Merritt.

"How goes the movie?" Merritt asked back.

"You tell me," Harper said. "You're here."

"I sure am."

"Is this Ava Brookhants?" Audrey asked. "Like adult Ava?" She was leaning forward, looking at a framed black-and-white photograph.

"If that's the picture I think it is," Merritt said. She stood to better see.

"She's stunning," Audrey said. "Just not how I pictured her."

As Merritt joined Audrey at the shelves, she took the bottle of wine back from her. "Yeah, that's her," she said, leaning in to look more closely. She said something to Audrey that Harper couldn't hear. Both of them laughed at whatever it was before Audrey whispered something back.

"Wait, wait—what is this?" Harper tossed what was left of her third slice back into the pizza box and joined them in front of the photo. "What's happening here? There are no secrets allowed in the Plain Bad Heroine Society."

"Oh, that's very rich," Merritt said.

"It's not a secret," Audrey said. "Merritt just made an observation."

"Something about me?" Harper said, smiling at them both.

"Does your vanity know no end?" Merritt said. "Run along now, Dorian Gray."

"That's my favorite-ever novel," Audrey said like it was the best thing.

"Really?" Merritt said.

"Yes," Audrey said. "For years. Since I first read it."

"I would never have guessed that," Merritt said.

"Wasn't she famous, sort of?" Harper asked, leaning between them to look at the photo. In it, Ava Brookhants glares at the camera, a cigarette poised at her lips, her cropped hair rolling with shiny finger waves. She looks both unamused and chic as fuck.

"Very," Merritt said. "In her way. For a while, she was even more known than Madame Verrett had been in her heyday. She advised all the Broadway weirdos first—and queers, naturally—until she worked her way up to Hollywood. Or is it worked her way down to Hollywood?"

"So unnecessary," Harper said.

"She would hold these massive séances for the stars, very exclusive. An Ava Brookhants reading was *the* invite, for a minute."

"And then what?" Audrey asked.

"Obsolescence," Merritt said, raising her eyebrows at them. "Maybe McCarthyism? Blacklists and baddies. People got spooked and her whole field went out of fashion."

"So she became the cat lady of Spite Manor?" Harper said.

"Give her a little credit," Merritt said. "I mean look at her. She married a count, moved back to France. She had never really lived here to begin with, I don't think, except for when she was a little kid and they made her."

"She did not marry a count," Harper said. "A fucking count?"

Merritt nodded.

"And she was what to Elaine?" Audrey asked.

"Some level of cousin," Merritt said. "Twice removed maybe? Harold Brookhants's youngest brother was Elaine's great-grandfather. But remember, that's only if you choose to recognize Ava as a Brookhants at all. Which many a Brookhants did not. Does not."

"Did the Packards ever claim her?" Audrey asked.

"No," Merritt said. "But I don't think she wanted them to. At least that's what she said in her book."

"I didn't know she wrote a book," Audrey said.

Merritt smiled a real smile. "Oh did she ever. It's kind of a mess, but it does have some sterling trash talk." She looked toward the stairs. "There's probably a copy here, somewhere, if you want to read it."

"I think I do," Audrey said.

They stood passing the wine bottle in front of Ava's photo, the ocean breathing its wet breaths outside and the house too still around them.

All of them now had wine-tinged lips, and Merritt's had extended up from her mouth into something unfortunately Hitler-ish.

"You have a little—" Audrey said, pointing at Merritt's mouth.

"What?" Merritt was immediately self-conscious.

"No, it's—" Audrey said. "Your mouth." She only just traced the top of Merritt's lip with her fingertip, a move Harper found enormously intimate—especially there, so close, in this small circle they'd formed with their bodies. "It's from the wine."

"Oh," Merritt said. The room was dim, but Audrey seemed to be blushing. Maybe. "If that's all." She reached for the bottle, drank again.

Harper wondered, if the two of them had been alone—Audrey and Merritt—if they might now be kissing. The potential for it thrummed the air, but would either of them have risked acknowledging that, acting on it? If it was just Harper with either of them, she would now be doing so. She *wanted* to do it. But as it was, it was the three of them, so . . . *So what?* What did that mean as far as kissing one of them was concerned? Or either of them? Both?

The thought of doing this, kissing both of them, all of them kissing—and then, if then—made Harper feel like she was floating up to that high ceiling and its umbrella undercarriage of rafters. She was floating and also not floating, still planted within this circle of three, the wine bottle being passed, their faces warm with its contents, their bodies close. Ava Brookhants looked on at them from behind her glass and frame, and maybe she could kiss one of them first, to start, and then, if she did maybe—

There was shouting out the windows, queer and out of place.

It was hard to say exactly what was being shouted because it was thin and lost in the ocean crash, but then came something that sounded like *Errrrrrrrrrrrrrrrr!*

By the time the three of them crowded at the windows to look out, the shouting was clearer: "Harp-errrrrrrrrrrrrrrrr!"

There were people on the beach below. Finding them in the fog took several moments, and then they'd be lost and reappear. And they weren't just any people but the three fans from the convenience store. They were now bringing a dinghy up onto the strip of sand in front of Spite Manor—Asha and Bryce out of the boat and pulling it ashore while Mackenzie stayed seated and worked the oars. "Harp-errrrrrrrrrrrr!" they screamed. "We love you!"

"This isn't ideal," Merritt said.

"So where's all this security?" Audrey asked.

"I'm sure they're coming," Harper said, though she did not feel at all sure of this. She pulled out her phone and tried to record the scene out the window, but between the fog and the darkness and the distance she might as well have been trying to film ghosts.

The fans had the boat fully ashore now and seemed to be trying to decide what direction to head in next.

"I can't believe they're here," Audrey said.

"You can't?" Merritt said. "They were here earlier."

"We'd better go say something to them," Harper said.

"You're joking," Audrey said. "There's no way I'm going out there."

"Well it's that or they're gonna head up here anyway. Or to the tiny houses—and then they'll know where we're sleeping."

"Fuck," Audrey said. "Fuck. I don't like this."

"It's OK," Harper said. "I've got this. I'll go talk to them."

The fans were really screaming now—all three of them. *Where are you? We came to find you! We loooooove you!*

"I'll come too," Merritt said. "Before they wake up Elaine."

"Well, I'm not staying up here by myself," Audrey said.

So they took the stairs together, Merritt again in the lead but this time carrying the open bottle of wine. They were hopped up on their task, rushing, and the staircase seemed even steeper on the descent. A couple of times, Harper had to work to keep from crashing into the back of Audrey. One of those times, she pushed a hand against the bookshelves to slow her momentum and knocked some books loose. Those flopping volumes tangled in their feet—Audrey's more than Harper's own—and made Merritt say, "Could you both calm your tits, please?"

Harper could hear the books sliding down the stairs, but no matter, they could get them at the bottom, since they were almost there. Merritt stepped into the foyer first, with Audrey right behind her, and then Audrey screamed.

She did not yelp or shout. Audrey screamed a sharp blade of a scream.

Harper soon saw why. Standing at the base of the stairs, two just-retrieved books in her hand, was Elaine Brookhants, looking like a phantom in her white satin pajamas and bed-mashed hair. Her face was smeared strangely with the remains of pearly night cream and it was difficult to read her expression. Audrey and Merritt had already moved past her. They were standing next to the hydrangea table, shoulder to shoulder like kindergartners waiting to be punished for a prank.

"I think you stole my line," Elaine said to Audrey. "Shouldn't I be the one screaming at the three galloping night stalkers in my home?"

"I'm so sorry, Lainey," Merritt said. "We didn't mean to wake you. There are people here who shouldn't be—out on the beach, I mean." Harper had never before seen Merritt without the right words.

"*What* people are here?" Elaine said with an iciness that would have chilled Harper had it been directed at her. Even without it being directed at her, she was chilled.

"Just like college kids," Merritt said.

"They followed us here. Earlier. We thought they left," Harper said, because she felt like she should help to explain.

"They're her fans," Merritt added, nodding at Harper. "Now they seem to have found a boat."

"How wonderfully industrious of them," Elaine said. "And so what is your plan for removing them?"

"We just wanted to check and see if, I don't know—what they want." Again Merritt seemed to be without her words.

"I think I can talk to them and get them to leave on their own," Harper said, starting toward the front door.

"I'm sure you're right," Elaine said. Her voice lifted in such a way that they could all sense the *but* coming. "But given our history here, I'd appreciate it if you'd let the professionals handle this. That is why we're paying them. Why *I'm* paying them."

Harper stopped.

Elaine set the books she'd collected on the table with the hydrangeas and pulled a cell phone from the lower front pocket of her monogrammed pajama shirt. She pressed the screen, held the phone to her ear, and said, while waiting for someone to answer, "Even if you're intent on terrorizing me, it's good to see you three together like this. And drinking my wine."

Our heroines didn't have to muster an immediate response to this because Carl was on the other end of the call and Elaine was now explaining the situation on the beach to him, something she did in a tone that moved from amusement to annoyance and back.

"He said he's already sent security," she said as she slipped the phone back into her pocket. "And he's driving over, too."

"I was just showing them the tower," Merritt said. "I really am sorry we woke you."

"You didn't," Elaine said. "I heard something outside. It must have been your fan club, but I couldn't see through the fog when I looked, so I was coming down to go up. That's the way in this house." She now peered up the tower stairs. "I thought maybe I was finally going to have to heft myself up this damned tunnel to get the full view."

She turned to Merritt. "I haven't even seen what they added up there for the shoot. How's it look?"

"It looks fine," Merritt said, distracted. "I showed you the app on your phone with the security camera feed. You can use that to see outside."

"It's not the same," Elaine said, shrugging her off. "The tower's got the full sweep of things."

"Do you not go up there anymore?" Audrey asked.

"Only rarely," Elaine said. "And never at night. Those stairs might as well be forty-seven tricks in a row, and me with only so many tricks left to spare." Her eyes glittered with what she was about to say next, which was: "I thought maybe Alex was feeling restless to-night, when I heard you three come down them like horses."

"Groan," Merritt said.

"Wait—do you mean, like, Alex's ghost?" Harper asked, waiting to be chided in Elaine's response.

But Elaine nodded.

"Do you really see her?" Audrey asked.

"Not always Alex," Elaine said. "Or not only Alex. And I don't always see her. Sometimes I only feel her. Or she plays little tricks on me—turning on lights and moving my things. She likes to hide my keys in the oven."

"But *you*, never?" Harper asked Merritt.

"No," Merritt said. "Never. I know how that disappoints you."

"Merritt gets very uncomfortable when I talk like this," Elaine said. "It embarrasses her."

"No, it does not *embarrass me*, Lainey."

"It does," Elaine said. "Always has. The stories you love, you *do* love them, but never as the truth, only ever as containers. You want it all put down in words and trapped in the maze of a narrative. But you don't ever want to contend with it in the actual."

"What exactly is there to *contend* with that you think I'm avoid-ing?" Merritt asked. "Here I am, standing in Spite Manor at the base of the tower stairs on a foggy night. And what?"

"And what?" Elaine asked her back, smiling.

"That's what I'm asking you," Merritt said.

"That's what I'm asking you," Elaine said.

Merritt shook her head, added a sigh at the end.

"I believe," Harper said. "In all of it."

"Ugh, don't be a sycophant," Merritt said.

"That's not what I'm doing," Harper said.

"You can see how uncomfortable it makes her," Elaine said as if Harper was now her conspirator. "Even now, even with the book written, she's still embarrassed by how messy and fleshy it is when I forget to keep it only in the past for her—the stink of it has her wrinkling her nose. That's history for you, my darlings. When you dig it up, it always carries a whiff of rot."

Hard knocking on the front door startled them all.

"Come in," Elaine called. "Nobody here but us ghosts!"

It was a security guard, tall and holding a walkie-talkie. She stood in the doorway, fog swirling behind her, not entering but ducking her head as she took them in. "Sorry to interrupt," she said, clearly confused by the strange party before her. "Just letting you know that we already got 'em—down on the beach, they were still trying to hide their boat so they hadn't had time to get anywhere."

"They *did* get to my beach," Elaine said.

"Right," the guard said like she'd rather skip this fact. "Well, there are three, oldest says she's twenty-one. All locals. We've got an officer coming to scare them about the trespassing—unless you want us to pursue something more . . . I don't think there was any grand plan at work. They just wanted to see how far they could take it, but the guy whose dinghy they borrowed may feel differently about pressing charges."

"I wouldn't blame him one bit," Elaine said. "Yes, fine, that's fine—if you scare them a little and let them go."

"It is the Brookhants way," Merritt said. "Always be sure to get the scare in first."

"Right," the officer said again, as if she was in on a joke she clearly wasn't.

FINALLY, SOMEONE TENDS TO
THOSE FUCKING PLANTS

....

Libbie stood at the doorway to The Orangerie. She was afraid to go inside.

"Shall I get someone else, Principal Brookhants?" Camille Andrews asked from behind her. That even Camille Andrews seemed afraid was more disconcerting still.

"No," Libbie said. "Thank you, Camille. You'd best return to class."

"Are you sure, Principal Brookhants?" the girl asked with none of her usual, *Beetle*-reading verve.

"Very," Libbie said. "Thank you for coming to find me."

Libbie watched the girl take one long, final look at the trouble that lay inside The Orangerie, clearly trying to commit it to memory. Camille said she'd been using the lavatory when she'd happened past. Libbie guessed that it was something more than that—likely she'd been dawdling, out of class and meandering the halls—but in either case: Camille was scared. She was out of breath and saucer eyed when she'd come running to Libbie's office to fetch her and bring her here. No doubt Camille would report this trouble to the whole of her geography class as soon as she returned to it.

Which meant that Libbie needed to make herself go inside right this moment.

She did.

Even from the doorway, the heat escaping The Orangerie had been heavy and wet. Now Libbie felt like she was being pulled under its waves. Her limbs slowed in response and her clothing sucked to her skin.

She had to hike her skirts to step high and over, and sometimes on top of, the many hacked limbs now piled on the floor. She might have been walking in the Tricky Thicket for all the growth strewn about. An axe had been used to chop down anything with a trunk thick enough to be felled by it.

Whether or not it was sentimental to say so, everywhere plants lay *bleeding* their green and yellow and clear whatever—whatever its correct name, for this was Alex's area, and not her own—until it ran down the sides of tables and pooled on the floor.

Everywhere planters had been overturned, their dirt cascaded and the life inside smashed or crushed. Or, she soon discovered, covered in chemicals. That explained the smell: floral and metal, fetid and astringent. She spotted various open containers of lye and kerosene. Even canisters of bluestone (technically sulfate of copper) with its crystals like cut gems. There seemed no rhyme or reason for what had been dispensed, or how it had been accomplished—none that Libbie could understand.

The results were the same, regardless: plants split open and melted in death.

At some point it seemed the axe had been abandoned as either too tame or too slow, and great swaths of vines and leaves, flowers and tendrils, had simply been torn at, by the handful—by the *clawful*, you would think, from looking at them now—ripped and shredded and thrown to the ground.

Near the center of the room, a mass of various blooms and pieces of fruit had been piled together, almost as if wine was to be made. They *had* been stomped into the floor. Only what remained was not wine; it was instead a stinking, bubbling, brown-and-green mash.

And though, individually, they flicked the air throughout the whole of The Orangerie, the fruit flies and bees, houseflies and, yes, yellow jackets that now swarmed above this pile were as dark and thick as a storm cloud. The closer Libbie went to this swarm, the various sounds these insects made—the buzz and whine and hum—seemed to condense into a singular note, one not unlike the unheeding plucking of a detuned cello string.

Libbie gave this sacrificial pile, for that is what it seemed to her, as wide a berth as was possible and headed to the far end of the room, where thin hairs of black smoke lifted from the chaos below.

Other than Libbie Brookhants, two things appeared to be left living in The Orangerie: the angel's trumpet tree, and beneath it, Alex the Flirt.

Alex, the singular cause of all this destruction, sat on a throne of leaves and stems and—even now, right now, as Libbie walked toward her—burned stereo cards, one by one.

"Alex," Libbie called softly, using the voice she typically reserved for the youngest Brookhants students when they were homesick or frightened. "What are you doing, my love?"

"Oh, but you're so early!" Alex said, her eyes still on the flaming card in her gloved hands. "I didn't expect you for another half hour. I know, I know it *looks* mad, Library! I *do* know it. But I couldn't wait any longer. And it will make sense to you, I know it will, once I get it all done."

Libbie moved closer, keeping her steps soft and even. "I'm sure you can explain it."

"Oh yes. I will. Let me—if I could just finish these first."

"Are you feeling alright, darling?" Libbie asked.

"Yes, so much better than before."

She did not look it: her hair was stuck with bits of plant, the sleeves of her dress as well, and the white pinafore she wore over it—Eleanor Faderman's pinafore, Libbie felt suddenly sure—was as soiled as it had been when Eleanor last wore it.

Worst of all was her eye, her left, swollen to nearly shut, puffed and pink, her view from it cut in half.

"Alex," Libbie said. "Darling, what's happened to your eye?" It was painful for Libbie to even look at it. Doing so somehow made her feel a sharp pulse within the bruise on her hip, the one she'd gained when she'd slipped against the tub, in the bathroom with Adelaide. It was a bruise that would not heal, even now, weeks and weeks later.

"These cards Sara brought you, they're tricky," Alex said. "Tricky-tricky like Sara—only I'm onto their ways. Something tried to escape one of them but it's fine, now. It will all be fine, soon as I finish."

"How did you hurt your eye, Alex?" Libbie asked again. Her hip seized and she winced.

"I was making my notes," Alex said, still watching the flame before her. "I was checking these cards, you know I have to, now, daily. In one, the yellow jackets clouded the room like smoke. As I watched, they splintered and one flew at me. I couldn't understand it! It came closer and closer, growing larger and larger, until it escaped the card and was on me." She looked up at Libbie, smiled a terrible smile, and said, "I burned that card first. I could hear the other yellow jackets left inside it hiss and pop as I did. They're only ashes now."

Libbie was holding her breath in disbelief, but if she kept that up in this heat she would faint.

"I know you can't see it yet," Alex said easily. "I know. I don't think you want to see it. You never have. But I can see it for both of us. And now I'm making such good progress! We just need to kill off the bad and start again. I do have the orchard left, and the thicket, but you can help with those, when it's time. We can cut it all down in its growing season. First, I'll explain it—you have to let me explain it to you—and then you'll help me, and then we'll set it right and start again. Start clean here, as we always should have done."

Libbie nodded. She tried to keep her face placid as a puddle.

But Alex shook her head like she was trying to knock something loose. "Adelaide will have to go. She'll go with Max, I don't know where." Her voice had turned into a flat singsong. "And Hanna and Caspar will go, too. None of Harold's people can stay when we start again. None of Harold at all."

Carefully, slowly, Libbie knelt beside Alex. The flame on the card

Alex was burning was at its bottom now, very little image left to go before it reached the soiled fingertips of her gloves.

"Careful," Libbie said.

"*So* careful," Alex said, laying the card in the ash pile so that it could finish its burning there.

"And all of these are wrong, too?" Libbie asked. She'd picked up the small stack of yet-to-be-burned cards.

"Oh do be careful," Alex said, taking them from Libbie as if they were lit dynamite. "These are the *most* corrupt. I've saved the worst for last. One even shows the book, plain as day." She looked around, her eyes glazed, at the downed leaves and plants. "I can show you. I thought I had the viewer here. It might be a risk to do it—I'm not sure—"

"You already did show me," Libbie said. She had to interrupt Alex. It hurt to hear this madness, to be steady and not show revulsion to it. "Yesterday, remember? We looked together yesterday, in my study."

Alex had shown Libbie the cards the day before, the day she was supposed to be home resting after the trifle incident of the previous evening, when she'd accused Adelaide of trying to poison her. (*With yellow jackets! It was lunacy.*) But Alex hadn't spent her day home resting: she'd spent it plotting.

When Libbie had returned from campus that afternoon, Alex had come to find her atop the tower—already a bad sign that she made that climb. She'd brought with her the stereo cards and her notes about them. Those notes were a jumble of indecipherability. But even if the things she had been writing were nonsensical, it had frightened Libbie to see Alex's typically measured penmanship switch from looping scrawl to minuscule scratch and back again.

But the cards themselves—and Libbie had made a point to view each of them, all fourteen—were the same images they had always been, exactly as Sara Dahlgren had brought them from France: risqué, still in poor taste, but hardly sinister. Alex went on and on about changes to the wallpaper or in the bouquet on table, but how could Libbie be expected to remember what these unimportant attributes had looked like in the first place? Who pays attention to the pattern in the wallpaper when two women in silk robes are fondling in the foreground?

Alex. Her Alex is who.

Now, through a nearby window revealed only because Alex had torn all the vines from it, Libbie watched their hulking black carriage come to a stop. They had only minutes, maybe not even so long as that, before students and faculty spilled from their classrooms and noticed this fresh horror in The Orangerie.

"Let's burn them all and be done with it," Libbie said, reaching into Alex's lap, the folds of her skirt, for the box of matches. "Quickly, now. So that we can get you home to do the rest."

"I'm not sure," Alex said. "I've been going one by one. Or—"

"*I'm* sure this is better," Libbie said, doing her best Principal Brookhants. She struck the match, its flame at the ready. "These are the worst, *you* said that, so we'll burn them together."

With some reluctance, Alex now fanned the remaining stereoscope cards and tipped them toward Libbie, who lit each along one edge. They caught at once, and encouraged by the surrounding flames, burned more quickly than they had in the singular. Soon only gray ash remained. Alex reached for a nearby watering container and poured its contents over the ash, streaming it away like gray worms.

Libbie didn't want to ask, but felt she must, before Alex brought it up herself or refused to leave. Gesturing to the angel's trumpet tree above them, she asked, "What about this? Shall I bring you the axe?"

"There's no need," Alex said, steadying herself against the zinc planter as she stood. "By morning it will be the most dead thing in the room. I opened its roots and fed it every poison on campus. It's drinking death even now."

Libbie nodded. She could hear the laughter of students out on the lawn. She and Alex needed to go.

Libbie struggled into her coat, a cruel task in such heat. She asked after Alex's, but Alex was no help in locating it. She stood still, slightly openmouthed, staring with good eye and bad at the sacrificial heap of plant mash and its humming fever of bugs.

Libbie pushed leaves and flowers with her feet, picked up piles of vines, and eventually found the coat dumped on a table. She cleared the bits of plant from it and shook it out. It was new that season, brown wool and flannel with leather trimmings. Libbie usually thought Alex looked particularly fetching in it. Today, though, Alex stuck out her arms at the sides and let herself be dressed like a sleepy child reluctant to leave for church on a winter morning.

Once she had the coat buttoned, Libbie took Alex by the hand—she didn't want to chance it—and said, "Come with me now, I'll take you home to rest." She then led Alex over and around the ruined plants, toward the exterior door. Through the windows she saw students, in clusters and duos, heading toward Main Hall.

"Soon as we're there, we'll find Adelaide," Alex said. Her words were slow and heavy, as if she were selecting them, one at a time, from a dream. "We'll have to speak to Adelaide. It won't be pleasant but it's in her now and she can't be allowed to stay even another night. Hanna and Caspar we might give a week or two, to make arrangements. But Adelaide goes tonight." She sounded like she might drift off to sleep even before she finished speaking.

"Yes, we'll speak to Adelaide," Libbie said, opening The Orangerie door. At once a blade of winter wind shoved them back.

"Good afternoon, Mrs. Brookhants," a few nearby students called. "*And* Miss Trills!" a few others hastily, amusedly, added.

"Good afternoon, girls," Libbie said, pulling Alex along, as quickly as she could. Alex seemed not to register the cold, the nonrotted air, the chattering of approaching students.

They walked quickly, Libbie still steering them, until they were up and into the carriage, the door latched, the wheels moving. Alex was asleep—her eyes closed, mouth in a frown—even before they reached the edge of the woods.

Libbie was grateful for the quiet and time to think—grateful not to have to, for the moment, continue to listen to Alex's awful theories. The hiccupping of the carriage hurt her bruise. She had not looked at it properly for a day or two, having been so preoccupied with Alex, and she worried about what she would find when she did. She knew she should be treating it, that it really should have healed by now, but when she did look at it, she remembered the night she'd gotten it, which she preferred not to do.

Libbie had settled on a story about that night and she was keeping to it: Adelaide had barged in, raving with fever, while Libbie had still been half asleep in the tub. The yellow jackets, the creeping blackness, the wrong things Adelaide had said, all of those were only figments of her then-addled mind. One additionally addled by Addie in such a state.* And it did no good to dwell on figments.

Besides, there was Alex to dwell on now, anyway. She was plenty addled herself. And so quickly! How could Libbie have known she'd unspool so quickly? A comment here, an accusation there, but this?

She watched Alex sleep. Even closed, her injured eye wept yellow trails of pus.

Libbie shuddered. Perhaps, if she'd told Alex about the book, if she'd done so right after Flo and Clara had died, if she'd said, "I gave it to them because I was so happy for the bright rush of their young love." What then? Could she have prevented this?

But Libbie already knew *what then*. Alex would have been aghast. She would have fixated on that act and its ties, however thin, to her imaginary rival: Sara Dahlgren. For days after she would have mooned about, blaming Libbie for endorsing those bad young heroines and their worse club by giving them her personal copy of its manual, a copy gifted to her by her former sweetheart. Alex would have pouted. She might have seethed.

And the truth was, she would have been half right to. Yes, Alex was too often jealous. And yes, sometimes Libbie gave her good reason to be.

The fact that she loved Alex, then and now—though differently— did not change the larger fact that Libbie never should have accepted Harold Brookhants's offer. Oh, she'd thrown herself into building

---

* Adelaide/Addled: Was there something to that, Readers?

the school and playing her part as the widowed principal, and she *was* sometimes content to spend her days and nights with Alex, but what she'd wanted most from Harold Brookhants was his promise that she would not have to bend her own life to the will of the one growing within her. And she got that. Mostly. Ava, as per Harold's instructions and arrangements, was in France, believing herself to be an orphan whose aunt Libbie would one day send for her to come attend her school.* Libbie had seen her child only a few times since her birth, one of those in a photograph.

The rest of it—the house on the ocean, the school, even the ever after with Alex—these were not Libbie's dreams fulfilled, not really.

As a schoolgirl, she'd pursued, and won over, Sara Dahlgren. As a young woman, she'd done the same with Alex. And there were others, lesser, in between. Then she'd been careless, found herself pregnant, and had reconnected with Alex only *one day* before Harold and Madame Verrett and the rest of her life being offered to her over lemon ice at the Palmer Hotel.

Libbie knew she should be grateful. She had so much to be grateful for, and yet . . .

She'd told Harold that she didn't want to be married, didn't want to be a wife. And it's true that she had not been *his* wife in any sense of that word other than title—and only that for a matter of months before he died—and yet, she *was* in a kind of marriage, here, with Alex. That's how Alex understood what they were to each other. And why shouldn't she?

Only, Libbie's feelings hadn't changed: she did not want to be a wife. Not to Harold Brookhants, certainly. But not to Alex, either. She wanted to belong only to herself.

She wanted. She wanted. She wanted.

If there was a curse at Brookhants, Libbie thought, it wasn't from a book. It was her own resentment and perpetual discontentment. How did Mary MacLane put it? *I am a selfish, conceited, impudent*

---

* Though Libbie still hadn't decided if she *would* send for the girl, despite what she'd promised to Harold by pen and by word.

little animal, it is true, but, after all, I am only one grand conglomera-tion of Wanting . . .

Alex stirred as the carriage slowed in Spite Manor's drive, its wheels clicking against the shells. As she'd slept, her stung eye had sealed shut with a layer of yellow crust, and now she had to wipe at it with her own spittle in order to get it open. It looked very painful, swollen now to purple, and it left her vision there down to a slit the thickness of a sheet of paper.

Nonetheless, as soon as she'd cleared the gunk from it, she again started in about Adelaide, talking to Adelaide, demanding that she leave at once. Her words were as jumbled and fuzzy as her eye. Libbie managed to get her in the door and up the stairs to the bedroom—not to the room they shared at night, but to Alex's own bedroom—telling her she needed to sleep before supper.

"We'll take care of it then," Libbie promised, first helping Alex out of her coat, then her shirtwaist and skirt. Throughout this process, Alex did not assist, but she did not fight, either. Soon she was in only her chemise, the look on her face as hollow as a rotten stump.

Libbie peeled back the bedding and said, "You sleep now and I'll wake you later and we'll talk to Addie together."

"Don't you go to her alone," Alex said, a twinge of panic still in her voice though her exhaustion was winning. "I know how she lures you and you let her. I know how you like it, but now it isn't safe."

Only once Libbie had agreed did Alex lay her head against the pillow.

"By tonight we'll have done the job," Alex said. "The ridding."

"Yes," Libbie said. She thought Alex meant Adelaide, that later that night Alex believed they'd be rid of Adelaide. But what Alex really meant was that they'd be rid of the trouble, the Devil, at Brookhants.

Either way, Readers, things did not go as planned.

NO MORE NECKS

....

"Cut!"

Bo Dhillon launched from his seat behind the monitors like he'd been pushed by a spring. He yanked his headphones down to hang around his neck. "Goddamnit! It's still there. I thought we fixed this. Isn't that what we were just doing for an hour?"

Various crew members crowded around him, including the AD, who shook his head at the images on the screens. They took turns looking into a camera, back at the monitor, into a camera, back at the monitor, and grumbling to one another, trading shrugs and shaking their heads when Bo had his face buried in a viewfinder.

Merritt watched all of this from an honest-to-God canvas-and-wood director's chair with *The Happenings at Brookhants* and her name across its back. She pushed her own headphones down to better hear whatever Bo might say next. Her laptop was open and resting on her knees. She read over the paragraph she'd just written, fiddled with one sentence, deleted another.

She did not hate it, what was there on her screen. And that was something.

She put her hands on the keyboard, thought a moment, and then wrote:

> The tendons in the director's neck were the yanked strings to the
> furious red kite of his face.

Well that was too much, clearly. But she'd work on it. She'd enjoy working on it.

"Audrey, can you come here a minute?" Bo called. At this mention of Audrey, Merritt looked up again. The troubles they'd been having on set this morning—and there had been several—were primarily technical, but Bo seemed out of sorts with Audrey today, too. Or with her performance, anyway.

"Uh-oh, Daddy's not happy," Harper's friend Eric singsonged from the chair next to Merritt. He was visiting the set and had also watched Audrey get called over.

"Don't you think this set is paternalistic enough without you actually calling him Daddy?" Merritt said.

"He can be my daddy," Eric said, sliding off the chair to his feet and stretching into a yawn.

"I feel like you're saying that without meaning it," she said. "Which is *my* specialty."

"Oh I mean it," he said. "I'm getting tea and Swedish Fish, you want?"

"No thank you."

Merritt studied Bo. She wrote:

The tendons in the director's neck were now the taut fuse to the red dynamite of his face.

Very bad. Very dumb. She deleted it. No more necks.

Merritt looked up again to see where the Audrey-Bo conversation was going. It wasn't. Audrey had joined him, but now she was waiting as he attended to whatever this camera problem was. She noticed Merritt looking at her and smiled.

Merritt smiled back and side-eyed Bo on her behalf. So there, Readers. So there. People can change. And after the stalking convenience store trio and pizza picnic in Spite Tower and Elaine being Elaine, after a night like that together and more days on set in between, Merritt had softened her once-hard feelings about Audrey.

This particular set was in the school's dormitory, which they'd partially reconstructed for filming, taking down walls and shoring up others until it was the Brookhants equivalent of a soundstage. Production had found the section of the building with the best bones and went to work. They laid flooring, replaced smashed win-

dows with new-to-look-old stock, and added all the dressing besides: rugs and nightstands, bookcases, beds and bedding, lamps
and desks and bric-a-brac.

Presto chango: a dorm room from 1902, only don't pan to the
side, or you'll see it's missing a wall.

The areas of the building that didn't get the movie magic treatment were still a mess: plaster crumbling into piles like crushed butter mints and ivy slithering through window gaps like the searching
heads of snakes. The floors were warped and bloated from the leak-
ing roof, the boards soft underfoot when you walked upon them.
Untrustworthy. Plus, the whole place stank of mold and damp.

In the scene they were trying, and thus far failing, to shoot today: Harper and Audrey—pardon me, *Flo* and *Clara*—convened
a meeting of the Plain Bad Heroine Society. This was not typically
an event best suited to their dorm. The PBHS preferred the cover
of the woods, but haste was the order of the hour as one of the
members had just received a letter from a girl whose relative lived
near to Fannie Corbin's apartment in Boston, and—or so the letter writer claimed—had seen Miss Mary MacLane and Miss Fannie Corbin walking together in the Public Garden. Walking arm
in arm in Public Garden.* Mary MacLane and the very anemone
lady of her heart (and her pages) together again. And in Boston no
less, right up the coast from where these girls in their nightclothes
now twittered.

It was a scene that explored the romantic delight of it all—the pin-
ing, the nascent desire—this while the Plain Bad Heroines tried to
keep their nonmember roommates unaware of these developments
and their excitement over them. Tried unsuccessfully, of course. That
was the scene's principal tension.

As such, this scene, and therefore this set, had many actors: eleven
Brookhants students and an interrupting adult faculty member as
well. Plus all the crew besides, and Eric and Merritt as onlookers. So

---

* I know I don't have to remind you about which city the Boston marriage was
named for, Readers.

there were lots of people milling around, waiting out this delay. Or trying to resolve the reason for it.

This meant there were also lots of people around to witness the next exchange between Audrey and Bo, who had finished whatever he was doing and was now in a huddle with her and Heather.

"It's *not* what you've been doing," Bo said to Audrey. "I'll play it back for you from yesterday, from three days ago. This is much more mannered and sounds it."

"Right now, it's sounding almost more, it's—I don't mean to overstate it—but it's almost like you're doing a kind of transatlantic accent à la Katharine Hepburn," this from Heather. "Half British meets all snob."

"That's right, that's it," Bo said, pointing at her in agreement. He did his own bad Katharine Hepburn impression to emphasize the point: *"The loons, Norman, the loons.* We don't need the loons, OK? The loons are hokey. And it's not the right era."

"I mean, I have been doing, like, a light transatlantic," Audrey said. "Since we started. It's what I worked on with Rachel. She called it pretransatlantic. They taught them to talk that way in some of the private schools so—"

"I'm sure there are shades of subtlety to this," Bo said, "but whatever you've been doing today's not working. It's over the top. You sound like you're doing an old-timey radio announcer."

"That's really embarrassing," Audrey said, though her face seemed to still not quite believe him. She paused, then said, "Can I hear what you're hearing? I don't feel like I was speaking any differently than I have been."

"I can get Rachel on the phone, if it'll help," Heather said.

"No, let's just let her hear how it sounds today first," Bo said. "We have the fucking time. Obviously." He leaned back toward the crew members doing complicated things with various cables and computer equipment. "Unless you have news for me? Have we fixed this? Have we even diagnosed it?"

They shook their heads no.

"See, we have all the time in the world to fix your suddenly wrong accent," he said with his hands in the air. "Jesus Christ."

When he was angry, as he was now, the director held his mouth like he'd just eaten a wedge of lemon, the bitter meat of it still threaded in his teeth.

Merritt liked this one better. She'd keep it for now.

One of the sound techs brought Audrey headphones and she and Bo and Heather listened together to her dialect. Merritt hadn't found it any more or less mannered than she'd found it over the last several days. It certainly didn't sound to her like Bunny Bixby starring in a Hal Roach production. But then, Merritt wasn't the person on set being paid to notice things like this, either.

"You hear it?" Bo was saying. He repeated his bad Hepburn impression, but this time using a few of Audrey's—Clara's—lines. "*We could go ourselves, if you really do have the address? Wouldn't it be like a dream to show up at her door, all of us together with our books?*" It sounded ridiculous when he did it, but that was the point: he wanted it to.

Only now Audrey was nodding and, Merritt could see, processing the direction she'd been given. Oh how Merritt knew that look, the look of someone thinking and thinking, working hard to hold back the contents of those thoughts from others. Merritt wished that she could right then see, scrolling across one of the faulty monitors, those thoughts of Audrey's. Did she agree with him? Did it matter? How would she reset when the next take came and push Bo and his Hepburn caricature out of her mind?

Audrey kept listening to herself Clara wrong, but Bo had again pulled off his headphones and was over at a camera on the other side of the room. Merritt couldn't hear what he was unhappily saying to the AD, but she could hear the crew at the monitors in front of her.

"It's almost like there's water in there."

"Water's not black, though. That would fog it, anyway. This looks like ink."

"Or mold. Fuck if I know. It is wicked damp in here, but I don't get how it would form instantly between takes."

"It's not mold. There's not suddenly gonna be mold in every camera in the room."

Bo was now removing the lens from one of the cameras while the DP hovered and worked through a collection of fidgets: putting his hands on his hips, taking them off, scratching underneath his baseball cap, returning his hands to his hips, crossing his arms over his chest.

Merritt wrote:

> The DP looked like he'd been asked to mind someone's precocious toddler without being given any authority to restrain him, this as the child attempted something spectacularly unwise, like climbing atop a kitchen counter to cut open a melon with a butcher knife.

"Godfuckingdamnit," Bo said to the lens in his hand. "Goddamnit! What is this?" Now he was showing it to the DP.

Merritt hadn't yet settled on fictional Bo's name, but she was playing around with the idea of a single-syllable first name, like Joe or Mo, paired with a two-syllable New England town like Newport or Salem.

A hand wagging a phone with an image of a white flower on its screen dropped in front of Merritt's laptop. She knew without looking up who that hand was attached to: Harper Harper. Last Merritt had noticed, Harper had been talking with some of the actors playing her fellow Brookhants students.

Now she was here, saying, "Eric wants me to ask you for a recipe."

"Why does he think I'm Rachael Ray?"

"More like Walter White." Harper took Eric's chair. "Did you know the angel's trumpet tree they have in The Orangerie is the real deal? Eric just confirmed it with somebody working down there."

"I thought he was at crafty," Merritt said. "He told me he was getting tea."

"That's what he wants the recipe for." Harper held up the phone again and this time Merritt saw that the flower on the screen was, in fact, an angel's trumpet.

"Oh come on," Merritt said. "Did you really read my book? Did *he*?"

"I think he did, actually," Harper said, her thumbs flying over a text. "He told me he was."

"It's not something I made up," Merritt said. "Eleanor Faderman is a person who in real life died right here, from eating angel's trumpet flowers. She died. Every part of that plant is poisonous."

"No, I know. I know. I told him. But Eric's gonna do Eric. He's been on a bunch of homeopathic forums reading about them. He's only focused on the shroomy effects."

Merritt blinked at her.

"Trippy hallucinations," Harper said.

"Violent, unpleasant hallucinations," Merritt said. "Delirium. Asthma-like symptoms. Loss of willpower. Loss of speech."

"Will you tell him all of this?" Harper asked.

"Yes, but so should you."

"No, I will," Harper said. "I have and I will."

"It's a terrible, dumb idea," Merritt said. "*D-u-m-b*: dumb."

"I know," Harper said. "I'll talk to him."

Outside, in the hallway, someone—Bo, it sounded most like—shouted something angry. It echoed down that long, empty space and spilled back onto set. The cast and crew still there made embarrassed or pleased-at-the-drama WTF faces at each other. Another shout. Then it was quiet.

A few moments later, both Heather and the DP returned to the set and the DP went to the camera equipment while Heather started working her way around the room's edges, talking to the waiting cast and crew. Audrey was in one of those first clusters and she now walked over to Merritt and Harper, pulling pins out of her hair as she said, "To your list of unexplained Brookhants phenomena please add black fungus in the camera equipment."

"Fuck yes I will," Harper said. "Is it bad?"

"Bad enough we just wrapped," Audrey said, three pins in hand and another on its way. "For the day. Heather said they can't fix this without help they don't have. I don't think they even know what they're fixing."

"It's not even noon," Merritt said. "For the rest of the day? You're sure."

Audrey nodded.

"Shit," Harper said. "No wonder Bo lost it."

"Yeah," Audrey said, shaking out her hair and stretching her neck. "So what were you telling me about the beach below our houses?"

"Oh, I like you so much," Harper said. "I really do."

Merritt wanted to make a note then, about the particular joy Harper's face held in that moment, but knew it was more important that she was with them for whatever happened next than it was for her to be here alone writing about what had already taken place.

TRICKY THICKET

....

Audrey hadn't slept, hadn't *really* slept—as in hours uninterrupted by nightmares, sleep that didn't fracture with the tick of her heart rate and the churn of her thoughts—in weeks. She'd climb into bed, exhausted, maybe even drift off, but it wouldn't last. She'd wake in cold jolts, certain that someone was watching her. She'd just catch their shadow slink away, eyes not fast enough. Or she'd hear buzzing inside the walls, a humming beneath her pillow. Or a breeze that should carry only the scent of the water would somehow be choked with rotten apple, too.

No, she wasn't sleeping. And she knew she was now showing its absence. Certainly, she was feeling it. Although Merritt couldn't be sleeping much, either. It was so dark where their tiny houses were perched that even from her bed—every night, well into the small hours—Audrey could see the phantom glow of Merritt's laptop.

The small, sleepless hours.

Audrey had been using some of that time to text Noel on the West Coast, where it was much earlier, although soon enough they'd be sharing a time zone. He was headed this way for a New England concert tour, one that would be culminating with a show in Providence, a show she would be attending. (And so would Bo's cameras.) Brookhants seemed to her now like some massive magnet pulling all parts of her life to it.

Or maybe that was dumb and she just needed to sleep.

This is why, as she now stood at the breakfast bar in Harper's cottage and watched Eric take several enormous, if wilted, angel's trumpet flowers from his messenger bag, Audrey started paying attention to his sales pitch: he'd just said something about them be-getting deep sleep.

"Yeah, as in indistinguishable from a coma deep sleep," Merritt had said.

Before they'd left Brookhants for their bonus beach day, Eric had harvested the flowers, and since then he'd been listing their poten-tial medicative and hallucinogenic properties, alternating between what he'd committed to memory and what he read to them off his phone. Merritt peppered this rah-rah with fear and loathing.

The two of them had been arguing—mostly good-naturedly and hypothetically, Audrey had thought—but here, in the tiny kitchen of this tiny house, the strength of Eric's intent was made much more real. Here were the flowers on Harper's counter, their sweet scent already emanating. And here was Eric filling her silver tea kettle with water. And here was Merritt picking up his phone and reading the screen and saying, "OK, so to be clear: you're willing to bet your life on advice given to you by total internet stranger the Shroom Savant?"

"Not only him," Eric said. "I know it kills you but I too have done my research on this subject."

"I'm not gonna be the one it kills," Merritt said.

He Dracula cackled at her.

"This is ridiculous," Merritt said. She turned around to Harper, who was on the love seat behind her. "Your friend is being ridicu-lous."

"All my life," Harper said.

Eric was now dropping the flowers, one by one, into the kettle. They were so large and delicate and white, he might have been drop-ping in silk handkerchiefs. He put in three, consulted his phone, and added a leaf from the same tree, honey, and a few orange spice tea bags. Then he put on the lid, placed the kettle on the stove, and clicked on the burner. While he washed his hands at the sink he said, in the voice of a teacher tired of reexplaining a fact, "Like I said, I'm not messing with the seeds or the roots, which are significant points of potency. I'm brewing a mild tea that I will drink only a lit-tle of to give me an introductory experience to this plant and its attributes. I have a lot of experience with introductions to substances. I am good at them."

"Has it occurred to you that maybe it's a little uncharitable for you to force us to babysit you during your drug trip?" Merritt asked.

"Who's asking you to babysit? I'm asking you to come along."

"That's the thing—nobody wants to," Merritt said.

"I mean—" Harper said.

"You're not serious?" Merritt said.

"I am curious," Harper said.

"Me too," Audrey said before she didn't. "The sleep part sounds really good to me." Harper smiled at her.

Merritt did not. "Not to me," she said. "No part of me. Are we going in the water?"

"I am," Harper said.

"It will be freezing," Merritt said.

"I'll keep you warm, girl," Harper said.

"Significant eye roll," Merritt said. That's what she said, Readers. I'll leave it to you to determine what she felt.

"I'll meet you down there," Eric said. "As soon as it's ready."

"Take your time," Merritt said. "Take all the time."

And so they left him at the stove brewing a flower potion in a tiny cottage by the shore.

There was something to the three of them walking the same wooden stairs down to the beach that Libbie and Alex and their sapphic squad had walked all those years before. Not *the same*, the same, of course—over the years boards would have been replaced, likely many times, salt water is so hard on things—but the path they took, the quality of the light, the roil of the waves: it was the same enough and there was something to it.

They spread their towels on the strip of sand, avoiding the stinking piles of seaweed and things washed ashore. Audrey had assumed they would sit for a while in the sun, talking or not, but looked up to find Merritt and Harper shedding their outer layers of clothing, down to their bathing suits. Audrey never went about things this way at the beach. She was not the type to immediately plunge into the water. She liked to acclimate, to take her time. But right then she needed to be a part of whatever they were doing.

They as in the three of them, the three of them together.

They walked in up to their ankles, the cold water aching their bones, all the way through their bodies to the roots of their teeth. It *was* freezing. And the floor was sharp with shells and stones. They went in a little farther, up to their knees, gritting their teeth. It was too cold and yet there they were in it. Smiling.

Harper did it first—crashed under the roll of a wave. Then Merritt. Then Audrey. The cold sucked away her breath. She'd forgotten how salty it was. She always managed to forget that.

They screamed from the cold, a tangle of seaweed in Merritt's hair until Audrey plucked it out and flung it at Harper. They came alive in this water. They had to—how else could they bear it? Splashing and dunking, touching each other freely because for now they were only playing in the surf like children. There was no weight to this kind of touching. It was open and easy, reciprocal, wanted and without agenda.

Above them loomed Spite Manor, and above it loomed its strange tower, that single arm blocking the sun and casting a long dark shadow down the terraces and over the rocks. But for now, they were happy on the beach below.

Time had become very slippery.

When they saw Eric on the stairs, they crashed out of the surf and back to their towels, their lips drained of color, their skin cold to the touch and rippling in goose bumps from the breeze. Eric was carrying a thermos and wore the proud smile of a parent at a dance recital.

"You're mermaids," he said. "And I've brought you an offering."

They formed a dripping knot around him as he twisted off the lid and steam rose from the container, along with the heady scent of angel's trumpets steeped in honey.

"Are we doing this?" Harper asked.

No one answered.

For a few moments, they stood in that knot and let the sweet steam swirl between them. Then Eric tipped the thermos to his lips and drank and swallowed and then once more. He passed it to Harper, who did the same, and then Audrey did so as well, when it was handed to her. Still no one had spoken.

Audrey offered the thermos to Merritt. She held it before her, looked down into its mouth, and said a thing that was, just then, the only thing that could be said. The words were Mary MacLane's: *There is something delirious in this—something of the nameless quantity.*

And then Merritt took a long drink. She passed the thermos back to Eric, who walked the few feet to the water and poured what remained into the bay.

"I'm surprised," Audrey said to Merritt.

"I didn't want to be left out," Merritt said. "I might already regret it."

"None of that," Eric said, walking back to them. "We have to set our intentions now for the experience we want to have. If you launch your ship in negativity, you'll spend your trip that way."

"So deep," Merritt said. "Deepak Chopra deep."

"There she is," Harper said.

"How long will it take?" Audrey asked.

"No idea," he said. "An hour?"

"How long will it last?" Harper asked.

Eric shrugged. "I mean, nobody drank very much."

"Oh Kind Devil," Merritt said. "What have we done?"

From a tall tree in the woods, a flock of birds lifted. They were noisy with their calls and the beat of their wings. This as the wind skipped over the water. Our heroines shivered.

"Is it worth getting in?" Eric asked them, tilting his head at the churning foam.

"It's freezing," Harper said.

"I know somewhere that's not," Merritt said.

Back at their houses, they provisioned quickly. Eric insisted they bring drinking water, so much drinking water, because they'd need it. Dry mouth was, he promised as he loaded a canvas shopping bag

with bottles, a guaranteed side effect. He also recommended chocolate to enhance their experience. Merritt said they'd want real shoes,
not flip-flops, for their trek through the woods. But they kept their
swimming suits on.

Audrey thought she'd like to sink into her bed and stay there, but
she'd like it even better if the others stayed, too. If they all took a
long, lazy, afternoon nap while they waited for the tea to do its work.
Maybe by then, when it finally kicked in, it would only serve to keep
them in sleep, throughout the rest of the day and night and on into
morning. She would have liked this best.

But there was a message on her phone—on her new, nonbroken,
production-provided phone—from Bo: Try to get Merritt talking about
the Rash brothers. Also, flat rocks—you'll see them—are best for hanging out
once there. Good angles. Please drink water! Lots!

They walked two by two, Harper and Eric trailing behind Audrey
and Merritt.

Audrey held her hands out to her sides and let her fingers brush
the reaching tips of the tallest ferns. She listened to the way their
footsteps fell. She listened to the way Merritt breathed next to her.
She tried to decide if she was already feeling something from the
tea, but she couldn't decide and anyway, Eric said it was too early
for that.

They'd hit one of those patches where cell service decided to
work, and an explosion of notifications landed on Harper's phone.
She stopped to scroll and Eric stopped with her, but Audrey and
Merritt kept walking, letting the gap between their foursome grow.

Audrey worked on a Rash brothers question, a lead-in that
wouldn't announce itself as such, but it was Merritt who spoke first.
"I thought Bo's Hepburn impersonation was unnecessary. Earlier."

Audrey was almost as surprised by this offering as she was by
Merritt drinking the tea. "Yeah?" she said. "Maybe. But his point
was valid."

"Was it?"

"I think so," Audrey said. "When I listened back, some definite cringe moments. There was so much else going on this morning with the delays, I wasn't focused the way I needed to be. I wasn't Clara, I was playing Clara."

"Is that really how it works for you?" Merritt asked. "That's what it feels like?"

"When it doesn't feel like anything is usually when it's going well," Audrey said. "But Clara Broward has a confidence I wish I had, so maybe I've been trying too hard to project that. I'm sure I have been doing that."

"For what it's worth," Merritt said, "for the very little it's probably now worth to you—I've been thinking the last few days that you suit her."

"It's not worth little," Audrey said. "Thank you." She almost didn't say the next thing but this afternoon, thus far, felt so peaceful to her. Easy. So she did say it. "I got the sense you weren't my biggest fan. I mean back in LA."

"Yeah, I act like that sometimes and then regret it after. I'm sorry. It wasn't really about you, if that helps."

"I think it was about me, actually," Audrey said.

Merritt smiled. "Yeah it was. But I've grown up since."

"What, are angel's trumpets a truth serum, too?"

"You joke," Merritt said. "Will you do me a favor?"

Audrey laughed in surprise. This she really wasn't expecting. "I mean, maybe," she said.

"If this gets intense, or if you feel like it's too much—or if you think I do, but I won't say it—will you stay with me? I know we're all together, but Harper and Eric have their whole history, so . . . will you be my trip buddy?"

"Yes," Audrey said. "If you tell me something."

"Oh God. What?"

"I'm sure it's not whatever you're thinking," Audrey said. "I wanna know—I mean, I've been thinking about it and wondering why you didn't put the whole story of the Rash brothers in the book, like not just as a footnote?" She felt a little guilty about using what had been a nice moment of connection between them to do Bo's bidding. But only a little.

"I think it's generous to have even given them footnote status. I don't care about the Rash brothers. Fuck the fucking Rash brothers!" Merritt now shouted into the trees.

Audrey laughed. That was enough for her. She didn't care if Bo wanted to hear more about the Rash brothers. She didn't.

Harper and Eric came charging from behind. "Who are we fucking?" Eric yelled.

"The Rash brothers!" Merritt yelled back.

"Oh, those cunts?!" This from Eric.

Were they feeling the tea now? Audrey tried, again, to tell if her reality had altered. She couldn't say for certain. It might have been the sunlight through the leaves and the scent of pine pitch and the permission granted by having an afternoon to do something like this in just the place for it. It might have been her lack of sleep.

Merritt pointed to the left, where, in the distance, there was a noticeable density to the understory, the brambles bramblier. "That's it," she said as she started in that direction. "Part of it."

"I mean, hold off on the mockery if you can, but should we be at all worried about yellow jackets in here?" Audrey asked.

"Probably," Merritt said, pulling back a branch to help them clear the entrance.

Audrey was the last one through and just after, her shirt was snagged by something. When she turned to look, she saw it was the thorny arm of a blackberry bush clustered with ripe berries. She picked and ate one and it was so sweet and fat with juice, so perfect an experience, that she did not want to pick and eat another and be disappointed by it.

Merritt and Harper were examining a stand of delicate pink flowers on thin stalks, which Merritt, of course, identified as "lady's slippers—a kind of wild orchid."

"I see lungs," Eric said.

"I see vulvas," Harper said.

"Oh, I'm switching to yours," Eric said.

"It's not a Rorschach," Merritt said.

"Everything in the world is a Rorschach," Eric said.

"Do you feel anything yet?" Audrey asked them.

"Maybe," Harper said. "I can't tell. This place is a trip on its own."

"You don't," Eric said.

Audrey couldn't help herself: she took another blackberry. Actually, she took several from the same cluster, popped them in her mouth and crushed her teeth against their ripe flesh. They were just as sweet, just as good.

They continued on, slowly, picking through bushes and pulling back vines, until Merritt said, "Here."

She knelt on a bank so thick with moss it might have been a sheet of green velvet, her hand tipped below the ledge where Audrey couldn't see until she came closer and saw the bend, the pool, the feathers of algae—Merritt's fingers floating among them like fish.

"I think we'll all fit," Merritt said. "Mostly."

There were the flat stones Bo had mentioned. They set their things upon them and shed their clothing like snakeskin. Merritt and Eric climbed in first, each of them squealing at the slimy floor, the heat of the water. Harper propped her phone, turned to video mode, in the V of a nearby branch and set it to record this experience for later uploading. Then she slipped into the hot springs next to Merritt, exactly next to her, their bare skin touching in places.

Audrey still hadn't gotten in. She drank water, half a bottle. She heard, she thought, voices from off in the woods and wondered if it was their trailing camera crew not being quite quiet enough.

"Hey, will you play music? Something?" Eric asked her. "You're the only one who still has dry hands."

Audrey chose a playlist and turned up the volume. She sat on the mossy bank and dipped in her feet and legs up to her knees.

"You're not getting in?" Harper asked like this was a personal affront.

"Eventually I will," Audrey said. For now, she let herself fall back onto the moss, which was cool and plush. Her feet and ankles stayed in the warm water. She could hear the three of them talking softly about something but soon their voices were no different to her than the hum of the bugs. She closed her eyes to sleep.

And she did sleep. She thought she might have slept for hours, a deep dreamless sleep, like entering a cave and the entrance closing behind her.

She woke when there was a dripping shadow over her. It might have been the shadow from Spite Tower, a blocking of the sun, but it was only Eric trailing slimy algae from his swim trunks. He was holding her phone.

"Sorry," he said. "We got tired of your playlist and I was finding something else."

She tried to lick her lips, but it felt like moving two pieces of Styrofoam against each other. And she had blackberry seeds in her teeth. She could feel them now, back in her molars and along her gums. She needed water. She sat up, reached for a bottle, and caught Merritt and Harper kissing. Or maybe she didn't catch them doing anything. They weren't hiding it.

If Eric wasn't here, she wondered, what then? Maybe nothing. Would she have wanted something?

Audrey unscrewed the cap, took a long drink of water, swished it around and around her mouth in an attempt to loosen those seeds and flush them out. Anyway, it didn't matter, because Eric was most definitely here, standing above her while dripping and complaining.

She drank again. The water was warm now and unpleasant tasting. It seemed to coat her mouth without solving her thirst. But she could at least feel it dislodge some of the seeds. She stuck a finger in her mouth and dragged it along her gums until she'd collected them.

At first, when she looked down at her fingertip, she thought she'd pulled out a chunk of blackberry that had somehow escaped her chewing, a fleshy section of three still-plump drupelets. But right before she flicked it away, she saw what it really was: the tiny, severed head of a yellow jacket, its empty eyes staring back at her.

The moss beneath her seemed to undulate as she took it in, as she tried to make the head turn back to being a blackberry segment.

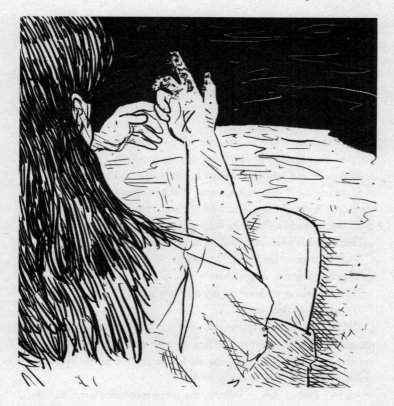

"The fuck's up with your phone?" Eric asked. He sounded so far above her he might have been in a tree.

Audrey did not answer. She stared at the head, tried to make it unreal. She could feel other things still in her teeth, even more than before. She dragged her finger along her wet gum trench again, pulled it out. She thought she might vomit, could feel it bubble in her throat. The yellow jacket head was still stuck to her fingertip but now it was there along with other chewed pieces of its body.

"What's wrong?" Harper asked, but she wasn't speaking to Audrey, she was asking Eric about the phone.

"It's really bizarre," he said. "It's—I think this is *your* feed."

"What does that mean?" Harper asked. "Like my Insta?"

Eric looked back and forth, back and forth, between the screen on the phone in his hand and somewhere off in the trees.

"Eric, what?" Harper asked again.

"No, it's like, I can't even figure out how this could be happening," he said. "What's up with your phone, Audrey? What kind of witchcraft you got going here?"

Now Harper was climbing out of the water to join him. She too dripped over Audrey as she made her way to Eric.

Audrey could still feel things in her teeth, along her gums. She thought maybe if she took another drink of water, but as she tipped the bottle it caught the light and she saw that it had things floating in it. She looked closer: they were slimy threads of black algae.

"How is this even possible?" Harper was asking.

"I don't know," Eric said. "I tried to clear this screen to see if it's an app, but it won't let me close it."

"Is it somehow picking up my phone's signal?"

"How would that work?"

"Why are we playing around with our phones right now?" Merritt asked. She was still in the hot springs and had pushed over to the mossy bank. "Oh gross," she said, noticing the bottle in Audrey's hand. "What's wrong with your water?"

Audrey looked down. Even in the mere moments since last she'd looked, scum had crept up the insides of the bottle and tinged the water yellow.

"What's wrong with her phone is the question," Eric said.

Merritt climbed out to see for herself and Audrey, legs shaky, also stood.

The buzz in the thicket had turned up and deepened. "Something's wrong," Audrey said. "I think something's wrong with me." Her voice sounded strange to her, almost as if rendered in the transatlantic accent she'd been scolded about that morning. But it didn't matter because nobody else heard her. They were all so focused on the screen in Eric's hand. Which now, finally, Audrey looked at, too.

It took her several seconds to understand what it was she was seeing.

"Jesus," Harper said. "Fuck."

Audrey looked off into the woods where Eric had been looking earlier. She saw Harper's phone still propped on that branch, still recording, and then she understood while not understanding at all: her own phone screen was playing the live video feed that Harper's phone was recording.

"How are you doing this?" Harper asked her.

"I'm not," Audrey said. "I can't imagine why it's doing that."

"Oh you can't imagine?" Eric asked in a sneer.

"Why are you talking like that?" Merritt asked Audrey. "Are you mocking me?"

"No. I'm not, I—" Audrey looked at Merritt to explain but when she did, she noticed that Merritt had algae slime threaded through her eyebrow piercings and almost dripping down into her eye. She really thought she might vomit. "Merritt, you have—" she started to say.

But Eric yelled, "Oh fuck, look. Look!"

Audrey whirled to look behind them, bracing for the jump scare, but he meant at the phone screen.

"This is the tea, right?" Harper said. "This is the trumpets?"

Audrey turned back around, saw what they were seeing: there was something now on the opposite bank. It was hard to tell quite what it was because the angle of the camera placed it only in the top right portion of the screen, but it seemed to be folds of fabric, like the pleats of a long, black skirt. She looked up from the phone screen to the bank across the springs from them, where someone, presumably in a long skirt, should have been standing. There was no one there.

"It moved!" Eric shouted. "It just moved."

"Wait, what are you seeing?" Merritt asked.

Eric held his finger on the screen, directly on the image, and as he did it grew larger and more complete. The woman, or the half of the woman they could see, now moved a step, then another, toward the water—and so more of her emerged within the frame. Her corset gave her black dress the much-desired wasp shape of the time. The whole look could have come straight from costumes and wardrobe. But still they could not see her head or face.

And still there was no one on the bank across from them.

"I'm not staying here for this," Audrey said. "I'm going back." The seeds in her teeth—they *weren't* seeds, she knew that now—felt like they were twitching. The dense hum-buzz of the thicket was filling her head with black scribbles.

"I can't understand this," Merritt said. "This doesn't—"

On the screen, the woman had started to bend toward the water, slowly, haltingly, and as she did—as her face came closer to an angle at which the camera, and they, would see it—the whole image began to cloud. Black algae crept from the corners of the screen and the image shuddered with it, almost like it was trying to shake it off.

The woman bent lower still, extended her hands toward the surface of the hot springs. They could see the top of her head now, her hair all pinned up, but her face was down, looking at the water. If she only looked up, they would see her—whatever face she might have, be it that of Mary MacLane, or inflamed from stings, puffy and bruised like a rotten apple. But the black spread of growth clouded the frame like smoke. Soon the image, the woman, would disappear in it.

Again, Audrey looked across the hot springs. But there was no one there. Except—in the thick growth beyond the bank: a movement, shuddering like a swarm. The seeds in her mouth came alive. Buzzing.

Audrey ran.

She left them looking at her phone and she ran through the Tricky Thicket as Clara Broward had once before her. It might have been her best performance yet, though even as she gave it, she wasn't sure if it was a performance at all. Branches and brambles tore at her clothing. Her feet twisted in the undergrowth and slipped over patches of moss. She stumbled. She lurched. She ran on.

"Audrey, wait!" Merritt called after her. "Wait for me!"

But Audrey didn't. She wanted to get free of the buzzing. Maybe Bo had hung speakers from the trees, because she couldn't seem to leave it behind, not even once she'd cleared the thicket and was back in open woods. She wasn't sure of the right direction, but she ran anyway. She could hear shouts behind her, but she did not slow for them.

Every few steps she'd spit, or try to, her mouth still so dry. But those seeds—they were not seeds!—were twitching in her teeth. She had to get them out. A squelch of mud shot up the back of her legs. A long branch scraped a line of skin from her arm. She did not stop.

Eventually, she could see their cottages growing larger through the trees. She ran to her own and in the door and to the kitchen sink, where she cupped water from the faucet and into her mouth and gargled and spit and did it again and again.

There, now swirling the drain, were legs and wings and a striped thorax, hopping in the sink like jumping beans. She spit out the stinger and her tongue went numb.

And she hadn't left the buzzing. It had followed her in from the woods and filled the house with its constancy.

She felt weak, scooped out.

She gripped the edge of the counter and bent backward to lower herself to the ground before her legs gave out, but somehow the edge of the counter gave out first. A chunk of it, as light as packing peanuts, broke off in her hand and she tumbled onto the floor still holding it.

What she held, she saw, wasn't wood at all. It was papier-mâché painted to look like butcher block, layers and layers shellacked together, and inside that: the hexagonal chambers of a yellow jacket nest.

Audrey looked up at the edge of the counter, where the piece had broken free, and saw more paper chambers inside. And now, she felt it—the thinnest flick of the air. A vibrancy. A hum.

And soon after she saw it, the searching head of a yellow jacket emerging from its chamber, twitching, looking at her. And now another right behind. And now another. They launched themselves into flight, chose a path over her shoulder, next to her ear.

She slumped back onto the floor.

From the front door of her tiny house, which she'd left open, she heard Merritt say, "Oh, Audrey. You really aren't feeling well."

And then her blurry vision gave up for black.

APPLE BRUISE

....

Libbie had so many things to do before Alex woke from her nap.

The first, and most important of these, she'd just finished: send Caspar to fetch the doctor. She'd been quite vague with him about Alex's symptoms, but Caspar Eckhart did not require details to do what he'd been asked. Right away, he'd headed out in the carriage with Max.

Now she needed to find Addie and Hanna and explain some of Alex's current delusion. Not so much as to embarrass Alex once she recovered, of course, but enough so that the women could be of assistance to Libbie if Alex attempted some additional act of lunacy before the doctor arrived.

She'd heard Hanna in the kitchen when they'd come in, and it was Thursday, so Adelaide was likely up in the tower, readying for their lesson. They'd have to skip it tonight. Addie would be disappointed, but that couldn't be helped, not with Alex in such a state.

Libbie just needed to change out of this sweaty skirt and blouse—which still held the rotten smell from The Orangerie—then she'd go find them.

And her bruise. She needed to look at her bruise—it was throbbing again.

In her bedroom, standing naked in a puddle of her skirt, Libbie tried to look down the length of her body at the bruise. But the way the light played on her skin, the sharp jut of her hip bone, the contours of her stomach—all of this made it difficult to properly see.

Instead, she looked ahead into the tall gilt-frame mirror along the wall, stepping forward into better light.

She gasped as she did. She could not help it.

The bruise was darker than when last she'd looked, purple black and the size and shape of an apple. A Black Oxford, Readers. It was even swollen so that it appeared convex like an apple, pressing out the side of her hip, almost as if you could slice her top layer of skin, peel it back, and pull it free from her body.

The more Libbie looked at it, the more it throbbed. It made her feel faint even to think of touching it, but something now compelled her hand. She knew it would hurt, when she did, oh the pain was certain to be unbearable, but she must trace her fingers over it.

She watched her reflection as her pale fingers drew nearer to it. It did not feel like she was moving her arm to make this happen, but she could see that she was, there in the mirror. Her hand hovered over the apple's surface when—

"Mrs. Brookhants," Adelaide said from the doorway. Despite all that had occurred between them these past months, or maybe because of it, Libbie moved her eyes away when they found each other in the mirror. "I'm sorry to startle you. I think you'd better come with me. Miss Trills is in the tower and she seems unwell."

"I left her sleeping," Libbie said unhappily, though she knew it wasn't much of an explanation. "I wanted to talk to you and Hanna both before she woke."

"She's awake now," Adelaide said. "And her eye looks very bad— what I could see of it. She wouldn't let me get near to her."

"You mustn't take it personally, Addie."

"She seems upset with me," Adelaide said. "More so even than usual. She wouldn't—I almost think she's frightened of me."

"She's not thinking clearly," Libbie said. "That's all it is." She felt pulled from a dream.

"Here, let me help you," Adelaide said. She went into the dressing room and emerged just as quickly with a simple day dress that did not require a corset. She stood behind Libbie, but when she went to help Libbie pull it on, she also saw the bruise and gasped.

"I know," Libbie said, both of them looking in the mirror at the black apple on her hip. "I can't see how it hasn't healed."

"Hasn't healed?" Adelaide said. "Oh, but it's gotten so much worse!" Without either of them quite understanding what was happening, Adelaide's fingers—only the lightest touch of the tips of one hand—were now upon the bruise, trailing against it. Instead of the pain Libbie expected, watching those fingers in the mirror before her, Adelaide's touch felt cool and welcome.

"You must tell the doctor, Mrs. Brookhants."

The doctor. That did it. That broke the spell. "There's one on the way," Libbie said.

Adelaide looked rather stunned by this news, and she pulled her hand back.

"For Miss Trills, I mean. Caspar and Max went to bring the doctor for Miss Trills. You're right that she's not well and what's wrong isn't only her eye." Libbie was now pulling on the new dress, the fabric tight and painful against her hip.

"Please don't hurt yourself rushing," Adelaide said. "Hanna's waiting with her up in the tower."

"Oh, she is?" Libbie said, feeling some relief. "Oh good." Now if she could keep Alex away from Addie until the doctor arrived with a sedative or some other plan. "Was she looking for me?"

"Hanna?" Addie asked.

"No, Miss Trills. Is that why she went up in the tower? She tends to avoid it if she can."

"I've noticed that," Adelaide said as if she was thinking. "But I don't think she was looking for you. She was after a photograph, she said, one of the late Mr. Brookhants. This was part of her agitation. It was the page from the book that started it, which was confusing to us, because we thought Miss Trills would be so pleased about us finding it."

This mention of a page from a book caught Libbie like a steel hook in the spine. "What did you find?" she asked, turning around even though Adelaide wasn't finished fastening her dress.

Libbie's interest in this topic seemed to further confuse the maid. She continued on, now more careful with her words. "It was really Hanna who found it, though I suppose I helped. We were dusting the shelves in the stairwell. I knocked loose some books—those shelves are so full, it's easy to do—and they came crashing down the stairs and then when we were gathering them, we found it. The page. We thought it had come from one of the books but when we looked it didn't match any of them. It must have only been—"

"Placed in a book it didn't belong to," Libbie said for her.

"Yes, that exactly," Adelaide said, nodding and speaking faster now. "And we both remembered during the blizzard, when Miss Trills had been so upset about the missing page in her book. So we thought, mightn't this be it?"

"Where is the page now?" Libbie asked. She was already crossing the room to the hallway, though her dress hung open in various places.

Addie was at her heel, attempting to pull the sash and close the back of Libbie's dress as they went along. "I expect Miss Trills has it with her. She came down looking for me—I think she was looking for me—and that's when Hanna showed it to her, and soon, she was shouting at me, she wouldn't be calmed. There were some markings on it, someone's notes. Those seemed to upset her."

"Oh no," Libbie said. "No, no, no."

The tower had never seemed farther away. Now Adelaide was like Libbie's shadow, the two of them moving through the too-quiet house in a swish of skirts and steps.

As they landed in the front hall, Libbie heard the hum of the yellow jackets.

It was as it had been that night in the bathroom, soft to start. Soft until they started up the dim tower stairs. Then the hum deepened, attaching itself to her body and reverberating there. Louder and louder as they climbed, Addie still too close, her breath wet and heavy against Libbie's neck, the tunnel of the stairwell dark and steep, the buzzing thick and awful and pounding in her bruise, making her wince.

They rounded the last turn.

Orange light spilled down from above. Each stair climbed brought more of the room into view. Libbie's desk, and right behind it, a flash of Alex, who was sitting on the floor against the shelves, bent over something in her lap.

"Stay behind me, Addie," Libbie said quietly.

Outside the sun was setting and throwing the last of its light in through the windows. As Libbie fully stepped up and into the study, her eyes took a moment to adjust. She had to walk a few feet into the room before she saw it clearly.

She turned to Adelaide, who hovered in the dark of the stairwell, watching. "Hanna's not here," she mouthed.

"She was!" Adelaide whispered.

Libbie continued across the room, stepping slowly, softly. But Alex did not notice her. Not yet.

Her back was against the shelves and her arms extended on either side, each hand gripping an edge of the long frame that lay across her lap. She had her head bent over it.

Libbie was now close enough to see what it was, this thing that had Alex entranced: the panoramic photograph of a séance at Harold's (in)famous redwood table. The photo hadn't hung in the tower since right after he'd died. Libbie had taken it down when she'd removed many of Harold's other photographs and prints. It was so large that she'd placed it at the very bottom of a stack, where it had, for years, collected dust on a lower shelf. (Even Hanna was not good about remembering to clean that pile.)

What could Alex want with it now? Libbie glanced again at Adelaide, who was still half hidden like a phantom in the darkness of the stairwell.

Libbie made herself speak calmly, even a touch brightly, as if her own false sunshine could rid this gloom. "Alex, what are you doing out of bed?" she asked. "You were going to sleep, remember? Sleep first and then, later tonight—"

"Oh, oh," Alex said. "*Now* you're here." She wrenched her head up from the panoramic to look at Libbie through her good eye—her other eye still swollen and actively weeping yellow gunk, which had built up and crusted like pollen. Libbie was relieved when Alex again dropped her face to the photo.

Carefully, slowly, Libbie knelt beside Alex, wincing at her apple bruise as she did. "I've been here. I thought we had a plan."

"We did have a plan! Such a charming plan. But the devil's in the details, isn't he, Library?"

"You don't know what you're saying, darling." She was still trying for calm.

"I do know!" Alex said. "I do finally know." She slid the frame on her lap forward to reveal the book, Libbie's copy of Mary Mac-Lane's story, and atop it the missing page, there in the folds of Alex's skirt.

While they'd been speaking, the buzzing had thinned, but as soon as Libbie saw the book, the page, the proof of what she'd done, it again threaded itself to her veins and thrummed insistently.

"You lied to me, Library," Alex said. "Again and again. Here we live in a thicket of lies."

Libbie nodded. She waited for what she deserved, Alex's listing of her misdeeds. Instead, what she got was:

"And I lied to you," Alex said. "Harold's awful bargain—oh how I wanted you to take it. I sold it to you for them, so that I could come here and be with you. So that we could be together."

"We are together," Libbie said weakly.

"Oh no. No, not here we aren't. Here the very trees and soil come between us."

Alex tapped the book in her lap with her pointer finger—*tap-tap.* "I wonder, did you forget that Sara had inked her provocations? When you gave this to the girls? Or did you mean for them to see her message to you?"

"Of course I didn't mean for them to see it. I would have told you—"

"And so did you intend to find a Harold for Flo and Clara, too? Was that your plan? Did you think you might introduce one or the other of them to a man with the correct sum to his name and a parcel of land? Tell me, Library: How would you have continued to advise them as they made their way, these girls in love?"

"Alex," Libbie started, but it was no use. "You're so tired and confused, darling—you're spinning all around."

"I'm no longer confused," Alex said. "Not even a touch. Why do you think the few students who remain here gather in the woods to talk of horror? Our whole world's gone dark and rotten, its belly bloated with worms, and *you* let the answer hide on a shelf in our home."

"What you're saying is madness."

"I'll show you the extent of my madness," Alex said, yanking Libbie's arm, hard, so she slid closer to Alex in the jerk of the rough movement. Alex then pulled the frame back to her lap, so that it again covered the book and its once-missing page. Libbie could see that the panoramic's glass looked freshly cleaned. There were no finger smudges, no dust, nothing to hide any of the séance's participants.

"Look here," Alex said, pulling until Libbie was bent down over the frame.

"You're hurting me, Alex," Libbie said.

Alex did not hear Libbie. Or if she did, she did not care. "Look at their faces," she said. "Who do you see? I want you to take your time. I won't show you. I don't need to because you'll find her. And then you'll know how they played us from the start."

Libbie couldn't concentrate. The buzzing filled the room, poured in her ears and thickened her thoughts. When she did look down at the photograph, it seemed to hover, almost as if she was viewing it through a stereoscope. The last of the daylight flashed against the glass, charging white spots across her vision. The buzzing was now so intense within her it seemed almost to toggle her vocal cords, as if *she* was making the hideous sound.

"I can hear it, too," Alex said.

"You can?" Libbie did not feel at all comforted by this.

"Of course. It's part of this, but you have to tune it out. Concentrate on the faces and you'll see. You'll see what I see."

From what seemed very far away, Adelaide asked if she should look for Hanna. Libbie had forgotten about her waiting on the stairs. She now looked up to find Addie standing just inside the room. She was rightly afraid to come closer.

"Never mind her," Alex said. "Look at the photo."

Libbie did as she was told. She started at Harold, who was easy to spot, his smile wide and proud. This was, after all, his grand gathering. She then worked her way around the table, studying each face as she encountered it. Madame Verrett was next. She was easy too, with her jewels and scarves. Then came a few friends of Harold's Libbie had met once or twice. A Spiritualist out of Baltimore. More men and women she did not know, at least she didn't think so— swooped hair and trim moustaches, eyeglasses and drooping jowls, starched lace collars, a thin, bird neck and a round face framed in curls, a man and a woman and a man and a face and a face and a face and no one she knew that surprised her, no one that meant anything at all. This was true all the way around the table until there, seated next to Harold on his other side, his right side, with features part in shadow—though there was no obvious cause for that and it affected no one else in the image—but still, was it, it might be . . .

The buzzing wrapped Libbie's heart and rattled her spine. She squinted again, shifted even closer to the photograph, which caused her breath to fog the glass, but—

"I've brought some water and a bandage!" It was Hanna, finally, there on the last stair with a pitcher and glass in hand. "And I think I heard them coming up the road with the doctor."

Her voice seemed to enter Alex like the thrust of a knife. "Stay back!" she yelled. "You stay away!"

Hanna, stunned, did not move from that final stair. So Adelaide took the items from her, set them on the edge of the desk, and rushed to the windows to look for the promised carriage.

Alex still gripped the picture frame at both ends and now pressed down on it with too much force as she moved to stand. The glass snapped, first with a crack and then with a scuttling spiderweb. The thin pasteboard backing gave too, snapping the long photograph in half. Alex seemed not to notice. She let go of the frame, took Mary's book in her right hand, and leveraged it against the ground to help push herself up. Shards of glass spilled from her skirts like salt and Sara's marked page fluttered to the floor to lie atop the glass.

Alex was now on her feet. "We know your tricks, Hanna Eckhart," she sang horribly across the room, the desk no longer blocking her view. She turned her good eye toward Hanna. "We see you now. I see you."

"Did you really hear the carriage?" Adelaide asked. She was still at the windows, scanning the ground below for the promised doctor. "I can't see it."

"That's because she lies," Alex said, triumphant. "She's only ever worked for Harold. Even now, she works for him."

"Are they really here?" Libbie asked Hanna. It seemed impossible that Caspar, Max, and the doctor should have arrived so soon from town.

As the others were speaking, Alex had crept her way along the wall toward the stairwell. Now she seized her chance, taking off, full force, toward Hanna. She had Mary's book held out before her, each hand gripping a side as if she were carrying a sign in a march. Her intention was clear, clear to Libbie and to Adelaide and especially to Hanna: Alex would shove her, hard, so that she toppled over like a chess piece and fell back down the stairs.

Alexandra Trills was only a blur of hair and flesh and book.

The buzzing had reached an impossible pitch. It was the air itself.

And then, the awful crash of bodies.

Except—

At the final moment, Hanna flattened herself against the stairwell wall, pressing her body into the books that lined it. She had to get the timing exactly right, and even then, it didn't seem like it should quite work, the stairwell was so narrow.

But it did work, Readers. Hanna made it work.

It was almost as if the books and shelves became something less than solid, something more like flesh, with enough give for her to press her body into their embrace. They let her in.

Alex, with her weeping eye, her skewed perspective, was now at the top of the stairs, but where Hanna should have been was a gap, empty space, humming air. There was nothing for her to collide with, and so instead she dove—outstretched book, then head, then body—down and down, into the twisting darkness.

The buzzing ceased at once, like the popping of a balloon.

Alex did not scream or cry out as she fell, but her body, hitting the walls and knocking loose volumes, careening the corners and bouncing on the stairs, made a terrible kind of gasping, thudding noise that drew quieter the farther it descended.

There was no doctor waiting for our Alexandra Trills when she crumpled into stillness at the bottom of the staircase. This was because the doctor had not yet arrived and would not do so for another hour.*

Alex, smart, strong, devoted Alex, of course did not survive her fall. Her neck had snapped on the first turn of the staircase. Not unlike the glass in the séance photo, first came the solid, murderous break, and then came a spiderweb of smaller cracks throughout her body's other bones—both wrists, a femur, several ribs.

By the time Spite Manor's gravity stopped her at the bottom, Alexandra Trills was no longer of our world. She'd drifted from it somewhere in the stairwell, fluttering up over the pages of the many books that lined her fall.

I will not linger here describing all that came next, such as the wailing sob that accompanied Libbie's harried slipping down the stairs, whereupon she flung her own body over that of her lover and stayed for so long that what they were to each other would never again be denied by anyone who saw.

When, much later, Hanna had tried to help her stand, Libbie screamed at her to get away. Even after Max had pulled his mother from the room, still Libbie screamed, on and on. She was in such a

---

* Libbie would not confirm this until later, but as she'd suspected, at the time Alex was making her running shove, Caspar and Max hadn't even reached the doctor's practice in town, let alone returned with him. To explain her error Hanna had said simply, "I was so sure I'd heard them on the road."

state of rage and terror that the doctor, who had finally arrived, gave her a knockout drop and had her carried to her bed. He hoped that rest would cure her shock.

But in the coming days, whenever she came to, Libbie would not let Hanna Eckhart near her. And even if Hanna stayed away, Libbie would soon grow so agitated at the thought of her somewhere on a floor below that the consulting physicians (for now there were several of them) felt they had no choice but to give her another sedative to quiet her fear. And then the process would begin again. Libbie would rest. Then wake. Then shudder, or scream, or lash about in a hysterical rage over Hanna and her evil machinations. For a week, she did this.

And then—

Adelaide caught our Libbie with a bit of lit kindling she'd pulled from the fireplace. Libbie was trying to light her bed on fire. She *did*, in fact, light her bed on fire, and the hem of her nightgown too, but they got it put out in time. And so they knocked her out again and sent for her brother, the senator, who was then down the coast in Washington. He arrived with the intention of escorting her back to Chicago, to convalesce with their parents, but when this was explained to Libbie, she again became so violent and unreasonable that the idea of sending her on a cross-country journey now seemed out of the question. (Perhaps it's worth noting that this was her least favorite brother.) At any rate, soon after she was committed to the Rhode Island State Asylum for the Incurable Insane, where she was further confined for more than a year.

But *this* ending is not Libbie Brookhants's ending, Readers. She'll have to wait for that.

So for the moment, let us leave her wearing a black mourning gown and sitting in a stiff chair, in a drafty room, while she stares at the crack in the plaster wall and tries not to hear the sound of the buzzing, tries not to see the twitching head, and now the cellophane wings and sticky legs, of a yellow jacket as it appears in that crack, tries not to remember all the things she'd prefer to forget. The doctor will be in soon enough and he'll make her remember, and worse, he'll make her speak those things aloud. And then he'll tell her they're only delusions, only figments of her own invention. He'll have one of the white-cap nurses with him, the kind who smirk but never smile, who pinch and scratch her when his back is turned. This while the doctor tries to tell her, calmly, so calmly, that these things she remembers are only delusions, only figments of her own invention.

This when she knows, when she *finally knows,* they are not.

UPDATES FROM THE SET OF
The Happenings at Brookhants
AS TOLD ONLINE

....

SEPTEMBER 27

ReelSkeeze nabbed these upsetting exclusive photos of costume supervisor Maya Barslonick being loaded into an ambulance at the troubled *Happenings at Brookhants* set, located at an abandoned boarding school in coastal Rhode Island that has long been <u>rumored</u> to be haunted.

Barslonick was reportedly sorting clothing in a storage container when it caught fire late Wednesday morning. In her own words, she had to "run through a wall of flames" in order to get out the door to safety. Barslonick was treated for second-degree burns at St. Anne's Hospital in Fall River, Massachusetts. A representative for Barslonick said that she is now "recuperating away from the production with friends." At this time, the cause of the fire has not been officially determined, but a preliminary investigation seems to point to faulty wiring. A spokesperson for *The Happenings at Brookhants* told Film Fever that over $65,000 in damage was caused by the blaze and that filming had been significantly delayed. Again.

As ReelSkeeze has already reported, <u>here</u>, <u>here</u>, and <u>here</u>, now only thirty-two days into its scheduled seventy-three-day shoot, the *Happenings at Brookhants* production has incurred more than its fair share of <u>strange</u> and <u>difficult circumstances</u>, leading <u>online commenters</u> to suggest one of two things: either an elaborate hoax meant to convince us that the film is cursed, or an <u>actual curse</u>. (Much like those said to have tainted films like *The Exorcist, Poltergeist,* and, the grand-devil of all supposedly cursed films, *The Omen.*)

While various <u>internet communities</u> are stridently divided on the subject, discussions about a possible curse began in earnest after one of the film's leads and producers, Harper Harper, posted a short video to her <u>Instagram account</u> on September 2 purporting to show a swarm of wasps that she (and <u>others</u>) claimed looked like a <u>beckoning ghostly figure</u>. Days earlier, Harper had posted a photo to her Instagram that showed several <u>small objects</u> that she claimed she and another crew member had discovered while helping to arrange props on set. Those figures have been <u>reported</u> to link to <u>lore</u> about the school's <u>troubled past</u>.

In the wake of these posts and rumors, TMZ is reporting that the *Brookhants* shoot is swarmed with fans and paranormal seekers hoping to get in on the action. The production <u>significantly increased</u> its security forces in order to keep people from the set, and even with these measures, they haven't been <u>entirely successful</u>.

Casie Fregg, a college student at nearby Roger Williams University, <u>nearly drowned</u> after attempting to swim to the shores of the *Brookhants* set so that she could meet Harper Harper and, according to an interview Miss Fregg gave with the *Providence Journal,* "just do a séance with her." Fregg was rescued by a quick-acting carpenter currently working for the production.

While most people associated with the film have been reluctant to speak to press, ReelSkeeze did manage to interview a camera operator who asked to remain anonymous but offered the following statement regarding the alleged curse: "I'm the definition of a skeptic, but with as many people as we've had get hurt already, at some point you have to start asking, *Is there something to this?* You know? Even if you feel dumb asking it—and I really do. Like, what is it worth to maintain my skepticism, though? For sure not my safety."

Thus far, veteran horror director Bo Dhillon has not made any on-record comments about the rumored curse, which has only <u>fueled speculation</u> that this is all a hoax intended to increase interest in the film and its story's supposedly factual basis.

If that's indeed the case, it <u>seems to</u> <u>be working</u>. Google searches with the film's title have increased over 1,000 percent since these rumors of a cursed set began making their rounds online.

UH-OH, IT'S MAGIC*

Merritt exchanged the word *equable* for the word *placid,* read the sentence again, highlighted it because she still didn't think she'd gotten it quite right, hit Save, and closed her laptop. Then she stretched her arms high overhead and popped her neck. It had already been a six-thousand-plus-word day. I say *already* because she thought she might take a break now, for several hours, and then start up again when she returned to her cottage later that night.

She was sitting on the pavers in front of the Brookhants Main Hall. They were filming inside. She leaned back against the fountain, slid her legs straight out in front of her in another stretch, this one to ease the cramps that came from sitting cross-legged on the ground and hunched over her keyboard for too long.

Earlier she'd pulled off her chunky-knit sweater—like a blanket, that thing, and too hot. Now she was grateful for the stone side of the fountain's basin, baking there in the golden sun of that October afternoon, and how it warmed her skin through the thin fabric of her T-shirt. She had it tucked into her mom jeans, high waisted and button front in washed-out denim. Harper had gifted the shirt to

---

* Lyrics from the song "Magic," a chart-climbing, 1984 single from the band The Cars.

her. She'd had one made for each of the three of them. It was black, and on its front, in all caps in a sans-serif white font, it read: *Mary MacLane*.

"Because we're with the band," Harper had said as she'd presented them. Merritt loved hers, but this was her first time wearing it and when she'd put it on that morning, she'd felt a little self-conscious.

At least until an hour later, when Harper surprised her at crafty. Merritt had actually been in the middle of receiving a compliment on the shirt from a lighting crew member. Harper witnessed this as she selected her banana. She smiled at Merritt from behind the compliment giver. And as he walked away, she said, "You look hot in my shirt," before walking away herself. You could've traced a line from those six words to Merritt's clitoris,* but she did manage to collect herself enough to yell after her, "I know!"

Even now she felt a surge just thinking about it.

The trees that rimmed the emerald lawn before her had begun their seasonal show. Several of the maples had patches of crimson and orange, like fire trying to take hold. For as far as Merritt could see, the sky was blue and brilliant, the sun a melting gob of butterscotch ice cream, though if she'd been at the top of Spite Tower, she would have seen a gauze of clouds building in the distance.

But she wasn't at the top of Spite Tower. She was here, in the sun near the fountain, her back warm from the heat of the stone.

There was that in the air which is there when something is going to happen. Though this fact was beginning to mean very little to Merritt. Things kept happening all the time now at Brookhants. Who could even keep up to write them all down?

She checked her alerts to read some of the latest posts about problems on set. There were three dozen from today alone. She didn't bother with them all, especially since most were regurgitations of others.

Since the news of the near-drowning student swimmer, fans,

---

* Too much, Readers? I was hoping that we'd come to a place in our relationship where you'd allow it.

skeptics, and attention seekers alike had gone to greater and greater lengths to not only crash the *Brookhants* set but document their attempts at doing so. It had become a *thing,* a viral thing, even for people who didn't care all that much about the actors, or the film and the true story behind it, even for people who could have accessed other film sets—in New York or Toronto or LA—much more readily. There's no explaining it, really: it just hit the exact right combination of factors to make it a thing certain people posted about themselves attempting on their social media feeds.

There were now two dozen full-time security officers working for the production, and even they couldn't stop all the crashers. They held it to a trickle but still the trespassers came, by land and by sea. And the more the disturbances were reported online, the more people wanted to see for themselves.

And they were having no shortage of disturbances on set.

In fact, right then one of the massive doors to Main Hall banged closed behind her and Merritt turned in time to see Bo coming down the stairs, his face angry. He had his phone on speaker, held up in the direction of his frowning mouth, and as he came closer he shouted into it: "How about you tell them I said right goddamn now? Unless they're ready to send me a check for three hundred and fifty thousand dollars."

He was already charging toward the production office set up in the dorm building when he turned around, took in Merritt—her laptop, her place in the sun—shook his head (in what appeared to Merritt as additional disgust), and then turned back around and continued on.

More of the cast and crew banged out the front doors too, including the first AD and Heather, who seemed to be following along after Bo, though not really in a hurry to catch him. Merritt watched as the script supervisor took off running onto the lawn in a sprint before managing three handsprings and a roundoff, much to the enjoyment of the various crew members who cheered this performance. Everyone was acting like they'd just been let out of detention, except Bo, the beleaguered schoolmarm.

Merritt brushed at a tickle at the back of her head, something slight twitching her hair. More crew joined the script supervisor in the lawn to do cartwheels, those who could do them, anyway. "See how many grills we can round up," one of them yelled to someone who jogged off toward catering. "I'm only in if we're for sure doing lobstahl!"

Merritt brushed at the hair twitch again and this time she thought her fingers might have glanced against something hovering there—something nonhair, like maybe a bug. Like maybe a yellow jacket.

When **Harper** walked out the double doors of Main Hall she saw that Merritt was right where Harper had left her hours before: sitting in front of the fountain. This was too perfect.

Harper pulled off her shoes and rolled her pants—tweed things provided by costuming—to the knees. And then she walked behind the fountain, and, quietly as she could, stepped over and into its cold water. She held a finger to her lips to shush one of the crew before they said something about what she was doing—which would announce her presence.

The floor of the fountain was slimier than Harper had expected, and the water colder. She stepped slowly, slowly, not sloshing any water because it would make too much noise, until she was behind Merritt. Then she bent over in a silent crouch and, with her mouth right next to Merritt's left ear, she whispered, *"There is that in the air which is there when something is going to happen."*

"Jesus fuck!" Merritt shouted.

Harper nearly fell over in her laughing delight.

"You're an asshole," Merritt added, reaching to dip her hand into the water and slosh it at Harper.

"Careful," Harper said, steadying herself with one hand on the fountain's rim in order to step out and down. One of her bare feet landed not on a paver but on a thick scab of the spongy green moss that grew between them. The sensation made her momentarily seasick.

"Careful why?" Merritt asked, flicking more water still.

"This particular look doesn't belong to me," Harper said, hopping away from the fountain and Merritt's reach while trying to avoid landing on moss as she went. Atop those tweed pants she wore a tight, ribbed, navy sweater in the style football players of 1902 might have worn, and like those players' sweaters, hers had a large white letter across its front: *B* for Brookhants.

"That look might not have been procured by you, but it absolutely belongs to you," Merritt said. And it was true, Readers. Harper certainly looked the part. "What happened in there?" She added, pointedly: "Today."

"Ghosts in the mics," Harper said, reaching into her back pocket for her cigarettes and lighting one as she spoke. (The vaping hadn't stuck, Readers.)

Merritt raised her eyebrows. Waited.

"Feedback," Harper said. "It was these truly bizarre noises—kind of like moans, at one point, but then it was like people talking fast from far away, so you couldn't really make out the words. They switched out a bunch of the sound equipment." She yawned, squinted in the sunlight, and took a drag from her cigarette. "Didn't help."

"I'm sure I'll be able to watch it online any minute," Merritt said.

"Probably," Harper said. "I didn't notice anybody with their phone out this time, though. Actually, Misha and Renae seemed scared today. Like genuinely scared."*

"But not you? I thought you were such a believer?"

"I don't know," Harper said. "I didn't really notice at first. I was going over this blocking issue with Bo and Audrey and it didn't seem like a big deal, just standard set-delay bullshit. But then when we all started paying attention, I did think the whispering part was creepy. And that they couldn't get it to stop, even with everyone trying everything. That was weird."

---

* Misha Reditch and Renae Gonzalez were actors with small roles playing fellow Brookhants students. There was good reason to believe that one or both of them had leaked footage they'd shot from their phones of a previous on-set alleged paranormal occurrence involving several crows smashing themselves into the windows of The Orangerie.

"Did it bother Audrey?"

Harper thought a moment before she said, "Yeah, I think so. A little. I mean, it *was* weird."

"So that's it for today? The whole rest of the day?"

Harper nodded like her head was on a slow bobble. Nodding and nodding, resigned to this perpetual state of delay. Again.

"That explains Bo," Merritt said.

"Did you see him?" Harper asked as she slid down to sit beside Merritt, their shoulders and hips brushing.

"Oh yes," Merritt said. "He came storming out."

"It's more than that," Harper said. "He had a total blowup. That's probably the part that'll leak."

Merritt looked at her. "Blowup like how?"

"Like throwing his headset at the wall. Then he kicked over a chair in video village. It was a full-on tantrum."

"Cool," Merritt said. "Profesh."

"Yeah," Harper said. "That's probably what bothered Audrey more than even the sounds. But I mean I get it, sort of. He can't seem to get this movie back on track."

"Is it possible that's because he's chosen the wrong track for it?" Merritt asked.

"What does that mean?"

"What do you think that means?" Merritt turned to the side to look at Harper's face and Harper did the same to her. They held that joined look, saying nothing, until Harper started to smile—until they both did, couldn't help it.

"Nerd," Harper said.

"Where's Audrey now?" Merritt asked.

"Changing."

"Not you, though?" Merritt reached to pluck at the sleeve of Harper's sweater.

"Never," Harper said. "When Flo goes andro, I go Flo."

"It suits you."

"Oh shit," Harper said. "Was that a compliment? Like a real compliment? I wasn't even ready. Can you start it again? Let me just get my phone out to capture—"

"Fuck off," Merritt said. "What's the plan for the rest of the day?" These delays had been happening so frequently that the crew members who weren't busy putting out fires* found other sources of entertainment. They'd played hours-long games of red rover and dodgeball. They'd held a pie-eating contest. For no discernable reason, they'd bought, filled, hung, and bashed to shit four different piñatas.

And for the last few days, they'd been filling their ample downtime by screening movies out on the lawn—projecting them on the side of Main Hall as soon as it was dark enough to do so.

"Movies and a clambake, I heard," Harper said.

"Which movie?"

Harper shrugged.

They'd been watching, predictably, horror films—or thrillers, supernatural dramas. Creepy stuff. The night before had been *Picnic at Hanging Rock*. Two nights before: the French film *Haute Tension*. That one had been scary enough that our heroines had ended up again crashing together after, in Audrey's tiny house.

Audrey had been grateful for that—even if she still didn't get much sleep that night. (Harper did. Enough to snore.)

Even without sleep, Audrey felt safer, and just generally better, with Merritt and Harper around, especially since their afternoon in the Tricky Thicket. She knew that it was unwise to feel this way, or at least counterintuitive. Things—scary things—were more likely to happen when the three of them were together than when it was just her alone. But she couldn't help it. She didn't want to be alone here.

Right now, she was cutting through The Orangerie on her way back from changing out of her costume. One of the suspended blooms of the angel's trumpet tree brushed her shoulder as she went along. Another touched the top of her head. The feel of their petals against her was almost like the terrible soft brush of a

---

* Sometimes, as you know, Readers, quite literally.

reaching hand, one that brought the memory of the tea and what happened after she drank it. Harper and Merritt seemed to have decided that they'd all been hallucinating that day at the hot springs, and Audrey was the unlucky one who'd ended up with the worst trip.

As explanations go, this one was so weak as to be barely plausible. Audrey was fairly certain that the phone production had given her had something to do with the *shared delusion* that appeared on its screen.

The day it happened, Harper and Merritt had helped her from her kitchen floor to her bed and then stayed with her as she slept it off. Or they said she slept, anyway. She couldn't remember—and she still felt so tired when she woke, hours later. But when she checked her kitchen countertop, while it was still broken, it was also still butcher block—solid and true, with nary an exposed yellow jacket chamber in sight.

Bo had called her later that night and asked if she wanted them to send over a nurse. She said no. She'd vomited, drank a bunch of Gatorade and some lemongrass soup. She was feeling better.

"You gave us a scare," he'd told her.

"That's funny," she'd said. "Isn't that what you want me to do?"

"Listen, I want you to know, again, that whatever was in that tea he made, it came from Eric, not from us," Bo said. "We told him that it's a real-deal angel's trumpet, but the tree we have in The Orangerie has all the potency modified out of it. Or it's supposed to."

"I don't know why you would think that's comforting to me," she'd said. "I want to believe that whatever happened was *because* of the tea."

"It certainly looked that way on camera."

"I really don't know if I can do this much longer," she said. "It's not good for me. I'm not sleeping. I haven't been."

"You're doing so great, Audrey. Really. What we're getting is phenomenal."

"I'm not sleeping."

"Nobody is," he said. "Do you think you can try to use that? Mine it?"

"I mean, I don't know what other choice I have," she said.

"I think you *can* use it. I think it's all part of this. I mean, tell me if it gets worse, of course—but really, I'm not sleeping much, either. Try to use it."

Now, Audrey could see out The Orangerie windows to Merritt and Harper together by the fountain, talking in the sun. She checked her face one last time in the reverse camera on her phone. She'd changed out of her costume dress and corset and wiped clean her full makeup, but she'd left her hairdo—piled and pinned into a kind of faux crop—as it was. That, plus the off-the-shoulder cut of her sweatshirt, made her neck seem extra long, just how Charles Dana Gibson (of Gibson Girl fame) would have liked it.

She cleared the camera app and opened her texts to reread her afternoon instructions. She had a chilled six-pack of a local hard cider in her bag, along with a blanket, an additional mic pack, and the prize item: the most ornate of the antique talking boards from Spite Tower and the planchette that went with it. She was supposed to now get Harper and Merritt to join her here, in The Orangerie, to use that board. Her backstory being that she'd managed to sneak it out of the tower the night they'd been up there, which no one would buy for a minute. But she did now have it, so . . . That much even Merritt couldn't deny. And if she tried to argue, well, Bo would like that better anyway.

The staging could be wonderful, sure. The three of them together on a blanket spread across the tiled floor, a shiver rippling through their bodies as they bent over the board and saw its message to them, while cameras, cameras everywhere watched something bad begin to happen. Keep happening.

As always, Audrey didn't know what that bad would be, but these arrangements were more elaborate than usual, so she guessed it would be something significant. Something terrifying. But not *real,* of course. Not that.

Even as she thought this, Audrey heard a noise like a whisper behind her in the plants. She turned to look but there was no one there but the flowers and leaves. Still, there was a shadow on the far wall she hadn't noticed before. Maybe a crouching body with a camera? Maybe a crouching body without a camera?

She didn't wait to find out.

She pulled the spare mic pack and the talking board from her bag and shoved them into a nearby planter. Then she took off the mic she'd been wearing and did the same with it. Finally, she turned off her phone completely.

She started to open the door, and in a moment of pure inspiration, turned around and pulled a cluster of orange blossoms off the nearest tree. She tucked them behind her ear and walked out the door and across to Harper and Merritt so that she could stand in front of them and say, before she lost her nerve: "Can we go to the orchard? We have time."

"Right now?" Merritt asked.

"Oh *fuck* yes," Harper said. She reached both arms up so that Audrey would help pull her to standing, which she did.

"OK," Merritt said like she was amused. "I'm game." She shoved her things into her bag and then held both of her arms up, just as Harper had, and the two of them pulled her to her feet as well.

Audrey spared one look behind her at The Orangerie, thinking maybe Bo would be on the other side of the windows, glaring back at her. He wasn't. There was no one there at all. No one except for the sunny wash of their own reflections in the glass. And that didn't count. Right?

They started off across the wide lawns toward the dark mouth of the orchard path. They didn't actually link arms, Readers, but they might as well have. They could feel the eyes of the various crew members upon them, and other eyes and maybe lenses, too.

They were being watched. **They** didn't care. **They'd** made a chain of three.

"Somebody just posted a new joke," Merritt said, reading her phone. *"What was the lesbian ghost tired of explaining?"*

"What?"

"That she's not a lesbian, goddamnit. She's boosexual."

"Boooooooooo," Harper said. "So dumb."

"I've got one," Audrey said. "What's the problem with a lesbian poltergeist?"

"What?" Merritt said.

"After one good fuck, she'll try to possess you."

Harper and Merritt laughed.

"Are those all on that thread?" Harper asked.

"Yes," Merritt said.

"I have to catch up with that. My own finsta at work,"* Harper said, referring to a comment thread beneath a photo she had posted of the three of them hanging out in The Orangerie, and after Eric (of course it had been Eric) had made a dumb orgasm-phantasm pun, many more lesbian ghost puns had followed.

"I told Noel," Audrey said. "I hope that's OK. He was coming up with a bunch. I can't remember them all—one of them was something about lesbian bed death. It's exactly his kind of thing to be into."

"For sure," Harper said. "I'll add him now." She pulled out one of her phones.

"Is he in Rhode Island yet?" Merritt asked.

"Yeah, they got here a few hours ago," Audrey said. "They're staying in this, like, artists' collective. Who knows with Noel. They might be squatting. He'd love that. I just know the show starts at ten and they're going with Newportmanteau as their name."

Merritt didn't hide her sneer.

"Really?" Audrey said to her, taking in the judgment of that face. "This one I like."

---

* In case you're not familiar, *finsta* is a portmanteau of *fake Instagram*. These are accounts created by celebrities or anyone who wants to lurk or post without feeling the need to perform for fans (or advertising dollars) or who wants to embody a fake persona while using the platform. Generally, the celebrity in question keeps the account set to private, not public, and only allows select people to follow it. Harper's finsta, at that time, was @RubyBoobyMcLintock (it referenced a private joke). That account had only 149 followers and itself was following only 28 accounts. (Audrey was one of its most recent followers, and she'd finally made her own private Instagram account in order to do so.)

"God, ten suddenly seems so late when your call time is seven hours later," Harper said.

"You're not bailing," Merritt said.

"Never, never ever," Harper said. "Just making an observation."

"You won't be starting your day at five if they don't get the ghosts out of the mics before morning," Merritt said.

Nobody answered her.

They were in the woods now, on the very same route Flo and Clara and stupid cousin Charles had traveled those many years before. Though they'd entered at the mouth of that path, by now they were well down its dark throat, the trees having swallowed them whole.

And as they moved still deeper into the woods, the scent of rot and soil lifted around them, while acorns fell like sporadic hail, heavy and hard. Above them, branches rubbed and leaves fluttered, sometimes making a sound like walking across old floorboards, others like the swish of rushing in a skirt.

It was as if the understory cast its own spell upon them.

And they wanted it to.

Merritt thought about her book and what she might write in it after this night.

Harper thought about the call she'd not clicked over to, the call from her little brother, Ethan, when earlier she'd been on the phone with her manager. And she still hadn't called him back.

Audrey thought about Bo and how she'd just fucked up his afternoon shoot. It was amateur hour, she knew, grossly unprofessional. She was acting like a disobedient child. A brat. But she really needed a few hours without being looked at. She was having a hard time separating her performances. Even what she'd just done—breaking the rules, asking them to come to the orchard—wasn't that more a Clara Broward than an Audrey Wells thing to do?

Whoever the action belonged to, in this moment, it felt good.

"I should've brought water," Merritt said.

"I have some," Audrey said. When she pulled out the heavy bottle—a metal one in green with *The Happenings at Brookhants* along one side—she also pulled out the six-pack of hard cider and held it up to the others.

"They're still cold, I think."

"I could kiss you," Harper said, plucking a bottle from the cardboard carrier.

"OK," Audrey said. (Clara said?)

The three of them looked at each other like there were perhaps other things to say about this, but they did not say those things just then.

Merritt drank some water, screwed the cap back on the bottle, and then took a cider of her own. Harper used the opener on her keychain to pop the tops, letting them fall to the path as their breadcrumbs.

On and on they walked and drank, tugging their shirts free of the snagging branches, pulling prickly seed pods from each other's backs and butts, their mouths fizzing with swallows of sweet, sharp cider.

At some point, Harper started humming, then singing, the yellow jacket song.

Just one sting will make us smart.
With two, we might be brave.
Three will buzz inside our hearts.
With more, we're in the grave.

After this verse, she stopped singing to ask, "Do you think the girls really let the yellow jackets sting them?"

"Supposedly three stings was the price of entry into the Plain Bad Heroine Society," Merritt said. "But I couldn't ever find any proof. And that song drifted out and away from here once the school shut down, so it's possible that verse is only an aftereffect—people adding lyrics to fit the story of the curse."

"Is there anything growing here they *weren't* using to get high?" Audrey asked.

"This is it," Merritt said.

It seemed like they'd reached a stand of overgrown lilac bushes, leggy and buggy, but Merritt knew how to cut through and around them until it was like she'd opened a door and they were standing on the edge of a large clearing, orderly rows of apple trees ahead.

These moments were charged in a golden light—they had managed, not at all by accident, to arrive at the orchard right as Brookhants tipped over into the magic hour.*

The Black Oxfords were just as they'd been promised: fat and ripe, shining purple and blue black on the branches, bending boughs with their weight. And on the ground, more apples, felled apples, like jewels in the grass, while above them buzzed yellow jackets.

Our three heroines might as well have entered an illustration from a fairy tale.

Except, of course, for the solar lights production had strung between a section of trees. And the ladders leaned against their trunks. And the metal storage containers hulking off to one side of the orchard. They had a Flo and Clara scene to film here in two days. One was *scheduled* in two days, anyway.

All around them buzzed yellow jackets, but *not* like a threat or a warning. Instead, their sound was like the hum of some ancient meditative practice, something to bind them.

Audrey-Clara felt words that were not her own build inside her. All she had to do was open her mouth to let them out. She did: "*Per-*

---

* Photographers call it the golden hour, too. Probably you know this already, especially since you can now use a filter to conjure the same effect. But if you're gonna be old school about it: you get two magic hours a day, when the sun is low on the horizon and the world appears as if dipped in honey.

haps it was because, in Paul's world, the natural nearly always wore the guise of ugliness, that a certain element of artificiality seemed to him necessary in beauty . . . that he was so moved by these starry apple orchards that bloomed perennially under the lime-light."

Harper took her hand and it didn't seem weird or corny, it seemed just right. So Audrey took Merritt's hand, and Merritt let her, and then she asked, "Is that from 'Paul's Case'?"*

"Yes," Audrey said. "I read it because you told me to."

"I didn't know you had," Merritt said.

"I read all the things you told me to read to prep," Audrey said.

"Yes, but you memorized it," Merritt said.

"I didn't mean to," Audrey said. "It stuck."

Together they walked through the orchard, dropping hands only when they'd decided to stop and spread their blanket. Harper used one of the ladders to climb into a tree and select apples for them, which they tried greedily—taking one bite and tossing the rest for the yellow jackets, and then doing it again because they could. They were rich in apples.

The three of them lolled on the blanket. If you were above them, filming, say, you'd have seen that their bodies made the figure of a broken star: Harper's head resting on Merritt's lap and Audrey's head on Harper's stomach.

The daylight drained quickly now, and what was left of the sun over the trees gilded their crowns—and when the wind blew their leaves tossed that gold around and made it glint.

"Is it really stupid for me to say that it feels like everything that isn't in this orchard has disappeared?" Harper asked. "Like if we walked back through those bushes right now it would all be smudged black, like somebody had erased a chalkboard and left streaks from what was there before?"

---

* A beautiful short story by Willa Cather. It was first published in 1905 and is now widely considered an examination of a young queer person's life of longing in a world that doesn't understand him. You should check it out, Readers.

"No," Merritt said.

"It's not stupid at all," Audrey said.

"Do you think this is what Flo and Clara did here before they died?" Harper asked.

"Yes," Merritt said.

"And more," Audrey said.

"Fucking cousin Charles," Harper said.

"I think I feel the sorriest for Alex, though," Audrey said. "Or maybe for Libbie."

"For *Libbie*?" Harper asked. "You're kidding."

"I mean sort of," Audrey said. "It's not like marrying Harold saved her reputation anyway—everybody just thought she was like a weirdo gold digger, especially when he died right away. His family hated her. Her family was creeped out by the whole thing. And she's stuck running a school she doesn't want to run in Rhode Island."

"Yeeeah, I dunno," Harper said. "Alex still gets the bulk of my sympathies."

"You know what I used to think about when I came here?" Merritt asked as she twisted strands of Harper's hair. "How close Clara was to her home—at least to her summer home. I mean, she probably could've swum there if she was desperate. But Brookhants might as well have been France, the way she lived here. I mean the way she gave herself permission to live here."

"Was it Brookhants or Mary MacLane that gave her permission?" Audrey asked.

"Or Flo?" Harper added.

"Yes," Merritt said.

"What I can't get over," Harper said, "is how Mary MacLane gave all these girls a model for thinking the things they thought, and then a few years later she took it back. I mean, what the fuck happened to her?"

"She grew up and the world was hard and her fame didn't fix it," Audrey said.

"She didn't take it all back," Merritt said. "She just—"

"She later called lesbianism a *warped predilection*," Harper said.

"Yes," Merritt said. "Despite that, she also continued to have relationships with women. And men."

"I want a T-shirt with *Warped Predilection* on it," Audrey said.

"Now I do, too," Harper said.

"You know she died in obscurity?" Merritt said. "Basically. Broke in a rooming house in Chicago."

"You know what's funny about that?" Harper said. "My grandparents are significantly more OK with me being a dyke now that I'm earning money from it."

"That's not *why* you're earning money," Audrey said.

"I mean—" Harper said.

"So you're saying you see that as a win for rainbow capitalism?" Merritt asked.

"I'm saying it's a win for me," Harper said. "I guess. Unless I think about it for too long."

Audrey sat up. "Wait, I have a toast," she said, reaching into her bag for the next three ciders since they'd already finished the others. Harper opened the bottles and passed them along until each had one in hand.

"To Mary MacLane and cultivating our elements of badness," Audrey said. They drank. It was unreasonable how reasonable this behavior seemed to them.

This world where they'd spread their blanket, this moment beneath the heavy apple boughs, in the golden light, was too beautiful by half. And it would not last. And our three heroines knew this.

It was Merritt who said, "I just really want to kiss you." She paused and then: "Both."

The answer they gave her was instant and shared. They smiled and slid closer, bunching the blanket between them as they did. And then they let her kiss them, and then they kissed each other.

You shouldn't think that the fact that it all felt like a dream made it somehow *unreal*. It was only more real this way—the last of the honey light in Merritt's hair, glinting her eyebrow rings like a wink, the scent of Harper's cigarettes on her clothes and the rich, earthy scent of apple rot around them; their mouths, when pressed together, as if still buzzing with cider fizz even though they'd already swallowed and set down their bottles in order to leave their hands free.

Not a one of them was personally familiar with the logistics of arranging three bodies for pleasure, but there was something so easy and right in the way they fit together, in the feel of a hand beneath a shirt and a thigh between two legs and a mouth on a neck, a mouth on a stomach, a mouth on a mouth on a mouth. It was not at all silly to them, but it wasn't at all serious, either. It just was: pleasure.

The yellow jackets snapped about them, flitting and hovering, their buzzing both a sound and a feeling. The only feeling, right then.

They were but a few steps into their desire, as if they'd entered the ocean up to their knees and were still gauging the waves, waiting for the best moment to dive in headfirst, when the solar lights strung about the trees twitched on above them.

Harper noticed this. And in noticing this, she noticed something else. "I think it's snowing," she said.

It could not be. They thought she must've misread the flutter of yellow jackets or parachute seeds. She *wanted* to see snowflakes, but surely it was only the drift of pine duff kicked up by the breeze—which now came to them heavy with the scent of wood smoke.

It could not be snow, but it was—slow, fat flakes that took their time on their descent, that made a show of it. The snow looked like confetti or soap flakes, but it was real.

The sky was dark and thick with clouds and it was snowing over the apple orchard at Brookhants, putting enough of a chill in the air to make Harper look around for her costume sweater and eventually find it near Merritt's head, off the edge of the blanket atop a mashed apple, where Merritt had tossed it after pulling it from Harper's body.

"Was it supposed to snow today?" Audrey asked, looking up into the trees in disbelief, the flakes sticking to her hair for only a blink before melting.

"*There was that in the air . . .*" Merritt said. She knew she didn't need to finish Mary's words. "It just is. It *is* snowing. I did want to kiss you."

"I wanted you to," Audrey said. She took in the loveliness of Merritt's expression and the way the static from the sweater lifted the strands of Harper's hair. Merritt took in the flush of Audrey's cheeks and the glow of the lights in the branches and the burn on Harper's neck from where her sweater had rubbed until she'd pulled it off. Harper took in the desire that still pulsed in her body and the smell of wood smoke drifting through the trees from campus.

They would remember these things, Readers, for the rest of their lives.

There was no rush to continue what they'd started, to follow their want to its end point, because it seemed like they would have so much time to do so, for days and weeks to come. And so they caught snowflakes on their tongues and shouted and kissed and twirled and gathered their things, their fingertips and noses and the tops of their ears red and burning with cold.

"Let's drive back for movie night," Merritt said, leading them out of the orchard and toward Spite Manor. They half ran in the dark through the understory, laughing and stumbling and turning to grab at each other as they went.

The tree canopy blocked the sky and they could no longer tell if it was snowing and so took bets that it wasn't, probably, or that it wouldn't be anymore, not by the time they got out of the woods.

But it was. It was still snowing.

So they went first to their tiny houses for their coats and gloves and hats and stood in the doorways of each other's production-stocked fridges to eat handfuls of berries and soft cheese on pretzel sticks and Nutella straight from the jar, ravenous and goofy and googly eyed.

When they were satiated, they walked to Spite Manor and Merritt alone slipped in the front door. Moments later, she returned with the keys to Elaine's vintage convertible, saying, "She won't mind at all. She'll love it." And then she backed it out of the garage before getting out again and insisting, with Harper's assistance, that Audrey drive them.

And, unbelievably, Audrey said, "Yes. OK."

It wasn't a car built for three, but Merritt and Harper made their bodies fit together on the passenger seat and Audrey, with a few lurches and false starts, drove them through the woods and over to Brookhants, top down, in the flying snow, on the very same road that Alex and Libbie traveled together each morning and night all those many years before.

Audrey took it slowly, of course, but with much laughing and instruction-giving from Merritt and Harper—and of course with no other traffic on the road to contend with, she did just fine. On and on into the night snow she drove them, the seep of wood smoke and grilling lobsters gaining in strength as they grew closer— that and the blue light of the movie projection glowing weirdly through the trees.

And then, faintly at first, they heard the song. This was their first clue—and the only one Audrey needed—to guess what was then being shown on the side of Main Hall:

I got a hold on you tonight.

"Uh-oh, it's magic!" Harper sang-shouted—awkwardly standing up in the car as she did, gripping the top of the windshield to steady herself.

Closer and closer they came to the source of that song. They were through the woods now, the wash of light from the projection re-vealing bodies in chairs and on blankets on the lawn, bodies being flaked in snow.

"I can't believe they're showing this," Audrey said, feeling shame in her chest where it didn't belong, where she didn't fucking want it to be.

"I can't believe we're getting back during this scene!" Harper yelled.

The film was *House Mother 2: She's Coming for You*. They were arriving during the opening moments of its infamous pool party scene.

The film, of course, Readers, was *House Mother 2: She's Coming for You*. And they were arriving during the opening moments of its infamous pool party scene. *The* scene.

Any second now, the twenty-year-old version of Audrey's mother would take off her bikini top (along with the other women playing buxom coeds) and then spend the next minute and forty-six seconds' bouncing around a blue pool, her breasts shot from every exploitative angle that could be imagined, lit, and captured on film—all while The Cars sang about magic on the soundtrack.

A few people on the lawn had noticed their approach and waved at them. Harper leaned over and pressed the car horn a few times to say hello back.

And now, there on the wall of a building on her own film set were Audrey's mother's breasts, projected to the size of—

She didn't even want to draw the comparison. As her cast- and crewmates drank beer and threw popcorn and shouted, laughing—*Don't look in the filter basket!*—Audrey tried not to let the feeling of the orchard drain away. She tried to keep it in her chest, through her limbs—the three of them together, what they'd done and said as *real* and as their own, as belonging just to them.

"What's in the filter basket?" Merritt asked, neck craned toward the projection.

"Dave's dick!" Harper shouted. "How have you still not seen this movie?!"

It was too late.

The feeling was gone. It was gone for Audrey, anyway. Now there was just this scene.

She'd never parked a car before, so Merritt and Harper had to yell at her to *brake!* She managed to do it right before running them into a production trailer.

---

* Then and still the record length for a single onscreen scene featuring multiple topless women in a slasher film.

"Are you OK?" Merritt asked, touching Audrey's arm.

"Sure," Audrey lied. "Just cold. And I've literally never done that before."

She wanted to ask if they could turn around and go back to their tiny houses together. Or back to the orchard, even. But she knew it wouldn't matter if they did. She knew it was over, that it had left them the minute they'd heard the first strains of the song.

And they couldn't go back anyway. Noel's band was playing in Providence—Bo had arranged for that to happen, and for some of the footage from that show to make it into the film. And for that to happen they had to go see the band. *She* had to go.

The crowd booed the action on the screen, the pound of piano keys indicating some lurking threat, some coming violence.

Audrey got out of the car and Harper and Merritt came around to join her, bundling her between them with their arms and bodies; she shivered and did not feel them there the way they wanted her to. Or the way she wanted to.

"Here comes Bo," Harper said. "He's smiling. He must've had a nap and a bottle."

"Wait, is that your mom?" Merritt asked.

"No way!" Harper said. "Is it?"

Audrey looked up to see that of course it was. Of course it fucking was. Caroline wasn't supposed to be here yet, not for another week, but here she was—striding across the lawn with Bo at her side. She was wearing one of those puffy, ankle-length winter coats that made her look like she was sheathed in a flayed caterpillar and was further silhouetted by the projection of her younger self, topless in a pool.

"Honey, were you just driving?" she called to Audrey. "That's so great!"

And where were the cameras now? Trained on this moment is where. They had to be. Audrey couldn't quite read Bo's face at this distance. Was he scowling at her? Was he smiling?

"I can't be here right now," Audrey said quietly. "Can we please go to Providence?"

"Now?" Harper asked. "Why, what's happening?"

"You really didn't know she was coming?" Merritt asked.

Now Bo and Caroline were there in front of them and Audrey was hugging her mom, because what else, and everyone was saying things that didn't matter and weren't real, like *What about this crazy snow? It's unbelievable.*

"What are you doing here?" Audrey asked.

"I came early!" Caroline said. "Surprise! This guy convinced me to." She tilted her head at Bo when she said it.

"Thought she was missing out," Bo said.

"He said you'd be happy about it," Caroline said, taking in Audrey's face. "I wasn't sure."

"Of course I am," Audrey said. "It's just that we have to go right now. We're going into Providence to watch Noel's band play." She did not look at Bo. She would not.

"I know, Noel told me," Caroline said. "Isn't that later, though? I'm going, too—it sounds like everyone's going."

"Yeah, the show's not until later, but I want to see him first. Beforehand." Until Audrey said it, this had not been the plan.

"You have to go right now?" Bo said with one eyebrow raised outrageously high—not that Audrey saw it. "You sure about that?"

"Yes, right now," Audrey said to the dark rim of woods over his shoulder.

"OK," her mom said easily, reaching out to squeeze her shoulder, which made Audrey bristle in a way she didn't like. "I can't wait to see your little house on the water! Everybody's telling me they're so cute. I really hope it warms up again while I'm here."

"OK, I love you," Audrey said. She felt relief turning away from them and handing the keys to Merritt, adding, "I can't be trusted on the highway yet, obviously."

Merritt and Harper looked at her, at each other, and then shrugged with semiconfused acceptance and Harper slid back in the passenger side and Audrey squished in beside her, shutting the door as if that was that. They were going. So Merritt put herself behind the wheel.

After Merritt had started the car, but before she began to back up, Caroline called to them, "You're not gonna put the top up? You'll freeze!"

"We like it this way," Merritt said.

"Be safe," Bo said.

As Merritt pulled the car past the two of them, standing there with puzzled faces in the glow of the film, Audrey said, quietly but not *that* quietly over her door, "Anything from the orchard's off-limits. I mean it. It's out or I walk."

AVA IN THE ORCHARD

....

Ava Brookhants was up in her favorite tree, watching.

Since she'd first come to Spite Manor the year before, Ava had climbed many trees. Enough to know, anyway, that this one was her favorite.

She almost always went up and up, past the first fork of limbs, reaching her feet out in a bizarre kind of geometry to find the best branches to carry her to a topmost perch where she liked to sit, sometimes for hours. There she had access to a hollow formed when a limb had crashed down during a blizzard.

This had happened, Addie had told her, during the year of the curse, the year that had sent her aunt Libbie away. They'd had a most terrible blizzard that year. (Though Adelaide hadn't phrased it quite that way. She'd only named the year. It was Ava who had done the calculations to confirm, for herself, that they were one and the same: the year of the terrible blizzard *was* the year of the curse.)

But now it was 1904 and the curse was no more.

And earlier today, her aunt Libbie had finally come home.

Ava's perch wasn't noticeable, especially if the tree was in leaf and you weren't looking for her, but her hollow was even more hidden than that. Because of this, she stored all kinds of important things within it. Just now she had a few of the pages-long letters her uncle Harold had written to her before he died, and a large moonstone she'd found on the beach, then cut and polished herself (well, with Max's help she'd done it herself), and the papier-mâché doll she'd made with Addie.

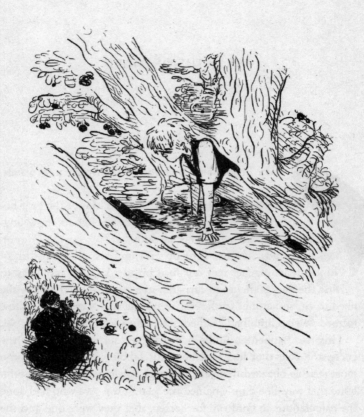

Ava also had a small knife hidden in a bone sheath that she used to cut slices from the apples around her. She often ate so many of these she'd get sick before climbing down. And she had two seashells she liked for no particular reason, and a piece of brown-sugar fudge wrapped in waxed paper, and, today, a book. (But only the one. Usually she had several books up in the tree with her.)

She pulled the knife, still sheathed, from the hollow and pinned it between her bony knees. Then she reached over and back, carefully, carefully, leaning out into the air to test the firmness of a fat purple-black apple she'd been eyeing. She plucked it free, managing to get the whole stem. Ava Brookhants was superstitious about not getting the whole stem. She shined the apple on her shirt, unsheathed the knife, and cut herself a slice. It was crisp and tart. Juice pink with lifted pigment dripped down her face, rolled off her chin, and fell onto the leaves below with the *pit-pat* of raindrops.

Even then, Ava had a vague sense that some of her interests, like tree climbing and stone polishing, were perhaps *unusual* compared to those of other girls her age. I say *a vague sense* because she hadn't yet spent all that much time with girls her own age. Not back in France, where it was only Ava and her careful caretakers, the Verretts—a family of sisters and their matriarch, the scarily glamorous Odette—expressly chosen by her uncle Harold to raise her, and certainly not here in Rhode Island, where, while waiting for her aunt Libbie's return, she was tended to by the doting Eckharts.

Only now Hanna Eckhart was dead, too. Ava had learned a new word as the cause: apoplexy. Of course, Aunt Libbie wasn't *really* her aunt, just as Uncle Harold had not been her uncle. Ava knew this because the Verretts had told her and Hanna had confirmed it. Harold Brookhants was her father and Libbie Packard Brookhants was her mother. This information made no difference at all to Ava, because at the time the Verretts were telling her this, Libbie and Harold were both only names to her. She did not know them, not as she knew the Verretts. What Ava did know is that her uncle-father Harold was already dead, but he'd written her long letters before his death, and her aunt-mother Libbie lived in America and was content to let the Verretts raise Ava in France. (And she'd never written Ava any letters at all.) So those things she knew.

The very important thing was that, for now: Aunt Libbie did not know that Ava knew any of this.

The other very important thing, at least according to Adelaide, was now that Aunt Libbie was back at Brookhants, she would probably again open her school, the Brookhants School for Girls, and at that time, or at least once she was old enough to do so, Ava could attend.

She'd been thinking a lot about this. What would it be like to attend a school with other girls her age and older too, which was even better—American girls who knew American things? She was both excited by this prospect and also unsure about it, about how she'd fare, how she'd get along, or not, with the other girls.

She cut another slice of apple, careful with the blade, which she always sharpened on the same stone Max used for his knives. Her hands were now so sticky with juice that if she pressed them against the trunk, flecks of bark stuck to her palms. She did not mind this. She liked the idea of wearing tree skin over her own.

The first of the yellow jackets found her then. Her cutting and chewing must have lured it from where it had been: buzzing among the apples rotting below the tree. This was only the first. Ava knew there would be others.

No matter. She cut another slice.

Ava had come to understand that some of Uncle Harold's ideas about her rearing, as carried out by the Verretts, had been, let's say, queer. That she was allowed, for instance, from the earliest age, to choose her own clothing. This would help to explain why she was wearing what she was wearing right now: wool knickerbockers and a striped Breton shirt. (When it was cold, she might add to this ensemble a wool fisherman's sweater and hat.*)

While the many maids Verrett wore diaphanous dresses in vibrant purples and blues, dresses that flowed like their very long hair, Ava was never inspired to follow their examples, and in fact kept her own hair cut quite bluntly (she took the shears to it herself when she deemed it too long). She did glean, however, from the novels she endlessly consumed (she could read in both English *and* French), that not only her own style, but even that of the Verrett sisters, did not precisely fit the expectations of the era where women and girls were concerned.

Indeed, Ava thought there was little about her that precisely fit those expectations.

------

* It's true, Readers, that in her way, young Ava Brookhants was not styled so differently than certain J.Crew models of today.

For instance, most people would likely find it peculiar that the Verretts had taught her not only geography, spelling, and mathematics, but also philosophies of ontology and mysticism. (As they had been directed by her uncle Harold.)

And she'd learned about various methods of spiritual communication in much more experiential ways, too. All of the Verrett sisters were mediums of different abilities, from channeling to clairvoyance. Germaine painted spirit portraits of the dead. And of course, Odette was one of the most famous trance lecturers of her time.

But as not a single of these subjects had ever before been included in the Brookhants curriculum, Ava sensed—correctly, Readers—that the specifics of her previous education might well set her even further apart from her classmates when and if her aunt Libbie's school reopened.

And so while she was excited about the pending arrival of so many girls, she was also a little frightened about the many changes afoot here in the only slice of America she'd ever known. A slice that, for a year, had been quiet, secluded, and populated only by the doting Eckharts and Addie and Max. A year during which her aunt Libbie had been merely a rumored phantom shut up nearby in a hospital for the insane. Ava had taken a few excursions into Newport and Providence, and one to bustling Boston, but otherwise, Spite Manor and Brookhants—empty, ghostly, deliciously cursed Brookhants—*were* America to Ava.

And she wasn't sure she wanted that to change just yet.

Of course, Ava hadn't wanted to leave France and the Verrett sisters, either, when the time had come to do so. She knew that Germaine must still wear a shoulder and neck of thick pink scars from the scalding tea Ava had thrown at her as they'd struggled over this mandate, but Ava *had* done it. Eventually. For here she was in America. And thriving, too.

The wasps were swarming now. In the time it had taken her to eat three-quarters of the apple they'd gone from one to dozens. They moved about her like drifting snowflakes, their hum-buzz the right vibrato to set her song to:

What's the racket, yel-low jacket?
At Brook-hants you roam!
You took the lives of all those girls—
but now I'm here and home.

So she'd made some lyrical alterations. What of it, Readers?

Ava had found the handwritten sheet of song lyrics folded and placed between the back pages of the book she right then had stuffed in her hollow.

She wasn't a stupid girl. She knew it was *the* book: the cursed book that had supposedly caused all the trouble. Ava had known, from the moment her hand touched the red binding, that this was the true copy of *The Story of Mary MacLane*. It was as if the book's very paper and ink had become heavy with its history. And, Ava believed, if she held her nose at the correct distance above its open pages—not too close, not too far—and sniffed, it still carried sweet notes of the deathly flowers once pressed inside.

She hadn't yet finished it, but truth be told, she didn't think a whole lot of it. She certainly didn't understand all the fuss over it. Or why girls all across this strange country had called themselves Mary MacLane devotees and formed clubs in her honor. (Why must Americans insist on always thinking they'd invented everything, including sentiment?)

Ava, after all, had already read all but the most recent of the Claudine novels. In French. (And she'd felt a curious pinch of attraction when she'd glimpsed the youngest Verrett sister, Marceline, nude and so fresh from a bath that the beads of water caught the light across her freckled back.)

I mean, if writing a book of this sort was all it took to inspire such devotion, then why didn't everyone do it? Ava thought *she* might. One day.

One day she would do so many things.

A mass of yellow jackets had pooled in front of her face. She took great pleasure in forming her lips into a tight O in order to blow out a strong stream of air and skitter them away. Ava was not afraid of the yellow jackets. She had sat, and even moved, in swarms much larger than this one—especially when she went into the woods to the hot springs. Adelaide had shown her the best paths to reach the springs and she had never once been stung. Not yet.

It was Adelaide who had also taught her about the intricate beauty of the yellow jackets' nests. These nests were, after all, nature's own elaborate and most literal works of papier-mâché: chewed pulp formed into a structure so spectacular they could live in it. Ava held a reverence for the yellow jackets and what they might manage when they worked together. (But she held even more reverence for their queen.)

She watched as those she'd just sent tumbling through the air tried to reorient themselves. A dizzy few of them headed away from her, in the direction of a large branch that currently held black apples and pink blossoms, *both*.

It was an old superstition, Ava knew, that an apple tree blooming out of season, especially after it had borne ripe fruit, foretold a death in the family. Germaine Verrett had taught her this when she was only five years old. Ava had been so thrilled to see their neighbor's apple tree—enclosed in a walled side garden—burst to bloom during a warm October that she'd stolen part of a low branch that hung over the garden wall. She brought it home, propped it in a jar of water. She thought she'd done something pretty and clever. She expected she might even be praised.

But when Germaine came in the door and saw it, she'd gasped. She asked Ava what she'd done and then slapped her before she could explain.

Only once Germaine had given the branch a salt burial beneath that same tree did she explain to Ava that apple blossoms brought indoors were sure to bring sickness on the house. *Especially* apple blossoms from a tree blooming out of season, which was an even worse predicament.

"You watch now, child," Germaine had told her. "One in their family will die. You watch."

She meant the family who owned the tree. So Ava had watched.

And maybe a week later, she was tossing pebbles into the well when she saw the neighbors emerge from their house in stiff mourning clothes and sweep into their carriage, all of them avoiding her eyes. And avoiding too, Ava thought, looking at their apple tree—which still stood defiantly full of out-of-season blooms: a pink cloud on a stick.

She ran to find Germaine then, who was reading cards in her bedroom. She said, without looking up, "I told you. His brother. Only twenty-two and so strong. Much too young for this death, but it came."

It was not a superstition that young Ava would soon forget.

Ava pulled out the book. Mary's book. And Clara's book. Flo's book. Eleanor's book. Alex's book. Aunt Libbie's book. (Or had it been Libbie's book? It might have been inscribed to her, given to her—but had it *been* hers?)

Ava again read the whiny entry from April 2:

> How can any one bring a child into the world and not wrap it round with a certain wondrous tenderness that will stay with it always!
> There are persons whose souls have never entered into them.
> My mother has some fondness for me—for my body because it came of her. That is nothing—nothing.
> A hen loves its egg.
> A hen!

"Ava!" her aunt-mother Libbie called.

Ava looked in the direction of the voice and saw that Aunt Libbie was only just entering the orchard and did not know where to look for her. She watched her search a wrong tree, then another. She turned back and forth to sweep her eyes over the ground. Ava had all the advantages. She could make her wait, if she wanted to.

"Ava!" Aunt Libbie called again. "Are you here?"

Ava didn't know what to make of Aunt Libbie. Not yet. She certainly didn't seem like a madwoman who needed to be locked away in a hospital. She seemed more like an orange squeezed of its juices: the life gone out of her. Anyway, how could Ava tell, after only a few hours spent in her company? She couldn't. Not really. Even if she did feel certain that she'd have liked Uncle Harold more. And she already *did* like Adelaide more.

Ava liked Aunt Libbie's friend Sara Dahlgren well enough. Sara had come to see her in France many times and had always brought such delicious presents: Parisian bonbons almost too pretty to eat (though Ava did eat them), a cut-glass paperweight with a flower pressed inside, and a kaleidoscope as big as her arm.

Sara Dahlgren's specialty seemed to be bringing things places. It was Sara Dahlgren who'd brought her aunt Libbie back from the hospital. She'd come all the way over from France to do it—and to attend one or two of the summer parties in Newport, so long as she was here. Though she hadn't wanted to stay with them at the house—Ava had overheard Aunt Libbie and Sara arguing about this earlier.

"Ava, is that you?" In her daydreaming, Ava had let herself be found. Aunt Libbie now stood at the base of the tree looking up, one hand held over her face to shade it from the sun so she could better see into its branches. "Why didn't you answer me?"

"I didn't hear you, Aunt Libbie," Ava lied. "Not until just now."

"I want you to come down from there," Aunt Libbie said. "I want to talk to you about something important."

"Can't I stay up here while we talk?" Ava asked. "I can hear you perfectly."

"No, you may not. I will not shout up the tree at you. Please come down."

Aunt Libbie shouldn't have been home for long enough to find occasion to be angry with her. Even still—Ava could tell that she was. She thought she might offer her aunt a gift *before* she had the chance to scold her; it had to be before, Ava had learned, or it wouldn't work. Maybe the moonstone? She hated to part with it but—

"Ava, I'm waiting," Aunt Libbie said.

Ava recalled some of the unkind, or sneaky, or generally thought-to-be-bad acts she'd done in the last few days and wondered which one of them she'd now have to account for. Is this how it would now be, with Aunt Libbie living here? Because it wouldn't do.

She flipped fast through the items remaining in the hollow, trying to find the moonstone, but there were too many things in the way. She pulled things out until she was holding the book, the knife, the letters, the papier-mâché doll. Finally, she could see it. Wedging the other items against her body with one hand, she reached in for the stone with the other.

Just exactly then, a yellow jacket poked its twitching head into the dark cave of her ear. It did not linger there, but its unexpected invasion startled her at precisely the wrong moment. Ava wobbled on her perch, and with both of her hands full, she could not properly grip the tree to steady herself.

First, she spilled her things: the book falling heavily onto the apple core she had dropped earlier, the other items following after.

And then Ava herself spilled.

Hers was not a clear fall. She crashed upon or snagged against branches as she went, which at least slowed her speed a little.

Still, it all happened in a matter of moments. Aunt Libbie tried to position herself to catch the girl, but Ava landed against her outstretched arms like a spilled suitcase. The force of this collision smashed them hard against the appled ground.

Other than oofs and groans, Ava's wan giggle was the first sound either made as they tried to untangle. And then, this also from Ava, "It was not the most graceful way to exit a tree, it's true."

"You poor girl," Aunt Libbie said, pulling herself, as gently as possible, out from under Ava's body so that she could get a look at her. Ava's forehead and cheek were gashed red, her shirt ripped at the neck, the skin beneath torn.

"What hurts the most?" Aunt Libbie asked.

"My arm," Ava said. "I'm sure it's broken. It feels it." She was able to squeeze her fingers, though. And in them she felt the moonstone.

"But I managed to keep hold of your present!" She opened her palm so Aunt Libbie could see.

"What a thing to worry about," Aunt Libbie said, though she made a point of carefully looking at the polished stone; round and iridescent, it flashed the pale spectrum of colors contained in the pack of candy wafers the child seemed to favor.

"Feldspar," Aunt Libbie said, the name floating onto her tongue without her trying for it.

"I thought it was a moonstone."

"Feldspar is its mineral group. Alex . . ." She seemed to stop herself. Then she said, "Alexandra Trills, the woman who lived here with me, she could have told you all about it."

"Addie already told me that it's lucky," Ava said.

"Only not so lucky today." Aunt Libbie moved to a crouch. She was clearly in pain—the shoulder that had taken the brunt of Ava, but also, and sharply, her hip. "Do you think you can walk, Ava, if I help to support you? If we can get close enough to home, we'll call out. When I came, Max was tilling soil in the winter garden. And he has the wheelbarrow with him."

"I can walk, Aunt Libbie," Ava said. Her arm throbbed—it already felt too big and strange, as if it was a pillow filled with air and blood, her bones floating around somewhere inside all of that. But her legs felt fine. "You won't need to bring the wheelbarrow."

"Let's try to get near to it and then we'll see." Aunt Libbie attempted to gather some of Ava's spilled items. She saw Harold's letters first. Then the knife.

"I can put that in my pocket," Ava said. She watched as Aunt Libbie reached the book, Mary's book. She watched as she hesitated before picking it up.

"*This* is what I was coming to talk to you about," Aunt Libbie said. She was looking at the book, not at Ava.

"I only took it from the stairwell," Ava said. "I find all my books there."

"You took it?" Aunt Libbie asked. "Or did someone give it to you?"

"Who would give it to me?" Ava asked in a sniff. "Everyone here acts like it's an illuminated manuscript. I've already read most of it and she's just a boastful girl convinced of her own genius. I think nothing at all of Mary MacLane."

"I see," Aunt Libbie said, tucking the book beneath her arm. "I'm sure you won't mind me taking it back, then? No point in your wasting more time with it."

Ava sensed the trick in this suggestion, but her arm was throbbing and she wouldn't dwell on it for now. Together they worked to get her standing. Then walking. Slowly.

Aunt Libbie was kicking apples from their path so the girl wouldn't roller-skate upon one when Ava remembered. "Oh, my doll!" she said. "She fell with me and I can't leave her. Would you look for her, Aunt Libbie?"

"What does your doll look like, Ava?" Aunt Libbie asked as she turned around.

"It's the one I made with Addie," Ava said. "The nesting doll. It took us so long to finish her."

Ava watched her aunt Libbie flinch at this answer.

There were many mashed apples beneath Aunt Libbie's feet as she bent low to look. Yellow jackets buzzed about them—not a swarm, but many. They seemed to prefer the most-rotten apples, the skin split, their inner flesh soupy and yellow like pus, and their coloring, especially the peels, which had deepened with their time in the sun, making them appear more like hunks of festering meat than apples.

"I'm afraid I don't see it," she called to Ava. "What if I send Max back for it later? We'll be sure to find it before it's dark."

"I'd rather have it now, though," Ava said. Her arm was really bothering her. Funny how quickly that had happened. It was hurting enough to make the rest of her weak with it. Maybe she would need the wheelbarrow ride after all.

"I know, darling, but I . . ." Aunt Libbie started, but then she seemed to see something on the ground. She moved toward it.

"Did you find her?" Ava called.

Aunt Libbie reached for something in the grass. She did so carefully, gingerly. "I think so." Her voice sounded strange. "You made this with Adelaide?"

"Yes, when I arrived," Ava said. "Addie said she wanted something for us to do together. I don't really play with her—I'm too old for that. I just like to have her with me. She's got so many versions of herself."

It seemed to Ava like her aunt Libbie wasn't really looking at the doll, like she was avoiding looking at it, even as she now held it in her hand, even as she walked with it, the doll's many selves clicking against each other as she went.

"You did find her," Ava said. "Thank you, Aunt Libbie. I don't like to be without her." She held out the hand of her noninjured arm.

"You'll have to be without her until we reach the house," Aunt Libbie said.

"But I can carry her fine," Ava said, her empty hand still waiting to be filled.

"You need to concentrate on carrying yourself," Aunt Libbie said. She would not relinquish the doll. She now held both it and the book at her side. "Come. Let's go now, slow as you need—you're a little pale. While we walk you can tell me all the other things Addie taught you while I was away. It will help take your mind off your arm."

Ava knew this was another trick, but right now she didn't care. She just wanted to get back to the house, where Addie would give her something good for her pain and maybe cookies or cake, too.

There was nothing her aunt Libbie could do about it now, anyway. Addie already had her loyalty. And Addie would keep it.

PROVIDENCE

Our three heroines were always going to wind up in Providence together, savvy Readers. I have to believe you saw this coming.

I mean, here they've been, trapped for pages on one estate in the tiniest state, when just thirty-five miles to the north, Rhode Island's capital city makes an industry out of its hauntings and its home-grown horror writers. Or at least one of them in particular.

I'm talking, of course, about H. P. Lovecraft, who was born in Providence, raised in Providence, and spent most of his rather short life writing weird and horrific tales set in and around Providence. You can't toss your crocheted Cthulhu* very far in that city without it hitting a building that Lovecraft once wrote about, lived in, or said something racist near.†

So while Bo Dhillon might have come to Rhode Island expressly to exploit the terrors of Brookhants, he was delighted to use Noel's band as an excuse to take a one-night detour in order to do his own

---

* One of Lovecraft's most lasting and influential creations: a mind-controlling entity that appears as a monstrous mash-up of octopus, dragon, and human. Ugh, all those dangling tentacles.

† Even more fucked up than his fictional monsters were Lovecraft's very real beliefs about white supremacy.

kind of storytelling in the city where, for better or worse, America grew one of its most influential horror writers to date.* How could he resist the chance to make a little (onscreen) terror in the place where so many nightmares had been launched?

He could not.

And Harper, Merritt, and Audrey—wind rattled and bone numb from their convertible ride—knew this. As they stood waiting for Noel on a too-empty street, their noses dripping, they each, to a heroine, knew that something rank and wrong was right now scuttling about this city and waiting for its chance to get at them.

Oh, they wouldn't have each phrased it this way, Readers, but their collective knowledge ran deeper than any syntax. There would be trouble for them tonight in Providence.

"I wish we'd stayed in the orchard," Audrey said.

"You wanted to leave." This from Merritt.

"Not the orchard," Audrey said. "I only wanted to leave movie night."

"We'll go back tomorrow," Harper said.

"We won't," Audrey said. "Not like we left it."

"You're sure the car will be fine here?" Merritt asked for the second time to no answer.

They were huddled together on a narrow sidewalk, the block crowded by looming redbrick factories turned lofts, the panes of their massive windows reflecting the wan streetlights. Near them a gingko tree seemed to have dumped all its leaves at once, and recently: the sidewalk beneath was a bright circle of yellow, as if someone had colored it in with a highlighter.

"He's coming down now," Audrey said, reading a text on her phone.

Harper pinched out the cigarette she'd been smoking and put it behind her ear as a group of laughing people pushed out the heavy door in front of them. The last one held it open. Our heroines

---

* The inscription on Lovecraft's gravestone in Swan Point Cemetery: *I am Providence.*

went inside to find Noel just a few steps from the bottom of a wide set of concrete stairs. He looked like he hadn't been awake for very long, wearing socks and Adidas slides, joggers and a too-tight blue T-shirt from his prep-school days, the logo peeling across its front.

"The Plain Bad Heroine Society," he said, grinning. "I'm right here where you are."

When Audrey hugged him, she nearly started crying into his shoulder. Even here in scuttling Providence, he was just so reliably, comfortingly Noel.

He led them up the stairs to a loft lit by strung bulbs that made geometric shadows over faces and left corners dark like caves. There was art, in all forms, everywhere—murals and sculptures and mosaics—even hanging from the rafters. The crowd was too cool to make an obvious thing about Harper Harper walking among them, and yet her presence crackled around the space until it had touched all surfaces. Soon she was flanked by a chatty group of graduate students, craft beers in hand, who shared their theories about ghosts and curses and, of course, filmmaking.*

Audrey scanned the space, still half expecting to find a B-roll crew, cameras up and on, hairy boom mics hovering. She hadn't yet made a move that Bo hadn't anticipated. Why should a stop in at this party be any different? (That she couldn't see such a crew didn't mean much where Bo was concerned.)

"I wish I had more time," Noel said. "I don't even know where half the band is, and we're supposed to be at the venue. Like now."

Merritt took this as her cue to let Audrey and Noel have a moment alone, and she headed toward a messy drinks table.

"No, I know you have to go," Audrey said. "I just wanted to see you before . . ." She let the unfinished part of that sentence do its work.

---

* The general consensus that night, Readers, at least from the loudest pontificators, was that all this Brookhants nonsense was just that: Bogus. Bullshit. A hoax of the dumbest order intended to froth the dim-witted moviegoing masses.

"The terror unleashes?" Noel scooped a carrot into a jumbo plastic container of hummus.

She nodded. "You don't know what he's got planned for tonight, do you? I mean, in specifics?"

"No," he said. "I wish I did. It'll be something when we're on-stage, but I hope he at least waits until we're a few songs in." He shrugged and added, "Bo Dhillon's nightmare circus."

"That's where I live now."

"I know. You do look—" He stopped himself, chewed his carrot.

"I do look what, Noel?"

He swallowed. "You look tired. You look really tired, kid." He peered closely at her face. "Unless that's just makeup for effect?"

"I wish. I don't sleep anymore."

"Audrey, that's not good."

"I know." She couldn't find the way to say it all so that he'd understand, not in a rush, not with him needing to leave. So instead she said: "In other news, I just had my first sort of threesome like two hours ago. Oh, and somebody's probably inspecting that footage for picture quality as I stand here."

Noel stopped mid-chew, looked hard at her. "Wait, what? Are you being serious right now?"

"I mean, we kept our clothes on. Most of them." She couldn't take the face he was giving her. It was too close to the face she would give herself if she was listening to this. "It's fine, Noel."

"It doesn't sound like you're fine. You did this on camera?"

"Maybe—I don't know. I wasn't really thinking about it at the time but it's possible. It's always possible there."

"OK," he said, but like it wasn't. "Are you OK?"

"No—yes."

He'd gone from looking sleepy to looking pained. "Are you serious that you've not slept at all since you got out here? At *all*? You haven't told me it's been that bad."

"I have told you."

"Not that it's been that bad," he said again. "Not like you're saying now. I just thought it was stupid-long hours and the work catching up to you."

She felt like he was missing the point. "I mean, I've slept some here and there."

"Audrey—"

She was too tired to have this conversation, even though she'd thought she wanted it. "It's not even that it's all been bad," she said. Trying to find the right words was like pawing through silt for them. "It's been really good, too. But I honestly, and I know how this sounds, but it's like we're under a spell there. Or I am—between the place itself and Bo."

"What do you mean *the place itself*?"

Now she was annoyed. "I mean what you think I mean."

He lowered his head and spoke slowly to her in a way that wasn't condescending but lived in its neighborhood. "That it's haunted?"

"You're not out there with us—you don't know what it's like with Bo tweaking every surface. I can't keep ahold of what's real. I literally don't know what is and what isn't."

"Yeah, that's called sleep deprivation," Noel said. "Fuck, Aud, you have to tell them this. Say it's cracking you in ways you couldn't have anticipated, and you can't keep doing it."

"I tried," she said. "Bo told me to *use it*."

"Then tell him again and tell Heather, too. And Gray—he should be telling them for you. Make them listen to you, it's their job."

"I will," she said. "I know." She did not mean this. "You should go, you're late."

"You have to tell them," Noel said again as he hugged her. "It's not worth it. Not if it's making you question your reality."

"Isn't that the whole point?"

"No," he said as he pulled away. "It's *not* the point for you. That's for the audience."

"Yeah," she said and did not believe.

They turned to look for his bandmates. One of them was on a couch next to Merritt, packing marijuana into a ceramic bowl that was sculpted and glazed to look like the folds of a vulva. When he finished packing, he performed basic party etiquette by passing first, in this case to Merritt, who now gestured to Audrey to come sit with them.

But Audrey shook her head no, told Noel she loved him, and walked along a wall until she found a bathroom crowded with leggy houseplants: the hipster's Orangerie. She went in, turned the lock, and was startled to see herself in the grimy mirror above the sink. *Was* it herself she saw, this sallow-cheeked Clara Broward imposter with circles under her eyes? Normcore Audrey Wells meets phantom? She sat almost crying, actually crying, almost crying on the edge of the dirty tub for a good while until someone who lived in the loft grew tired of waiting to use the only toilet and banged on the door, saying, "Can I please shit in my own bathroom, now?"

When Audrey came out, the number of people at the party had more than doubled and she could no longer spot Merritt among them. She did see Harper leaning against a wall mural of James Baldwin dressed in a 1990s-era white-and-red Michael Jordan Chicago Bulls uniform.* Harper had her sweater sleeve rolled on one arm so that she could show off her yellow jacket tattoo to the willowy person in floral coveralls who was now hanging on her.

Audrey's phone buzzed in her pocket. She looked. It was Merritt. No message, only a link. She clicked it with dread. She knew it would send her back to the three of them on that blanket in the orchard: footage captured by some set crasher or even just by Bo's instructions. She knew it.

The link did lead to a video. But not to that one.

Instead, it was of the side-of-the-wall screening of *House Mother 2*, with Caroline and Bo standing in the frame in front of the projection, smiling, their bodies washed in blue light and their shoulders and hair cluttered with snowflakes. It did look pretty magical, the internet commenters seemed to—for now—agree. And *so good* that Caroline Wells was cameoing in the movie as Audrey's mom.

And *so good* that it had snowed in Little Compton that night—the only place it had snowed in Rhode Island.

Audrey felt someone move close behind her. She thought it was

---

* The artist had made this necessary distinction clear by painting the words *James Baldwin* next to the mural's head with a helpful arrow.

just a party shove, the space too full of people. But then that someone touched the small of her back and left their hand there. She
turned. It was Merritt, who said, "What's happening with you right
now?"

Audrey shook her head.

"Tell me," Merritt said. "You can say it."

Audrey shook her head again. "I can't," she said.

Merritt thought Audrey looked, just now, like she had the whole
queer collection of Brookhants ghosts about her: sitting on her
shoulders, hanging off her back, curled like toddlers around her legs.
"Let's go back to Brookhants," she said. "I'll get Harper."

"I can't do that to Noel."

"Really?" Merritt asked. "This is about Noel?"

"What do you mean?"

"You're here right now for Noel?" Merritt asked again.

Audrey chose her words carefully. "Yes. He's my best friend and
he's playing a show that Bo agreed to shoot for him. Plus Harper
will get it trending. There's already press there."

"Okeydokey," Merritt said.

"What are you talking about?"

"I guess I'm talking about Noel's big moment. We should go."
Merritt was all business as she went to find them a ride since she
was no longer OK to drive.

It took another half hour, but eventually someone named Danny
drove Merritt and Audrey in Elaine's car the not-all-that-many
blocks over to Broadway, where the Columbus Theatre was, its old-
fashioned marquee lit up with red letters: NEWPORTMANTEAU—SOLD
OUT! (Merritt and Audrey weren't sure who Harper ended up riding
with. By the time they left the party they couldn't find her.)

Concertgoers spilled out the theater's front doors and pooled
onto its sidewalk. Scattered among them were camera crews from
various press outlets or maybe hired by production. Audrey and
Merritt were spotted immediately, and the camera lenses made a
hall of mirrors around them as they entered the lobby. It was a the-

ater from another time repurposed for this one: marble tiles and gilt moldings and a curved ceiling like in a European cathedral, a line of brass-and-glass chandeliers with fixtures shaped like angel's trumpet flowers.

And a stained red carpet, spongy as Brookhants terrace moss, beneath their feet.

Their wrists were cuffed with yellow VIP bracelets as Noel texted to tell them to come backstage, and how, but the lobby was jammed with bodies and they had to pick their way through slowly.

Audrey felt trapped in the crush of winter coats, the chatter and anticipation about them its own kind of buzzing. She worried she might faint and kept close to Merritt, who now said, unhappily, "Wasn't enough to beat us over here, she already had time to find the bar."

"And a date," Audrey said when she also saw what Merritt was seeing: Harper very comfortably chatting up someone in a black-and-gold dress.

"What else?" Merritt said as she steered them in that direction.

The person in the dress was Annie Meng. After cursory introductions, Harper explained that she had been in the area—*in Boston, actually*—and had decided to *drop down* for the night and probably come to the set tomorrow, too.

"Well, and since I spent, like, three months making papier-mâché, I thought I should at least see how it got used," Annie said. "It made me feel like a toddler working with Play-Doh. Turns out wasps don't really consider my needs when they're chewing up wood pulp for their nests."

"I don't think they've used most of what you made yet," Harper said. "It comes later."

"I didn't know you were working on the film," Merritt said, her face a beige wall.

"Barely," Annie said, waving her hand as if it was nothing. "Just a few projects Harper thought I was right for. Bo bought three of my paintings last year, so how could I say no when he asked?"

"How could you?" Merritt said like some robot myna bird.

"Should we get a drink before we go in?" Harper asked, signaling to the bartender even before anyone had answered her. The night's two signature cocktails? The Mary MacLane* and The Orangerie, which came complete with citrus blossoms floating on top. Of course it did, Readers.

Audrey drank hers without thinking. She didn't want it, really, but one had been passed to her, the glass sweating in her hand, and eventually she brought it to her mouth, and then again, a thing to do. It had the kind of herbaceous aftertaste that made her take another sip to clear it, only to start the cycle again.

A broad-shouldered member of the security staff approached. He'd been sent to bring them backstage and away from the crowd, who had been alerted to their presence, particularly Harper's. People were now gathering even more thickly around them, phones up and shooting.

They weaved through the crowd, sloshing their too-full Mary MacLanes as more security flanked them. Audrey felt like she was slipping in and out of time. There were so many people, their conversations too loud, bodies too close. The knot of dread in her chest pulled tighter.

Backstage they found Noel with his band. He was in a rust-colored velvet suit and seven pounds of gold eyeliner and he looked about perfect, Audrey thought. She forced a big smile and kissed his cheek and told him to *kill it out there*. His bandmates were giddy with the size of the crowd, the press, all of them humming with preshow energy. Foreboding twisted in Audrey's gut.

Something bad was about to happen. Was happening?

She couldn't feign additional chitchat. Without waiting for anyone else to join her, or even checking to see if they were following, Audrey headed through the nearest doorway (that didn't lead back to the lobby) and found herself in a different dark hallway, one that eventually deposited her, after a wrong turn, at the front of the theater, to the left of the stage.

---

* They used the same recipe as at least one of the cocktails named for MacLane at the height of her popularity.

The theater proper was its lobby writ large: a cathedral built for vaudeville acts and silent films, with Greek-inspired frescoes on its arched ceiling and more gilt in its ornate moldings and columns. The main floor was already half full and the balcony was stuffed to capacity. Audrey took one of the front-row-center seats (where Bo wanted her). She was still holding the watery remains of her cocktail and so she reached to set the glass under her chair. While her hand was there, she felt around for some sort of William Castle rigging meant to jolt her at the proper time. There was none. But there was *something* on the underside of her seat, something that made her fingers curl away in revulsion when they brushed against it. It felt fuzzy, almost like moss.

Merritt and Harper (and Annie, too) had followed her and they now stood in front of their seats and scanned the crowd behind. "Your mom just came in with Bo," Merritt said, doing the play-by-play though Audrey hadn't asked her to. "People are losing their minds."

Audrey looked to see Bo guide Caroline onto an elevated platform in the center of the theater, where the camera crew was situated to best film the show. One of the camera crews, anyway.

"Oh, she sees us," Harper said, waving in that direction.

Audrey did not join them in waving at her mother. Instead, she turned back around to face the still-empty stage. Her brain felt gummy and thick. She closed her eyes and tried to let the crowd become a hum. It felt good to close her eyes, but it didn't work to shut them out.

Next to her, Harper said, "Look at all these badasses who dressed up."

"Brookhants cosplay," Annie said. "Are they extras?"

"I think just fans," Harper said.

Audrey felt compelled to look. She couldn't say why, only that it was part of this. It was all part of this. She opened her eyes and again turned around to see. There were several pockets of people in period costume, puffed sleeves here, a boater hat there. Even coming down their own aisle, three smiling women who might have stepped out of a John Singer Sargent painting: skirts and shirtwaists with lace trimmings at their high necks, fitted jackets cinched with belts of the same material, their hair in simple chignons.

The one wearing a toque perched atop her head like a tilted cake took the seat next to Audrey, nodding hello as she did.

"You nailed the look," Merritt said to the woman. "That hat's a dream."

"I would dress like this every day if I thought I could pull it off," the woman said.

"You could," Merritt said.

Audrey felt like she wasn't even there between them as they spoke. She didn't want to be.

The houselights dimmed, just as they do at every concert ever, but it still sent whoops and shouts up from the crowd. Kelsi, the band's drummer, walked onstage and settled at her kit.

"You're not really going to sit for Newportmanteau," Merritt said, leaning her mouth close to Audrey, her breath hot and wet and a little bit gross in her ear. "Are you?"

Audrey stood, though she didn't feel inside her body as she did. Her view of the stage had been lower. Now it was higher. She let Merritt take her hand. Why not? Who cared? None of this meant a thing.

The shadows at the wings of the stage were twitching. Weren't they? Was it something they were doing with the lighting? If they kept this up the whole show she'd throw up. She knew she would. It was like a strobe light but for shadows: hopping and blinking and making her sick.

Next to her, the three women in period costume whispered something to each other. They were talking about her. Audrey could feel their eyes on her. She chanced a look, to scowl at them. Didn't they know it was rude to stare? The one on the end, farthest from her, could she be one of those from that night at the convenience store? Who stole the boat to chase them? She might be. Harper knew her name. She'd talked to her the most. It *was* her, wasn't it? She'd dressed in a disguise to fool them. But Audrey wasn't fooled.

Why did the red stage curtains look dipped in black ink and still wet with it? They didn't. They didn't. Ignore them.

Something was happening. It wasn't about to happen. It already was.

Noel did a series of slides and glides to take his place onstage, as if he was ice-skating across it. He'd perfected these moves since Audrey had seen him do them last. Kelsi ticked off the count and they started their first song and it was loud. So loud. Audrey thought she should have recognized it but for her fumbling brain and God it was loud. Did Noel sound OK? She thought he must, the crowd seemed into it, and he looked the part, but it was hard for her to tell. Their guitars were screaming at her and those shadows in the wings kept sputtering. Camerapeople emerged from them to capture these moments from all the angles. The song went on and on and shouldn't she know these lyrics? Harper was jumping up and down like she was on a spring and Audrey could still feel the eyes of the trio of women beside her. Why wouldn't they look at the stage like they were supposed to? The band's fucking playing, idiots. Look at the band! They're the ones on the stage wanting to be looked at.

What were the lyrics? It was Noel's mouth that was open, but it was Mary MacLane's words coming out: *I am not strong. I cannot bear things. I do not want to bear things.*

Audrey would learn, later, that Newportmanteau's set list that night was comprised of covers, like usual, but they were not the band's *usual* covers. Instead, they were all songs about ghosts or curses.˙

˙ Set List for Newportmanteau: October 11, 20—:
"Walking with a Ghost," Tegan and Sara
"Cry Like a Ghost," Passion Pit
"It's a Curse," Wolf Parade
"Ghost," Halsey
"I Put a Spell on You," Screamin' Jay Hawkins
"The Ghost of Tom Joad," Bruce Springsteen
"Seven Curses," Bob Dylan
"Ghost Town," Kanye West
"In the Fog," Azure Ray
"Registered Ghost," Portastatic

Harper leaned across Merritt to shout at Audrey over the song, "They sound awesome tonight!"

Audrey nodded in response. Was there something in Harper's grinning tooth gap? Something that shouldn't be there? Maybe just some bit of flower deposited from her cocktail. Or something worse: a stuck worm; a string of seaweed. Audrey swallowed bile. Merritt's hand now felt funny in her own, like something was pressed between their palms that wasn't their skin. It was—

The song ended and the crowd lost it. The strength of their applause seemed to surprise even Noel. It was too much, ravenous and pounding. A camera on a rig panned the stage in a wide arc. Audrey looked up to watch its path and noticed the gilt molding that edged the ceiling tremble with the noise. Didn't she see it tremble? Maybe it was only another hollow trick of Bo's: Styrofoam meant to come crashing down on cue.

Maybe it was made of the paper chambers of a yellow jacket nest.

Audrey pulled her hand from Merritt's in order to join in the clapping. She had to do it; she was right up front: Noel was looking at her. But her hands didn't make the correct sound when she put them together, and wet sludge flew from between them and landed on her cheek. She brought the hand she'd held to Merritt's to her face. Its palm was smeared with yellow mash. It smelled of rotten apple. Merritt was acting like nothing was wrong, taking a selfie with Harper. Everyone was acting like nothing was wrong. The band was already on to their next song, even as the shadows from the wings skittered out across the stage to claim them.

Audrey felt swoony, stars and black across her vision. She sat down hard in her seat, only to find the arm of her chair scabbed thick with moss. She jerked her hand away as the woman next to her, the one in the cake hat, leaned down to ask if she was OK. "You seem like you're really having some trouble," the woman said, her mouth twisting into a terrible, searching smile.

"I'm fine," Audrey said, dropping her eyes from that awful stretched mouth just in time to watch a yellow jacket climb up from inside the high neck of the woman's shirtwaist and cling its sticky legs along the ruffled edge of the fabric to hum in the air between them. The woman acted like it wasn't there.

Another yellow jacket emerged from the cave of feathers on her hat. "If you're sure," the woman said, straightening to join her friends.

Audrey turned around in her chair, hoping to signal to Caroline on the platform. If she could just calm down enough to get her thoughts right, but she didn't even manage to cast her eyes far enough back into the theater to find her, because for rows and rows back, all the rows, there were smiling concertgoers from the past.

Not pockets of them. Not a smattering here and there. It was like looking around the redwood table in Harold's séance panorama: everyone dressed and styled like Flo and Clara and Eleanor and Libbie and Alex and even wretched cousin Charles, too. An audience of Gilded Age phantoms singing along to the screaming song and batting their faces for yellow jackets.

She was going to be sick. She caught the lurch of it. Swallowed it back and made herself stand. She had to push up on the arms of her chair to do it. As she did, she felt the moss wedge under her fingernails.

Audrey walked careful steps through the vibrating shadows, one after the next, to the end of their row and out the way she'd entered from backstage, into the dim passage, its walls skinned in gold paper with fuzzy maroon patches, its sconces dead ringers for those in Spite Tower.

It is a dim, dim light and there's a treachery in it.

She made it to where the hallway curved around the stage and pressed her palms against that fuzzy paper to lean forward and spew an arc of vomit up against the wall. Though it didn't smell of vomit: it smelled of rotten apples. The smell alone made her heave again.

The music pounded like a pulse through the wall and into her hands and body—the big show happening just on the other side, the show she'd agreed to: the one she'd helped make happen. She felt flushed and put her cheek against the fuzz, closed her eyes.

At the end of the hallway, she heard someone enter from the theater.

Someone was walking toward her. Audrey didn't even care. She wouldn't even open her eyes to see.

"Are you OK?" It was Merritt, now right next to her. "Oh," she added, when she noticed the vomit. "So you're not."

"No, I'm not," Audrey said to the wall. There was a choke in her throat that embarrassed her.

"Just breathe for a minute," Merritt said. "Maybe you should try to sit. I can go get you some water."

Audrey opened her eyes at that and said, "Don't go. I know we have to get back in there, I just need a minute."

"We don't have to get back in there," Merritt said.

"Yes, we do." Audrey closed her eyes again against the thought of walking back into that theater with that crowd. The band had just ended a song and the applause kicked on high. Behind her, she heard Merritt move to the opposite wall and slide down against it.

When Audrey opened her eyes and turned to look, Merritt was sitting on the floor, looking up at her. She looked like she was settling in. Now Bo would be mad at her about this, too. She was ruining the scene. Had ruined it. Again.

"I'm really OK," Audrey said, taking a deep breath and turning fully around. "I just needed to puke, I think."

"You're not OK and you know it," Merritt said, patting the floor next to her. "Come sit. I thought we were going to do this earlier, but then you didn't want to, so let's do it now. I bet Harper will come join us any minute."

"Do what?" Audrey asked, though even as she said it she thought—

"Seriously, come sit down," Merritt said again, patting the floor beside her. "Bo's not gonna rattle all the chains without two of his leads in place. Who's he gonna drop the chandelier on if we're not out there?"

"What?" Audrey asked again, though she knew. She *did* know. The truth scuttling through her like a spider.

"You heard me perfectly," Merritt said, casting her eyes to the ceiling for cameras. "As I'm certain Bo did, too."

Audrey steadied herself against the wall; the floor couldn't be trusted and she couldn't be trusted to stand on it. She spoke carefully—everything felt like a trap. "Is that what he's doing tonight? Making a chandelier come down out there?"

Merritt seemed confused. "Oh, I mean—sorry, no. Is there even a chandelier? I just meant whatever it is, he'll wait for us to do it."

Audrey couldn't assemble the right reaction to what she was feeling. Merritt was being so matter-of-fact, so blasé. She was acting like they'd already had a conversation they'd never actually had. This made Audrey speak calmly, too. Even if she didn't feel calm. "Does Harper know?"

"I mean, what do you think?"

"But you don't know for sure that she does?"

"Well, I knew about you."

Why were they talking in riddles when there was so much to say? "*How* did you know about me?" Audrey asked. "Because Bo told you? Or was this your idea? I mean, to film it this way?"

Merritt rolled her eyes. "Does this seem like my idea? I knew the same way you knew. I guessed. I put it together."

"I didn't know," Audrey said.

"Yes, you did," Merritt said. "I think you did."

Audrey sighed. "I mean, I wondered. A bunch of times I wondered—it seemed possible, one of you would say something, but then I thought, *No way.*"

"You knew," Merritt said. "You just didn't want to know. But I can't really decide: Does it make it cheaper that we all know or less cheap?"

Audrey felt like she might cry. Whether from relief or shame, she wasn't sure. Both? "God, I feel really fucking stupid." She leaned her head back against the wall. "When did he tell you this is what he wanted?"

"After you signed on and I'd quit," Merritt said. "He called me. He said that you and Harper would be in the dark. I was the one who had to keep it all together."

"I got the same pitch. Like exactly the same."

Merritt shrugged like this was not a surprise to her. She started to say something, but the door at the end of the hallway opened and they waited to see who would emerge from the long shadow now moving toward them.

It was Harper.

To her credit, she didn't pretend not to know what was being discussed in this hallway without her. There was no casual approach, no feigned confusion about where they'd gone off to and why. She knew. She wasn't confused at all.

"Hey, are you OK?" she asked Audrey.

"Not really."

"Do you think you can make it through the rest of the show, or do we need to take a break with the whole thing?"

"What's *the whole thing,* Harper?" Merritt said like Merritt would.

"Listen, if you're still sick, we should deal with that," Harper said to Audrey. "But otherwise, we all need to get back out there. If we just get through the concert, we can do this whole part later, when we have time. Back at Brookhants."

"Well there *are* more cameras there," Merritt said. "Better angles."

"I'm being serious," Harper said. "Please? We flew in an effects crew from Germany and now they're waiting on us to do some hologram-smoke thing."

"God, look at you *producing,*" Merritt said. "You're producing so hard right now."

"They're really good," Harper said, ignoring her. "And really expensive. I'm sure it will be worth it, whatever they do."

"I don't think I can," Audrey said. "I don't have that take in me." This was true.

"I'm with Audrey on this one," Merritt said.

Only now, Audrey thought, did Harper seem to realize how much ground she had to make up. Impossible ground. "We can do this part," she said, "this whole talk-it-out part. I think Bo wants us to. I mean eventually. Can we just not do it right now?"

"Oh my God," Merritt said, like a puzzle piece had snapped in place for her. "He *wants* us to have it out over this, right? To what, like, confront each other about it?"

But Audrey was stuck on something else. "Was this *your* idea?" she asked Harper. "To make the movie this way?"

"No," Harper said.

"But you knew about it," Merritt said. "From the start. You helped plan it."

To this, Harper said nothing.

"She did," Merritt said to Audrey. "You did," she said again to Harper. "You've been back there pulling the strings with him all along. Is your tattoo even real?"

"What are you talking about?" Harper flipped her arm over, shoved up her sleeve. "It's real."

"That doesn't mean anything, though," Merritt said, barely glancing at it. "In the scheme of things."

"It hasn't just been Bo pulling the strings," Harper said. She reached for the cigarette at her ear, put it between her lips.

"No, we know that," Merritt said. "I just said you were back there, too."

"It was Elaine," Harper said, matchbook now in hand. "This was Elaine's idea, this whole found-footage approach." The spark of the match, the puff of flame as she lit her cigarette: all of it like the flourish at the end of a magic trick.

"That's not true," Merritt said. Her face said the opposite.

Harper took a long drag. Then she said, on her exhale, "It is. Ask Bo."

Merritt snorted. "Why would I trust any answer Bo ever gives to anything?"

"Then ask Elaine," Harper said, "but it doesn't matter whose idea it was, anyway. She was right. Something else is happening, something worth getting on camera. Today in the orchard wasn't anybody pulling our strings."

"I mean, how wasn't it?" Audrey asked. "The snow?"

"They didn't make it snow," Harper said. "And they didn't film any of that, anyway."

Audrey shook her head. This couldn't be true. "How do you know?"

"Because I told them not to."

"Forgive me if I don't put much stock in that," Merritt said. "Even if it's not on camera, it was designed to be. This whole thing is designed to be."

"Nobody was *designing* the way I felt there but me," Harper said. She turned to Audrey. "Didn't you just recite us something about there being more beauty in the artificial than in the natural?"

"Oh don't," Merritt said before Audrey could get any words out. "Don't be cheap, Harper. That story was written in 1905 and its hero kills himself at the end because he's depressed and alone and his queer ideals have no place in his world."

"But that's only *part* of that story," Harper said. "That's what I'm saying—it's not all one or the other. Even if I sometimes knew more than you did, that doesn't automatically cancel out everything that's happened between us or make it fake. Not for me."

"I don't know if I can believe that now," Audrey said.

"You shouldn't," Merritt said. "It's all been smoke and mirrors. And we were plenty happy to dress up and play along."

Audrey looked at her, there on the floor, smug and cool and trying to act like she was above all of this now even though she was as much a part of it as they were. "Why are you even here, then?" she asked her. "If you figured it all out ahead of time and you think it's so terrible, why did you come?"

"Because she's writing about it," Harper said. "Right? You're making a book out of this, starring us."

Readers: if Audrey was surprised by this, and she was, so was Merritt.

"Are you?" Audrey asked.

"It's fiction," Merritt said dismissively. "A novel with biographical underpinnings."

"It's about this," Harper said. "Wait for the scene in the creepy hallway backstage at the Columbus."

But Audrey was disappointed. Again. "Is that really the only reason you came here?"

"Which one would you prefer?" Merritt asked.

"I don't know," Audrey said, feeling just so stupid. "I can't believe how much I wanted this to mean something. It's embarrassing how much."

"*I consider calmly the question of how much evil I should need to kill off my finer feelings,*" Merritt said.

"Please stop *fucking* quoting Mary MacLane," Audrey said. "You're not Mary MacLane, Merritt."

Merritt seemed a little stunned, but she gathered herself to say, "How about I stop when *you* stop pointing your finger at us, Audrey."

"I'm not pointing my finger, I—"

But Merritt was spitting, now. "Oh you are. You are. You keep asking what this is—like you don't already know and it's for some reason our job to tell you. We did it because not one of us is a single ounce better or wiser than Mary MacLane, even if we've had a hundred and twenty years to be. January fourteenth: *I wish to acquire that beautiful, benign, gentle, satisfying thing—Fame. I want it—oh, I want it! I wish to leave all my obscurity, my misery— my weary unhappiness—behind me forever. I am deadly, deadly tired of my unhappiness.* March twentieth: *Fame, if you please, Devil. One may wander over the face of the earth. But Fame is herself a refuge. Oh, kind Devil, I entreat you, let me have that!* That's why we did it. That's why *I* did it. In the hallway with the wrench."

They looked at each other in that dim hallway with its gold-and-blood wallpaper until Audrey said:

"That makes me really sad."

"I am sad," Merritt said. "I'm a sad person who does sad things. And I am deadly, deadly tired of my unhappiness."

Light shifted at the entrance to the theater, the sound of the band and the crowd swelling and dimming. Someone else was walking toward them, two someone elses, in fact, shadows growing and growing around the corner until Bo and Heather appeared.

"Look at that," Merritt said. "It's almost like you could hear what we're saying."

"Merritt, I need to talk to you," Bo said, his face grim and distorted. He looked at Audrey and Harper. "Can you two give us a minute?"

"It's OK, captain," Merritt said. "You can just say it to all three of us now. We pulled back the curtain."

"This isn't about the movie," Bo said. He looked, could it be pained? "You should look at your phone."

"Did I miss my cue?" Merritt said, though her voice had lost some of its edge and she was now reaching into her jacket pocket for the phone, pulling it out, scanning its screen of notifications. "We were discussing our characters' motivations for this scene."

Bo seemed to know at least some of what she'd be reading on that phone screen, because now he said, "I don't know who sent you what, when, but they've already got her in the ambulance. I just talked to Carl before I came to get you."

"What did you do to her?" Merritt asked, fumbling to stand and join them, no longer casual in the least.

"What's happening right now?" Harper asked. "Who's in an ambulance?"

"I'm sorry to be the one telling you," Bo said to Merritt. "We can meet them at the hospital if we go now."

"What did you do, Bo?" Merritt asked again.

He shook his head like he somehow expected this accusation. He said, "I guess she forgot something on the stove. She went upstairs with it still on and after the fire in The Orangerie, she'd put in those alarms with the strobe lights. She was coming back down when the smoke set them off—it was too much, it startled her."

"Which stairs?" Merritt asked, though they all knew the answer.

"Spite Tower."

"Oh my God," Audrey said. She held the wall to keep standing.

"She told us she never went up there," Harper said.

"Oh my God," Audrey said again. She didn't mean to. How could she be both in shock and not at all surprised? How could something so awful feel so perfectly inevitable?

"She's still alive?" Merritt asked. "You're sure?"

"She was, *yes*," Heather said quickly. "When they took her in the ambulance she was."

"Carl was right there," Bo said like he was happy to have this, at least, to say. "He got to her almost as soon as it happened."

No one had to ask how they'd gotten to Elaine so quickly, how they'd known just what had happened and where to find her. There were cameras all over Spite Manor.

"Do you want us to come with you?" Harper asked as Merritt followed Bo back down the hallway.

"I don't see why you would," she said. "Unless you know something I don't."

ELAINE BROOKHANTS,

SOCIALITE AND PHILANTHROPIST,

DIES AT AGE 81

....

Little Compton, RI—American heiress, philanthropist, writer, and late-in-life Hollywood film producer Elaine Brookhants died October 11 at Newport Hospital at the age of eighty-one, a spokesperson for the family told the *Providence Journal* in a telephone interview. The cause was complications stemming from a fall at home.

Effortlessly elegant and never far from her sharp wit, Elaine Brookhants and her various exploits first captivated New York society pages, and then, for years after, the churning Rhode Island rumor mill. (Which certainly hasn't been quieted by her death.) She was the most recent Brookhants to occupy the "cursed" family estate: Breakwater, in Little Compton—better known to locals as Spite Manor. The home was built by her eccentric great-grand-uncle, steel tycoon and Spiritualist Harold Brookhants.

She was born Elaine Elizabeth Bishop Brookhants in New York on June 21, 1934, to railroad heir Arthur Ryan Brookhants and his second wife, Valerie Bishop Brookhants. Arthur was a self-styled adventurer who sank much of his inheritance into wild and sometimes unlawful searches for objects of interest around the globe. Largely as a way to legitimize these pursuits, he founded the Brookhants Museum in Providence in 1939. He died of a heart attack in 1948, leaving his daughter with a rumored inheritance of $13.7 million. Valerie Bishop was a jet-setting photographer whose candid shots of her society friends would become some of the most iconic of the era. However, she is perhaps best known now for her series of stark self-portraits, taken while she was hospitalized after a suicide attempt in 1950, while Elaine was away at boarding school. In the coming years, Valerie would spend significant time receiving treatment for depression and *neuroses* in mental hospitals in New York and California. She died from an overdose of sleeping pills in Los Angeles in 1955.

Elaine was educated at the Wheeler School in Providence, where she was first nicknamed Lainey (a name she continued to use throughout her life) and garnered a reputation as both a gifted writer and a prank-playing troublemaker. However, despite the pranks—or because of them—she was wildly popular with her fellow classmates, occasionally hosting what she called "Spooky Weekends" away for them at her family estate. The caption in the school annual from her junior year describes her thusly: "The only curse our Lainey has to worry about is her mouth and what too often comes out of it."

In 1951, Elaine entered Vassar, planning to study art history. However, she dropped out to be with her mother after completing only one academic year. Back in Manhattan at age nineteen, Elaine emerged as a youthful new addition to its shifting high society. She forged friendships (and rumored romances) with film stars and her fellow heirs *and* heiresses alike. Although he typically ran with a crowd closer in age to her mother, Truman Capote wrote this regarding Elaine's reputation as a desirable match: "Lainey Brookhants might be catch of the day, but unlike a few others of which the same is said, she won't stink up your kitchen come morning. This particular flounder won't."

For a time, Elaine seemed to enjoy mocking social customs as much as she did participating in them. However, after her mother's suicide and the fervent publicity that followed, she withdrew from the social circuit and developed the reputation for fierce loyalty that she maintained throughout the rest of her life. She also used part of her inheritance to found the Valerie Bishop Clinic in Manhattan, which provided counseling and other psychological services to women of all means. In the 1980s, the endeavor expanded into the Valerie & Eleanor Foundation, with a mission to fund research in mental illness. When she was honored for this work in 2007, Brookhants said, simply, "It's what my mother would have wanted. And what I wanted for her."

In 1963, while on vacation in San Francisco, Brookhants met political cartoonist Taylor Behrens, who was then fifty-five to her twenty-nine. The two married just four months later and settled in Little Compton at the family estate. There, Brookhants wrote *Mrs. Mittens Invites You to Tea,* the first of three macabre (children's) books of simple rhymes about the strange and guileful Mrs. Emily Mittens and her neighbor (and implied lover) Gladys Glovely. A sample: *Mrs. Mittens had five kittens, but then she ate just one. Now Mrs. Mittens has four kittens—but Mrs. Mittens isn't done.* Taylor drew the fearsome pen-and-ink illustrations for the books, which were initially printed as amusing Christmas presents for friends. One of those friends, who was then an editor at Troubadour, convinced Elaine that there was a wider market for the books and published the first the following year. *Mrs. Mittens Takes Up Fisticuffs* and *Gladys Glovely Isn't Lovely* followed. The books sold well for several years, despite often being panned (and banned) by those who felt their messaging wrong for children. (All three are now out of print.)

In 1977, Taylor Behrens died of colon cancer at the age of sixty-nine. Shortly thereafter, Elaine moved to the South of France and remained living there until the early 2000s. She disappeared almost entirely from public life during these years.

In 2011, Elaine purchased the film rights for the nonfiction book *The Happenings at Brookhants,* which details the history of the real deaths and supposed curse attached to the Brookhants School for Girls, a boarding school founded by Harold Brookhants and still remaining, though long abandoned, on the northeast corner of her Little Compton estate. *The Happenings at Brookhants* was written by then-sixteen-year-old wunderkind author Merritt Emmons, who credited Elaine with not only convincing her to write it but also significantly assisting in her research.

Horror film director Bo Dhillon became attached to the project in 2014, with rising star Harper Harper cast as one of the leads and

Brookhants remaining on as executive producer. Principal photography began in September at the Little Compton estate, and almost immediately rumors began online regarding supposed bizarre or ghostly occurrences on set. Elaine herself commented on the rumors in an interview with the *Providence Journal* just two weeks ago, saying, "Everyone involved wanted to make the film here *because* it's a place full of tricks like these, so we can't act surprised now that they're being played on us. But it's also a place full of treats. When you see it all captured on the big screen, you'll know what I mean."

ESSE QUAM VIDERI

....

When at Brook-hants, mind the hour,
for here time is queer.
If you think you hold the power,
death will draw you near.[*]

As soon as she was certain Ava was sleeping in her bed—her
wounds dressed and her broken arm set in a cast by the doctor—our
Libbie did not wait one moment more to do what she'd come back
to Brookhants to do.

What she'd pretended, for far too long, needn't be done.

She gathered the book and the awful doll, too. She bundled them
in a feed sack she'd taken earlier from the barn. Then she packed
a valise with a few items of clothing—she could send for the rest
later—and told Caspar to ready the carriage because she'd want him
to take her over to Newport as soon as she finished a chore.

What gall, Readers, to call what she had to do a chore.

And what gall to think she would ever finish it.

Since nightfall, Libbie hadn't been able to account for Adelaide's
whereabouts and that *did* trouble her. But she was already so trou-

---

[*] The stanza used most often to end the unofficial ballad of the Brookhants School
for Girls.

bled. What did it matter, really? Addie would find her, when she wanted to. Or she wouldn't. No matter which, Libbie had things to do until someone or something stopped her from doing them. She herself would no longer be that someone.

She headed out into the dark, across the terraced lawns to the wooden stairs, slick with mist and algae, that would take her down to the water's edge. She took each step carefully, holding the railing with her free hand. No need to create cause for an accident when Spite Manor specialized in them.

She cleared the final stair and her footfalls sank into the wet sand. The dark water flashed white in its crashing surf, like the ocean baring its sharp teeth again and again, its mouth rolling open and closed. As she walked, wind whipped sand into her own mouth. It crunched between her molars and tasted of rot. The beach was colder than she'd expected, than she remembered. Her time in the asylum had been like being buried beneath this sand: only the world in her head had felt real to her there. The doctors tried to reach inside it but she wouldn't let them. And though it was a dark and lonely world, one built from her own guilt and fear, she hadn't minded. Not entirely. It gave her somewhere safe to wait while she plotted. While she puzzled and repuzzled the events that had ended with her Alex at the bottom of the Spite Tower stairs. When Libbie apportioned the blame for this, she always took the biggest helping. Even still: there was plenty left to go around.

And then Adelaide had written to tell her that Hanna was dead.*

This news hadn't made Libbie feel consoled so much as curious. And maybe a little bit brave. If Hanna's death wasn't a sign that it

---

* It wasn't a trick of light or a shared hallucination that night in the tower, Readers. It *was* Hanna Eckhart seated next to Harold in the panoramic séance photo. Hanna might have long been a member of Harold's house staff, but she was also a person with a keen interest in the afterlife, and Harold was only too delighted to push that interest in the directions he most favored. However, the plain fact that Hanna Eckhart sometimes participated in Harold's psychic pursuits does not *necessarily* mean that any of the other terrible things our Alex (and after, at least for a while, our Libbie) believed about her were true. Remember this for what comes next.

was time for her to act, what would be? Libbie was someone who put much stock in signs, now.

So she'd stopped hiding.

And just this morning, she'd come back to Brookhants.

Sara Dahlgren told her plainly that it was mad for her to do so, even for only one night. In fact, Sara said, it was the kind of idea that belonged to someone who should stay in the asylum until she no longer had it. You must have guessed that it would be Sara Dahlgren, Readers, who would call in several significant favors from her coterie of well-connected double-dealers in order to bypass Senator Packard's wishes and to hasten Libbie's release. For now.

Sara said she wanted to get them (and Ava) on a boat back to France as soon as she could make the arrangements. (And maybe after she'd also attended one or two parties in Newport. You know how it is, Readers: when in Rhode Island . . .)

But Libbie had no such plans. When their carriage had rounded the Spite Manor drive earlier that day, and passed through the tower's shadow as it stretched over the road, she knew she'd likely never leave again.

"It's as ugly as it's ever been," Sara said, as they pulled up to the house.

"Worse," Libbie said as a reward to Sara for getting her here.

Sara had been anxious, distracted, saying, "Promise me you'll pack *only* a few things, for now, and we'll send for the rest later. We'll go over to Newport for a week or so—*if* we make the ferry—just until you remember what it's like to be a person with other people. And then on to Boston and out of Puritanical New England for good."

Libbie wasn't even paying attention because there was Ava, already there she was, out on the porch to greet them with Adelaide close behind. (And with Hanna dead and gone besides.)*

---

* Hanna Eckhart was buried in the Little Compton cemetery. Libbie was certain of this. She had asked to stop and see the headstone on their way to the house. She had touched it, the stone cold even in the sun. And when Sara's back had been turned, Libbie spit on the grave.

"She's bigger than I imagined her," Libbie said. Though she hadn't imagined her very much. She thought she saw something of Harold in this girl now staring at their carriage from beneath the shade of the low porch roof. Maybe she even saw, strangely—*impossibly*—something of Alex. But Libbie saw nothing of herself.

"Oh, she is a weed, isn't she?" Sara said, looking, too. "France is more her home than America will ever be—clever girl. She'll be happy to go back, I know it. And you'll be happy again. Finally." Sara had then turned from the window to look at Libbie. "Oh, Library, you look so old." Were those tears in her eyes? Was it possible, Readers?*

Sara Dahlgren was still Sara Dahlgren. There was some comfort in that. But Libbie didn't want to be comforted. She'd only wanted to use Sara to do what had now been done: to return to Brookhants. She wouldn't explain herself. She knew she couldn't.

So Libbie and Sara had argued. And then Sara had left, saying she couldn't miss the ferry over to Newport or she'd be stuck here, but that she'd come back for them on Monday. She'd give Libbie the weekend to get acquainted with Ava and to pack her things, sort her affairs, but she would not leave without her. Sara knew Libbie would change her mind, she said. She knew Libbie would see her way to reason.

But our Libbie no longer dealt in reason, Readers. She dealt in signs and omens. And this afternoon, in the orchard, she'd had plenty of those.

Now, she walked on, thirty, maybe forty yards down the cold beach, to the area she and her friends had once favored for splashing about in their new bathing suits, the same place Alex had kissed her brazenly in the surf and Libbie had let her and everyone had cheered.

Libbie was not surprised to hear the sound of the yellow jackets

---

* It was.

begin in a low hum and then ramp up to a deep and throbbing *whir* as she went. She had expected this. Though the pain in her hip, where the apple bruise had been—and where it hadn't been for more than a year—that did catch her out.

She knelt in the fine, wet sand near the shoreline and began digging with her hands. The silt wedged up under her fingernails and the crashing black water sprayed until her dress was sopping and heavy. She shivered but continued on. She had a job to do, one she'd neglected for too long—unforgivably too long. She finished one hole, judged its size as correct, and pulled the sack of items toward her. She took out the matches first, then the awful doll. Perhaps *charm* was more accurate? Or *talisman*?

Alex, her Alex, had been right: fire was the thing. Burn these cursed items to ash and then let the tide carry them out and away from Brookhants. She would set fire to each of the doll's selves on its own, just as Alex would have.

And then she'd burn the book, each page. And then the orchard, every tree.

And finally, if she had time, if nothing stopped her: the tower.

This was her plan. And now to accomplish it.

The wind took the life from the first match as soon as she struck it. It did the same to the next.

She cupped the third until it caught and lasted, and then carried that cupped palm to the largest doll, the one with blackberry brambles wrapping her throat and a pile of stripped flesh at her feet. It took the fire as soon as she pressed the match to its side.

As it burned, it produced flames of purple and green among the orange. It hissed and writhed in the silt hole where she'd dropped it, as if in death throes, until only a mound of black ash remained. Libbie swept more silt over that ash, filling the hole until it wasn't there any longer. And now the waves could do their work.

She dug another hole in the silt for the next doll, the Clara lookalike. Her fingers ached with cold.

As she worked, she thought of the story she'd never told Alex. She'd never told anyone.

When Harold had told *her* the story, which he'd done the first time he'd brought Libbie to Brookhants, she had dismissed it as silly and false: a relic from an unenlightened age. Or she'd wanted to do this, anyway. She'd told herself that's what she had done.

But the story didn't care about that. It simply was, whether or not she chose to believe in it.

The curse at Brookhants, Libbie knew (and now believed), had not started with Flo and Clara and a book by a provocative girl from Montana. It traced much further back than that, to the Rash brothers and their Spite Tower, though not as in the historically sanctioned version of that story, the oft-repeated anecdote. That version, as with so many of the stories we tell about our history, erased a woman*—a plain, bad heroine—in favor of a less messy and more palatable yarn about two feuding brothers from New England.

According to Harold, there had long been gossip about this woman, since even before the arrival of the brothers. These were enigmatic accusations, whispered primarily by locals on the rare occasions when they spotted her. (Or when misfortune fell upon them.) The kinds of things insinuated about her were exactly what you would expect to be said of an unmarried woman living alone in that era.

She lived in a cottage on what is now Brookhants land, though back then it was her land. After the death of her parents, the entire estate had been (quite unusually, for the time) left to her and her alone. The girl's parents were French immigrants and they had no close relations in America. (And were never very eager to discuss those that they'd left behind in France.)

---

* I'm very sorry that I cannot give you the name of this woman, Readers, but it's been lost to time and mansplaining, while, of course, the names of the Rash brothers have stayed firmly affixed to their dumb tale.

The small family lived happily and peacefully in the cottage on the water that the parents, *both* parents, had built by hand. The girl grew. She was bright and passionate. She was educated by *both* of her parents about things near and far, but what she cared most about in the whole of the world was this land on the water where she lived. And about this place she knew every single thing, everything there was to know.

Years later, one of her parents died and the other too soon followed. It would be cliché to tell you that it was of a broken heart, and yet . . .

After, the woman's world remained as small or as large as that. She had no siblings and did not seek a lover. She lived simply in her cottage. She fished and hunted, sewed and painted, read and wrote and thought, and made her way alone. Sometimes she went into town to buy or barter for things she needed, but most often she did not.

She was not unhappy. But she was alone.

Her parents had once seen so much of the world, they had *lived* in it. But when they'd taught her about what they'd seen and done, it had not made their child want to seek it out for herself. She was content in this cottage on her own land by the water.

Into this picture, enter the Rash brothers: Samuel, the elder and more pragmatic, and Jonathan, the more ambitious and with a temper to match. The brothers were full of belief in themselves and their masculine industriousness. Fueled by a generous allotment from their own father's estate, they moved to the area expressly to buy and cultivate two large parcels of land adjacent to the woman's property.

And seeing as her property was wedged like a splinter between those parcels, the brothers thought they might offer to buy hers as well. As a condition of their offer, they would allow her to continue to live in her cottage as long as she wished.

A few of the locals warned the brothers not to do business with this woman, that her lineage was *unnatural* and that she was not to be trusted. (That she was, maybe, even worse than that.) The Rash brothers scoffed at such old-fashioned superstition. They joked about how amusing it was for two farmers from Connecticut to be the men to finally bring modernity to the region. Samuel even made reference to the lessons of Salem.

And so undeterred by local nonsense, they visited the woman at her cottage and she greeted them warmly, invited them in. Her rooms were small and spare but clean and warm—the cottage had a good fireplace. There were bookshelves on one wall and books on those shelves. She served them tea with honey and milk. She was much more refined in her manner than they'd been led to expect, and also, in the firelight, less plain and dour.

Their mugs drained, the brothers made their offer. The woman listened carefully and asked to consider it for three days. Jonathan and Samuel agreed to grant her the time she wanted and said their goodbyes.

It is as good as done, they told each other.

Three days later they returned to her cottage. The woman was, perhaps, a bit chillier toward them than during their previous visit, though still polite when she invited them in. She did not offer tea. Instead, she asked if they had offered her a fair price. They said yes, they had. She then asked if it was the same price they'd have offered her if she was a man. The brothers said of course, just the same figure.

The woman considered this answer for several silent moments. She then told the brothers about her parents and how much they'd loved this cottage, how they'd picked this place for its views of the glittering water and the lush surround of the trees. She told them how happy they'd all been here.

The brothers listened without hearing.

When she was finished, she asked them, a final time, were they sure they had offered her the fairest price for her land? An honest price?

The Rash brothers said, *Yes, yes we certainly have. We would not cheat you. We are honest men.*

Then I cannot sell to you, she told them. *You've lied to me. And still you lie.*

They insisted that this was some misunderstanding, that they were honest men and true to their word, but the woman would not hear these insistences. She showed them to her door and wished them well in their work. Eventually, and with Jonathan still sputtering protestations, they left.

Of course, you already know, Readers, that the brothers had not given her the fairest price. In fact, they'd purchased a lesser piece of land for almost twice what they'd offered her. It was good business, after all, to try to get the best deal.

It's also true that the woman could have simply told them that she knew this and asked for more money.

But she *had* asked for something: the truth. And they had not given it to her.

At first, the Rash brothers were angry, Jonathan most of all. But they had too much work to do to dwell on their anger for long. They consoled themselves with the belief that while they were sure to thrive in this new venture, the woman who had refused them would only grow weaker and more alone in her old age. Once their farms were prosperous, this same woman might even come begging them to buy her land. And when that time came, Samuel told his brother, they should take pity on her, for they were not only wise and strong, they were decent and God-fearing men who wouldn't turn away a feeble old woman unable to care for herself, even if she had turned them down first.

Jonathan was, for a time, appeased.

The brothers were busy. Their undertaking was large and difficult. For more than six months they lived peacefully with their sandwiched neighbor as they cleared large swaths of woods for their crops, dug their wells, and built their houses. They would see her often but not always and she was unfailingly polite. Her own cottage she kept immaculately, every repair in order. And her gardens, though meager in comparison to their grand own farming plans, were lush and healthy. She gave them useful tips on clamming at the rocky beach and both Jonathan's and Samuel's wives found her pleasant and harmless if also rather odd, but then wasn't that to be expected given her unusual circumstances?

In the fall she brought them a crock of her blackberry jam, which was delicious. During that visit, she also gave each of their children small papier-mâché figures she'd made: an apple and a tree, a yellow jacket and a flower. They were beautifully constructed and painted, delicate and fine—it was clear she was an artist. The children loved these objects and treated them with care. Samuel returned the woman's kindness with a gift of smoked pheasant.

For six months all was well enough. Or so it seemed, though perhaps Jonathan Rash had been silently stewing the entirety of those days.

He was the brother who had been the most unhappy about the woman's refusal to sell her land. And by the following spring, as the days grew longer and their work more challenging, he began to blame every other setback or delay on this refusal.

For instance, they'd been forced to build the service road between their two parcels of land out beyond the farthest edge of the woman's parcel, which extended their travel time between. This was something Jonathan found particularly aggrieving at the end of the day, when he had been working Samuel's land and was now heading home to his own.

Jonathan also saw that the woman's land contained what could be better grazing meadows for their cows, and richer soil, and generally more favorable conditions—and yet she wasn't even taking advantage of those conditions. She let most of her land sit feral, and wasn't that itself an affront to God: to waste the resources He'd provided?

Jonathan came to talk so much about this that Samuel began to tease him, saying that since he'd already made the woman's land the Garden of Eden in his mind, he might do well to remember the snake that lived there.

Soon, Jonathan refused to travel the service road after finishing his workday at Samuel's farm. Instead, he cut across the woman's land. Twice the woman saw him do this and he saw her. Both times she said nothing. After that, Jonathan only traveled via this shortcut and encouraged his brother to do the same.

One night, in the silvery dark of dusk and after a particularly trying day, Jonathan was taking the shortcut when he glimpsed the woman moving through her woods toward the hot springs, which was yet another feature of her land that theirs did not share.

He froze in place to watch her. This time she had not seen him.

She was carrying a lantern and a cloth and he could guess her purpose: a starlight bath. Jonathan was tired and hungry, dirty and worn thin with stress over this grand endeavor that he and his brother were pursuing. Earlier that afternoon they'd had a plowing incident that had damaged two valuable machines: a plow and a horse. These damages would cost both time and money, neither of which they had to spare.

In the wake of this day of disappointments, the woman's peaceful freedom, her seeming self-possession and purpose, enraged Jonathan.

So he followed her at some distance, through the woods to the springs, where she soon removed her dress under what she must have assumed was the cover of darkness on the privacy of her own land. Steam swirled from the hot springs as she slipped into the water.

He moved closer.

The woman was singing to herself, a song in French like a lullaby.

Jonathan recognized the song. A week or so before he'd come home early with an injury and found the woman laughing in his own vegetable garden with his wife. The woman had been offering her advice on how best to arrange the string beans for success, advice his wife had seemed pleased to take despite the fact that he, Jonathan, was the farmer. The next day, he'd heard his daughter singing the song and he'd wondered where and how she'd picked it up.

Now he knew.

The woman had brought a bar of soap with her and Jonathan watched her use it. He was fully aroused, and this made him hate her more. She kept humming her song.

He stepped out from behind the tree that had hidden him and strode, as loud as he pleased, to the water's edge. The woman shrieked in shock and embarrassment. She cowered, trying to cover herself with her hands.

At first, he talked softly and awfully to her, telling her that he'd seen her watching him, wanting this. But when the woman screamed and screamed and demanded that he leave, he called her a whore and a temptress and crashed into the water, grabbing her and forcing his kisses and hands upon her.

As he worked to unbuckle his pants, the woman, with a strength he could not fathom, clawed his eyes and kneed him, and as he doubled over she pushed him into the water and climbed out onto the bank, hastily covering herself and telling him, as she turned to leave, to *never cross her land again.*

Jonathan Rash arrived home that night wet and muddy, with a scratch across his face and blood in one eye. He gave his wife a stupid story about an unruly goat near a stream. He then ate his supper in silence, plotting against the woman. He went to bed plotting and dreamed in revenge: plots that curled and twisted into each other like a cave of poisonous snakes.

When he woke in the morning and went outside, the woman was, as he expected she would be, on her slim wooden porch watching the sunrise over the water. The woman loved to look at the water. She especially loved the sunrise and sunset, but at all times of day she favored the view from her cottage. She stood still and breathed it in.

Jonathan Rash hated this about her, her stillness, her peace, as the first or last rays of light found her on that porch. And so he had made his decision: he would take this from her.

He could do so, he knew, if he built a structure just so. Her cottage was situated up and away from the water. Which meant that the view she enjoyed looked out over Rash land.

He could take the woman's view and at the same time give himself the best one for miles.

That morning, plain as day, Jonathan went to her cottage to ascertain the angles that would favor him and hurt her. The woman hurried inside, barred the door, and was silent behind it. He ignored her, climbing onto her porch and lingering there while he took in the view he would soon be erasing.

He started his construction of the tower that same afternoon. He *did* explain what he was building to Samuel, but when pressed for a reason for the construction of such a folly, and why so suddenly, Jonathan would say only that he had now lived next to the woman for long enough to judge her wicked, and that if she would not sell them her land through reasonable means, she must be convinced through unreasonable ones.

Samuel (and also Jonathan's wife) thought the tower was a waste of time and resources, but Jonathan would not be dissuaded. Eventually Samuel, who was plagued with his own burdens—including his father's voice in his head telling him that he shouldn't have entered into business with his hotheaded brother to begin with—decided it was more pragmatic to let Jonathan finish this madness quickly and be done with it than it was to keep arguing with him about it and getting nowhere.

But the brothers had no idea what was to come.

Jonathan finished the tower's foundation, and the very next day, a field of soil that had been tilled and ready for planting was as solid as a floor of bricks and full of thick roots and weeds.

Jonathan built the tower's first walls, and crops that had been thriving withered as if they'd been cut down by harsh frost (this in summer).

Jonathan built higher and higher, the tower taking its shape, and their new wells ran dry. And when more were dug, the water in them was unsuitable for use: brackish and filled with black algae.

Livestock disappeared or grew sick with strange symptoms—skinny white worms spilling out of their mouths and noses when they died. Or even before they died, when they were stretched and bloated skin sacks showing bones. Hens stopped laying, or worse, laid eggs filled with blood, dozens at a time. And once: an egg filled with tiny green snakes all knotted together.

The brothers fought constantly, and newly, with their wives and children. And those children, too often sick and improperly growing, sometimes saw strange and terrible things in the woods that left them unable to sleep at night, so they grew weaker and sicker still.

Worst of all—or so said Harold Brookhants, when he'd told this story to Libbie—was the plague of yellow jackets. Every time the brothers cleared a new field, they'd run into another nest, and then another. Several workers were stung so badly they would not return to work, and those who remained refused to tend certain sections of the fields or demanded wage increases for doing so.

And it wasn't only the swarms of yellow jackets, the drifting, whirring black clouds that sometimes descended to kill a cow or a goat, it was how they littered the air like dandelion fluff. They were never not around: humming, buzzing, flicking about.

They seemed to be watching, the workers said. They said this especially when they visited taverns at night, or gathered on church lawns Sunday mornings.

Of course, some of this can be explained as part and parcel of the standard setbacks of the Rash brothers' profession. It was hard work, and they were the men to do it. No profit without labor. God smiles upon the industrious. But as their troubles grew, week by week—never dwindling, always increasing—Jonathan's conviction that the woman was at the root of them became more difficult for Samuel to dismiss. Especially when Jonathan began simply inventing things about her, such as claiming that one night he'd seen her spread a ring of salt around her cottage, salt she'd harvested from the bay.

Their children and marriages and crops failing, the Rash brothers finally took their queer troubles out for a drink amid the ears, and mouths, of sympathetic locals. They had never relied on spirits before, but this night they accepted pours from neighbors happy to ply them with more outlandish stories about the woman. And even happier to hear the brothers' fresh tales of her.

Their reasoning was hateful and fearful and fully indulged in by the tavern's patrons. Oh yes, they agreed: *That woman has got the devil working for her, always has—and now he's working against you.*

The Rash brothers left that tavern drunk. And furious. And more frightened for their futures than they'd ever been before. It was very late once they returned to their land, *her* land, and the liquor had helped them grow brash in their fear and rage.

It was in that drunken rage that they found her, not at her cottage, but at the base of the tower, attempting to burn it down. And they acted. Together, the Rash brothers acted. She'd been able to fight off one, but both brothers, and in such a fury, were too much for her.

She ran into the woods.

They chased her.

Near the hot springs, they caught her and strangled the life from her.

Then they buried her there, right where they'd killed her.

Soon after, the troubles plaguing the Rash brothers ceased. The work went better, day by day. Their children again grew healthy and strong. Their laborers were mostly content, and the fog of yellow jackets diminished to only reasonable encounters now and again.

When the woman was infrequently asked after (before she was forgotten about), one of the brothers might say that he believed her to be visiting friends in a neighboring state. And once that rumor was spread and accepted, it didn't take long for it to become she had moved away to Massachusetts, or Connecticut, or even sometimes to Delaware, to be with her only living relatives. And that was that. She was not particularly missed by anyone except for maybe one or two of the Rash children, and even then, it was only ever occasionally.

Things continued on.

Except now, between the two brothers was buried a rancid secret. And it was this secret, black and rotting, that fueled the feud between them. The local storytellers and their tales about Spite Tower got it both right and wrong. Jonathan Rash had not built the tower to block his brother's sight lines, but the brothers *had* fought over it. Eventually they had. Once their lie about the woman's departure was established, and she was no longer asked after, Samuel wanted the tower torn down. Jonathan refused to do so.

And from there, our lay historians' tale of the Rash brothers is close enough.

Of course, they've left out so much to get *there* that they might as well be telling a different story entirely.

It was never Spite Tower itself, or its rather silly and certainly incomplete local lore, that had interested Harold Brookhants. Instead, it was the bloody root of the brothers' feud that lured him to this place, the act of murder that linked those men to a woman who once lived alone in a cottage by the water.

A woman, Madame Verrett had explained, with a mysterious and powerful lineage.

Once he'd acquired the land, Harold Brookhants had conducted all manner of occult practices in order to better understand that power. He consulted spirit guides *and* historians, geologists *and* diviners. (Harold had never had any compunctions about mixing his methodologies.) He'd even tried, on several occasions, to find the woman's unmarked grave, but the mass of growth in the Tricky Thicket, and the yellow jackets that swarmed there, had thwarted those efforts.

Harold Brookhants believed that some of that woman's power remained in the land that she had loved, the land where she had died too soon and violently. And he wanted to not only understand that power, but claim it for himself. (In this life and in any others to come.)*

There was now only one of the Matryoshka dolls left to burn: the smallest. The Ava look-alike. And Libbie had already dug its silt grave.

Her fingers were so stiff that she could scarcely make them work to strike the final match. She fumbled with the box.

"Mrs. Brookhants?" Adelaide's soft voice was like its own set of cold fingers, fluttering over the base of Libbie's spine.

---

* If you guessed, Readers, that Harold's interest in Libbie's child—in other words, his interest in obtaining a child (or vessel) that could be reared in exactly the manner he prescribed—had something to do with these beliefs, you'd be right. I won't attempt, here, to summarize his complicated thinking about the insignificance of corporeal death when compared to the realms one's spirit might live on in, but you can read it in Harold's own words if you can track down copies of the letters he left for Ava.

Between the digging and the burning and the ocean crashing, the yellow jackets' hum, Libbie hadn't noticed the maid's approach. She looked up now to find Adelaide standing before her, over her. Too close. Adelaide was much too close.

"I do not require your assistance tonight, Adelaide," Libbie said, keeping her voice steady. "Nor do I want it." Libbie had not yet managed to burn this last doll, but for now, she buried it in silt so it stayed hidden from Adelaide's view.

Libbie stood, Mary's book in her hand. She backed away from Adelaide and her hip throbbed as she did. Her skirt was so heavy with water and sand that it seemed to pull her back to the ground.

"I spotted you from the tower and grew worried," Adelaide said, coming closer, the exact amount that Libbie had moved away.

"I am no longer under the province of your worries, Adelaide."

"Why are you being so cold to me? I only came to see if I could help you." She stepped closer still. "Mrs. Brookhants?" She tried again. "Libbie?"

"Stay back!"

Adelaide looked like she'd just been slapped. And even now, knowing what she did—or thought she did, at any rate—Libbie was embarrassed to have shouted at her.

Libbie was still walking backward and without meaning to had drifted closer to the water, so that she was now in its thinnest edge, though right then she did not feel it soaking her boots.

She kept her eyes on Adelaide and made her voice as level as she could. "Please stay back. There are things I have to do tonight and if only you let me do them, then I'll be gone from here forever and you can stay on as you like. For as long as you like."

"What do you mean, you'll *be gone*?" Adelaide asked, her eyes wide and confused. "You've only just returned! You're to be better, now. And how would I stay here without you? Why would I?" She was still advancing, and so Libbie was walking backward, now sloshing through the foamy water as she went. "I thought we shared—"

"I share *nothing* with you," Libbie said.

"But, Mrs. Brookhants, you know that isn't true."

Libbie could not counter this. She had shared things with Adelaide, intimate things, up in the tower during their tutoring sessions. She'd shared complaints about what she'd then chosen to classify as Alex's increasing delirium, and her many worries about the school, and her sorrow to be missing the life Sara Dahlgren was leading. Even her regrets about Ava.

She had told Addie the truth about Ava. And Harold. And how she'd come to live at Brookhants. She had told Addie so many truths up in that tower, private truths, with Alex stewing away down below. Wonderful Alex, *her* Alex. And she had done more than talk to Addie, she had let Addie kiss her. And she had wanted to do much more than only that. Not since Alex's death, at least, had she wanted this, though she knew that if she stayed, if she let herself live here with Adelaide, then perhaps . . .

"Please come back with me now," Adelaide said. "We'll warm you up, get you out of these wet clothes, and then we'll talk. We haven't had the chance to talk, really talk as we should, as we once did, since the awful night when Alex—"

"Don't you say her name! You keep it from your mouth."

At this, Adelaide stopped approaching. Libbie stopped, too. They looked at each other. Strands of Addie's hair tossed about in the cold wind and Libbie felt the hum of the yellow jackets vibrate through the sand, up through her feet, and into her legs and core.

It was as if, in a collection of mere moments, Adelaide's whole countenance changed. Gone was any pleading affect, warmth or confusion. It was replaced by a coldness that cast itself over Libbie like a shadow. Libbie shuddered. Adelaide was clearly now the one in charge. Perhaps, Readers, this had always been the case, since the day she'd arrived at Spite Manor.

Adelaide turned around for a moment, her back to Libbie as she looked down the beach from where they'd come. Something about how purposefully she did this made it more awful still. She had no need to hurry.

She turned to face Libbie again. "Ava's doll took me weeks to make. She says she helped, I know, but really she only got in the way. She has no talent for that particular art. Not yet. But I do know she'll be very upset to find it missing. What reason will I give her for its disappearance?"

"I'm sure you'll find one that suits you."

"I'm sure I will," Adelaide said. "I could even tell her right now, if I wanted to. If she'd only open up to listen to me. But she's young and still learning."

"Do not say these things to me!" Libbie shouted. She had to shout over the terrible buzzing of the yellow jackets. They might now *be* the sand: millions of yellow jackets piled atop each other like humming grains of quartz. "I won't listen."

"I don't think you have much choice," Adelaide sang. "You *can* still come with me, sweet Library. Come and be with me. Everything here is ready for us to be together. The school could open again, little Ava is here. Come and let's see how this might be for the three of us." She extended her hand toward Libbie.

It was too close; she was too close—Addie's twitching worm fingers nearly against her dress. In her haste to get away, Libbie twisted her foot in a dip and crashed backward, hard, landing in the cold water.

The surprise of this fall knocked the wind from her and made her see stars—though that might have only been because the sky was now full of them and she was looking up. She felt as if she'd slipped off the edge of the planet and not just a few feet to the ground.

But then she saw Adelaide still standing there, reaching out toward her. Libbie cowered, ducking her head into her shoulders. She waited for Adelaide to come down upon her, to consume her.

But this did not happen. Adelaide only took the book from her— Mary's book. Libbie had forgotten she was still holding it. And now she wasn't anymore.

"It's certainly the worse for wear, isn't it?" Adelaide said, turning it over in her hands. "It was pristine when I sold it to her. What a flash, your Sara. I wish you'd been able to convince her to stay tonight. We might have avoided this, the three of us together. Of course, we might have ended up here anyway. Who can ever say, at Brookhants?"

Libbie couldn't understand. She did not want to. The buzzing now so loud that the crash of the waves was muted inside it. She was wet and shivering and her heart pounded. Horrid white snakes of sea-foam swirled around her. She could not understand what was to happen next, or why Adelaide was not upon her.

"I can hear you, too, Libbie," Adelaide sang. "I can hear the thoughts you think are yours alone."

"Stop it! Please, stop talking to me."

"You don't think this book is what's to blame here, do you? You'd really give a child's diary the credit when Brookhants has its own story, ripe as a peach? It certainly doesn't need Mary MacLane's."

"Please stop," Libbie said, now in tears. The sand *was* made of yellow jackets, she was sure of it—writhing and buzzing beneath her, so cold they stung her hands and made her shiver.

Adelaide knelt in that buzzing, so their heads were level. But still she did not touch Libbie. She said, "Your husband did not know her name, the woman who lived here. But I do.* She was called Simone. You're right to think of her tonight. Though poor Harold never had her story quite correct. He was such easy meat, your Harold. He so wanted to believe that he forgot to ask questions. Or never the right questions, at any rate."

"I don't believe you."

"Oh, but you do." Addie looked off toward the dark rim of woods, as if she saw something there, then she again looked at Libbie, who cringed beneath that gaze. "People said the girl, Simone, came here with her parents. Like everyone else, Harold assumed that meant a mother and a father. Not so. Simone lived with her mothers— two mothers—only one sometimes dressed and acted as a man because the world didn't understand her when she did not do so, especially when she was with her wife. They had tried to live that way back in France and did not find it at all successful. And so, they got on a boat and left to make a new life. Sim-

---

* OK, OK—so I lied, Readers. I did know her name. But *Harold* didn't, and that was the point.

one's mothers *both* built the cottage here. Simone's mothers *both* made their life here with her. And it was a very happy life. Until it wasn't."

"Oh, I can't," Libbie said, the sand still stinging and the foam snakes swimming about her sopped skirts. "Please, I don't want to know. You don't need to tell me."

"You do want to know," Adelaide said. "And I do need to tell you. Is it worse, do you think, to not tell her story at all than it is to tell it poorly, to start it at the wrong place? Why give it over to the brothers Rash? Yes, they killed her, but *who* did they kill? The real trouble, the trouble that claimed this place and claims it still, was that one of Simone's two mothers had left a family of diverse and powerful talents back in France. You can say that she escaped that family, if you like, but in any case, its remaining members were not happy when one of their own absconded to America to make her life anew and raise her child here without their guidance. That is not what members of the Verrett clan did. That is *still* not what we do. Not without permission."

"I can't," Libbie said again. She could not look at Adelaide, who was then grinning horribly. Instead, she looked out across the water at the glinting lights of Newport. She thought of Sara at a party there, she tried to make her mind speak—

"Just now, Sara Dahlgren is drinking gin and flirting with a Rockefeller. I'm sure you can guess which one. She can't hear you. She doesn't want to, anyway."

Libbie closed her eyes to this mad talk. She felt the buzzing enter her body and hum there.

Adelaide continued on. "What story might I tell *you*, now? Which will make you contented as a fat baby in a crib with jam on your lips? None of these stories, alone, are the truth, but they do add up to something close to it. For instance, I could tell you that I tried to warn your Alex at the fair. I *did* try, with the doll. I wanted to scare her, too—just a little, you know, for sport. But I did try to warn her as well. I liked her. I thought she could do better than you."

"She could have," Libbie said.

"It didn't matter in the end—my warning. They got to her on the train. Did you know that?" Adelaide wrinkled her face like she was thinking. "I can't remember if you *do* know that. Harold and my aunt—they got to her to get to you, two worms in your apple before you even took the bite."

Libbie tightened the close of her eyes to shut her out. It didn't help. Adelaide had waited to deliver this soliloquy. And she would now take her time in full.

"Or I could tell you about Simon Everett, if you like. Tell me, does that name strike you as more or less familiar, Library, than it did a moment ago? Do you remember your night at the fair with him? Simon Everett, Simone Verrett?" Adelaide laughed as though what she'd said was funny. "I know you're wondering about the extra *r*. It is, perhaps, a question worth asking—but you make such a mess of your French anyway. We didn't think you'd mind."

"You don't need to tell me," Libbie said. "I believe you. I believe all of it."

But Adelaide wasn't finished. "You shouldn't blame yourself as you do, Library. You were only ever a means to an end. Swarms of yellow jackets, poisonous flowers, a too-steep staircase built by a brute out for vengeance? I should think there's ample room for accidents in each of those."

They were not accidents! Libbie thought like a scream. Adelaide heard this thought perfectly.

"You're right about that," she said.

Libbie's whole self buzzed.

"Come with me, Library," Adelaide now whispered. "Take my hand and come and I'll tell you this story as it wants to be told, in each of its variations. I'll write it on your body with my tongue so that you'll always remember. You won't be able to forget. None of the dead girls are gone from here, not really. You just don't know how to see them. We could be three here, again—in our house by the sea. Two mothers for little Ava."

At this fresh horror, Libbie opened her eyes and tried one final time: "Please, please—I don't want to be here a moment longer. Please."

Adelaide, with, was it a glance of sorrow—could it really be that?—stood and brushed the sand from her skirts. "I know you don't. And that being true, I suppose it is now time for a bath, Mrs. Brookhants. And oh, I'm sorry about that. I've been watching for such a long time—but I did like watching you best. I think you know that."

She gave Libbie a final, appraising look, almost a shy sort of smile, and then she turned and began to walk back down the beach toward the wooden stairs that would lead her up to the house and away. Her steps were unhurried and light as air. Indeed, she seemed to walk atop the sand without sinking into it at all.

Libbie did not understand how she had escaped, or why. For now, she cared only that she had been left alone and alive.

She waited until Adelaide was ten yards away, twenty, twenty-five—far enough so that Libbie would be able to run with a good head start if Adelaide turned back toward her. Only then did our Libbie move to stand.

She could not.

It wasn't painful, at first, only confusing.

She tried again to push her palms down into the sand—which was again sand and not yellow jackets—and to situate her legs beneath her. But her body refused her efforts. She could move her head and neck, and she could still *feel* her limbs as if they belonged to her, but they would not do the things she was telling them to do. It was as if her body was now a marionette that she did not fully control. She tried again and then again. Again. And now her futile efforts did feel painful, until she was wincing and panting with them, and still no movement came.

It was then that she felt the first tickle of black seaweed pushing against her, its rotten stink clouding the air.

Once again she worked to stand and once again found she could not. She refused to scream the scream now reaching up her throat. More tangles of black seaweed, those awful nests of hair or snakes, floated against her, around her.

Soon the seaweed was wrapping around her and tugging her out. Libbie did not notice this at first, that she was drifting away from the land. She was so consumed by her immobility, and the mounting horror of the seaweed, its stench and increasing presence, that she did not sense this larger movement around her.

She could not tell, at first, that the shoreline was no longer beneath her.

She was being pulled out to sea, but her body still faced her house and its tower. And the woods. And the school that lay beyond those woods.

Too soon she felt the water creeping higher and pushing harder, and now she was in the breakers, the waves with their white teeth smashing up into her nose, salting her eyes, black water and white foam collapsing upon her so that she had to remember to catch and hold her breath, and then to breathe in ragged chokes when her mouth at last found air. And then to do it again. And again.

This was the only thing she *could* do, Readers, the only thing she could control. She might as well have been Houdini in a straitjacket giving an ocean performance, for our Libbie still could not move a thing but her head and neck. She was pushed under, her face smashed hard against the sand, the bay bottom filling her ears and a piece of stone gouging an eyebrow, before she was rolled back up to breathe and glimpse the sky and then be smashed again.

She grew so waterlogged and delirious that she felt she wasn't in the water at all, but somehow inside the yellow jacket buzz—as if that noise, that awful noise, was the thing churning her around and smashing her about and filling her up with its blackness.

But the stinking seaweed she was tangled in tugged on, pulling her body farther out, and eventually Libbie cleared the breakers and was again upright, drifting, bobbing, rocking up and down on the cresting black waves.

She was like a bobber, now, floating upright and mostly atop the waves, out and out and out into the dark—black sky, black water, black weeds wrapping her like a package sent out to sea. Death was certain, but it was not imminent.

She did not scream. She did not even try to do so.

It may be that our Libbie accepted this fate as punishment for what she knew to be her previous inaction, or perhaps as something foretold by a curse that she now believed in her very marrow she could not outrun.

It also may be that she was only trying to save her breath.

Either way, it is a horrible ending for our Libbie Packard-~~Brookhants~~. (No more horrible than any of the other endings you've endured in this story, it's true, but plenty horrible nonetheless.)

Oh, Readers, I know you'll cling to this next thing I tell you. You'll want to tether all your hopes to it.

I'll let you.

Libbie Packard's drowned and lifeless body should have drifted over to at least Portsmouth, maybe all the way over to Newport, to shoreline belonging to one of the gilded summer cottages there, perhaps to then be spotted by the member of the house staff sent to rake the beach early the next morning.

But this did not happen. Our Libbie disappeared that night, it's true, never to return to Spite Manor. But her body was not found. Not the next morning, or the one after that, or even to this day.

Is it possible that Libbie Packard did wash up somewhere, and upon reaching this non-Brookhants land found that she had regained the use of her body and so now used it to simply shed the black seaweed like it was snakeskin and walk up the sand and into a new life far away?

Almost certainly not.

And yet . . .

There is a known photograph of Sara Dahlgren in Paris sometime around 1920. In it, a group of women are gathered in some elegant apartment with high ceilings and mullioned windows flung open to the sidewalk trees and sun. They are joyous, these women. Some of them are kissing each other. One is sitting in the lap of another. They are, almost without exception, smiling for whomever is taking their picture.

The woman who makes the exception is one near the back of the group. She is not smiling. She is not scowling, either, but was in the midst of turning her head when the photo was taken. Turning her head and beginning to raise a hand to shield her face. She was not quite fast enough to escape the camera, though. It caught her. She is lovely, this woman, likely somewhere in her forties, maybe fifties, and very elegant. She is standing beside Sara Dahlgren.

And she looks more than a little like Libbie Packard's mother in photos of Mrs. Packard at that age.

This photo is one in a series of photos from that gathering of women in that apartment that day. But the woman in question, this aged Libbie look-alike, appears only in the photo I've described.

Make of that what you will, Readers.

One thing I do know is this: as she drifted out and away from Brookhants, if our silent, bobbing Libbie had looked not at the black weed and water around her, or at the stars above, but instead back up the beach, across the terraced land, to the house with the reaching arm of Spite Tower, she would have seen her own Ava in one of its lit windows, looking down at her.*

---

* Readers, as you may know, we do have Ava Brookhants's own account of this scene from her 1964 memoir, *Seer: The Ava Brookhants Story.* The book was neither a critical nor a commercial success, but her rendering of these moments is both beautiful and terrifying (a combination favored by our own Bo Dhillon). In the passage, Ava writes that she did not understand, as a child—one who had recently been given a dose of heroin for the pain of her broken arm (yes, you read that correctly)—what she was seeing. She could not fathom what Libbie was doing in the water with all her clothes on at night, or if she should even believe that Libbie was there at all, given her state of mind. And soon, Adelaide came to find her and tuck her back into bed, anyway. Ava accepted her mother's departure as readily as she had accepted her return: with disinterest.

Death was certain, but it was not imminent.

THE RED CARPET AFTER

··················

It's a terrible story, and one way to tell it is this: two girls in love and a fog of yellow jackets cursed the place forever after.

Maybe you think you already know this story because of ~~the movie they made about it~~ the book you read about it. Certainly, it's true, Readers, that you now know more than many of those who have chanced upon only a portion of this tale, one curling bramble of its understory.

You now know just how tangled and thorny that understory is.

However you think of this book—if you do think of it—I hope you'll remember to remember the yellow jackets. I hope you'll remember their dedication to their ilk and the steadfastness of their purpose. Perhaps one night, when you wake dry-mouthed and shuffle to the bathroom to cup your hand beneath the faucet for water, you'll startle to feel the flick of them about you, the brush of their wings near your ear, their sticky-footed landing in your hair, against your neck, the pulse of their buzz through these pages seeping into your skin, their humming constancy: the vibrating life of them as they go about their days sucking sweetness from the rot.

Maybe on a sidewalk in the afternoon sun you'll hear leaves flutter in branches spread above and you'll mistake that sound for the rustle of skirts on stairs, bodies rushing up or down. Bodies falling. Or you'll smell orange blossom when you open your closet door, and the scent of apple mash and wood smoke will pour from your AC vent.

Or it will snow when it should not.

Or there will be ripe berries in the winter woods.

Or a tune will trickle in the window and you'll be almost certain that it's "Annie Lisle."

But I did tell you that the yellow jackets were the thing, Readers. I told you that at the start.

In fact, just now one of them is trailing **Harper Harper** as she works the red carpet for the *Happenings at Brookhants* premiere at the Festival de Cannes.[*]

Harper hasn't noticed it yet. She's busy finding her angles, of which there are too many good ones to count. She's in a navy tux that looks like it was made to fit her because it was, the slim-pleated white shirt beneath its jacket unbuttoned nearly to her navel so that her pink satin bra frequently peeks out its gaps: a perfect nod to late-80s Madonna.[†] And because of her recent buzz cut (a requirement of her current role in a big-budget franchise about a world without gender but with robot monsters) her face is right now more about her sculpted brows, Hollywood-blue eyes, and cutting cheekbones than ever before—which is really saying something where Harper Harper is concerned.

"Harper, here!" a photographer calls. She looks at him there behind the rope line. In fact, she gives him a bunch of looks to choose from. She gives them to all the media around him as well: both hands in her pockets, one hand in her pocket, her head tilted, a smile with teeth (and tooth gap), no smile, a sort of smile with no teeth (and so no tooth gap).

"*Regarde-moi!*" another calls. So Harper looks at this one. She looks at them all: they're all she can see, this swarm of people with cameras in front of their faces or microphones directed at her, so

---

[*] Otherwise known as Cannes, the film festival held annually in the spring in Cannes, France. Did you really think, Readers, that this film could premiere anywhere other than France? (Except for maybe Brookhants, but what would be the point of telling this story back to itself?)

[†] Word was that Harper was seeing her tuxedo's designer, Annicka Barris, until word was that she was not.

many stemmed mics in some places along the rope line that they look like a thicket of mechanical cattails.

Harper smiles into a laugh, as though something one of the camera faces has yelled has struck her as funny. It hasn't, but she knows from having done this before—a lot of times before, and there will be even more after this time, too—that everyone loves moments that seem genuine and spontaneous on the red carpet. (Cameras especially love them.)

She feels a flutter at the nape of her neck, which is all the more sensitive now that she hasn't even an inch of hair to cover it. She turns, surprised. It's only Esther, her stylist, having peeled from the background to adjust Harper's shirt collar.

"Just finessing this—no big," Esther says as she pinches and tucks. "You look goooood."

Harper smiles at her, and then again at the camera faces. "Thank you, Esther."

Esther takes a couple of steps backward, ready to return to the pit crew, as it were, but then she suddenly steps forward again, swatting her hand through the air near Harper's left shoulder.

Harper pretends, in an overdone way, to shrink back from this violence, which shivers a laugh through the crowd. (The reaction she wanted.)

"What the hell?" she says to Esther, her very pink lips sliding over her teeth in a real smile.

Esther swats again. "Sorry. There's, like, a bee chasing you."

Even before she sees it, Harper knows that it is *not* a bee. But to Esther she says, "That's how sweet I am."

"You're corny and you're about to get stung," Esther says, swatting again. Harper likes that Esther does not go in for any of her bullshit. Esther has a wife who's a lawyer for a climate change nonprofit. They have a kid and another one coming and a house in Silver Lake.

Esther represents a kind of adult ideal to Harper, who feels in need of ideal adults.

"I think it's buzzed off for the moment," Esther says. She returns to the sidelines.

Harper keeps moving forward. She answers a few questions from the microphone wielders before she notices that the yellow jacket is still following her. In fact, Harper's pretty sure there are now a few of them following her—or one of them that sure gets around: her left shoulder, her right hip, up against her temple.

There's so much noise and chaos around her, the glint of camera lenses, the blood red of the carpet, which is weirdly squishy (it rained hard that morning and the carpet is still soggy with it), the Cannes handler scooting in to tell her where to look and what outlet this person represents, but she can still feel the flick of the yellow jacket: the pulse close to her skin, the vibration in the air about her.

It's like winding the dial on the dread inside her.

She looks back along the carpet from where she's just come. Audrey is now working the rope line as well—and Bo is out, too. The plan is for them to meet up soon, here toward the middle, and pose together for some shots, answer questions as a trio. People will like that, so they'll be sure to be extra about it. Of course people would like it even better if Merritt was here too, but Merritt isn't coming.

Until fifteen minutes ago, when they were together in the staging area, Harper had seen Audrey only a few times (twice to do soundstage stuff in LA) since their last day shooting at Brookhants. And those last days at Brookhants—those last weeks, really, everything that came after Elaine's fall on the Spite Tower stairs, and her death—had been so strained between the three of them. In the immediate aftermath, with production shut down, it had seemed like maybe they wouldn't finish the film at all. While estate lawyers sorted the details and press reported endlessly, Audrey had moved out of her tiny house and into an offsite hotel and Merritt had disappeared. Basically, she had. I mean, they saw her at the funeral, but . . .

It had seemed, then, like that might be that. The press was everywhere, saying nothing good. Nobody knew if they could finish the film. Or should finish it. Harper had another movie to get to, one starting in Montreal the following month, and she'd been hoping for some time off in between. Plus, she didn't want the stink of this one to land on that one. She'd been ready to call it and head back to Los Angeles for a while. Or maybe Montana, to check in on things.

But then Bo had texted that it was all sorted. They could reassemble at Brookhants to finish telling the story of Flo and Clara, and what had happened to them all those years before. The story from the past, that is. *That's* the story they could finish. So they had.

There were no more strange occurrences, no more delays. They were now as rigidly on schedule as they'd once been off it. Audrey, Harper had noticed, thrived under these conditions. Actually, everyone on set had noticed this. It was like she had finally given herself permission to be as good as she could be, and then she was. But they never discussed this fact among the three of them because, for those last weeks of shooting, there was no longer a three of them. (And some of the things they'd said to each other the night of Noel's concert made it seem like maybe there never had been to begin with.)

But now, for the next few weeks anyway, Audrey and Harper will be together a lot, doing press for this film, selling their story to the people in practically any way the people would want to receive it.

Truth be told, Harper had been really glad to see Audrey come into the staging tent with Caroline at her side. They didn't have much time to talk, and there were too many people around them to do it properly, anyway, but when they hugged—carefully, because of their makeup and hair (well, Audrey's hair) and couture—Harper said, "Oh my God I'm glad you're here. I'm so fucking happy to see you." And that was true, Readers.

"I'm happy to see you, too," Audrey said. Harper didn't know if that was true or not. She hoped it was.*

Harper has wanted to talk and talk about the things they've not said to each other, or to anyone, about what really happened to them at Brookhants. She especially wants to talk about the things that have happened—happened to her, at least—since they all left Brookhants. Harper wants to talk to Merritt about these things too, but since the splashy announcement of her bidding-war book deal (which neces-

---

* It was.

sarily lit up Harper's own Google Alerts), Merritt has dropped off all social media and appears to have changed her phone number.

At first Harper's texts and congratulatory calls weren't returned, but the last two times she tried they wouldn't even go through. And she's too embarrassed to ask anyone who might have Merritt's new number, the working number, to give it to her. Harper doesn't even know if Merritt's seen the movie yet. She didn't come to any of the cast and crew screenings in LA.

"Harper! Do you like the film?" This from a rope liner with mirrored sunglasses and a pink-stemmed microphone.

Harper looks in the general direction of that microphone. The swarm of camera faces look back. "Yes! I think it's terrifying."*

"But is it the film you thought you were making? Were you in on it?"

She pauses. She's practiced for these questions, has some lines memorized. "Yes and no," she says as if she's thinking. "Movies are always something else, something different, when they're finished than when you're making them. I had a sense of Bo's vision for this film, but not the specifics of how he would piece the timelines together."

"Isn't it a bit of a cheat for him to cast himself as the villain, though?"

"Why is that *a cheat*?" Harper asks. She hadn't known, before she saw the first cut, how much Bo Dhillon would appear in his own film, how willing he was to show himself unflatteringly pulling the strings. (Though she's pretty sure Bo knew that's what he would be doing the whole time.)

"Isn't that choice meant to absolve him of any objections about how he made the film—if he's portraying himself as the villain *within* its story? Now he can call it all a performance?"

"I don't think he's doing that," she says. "I think he used the film

---

* This is true. Harper does really like the movie that Bo made from the Brookhants wreckage. It's also true that she thinks Audrey is its breakout star. Audrey's is the performance they'll be talking about most.

to interrogate his own acts of manipulation, to question the nature of narrative film, of horror as entertainment." (This is one of the answers she's memorized.)

Another reporter: "Audiences are supposed to believe that you were really frightened to be on location there. Were you?"

"Definitely," she says, feeling the flick of the yellow jacket at her ear. "The whole time."

She does not say: *I still am.* (But she thinks it, Readers, and sometimes that means more, the things you think and don't say—especially when you're on a red carpet.)

She feels the tap of the yellow jacket against her scalp. It is not possible, but she now smells lilac, too. It's a waft of fresh scent—not a perfume, not a spray—descending like a draped sheet over the whole area. The microphones are buzzing, buzzing. The glint off the hundreds of glass lenses around her might actually be the flick of advancing yellow jackets, more and more, or maybe the first flakes of falling snow, here in the May sun on the French Riviera.

She feels a touch dizzy, her steps still sinking in the red sog of the carpet. Its springiness reminds her of something. Moss? Like the thick scabs of moss that grew between the stones near the fountain at Brookhants. Or the sand there on its strip of beach? These thoughts make bile rise in her throat. Her next step sinks weirdly into the moss carpet. The sand carpet. And the next. She should have eaten more of that yogurt parfait they'd brought her while she was getting her makeup done. She needs to get water or—

"*Sorridi, bella!*" a camera face from an Italian magazine yells. The glint, the flick, the lilac—Harper cannot tell who's yelled this. Can she even lift her foot for the next—

"*Sorridi!*"

And now someone shouts from down the carpet, "Don't fucking bark at her to smile, asshole."

Harper turns. It can't be, but it is: Merritt. Merritt, who wasn't supposed to be coming, who maybe hasn't even seen the movie, but who is now here on the carpet looking hot as fuck in her own suit with a satin stripe down the leg. Only paired with hers, beneath her jacket, is a T-shirt with *Warped Predilection* on it.

Now she's got Audrey by the hand and together they're walking toward Harper. They're not working their angles. They're not stopping for the camera faces or answering questions or doing it at all like they're supposed to. Hovering people with earpieces and tablets, the Cannes handlers, seem perturbed by this traffic violation, but Merritt is not stopping for even a one of them and Audrey seems content to let herself be pulled along.

They are hand in hand and they're coming for her and Harper is glad.

When they reach her the three of them pull into a group hug that is not at all like the one Harper shared with Audrey in the staging tent fifteen minutes before—as grateful as Harper was to have that hug then. This is something else entirely: it's a coming together. It's being able to arrange and rearrange themselves however they choose to allow someone to always be in the middle, flanked on either side.

From a microphone wielder: "Should you even be here screening this film? Promoting it? When a woman died."

Harper, as she pulls out of the hug, runs over scripted lines, but before she can offer any of them Merritt steps forward and answers: "The *woman's* name was Elaine Brookhants. You didn't know her, I did, and nobody wanted this movie to be made more than she did."

"Is that enough of a justification?"

"You tell me," Merritt says. "I haven't seen it yet."

"The camera loves her in it," Harper says quickly. She doesn't know quite why she's said this. It's a little desperate and she doesn't do desperate.

"Oh fuck off," Merritt says to her while Audrey takes a question.

"I can't believe you stole Audrey's shirt idea," Harper says.

"I didn't steal it," Merritt says. "I had one made for her, too."

This news hits Harper funny.

"Look at me, ladies!" another camera face yells. The three of them wrap their arms around each other until they're a locked chain—and then they do look, and they smile.

"I heard you owe your publisher two more books," Harper says to Merritt while they continue to smile, and turn, and pose—still bound together in their line. "Is that true?"

"That's what I heard," Audrey singsongs.

"It is a very ill-advised thing they offered me," Merritt says. "So I accepted. I mean, if they're going to offer it . . ."

"Who you gonna write those books about?" Harper asks.

"I'm waiting to see what happens on this press tour."

"So you're doing it?" Harper asks. "The whole tour and not just tonight?"

Merritt shrugs.

"That's really why you came? So we can be your content farm?"

Merritt shrugs again.

"I don't believe that," Harper says. But she isn't sure. Maybe she does believe it.

They unchain themselves to pose in different ways, move down the line a little, answer more questions.

Harper tries one final question and delivers it as lightly, as casually, as she can: "So are you gonna let me read it early or what?"

"I wasn't planning to," Merritt says. "I saw what they're paying you for *Ripe Planet*—you can afford to buy your own copy. That title, though? Shudder."

Harper ignores that last bit. "You don't think Capote Capote is a little on the nose for your heroine?"

"I told her that," Audrey says, grinning. She looks at Merritt. "I *did* tell you that."

"Who told you Capote Capote is the protagonist?" Merritt asks Harper. "Alluring but enigmatic love interest, yes. A very bad heroine to be sure—but *the* heroine? You've been misinformed."

"Have you read it?" Harper asks Audrey, thinking there's no way this could be, but she's sensing a certain new camaraderie between them—the T-shirt thing, their winking comments.

"Months ago," Audrey says, turning so that a photographer can capture her cream gown—one not unlike an angel's trumpet—from the side. "While she was still editing. I had to help her get a certain character's motivation right." Audrey smiles.

"Those were early days," Merritt says. "You've read it more recently than that."

Harper is bothered by this news and she does not do a particularly good job hiding this fact on her face. "Really?" she says, again feeling a little like she's sinking into the carpet. "What's the secret to getting inside the locked vault?"

"She was over," Merritt says, tilting her head toward Audrey, casual as a trip to the grocery store. "She drove herself over—in her own car."

"Good for you," Harper says, still so confused.

"And the galleys had come in the mail like the day before, so they were sitting out and she kept whining about reading it until I gave her one."

"I'm sure they just happened to be sitting out," Audrey says. "You couldn't have possibly found two minutes to put them in a closet before I came."

"Certainly not," Merritt says.

The smile they share in this moment bothers Harper even more. "You just happened to be in Connecticut?" she asks Audrey.

"Merritt's in LA now," Audrey says like it's common knowledge. "She's gonna get taken out by an earthquake-mudslide-brushfire with the rest of us."

"Since when are you in LA?" Harper asks. She is disoriented by all these true facts that have been unknown to her before these moments. She also feels like she's now up to her ankles in red carpet, her feet buried in it like they're in silt.

Glint, glint, pose, smile, step, buzz. "Here, please!" Smile again.

"January," Merritt says. "Basically February—I moved in at the end of the month."

Harper aligns this chronology with all of the press about Merritt's book deal, the change in her phone number: everything happened around then, the end of January.

"I wish I'd known," Harper says.

"Why?" Merritt asks.

"So I could've brought you a cactus," Harper says. "As a housewarming gift." She's proud of herself for being this quick, especially since she still feels dizzy and hears the buzzing, and especially because it's Merritt she's saying it to.

But Merritt doesn't want to do the thing with her, the flirting thing that they've always done before. "Better that you didn't. I'm sure it would be dead by now."

This is not the place for intimate moments, but Harper cannot stop herself from saying, "I've really missed you. I keep wanting to talk to you. Both of you, I mean. We left it in such a weird place."

"Left what?" Merritt says.

"I think you know what," Harper says.

Audrey had pulled away from them. She's been answering a question at the rope line and only catches the end of this statement, but as she turns back, she says, "I know what. I have things to say to you both. And I want to ask you about . . . things—" She does not finish this.

"Me too," Harper says fast. She will not let embarrassment or shame stop her from admitting this. She won't let the cameras or the microphones or the red carpet stop her, either. She knows Audrey's talking about the months since they were last together—the things that feel like innocuous loose threads, until you go to pull one and find that it's not loose at all—it's attached, and if you follow it, it reaches back and back to Brookhants.

"I keep calling it all coincidental," Audrey says. "But I don't really think it is."

"It's not," Harper says. "Not the stuff that's been happening to me—it's still happening. I can't turn it off."

"It's more like a love letter to *Answered Prayers* than it is a true completion of Capote's novel," Merritt's saying to a reporter who has asked about her book.

"And they're both in it?" the reporter asks, gesturing at Harper and Audrey.

"Oh no—it's a work of fiction," Merritt says. "Any resemblances to persons living or dead are incidental." And then she winks—which is a textbook Harper Harper move, Readers.

Harper can't tell if it's the sand dune red carpet that's to blame for how seasick she's feeling. But she doesn't think so.

They pose again, the three of them with their arms about each other.

The buzzing has swelled and deepened without Harper's registering of it. Its volume has simply turned up and now emanates from the crowd, the air. She feels it vibrating through the soles of her shoes, up and up through her body.

Now Audrey pulls away to be shot alone.

Harper thinks she might pass out. When she's near swoon, she catches Merritt's eye. The buzzing is thick around her, inside her.

"I can hear it, too," Merritt says, taking Harper's hand. Harper looks at her, unsure. Merritt nods, she's calm. "Stay here with me. We're OK. Anchor yourself to me."

Harper does, gripping Merritt's arm as she steadies herself, tries to slide back into her body.

"Get Audrey's hand, too," Merritt says.

Harper doesn't hesitate, she reaches out for Audrey's hand—and even though she's still in midpose, Audrey gives it. They're almost at the end of the carpet anyway. All they have to do now is climb the wide red stairs—which, I mean, is itself a thing. There are a lot of them to get up, but they've made it this far. Although the Cannes people around them with earpieces seem less than thrilled with how they've performed on this latter portion of their walk.

But, Readers: fuck those people.

"Wait here for Bo Dhillon, please," one of the handlers now says.

"We'd rather not," Merritt says. "He'll catch up." She turns. Harper and Audrey turn, too—to face the stairs. They again join hands and climb a couple of them. Harper is still struggling with her footing and she's glad to be between the two of them.

They climb another few stairs and Audrey says they should probably turn around to pose again.

"Did you know Mary MacLane was in a movie?" Merritt says as they do. "A silent film. They think it's been lost to time."

"Of course it has," Audrey says.

"*Men Who Have Made Love to Me,*" Harper says, looking at Merritt. "Right? That's what it was called?"

"Well look at you," Merritt says. "I'm impressed."

"What about all the women who made love to her?" Audrey asks.

"Much too queer for the censors of the day," Merritt says.

"Too queer to be believed," Audrey says.

"Planet Lady Love," Merritt says. She is smiling, Readers—for real. They all are.

"I think they expect us to climb more of these, now," Audrey says. "Bo's gaining on us, so if we wait, we're gonna be stuck with him."

It's true that Bo-in-tux is coming fast behind.

He looks up at them now and waves and grins and they all smile and wave back, but given their position on the stairs, the line of them: it's like a royal court acknowledging one of their subjects. (Or at least that's how it looks in the many photos taken of that moment and later shared in various places near and far.)

Again they climb, hand in hand. Again they turn to pose. But no matter how many times they are asked, how many times they are, in fact, *directed* by handlers to separate so that they may be captured in individual photos, they refuse to do so.

"You know why I moved to LA?" Merritt asks.

"No," Harper says. "I didn't even know that you had until a minute ago."

"Why did you?" Audrey asks.

"Somebody once took me on the best date there," Merritt says. "Like it was so good it was unreal. It couldn't have been real. Until the end, that is, which was very real."

"It was a good date," Harper says.

"You know what I think about all the time?" Audrey asks. "You know what I dream about?"

"The orchard and the snowstorm and whatever else that was," Harper says.

"Yes," Audrey says.

"Me three," Merritt says.

"I can't get clear for myself if it really happened," Audrey says. "Because of everything else around it, I mean—everything that wasn't real."

"It happened," Harper says. She also wants this to be true.

"What if we hadn't driven away from it?" Audrey asks. "What if we'd made ourselves stay?"

"We didn't," Harper says.

"We still could," Merritt says. "We could try it again."

"*Brookhants 2: We're Not Through with You*?" Audrey says.

"Spite Manor is mine." Merritt says this like it is not at all the thing she's just said. She tries to turn them around again, in order to climb more stairs. But Audrey and Merritt do not turn with her. "I guess that means the orchard, too," Merritt says, still facing up the stairs even though she's the only one of the three doing so. "Though when it comes to land and Brookhants, I think it's best not to think you own anything—even if a piece of paper says otherwise."

"Elaine gave it to you?" Harper asks as if it's the most obvious thing in the world. She knows that Brookhants logic works like this.

Merritt nods.

"Jesus," Harper says. "Fuck."

"You just found out?" Audrey asks.

"No," Merritt says. "I've known for a while. I knew right away, actually. I'm the one who gave permission to finish the film there."

"What?" Audrey asks. "Why didn't you say anything to us then?" She seems a little wounded.

"I don't know," Merritt says. "You saw how I was then. I couldn't think about it."

"Fuck," Harper says again.

"Yes," Merritt says. "That. Can we climb the rest of these stairs now, please?"

Neither Harper nor Audrey answers, but both turn around and start doing so.

"I can't believe you didn't tell me any of this," Audrey says, talking across Harper to Merritt.

"I know," Merritt says. "I didn't feel like I could talk about it before."

"Before what?" Audrey asks.

"Before this. Before now, I guess, with the three of us."

"What are you gonna do with it?" Harper asks. "It's so much."

"I have no idea," Merritt says. "I think a lot about bulldozers and wrecking balls and flamethrowers."

"*Those* I would come back for," Harper says.

"It's not the right thing, though," Audrey says. "That doesn't feel right to me."

"You do have a little headmistress in you," Harper says to Merritt. "More than a little."

"I don't particularly care for children," Merritt says. "Plus, do we really think anyone should try to run a school there ever again?"

"Queer artists' colony?" Harper says.

"Old-timey apple picking and haunted hay ride?" Audrey says.

"For sure that one," Merritt says.

"I feel better knowing that it's yours now," Harper says. Is this true?

"I'm not sure that I do," Merritt says.

"We should go in," Audrey says. They've reached the top of the stairs. They've actually been there for a while. They look at the glass doors but don't move toward them. And then there is a commotion behind them, down the stairs, back on the carpet at the rope line.

They turn, in a row, to find tuxes and gowns scattering. Bo has his hand pressed up to his neck. The camera faces are turned away from everyone else currently on the carpet and directed at him, their lenses glinting. The white lights wrapping the trunks of the palm trees have been turned on and a breeze blows the smell of ocean and smoke and blossoms through the crowd, which is murmuring and pointing at Bo.

"He just got stung," Harper says, watching Bo continue to cup his neck and try to joke it off. She knows this to be true without anyone confirming it, but someone, a Cannes handler coming fast up the side of the stairs, *does* confirm it.

"A wasp—just now," she says, looking at Harper. "I'm going for ice."

"You can both hear the buzzing," Audrey asks. "Right?"

"A yellow jacket," Audrey calls after her.

Bo turns and looks up the stairs at the three of them. He shrugs. It's a cross between *What, me worry?* and something more genuine, something like *Did this just happen?*

"Now let it sting you twice more," Merritt yells down at him. "That's how you get hiiiiiiigggghhhh!"

Audrey, Merritt, and Harper laugh. Bo can't hear what she's said. Or at least he pretends that he can't. He turns back to the camera faces.

The red carpet stretched out before them could be a clown's tongue or a river of blood. It could also be a rain-soggy red carpet at a movie premiere. There are things floating in the air around them that might be pollen or yellow jackets or snowflakes. Or Hollywood fairy dust.

Merritt sneezes. And again. Photos of her midsneeze will wind up on many more pages than necessary.

"You can both hear the buzzing," Audrey asks. "Right?"

Harper and Merritt nod. They all squeeze hands. They have to go in now. Because what else?

"*I have read of women who have been strongly, grandly brave,*" Harper says as they turn toward the doors.

"*Sometimes I have dreamed that I might be brave,*" Merritt says.

"*The possibilities of this life are magnificent,*" Audrey says.*

---

* March 15 entry in *I Await the Devil's Coming*. But then you knew that already, didn't you, Readers?

Fin

ACKNOWLEDGMENTS

....

Oh, Readers, where to begin when my gratitude for those who helped to make this big, queer novel is so deep and wide? When this book wouldn't exist without the support of everyone from the lifeguards at my neighborhood Y, who (usually) managed to stay awake to watch over my early-morning lap swims—a meditative time during which I sorted plot elements—to the antiques dealers who sold me sapphic stereo cards and flower dictionaries, ostensibly for research, but also for sheer delight?

To my agent, Jessica Regel, who sat with me at a sticky dining table in a rented ski condo filled with my loud (and tipsy) family members, a snowstorm outside, and who told me to stop hemming and hawing and to write this book exactly as I thought it should be written, even if that meant complicating a lot of other things. Jessica, thank you for your years-long belief in my words. (Also, thanks for sharing twin bunkbeds with practical strangers and for being so damn chill about it.)

To my tireless editors, Jessica Williams at William Morrow and Carla Josephson at Borough: thank you for seeing the much better novel in that monstrous early draft and for pushing me to write and revise toward that end. I'm so glad we figured out, together, how to *fill the holes* while staying true to my weird vision. This book was so improved by your careful attention and good humor along the way.

Sara Lautman, thank you for sending that first *hello and how are you* email all those years ago, and for sticking with this unwieldly story during all the years since. (I know how slow I work, especially when compared to your usual output.) When I wasn't sure what this novel was, or what it could be, I felt so lucky to have your illustrations there to help inspire me. (And we got our map!)

I have so much gratitude for the brilliant teams at HarperCollins US and UK that work so diligently, and with such good cheer, to make books and authors shine: Julia Elliott, Leah Carlson-Stanisic, Ploy Siripant, Ryan Shepherd, Shelby Peak, Eliza Rosenberry, Liate Stehlik, Jennifer Hart, and Kelly Rudolph at William Morrow; and Fleur Clarke, Ann Bissell, Isabel Coburn, and Andrew Davis at Borough Press.

I am in debt to my early readers for their thoughtful notes and questions and their creative insights and enthusiasm. Thank you to Marissa Neilson, Carrie Shipers, Malinda Lo, and Alessandra Balzer (who took a chance on a very different version of this novel back when it was just a few pages and who, for a time, helped to guide it). Thanks, too, to Rebecca Rotert and Timothy Schaffert, who let me vent and kvetch and who gave me back such calm understanding and wisdom (and jokes!) in response.

Much love to Ben Chevrette and Scott Humphreys. Thank you, always, for your friendship and support, but in specific: thank you for those long beach weekends. If you hadn't been so willing to keep hauling that cooler with cheap champagne and stemware across the dunes for literal miles, I might not have fallen so in love with the Rhode Island coastline and its many charms. We'll always have [name of beach redacted to keep away the summer people].

Thank you to my former colleagues in the English Department at Rhode Island College for your early support of this novel—and of me—and to the MacDowell Colony for time, space, and those fantastic picnic basket lunches.

Thanks to every single reader and family member and friend who has asked about this book along the way to get here (*when's it coming?!*). I feel so lucky that you're out there.

Thank you to my mom, Sylvia Danforth, who is one of the most dedicated and enthusiastic readers I know (three book clubs!) and who, over the long course of my working on this novel, so often fed our dogs and did the dishes, baked muffins, cooked dinners, arranged vases of flowers, and, in general, let me submerge myself in Brookhants for hours on end, and then was always excited to ask me about how things were going once I came up for air. (Even if I didn't always feel like saying.)

Last and most and always, to Erica Edsell, my Erica Edsell: my very favorite person ever.

(Oh, and of course: to Mary MacLane, and not just for what she wrote, but for who she was.)

ABOUT THE AUTHOR

....

emily m. danforth is the author of the highly acclaimed young adult novel *The Miseducation of Cameron Post*, which was adapted into the Sundance award-winning feature film of the same name. emily holds an MFA in Fiction Writing from the University of Montana and a PhD in English-Creative Writing from the University of Nebraska-Lincoln. She lives in Rhode Island with her wife Erica, her mother Sylvia, and her two fairly terrible dogs, Kevin and Sally.

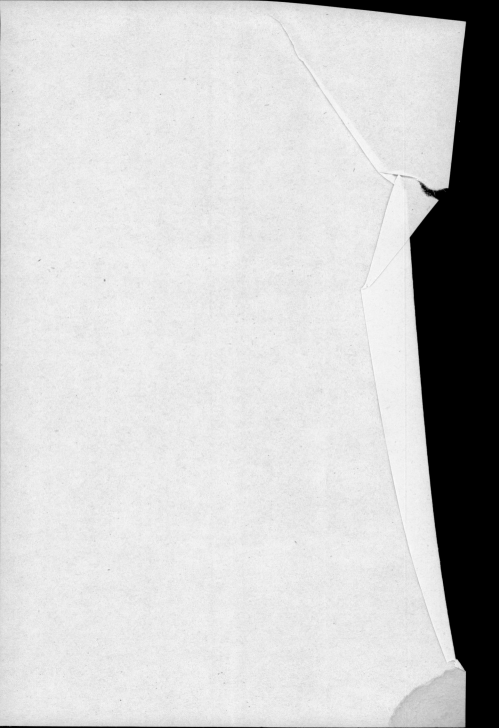